HILARY MANTEL

A CHANGE OF CLIMATE

VIKING

VIKING

Published by the Penguin Group
Penguin Books Ltd, 27 Wrights Lane, London W8 5TZ, England
Penguin Books USA Inc., 375 Hudson Street, New York, New York 10014, USA
Penguin Books Australia Ltd, Ringwood, Victoria, Australia
Penguin Books Canada Ltd, 10 Alcorn Avenue, Toronto, Ontario, Canada M4V 3B2
Penguin Books (NZ) Ltd, 182–190 Wairau Road, Auckland 10, New Zealand

Penguin Books Ltd, Registered Offices: Harmondsworth, Middlesex, England

First published 1994
3 5 7 9 10 8 6 4 2
First edition

Typeset by Datix International Limited, Bungay, Suffolk
Filmset in 12/16 pt Monophoto Bembo
Printed in England

A CIP catalogue record for this book is available from the British Library

ISBN 0–670–83051–8

To Jenny Naipaul

NOTE

All the characters in this book are fictitious, except that of the Archbishop of Cape Town, which is based on his real-life counterpart, Geoffrey Clayton. I have used some of his words, taken from writings and sermons.

The settlement of Mosadinyana is fictional. The township of Elim is invented too, but I am indebted to the memoirs of Hannah Stanton, who served in the township of Lady Selborne.

Cases similar to that of the Eldreds may be found in the Law Reports of Botswana.

Charles Darwin, *The Descent of Man*, 1871:
'We are not here concerned with hopes and fears, only with the truth as far as our reason allows us to discover it. I have given the evidence to the best of my ability . . .'

Job 4:7:
'Consider, what innocent ever perished, or where have the righteous been destroyed?'

1970

SAD CASES, GOOD SOULS

One day when Kit was ten years old, a visitor cut her wrists in the kitchen. She was just beginning on this cold, difficult form of death when Kit came in to get a glass of milk.

The woman Joan was sixty years old, and wore a polyester dress from a charity shop. A housewifely type, she had chosen to drip her blood into the kitchen sink. When Kit touched her on the elbow, she threw down the knife on to the draining board and attempted with her good hand to cover Kit's eyes.

By this stage in her life Kit was not much surprised by anything. As she ducked under the woman's arm she thought, that's our bread-knife, *if* you don't mind; but she said, 'You shouldn't be doing that, Joan, why don't you come away from the sink, why don't you sit down on this chair and I'll get the first-aid kit?'

The woman allowed herself to be led to a chair at the kitchen table. Kit pulled a clean tea-towel out of a drawer and wrapped it around Joan's wrist. The towel was a checked one, red and white; Joan's reluctant blood seeped black against the cloth. Her cuts were light, early, indecisive: the practice cuts. 'Just wiggle your fingers,' Kit said, 'make sure you haven't done any damage.' The woman looked down at her hand in dry-eyed dread, while the child scrambled on a stool and brought down a box from a cupboard.

'Lucky it's half-term,' Kit said, unpacking the bandages and the round-ended scissors. 'Otherwise I wouldn't have been here. I was upstairs. I was reading a book. It's called *Children of the*

I

New Forest. Have you read it? It's about a family like ours, two boys and two girls, but they live a long time ago, in the olden days.'

I'm all fingers and thumbs, she thought. She heard her voice, running on. She was learning first aid at school. They told you, 'Reassure the patient.' 'They live in the forest by themselves.' Joan nodded: again her dumb dazed nod. 'They're Royalists. They have to hide from their enemies.'

Kit was afraid that Joan might faint, dropping as a dead weight to the flagstoned floor. 'I'll get you a glass of water,' she said. 'Or I dare say you could have hot sweet tea.'

She thought, poor Joan. Perhaps dead is what she wants to be. It's just as Dad always says: you can never find a sharp knife when you need one.

As she stood filling the kettle, she heard her mother's car. She knew the crunch and scrape and wheeze of it, as it lurched up the drive. Relief washed through her body, turned her legs to water. She put the kettle on the hob, and was wiping out the sink with disinfectant when her mother came in.

Anna put her bags down on the table. She saw, more in sorrow than in surprise, Joan's figure slumped across it. 'Tea for me as well, Kit,' she said.

That night Kit caught the tail-end of a whispered conversation: 'You didn't *say* she was a suicide risk, Ralph.'

'I didn't say because I didn't *know*.' She closed her bedroom door; she didn't want to listen to her parents' private thoughts.

Three days later, she came into the kitchen and found her mother on her hands and knees by the sink, working on the flags with a scrubbing brush. 'The blood's gone,' Kit said, puzzled. 'I wiped it up.'

Anna didn't answer her, but rose from the floor, lifted the bucket and threw the soapy water into the sink.

By this time Joan had left, taking everything she owned in the two carrier bags with which she had arrived. Sudden exits were not infrequent among their visitors; they were not like the visitors that other households get. Ralph made inquiries of the police, the Salvation Army, and the Department of Health and Social Security, but he drew a blank. When Anna came to check the first-aid kit – restocking it was one of her responsibilities – she noticed that Joan had taken an extra bandage with her. They saw this as a hopeful sign.

In those years, when the children were growing up, the house was full of people like Joan. Ralph brought some of them from the hostel in London, which was maintained by the charitable trust for which he worked. Others he took in when Social Services didn't know what to do with them, or when there were no beds at the local psychiatric hospital. Sometimes they turned up of their own accord, crouching out of the wind in one of the outhouses until he came home. 'So-and-so's a sad case,' he would say; and over the years, this was what the family came to call them: the Sad Cases. Other people he called Good Souls. 'Your Aunt Emma is giving so-and-so a lift to her drugs clinic in Norwich – she's a good soul.'

And this was how the world was divided, when Kit was growing up – into Good Souls and Sad Cases. There was no wickedness in it.

ONE

On the day of Felix Palmer's funeral, his wife, Ginny, met his mistress, Emma. They had met before, of course. The county of Norfolk is not so populous that they could have avoided each other. Their conduct at these meetings had been shaped by Ginny's lofty and wilful ignorance of the situation: by Emma's sang-froid: by Felix's natural desire to maintain an arrangement that suited him.

Over the years they had coincided in draughty parish halls, in charity committee rooms and at the caucuses of local groups concerned with the protection of what, in the decade just beginning, would be known as 'the environment'. They had bumped into each other in Norwich, shopping in Jarrold's department store; they had exchanged small-talk at exhibitions of craftwork, and occupied neighbouring seats at the theatre.

Once, travelling to London, they had found themselves sole occupants of a first-class carriage. For half an hour they had found enough that was anodyne to pass the time. Then Ginny, excusing herself with a smile, delved into her bag and pulled out a fat paperback book. She retired behind it. Emma examined its cover. A svelte woman, with a small crown perched upon her wimple, stood before a manor house with anachronistic chimney-stacks. The title was in florid gold script: *Wyfe to Crookback*. Emma looked out of the window. The landscape was a sad East England green; crows wheeled over the fields. As they moved from the edge of England to its heart, Emma herself took out a book.

They parted at sooty Liverpool Street with a nod and a smile. London forced no collusion on them, but Norfolk did. A handful of farming and professional families played host to both. At a round of weddings and christenings they had made polite, even warm conversation. At a dozen New Year's Eve parties they had wished each other luck and happiness: and sometimes almost meant it.

Now, on this February morning, Ginny stood surrounded by a knot of mourners. Friends and business associates had turned out for the occasion; Felix had been well-liked in the district. The church occupied high ground, and a ripping wind billowed coats and snapped at woollen head-scarves and brought a flush to aching faces. The mourners could sense the presence of the sea, hidden from them by a belt of pines.

Some of them lingered in the church porch, reading the notices about flower rotas, dusting and brass-cleaning; others stood among the gravestones, looking depressed. They had double-parked in the open area beyond the church gate, and would have to wait their turn to get away. Ginny, leaning on the arm of her son, moved from group to group, offering a few tactful words to soothe their feelings; she understood that death is embarrassing.

Her own family – her son Daniel, who was an architect, her daughter Claire, who was a buyer at Harrods – had been as gentle and as careful of her feelings as anyone could wish. But – even as she deferred the moment – Ginny felt that it was Emma to whom she wished to speak, to whom naturally she should be speaking. Patting her son's arm, smiling up and dismissing him, she made her way across the grass with a short, precisely regulated stride, her high heels spiking holes in the ground like some primitive seed drill.

Ginny Palmer was a sharp, neat, Wallis Simpson sort of woman, to whom black lent an added definition. As she advanced on Emma, she took from her pocket a crisp lace-edged handkerchief, folded it very small and polished the tip of her nose: a gesture quite unnecessary, but somehow drawn out of her by the occasion. You see me, the widow: fastidious but distraught.

Emma Eldred kept her hands in her pockets; she had forgotten her gloves. She wore the coat that she had worn for years, to go out on her doctor's rounds, to go shopping, to go out walking and to meet Felix. She saw no need for any other coat, in her ordinary life or on a day like this; it was dark, it was decent, and – she felt obscurely – it was something Felix would have recognized.

Emma Eldred was not a large woman, but gave the appearance of it: forty-eight years old, her face innocent of cosmetics, her broad feet safely encased in scuffed shoes decorated by leather tassels which somehow failed to cut a dash. Emma had known Ginny's husband since childhood. She might have married him; but Felix was not what Emma considered a serious man. Their relationship had, she felt, borne all the weight it could. As Ginny approached, Emma shrunk into herself, inwardly but not outwardly. A stranger, only partly apprised of the situation, would have taken Ginny for the smart little mistress, and Emma for the tatty old wife.

The women stood together for a moment, not speaking; then as the wind cut her to the bird-bones, Ginny took a half-step closer, and stood holding her mink collar up to her throat. 'Well, Ginny,' Emma said, after a moment. 'I'm not here to act as a wind-break.' She drew her right hand from her pocket, and gave Ginny a pat on the shoulder. It was a brusque gesture, less of consolation than of encouragement; what you might give a weary nag, as it faces the next set of hurdles.

Ginny averted her face. Tears sprang into her eyes. She took out her tiny handkerchief again. 'Why, Emma?' she said. She

7

sounded fretful, but as if her fretfulness might turn to rage. 'Tell me why. You're a doctor.'

'But not his doctor.'

'He wasn't ill. He never had a day's illness.'

Emma fixed her gaze on the tassels of her shoes. She imagined herself looking right through her dead lover; through his customary tweed jacket, his lambswool pullover, his striped shirt, through the skin, through the flesh, into the arteries where Felix's blood moved slowly, a dark underground stream with silted banks. 'No one could have known,' she said. 'No one could have spared you this shock, Ginny. Will you be all right, my dear?'

'There's plenty of insurance,' Ginny said. 'And the house. I'll move of course. But not just yet.'

'Don't do anything in a hurry,' Emma said. She had meant her question in a broad sense, not as an inquiry into Ginny's financial standing. She raised her head, and saw that they were being watched. The eyes of the other mourners were drawn to them, however hard those mourners tried to look away. What do they all think, Emma wondered: that there will be some sort of embarrassing scene? Hardly likely. Not at this time. Not in this place. Not amongst people like ourselves, who have been reared in the service of the great god Self-Control. 'Ginny,' she said, 'you mustn't stand about here. Let Daniel drive you home.'

'A few people are coming back,' Ginny said. She looked at Emma in faint surprise, as if it were natural that she would know the arrangements. 'You should come back too. Let me give you some whisky. A freezing day like this . . . Still, better than rain. Claire's staying on over the weekend.' Ginny raised her hand, and twitched at her collar again. 'Emma, I'd like to see you. Like you to come to the house . . . Mrs Gleave is making vol-au-vents . . .' Her voice tailed off entirely.

Emma's brother, Ralph Eldred, loomed purposefully behind them: a solid figure, hands scrunched into the pockets of his dark wool overcoat. Ginny looked up. The sight of Ralph seemed to restore her. 'Ralph, thank you for coming,' she said. 'Come back with us and have some whisky.'

'I should take myself off,' Ralph said. 'I have to go to Norwich this afternoon to a meeting. But naturally if you want me to, Ginny . . . if I can be of any help . . .' He was weighing considerations, as he always did; his presence was wanted on every hand, and it was simply a question of where he was needed most.

'Why, no,' Ginny said. 'It was a courtesy, Ralph. Do run along.'

She managed a smile. It was her husband's under-occupation that had freed him for his long years of infidelity; but Ralph's days were full, and everybody knew it. There were advantages, she saw, in being married to a man who thought only of work, God and family; even though the Eldred children did look so down at heel, and had been so strangely brought up, and even though Ralph's wife was worn to a shadow slaving for his concerns.

Ralph's wife Anna wore a neat black pillbox hat. It looked very smart, though it was not remotely in fashion. Lingering in the background, she gave Ginny a nod of acknowledgement and sympathy. It was an Anna Eldred nod, full of I-do-not-intrude. Ginny returned it; then Ralph took his wife's arm, and squired her away at a good clip towards their parked car.

Ginny looked after them. 'You wonder about marriage,' she said suddenly. 'Are marriages all different, or all alike?'

Emma shrugged, shoulders stiff inside her old coat. 'No use asking me, Ginny.'

Inside the car, Ralph said, 'It's not right, you know. It's not, is

9

it? For Emma to find out like that. More or less by chance. And only when it was all over.'

'It was all over very quickly,' Anna said. 'From what I gather.'

'Yes, but to have no priority in being told —'

'I expect you think Ginny should have rung her from the hospital, do you? Just given her a tinkle from the intensive-care unit?'

'— to have no right to know. That's what galls me. It's inhuman. And now Ginny gets all the sympathy, all the attention. I'm not saying she doesn't need and deserve it. But Emma gets nothing, not a word. Only this public embarrassment.'

'I see — you think that as Emma was the *maîtresse en titre*, she should be allowed to put on a show of her own?' Anna sighed. 'I'm sure Felix has left her some fine diamonds, and a château for her old age.'

A contractor's van drew up in front of the Eldreds' car, adding to the traffic jam; restoration work was going on at the church. Two workmen got out, and began to untie a ladder from the roof-rack. A lesser man with Ralph's schedule would have fretted at the delay. But Ralph showed his impatience only by a little tapping of his forefinger against the steering wheel. There was a school nearby, and the voices of children drifted from the playground, carried on the wind like gulls' cries.

The couple who blocked them drove off, nodding, raising hands in a stiff-fingered wave. The contractor moved his van. Ralph pulled out on to the road. Anna saw the children dashing and bumping and careening behind a fence: bullets trussed in duffle coats, their faces hidden under hoods.

The route home lay inland, through narrow lanes between farms: flat airy fields, where tractors lay at rest. Ralph pulled up to let a duck dawdle across the road, on its way from a barnyard to nowhere. 'I'll tell you,' he said. 'I'll tell you what's the worst of it. Emma's got nothing. Nothing. She's given twenty years to Felix and now she's on her own.'

'Emma's given something,' Anna said. 'I think to say that she's given twenty years is being melodramatic.'

'Why is it,' Ralph said, 'that women manage to be so cool in these situations? What's all this keeping up a good front? Why do they think they have to do it? I heard Ginny talking about *insurance policies*, for God's sake.'

'I only mean, that Emma's life has suited her. She had what she wanted – a part-time man. Felix didn't use her. The reverse, I think. She could have married. If she'd chosen to. She didn't have to wait on Felix.'

'Married? Could she?' Ralph turned his head.

'Look out,' Anna said, with a languor born of experience. Ralph put his foot on the brake; a farm truck slowly extruded its back end from a muddy and half-concealed driveway.

'Sorry,' Ralph said. 'Could she? Who could she have married then?'

'Oh Ralph, I don't mean any one person, not this particular man or that particular man . . . I only mean that if she had wanted to marry, if that had been what she preferred, she could have done it. But marriage entails things, like learning to boil eggs. Things that are beyond Emma.'

'I can't see men beating a path to her door.' Ralph edged the car painfully down the lane, squeezing it past the truck, which had got stuck. 'Not Emma. No beauty.'

'Felix liked her.'

'Felix was a creature of habit.'

'Most men are.'

Ralph fell silent. He was very fond of his sister; no one should think otherwise. Emma was kind, clever, wise . . . and lonely, he'd supposed: a little figure glimpsed on a river bank, while the pleasure craft sped by. This notion of her as a manipulator, of Felix as a little fish that she played at the end of her stick and hook . . . Seems unlikely to me, he thought. But then, what do I know?

The journey took them a half-hour, through back roads and lanes, through straggling hamlets of red brick or flint cottages, whose only amenity was a post-box; between agri-business fields, wide open to a vast grey sky. Ralph pulled up with a jolt at the gate of their house. Anna shot forward, one hand on the dashboard and one on her hat. 'Can I leave you here? I'm late.'

As she unravelled her seat-belt, Ralph turned to look at her. 'Those people at the funeral, all those friends of Felix's, how many of them do you think knew about him and Emma?'

Anna took her house keys from her bag. 'Every one of them.'

'How did Ginny bear it?'

'Easily. Or so everyone says.' Anna swung her door open and her legs out, setting her high heels daintily into the mud. 'What time will you be back?'

'Seven o'clock. Maybe eight.'

Nine, then, Anna thought. 'Everybody knew except you,' she said. 'I suppose you still feel a fool.'

'I suppose I do.' Ralph reached over to close the passenger door. 'But then, I still don't see why I should have known. Not as if their affair was the flamboyant sort. Not as if it was . . .' he searched for the word, '. . . torrid.'

Torrid, Anna thought. She watched him drive away. Interesting how our vocabulary responds, providing us with words we have never needed before, words stacked away for us, neatly folded into our brain and there for our use: like a bride's lifetime supply of linen, or a ducal trove of monogrammed china. Death will overtake us before a fraction of those words are used.

TWO

Anna, as Ralph vanished from view, plucked the afternoon post from the wooden mail-box by the gate; then picked her way over rutted ground to the front door. The drive was more of a farm track than anything else; often it looked as if a herd of beasts had been trampling it. The mail-box was something new. Julian, her eldest boy, had made it. Now the postman's legs were spared, if not the family's.

The Red House was a farmhouse that had lost its farm; it retained a half-acre of ground upon which grew sundry bicycle sheds, a dog kennel and a wire dog-run with the wire broken, a number of leaning wooden huts filled with the detritus of family life, and an unaccountable horse-trough, very ancient and covered with lichen. Recently, since Julian had been at home, the hedges had been cut back and some ground cleared, and the rudiments of a vegetable garden were appearing. The house and its ramshackle surroundings formed a not-displeasing organic whole; Julian's attempt at agriculture seemed an imposition on the natural state of things, as if it were the bicycle sheds that were the work of nature, and the potatoes the work of man.

The house itself was built of red brick, and stood side-on to the road. It had a tiled roof, steeply pitched; in season, the crop-spraying plane buzzed its chimney-stacks and complicated arrangements of television aerials. There were a number of small windows under the eaves, and these gave the house a restless look: as if it would just as soon wander across the lane and put down its foundations in a different field.

Two years before, when it seemed that the older children would shortly be off their hands, Anna had suggested they should look for a smaller place. It would be cheaper to run, she had said, knowing what line of reasoning would appeal to Ralph. With his permission she had rung up Felix Palmer's firm, to talk about putting the house on the market. 'You can't mean it,' Felix had said. 'Leave, Anna? After all these years? I hope and trust you wouldn't be going far?'

'Felix,' Anna had said, 'do you recall that you're an estate agent? Aren't you supposed to encourage people to sell their houses?'

'Yes, but not my friends. I should be a poor specimen if I tried to uproot my friends.'

'Shall I try someone else, then?'

'Oh, no need for that . . . If you're sure . . .'

'I'm far from sure,' Anna said. 'But you might send someone to look around. Put a value on it.'

Felix came himself, of course. He brought a measuring tape, and took notes as he went in a little leather-bound book. On the second storey, he grew bored. 'Anna, dear girl, let's just say . . . a wealth of versatile extra accommodation . . . attics, so forth . . . an abundance of storage space. Leave it at that, shall we? Buyers don't want, you know, to have to exercise their brains.' He sighed, at the foot of the attic stairs. 'I remember the day I brought you here, you and Ralph, to talk you into it . . .' His eyes crept over her, assessing time's work. 'You were fresh from Africa then.'

I was tired and cold that day, she thought, tired and cold and pregnant, rubbing my chilblains in that draughty wreck of a drawing room; the Red House smelled of mice and moulds, and there were doors banging overhead, and cracked window glass, and spiders. To pre-empt his next comment, she put her hand on his arm: 'Yes, Felix. It was, it was a long time ago.'

Felix nodded. 'I remember saying to you – it's the sort of place you come to grips with in your own good time.'

'And we never have.' She smiled.

'You filled it with children. That's the main thing.'

'Yes. And for all their presence improved it, we might as well have stabled horses. Well, Felix – what's the verdict?'

'There'd be interest,' he said cautiously. 'London people perhaps.'

'Oh – fancy prices,' Anna said.

'But consider, Anna – do you really want to do this rather drastic thing?'

Felix closed his notebook and slipped it back into his pocket. They went downstairs, and had a glass of sherry. Felix stared gloomily over the garden. Slowly the conventions of his calling seemed to occur to him. 'Useful range of outbuildings,' he muttered, and jotted this phrase in his book.

That evening Felix telephoned Ralph. 'Why don't you hang on?' he said. 'Prices are going up all over East Anglia. A year from now you might make a killing. Tell Anna I advise staying put.'

'I will.' Ralph was relieved. 'I take her point, of course – Kit and Julian away, Robin will be off in a year or so, and then there'll be just the two of us and Becky, we'll be rattling around. But of course, it's not often that we're just the family. We get a lot of visitors.'

'You do, rather,' Felix said.

'And we have to have somewhere to put them.'

Two days later, while Ralph and Anna were still debating the matter, their boy Julian turned up with his suitcase. He wasn't going back to university, he said. He was finished with all that. He dumped his case in his old room in the attics, next door to Robin; they had put the boys up there years ago, so that they could make a noise. Julian offered no explanation of himself, except that he did not like being away, had worried about his family and constantly wondered how they were. He made himself pleasant and useful about the house and neighbour-hood, and showed no inclination to move out, to move on, to go anywhere else at all.

Then Kit wrote from London; she phoned her parents every week, but sometimes things are easier in a letter.

I'm not sure yet what I should do after my finals. There's still more than a term to go and I have various ideas, but I keep changing my mind. It isn't that I want to sit about wasting time, but I would like to come home for a few weeks, just to think things through. Dad, I know you mentioned to me that I could work for the Trust for a year, but the truth is I've had enough of London – for the moment, anyway. I wondered if there was something I could do in Norwich . . .

'Well,' Ralph said, re-reading the letter. 'This is unexpected. But of course she must come home, if she wants to.'

'Of course,' Anna said.

Her perspective altered. She felt that she must settle to it, give way to the house's demands, perhaps until she was an old woman.

When on the afternoon of the funeral Anna let herself into the wide square hall, she peeled off her gloves slowly, and placed them on the hall-stand, a vast and unnecessary article of furniture that Ralph had picked up in an antique shop in Great Yarmouth. 'No other family in the county,' she had said at the time, 'feels they need an object like this.' She looked with a fresh sense of wonder and dislike at its barley-sugar legs and its many little drawers and its many little dust-trapping ledges and its brass hooks for gentlemen's hats, and she saw her face in the dim spotted oval of mirror, and smoothed her hair back from her forehead, then took off her coat and threw it over the banisters.

The Norfolk climate gave Anna a bloodless look, tinged her thin hands with violet. Every winter she would think of Africa; days when, leaving her warm bed in a hot early dawn, she had felt her limbs grow fluid, and the pores of her face open like petals, and her ribs, free from their accustomed tense gauge, move to allow her a full, voluptuary's breath. In England she never felt this confidence, not even in a blazing July. The thermometer might register the heat, but her body was sceptical. English heat is fitful; clouds pass before the sun.

Anna went into the kitchen. Julian had heard her come in, and was setting out cups for tea.

'How did it go?'

'It went well, I suppose,' Anna said. 'We buried him. The main object was achieved. How do funerals ever go?'

'How was Mrs Palmer?'

'Ginny was very much herself. A party of them were going back to the house, for vol-au-vents provided by Mrs Gleave.' Anna made a face. 'And whisky. She seemed very insistent on the whisky. If you'd have asked for gin – well, I don't know what!'

Julian reached for the teapot. 'Nobody would have gin, would they, at a funeral?'

'No, it would be unseemly,' Anna said. Mother's ruin, she thought. The abortionist's drink. A mistress's tipple. Flushed complexions and unbuttoned afternoons.

'And how was Emma?'

'Emma was staunch. She was an absolute brick. She turned up in that old coat, by the way.'

'You wouldn't have expected her to get a new one.'

'Oh, I don't know. A lesser woman might have hired sables for the day. And implied that Felix had given them to her.'

Anna smiled, her hands cradling her tea-cup. 'Your old dad and I were talking on the way home. About how he went on for so long, without knowing about Felix and Emma.'

'Twit,' Julian said.

Some three years earlier, the year before Kit went to university, Ralph Eldred had been in Holt for the afternoon. It was a Wednesday, late in the year; at Gresham's School, blue-kneed boys were playing hockey. The small town's streets were empty of tourists; the sky was the colour of pewter.

Ralph decided – and it was an unaccustomed indulgence on his part – to have some tea. The girl behind the counter directed him upstairs; wrapped in bakery smells, he climbed a steep staircase with a rickety handrail, and found himself in a room where the ceiling was a scant seven foot high, and a half-dozen tables were set with pink cloths and white china. At the top of the stairs, Ralph, who was a man of six foot, bent his head to pass under a beam; as he straightened up and turned his head, he looked directly into the eye of Felix Palmer, who was in the act of pouring his sister Emma a second cup of Darjeeling.

The twenty minutes which followed were most peculiar. Not that anything Emma did was strange; for she simply looked up and greeted him, and said, 'Why don't you get that chair there and put it over here, and would you like a toasted tea-cake or would you like a bun or would you like both?' As for Felix, he just lowered his Harris tweed elbow, replaced the teapot on its mat and said, 'Ralph, you old bugger, skiving off again?'

Ralph sat down; he looked ashen; when the waitress brought him a cup, his hand trembled. The innocent sight that had met his eyes when he came up the staircase had suddenly and shockingly revealed its true meaning, and what overset Ralph was not that his sister was having an affair, but his instant realization that the affair was part of the world-order, one of the givens, one of the assumptions of the parish, and that only he, Ralph – stupid, blind and emotionally inept – had failed to recognize the fact: he and his wife Anna, whom he must go home and tell.

Ask him how he knew, that moment he swivelled his head under the beam and met the bland blue eye of Felix: ask him how he knew, and he couldn't tell you. The knowledge simply penetrated his bone-marrow. When they brought the toasted tea-cake, he took a bite, and replaced the piece on the plate, and found that what he had bitten turned into a pebble in his mouth, and he couldn't swallow it. Felix took a brown paper bag out of his pocket, and said, 'Look, Emma, I've got that wool that Ginny's been wanting for her blasted tapestry, the shop's had it on order for three months, I just popped in on the off-chance, and they said it came in this morning.' He laid the skein out on the white cloth; it was a dead bracken colour. 'Hope to heaven it's the right shade,' he said. 'Ginny goes on about dye batches.'

Emma made some trite reply; Felix began to tell about a church conversion over in Fakenham that had come on to the firm's books earlier that week. Then they had talked about the salary of the organist at the Palmers' parish church; then about the price of petrol. Ralph could not make conversation at all. The loop of brown wool remained on the table. He stared at it as if it were a serpent.

Ralph arrived home alone that evening – which surprised Anna. No cronies, no hangers-on, no fat file of papers in his hand: no rushing to the telephone either, no flinging of a greeting over his shoulder, no distracted inquiries about where this and where that and who rang and what messages. He sat down in the kitchen; and when Anna came in, to see why he was so subdued, he was rocking on the back legs of his chair and staring at the wall. 'You know, Anna,' he said, 'I think I'd like a drink. I've had a shock.'

Alcohol, for Ralph, was a medicinal substance only. Brandy might be taken for colic, when other remedies had failed. Hot whisky and lemon might be taken for colds, for Ralph recognized that people with colds need cheering up, and he was all for cheerfulness. But drink as social unction was something that had never been part of his life. His parents did not drink, and he had never freed himself from his parents. He had nothing against drinking in others, of course; the house was well-stocked, he was a hospitable man. When the tongue-tied or the chilled called on him, Ralph was ready with glasses and ice-buckets. His eye was inexpert and his nature generous, so the drinks he poured were four times larger than ordinary measures. A local councillor, upon leaving the Red House, had been breathalyzed by the police in East Dereham, and found to be three times over the legal limit. On another occasion, a female social worker from Norwich had been sick on the stairs. When these things happened, Ralph would say, 'My uncle, Holy James, he was right, I think. Total abstinence is best. Things run out of control so quickly, don't they?'

So now, when Anna poured him a normal-sized measure of whisky, he judged it to be mean and small. He looked at it in bewilderment, but said nothing. After a while, still rocking back on the chair, he said, 'Emma is having an affair with Felix Palmer. I saw them today.'

'What, *in flagrante*?' Anna said.

'No. Having a cup of tea in Holt.'

Anna said nothing for a time: then, 'Ralph, may I explain something to you?' She sat down at the table and clasped her hands on the scrubbed white wood. It was as if she were going to pray aloud, but did not know what to pray for. 'You must remember how Emma and Felix used to go around together, when they were young. Now, you know that, don't you?'

'Yes,' Ralph said. He stopped rocking. The front legs of his

chair came down with a clunk. 'But that's going right back –
that's going back to the fifties, before she was qualified, when
she was in London and she'd come up for the odd weekend.
That was before we went abroad. And then he married Ginny.
Oh God,' he said. 'You mean it's been going on for years.'

'I do. Years and years and years.'

'Would it be . . . for instance . . . when we came back from
Africa?'

Anna nodded. 'Oh, yes. It's so many years, you see, that
people no longer bother to talk about it.'

'And you knew. Why didn't I know?'

'It's hard to imagine. Perhaps because you don't notice
people.'

'But people are all my life,' Ralph said. 'God help me.
Everything I do concerns people. What else do I ever think
about?'

'Perhaps you don't think about them in quite the right way.
Perhaps there's a – gap – in the way that you think about
them.'

'Something missing,' Ralph said. 'Well, there must be,
mustn't there? If that's the case I'll have to sit down and talk to
myself and try to examine it, whatever it is, this lack, won't I?
Otherwise it's obvious I'm not fit to be at large.' He shook his
head. 'I'll tell you what puzzles me, though. There's Emma
living in her cottage right on the main street in Foulsham, and
there's Felix over at Blakeney, and since we know innumerable
people in between –'

'Yes, we know people. But it's as I say, they don't talk about
it any more.'

'But why didn't somebody tell me?'

'Why should they? How would they have broached the
topic?'

'Why didn't *you* tell me?'

'What would you have done with the information?'

Ralph was still shaking his head. He couldn't take this in – that his discovery, so exciting to him, was stale and soporific to everyone else. 'What I can't understand is how in a place like this they could conduct what must be so blatantly obvious – I mean, the comings and goings, she can't go to Blakeney I suppose so he must come to Foulsham, his car must be parked there, all hours of the night –'

Anna smiled.

'No,' Ralph said. 'I don't suppose it's like that, is it? I suppose they go to teashops quite a lot. I suppose it's a – mental companionship, is it?'

'I think it might be, largely. But people like Felix and Emma can get away with a lot, you know. They have everything well under control.'

'It's never damaged their standing,' Ralph said. 'I mean, their standing in the community. Do the children know?'

'Kit knows. The boys know, I suppose, but they never mention it. It wouldn't interest them, would it?'

'What does Kit think?'

'You know she always admires her aunt.'

'I hope her life won't be like that,' Ralph said. 'My God, I hope it won't. I don't want Kit to turn into some plain woman driving about the countryside in a tweed coat to share a pot of tea with some old bore. I hope somebody flashy and rich comes and carries her off and gives her diamonds. I don't mind if she isn't steady. I want Kit to have a good time.'

'How old-fashioned you are!' Anna laughed. 'You talk about her as if she were a chorus girl. Kit will buy her own diamonds, if it crosses her mind to want any.' Anna looked down at the minute solitaire that had winked for twenty-five years above her wedding ring. 'And Ralph, there is no need to insult Felix. You like him, you always have, we all like him.'

'Yes. I know. But things look different now.'

He put his empty glass down on the table. This is more than a failure of knowledge, he thought, it is a failure of self-knowledge. Anna poured him another whisky. He ignored it, so she drank it herself.

Sitting at the kitchen table, Julian said, 'I thought Kit would have come home for the funeral.'

'It was mainly our generation,' Anna said. 'There were a lot of people there. I think three Eldreds were enough.'

'An elegant sufficiency,' Julian said.

His mother laughed. 'Where did you get that expression?'

'I heard Kit say it. But didn't you think she'd have wanted to be there? As she's so friendly with Daniel Palmer these days.'

Felix's son, the architect, had a flat above his office in Holt. He was interested in Kit; he had taken her to the theatre, and out to dinner, and invited her to go out in the boat he kept at Blakeney. Anna said, 'I think Kit regards Daniel as a provider of treats. A funeral is not a treat.'

'When will she be coming home, then?

'Not till Easter. She's got her exams in a matter of weeks, you know.'

'Yes, I do know. You don't have to keep mentioning things like that. Terms. Exams.'

'We have to talk about you, Julian. But perhaps not this afternoon.' She looked over the rim of her cup. 'What have you done today?'

'I started putting in those poles for the back fence.'

'And have you seen your girlfriend?'

The slight vulgarity and childishness of the expression struck Julian. It was as if his mother had spilled her tea on the table, or put her fingers in the sugar bowl.

'I'm going over tomorrow. I just wanted to get a start on

that fence, as the rain was keeping off. I wish Kit would come home soon. I want her to meet Sandra's mother. I want to know what she'll think of her.'

So Sandra will be with us for another summer, Anna thought. With Julian you had to glean things, here and there.

A few days after the funeral, Emma went to the shrine at Walsingham. She was not sure why; her faith, if it still existed, was not something she displayed in public. But when you cannot cope with grief, she reasoned, you can do worse than observe the forms that have helped other people cope with it. At Felix's funeral the minister had said that, even in the depth of misery, the familiar forms of prayer can lift the heart towards Christian joy. Very well, Emma thought grimly, let's try it. Something is needed. For Ginny, there were undertakers. There was the question of probate. There was the business of organizing Mrs Gleave and the vol-au-vents. But for me there is nothing. An empty space. A lack of occupation. It is as if I have been told of a death that has taken place in a distant country. It is as if I have no claim on sympathy, because I have heard of the death of a person my friends do not know. There is no body. There is no corpse. Just this absence, this feeling of something unfinished.

Skirting Fakenham, taking the back roads towards the shrine and the sea, she found her car alone on the road. Across the flat fields towers spiked the snow-charged sky, the clouds pregnant and bowed with cold; Norfolk is a land of churches, some open to the sky, their chancels colonized by nettles, their naves by blackthorn and brambles. In those not yet redundant, congregations dwindle; the Samaritans' notices, flapping in the porches, attest to the quality and frequency of rural despair.

In Walsingham, the car park was empty. The streets were devoid of tourists and pilgrims, and the old buildings – half-

timber and brick and stone, steep roof and Dutch gable –
seemed to have moved closer together, as if the town were
closing itself down for the winter. By the Anglican shrine,
plaster saints looked out from shop windows: and woven saints,
with tapestry eyes. Touches of gilt glinted here and there on a
cardboard halo; postcards were for sale, and prayers printed in
mock black-letter on mock scrolls. You could buy candles,
which you might put to secular use; other windows displayed
recordings of plainchant, and pots of honey in stoneware jars,
and boxes of Norfolk Lavender soap. Walsingham tea-towels
were on offer, jars of chutney, tins of shortbread, Earl Grey tea-
bags in cod Victorian packaging; and there were herb pillows,
Olde Englishe Peppermint Lumps, pot-pourri and fluffy toys,
wall-plaques, paperweights and scented drawer-liners – all the
appurtenances, in fact, that you would expect to find at an
ancient pilgrim site. Trade was poor. The only visible inhabitant
was a woman with a shopping basket over her arm and a pug
dog on a lead. She nodded to Emma and walked on, huddling
into the shadow of the Abbey's wall.

Emma went up the path to the church. It was a building put
up in the 1930s, and its exterior, disappointingly plain, hid its
dim papistical contents: devotional candles blinking, sad-eyed
virgins pouting in gold frames. She asked herself, what would
my father have said, what would my father have said to a
bauble-shop like this? Matthew Eldred seemed very far away,
very old and dead and gone. Not so Felix. Alone in her cottage
in Foulsham, she still listened for the sound of his key in the
lock.

Emma lurked about towards the back of the church, away
from the altar. Finally she sat down on a chair at the end of a
row. She gave herself permission for tears, but she was not able
to cry. Like her sister-in-law Anna, she had trained herself out
of it. The thought of Felix lay like a stone inside her chest.

Outside, some sort of building work seemed to be going on; she could hear the monotonous thump of hammers and the whirring of drills. In my family, she thought, we practise restraint and the keeping of secrets, and the thoughts we respect are unvoiced thoughts; even Felix, an open secret, was a secret of a kind. But our secrets do not keep us. They worry at us; they wear us away, from the inside out.

On the back wall were wooden plaques, names and dates: thanks given, intentions stated. *Thanks for preservation in a motor accident, 1932. For reunion of husband and wife, after prayer at the shrine, 1934. Success in an examination, Thanks, 1935.* What minute considerations we expect God to entertain, Emma thought. *Thanks for a happy death, prayed for at the Holy House.* Who put that here, and how did they know it was happy? Some plaques gave nothing away. Upon these the visitor might exercise imagination: *Prayers Answered.*

Near these plaques, the water from the Holy Well was made available in buckets. Pilgrims might help themselves, by dipping with assorted vessels; a table, stacked up with prayer books, held also the abandoned top of a Thermos flask, some paper cups of the kind tea machines dispense, and some beakers of moulded plastic, each one frilly at the rim, as if it had been gnawed. Emma thought the arrangements unsanitary. She went out, her gloves in her hand.

In the porch was a vast book, well-thumbed, its pages ruled into columns. A notice promised ALL WHOSE NAMES ARE INSCRIBED IN THIS BOOK WILL BE PRAYED FOR AT THE SHRINE.

Emma took her pen out of her pocket, turned to a clean page and wrote down the date. She did not put Felix's name in the book, because she believed that energy should be directed towards the living, not the dead. She did not put her own name, because she believed she would manage well enough. But she wrote the names of her brother and his wife:

RALPH ELDRED

ANNA ELDRED

Beneath she wrote:

KATHERINE ELDRED

then hesitated, and skipped one line, before

JULIAN ELDRED

ROBERT ELDRED

REBECCA ELDRED

It was half dark when Emma left the porch. Between the church and the road there was no pavement; she crept uphill by the high wall, protected only by heaven's benevolence from the cars behind her. Eddies of sleet swirled in a huddle of stone and flint, slapping at window glass and melting underfoot. Sitting in an almost empty café, her hands around a mug of hot chocolate, she thought of that other frozen afternoon, when Ralph's curly head emerged up the staircase of the Holt tea-room, and dipped under the beam, and swivelled, gaze focusing . . . If Ralph had not come upon them that particular day, his sensibilities skinned by the cold, he would have continued in his obstinate and peculiar ignorance; when Felix died, they would have stood at his graveside as two old family friends, and Ralph would have given her not a word of sympathy except that due between decent people when a contemporary has quit the scene. And that, she thought, would have suited me.

Lines of poetry ran through Emma's head. Auden, she thought. She was pleased at being able to identify it, because she was not a literary woman. They were insistent lines, stuffed with a crude menace.

The glacier knocks in the cupboard,
The desert sighs in the bed,

> And the crack in the tea-cup opens
> A lane to the land of the dead.

Emma shared the café with one be-skirted cleric, who was reading the *Daily Telegraph*. An oil stove popped and hissed at her back. She thought again of crying, but she was afraid the man might put his newspaper down and try to console her. Instead she buttoned her coat, and braced herself for the twilight and cold, the drive home to Foulsham. I hardly know what I am any more she thought: a Good Soul, or a Sad Case.

> O look, look in the mirror,
> O look in your distress;
> Life remains a blessing
> Although you cannot bless.

THREE

Kit sleeps, blanketed in heat. She rolls on to her back. Her lips
move. What is she saying? Mama, mama: milk, milk, milk. Her
wrist pushes her hair back from her forehead. She turns over
again. The sheet creases beneath her, damp from her body. An
institutional counterpane slides to the floor.

Kit's hand clenches and unclenches – fat baby fist. The air is
too hot to breathe. Soon Felicia will come, in her blue scarf,
and lift her out of the mist of mosquito nets.

Her eyes open to an expanse of white wall. She turns her
eyes, and sees the polished floor and the fallen bedcover, and her
own bare arm dangling from the sheets, like someone else's
limb. It is 7.30, a dirty London morning, traffic building up.
There is a hint of spring in the air.

In her dream, she has been to Africa.

She sits up slowly, pulling the top sheet across her breasts, as
if someone had come into the room. She is in her term-time
lodging, a women's hall of residence. Her little gold watch ticks
away on top of a pile of textbooks. Her jeans and warm plaid
shirt are folded on a chair. Outside in the corridor her fellow
residents are going in and out of bathrooms in their towelling
robes, their hair in various arrangements of turbans and pins.
They stop to exchange words, to say that the central heating is
ridiculous, it is like being in the tropics, a complaint will
definitely have to be made. Lavatories flush. From the basement
drifts the aroma of breakfasts seething on a range, pallid scraps
of bacon, mushrooms stewed black. Toast hardens in its racks.

29

In Norfolk, at the Red House, her mother Anna dreams of a cell. She feels against her bare legs the rasp of a prison blanket, and under her hand the metal of a prison bedstead. A woman's voice tells her, 'The colonel has refused your request for a mirror.' Anna wakes.

The room is cold. Ralph has pulled the blankets over his head. She sits up, massages her temples with her fingertips. With little circular motions, as if it were vanishing cream, she rubs the dream away. She forgets it. Forgetting is an art like other arts. It needs dedication and practice.

As for Kit – she washes and dresses and goes down the big carved staircase, down the corridors smelling of parsnips and polish. On her way from breakfast she plucks a letter out of the pigeonhole marked 'E'.

The letter is from her father. Ralph is a good correspondent – whereas in other families, as she knows, fathers never put pen to paper. She slides the letter into the pocket of her jeans, to read at lunchtime over her salad roll and yoghurt; jogs out across the dappled dampness of Russell Square, towards the Tube and the Thames and an airless lecture room.

Her dream trails after her, contaminating her day.

Julian, with no reason to wake, sleeps till half-past eight. Bright letters float from a summer sky, and form themselves into nonsense words. It is his usual dream; deprived of the terror it once held, it still carries its component of frustration.

Emma does not dream. She has taken to insomnia, walking the rooms of her cottage in the small hours, the hours of deep rural silence. She does not draw the curtains; outside her cottage a street light burns, and shines on her medical books in their orderly shelves, and the washing-up she has left in the sink.

★

Ralph dreams of his father.

This is the town, the date, the place, to which his dreams return him: Ralph walks on cobblestones, his wrist manacled in his grandfather's hand, his eyes turning upwards to scan the column of his grandfather's body. Wind soughs around the streets and the high stony houses and their chimney-pots. Ralph is three years old. His grandfather lifts him into his arms, and wraps him in his coat to keep out the cold.

'In my day, Ralphie,' he says, 'we used to have donkey races round the market-place. And in my grandfather's day, they used to have pig-hunts, and chimney sweeps dipping for pennies in a basin of flour. And then they used to have fireworks after, and burning of Boney.'

His Uncle James says, 'Poor Ralphie! He does not know who Boney is.'

Ralph turns his head, against Grandpa's woollen shoulder. He lifts his chin and wriggles his body, trying to turn in Grandpa's arms. There is his father, Matthew Eldred, one step behind them. But the shoulder blocks his view; or perhaps it is Uncle James who stands between himself and Matthew. His father is there, he knows; but Ralph cannot see his face.

This is Ralph's first memory: the cobbles, the deep moaning of the wind, the thick cloth of his grandfather's overcoat sawing against his cheek.

The Eldred family belonged to the country which is called the Brecklands; it is a country bounded by chalk and peat, but covered by a mantle of shifting sand. Its open fields are strewn with flint or choked with bracken; they are edged by fir trees twisted into fantastic forms. It is a country of flint-knappers and warreners: latterly of archaeologists and military personnel. There are barrows and mounds, tumuli and ancient tracks; there

31

are oaks and elms. The Romans have left their coins, their skeletons and their fragments of terracotta; the military have set down their huts and wire fences among the ruins of monasteries and castles. Everywhere one senses the presence of standing water, of wading birds, of alders and willow, and of swans rising against the sky.

This is meeting-house country, chapel country; the churches are decayed or badly restored, and the sense of the past is strong, seeping and sinister. Halls and churches have perished, fire eaten thatch, air eaten stone; buildings rejoin the landscape, their walls reduced to flint and rubble strewn across the fields. Some artefact you drop tonight may be lost by morning, but the plough turns up treasure trove. In this country, man's work seems ephemeral, his influence transitory. Summer scorches the heath. Winter brings a pale damp light. The sky is dove-coloured; the sun breaks through it in broad glittering rays, like the rays which, in papist prints, signify the presence of the Holy Spirit.

Matthew Eldred, Ralph's father, was born near the market town of Swaffham in the year 1890. His family were printers, lay preachers. His grandfather had printed pamphlets and tracts. His father had printed handbills and auction catalogues and stock lists, and the privately financed memoirs of clergymen and schoolmasters. Their homes, and the homes of their friends, were temples of right-thinking, of inky scholarship, sabbatarian dullness; their religion was active, proselytizing, strenuous and commonsensical. They saw no need to inquire into God's nature; they approached Him through early rising, Bible study and earnest, futile attempts at humility. The Eldreds were as clever in charity as they were in business – casting their bread on the waters, and rubbing their hands in anticipation of the plump milky loaves that would come back to stack upon the shelves of their family and friends.

Matthew Eldred's brother James, who was four years his junior, was ordained in the Church of England just after the end of the Great War. He left almost at once for the African missions, and so he missed Matthew's wedding; Matthew married a grey-eyed girl called Dorcas Carey, whose father was a local wood merchant, and whose connections outside the county – her elder sister had married a Yorkshireman – had been examined and then forgiven.

James reappeared a decade later – thinner, cheerful, somewhat jaundiced – for the baptism of his brother's first child, Ralph. Dorcas wore a look of bewilderment; after a decade, she had got something right. Another baby, a daughter, followed two years later. James was still, as he termed it, on furlough, but he was not idle; he was working in the East End of London in a home for derelicts and drunks. When Ralph was four years old, Africa opened and swallowed Uncle James again. Only letters came, on tissue-thin sheets of paper, and photographs of naked native children and round thatched huts: of unnamed clergymen and lady assistants with large teeth and white sun-hats: of catechumens in white gloves and white frocks.

Ralph has these photographs still. He keeps them in brown envelopes, their subjects named on the back (when Uncle James' memory has obliged) in Ralph's own large, energetic handwriting. And dated? Sometimes. Uncle James peers at some fading spinster, weathered by the African sun; at some wriggling black child clothed only in a string of beads. 'How would I know? 1930?' Ralph makes the record on the back of each one; makes it in soft pencil, in case Uncle James should reconsider. He has respect for dates; he cares for the past. He files the envelopes in his bureau drawers. One day, he thinks, he might write the history of his family. But then his mind shies away, thinking of what would have to be omitted.

His father and mother stand in pewter frames on his bureau,

watching him as he works. Matthew Eldred has grown stout; his watch chain stretches across his belly. Self-conscious before the photographer, he fingers his lapel. In middle age, Dorcas has the face of a Voortrekker or an American plainswoman: a transparent face, that waits for God to do his worst.

When Ralph was eight years old and his sister Emma was six, Matthew moved his family and his business from Swaffham to Norwich. He began by printing ration books, and ended by growing rich.

The war came. 'Do you wish,' Emma asked Ralph, 'that you were big enough to fight?' Emma doubled up her fist and pounded at the drawing-room sofa, till her fist bounced back at her and dust flew up, and her mother came from the kitchen and slapped her.

A year or so later, they heard talk behind closed doors. 'Yarmouth Grammar School moved to the Midlands ... Lowestoft evacuated yesterday ...' They had visited the seaside – a pointless excursion, the children thought, because the beaches were mined – and seen the first wave of London evacuees, decanted from pleasure steamers, fetching up in coastal villages with their gas masks. They stood by the road and stared, these children, stubble-headed and remote. Now the children were moving on again, deeper into England.

Emma turned her eyes on Ralph. 'What is it like, evacuated?' she hissed.

He shook his head. 'It won't happen to us, I don't think. It's the ones from the coast that are going.'

'I mean,' Emma said, 'how do you fix it?'

He put his finger to his lips. He did not think, then or later, that his parents were cruel: only staid, elderly, without imagination.

When the war ended, there was more whispered discussion.

34

His parents debated taking in an orphan – perhaps the child of some local girl who had given way to an airman. Or an older child, a companion for Ralph ... They had heard through some church connection of a most unfortunate Lowestoft case, a boy of Ralph's age exactly: whose father, a gas-company worker, had been killed when the bomb fell on Lorne Park Road, and whose mother had died when Waller's Restaurant received a direct hit. 'What was she doing in a restaurant, that's what I'd like to know?' Mrs Eldred said. There was some suggestion that the child might have lived a giddy life before his bereavement. The project was dropped; Ralph's companion faded away, into the realms of might-have-been.

For when you surveyed – his father said – when you surveyed the want in this world, when you peered into the bottomless pit of human improvidence and foolishness, it occurred to you that if there was to be charity it must be systematic.

Much later rationing ended. In the Eldred household it continued. 'There's nothing wrong with economy,' his mother said. If you wanted anything nice to eat, you had to eat it outside the house.

When Ralph was fifteen years old, he went to stay with his aunt in Yorkshire. The Synod of Whitby, his Uncle James called the Yorkshire set; they were too dour, cramped and narrow for James' High Church tastes. The trip north had been intended as a holiday, Ralph supposed; by now he was beginning to be critical of his family, and it seemed congruent with everything else in his life that a holiday and a penance should be so very alike.

The Synod occupied a dark house, and inside it were brown shadows. It contained an unreasonable number of upright chairs, with seats of slippery polished brown leather; it was as if preparations were constantly in hand for a public meeting, a chapel get-together. In the dining room the chairs were high-backed and unyielding, of a particularly officious type. Small meals were sanctified by a lengthy grace. The bookcases had glass fronts, and they were locked; upon the sideboard stood vases of dark glass, like cups of blood.

His cousins crept on slippered feet; clocks ticked. His uncle sat at his desk, making up accounts; his aunt slid her knitting down the cushion of her chair. She sat and stared at him, a bloodless woman the image of his mother; her pale lips moved. 'You should get out, Ralph. Go on the bus. Go up the coast a bit. A boy needs fresh air.'

Ralph left the house. He took the first bus he saw out of the town. It was a normal, hostile east coast day; no one else was on a pleasure jaunt. There were points where the road hugged the coast; a few isolated houses tumbled away towards a sea less glimpsed than felt, towards an impression of sliding subsiding rocks, of coal boats and fishing boats, of salt and chill.

He got off the bus. The place was nowhere he knew. The weather now was overcast but blustery; chinks of blue sky showed here and there, like cracks in a thick white basin. He fastened his coat, as his aunt, if she had seen him, would have enjoined him; and he wrapped his despised muffler around his throat. He descended a hill, one-in-four, and saw before him the cold sweep of a bay.

The tide was going out. A solitary walker picked his way along the cliffs. In the middle distance were other figures, with rucksacks and boots; their heads were down, their eyes searching the sands. Ralph, too, lowered his eyes to his shoes, and threaded his way among the seaweed and rock pools.

Ralph had gone twenty yards towards the ocean. Its sound was subdued, congruous, a rustle not a roar. He bent down and plucked from the sand at his feet what he took to be some muddy stone. A sharp pang of delight took hold of him, a feeling that was for a moment indistinguishable from fear. He had picked up a fossil: a ridged, grey-green curl, glassy and damp like a descending wave. It lay in his palm: two inches across, an inch and a half at its crest.

He stood still, examining it and turning it over. Inside it was a gentle hollow; he saw that it was a kind of shell, smoothness concealed beneath grit and silt. He looked up across the beach. The melancholy and windblown figures wheeled towards him, and came within hailing distance. They closed in on him, with their ribbed stockings and their cold-weather complexions.

There was a woman among them, her sharp nose scarlet above a swaddling of scarves. She stared at the fossil in his hand; she pulled off her gloves, hauled them off with her teeth. He dropped the fossil into her hand. She turned it over and back again, ran her forefinger down its mottled curve, feeling the ridges. She laid it against her face; she tasted it with her tongue. '*Gryphaea*,' she said. 'Don't you know?'

He shook his head; stood before her, like the dumb unconverted heathen. 'It's a bivalve – like an oyster, you know?'

'Oh, yes.' He was disappointed; something so ordinary after all.

She said, 'It's a hundred and fifty million years old.' He stared at her. 'You know how an oyster lives in its shell? This is the ancestor of oysters.' He nodded. 'It lived here when the sea was warm – if you can imagine that. Here was its soft body, inside this shell, with its heart and blood vessels and gills. When it died all those soft parts rotted, and the sand filled up the cavity. And then the sand compacted and turned into rock.'

There was a circle of people around them, their breath streaming on the air, eyes fixed on her hand; they were coveting what he had found, as if it were a jewel. 'The sea moved,' a man said. His face was a raw ham beneath a bobble hat. 'I mean to say, what had been sea became land. But now the sea's eating away the land again – all this east coast,' he waved his arm, gesturing towards the Wash – 'you can see it going in your lifetime.'

A man in a balaclava – green, ex-army – said, 'I served with a bloke from Suffolk whose grandfather had a smallholding, and it's in the sea now. Whole churchyards have gone down the cliff. Whole graveyards, and the bones washed out.'

The woman said, 'You've stopped this little creature, my dear. On its way back to the sea where it came from.'

'When it was alive –'

'Yes?'

'What did it eat?'

'It cemented itself on the sea-bed, and sucked in water. It got its nourishment from that, from the larvae in the water, you see. It had a stomach, kidneys, intestines, everything you have.'

'Could it think?'

'Well, can an oyster think these days? What would an oyster have to think about?'

He blushed. Stupid question. What he had meant to say was, are you sure it was alive? Can you truly swear to me that it was? 'Are these rare?' he asked.

'Not if you want a smashed-up one. Not if you're content with fragments.'

The woman held his find for a moment, clenched and concealed in her fist; then put it into his outstretched palm, and worked her fingers back painfully into her gloves. She wanted the fossil so much that he almost gave it to her; but then, he wanted it himself. Bobble-hat said, 'I've been coming here man and boy, and never got anything as good as that. Two-a-penny brachiopods, that's what I get. Sometimes I think we're looking so hard we can't see.'

'Beginner's luck,' the balaclava said. He stabbed a woolly finger at the object he craved. 'Do you know what they call them? Devil's toenails.' He chuckled. 'I reckon you can see why.'

Ralph looked down at the fossil and almost dropped it. Saw the thick, ridged, ogreish curve, that greenish, sinister sheen . . . All the way home in the bus he forced himself to hold the object in his hand, his feelings seesawing between attraction and repulsion; wondering how he could have found it, when he was not looking at all.

When he arrived at the house he was very cold and slightly nauseated. He smiled at the cousin who let him in and said he had better go upstairs right away and wash his hands. 'Did you enjoy yourself, love?' his aunt asked; he gave a monosyllabic reply, a polite mutter which translated to nothing. The ticking of the parlour clock was oppressive, insistent; he could imagine it buried in the earth, ticking away for a hundred and fifty million years. He took his place on one of the leather chairs, and wondered about the animal whose back the leather had adorned: what skin, what hair, what blood through living veins? His aunt quibbled about how the table had been laid, twitching the fish knives about with her forefinger. Smoked haddock came, with its thin-cut bread and butter, a pale juice oozing across the plate. He ate a flake or two, then put down his fork. His aunt said, 'No appetite?' He thought of the bones spilled down the cliff, into the salty whispering of the tides; *Gryphaea* sucking in its nourishment, the aeons rolling by, the devil walking abroad.

His mother made Satan into the likeness of some strict schoolmaster: 'The devil finds work for idle hands to do.'

The toenail was upstairs, locked in his suitcase.

When Ralph came home from Yorkshire, he and Emma played their Bible games. They always played them when they had some decision to make. Now Emma said, 'I want to decide whether when I grow up I'm going to be a doctor or a lawyer, or just a broody hen who stays at home like my mama.'

You were supposed to pick a verse at random, and it would give you guidance; but you needed a keen imagination to make anything of the verses they turned up. 'Try this one,' Emma said. '"And thou shalt anoint the laver and his foot, and sanctify it." Exodus 40:11. Very helpful, I'm sure.' She began to sing a hymn of her own composition: *'How daft the name of Jesus sounds . . .'*

Ralph took out the fossil from his coat pocket, where he was keeping it for the while. 'Look at this,' he said. 'It's the devil's toenail.'

Emma gave a startled wail. 'It's horrible. Whatever is it?'

He told her. Her face brightened. 'Give it me.' He dropped it into her cupped hand. 'Can I take it to school to frighten girls with?'

'No, you certainly can't. It's valuable. It's mine.'

'I'm an atheist,' Emma said.

'Not an atheist a minute ago, were you?'

These were the books on their shelves, old, crumbling: *The Christian's Secret of a Happy Life.* And dusty, brown: *Christ is All*, H. C. G. Moule, London, 1892. Slime-trailed, musty: F. R. Havergal, 1880: *Kept for the Master's Use.* Earwiggy, fading: *Hymns of Faith and Hope.* And *A Basket of Fragments*, R. M. McCheyne, published Aberdeen, no date, pages uncut.

A year later Ralph went back to Yorkshire. His request surprised his family, and gave some pale gratification to the Synod, who had found him a quiet boy who offered no offence, and were glad that someone in the family seemed to like them. He spent his days on the beaches and in the town museum. He did not speak of his discoveries at home, but he found a schoolmaster to encourage him – a man whom, he realized later, he should have enlisted on his side when the quarrel came. He studied alone after school, sent for books with his pocket-money and puzzled over geological maps; he walked fields, hills, coastal paths, examined ditches and road-cuttings. When he was tired and discouraged and there were things he could not understand he thought of the woman on the Yorkshire beach, putting out the purple tip of her tongue to taste the fossil, its silt and grit, its coldness and its age.

There was a trick he had to perfect: to look at a landscape and strip away the effect of man. England transforms itself under the geologist's eye; the scavenger sheep are herded away into the future, and a forest grows in a peat bog, each tree seeded by imagination. Where others saw the lie of the land, Ralph saw the path of the glacier; he saw the desert beneath copse and stream, and the glories of Europe stewing beneath a warm, clear, shallow sea.

Today his fossil collection is in cardboard boxes, in one of the attics of his house. Rebecca, his youngest child, had nightmares about them when she was five or six. He blamed himself, for not giving a proper explanation; it was Kit who had told her they were stone animals, stone lives, primitive creatures that once had swum and crawled. The baby saw them swimming and crawling again, mud-sucking and breathing at her bedroom door.

But in those days, when he was a boy, Ralph kept his finds in his bedroom, arranged on top of his bookcase and on the painted mantelpiece over the empty grate. Norfolk did not yield much for his collection. He combed the Weymouth and Cromer beaches for ammonites and echinoids, but his luck was out; he had to wait for the summer, for his exile to the slippery chairs. He endured all: his uncle's homilies, the piano practice of his female cousins. His mother dusted the fossils twice a week, but didn't understand what they were. 'It's Ralph's interest,' she told people. 'Old bits of stone, and pottery, things of that nature, little bits and pieces that he brings back from his holidays.' Geology and archaeology were thoroughly confused in her mind. 'Ralph is a collector,' she would say. 'He likes anything that's old. Emma – now, Emma – she's much more your modern miss.'

Emma said to her brother, 'Ralph, how can you talk so casually about 500 million years? Most of us have trouble with . . . well, Christmas for example. Every December it puts people into a panic, as if it had come up on them without warning. It's only very exceptional people who can imagine Christmas in July.'

Ralph said, 'What you must do is to think of yourself walking through time. To go back, right back, to the very beginning of geological time, you'd have to go round the world forty-six times. Suppose you want to go back to the last Ice Age. That's very recent, as we think of it. It would be like a cross-channel trip. London to Paris.'

'I wouldn't mind a trip to Paris,' Emma said. 'Do you think it's any good me asking?'

'Then, to reach the time of the dinosaurs, you'd have to go right around the world.

'I feel confined, myself,' Emma said. 'To the here and now.' She sat twisting at one of her plaits, pulling at it, finally undoing it and combing her fingers through her heavy brown hair. She glanced at herself covertly in mirrors these days. 'Geese turn into swans', her mother said; she meant well, but it was hardly science.

A frieze of evolution marched through Ralph's head. Each form of life has its time and place: sea-snail and sea-lily, water-scorpion and lungfish, fern tree and coral. Shark and flesh-eating reptile; sea-urchin and brontosaurus; pterodactyl and magnolia tree; cuttle fish and oyster. Then the giant flightless bird, opossum in his tree, elephant in his swamp; it was as clear in his mind as it might be in a child's picture book, or a poster on a nursery wall. The sabre-toothed cat, the little horse three feet tall; the Irish elk, the woolly mammoth; then man, stooped, hairy, furrow-browed. It is a success story.

At seventeen Ralph could be taken for a man, but not of this primitive textbook kind. He was tall, strong, with a clear skin and clear eyes, like a hero in a slushy book. Sometimes women looked at him with interest on the street: with a speculative pity, as if they feared other women might exploit him.

Ralph would go back to the Brecklands, in those years after the war, threading his bicycle along the narrow roads, between concrete emplacements and through lanes churned up by heavy vehicles. What he saw was victory: fences broken, orchards cut down, avenues of trees mutilated. Gates hung from a hinge, posters flapped on walls. Everywhere was a proliferation of little huts made of corrugated iron – rusting now, and without their doors. Farm workers ran about in scrapped jeeps they had salvaged. Heaps of rubbish festered amid the pines. The wind was the same, its low hum through the stiff branches. The thread-like trunks of birch trees were the same, viewed across tussocky fields; herons flapped from the meres.

The Ministry of Defence did not mean to relinquish its hold on the district. Its fences and KEEP OUT notices divided the fields. Ralph would pull his bicycle on to the grass verge, while a convoy rumbled past. Once, holding his handlebars and standing up to his knees in damp grass, he reached down for what caught his eye; it was a flint arrow-head. He turned it over in his palm, then put it in his pocket. He remembered the moment when he had found the fossil; here was another secret, buried life. He need not take it to a museum; these things are common enough. He took it home and put it on his mantelpiece, meaning to save it for his Uncle James to see when he was next in England. 'Ah, an elfshot,' his mother said, and smiled.

'You like that old country, Ralph,' his father said; the thought did not displease him. Matthew himself had kept friends in the area, church people, other businessmen of a charitable, socially responsible bent. These were the days of meeting-room hysteria and sudden conversion, of dipping people in rivers and calling it baptism. American preachers had come to the bases to service the raw spirituality of their compatriots, and found a ready audience in the poor, cold towns. 'A plain font is requisite,' said Matthew. 'Nothing else.' He hated display: Roman Catholic display, evangelists' display, emotional display. A plain mind is requisite: nothing else.

Emma said she wanted to be a doctor. His father said, 'Yes, if you wish to, Emma.'

Everything was permitted to her, it seemed to Ralph. She was a decisive girl, bossy, full of strong opinions strongly expressed. When Emma's opinions cut across those of her parents, they saw contrariness; they saw a defect of character. They tried, therefore, to correct her character; it did not seem important to them to correct her opinions, for Emma was a female, and what influence could the opinion of a female have in the real world? Her opinions might damage her, and she would then revise them – but they would not damage the social order.

At least, that was how Ralph supposed they thought. For when it came to his opinions, his desires, it was a very different story.

'So you don't want to go into the business, Ralphie.'

This was how his father joined battle: obliquely, from the flank. He made it seem that there were only simple issues at

44

stake, a change in family expectations. But soon enough, his weighty battalions were deployed. The issues went beyond the family. They became larger than Ralph had bargained for. They became universal.

First his father said: 'Ralph, you've never given me any trouble. I thought you believed in the religion that you were brought up in.'

'I do,' Ralph said.

'But now you are setting yourself up against it.'

'No.'

'But you must be, Ralph. We believe that God created the world, as is set down in the Bible. I believe it. Your mother believes it.'

'Uncle James doesn't believe it.'

'James is not here,' his father said flatly. It was incontrovertible; James was in the Diocese of Zanzibar.

'I believe it as a metaphor,' Ralph said. 'But I believe in evolution too.'

'Then you are a very muddle-headed young man,' his father said. 'How can you entertain two contradictory beliefs at the same time?'

'But they aren't contradictory. Father, most people got all this over with by the turn of the century. Nobody thinks what you think any more. Nobody thinks there's God on one side and Darwin on the other.'

'When I was a young man,' Matthew said, 'I attended a lecture. It was given by a professor, he was a distinguished scholar, he was no fool or half-baked schoolboy. He said to us, "What is Darwinism? I will tell you. Darwinism is atheism," he said. I have always remembered those words. I have seen nothing in my life since to convince me that he was wrong.'

'But if you thought about it now,' Ralph said, 'if you thought about it all over again, you might be able to see that he

45

was wrong.' Something bubbled inside him: intellectual panic? 'What's the point of just repeating what you were told when you were a boy? You can be an evolutionist, Darwinian or some other kind, and still believe that everything that exists is intended by God. It's an old debate, it's stale, it was never necessary in the first place.'

'My own beliefs,' his father said, 'have never been subject to the vagaries of fashion.'

Days of war followed. Silences. Ralph couldn't eat. Food stuck in his dry mouth; it was like trying to swallow rocks, he thought. He hated quarrels, hated silences too: those silences that thickened the air in rooms and made it electric.

Matthew closed in on him, and so did his mother: a pincer movement. 'Are you going to take evidence, what you call evidence, from a few bones and shells, and use them to oppose the word of God?'

'I told you,' Ralph said, 'that there is no opposition.'

'There is opposition from me,' his father said: shifting the ground.

'It is impossible to have a discussion with you.'

'No doubt,' Matthew said. 'I am not a scientist, am I? I am so backward in my outlook that I wonder you condescend to talk to me at all. I wonder you condescend to stay under my roof. Good God, boy – look around you. Look at the design of the world. Do you think some blind stupid mechanism controls it? Do you think we got here out of chance?'

'Please be calm,' Ralph said. He tried to take a deep breath, but it seemed to stick half-way. 'It's no good waving your arms at me and saying, look at God's creation. You don't have to force it down my throat, the miracles of nature, the design of the universe – I know about those, more, I'd say, than you.' (More than you, he thought, who have lived your life with your eyes on your well-blacked boots.) 'If I believe in God I believe from choice. Not because of evidence. From choice. Not because I'm compelled.'

'You believe from *choice*?' Matthew was revolted. 'From choice? Where did you get this stupid notion from?'

'I thought of it myself.'

'Can you believe in anything you like, then? Can you believe the moon is made of green cheese? Is there no truth you recognize?'

'I don't know,' Ralph said quietly. 'We used to go to sermons that said the truth was what God revealed, that you don't find the truth by looking for it. At least, that's what I think they were saying. Well – not to put too fine a point on it – I can't wait around all my life. If I've been given the faculty of reasoning, I may as well use it to dig out what truth I can.'

'You'll kill me, Ralph,' his father said. 'Your pride and your self-regard will kill me.'

Ralph was afraid his father might ask, with one old divine, 'What can the geologist tell you about the Rock of Ages?' He spared him that, but not episodes of choking rage, which terrified Ralph and made him regret what he had begun.

His mother took him aside. 'You are making your father very unhappy,' she said. 'I have never seen him more miserable. And he has done everything for you, and would give you anything. If you do this thing, if you insist on it, if you insist on this as your life's work, I'll not be able to hold my head up before our friends. They'll say we have not brought you up properly.'

'Look,' Ralph said, 'what I want is to go to university. I want to read geology. Just that, that's all. I didn't set out to upset anybody. That was the last thing on my mind.'

'I know you have your ambitions,' Dorcas said, with that frayed sigh only mothers can perform. 'But your abilities, Ralph, are not for you to enjoy – they are given to you to use for the Christian community.'

47

'Yes. All right. I will use them.'

'You've closed your mind,' she said.

Astonishment wrenched him out of his misery. She left him incoherent. 'Me? I've closed my mind?'

'You spoke to your father of reason,' she said. 'You'll find there is a point where reason fails.'

'Stop talking at me,' he said. 'Leave me alone.'

His mother left him alone. Her mouth drew in as though she were eating sour plums. If James were here it would be different, Ralph thought; he wanted to cry like a child for his uncle, of whom he knew so little. James could talk to them, he believed, James could ridicule them out of their caution and their scruples and their superstitions, James could talk them into the twentieth century. James is not like them, he knows it from his letters; James is liberal, educated, sympathetic. Ralph saw himself losing, being driven into the ground. All he believed, all he wished to believe – the march of order, progress – all diminished by his father's hard deriding stare and his mother's puckered mouth.

Why didn't he fetch in the schoolmaster who encouraged him? Why didn't he appeal to his headmaster, who knew him to be a bright, studious, serious boy? Why didn't he get some other, reasonable adult to weigh in on his behalf – at least to referee the argument, make sure his father obeyed the laws of war?

Because he was ashamed of his father's stupidity, ashamed of the terms of the quarrel. Because in families, you never think of appealing for help to the outside world; your quarrels are too particular, too specific, too complex. And because you never think of these reasonable solutions, till it is far too late.

'Ralph,' his father said, 'be guided by me. You are a mere boy. Oh, you don't want to hear that, I know. You think you are very adult and smart. But you will come to thank me, Ralphie, in the days ahead.'

Ralph felt he was trapped in an ancient argument. These are the things sons say to fathers; these are the things fathers say to sons. The knowledge didn't help him; nor did the knowledge that his father was behaving like a caricature of a Victorian patriarch. His family had always been cripplingly old-fashioned; till now he had not realized the deformity's extent. Why should he, when all his family's friends were the same, and he had spent his life hobbling along with them? They were churchgoers; not great readers; not travellers, but people who on principle entertained narrow ideas and stayed at home. He saw them for the first time as the outside world might see them – East Anglian fossils.

'There will be no money for you, Ralphie,' his father said. 'And you will hardly be able to support yourself through your proposed course at university. You may try, of course.'

'James will help me,' Ralph said, without believing it.

'Your Uncle James has not a brass farthing of his own. And you're quite mistaken if you think he would set himself up against his own brother.'

'Of course, I could see it coming,' Emma said. 'After all the fine theories and pieties have been aired, what it comes down to is their hand on the purse-strings. That's their final argument.'

Ralph said, 'It isn't God who's diminished by Darwin's theory, it's man. Man isn't any more lord of the universe. He's just a part of the general scheme of things. But there is a scheme of things, and you can put God at the top of it if you like.'

'But you don't like,' his father said. Another flat statement. It was not evolution that was the issue now, it was obedience. Even if his father had taken that last point, Ralph thought, he had done himself no service by raising it. If Man was diminished, then Matthew Eldred was diminished: a lord of the universe was precisely what he wished to be.

'If you like,' Ralph said, 'and I do like – you can still believe that Man has a unique place in creation. You can still believe that he has a special dignity. Only Man is rational. Only Man is an intellectual animal.'

'Bandying words,' his father said. He seemed satisfied with the phrase, as if he were a doctor and this were his diagnosis.

I except you, Ralph thought. I wouldn't call you rational, not any more.

When the conflict was at its height – when the family were barely speaking to each other, and a Synod-like hush possessed the rooms – Matthew absented himself for a night. He went to King's Lynn, to discuss with some of his business cronies the charitable trust that they were setting up. It was to be an ambitious enterprise, with broad Christian interests: money for the missions, money for the East End doss house with which James kept a connection; money above all for the deserving poor of Norfolk, the aged and indigent farm labourers, those church-going rural folk who had been mangled by agricultural machinery or otherwise suffered some disabling mischance.

It was to be called the St Walstan Trust; Walstan is the patron saint of farmers and farm labourers, and his image is found through the county on screens and fonts. The suggestion came from William Martin, a shopkeeper at Dereham; it was a little High Church for Matthew's taste, but Martin was generally sound, very sound, and the county connection pleased him. Matthew was a local patriot now, a sitter on committees, treasurer of this and chairman of that. Ralph said to Emma, 'I wish that charity would begin at home.'

That evening, the event took place which broke Ralph's resolve. His mother came to his bedroom, upstairs on her noiseless feet. She tapped at the door, and waited till he had asked her to enter; this arch, stiff politeness had come upon the family since the row blew up.

Ralph looked up from his books, adjusting his desk lamp so that it cast a little light into the room. It pooled at his mother's slippered feet as she sat on the bed. She wore her cardigan draped over her shoulders; she took the cuffs of the empty sleeves in her hands, and twisted them as she spoke. Her wedding ring gleamed, big and broad like a brass washer. She had lost weight, perhaps, for it hung loose on her finger, and her knuckle bones seemed huge.

Ralph listened to what she had to say. If he would not capitulate, she said – but she did not use that word – if he would not fall into line, fall in with the plans his father had formulated for him, then she could not say what his father would do about Emma. He might think that as Ralph had gone so badly off course, Emma needed guidance. He might like to have her at home, under his eye. There might, in fact, be no medical school for Emma at all.

His mother sighed as she said all this; her manner was tentative, and her eyes travelled over the peg-rug and the bookcase and the desk, they roamed the wall and flickered over the dark window at which the curtains were not yet drawn. But she was not afraid; and Ralph understood her. She had volunteered, he believed, for this piece of dirty work; she and her husband, his father, had planned it between them, so that there would be no more shouting, no more scenes, only his certain silent defeat.

'Emma might like to be a nurse, perhaps,' his mother said. 'Your father might let her do that, but I only say might. His frame of mind so much depends on you.'

Ralph said, 'You are a wicked woman.'

He didn't know that she was sick then, and that within a few months she would have the first of her many spells in hospital. Despite her sufferings she would have a long life. He was never sure that he forgave her completely. But he tried.

★

After his capitulation, his father began to backtrack at once. 'For a hobby, Ralphie,' he said. 'Keep it for a hobby. But not for what you are seen to do in the eyes of the world. Not for your life's work.'

'I don't want the business,' he told his father. 'I want my own life. I don't want anything to do with all that.'

'Very well,' Matthew said equably. 'I'll sell – when the time is right.' He frowned then, as if he might be misunderstood. 'There'll be money for you, Ralph. And there'll be money for your children. I'll put it in trust, I'll arrange it all. You'll not be poor.'

'This is premature,' Ralph said.

'Oh, you'll be married and have children soon enough, the years go by . . . you could be a teacher, Ralphie. You could go to Africa, like your uncle. They have a great need of people, you know. I would never try to confine you. I would never sentence you to a dull life.' He paused, and added, 'But I hope one day you will come home to Norfolk.'

For months afterwards Ralph never seemed to smile; that was what Emma thought. He kept his shoulders hunched as he walked, as if he wore disappointment like a tight old coat. 'Why did you give in to them?' she asked. 'Why didn't you stick by your principles, why didn't you stick out for the life you had planned?'

He wouldn't talk to her; occasionally, he would just remark that things were not as they seemed, that he saw there were hidden depths to people.

She did not know how he had been defeated. He made sure he did not tell her.

He had his National Service to do; it would fail to broaden his horizons. He would spend it behind a desk, employed in menial clerical work; or in transit in trucks and trains. He began to recognize his character, as it was reflected back to him by other people. He saw a solid, polite, always reasonable young man, who would sort out problems for the dim and timid, who kept his patience and who did not patronize or sneer; who never cultivated his superiors, either, who seemed to have no ambition and no idea how to make life easy for himself. Was he really like that? He didn't know.

He was not excessively miserable. It seemed to him that the boredom, the routine discomforts and humiliations, the exile from home, the futility of his daily round, were all simple enough to endure. What he could not endure were the thoughts of his heart, and the frequent dreams he had, in which he murdered his father. Or rather, dreams in which he plotted the murder; or in which he was arrested and tried, when the murder was already done. The bloody act itself was always offstage.

When he was twenty years old these dreams were so persistent that the memory of them stained and dislocated his waking life. By day he entertained, he thought, little animosity to Matthew. Their quarrel had not affected what he believed, it had only affected the course of his career; and one day Matthew would die, or become senile, or concede the point, and he could resume that career. He must be the winner in the long run, he thought.

So these dreams, these inner revolts, bewildered him. He was forced to concede that large areas of his life were beyond his control.

On one of his leaves, instead of going home to Norwich, he went to London with a friend. They stayed at his friend's sister's house, Ralph sleeping on the sofa. By day, he went sightseeing; he had never been to London before. One night he lost his virginity for cash, in a room near one of the major railway termini. Afterwards he could never remember which station it had been, or the name of the street, so that in later life he couldn't be sure whether he ever walked along it; and although the woman told him her name was Norah he had no reason to believe her. He did not feel guilt afterwards; it was something to be got through. He had not embarrassed himself; there was that much to be said about it.

On his next leave he was introduced to Anna Martin, only child of the very sound shopkeeper from Dereham.

Three years later, Ralph was teaching in London, in the East End. James had come home and was director of what had been the doss house and was now St Walstan's Hostel. Ralph went there most weekends. He slept on a folding bed in the director's office, and was called during the night to new admissions banging on the door, to men taken sick and to residents who had unexpectedly provided themselves with alcohol first, and then with broken bottles, knives, pokers or iron bars. He arbitrated in disputes about the ownership of dog-ends, lumpy mattresses and soiled blankets, and became familiar with the customs and rituals and shibboleths of welfare officers and policemen.

On a Sunday night he collected the week's bedding, and listed it for the laundry, counting the sheets stained with vomit and semen, with excrement and blood. On a Wednesday evening he would drop by for an hour to count the linen in again. The sheets were patched and darned, but stainless. They smelled of the launderer's press; they were stiff and utterly white. How do they do it, he wondered; how do they make them so utterly white?

He became engaged to Anna. They planned to marry when she graduated from her teacher-training college, and go straight out to Dar-es-Salaam, where a dear friend of James was a headmaster and where a pleasant house would be waiting for them, and two jobs as teachers of English to young men training for the ministry. Sometimes, on the London pavements, Ralph tried to imagine himself translated to this alien place, to the heat and colour of this other life. Letters passed to and fro. Arrangements were in hand.

Anna received all this with equanimity. She was planning the wedding, the quiet wedding. A quiet girl altogether; she wore grey, charcoal, dark blue, simple clothes with clear lines. Ralph thought she was setting herself apart, cultivating almost a nun-like air. They did not discuss their religious beliefs; a certain amount was implied, understood. She had taken on the prospect of Africa without demur. 'She hasn't really said much about it,' Ralph told James.

James said, 'Good – I suspect enthusiasm.'

The kind of person not wanted in those climes, he said, was someone who rushed with open arms to embrace the romantic deprivations of the life. Anna's reasoned agreement was a better foundation for their future than constant chatter about what that future might hold.

Later Ralph would think, when we married it was a leap into the dark: we didn't know each other at all. But perhaps when you are so young, you don't even begin to comprehend what there is to know.

As for those nun-like clothes – when he had seen more of the world, and was more accustomed to looking at women, he realized that Anna's style was deliberate, ingenious and contrived by the exercise of a stifled artistic talent. She had made her own dresses in those days; she could not buy what she wanted in Norfolk, and with her tiny means she would not have dared to enter a London shop. She spent what she had on fabric, buttons and trimmings; she cut, pressed and stitched, obsessively careful, tyrannically neat. And so what Anna possessed was unique among the people he knew – it was not sanctity, but chic.

★

'Freud said,' Emma told him, 'that religion is a universal obsessional neurosis.' She looked at him over her glasses. 'Tell me now . . . what happened to the dinosaurs, Ralph?'

'Their habitat altered,' he said. 'A change of climate.' She smiled crookedly. He saw that she hadn't expected an answer. 'The trouble with our parents,' she said, 'is that their habitat doesn't change. It hardly varies from one end of the county to the next. Give them a pew, and they're right at home.'

Emma had got her wish. She was at medical school; and home now for Ralph's wedding, her book open on her lap and her feet up on the old sofa that she had thrashed so thoroughly in 1939. Emma had grown heavy; the hospital food, she said, was all dumplings, pastry, suet, and that was what she was turning into, dumplings, pastry, suet. Despite this, she had a suitor, a smart local boy called Felix, not one of their Bible-study set. She dealt with him by ignoring him most of the time, and did not always answer his letters.

She had grumbled with vigour about the business of a new frock for the wedding, even though her father had paid for it; she would pay herself, she said, if Matthew would go and choose the thing, converse with shop assistants and track down a hat to match. Emma resisted the attentions of hairdressers. Anna, the bride-to-be, offered to take her in hand and see that she got a perm. Emma swore when she heard this, so violently that she surprised herself.

'So, Ralph,' Emma said, 'the news from Freud is not all bad. "Devout believers" – that's you and Anna – "are safeguarded in a high degree against the risk of certain neurotic illnesses: their acceptance of the universal neurosis spares them from the task of constructing a personal one." In other words, one sort of madness is enough for anybody.'

'Do you think it is madness?' Ralph asked. 'Madness and nothing else?'

'I don't think it has any reality, Ralph. I think faith is

something people chase after, simply to give life meaning.'

She spoke quite kindly, he thought later. 'And doesn't it have meaning?' he asked.

Emma reserved judgement.

That night his father took him aside. 'I want to talk about the arrangements,' he said.

'It's all in hand. All done. You don't have to concern yourself.'

'I don't mean arrangements for the wedding. Why should I concern myself with the women's business?' His father slid out a drawer of his desk, took out some papers, looked through them as he spoke; this was a family whose members no longer met each other's eyes. 'I mean the arrangements for the future. I have taken advice, and I am going to sell the press. I have a good offer from a publisher of educational books.' Unable to find anything of interest in the papers, he turned them over and stared at their back. 'Education, you know – it's the coming thing.'

'I should hope it is,' Ralph said. He felt at a loss. He ought to be able to give an opinion. 'Well, if your accountant –' he began.

Matthew cut him short. 'Yes, yes, yes. Now then, I propose to invest a certain amount, the interest to be paid to Walstan's Trust.' He had managed to drop the Saint, Ralph noticed. 'I propose to place a smaller amount into a family trust for yourself and Anna and your children. When you come back from the missions, you will sit on the committee of Walstan's Trust, which five years from now will need a full-time paid administrator. If you seem fit for it, you will be able to fill that position.'

'Other people may have claims,' Ralph said. This was all he could do – raise small objections. He could not imagine himself in five years' time. He could not imagine what kind of man he might be, or imagine these notional children of his. I might die in Africa, he thought. There are tropical diseases, and all sorts of strange accidents.

'Well, they may,' said his father. 'But I cannot see very clearly who they would be. Your Uncle James will be wanting a rest by then, and the children of my colleagues on the committee are pursuing their own paths in life.'

'It seems to be looking too far ahead,' Ralph said.

'Oh,' Matthew said, 'I thought the millennia were as naught to you. Really, you know, to plan five years or ten years ahead is nothing. All businessmen do it. We do it when we invest money – though you would know nothing of that.'

'I suppose I wouldn't.'

'My object, my plan – and here I may say the other trustees agree with me – is that the Trust should be forever administered from Norfolk, no matter how wide its interests may become. It is local money that has set it up – and we must keep our feet on the ground. So you will want to base yourself here in Norwich, or elsewhere in the county if you prefer. When you return I will buy you a house, because you will make no money while you are out in Africa. That goes without saying.'

If that is so, Ralph thought, why say it? He said, 'Had you any particular house in mind?' But he could not summon the strength of purpose to put venom into his tone.

'I want the Trust to benefit my own countrymen,' Matthew said, 'not just James' collection of drunks and wastrels. Don't mistake me – I have respect for James' work –'

'Yes, I understand you,' Ralph said. 'You don't have to talk to me as if you were addressing the County Council.'

He thought, from now on I shall take control, I shall order my own life, just as I like. I am going to Africa because I want to go, because Anna wants it. When I return I shall be my own man.

58

He did not feel demeaned when his father wrote out a cheque for a wedding present and put it into his hand. Payment was due, he reckoned, a tribute from the past to the future.

Four days before the wedding James telephoned from London to say that there was a spot of trouble, could Ralph possibly get on the train and come right away? He was due to appear in court as a witness, one of his inmates having assaulted a police constable; his assistant appeared to be having a nervous breakdown, and there was no one but Ralph who could be trusted to oversee the hostel for a day.

Ralph said, 'What will you do when I go out to Dar?'

His uncle said, 'That's another thing – I want to talk to you about that. Don't hang about – take a taxi from Liverpool Street. St Walstan will pay.'

Ralph picked up his coat and hat and strode off to the station. He feared the worst. His uncle was going to tell him that he was needed here, in the East End; that the tropics could wait, and that he and Anna should see about renting some rooms a bus-ride from the hostel. He wondered whether he would say yes and supposed he would. Anna would have to unpack her cotton dresses and put them in mothballs, and begin her married life as an East End housewife visiting street markets with a basket over her arm. He rehearsed some inner rebellions: let James sacrifice himself, James is a clergyman, he has no life of his own. He bought a cup of tea in a café near Liverpool Street. He thought of going back into the station and taking the next train back to Norwich; or alternatively, the next train to somewhere else.

It was half-past five when James came back from court, and the hostel was almost full that night, so before he had any conversation with his nephew he took off his jacket and rolled up his sleeves and began to help with the day's last meal. It was stew – it usually was stew of some sort – but there was all the bread to be cut and margarined. The inmates always wanted bread, three slices per man, whatever the rest of their meal was. They grumbled if they did not get it, as if their rights had been violated.

When the meal was over and the men on the washing-up rota had been identified and corralled and set to their task, James with a twitch of his head beckoned Ralph into his office. They closed the door and with a single purpose, without a word, heaved a filing cabinet at the back of it; they knew from experience that it was the only way they could get a minute without interruption.

'Is it about the posting?' Ralph asked. 'Is there a problem?'

'No, no problem.' James sat down at his desk, and found space for his elbows among the unpaid bills and begging letters and rubber bands. 'Why do I have these rubber bands?' he wondered. 'What are they for? No, Ralphie, there is no problem with Dar-es-Salaam, it is just that something more urgent has come up, and I thought that you should have the chance to consider it.'

Here it comes, Ralph thought: my future on the Mile End Road.

James said, 'Would you like to go to South Africa?'

On the outskirts of Swaffham today there is a goodly selection of dinky bungalows. They have wrought-iron gates and birdbaths, trellises, hanging baskets, shutters and dwarf walls. They have raw brickwork and shining windows, and scarlet floribundas in well-weeded beds. Their carriage lamps are the light of the twentieth century. In the market-place Ralph hears the broad drawling accent in which his grandfather spoke moderated to the foul contemporary tones of middle England.

These bungalow dwellers repopulated the villages of

Breckland, which were empty when Ralph went to Africa. Between settlements, there are still tracts of heather and furze, and black pine plantations: barren, monotonous, funereal, like the contents of an East European nightmare. But the bowed, arthritic pines that line the roads creep to the edges of the small towns, intruding themselves among the DIY merchants and filling stations and furniture warehouses; they gather round the new housing estates, like witches at a christening.

It is only in the land marked off by the military's fences that the old country can be seen. 'Danger areas,' they are called on the map. It is said the army builds models there, of life-sized Belfast streets, and that snipers and marksmen creep behind empty windows and false walls. From the roads you can see Nissen huts, like slugs in formation. Signs read 'No Entry without Permit – Ministry of Defence Property'. Vegetation creeps like serpents around their metal poles. The wind topples them.

To the east, where Ralph and his children now live at the county's heart, the great wheat fields roll on to the horizon, denatured, over-fertile, factory fields. A farm that employed eighty-five men now employs six; the descendants of the other seventy-nine have delivered themselves from rural squalor, from midden and rotting thatch, and live in the bungalows, or in red-brick council houses with long gardens. In spring, primroses struggle in the verges. In June, there are dog-roses in such hedgerows as remain.

Ralph dreams; again, he is three years old. Somewhere behind him, unseen, his father walks, and Uncle James. He curls down inside his grandfather's coat.

They are going to the church. His grandfather will show him the angels in the roof, and the Pedlar of Swaffham carved on a stall end, and the pedlar's dog with its round ears and big chain.

The Pedlar of Swaffham: John Chapman was his name. He dreamt one night that if he went to London, and stood on London Bridge, he would meet a man who would tell him how to make his fortune.

The day after this dream, Chapman put his pack on his back and with his dog set off to London. On London Bridge he stood about, until a shopkeeper asked him what he thought he was doing. 'I'm here because of a dream,' the pedlar said.

'Dream?' said the shopkeeper. 'If I took any notice of dreams, I would be in some country place called Swaffham, in the garden of some yokel called Chapman, digging under his damn-fool pear tree.' With a sneer, the fellow retreated to his merchandise.

John Chapman and his dog returned to Swaffham and dug under the pear tree. There they found a pot of gold. Around the pot ran an inscription. It said, 'Under this pot is another, twice as good.' The pedlar began digging again, and found a second crock: and now his fortune was made.

John Chapman gave candlesticks to the church, and rebuilt the north aisle when it fell down, and gave £120 to the steeple fund. His wife Cateryne and his dog were carved on the stalls, the wife with her rosary and the dog with his chain. John Chapman became a churchwarden, and wore an ermine gown.

But Ralph's dreams? He has shelved them: packed away his specimens and consigned his maps and monographs to a space under the eaves of his father's house in Norwich. He has consented to another kind of life from the life he had planned for himself. It happens to people at Ralph's age, at twenty-five, you realize you are no longer the person you were, and will never become the person you meant to be. But he thinks, after all, there is a living to be made; there is a row to be hoed, and at least I am not a clergyman. He is serving God – a bit – and

Mammon — a bit; his father's friends say he has not *committed* himself, not *wholly*, and he knows he has very little money in the bank. He comforts himself that he understands something of the nature of life, of the nature of hidden things: at least, he has classifications for what lies beneath the surface, he has categories and terms.

From a jelly speck to man the line improves, edging nearer all the time to the summit of God's design. As the species has evolved, the child in the womb grows, grows through its gills and its fur and becomes human. So society creeps forward, from savagery to benevolence: from cold and hunger and murder, to four walls and hearth stones and arts and parliaments and cures for diseases. At twenty-five Ralph believes this; he believes too in the complex perfectibility of the human heart.

FOUR

Lucy Moyo took a bunch of keys out of the pocket of her apron. She was six foot tall, imposing, solid, like a black bolster inside her print frock; the bunch of keys lay in her hand like a toy.

'This is the key for your office,' she said. She held it up. 'These little ones are for your desks and cupboards. This is for the cupboard where we keep the first-aid chest. This one is for the chest itself. Friday nights, Saturdays, you will be wanting that. These keys are for the inside doors of your house. This one is for the pantry and these are for the store cupboards inside the pantry.'

'Are they really necessary?' Anna asked. 'Every one?'

Lucy smiled remotely. 'Mrs Eldred, you will find that they are. This key is for the woodshed where the tools are kept. The baas must be sure that anything to stab and cut, anything with a sharp edge, you understand me, is shown to him or to you or some good person at the end of the day when it has been used and then it is locked up till it is wanted again.'

Lucy pressed the keys into Anna's palm. She folded Anna's fingers over them. 'You must keep all these doors locked. These people are thieves.'

Her own people, Anna thought. And how casually she says it. 'Is Lucy a cynic?' she asked later.

'I don't think we ought to criticize her,' Ralph said. 'She's kept the place ticking over.' His hands moved over his desk, bewildered, flinching. 'She probably knows what she's talking about. It's just the way she puts things, it's a bit bald.'

Lucy said, 'Mr and Mrs Standish, who were here before you, used to sit after their supper most nights and cry. It made me sad to see such old people crying.'

The voyage to Cape Town had taken three weeks. It had allowed Anna a pause for thought, a period of grace. Until the last year of her life, nothing had happened. Then everything had happened together. When she was thirteen or fourteen, she had made up her mind to go to a foreign country: preferably a distant one. Her idea was that she would say goodbye to her parents, and write to them twice a year.

Ralph understood her parents – which was a good thing, because of the time it saved. It would have been a lifetime's work to explain them to someone who had been brought up in a different fashion. In families like yours and mine, Ralph said, it's the girls who have the harder time. He knew, he said, what his sister had gone though. Anna reserved judgement. It seemed to her that Emma was not unduly marked by suffering.

The truth was that Emma frightened her; even her small-talk was inquisitorial, demanding, sarcastic. Without a word but with an impatient toss of her head, she implied that Anna was decorative but useless. At least, Anna took this to be the implication. Nothing could be less true. Her hands had never been idle.

Anyway, she was putting thousands of miles between herself and Emma. If she had stayed in Norfolk people would have expected them to be friends, they would always be saying, Anna and Emma, Emma and Anna. It was not a harmonious combination – not to her ear. As a child, it was true, she had sometimes wished for a sister. Any companions had to run through a parental censorship, an overview of their lives and antecedents. By the time a prospective friend was approved, the attraction had waned on both sides.

Her mother and father were shopkeepers, with the grocer's

habit of measuring out everything: especially their approval. Nothing is free; they stressed that. God has scales in which he weighs your inclinations against your actions, your needs against your desires. Pleasure is paid for in the coin of pain. Pay in the coin of faith, and God may return a measured quantity of mercy. Or then again, he may not.

Anna had been a great reader, as a child. Her parents gave her paper pamphlets, containing tales of black babies and Eskimos and how they came to Jesus. But what she liked were school stories, where the pupils lived away from home in a mansion by the sea, and played lacrosse and learned French from Mam'selle. Her parents said books were a good thing, but when they picked one up to inspect it – to permit or not permit – their faces expressed suspicion and latent hostility.

They eschewed the cinema and the theatre – they did not forbid them, but they knew how to make their views known. No alcohol passed their lips. Women who wore make-up – at least, any more than a smear of tan face-powder – were not their sort. Mr Martin looked at the newspaper, so his wife did not need to bother. She received each day a used opinion from him, just as she received a shirt for laundering, tainted with the smell of smoked bacon and ripe cheese.

Later, when she grew up, Anna realized that her parents were afflicted not simply by godliness, but by social snobbery. It seemed difficult for them to distinguish between the two. They looked up to those customers with big houses, to whom each week they delivered straw-packed boxes containing glacé fruits and tiny jars of chicken breasts in nutritious jelly. They looked down on ordinary customers, who queued in the shop for bags of sugar and quarters of tea. The former paid on account; of the latter, they naturally demanded cash. They were among the first in their district to get the ingenious, time-saving, pre-printed notice, which encapsulated so neatly their philosophy of life:

PLEASE DO NOT ASK FOR CREDIT,
AS A REFUSAL OFTEN OFFENDS

All through her teens, Anna had been tormented by this notice, and by this thought: what if I fall in love, what if I fall in love with someone *unsuitable*? She knew the chances of this were high; there were so many unsuitable people in the world. But when she came home and said that Ralph Eldred wanted her to get engaged, the Martins looked in vain for a reason to oppose it. It was true that the boy's future was unsettled; but then, his father was a county councillor.

Anna had been a compliant daughter. She had tried to do everything she could to suit her parents, while knowing that it would not be quite enough: *please do not ask for credit . . .* Some unhappy children have fantasies that they are adopted; Anna always knew she was theirs. In adolescence, she fell into reveries, irritating to the people about her, productive of sharp words from her mother. She dreamed of ways of being as unlike her parents as possible. But she didn't know any ways. To despise them was one thing; to free herself from them was quite another.

And she wondered, now, as the ship moved south, whether she was sailing away from them or towards them. After all, they were such charitable people; weren't they, in their own way, missionaries at home? There were no luxuries in their household; money was always needed for good causes. Besides, it was wicked to have luxuries when others had not the necessities: unless you were an account customer, of course.

And if the charity did not proceed from love, but from a sense of duty, did that matter? Were the results not the same?

Anna used to think so. The starving eat, whatever the motive of the bread's donor; perhaps it does not become the starving to be nice about motives.

Ralph saw the issue differently. The Eldreds and the Martins, he said, acted from a desire to make the world conformable. Grocer Martin would like to raise all tramps to the condition of account customers; Betty the grocer's wife would like to see chain-smoking unmarried mothers scrub their faces and take communion monthly. Cold, poverty, hunger must be remedied because they are extreme states, productive of disorder, of psychic convulsions, of demonstrations by the unemployed. They lead to socialism, and make the streets unsafe.

Ralph passed judgement on his father, and on hers. He knew a poem; he would laugh, and say:

> 'God made the wicked Grocer
>   For a mystery and a sign.
> That men might shun the awful shops
>   And go to inns to dine.'

There it was – Ralph hated nothing more than meanness. It seemed to her that he had a spontaneous, uncalculated kindness. She was looking for no more and no less. She slept with him before – just before – the engagement ring was on her finger.

It was she who had made him the offer. When the time came – the one occasion, perhaps in a year, when they had the house at Dereham to themselves – she was seized by fear. Even the touch of his warm hands made her shiver. But he was a young man with little experience – or none, as she supposed – so perhaps the difference between terror and passion was not readily apparent to him.

After the deed was done, she worried a good deal about whether she might be pregnant. She thought of praying not to be, but she did not think she would have God's ear. And besides, in the one way, disgrace would have delivered her. 'I'll look after you,' Ralph had said. 'If that happened, we'd just bring the wedding forward.' When her period came – four days late, late enough to put her into a daze of panic and hope – she leaned against the freezing wall of her parents' bathroom, against the hostile dark-green paint, and cried over the chance lost.

After this she seemed to lose her equilibrium; she had not thought of herself as a complicated person, but now all sorts of wishes and fears were fighting inside her head. Ralph suggested that they should bring the wedding forward anyway; marry as soon as she left her teacher-training college, not wait until the end of the summer. Uncle James came to meet her parents, and talked about this very interesting post that was going in Dar-es-Salaam.

Her mother thought that the climate might be unsuitable, but conceded that Anna had never had a day's illness and had not been brought up to be a shirker. Betty thought, further, that the natives might not be nice. But what surprised Anna was how easily they fell in with James' suggestion, how quickly they agreed that though the engagement had been unusually short the marriage might as well be in June. For the first time it occurred to her that they might be glad to have her off their hands. Think of the expenditure of emotion a daughter entails! With their daughter married, and at the other side of the world, they would have more energy for the affairs of strangers.

Of course there was something improbable, even hilarious, about the idea of being a missionary in Africa. She said, 'I won't have to wear a sola topi, will I? And be boiled in a pot?'

Ralph said, 'I don't think so. Uncle James has never been boiled. Not so far, anyway.'

Then Ralph came to her with the change of plan. If she agreed, they were not to go to East Africa at all. A job was waiting for them elsewhere, in a township called Elim. It was near Johannesburg, north of the city – not far from Pretoria either, he said, as if that would help her place it. He brought a book, newly published, called *Naught for Your Comfort*. If she would read it, he suggested, she would know why people were needed and why perhaps if they valued their own comfort they ought not to go. Then she could weigh up the options, think what was best for them. 'And best for other people, of course,' she said. At that time – the spring of 1956 – she could say such a thing with no ironical intent.

She read the book at once. It painted a picture of a hungry, bloody, barely comprehensible world. She felt ready to enter it. She did not know what use she could be, but Ralph seemed to think their work was cut out for them. And after all, comfort had never been one of her expectations.

She had dreamt about the book too, those last nights before they left England. The dreams seemed to heighten but not betray the text. Policemen strutted in the streets with machine-guns. Acts of Parliament were posted up on every street. The populace was cowed.

When she woke, she shuttled these nightmares out of her head. For one thing, the dream-streets of Elim were too much like the streets of East Dereham. For another thing, they had to jostle for space in her imagination with the images already there: missionaries' tales and childhood geography texts, smudgy photographs of mean proportions; women with their teeth filed sharp, men with cicatrized cheeks. Some other part of Africa, no doubt. Some other time. Still she imagined savannah, long horizons, thatched rondavels standing in kraals: a population simply religious, hymn-singing, tractable. In real life, she had almost never seen a black man.

Ralph had said to Uncle James, 'I hardly think my work at the hostel is going to have prepared me for Africa.'

Uncle James had said cheerfully, 'Don't worry. Nothing could prepare you for Africa.'

Her mother had given her a book called *The Sun-Drenched*

Veld. She could read it on the ship, Betty advised. 'One of the *Windows on the World* series, Anna. It cost 9/6.' She picked it up on the day they quit Las Palmas, flicking its pages as they moved through waters where flying fish leapt.

It bore little resemblance to Father Huddleston's text; but no doubt it was true, in its way. 'In descriptions of African wildlife the zebra is often mentioned only in passing. Yet he is a lovely creature; a compact, sturdy little horse with neat mane and flowing tail. And no two of his kind are patterned alike! Having drawn his outline you can paint in the stripes as you please.'

When the sea made her dreamy, unable to concentrate, she gave up on the text, let the book close in her lap and rested her eyes on its cover. It beckoned the reader through arches of the coolest, palest peppermint, into an other-worldly landscape – pink and gold in the foreground, green hills rising in the middle ground and beyond them the lilac haze of mountains. She wondered if the illustrator had confused it with heaven; got his commissions mixed up, perhaps. But then she remembered a book she had seen on Ralph's shelves – a book from his years as a fossil-hunter. The picture on the cover was much the same – strange, impossible colours. She had turned to the inside flap to see what was represented: *On the shores of a Jurassic lagoon*, the caption said. Amid the startling viridescence of the palms, Archaeopteryx flopped and swooped, feathers glowing with the deep autumn tints of a game bird. A little dinosaur, glinting like steel, scurried on spindle legs. The sky was a delicate eggshell. In the background shone a deeper aqueous blue-green – some vast and primitive ocean, with shores that had never been mapped.

But now, how small the sea appeared: a metallic dish, across which they inched. After dark the people who were sailing home stood at the rail, looking for the Southern Cross. And one night it appeared, lying just off-south, exactly where everyone had predicted it would be. Anna saw four dull points of light,

71

pale, hardly distinguishable from the meagre scattering of stars around. She would not have noticed it, she thought, if it had not been pointed out.

They came into Table Bay in the rain, in drizzle and cloud which lifted from moment to moment, then descended again. Through the murk a solid dark mass became visible. 'Table Mountain,' someone told her. A pancake of grey cloud lay over it. The sun broke through, gleamed, was gone – then sent out another searching ray, like an arm reaching into a tent. She could see the contours of the mountain now – its spines of rock, and the ravines and crevices steeped in violet shadow.

What had she expected? Some kind of municipal hill. 'Look there,' a man said. 'That's Devil's Peak.' The cloud was moving now, billowing, parting. The sun was fighting through. The stranger took her arm, and turned her body so that she saw a wisp of cloud, like smoke, rising into the sky.

The Archbishop of Cape Town said, 'You're not like your Uncle James. You're more of a muscular Christian.'

'Oh, James,' Ralph said. 'No, he's never looked strong.'

'But he has endured,' the archbishop said. He seemed to relish the phrase. It gave a heroic quality to James' life. Which, Ralph supposed, it really did possess. From some points of view.

He wished he could have avoided this interview. They did not merit a prelate; only James' letter of introduction had brought them here. They could have gone straight to Johannesburg by rail, and on to Elim. They could have been briefed by an underling from the Pretoria diocese. Or not briefed at all. Frankly, Ralph had expected he would have to muddle through. It was the usual way.

'I wanted James here with me,' the archbishop said. 'Some seven years ago. When I was raised to this – ah – dignity. We had here, at that time, everything one could require. Churches, schools, hospitals, clubs. We had the money and the men. We had the blessed opportunity of leadership. Well, perhaps James saw what would come of it. I cannot claim I did.'

The archbishop limped across the room, setting up little vibrations in the furniture, making the tea-cups tremble. He was a vast, heavy man, seventy years old or perhaps more. He handed himself to a sofa; grunting with effort and pain as he lowered himself, he manoeuvred his stiff leg and propped it on cushions as if it were a false limb, or as if it belonged to someone else. It was a moment before he spoke again. 'We set out with high ideals,' he said. 'The things we wanted have not happened. Well, there was no promise that they would.'

The archbishop seemed shy. Could an archbishop be shy? He spoke gruffly, in short, broken phrases; the phrases were, none the less, well-planned.

'A year before I was enthroned,' he said, 'the electorate threw out Smuts and put the Nationalists in. Then certain laws were enacted, which I presume you know everything about – or if you do not, you will know shortly. You will learn the theory. You will see the practice. You will see that we have come, in effect, to be a police state.' He broke off, waiting for Ralph's reaction. 'Oh, be sure I did not always talk in this fashion. I gave the elected government what leeway I could, for one tries to play the statesman. I understood the machinery of their laws, but I did not know how they would operate it.'

'Apartheid is hard to believe in,' Ralph said. 'I mean, you'd have to see it to believe it.'

The archbishop grunted. '*Separateness*, they used to say. It is the change of language that is significant – it is rather more than the evolution of a term. But I said to myself, when Daniel Malan came in, he is not an oaf. He is a cultured man. He has a doctorate,' the archbishop broke off and gave a short laugh, 'which he got from the University of Utrecht, with a thesis on

Bishop Berkeley. Malan has still some regard for public opinion, I told myself. Then behold, out goes Malan, in comes Strydom, who as you may know was at one time an ostrich farmer. Educated where? Stellenbosch and Pretoria. He is a man from the Transvaal. You will learn what that means. When J. G. Strydom came in I had my moment of despair. That was three years ago now.'

Anna made a tentative movement, in the direction of the tea tray. The archbishop nodded to her, then turned and addressed himself to Ralph.

'You have heard of the Bantu Education Act. They have put you in the picture in London, I hope. You know our pre-eminence in education; the churches have done everything, the government nothing. It is we who have educated the African. We did not know, when we were doing it, that we were going about to embarrass the government. All we have achieved, as they see it, is to create a threat to them. By this Act they mean to remove the threat.'

'I find it difficult to get my mind around it, I suppose,' Ralph said. 'Education is progress, would you not think, it is civilization? I can't imagine that any government in the history of the world, until now, has set out to make time run backwards.'

'Oh, I don't know,' the archbishop said. 'There would be some. It doesn't do to generalize. But you see why they've done it, don't you? Education for the non-Europeans is now put into the hands of Dr Verwoerd, at the Native Affairs Department. Dr Verwoerd's reasoning is, what is the use of teaching mathematics to an African child? A labourer doesn't need mathematics. Give him mathematics, he will begin to think he might try to be a little more than a labourer. Well, Dr Verwoerd would not want him to make that mistake.'

Anna brought the tea. The archbishop tested it. 'Very good, my dear,' he said, 'Such a pleasure, tea, isn't it?' He looked,

Anna thought, as if his pleasures were few. She melted away, back to her tapestry stool.

'The notion is to bring in a new kind of education,' the archbishop said, looking into his cup. 'An education to create coolies and houseboys and fodder for the mines. Two and a half hours a day, taught by little girls who have scraped through their Standard VI. This is not merely the prescription for the children of the illiterate, this is for all – for the children of our brightest mission boys and girls, for the children of university graduates from Fort Hare. The parents have to contain themselves in patience while they see their children stultified.'

'It seems to cut off hope for the future,' Ralph said. 'You can repeal other laws, but how will you undo the effect of this one?'

'Precisely,' the archbishop said. 'In twenty years' time, or in forty years' time, when this idiocy is over, how will you put wisdom into heads that have been deprived of it?'

The archbishop's hand shook a little now. The tea-cup seemed to be too much for him, as a delicate piece of china might be too much for a bear. Anna darted forward, took the cup, returned it to the tray. He did not appear to notice her.

'And so now, how are the churches situated?' The old man turned his head towards Ralph. 'We sit before the government "like the rabbit before the cobra", as Father Huddleston has so memorably expressed it.' His voice was dry. 'Father Huddleston has a gift for the vivid phrase, has he not? Some people say we should close all our schools rather than take part in this fantastic scheme. Others say that any education is better than none. Father Huddleston, if I may quote again, calls that sentiment "the voice of Vichy". Mrs Eldred,' he turned his head again, stiffly and painfully, 'although you are a trained teacher, you will find yourself engaged in amusing children rather than teaching them. We have to try to get them off the streets, where they will get into trouble. This place, you know, Elim –

well, it is not in my cure, but I can tell you something of what to expect. Elim is what they call a freehold township. Africans have been settled there since the turn of the century. They have built houses, they own them. Generations have grown up in Elim. There would be, I don't know, 50,000 people?'

'About that,' Ralph said.

'And now there is no security any more, no guarantee of what succeeding years will bring. They are knocking down Sophiatown, and Elim may be next.'

'Where will they put the people?' Anna said.

'Ah, this is the essence of the apartheid policy, my dear. The government wishes to return them to their tribal areas.' Turning his head again, he spoke with grave, weary courtesy, as if he were addressing the President himself, and giving him all the credit he could muster for a foolish scheme. 'Well, you will grasp the situation better when you arrive there. But you must understand that for the people you are going to live among everything has become hazardous, impermanent. It is hardly possible for them to step out of doors without wondering if they are falling foul of some new law. And they feel that their futures have been taken away.'

'I hardly feel equal to it,' Ralph said. 'To such a situation.'

'Then why did you come?'

He didn't know what to say. He couldn't say, to get away from my family. 'I thought it was my duty to try to do something. We both thought so. But we have so little experience.'

'Oh, you have youth,' the archbishop said, 'therefore you have resilience. That is the pious hope, at least. May I advise you? In your work, try to relate everything to God. Try to work on the scale of eternity. Do you see? Otherwise you will be fettered by trivia. The daily frustrations will cripple you.'

'That seems excellent advice,' Ralph said. 'Good advice in any circumstances. If one could follow it.'

Anna said, 'If I were a black person in this country, I'm not sure I would believe in God. Particularly.'

The archbishop frowned.

Ralph said, 'People may think that when they are so oppressed, when they are told that their nature is somehow inferior, when they have suffered so many misfortunes, that they no longer matter to God. It would be a natural thing for them to think.'

At this the archbishop gave vent to his sentiments, in short bursts of rhetoric, like barks. He referred to 'feeble secular humanism' (which he supposed to be a temptation to Ralph) and to the Christian faith as 'the charter of man's greatness'. It was clear that these were phrases from a sermon he was writing, or from one which he had already delivered. Anna looked sideways at Ralph, from under her eyelashes. She didn't know how either of them had dared say what they had said. They would do anything, she supposed, now that they were so far from home.

When the archbishop had finished barking, she put in a feeble, conciliatory word. It was only that they were inexperienced, she said. They were apprehensive – here in a new country, in their first real jobs.

'Do you also not feel equal to it?' the archbishop inquired.

'I am not sure anyone could be.'

This was a good answer. 'Well, I know I am not,' the archbishop said. 'There are two things – no, three things – I ask of you, particularly. Try not to despise your opponents; try not to hate them. It will probably be quite difficult for you, but for a Christian the effort is necessary. And try not to break the law. You have not been sent here to get yourselves into the newspapers or the magistrate's court. I hope you can remember that.'

'The third thing?' Ralph said.

77

'Oh yes. When you write home to England, ask your people not to make hasty judgements. It is a complicated country, this. I comfort myself that there is little real wickedness in it. But there is so much fear, fear on all sides. Fear paralyses the sympathies, and the power of reasoning. So it becomes a kind of wickedness, in the end.' The archbishop looked up, nodded. The interview was over. They rose. Unexpectedly he smiled, and patted at his leg, lying before him painful and inert. 'Do you know what I did last year? I went to Tristan da Cunha. I expect you did not know my diocese ran so far. They had to tie me into a chair and run me down the side of the frigate on ropes. Then I had to lie in a little boat with a canvas bottom, and they paddled me ashore. Your Uncle James wouldn't have believed his eyes. But you know, I don't think I'll go again. I hardly think I'd weather it, do you?'

He didn't expect an answer. A secretary ushered them out. He was picking up papers to read as they left the room.

Outside Anna said, 'The Winston Churchill imitation, do you think it's deliberate? Do you think he's studied from recordings?'

'I'm sure.'

'He practically accused us of not being Christians.'

'We are, though,' Ralph said. 'Despite provocation.'

'His heart's in the right place,' Anna said.

'His heart's irrelevant, I'm afraid.'

At Cape Town Station, the signs said *Slegs vir Blankes*. The non-European carriages were tacked like an afterthought on to the end of the train.

At stations up the line, children gathered around the carriage doors, their hands cupped for small coins.

At Johannesburg, the station was bustling with black men in

slick suits with cardboard briefcases, and with florid white farmers come to town. Their hair seemed insufficient to cover their great heads. Their bellies threatened to burst the buttons of their shirts. Great rufous knees, exposed beneath khaki shorts, butted at the future. Beneath the pavements, Ralph said, were diamonds and gold.

It was cooler than Anna had expected, and the air seemed thin. She shrank away from the hooting and snarling of the traffic and the mosaic of faces in the street. At midnight a noise brought her to the window of their modest hotel. Hailstones – frozen chips of ice, an inch and a half across – rattled at the glass. The bombardment lasted for five minutes. It stopped as suddenly as it began. For an hour, deep in the watches of the night, the city was quiet, as if holding its breath.

The Mission House stood on Flower Street. It was set back from the road, in a kitchen garden in which grew mealies, potatoes, cabbage, pumpkins and carrots. There were three steps up to the veranda, which was netted in against flies. There had been shade at one time, but the big trees had been cut down. Inside the rooms were small and hot.

Everything had been refurbished, Lucy Moyo said, refurbished in anticipation of their arrival. The linoleum on the floor, polished till it gleamed, was offensively vivid: irrepressibly jazzy, zigzagged, sick-making. No expense had been spared – or so Lucy claimed – on providing for the sitting room nylon-fur cushions with buttoned centres, and a coffee-table which splayed its legs, like a bitch passing water. With all the vicarious pride of careful stewardship, Lucy showed off a magazine rack of bent gold wire, tapping with the cushion of her finger at its little rubber feet. In the kitchen was an acid-yellow table with a chromium trim and white tubular legs. There were chairs to match.

The town was set on a height; every day there was a breeze. On clear days you could see the prosperous suburbs of Pretoria – white houses sprawling across green lawns, avenues lined with jacaranda trees. Down there, public monuments, Boer pride: up here, *swart gevaar*, the black peril. Yet what unfolded to the view, at Elim's centre, but a vision of clipped, cold-water respectability: wide roads on a grid plan, well-fenced playing fields, neat brick houses? The houses, true, differed as to the state of their repair. The best were freshly painted; and outside them, in regular rows, grew pot-plants in old paint tins. They were not exactly pot-plants, not strictly. They were things that would have grown just as well, and more naturally, in the soil. But these sprigs had been singled out for special treatment. They bespoke ownership. They were nature tamed. They were a form of civic pride. Everyone seemed proud in Elim. 'We live here as neighbours,' Lucy explained. 'Not as tribespeople. We all agree together.' This was not quite true, of course. But it was a pleasant idea, and could be entertained for some of the time.

In their first few days they were shepherded from house to house, welcomed in the homes of churchgoers and parish workers. Cups of tea were provided; there were needlepoint footstools, framed photos, lace curtains. There was no artefact that did not rest upon its little crocheted mat.

The price of this fussiness, in labour, was clear at once. Water was fetched in buckets, cement floors scrubbed every day on hands and knees. By a servant, perhaps; even the poverty-stricken can afford to employ the destitute. Every morning, in the backyards, clothes were slapped and wrung in tin tubs.

But on the fringes of Elim the houses were overflowing. There were families living in sheds, in less space than a farmer would give an animal. Lucy explained all this; rents were high in the neighbouring locations and when families could not pay them and were turned out they came to Elim. And then, relatives came from the bundu all the time, and you couldn't turn them away, people had to live somehow; perhaps you might build a lean-to at the back, with whatever came to hand, and hope it would withstand the wind and rain; if not, build it again. She indicated dwellings constructed of sheets of tin leaning against a wall. Naked children – naked except for a string of beads around the waist – played in the dust. Lucy stood before them, cajoling till they answered her, her bag matching her shoes, and her Sunday petal hat planted on her close-curled head. Sanitary arrangements? Better not to think about them. Even the Mission House, after all, had only its huts and buckets, emptied every day by Jakob Malajane, also employed as the gardener.

The Indian and Chinese shops were well-stocked and orderly, Lucy pointed out. There were several where she knew the proprietors, they were not bad types all of them, they would sometimes put things under the counter for you till you could pay. Every so often, though, the bad boys with knives and coshes came in, left the proprietor bleeding and took what they wanted. 'Not all these tsotsis are boys whom you can discipline,' Lucy said. 'Some of them are grown men.' She shrugged; she wanted to warn the Eldreds, whom she thought pitiful children, but she did not want to dwell upon this side of life. There was no need either to mention brothels and shebeens. After all, Mr and Mrs Standish had got by without talking about them.

So she marched them off to meet church-choir contraltos, a saxophonist in Elim's jazz band, a neat-waisted coloured woman who ran a Girl Guide troop: all good people, she said, all family people. Down the road walked a stately, very black man, robed and bearing a crozier. His wife walked arm in arm with him, her purple frock sweeping the dust; she wore a necklace of bones. 'Oh, Mr and Mrs Bishop Kwakwa,' Lucy said. 'Zionist Mount Carmel Gospel of Africa. Not at all a real church.'

★

81

The day in Flower Street began at six o'clock; but they woke earlier. The bedroom curtains were thin. Their background colour was tan, with a design of purple sunbursts. They did not quite meet across the glass. Each morning a shaft of sunlight, thin as an axe-blade, struck across their pillows and their eyes.

Already the kitchen was busy, the mealie-porridge bubbling on the range. Jakob chopped the wood, then ambled to his garden duties. He was a country boy: his face was battered like a boxer's. He had, Lucy told them, the falling sickness. The people of his village used to throw stones at him when he fell down in a fit, to drive the devil out. They were illiterate people, Lucy explained, in her lofty way.

They would walk to Matins: the church was five minutes away. Father Alfred would shake their hands, though he would be seeing them perhaps twice before lunch, most days, and twice after lunch, and whenever he felt the need. Father Alfred was a little, anxious man. He smiled perpetually. His eyes in his brown face had an air of faded surprise.

After Matins it was time for Anna to talk to the cook, Rosinah, about the day's meals. Quantities must be approximate, they must stretch to accommodate whoever might come by. No one could say what the day would bring.

There were a large number of servants at the mission, none of them overworked. They were people with spectacular bad-luck stories, and they were engaged on the basis of these, rather than of any aptitude or proficiency for their work. Jakob, who slept under a tree for most of the day, had an assistant, a young boy with no parents, seemingly no kin of any kind except some shadowy relatives in Durban who could not be traced. He passed his day listlessly raking the ground, and manufacturing elaborate besoms. He was permanently in rags, a disgrace to the mission. Whenever Ralph gave him any clothes, he would sell them. It seemed that his ambition was to be a walking sign, a symbol of wretchedness.

The cook Rosinah sat with her chair wedged into a corner near the stove. The back door was always open, so that her cronies could drift in and out. There was a constant procession of them, rolling through the kitchen and out again, squatting on the floor to exchange gossip. When Anna passed, she smiled and greeted them, but she could not help noticing that they were usually eating something. It disturbed her that the half of Elim that claimed acquaintance with Rosinah was better fed than the half that did not.

Rosinah had been known to chase people out of the kitchen and across the yard, with some offensive kitchen weapon: sometimes a thing so relatively benign as a wooden spoon, but once at least a small meat-cleaver. There seemed no reason for these outbursts of hers, nothing especially which brought them on. The victims would be back after a few days, squatting nervously on the threshold, drawn by the chance of a handout of a bowl of porridge or the heel of a loaf.

No one knew Rosinah's own particular bad-luck story. She never spoke of her past, but something must have soured her temper, something out of the ordinary run of fire and disease and sudden death. Day to day the chief victim of her wrath was a girl called Dearie, her assistant. Dearie was a frail young woman with rickety legs; pregnant, and with a sick baby bound always on her back.

Dearie's babies died, Anna was told. This was the third or maybe the fourth, and each one was weaker than the last. Anna decided that this current infant would not die on her: she would fathom the mystery, she would keep Dearie under her eye. She suggested the doctor; Dearie, head bowed, suggested in her monosyllabic way that she saw a doctor of her own.

Anna did not dare insist. She provided powdered milk and rusks, peered anxiously at the small wizened face. The babies slipped away in the night, breathed out the last of their lives while everyone else slept. At least, that was how it appeared to be; Rosinah, in her rages, suggested that Dearie murdered them. There was no husband, and it seemed there never had been. Lucy Moyo said, for one slip you can forgive a girl, but that Dearie, she is a walking outrage. Anna said, I thought we were supposed to forgive seventy times seven? Lucy glared at her. Anna thought, perhaps I have got my Scripture wrong. Perhaps it is God who does that.

A woman called Clara cleaned the house and washed the clothes. She was a mission girl, had passed her junior certificate. She was ashamed to do such work, and Ralph and Anna saw that it was demeaning for her. Whenever she asked them, they wrote her a glowing reference, recommending her for some job in a store, or a post as a hospital orderly. But employers turned her away. She came back to the house, stony-eyed, and picked up her brush to sweep the rooms out.

Clara had once had a husband, but he had disappeared, leaving her with four small children. Her expectations of these mild babies were ferociously high: silence, industry, a useful occupation at all times. Each evening she called them to recite Bible verses; if they failed, she told them to bring her the cane. Their little cries, like the mewing of cats, punctuated the evenings. But who could tell Clara not to do it? They must not be like their father; and she believed that only the weals on their legs stood between them and a life of drink and misery, with hell at the end of it.

It was not difficult to understand why employers turned Clara away, but it was difficult to put into words. She had some quality that stirred unease. It was not an overt violence, as in Rosinah's case. It was an emptiness; you did not care to think how it might be filled up.

Each morning at Flower Street, Ralph went into the cubbyhole he called his office to deal with letters and the accounts –

recording minutely, faithfully, the futile expenditure of tiny sums. Anna went to the nursery school to supervise the local helpers. It was not a small enterprise; there were a hundred and fifty children, organized by twenty or thirty volunteers, who came and went by some bewildering rota that they understood and Anna did not.

Each morning they put the children into their blue overalls, smocks which fastened at the backs of their necks; this was the day's first task, feeding squirming arms into sleeves. They employed two women to wash the overalls at the end of the week, and another woman to make the mealie-porridge for midday. The children had to have their porridge scooped into their mouths; they had to be put down for an afternoon rest, supervised on the swings, slides and climbing frames; they had to be weighed and measured and told stories. There was a waiting list, bigger by far than the current enrolment.

Once the children were seven they could not keep them at the nursery. They sent them into the dangerous world, for the two and a half hours of education that the new laws allowed them. This period over, the children were at the mercy of circumstance. If their mothers managed to find any kind of work, they took it, leaving the children to the fitful and reluctant supervision of relatives, of older brothers and sisters. Where the supervision failed, they were out on the streets.

For a few of these outcasts, the mission ran what they called a 'play-group'. They gave the children soup and bread, and fruit when they could get it. They didn't give them books because that would have been breaking the law. They tried to keep them amused with games and handicrafts, making sure they did not set their feet on any path that could lead anywhere.

And were they enforced, these absurd laws? Oh yes. 'This town is full of people who will run to the police,' Lucy said calmly. 'They will do it for a few pennies. Mrs Eldred, you must understand that.'

Anna would ask for nothing for herself, but the sight of the children made her bold. She pleaded with shopkeepers in the white suburbs to help them eke out the daily ration; she petitioned vegetable stores for bruised apples, and bakers for yesterday's bread. She searched for donors to support children whose parents couldn't afford the small monthly fee. Every day she set herself a target: so many pieces of effrontery, so many crude demands. She found it hard to work in the house because people were constantly walking in from the stoep, coming to ask her foolish questions or use the telephone; an hour could go by with nothing accomplished.

One of the nursery classrooms had a storeroom – a large broom-cupboard really. She took it over. She had to edge around the trestle table that formed her desk, ease herself behind the table, squeeze her narrow body against the wall. She stabbed with two fingers at a rusty typewriter: stabbed out her begging letters.

The fact is, Ralph said, this job reduces us entirely to beggars. You can almost never just buy something, no matter how much you need it. You have to plot for it, appeal for it, arrange to borrow it, coax someone else into paying for it.

Up at the house Ralph had his office door wedged open by a stack of papers. Other papers were stacked on every surface, in dangerous sliding piles. 'Do you think the diocese would buy me a filing cabinet?' he asked Anna. 'But no ...' and he dismissed the thought at once. 'There are more urgent needs.'

Often, at the end of the day, there were nursery babies uncollected. They were forgotten – or, rather, the complicated arrangements which underpinned family life had come adrift. Anna would gather up the children, who were wailing or dumb with bewilderment; she would take them to the house, give them biscuits, comfort them, send a messenger to find out what had gone wrong at home. Sudden illness? Arrest?

At this time of day, Ralph was usually at the police station. Every morning the police appeared on the streets, picking up their quota of pass offenders, herding them together on the street corners, handcuffed two by two; then a van came to collect them. African policemen performed this chore. At first Ralph thought, how can they do it? Soon he realized that they had a living to make. A white sergeant at the station told him wearily, 'Mr Eldred, we all have a living to make.'

In the afternoon the relatives of those who had been arrested would come to the mission, telling their stories: our son, he just went out to see a neighbour, my sister, she went to buy food and left her pass at home. Ralph would go down to the station, to bail people out, pay their fines. 'Next week,' he would say to the relatives, 'you must pay me the money back, you understand?' He had to recover the money, or the mission would be out of pocket, and some other head of expenditure would have to be cut. But Ralph could only urge people to remember to take their papers, whenever they stepped out of doors.

He did not like to cooperate with the government in this way. But he was not sent to Africa to encourage people to break the law, and James' letters reminded him of this. He was not required to be a hero or a martyr, only to go on doing his best in the circumstances in which he found himself.

People are not starving, he wrote to James. The poorest can just about feed and clothe themselves. But they live on the brink of an abyss. A few days' sickness pushes them over the edge: the loss of a few pence in the week. Women struggle to bring up their children clean and with good manners, literate. They hope there is a future for them, but from the children's eyes you can see they are wiser than their parents to the drift of events.

Naught for your comfort, Anna thought. Only a long little-ness consoles you – putting another stitch, then another row, into a blanket square. As winter approached, the women's knitting became zealous and purposeful. On Wednesdays there was a sewing circle, too, and Anna felt she must put in an appearance; Lucy Moyo, or some other woman with a strong voice, read from the New Testament while their fingers flew, and faith stiffened their spines. Compare them to these people, and the Norfolk families were atheists; the Martins of East Dereham were godless hedonists, the Eldreds of Norwich were heathens, and debauched.

Thursdays was the day for the women's church meetings. The Mothers' Union wore starched white blouses and black skirts, with their special brooch pinned to their blouses and black cotton kerchiefs on their heads. Unmarried mothers – if they were penitent – could wear the uniform. But never, ever, the brooch.

The Methodist ladies wore red blouses and black skirts. The Dutch Reformed wore black skirts and white blouses with broad black collars. They made the Methodists look skittish.

Dearie, every Sunday, went missing for hours. Anna was concerned. 'Don't fret, Mrs Eldred,' Lucy Moyo told her. 'She is attending Bishop Kwakwa's church, all day singing and dancing. She is going there for wearing a uniform with braid, and whooping and making an unseemly spectacle. And their tom-fool pastor going about with blessed water in a bucket.'

In the afternoons at Flower Street, there were meetings of various welfare committees. These concluded, Anna and Ralph went out together to see people who were sick, bouncing over the rutted roads in the mission's car. Four o'clock, sinuous shapes melted into the walls; the young boys, who had run wild on the veld all day, had come back to town.

By five o'clock they had taken up their station, these boys: they lounged outside the cafés, sometimes passing a cigarette from hand to hand. They gave off a palpable air of dis-ease; they were waiting for dark. It would be sunset when Ralph and Anna arrived home. As they rattled along to the corner of the street, as they approached the corner that would bring the Mission House within view, Ralph felt Anna in the passenger seat grow pale and still with tension. In summer she would be hot and dusty, in winter chilled to the bone. She wanted to wash and eat her supper, just that; but she could not know, until they turned the corner, what was waiting to frustrate her.

What she dreaded was the sight of a half-dozen men collected on the stoep, waiting for them with some problem they would not be able to solve. The only worse sight was that of a whole family, waiting with a problem they would not be able to solve. If it was a group of men, possibly Ralph and Anna would have to climb back into the car and jolt to the police station for some verbal conciliation and a pay-out; but if it was a family, they would need food, and they would need shelter for the night, at the very least. When Anna saw that the stoep was occupied, that they were expected, she felt her pulse rate rise, and a bitter taste, like bile, swim into her mouth.

Evening at Flower Street: Anna had hardly any time with Ralph. They never sat down to a meal alone; Father Alfred would be in, or some of the nursery teachers, or committee people with unfinished business. By bedtime they were often too exhausted to make love, and always too exhausted to talk; sometimes they had no thoughts they cared to voice. And the nights were often broken. A woman had been taken ill, or there had been an accident, or a young man had been hurt in a drunken fight.

When night fell, there were beatings, stabbings, robberies, rapes. Each of these incidents caused the men in the Department of Native Administration to shake their heads and talk of 'a trouble-spot', and 'the breakdown of law and order'. They did not see the Mothers' Union, in their starched blouses; they saw only gallows-bait. The vogue weapon of the gangs was the sharpened bicycle spoke. Approaching their victim from behind, they would stab the spoke into his thigh, and empty his pockets while he was frozen with shock and pain.

It was onerous, the nightly routine of locking up the Mission House: keys, bolts, bars, clanking from room to room. Futile, really, because if anyone comes knocking you have to let them in. You can shout through the door for their name but if their name means nothing to you that isn't a reason to keep them outside.

On Saturday mornings Ralph and Anna gave out supplies from the back porch: vegetables, sacks of mealie meal, sugar poured from sacks and bagged up, and whatever tinned food and clothing had been donated by the white charities in the last week. They trusted that no one would come for food who did not need it, but they knew they trusted in vain; they must endure Lucy Moyo's impatient clucking, the turning up of her eyes to her God. On Saturday afternoons there were funerals; hymn-singing, ululation. Charity filled the grumbling stomachs of the mourners.

Ralph would say:

> 'But who hath seen the grocer
> Treat housemaids to his teas
> Or crack a bottle of fish sauce
> Or stand a man a cheese?'

Saturday at sunset, funerals and parties merged. Enamel mugs of sorghum beer were passed from hand to hand: beer that looked like baby-vomit. The hosts played gramophones in their yard. There was drumming and dancing far into the night. When the guests had had enough they rolled up in their blankets, and slept on the ground.

Sunday mornings there were church processions, the women in their uniforms, their sons in suits with polished faces. Later the small girls tripped into Sunday school, their hair braided and tied up in ribbons. Their frocks were from the Indian store, and had stiff net skirts, with which they scratched each other's shins and calves. They had white gloves, and pochettes hanging over their skinny wrists. In a year or two they'd be saving up for skin-lightening cream. They'd be begging their parents, for a birthday treat, to find the money to send them to the hairdressers to get their hair straightened. 'When you are older,' parents say. 'Wait till you are fifteen, then we will see.'

On Sunday mornings, after church, the men of Elim visited the barbers who set up shop under the trees. On Sunday afternoons there were football matches. Anna and Ralph entertained Father Alfred to tea, and the Sunday-school workers too. Anna could see in her face what opinion Lucy Moyo held of her baking; her scones were flat, and fizzed in the mouth, unlike the scones of Mrs Standish.

After the tea party was over, they were, briefly, alone. Ralph held her in his arms as she swayed with fatigue, whimpering against his shoulder. 'I shouldn't have brought you,' he whispered to her. 'But we can't go home now.'

Only weeks, months had passed; they were sealed so securely inside Elim's bitter routines that they could not imagine any other kind of life.

Anna forgot sometimes what lay beneath the surface. She saw the baked soil and red cement floors, the ant-trail and the cockroaches' path. But Ralph was there to remind her of the truth: she was walking on diamonds and gold.

Every evening, at dusk, the women lit braziers. The smoke

rose into the darkening sky, and lay over the township in a haze: blue and fine, like the breath of frigid angels. Every evening, when the women lit the braziers, some two-year-old would fall into them.

There were hospitals in Elim, but casualties came to the mission: walking, or carried in their mother's arms, or limping between two friends and dripping blood. Mrs Standish had been a nurse, and people could not grasp that Anna had not the same skill. 'We have to know our limitations,' Anna said. 'I'd feel easier in my mind if we had a doctor on call.'

Ralph said, 'Koos is on call. In effect.'

Koos had his surgery on Victoria Street, in a dusty single-storey building with a tin roof. There was a waiting room and a consulting room, and another room at the back where Koos slept on a camp-bed. In the yard were two shacks, one for cooking and the other fitted out as the laboratory and sometime cat-house of Koos' dispenser, Luke Mbatha.

Koos might have been thirty, might have been forty. He had straw-coloured hair and a worried face; his smile was rare though his general disposition must, one supposed, be benevolent. He wore stone-coloured shorts; his legs were mottled and stringy, his knee-joints large and starved. His face and arms were red from scrubbing with a fierce antiseptic soap. Ralph washed his hands once at Koos' place, and felt that the skin had been taken off them.

Koos had a vast number of patients. He treated them for a few coppers. 'But they must pay,' he told Ralph. 'If they don't pay for their treatment they don't believe in it, you know? If you just give them the medicine, they think, this thing must be rubbish, if he is *giving* it to me. They go out and pour it in the road.'

Ralph said, 'Anna's trying to persuade our kitchen girl Dearie to bring the new baby down. Anna's worried about him, she says he's not gaining weight. Dearie won't admit there's anything wrong, but I suppose she must care, mustn't she? We can't work out what she's up to. She's got coloured strings tied round his wrists and his ankles. Yesterday, Anna thought he'd been dropped and got a big bruise on his head, but it turned out to be some ash he'd been rubbed with.'

Koos said, 'She's been to see one of my rivals.'

'No harm, I suppose,' Ralph said.

'Except it makes for delay.' Koos shrugged. 'Then, you see, perhaps she thinks it's some African disease.'

'Are there such things?'

'In people's minds,' Koos said. 'They think there are diseases that white people can't understand. It's right, up to a point. If I get a woman in here complains of palpitations, fainting, short of breath, I can listen to her chest and send off a blood sample, but sooner or later I have to say to her, look, what's your church that you go to? Have you been dancing at your church? Have you got possessed by a spirit?'

'They're not barbarians,' Ralph said, needled.

Koos' sandy eyebrows shot up. 'No? So quick to learn, man. Do you know what I think? I think we're all barbarians.'

Ralph always wanted to ask Koos, why are you here? It was like meeting a man with only one leg: you feel desperate to know what has happened to him. Accident? Illness? You want to ask, but you can only hope he'll tell you.

Six months in Elim. Ralph wrote to his Uncle James:

We could manage better if there were thirty hours in a day and nine days in a week, and yet I wonder if we are usefully employed at all. We don't have much time to stop and think, and I don't know whether that's bad or good. But every week we have to make some decision which seems a matter of

93

principle rather than of procedure, and there's no one we can go to when we want to talk things over. My nearest approach to a friend is our Afrikaner doctor, but though I think he is a good man and he has a lot of experience he looks at the world so differently from us that I can't go to him for advice, because I probably wouldn't understand the advice he gives me.

Most of these matters of principle we call 'blanket problems' – this is our shorthand for anything that derails us, in the ethical line. Now that the cold weather is here, some of the poorest people come to the door every day to ask for blankets. We have or can get or can knit blankets, but it seems that Mr and Mrs Standish, after they had given them out, would visit the recipients in their homes to check that the blankets were really needed and that they had not been sold. Anna and I, we feel terrible about this. It seems demeaning to all concerned. Yet Lucy Moyo says that if we don't do it, it will be widely understood that we are fools.

What should I do? I feel that, if I had had some training in England, I would have been aware that I would meet such problems of conscience – or am I dignifying them, are they indeed just problems of procedure? I keep saying it: I wasn't ready to come to Africa. Anna says, what is the use of all this effort? There is nothing an individual can do against a political system which, it seems to us, becomes more regressive and savage by the day. I try to urge people to think ahead, to show initiative, to help themselves, but what's the point when we know that in five years' time our town will no longer exist?

Lucy Moyo explained Koos, in her usual easy manner: 'The doctor went with some bad type of coloured girl.' She laughed. 'She thought it was for payment. He thought it was for romance.'

Anna reported it to Ralph. 'The coloured girl had a baby. A

small-town scandal, you know?' She had picked up some Afrikaans now, and her voice had taken on the local accent, the lilt. When she saw something pretty and helpless – a child, a kitten – she spoke in chorus with Lucy and Rosinah: 'Ag, shame!'

'Yes, I think I do know,' Ralph said. 'And I suppose that it happened in the days when it was only a disgrace, not a crime.' He shook his head. 'What happened to the woman and the child, does Lucy know?'

Anna was back to herself, her English tone: 'Oh, Lucy wouldn't stoop to know a thing like that.'

He thought of the doctor scrubbing himself, scouring his hands with the blistering soap. Had Koos a home, other than the back room with the camp-bed? Seemingly not; not any more.

Uncle James wrote back:

My dear Ralph, of course you were not ready to go to Africa. You went out of your own need, not out of the need of the people you were supposed to serve. Don't blame yourselves for that. It is the usual European way. When we find we lack a sense of purpose at home, we export our doubts; I have known people who – misguidedly, in my view – have gone to China to save their marriage.

The problems of our own country seem so complicated, that intelligent people wonder if it can be right to take a stance. It seems a thing only professional politicians can do – as we pay them, they can bear the burden of being simple-minded. But when we think of other countries, we imagine their problems are easy to solve – they are clear-cut, and we are so sure of the right moral line. Why do they make such a muddle of it? It is so obvious what ought to be done.

How clear-sighted we are – how benevolent! Until we arrive, of course, and see the reality.

Men and women working in the mission field are supposed to sort out their own notions before they try to foist them on others. But in my experience, when they arrive at their posting, they become – if they are worth anything – more confused than anyone else around them.

So do try, Ralph, not to burden yourself with a compulsion to be better than other people. Just do your best, can't you? I am aware that this sounds like a nursery nostrum, but it is the only advice I can give. You say you doubt (or Anna doubts) the power of the individual to achieve anything. But what if all the individuals give up? There will be precious little then for the people you are trying to serve. God will not provide, you know. You need not think it. His method is never so direct.

Every day brings a fresh problem to solve. Some people might argue that if you had a settled faith, you would not experience such turmoil. Myself, I have never believed in settled faith; there is always some emergency, God-given or otherwise, to undermine whatever certainties you have established for yourself. You could not take on, uncritically, your father's beliefs. You have had to find your own way. Conflict is not, in itself, a sign of lack of faith. It may be a sign of – dare I say it – spiritual insight, development. And at the very least – if what faces you is only a mental conflict, and an administrative problem – it shows you are beyond thinking of the world as a simple place, where good intentions are enough.

As for your problem about the blankets – of course you must go and see the people in their own houses. Has it occurred to you that the blankets may be a pretext? The people who apply to you may need far more than blankets, but find it difficult to draw your attention to this fact. And it may be that not all their needs are material.

Yes, Ralph thought, laying the letter aside; but who am I to diagnose these needs?

Anna came in. 'Am I interrupting you?'

'No. A letter from James.'

'I'll read it when I've a minute.' She wanted to tell him the news. The play-group children were going to give a concert. A ladies' charity from Jo'burg had donated a secondhand sewing-machine, and Anna would make costumes. She had been already to beg remnants from Mr Ahmed, on Nile Street.

For the next week, the machine's whine cut through his evening. Rain drummed on the roof, and the streets ran with red-brown water.

One week on, he found Anna running her hand, covetously, across a roll of cloth: it was a soft, limp fabric, a paisley pattern in a faded, near-mud green. 'Mr Ahmed sent this,' she said. 'It's got a big flaw in it. But I wouldn't mind – I could make wonderful curtains, if I could get some thick lining material. I mean,' she added, 'if I could persuade Mr Ahmed to give me some.'

'Why don't you do it? You've nearly finished the costumes now. You could start after supper, if you're not too tired.'

Anna shook her head. 'We have curtains already, don't we? Lucy Moyo sewed them with her own hands, those purple efforts with the sunbursts. The Sunday-school teachers had a collection among themselves to buy the material.' She looked up. 'Is it wicked to care about the way things look?'

'Of course not.'

'But the way people feel is more important, I suppose.'

So that was the end of the paisley curtains. Anna cut three yards off the bale, where the flaw showed least, and made herself a flowing calf-length skirt, gathered softly into the waist. 'Oh, Mrs Eldred,' Lucy said. 'Such a good seamstress you are. If you had your outfit made in Paris it couldn't fit you better. But that fabric – shame, so dull! Still, we must use what the Lord provides.'

Anna smiled. The weather cleared. Each morning the sun woke them, slashing through the inch where the curtains didn't meet.

Ralph wrote to James:

> How do you live? What is the proper way? The idea is gaining ground – and I find it is not without its appeal – that you should live like the people you work among, that for a Christian that is the only way. Why should you have more money and more comforts than they do? How can you mean anything to them, if you keep yourself apart?
>
> And yet, I can see that the idea might have disabling consequences.

He thought of Koos, with his dinner of mealie-pap and gravy.

> I am not sure I am brave enough to try to put it into practice.

James wrote:

> Do you have so much, Ralph, for people to envy you? Do I need to tell you that you are 7,000 miles from home? (You might, I realize, think it not much of a sacrifice – but let me tell you, if you do not miss us, we miss you, your sister and I, and we talk of you very often.) In one breath you complain to me of your life, your hardships and frustrations – and in the next you complain of your luxurious standard of living!
>
> Suppose you join the people you work amongst, and move into a lean-to in someone's backyard. What conceivable good will it do to anyone? It may make you feel better, for a week or two, but are your feelings the issue? When that life becomes unbearable – as it quickly would – you could escape. It would be, at best, only a well-intentioned experiment. The people around you cannot escape; there is no term put to their sentence. And so, you see, any gestures you might make in the direction of the equality of man are an insult to them. You are free to go, and they are not.

You have your education. You have your white skin, in a country where that means everything. Even the resources of your well-fed body mark you out as different. How dare you think you can become one of them? Privilege cannot be undone, once it has been conferred.

Ralph put his uncle's letter in the drawer. Again he thought of Koos, trying to scrub his skin away.

'I had another talk with Dearie,' Ralph said to the doctor. 'Anna had a talk too. We keep wondering if we should just grab the baby one day and bring it down to you, but that doesn't seem fair on Dearie, she's an adult after all. Or maybe you could come up to the mission. Though I don't know how we'd get him away from Dearie, for you to examine him. She keeps him fastened on her back the whole time. As far as I can see, he'll die there.'

'Promise her an injection,' Koos said. 'That's my last offer.'

'For her, or for the baby?'

'Both,' Koos said. 'Let's – what's the expression? – let's push the boat out. The people here, they love injections. Injections are the main thing with them. And I give so many, because if they don't get one from me they'll go and get jabbed with God knows what by God knows who, and pay a fat price for it.'

'It's not real medicine, is it?' Ralph was uneasy. 'Just giving your patients what they want.'

Koos tapped his forehead. 'Up here, Ralphie – that's where the battle's fought. You know, they have no confidence in me, these people. The girls want to find out if they're pregnant, and so they go to a diviner the day after they're late, and the diviner tells them what they want to hear, yes or no as it suits. If he's wrong, the girls somehow manage to forget it. But they come to me and I say, I can't tell you now, visit me again after two months. They look at me like – man, he's stupid, this Boer.'

Ralph glanced up at him. Koos wanted to talk; there was so much that he bottled up inside himself every day, and he would talk about anything, anything except what ailed him. 'Your girl, Dearie,' he said. 'You need to find out why she thinks her babies are always sick. You know, in this part of the world, we don't have misfortunes plain and simple. If something goes wrong you need somebody to blame. Who's done this to me, you ask? Who's put this sickness on me? It might be, you see, your ancestors. It might be some enemy of yours. But it's not just plain fate. It's not the hand of God.'

'I suppose that's comforting, in a way,' Ralph said.

'Is it?'

They both wondered, whether it was comforting or not: in the silence, cattle-flies buzzed and dashed against the wire-mesh window. Koos said, 'It sounds to me that what your girl needs is to call on Luke Mbatha, my dispenser. You've met Luke? You've seen Luke, Saturday night, in his zoot suit, with some Jo'burg shebeen queen on his arm? You think he bought that on what I pay him?'

'What, the suit or the woman?'

Koos was bowed by his amusement; his red hand knuckled his head. 'Both cost, Ralphie, suit and cunt. No, Luke – he does a good trade in cats' livers and lizard skins and python fat. You ought to go and see him in the backyard there. A lot of his mixtures you don't swallow, thank Christ, you just put the bottle on a string and hang it round your neck. Might suit your girl Dearie. He does business by mail, too. Love potions. Maybe other kind of potions – murder ones – but I don't ask him. A man came in last week and said he had beetles in his bowels. I sent him straight through to the back. If he believes that, it's Luke he needs, not me.'

Ralph no longer bothered to get on his high horse; to say, they're not barbarians. He knew Koos was not passing judgement. He was implying that there is another view of the world that you could entertain: and that he did not entirely despise it. 'Still,' he said, 'you have to keep your eye on Luke, I suppose. To see that he's not harming anyone.'

'He does less harm than some. Have you seen these things the blacks use?' Koos took a little box out of his desk drawer and skimmed it across at Ralph. *Extra Strong Native Pills*, he read. 'Extra Strong is an understatement,' Koos said. 'Almost, if you had beetles, you'd blast them out. And worms – I tell you, man, they're always deworming themselves, and killing themselves in the process. I've seen it – I've had people crawl in here and die on me slowly. Certified worm-free, but unluckily for them their blerry worm-free liver's packed up – and you need to see people dying at that speed, Ralphie, because when the liver's gone, a person's life continues three days, and the only pain-relief's a bullet in the brain.' Koos shifted in his chair. 'So I let Luke get on with it. It's like these churches, isn't it? You wish your mission servants would come to your church – but you know they go to more exciting types of services. What I do is, I go in there every month or so, have a look around among Luke's stock. Just make sure there's nothing human, that's all. Anything human, and – I've warned him – I go to the police.'

'What do you mean, human?'

'People disappear, you know? We always say, they're lost into Johannesburg, but sometimes they've gone a lot further than that. There is a trade, you can't deny it. In bodies, live ones. They take the eyes, the tongue, whatever they need for medicine at that time. It's a big problem for the police as to who's guilty – and of course they feel they shouldn't have to handle it, it's a native problem. The reason why it's so difficult to pin blame is that gangs do these things, networks, and how can you pick out who's responsible – who can you say is the killer, if a person's been cut up by different hands? And of course, if you cut people to pieces, they do die in the end.' Koos looked up, and saw the expression on Ralph's face. 'All right, don't believe me,' he said. 'I don't like to think about it either. Who wants to admit such things go on?' He jerked his thumb in the general direction of Pretoria. 'It gives encouragement to *them*.'

When the new year came, the bus fares went up, and the bus boycott started. Ralph got up at four each morning to pack the mission's car with more people than it should hold, and to edge the complaining vehicle out of Elim, downhill towards Pretoria. The people who had permits to work in the city needed to keep their jobs; every taxi in Elim was commandeered, but still they passed silent convoys of men and women, walking downhill in the smoky dawn. The headlights of other cars, going uphill, crept by theirs; there was some sympathy in the liberal suburbs of Johannesburg, and there were men and women willing to drive through the night to help the people from the townships. Ralph had his name noted, at road-blocks. He was questioned, roughly, in Afrikaans. His lack of understanding drove the policemen into a fury. 'We've got your number, man,' they said. 'You must be a communist, eh?'

I want, he thought, to put into practice a different kind of Christianity from my father's: one in which I don't pass judgement on people. I don't judge Lucy Moyo, or Koos, or (without evidence) Luke the dispenser whose trade is so dark; I don't judge the President, or the police sergeant who has just cursed me out. 'But if you don't judge,' Anna said, 'you certainly institute some stiff inquiries into people's motives. I am not sure that is always quite separate from the process of passing judgement.'

She knew him better, by now. That kindness of his, which she had taken so personally, was essentially impersonal, she saw.

That morning at the road-block, the policeman said to Ralph, *kaffirboetie*. Black man's brother, or dear friend. 'I would like to be,' Ralph said. 'But I wouldn't make the claim.' The policeman spat into the roadway. Only his upbringing prevented him from spitting in Ralph's face.

On the day of the public meeting, the day of the baton charge, Koos opened his hospital in the nursery school's hall, rolling up his shocked and bloodied patients in blankets, speaking in five languages to ban the hot sweet tea and ask for water, just water; for bandages – anything, any rags; for anyone with a steady hand to help him swab and clean.

Ralph gave a thought to a dusty office in London, an eyrie in Clerkenwell, the headquarters of the organization that had sent him here; and he thought of the churchgoers of Norfolk, passing the collection plate; he heard them say to him, you have no right to misappropriate funds in this way, misuse mission property: to press the blue smock of a nursery-school angel to the bleeding mouth of a township whore who has been smashed in the face by a baton. It was the cook, Rosinah, who of all the mission staff had witnessed the police charge; Rosinah, who seemed to have no life outside her dictatorial kitchen practices. Now she rocked herself in a stupor of grief, telling how it was peaceful, baas, hymn-singing, a speech, and now the police have chased the young women and beaten them on their breasts, they have done that thing, they know where young women are weak.

Ralph knew that on the scale of atrocity it was small. It was not, for example, Treblinka. Koos showed him what a sjambok cut looked like, administered by an experienced, determined hand. He learned something about himself; that the presence of evil made him shake, like an invalid or octogenarian.

Next day he was able to piece together a little more of the

story. It had been a peaceful meeting, as Rosinah said, on a patch of waste ground he knew, a mile away from Flower Street; but this was a typical thing in Elim, that there was no line of communication except an underground one, there was no knowledge, a mile away, of what was occurring on the waste ground; there was no mechanism by which he and Anna could have been warned and told to stand by for casualties. The meeting was to decide strategy for the bus boycott. At the last minute the police had demanded it be called off. A few children had started throwing stones, and the police had charged before the crowd could disperse. A great number of those injured appeared to be passers-by. They were dazed and weeping, their shaved and stitched scalps still oozing blood and clear fluid; they said that they had not known anything, not known there was a meeting at all.

Ralph walked over the site of the catastrophe. A few odd shoes had been left behind in the scramble to escape the batons and whips. He saw a straw shopping-bag, decorated with a swelling, pink straw rose; it lay on its side, and its contents were by now on someone else's shelf. The ground had been picked over pretty well, he saw; he thought it was a strange form of looting. It was hard to know who was worse; the policemen who had done what they said was their duty, or the scavengers who had taken from the housemaid's bag the half-loaf, the two ounces of green tripe, perhaps the soap-ends or old cardigan some Madam had given, some well-meaning idiot woman down in the white houses, the jacaranda groves.

'Can you do anything, Mr Eldred?' Lucy Moyo said. 'Anything to help us?'

'I can try,' Ralph said.

He went back to his office and rifled through his papers for the list he had been compiling: the names, addresses, telephone numbers of the senior policemen within a hundred miles. He picked up the telephone receiver and began to work his way through the list. These calls did not last long, in most cases; when the policemen heard his English accent, and learned that he lived in Elim, they put the phone down on him.

He sat up for most of the night, writing to the newspapers. 'You saw the casualties,' he said to Koos. 'You know what happened here, better than anybody. Put your name on these letters with me.'

Koos shook his head. 'Better not, Ralph. I have my patients to think about. What would they do without me?' He shrugged. 'A lot better, maybe.'

After the baton charge, their situation changed. They were invited to houses in Elim they had never entered before. People who were not churchgoers came to the Mission House. The local organizer of the ANC called on them; and on the same day came a man from Sophiatown, a black journalist from *Drum* magazine. He sat leaning back on one of the metal-legged kitchen chairs, so that its front feet were in the air. He found things to laugh about.

Rosinah's apprentice served him tea in an enamel mug. Anna said sharply, 'The cups and saucers, please, Dearie.' Dearie brought a cup and slapped it down on the table. She scowled. Cups were for whites, enamel mugs were for Africans; this Madam had instituted different practices, which proved she knew nothing. She thought this black man was above himself, putting on airs, in his lightweight blue suit with the sharp creases in the trousers. Trouble came of it: in her opinion.

'Pretoria wants to grow, grow, grow,' the handsome boy said, lolling back on his chair. 'The Nats want this place cleared. They will find these people somewhere else, some piece of the veld where they can put them and forget them. Some place with no water and no roads. So that their children can grow back into savages.' The young man laughed, a satirical laugh. His eyes were distant already, and it could be seen that he was on his way to a scholarship abroad: Moscow, perhaps, and who could blame him? 'I can tell you, Mrs Eldred,' he said, 'it is hardly possible for an African to live and breathe and be on the right side of the law.' He looked deeply into Anna's eyes; indicating, one, that she attracted him and two, that he would not think to take any trouble over her.

It was after midnight when the handsome boy left. Next afternoon, a white police sergeant sat on the same chair: its legs now foursquare and grounded. 'Makes a change, Mr Eldred, for me to come and see you. Usually it's you comes to see us.'

The sergeant was fair-haired, meagre, not a big man. But he sat like a true Afrikaner: legs splayed, as if to indicate that in no other way could he ease his bull-like endowment. Ralph did not, at once, dislike him, perhaps because he was of the same familiar, freckled, physical type as Koos, and anxious too, nervously smiling; his nails were bitten down to the quick.

The sergeant had not refused tea. Dearie gave him a cup, of course, and a saucer too. He just wanted Ralph to know, he said, as he helped himself to sugar, that the police were aware what kind of visitors he'd been getting. 'You're a stranger here,' the policeman complained. 'You're new to South Africa. You ought to make *nice* friends.'

In passing, Ralph felt sorry for him. He was nervous, a chain-smoker, offering his pack each time to Anna; sometimes a fleeting spasm crossed his face, as if he were in pain.

'I didn't catch your name,' Ralph said, when the sergeant wiped his mouth and stood up to go. 'Why don't you just call me Quintus,' the man said. 'Because I expect we'll be getting to know each other.'

'I think he must have beetles in the bowels,' Ralph said after he'd gone. 'Needs to go to Luke Mbatha for some python fat.'

Ralph told Koos that the more stupid the white policemen were, the worse they treated him – except maybe this Quintus, who was well-intentioned in his way.

Koos rubbed his red hands through his scrubby pale hair; and Ralph, who had been learning anatomy among other things, felt he could see afternoon light flash between radius and ulna. 'Be over to his braai, soon, Ralphie. You drink his beer, man, you eat up his scorched flesh-meat.'

'No. I don't see we'll be on those terms.'

'Ah,' Koos said. 'But you soon learn to like those motherfuckers. You like me, don't you? And I'm one of them. Something sweet and simple about us, isn't there? Something pathetic? Always trying to be liked. Well, there's this thing we have, a kind of – hospitality. If a man comes by you make him comfortable; it's an African thing, the blacks have it and so do we. Do you think that while you've been in this township you have learned anything at all about what goes on here? Because if you do, man, you're more imbecilic than I took you for.'

Later, in a more sober mood, Koos said: 'You have to try to understand these – my lot, I mean. The British put their women and children in concentration camps. The Zulu smashed the skulls of their babies against their waggon wheels. They have long memories, Afrikaners. Memory is their speciality.'

Ralph was struck by how he said 'these people'. Just as Lucy Moyo did, when she talked about her friends and neighbours.

'All I hope,' Ralph said, 'and it's a fairly faint hope, I know – is that the country will grind to a halt under the weight of its own ludicrous bureaucracy. You can hardly see a gap where a man can slip though.'

'There's no slipping through,' Koos said. 'Everybody's watching everyone else. This country is like that. My home town, my people – Jesus, man, you can't imagine.'

'I think I can,' Ralph said.

'My father believes the world was made in seven days. It's in the Bible, he says.' Koos laughed.

In the new year the early-morning raids began. They happened over three days. On the first morning, the police entered the township at five o'clock. They had armoured vehicles, and they came in force. They cordoned off the area they had chosen and went from house to house, kicking in the doors. Next day, when people came down to the mission to give their accounts, this as much as anything gave rise to indignation: that they had shouted out that they were police, that the doors must be opened, but then they had given no time for the householders to obey them. 'As if we were animals,' a woman said, 'who would not understand.'

They were looking for liquor, the police said, for evidence of illicit stills. They were also looking for arms; there was a rumour current, which Ralph wished he had not heard, that *matériel* had been brought into Elim by night, and stowed away against a braver age.

Since the riot — the so-called riot — the atmosphere had been restless and strained, and the corner boys had a sullen, knowing look. He no longer allowed Anna to go out alone. Where people knew them, they were safe enough. Where they were unknown, a white face had become a provocation.

Those nights of the raids, Ralph found it impossible to sleep. There was the fear that some wider kind of trouble would blow up; that forewarned of the police action a crowd would gather, young boys heedless of the consequences, with sticks and bottles and, God knows, perhaps these mysterious arms; then there would be a replay of the baton charge, or perhaps much worse, perhaps bullets. He felt foolish, helpless, inconsequential, as he lay on his back staring up at the ceiling, an orange light insinuating itself through the gap in the curtains.

It had become necessary to fix these lights around the mission compound. A week ago, the nursery school had been broken into. There was no money for the thieves to take, no food; they had kicked the little tables about, torn up some books, ransacked Anna's broom-cupboard office and made a small fire in there. It could, of course, have burned down the building, if Father Alfred had not seen the flames from his bedroom window.

Then, on Sunday, when the mission workers were at their various services, a sneak-thief had entered Rosinah's single-room house, taken her clothing, including a woollen hat which belonged to Dearie and which Rosinah had extracted from her on a forced loan. The cook's retching sobs had been out of all proportion to the loss. They had – himself and Anna, Dearie, the gardeners – spent an hour trying to coax her to stop crying. Clara, the educated washerwoman, stood by the door not speaking. There was no expression on her face. She looked like a woman who might have lost everything, many times over.

Hence the security lights. Their sleep had been broken since. His wife's tension seemed to communicate itself to Ralph through the sagging springs of the bed. Towards dawn he dozed. Phrases ran through his head, the phrases that he lived with each day: *Thirty shillings or ten days. My husband, baas, is whereabouts unknown.*

And towards dawn on the third day the police came to the mission. It was almost a relief to hear them pounding at the door. He and Anna were both out of bed in a moment; their faces peaked in the grey light, they understood the extent of each other's wakefulness. Ralph pulled on the trousers and shirt he had left folded by the bed. Anna belted her dressing-gown over her long nightdress. What was the point of rushing? The police would break the door down anyway.

In the event, the police checked themselves; as if, here on the mission steps, some notion of civility still held sway. 'It's you,'

Ralph said, opening the door; Quintus stood there. He had feared unknown faces, Special Branch perhaps. Half a dozen men trooped in. Quintus introduced his colleague, Sergeant van Zyl. They had hardly got through the pleasantries when the men began to stomp through the house, looking in the cupboards and under the bed. 'Of course, Sergeant,' Ralph said, 'you spotted at once that I'm the type to run a still. Me and my wife, aren't we just your typical shebeen-owners?'

Sergeant van Zyl said, 'We are looking for a person we have reason to believe may be on your premises.'

'What person? Dr Verwoerd? Mickey Mouse?'

Van Zyl looked baleful. He was a big man; hitching his thumbs into his belt, he moved the burden of his belly a little. 'You wrote a letter to the *Pretoria News*, Mr Eldred. Don't do that again.'

Let's stay calm, Ralph said to himself. 'My letter was only to tell people what really happened the day of your baton charge. I wrote to invite people to come up here and look at Elim for themselves. To look at our churches and our schools, and ask themselves if we are the hotbed of vice and crime they are constantly told that we are. To look at what we do here, and ask themselves if we deserve to be destroyed.'

'We know what your letter said,' van Zyl told him. 'We have read it ourselves in the newspaper. The brigadier doesn't like your tone, Mr Eldred.'

'Well, if it's only my tone,' Ralph said easily. 'The content doesn't trouble him?'

'You'd have more idea about crime,' van Zyl said, 'if you spent some time with us at the police station.'

'But I do spend time. I could hardly spend any more. Unless I moved in with you.'

'I suppose that might be arranged,' van Zyl said.

The police had given up on the mysterious person, whoever

he was. They were in Ralph's office, rummaging through his papers. Sergeant van Zyl settled on his desk. Again he twitched at his belt, settling his bulk comfortably, as if his gut were something apart from him, a pet animal he kept.

'If I knew what you wanted,' Ralph said, 'I could perhaps help you out.'

'Help yourself out, man,' van Zyl said. 'Keep out of our way.'

Quintus attempted covert signals. He looked sick. Ralph would not meet his eyes. His clear meaning was, be careful, for van Zyl is not your decent type of policeman. And that was evident; there was no need to collude on it. If Quintus felt bad, let him quit; he, Ralph, was not going to do anything to ease a policeman's conscience.

The search was a perfunctory one, but as messy as could be contrived. They had done it for the nuisance value, Ralph thought. Even so, he knew that Anna, standing against the wall, was trembling. He would have liked to turn to her, hold her in his arms, but he did not want to take his eyes from van Zyl's eyes. He would not be the one to look away first.

Quintus ushered them from the office, grumbling. 'I don't know how you find anything in this place.'

'We've always managed,' Anna said. 'But I don't suppose we'll manage now.'

Her voice was cool. Quintus shook his head. He spoke in Afrikaans to his colleague. Enough's enough, he seemed to be saying. The men trooped out. They were left alone, with their papers scattered about the Mission House, as if a gale had blown through, or some apocalyptic wind.

The same day, late afternoon, Quintus turned up with a truck. 'Got something for you,' he said, smiling as if he had not seen them earlier that day.

Two black boys leapt down from the back of the truck, and manoeuvred on to the stoep a large filing cabinet, battered and scratched, dark green in colour. 'Just what you need, eh?' Quintus said.

'Oh, Quintus, a donation,' Anna said. She smiled, as if deeply touched.

Quintus did not know the difference between affectation and reality. 'No need to thank me, man,' he said modestly. 'It's just scrap metal. We were throwing it out. A drawer fell out and broke the brigadier's toe, that's why.' He addressed Ralph. 'So you take care and don't be rough when you pull it out.'

'Cup of coffee?' Anna said. Like Ralph, she felt a sneaking pity for the man. Quintus sat down at the kitchen table. He said, 'I know you don't like me coming round here. But we've been told to keep an eye on you. Look, there are worse people in the force.'

'I know. We've met him,' Ralph said.

The sergeant sat brooding over his cup. 'Hell, man, you think I *like* my job? A man's got to earn a living.'

'I get tired of hearing that,' Anna said. 'There are other ways, surely?'

The sergeant reached into a pocket of his uniform, took out his wallet. To Ralph's deep embarrassment, he drew from it a family snapshot. 'My girls,' he said.

Ralph looked at it. Three daughters. Twelve, ten and eight they might be. Graded by height, the arms of one sister around the waist of the next, blonde heads leaning back on to the shoulder of a woman slighter, more modest than they, scarcely taller than the eldest girl. Filaments of hair escaped from their plaits, and stood out like haloes as they smiled into the sun. Hitler's wet-dreams, he thought. He handed the photograph to Anna. 'Beauties,' he said. 'Your wife, Quintus, she looks a lovely girl.'

'When you're a family man you'll understand a lot you don't understand now,' the policeman promised. 'You think about them all the time, Jesus, you *worry*. What sort of a world are they going to grow up in? Are they going to marry kaffirs?'

'We don't use that word here.'

'Oh, words,' the sergeant said. 'That's what gets to me about you people. Words.'

He didn't explain his objection; he stood up, said he must be going. 'Next time we come,' he said, indicating the filing cabinet, 'you'll have everything in the one place for us?' Tentatively, he touched his uniformed chest and winced. 'Mrs Eldred, could I trouble you? Have you got anything to take the acid off my stomach?'

'Quintus wants to be human,' Anna said, when he left.

'He must get another job then.'

That evening Koos came to the back door. Just for a few minutes; he wouldn't eat with them. Couldn't, really, he said. His jaw was swollen. He had lost two teeth. The police had called on him too. They had smashed their way through the front of his surgery, smashed in the windows – though everybody knew he slept in the room at the back. They said they wanted to talk to Luke Mbatha, the dispenser. They'd given Luke's shack a going-over, and taken Luke away in a van.

Koos wanted Ralph to come down to the station, bringing what money he had by him, to try and bail Luke out. 'God knows he's no innocent,' Koos said. 'But you know what happens to black men in police cells.' He had, he explained, no money of his own. The matter was urgent, he said, looking away. Otherwise he would not have come. They might have taken Luke Mbatha down the hill to Pretoria by now, and perhaps they would never find him again.

'Why didn't you come before?' Ralph said.

'Because I can't walk when I'm unconscious,' Koos said. His

pale eyes were bloodshot, and his hands shook. One of the policemen had hit him in the face with a pistol butt, and then presumably hit him on the head, because he had come to at the house of one of his patients, lying on a pallet and covered with one of Anna's knitted blankets. 'A good blanket,' he said. 'Very warm. Thank you, Anna.' He couldn't remember much of what had happened. The policeman who hit him had called him a white kaffir. That sergeant, he said – not van Zyl. The thin one. The other. Quintus Brink.

They realized, over the next few days, that it was no longer safe to make telephone calls. They knew there was nothing seditious in their conversation. But anything could be twisted, and would be, and they knew that there were listeners on the line.

Van Zyl came by again – just visiting, he said – and it went badly. He stared at the filing cabinet as if he knew it from somewhere. 'Any visitors last night?' he said.

'No.'

'You surprise me. You're sure no visitors after dark?'

'I'm quite sure.'

'Any visitors in your servants' quarters?'

'I can't help you there. But I'm sure no one was on the compound whom you would be interested in.'

'Luke Mbatha has given them the slip,' Anna said from the doorway. She spoke derisively. Van Zyl was not pleased.

'Where did you hear that rubbish?'

'It's not rubbish. I heard it on the street. Everybody knows it. How did he get away, Sergeant? Did he bewitch you? Did he bewitch the brigadier?'

Van Zyl got up from his chair, and tossed his paunch threateningly. 'Tell your woman to watch her mouth,' he said. 'Or she'll feel my hand across it.'

'Out,' Ralph said. '*Voetsak*, Sergeant. Out of this house.'

It is the word you use to a dog, and only then if it is a dog of bad character. But van Zyl would not hesitate to use it, to a man of inferior race; Ralph believed now that there were inferior races, distinguished not by culture or genes, but by some missing faculty of pity. '*Voetsak*, Sergeant,' he said again, and moved towards him as if to push him out of the front door, across the stoep and down the steps into the yard.

Sergeant van Zyl knew he should not fight; he had received warnings about his excess of zeal. He attempted some sort of lumbering side-step – so when Ralph did push him, he was not truly on course for the door. 'You must be a stinking Jew,' the policeman told Ralph. 'In my opinion, Hitler was right.' Ralph's fists against his belly, he careered backwards. His right arm flailed out, swept to the floor the papers from Anna's temporary desk. He backed his calves into the wastepaper basket, overturned it: and, attempting to regain his balance, trod in it. Ralph would never forget the feeling of his hands sinking into the sergeant's flesh. It gave him a shock, how easy it was to topple that great bulk.

The Special Branch came at three the following morning, and took them both away.

FIVE

Anna heard Ralph talking on the telephone. '. . . I do grasp,' he was saying, 'that you raised £132 from the harvest supper and gave the same amount to the Mission to Seamen, but I'm afraid you will confuse the auditor if you don't show them in separate columns. Leave aside for the moment the question of the rector's expenses . . .'

Anna swore mildly under her breath as she side-stepped through the bales of newspapers stacked up in the hall. When Ralph came out of his office she said, 'There are more papers here than when I went out. People are delivering these bundles at all hours of the day and night.'

'Not quite,' Ralph said, frowning.

'Couldn't you ask them to call between set hours?'

'It might put people off. I'm relying on their goodwill. Why don't you get the boys to carry them up to the attics?'

'What's the point? They'll only have to come down again. And when you try to move them the bundles fall apart and the damn things are all over the place.'

'It's true,' Ralph said. 'People don't seem to know how to tie up bundles.'

'Perhaps it's a lost art,' Anna said, 'like broadcast sowing. Can't they go in the bike shed?'

'No, nor in any other shed. They might get damp.'

Anna sighed. The newspapers benefited the parish church's restoration fund in some way: clearly only if they were dry, not if they were damp.

116

'I have to go out,' Ralph said.

'But Kit will be here soon. I was hoping –'

'It's the new committee. For the homeless in Norwich.'

'I hardly knew there were homeless in Norwich,' Anna said. 'There seem to be enough council estates.' Ralph vanished back into his office. Anna was left with her bad mood. 'Perhaps,' she muttered, 'some of them could come and live in our hall-stand.'

Ralph had almost finished his letters for the day. He had been interrupted by several telephone calls from elderly people within a ten-mile radius, all of them complaining about their Meals-on-Wheels; he had nothing to do with this service, but found it hard to convince them of that. Mobile libraries, too, had been much on his mind. He had received a request for the Trust to support a Good News Van, which planned to jolt around the countryside taking the latest Christian paperbacks to the house-bound. 'We have known people who have not read a book in years,' the letter told him, 'but whose lives have been transformed by thrilling new stories of what God is doing all over the world.' Ralph gave the letter a file number, and scribbled on it, 'I suggest we turn this one down. The house-bound have enough to put up with.' He dropped it in the box for the next meeting of the Trust committee.

The Trust was not rich any more, and it was necessary to be selective; need seemed always to increase. He had his procedures: he tried to avoid subsidizing anything too doctrinaire, or anything involving volunteers playing the guitar. Initiatives for the young attracted his interest, but he rejected applications from any group with 'Kids' in the title.

The hostel in the East End had changed its character now. Some time in the sixties it had stopped being St Walstan's and become Crucible House. In those far-off days when Ralph had reported each weekend to count the laundry out and returned mid-week to count it back in, the task had been shovelling old men up off the street and drying them out and sending them on their way a week or two later with a new overcoat and a hot breakfast inside them. Or finding a bed for an old lag who was between prison sentences: or a quiet corner for somebody who'd gone berserk and smashed all the crockery in the Salvation Army canteen. But nowadays the clients were young. They were runaways, some of them, who had fetched up at a railway terminus with a few pounds in their pockets, played in the amusement arcades till their money ran out, and then slept on the streets. Some of them had been 'in care' – you would think that was a complete misnomer, Ralph would say, if you could see the state of them.

These young people, boys and girls, had something in common, a certain look about them: hard to define but, after a little experience, easy to spot. They were often unhealthily fat: puffed up with cheap carbohydrates, with the salt from bags of crisps. When they were spoken to they answered slowly, if at all; they focused their eyes at some point in the middle distance, beyond their questioner's shoulder. Large bottles of prescription drugs clanked in their pitiful luggage, which was often made up of Tesco bags – though Ralph always wondered where they got the means to go to Tesco.

The volunteers who staffed the hostel had changed too. The present director, Richard, was an intense young man with a higher degree. Before his time, in the days when the last of the old men used to shuffle in and out, the volunteers had been clean-cut young men in crew-neck sweaters, and girls with good accents, who had a way of talking to the clients as if they were recalcitrant beagles or pointers. But now it was hard to tell the workers and the clients apart. They had a lost air, these modern volunteers: children filling in a year before university, lured by the promise of pocket-money and full board in a room of their own in London. They wore clothes from charity shops. They read no books. They seldom spoke, except to each other.

Ralph invited them to Norfolk sometimes, for a week's country air. He would bring the clients too, packing them carefully into his car with their Tesco bags and driving them through Essex and Suffolk towards a warm family home – though because of the state of the central heating, 'warm' was only a figure of speech. Anna, he believed, liked to see new faces. The children were used to what they called Visitors. But nowadays they would look at the arrivals, and affect a greater bewilderment than they felt: 'Is she a Sad Case, or a Good Soul?'

There were nights when Ralph sat up till dawn, talking on the telephone to some suicidal adolescent in London; there were nights when he would jump into the car and roar off – this too being a qualified term, considering the state of the Citroën – to deal with some catastrophe that Richard's jargon was not equal to. Ralph had a plainer way of doing things than Richard could imagine. He was calm and patient, he expected the best from people, he never gave up on them. They recognized this; and often, from plain weariness in the face of his implacable optimism, they would decide to live, and to behave better.

Sometimes, rude questioners would ask him why the Trust didn't move its entire operation to London, since the need was such a crying need. Then Ralph would talk about the glum, silent forms of rural deprivation: the bored teenagers kicking their heels at a bus stop waiting for a bus that never came; the pensioners in isolated cottages by overgrown railway lines, without telephone and heat and mains drainage. He would talk so long and hard about branch-line closures that his questioner would wish he had never opened his mouth.

The fact was – he was the first to admit it – Ralph and the dwindling resources he could command were wanted in too many places. He was torn, divided. The demands of the world dragged on his conscience; but did he do enough for his own family? Sometimes he felt a strange physical force – little hands pulling at him, invisible hands plucking at his clothes.

So, today – he had just one more letter to do: Church of England Children's Society. Then Norwich for the committee – and then he would race back for dinner, because Kit was coming home, and Anna was cooking a big meal, and Julian would be bringing his girl over from her farm near the sea.

He applied stamps to his letters. Yawned. But, he told himself, don't despise these little things; they add up. A tiny series of actions, of small duties well performed, eventually does some good in the world.

That's the theory, anyway.

Mid-afternoon, Emma collected her niece Kit from the station in Norwich. Kit ran across the forecourt with her bag; an Easter breeze lifted her hair, fanned it out around her head. Jumping into the car, she shook it like a lion shaking his mane. She kissed her aunt, squeezed her shoulders. Her eyes were leonine: wide, golden and vigilant. How handsome she's become, Emma thought: a heartbreaker. She remembered Ralph in his National Service days, coming home on leave. Ralph had been too remote to break hearts.

'You can have tea with me,' Emma said. 'Then I'll take you home. Oh, don't worry, I've bought a shop cake. I haven't launched myself on anything ambitious.'

Emma lived in a neat, double-fronted, red-brick cottage, which stood on the High Street in Foulsham. Foulsham is not a town, by the standards of the rest of England: it has a few small shops, a post office, a church, a Baptist Chapel and a number of public houses. It has a war memorial and a parish magazine, a village hall, a Playing Fields Committee, a Women's Institute and a mobile wet-fish van. A hundred yards from Emma's house was the school Kit attended when she was five; fifty yards away was the shop where she used to buy sweets after school on her way to her aunt's house.

In those days Emma seldom held an afternoon surgery; she put in the hours at other times, evenings and weekends when her partners wanted to get away. At four o'clock she had been there to open her front door to the children, to bring them in, listen to the news of their day and give them lemonade and a plain bun and then drive them home. Often Mr Palmer the Estate Agent was leaving just as Kit arrived. He was, she knew, a very great friend of Aunt Emma's; she suspected him of getting there before them, to eat buns with icing, have treats that children were denied. Sometimes Mr Palmer was exceptionally happy. He would throw her up in the air, toss her – giggling, hair flying – to the ceiling, and then give her a two-shilling piece. She'd got quite rich, out of Mr Palmer. Her small brother Robin, when he started school, complained he didn't get the same money. Mr Palmer would ruffle his hair and give him sixpence. Well, she said to Robin: you don't know, perhaps he's fallen into poverty. People do. It's in books.

Now fifteen years had passed, and she put make-up on and went out to eat oysters with Mr Palmer's son.

Emma, though not fifty, now described herself as 'semi-retired'. You'd want to steal away, she said to Ralph, after a lifetime of pallid pregnant wives, and screaming mites with measles spots, and old men wheezing in: 'Missus, the old chest – I'm bronical.' She filled in for holidays and weekends off, kept up with the medical literature, and took the occasional family-planning session. This last had always been her interest. She would turn up at outlying cottages, and talk in blunt terms. They would call her in to attend to shingles or lumbago, and she would leave them with some rubber device. Robin had once introduced her to a schoolfriend as 'My Aunt Emma, who has done so much to depopulate East Anglia'. She was in demand these days for talks in schools and colleges throughout the county. Heads liked her because she talked straight, but did not embarrass their young people. After all, she was old. They did not have to think of her *doing it.*

Emma's house was warm and tidy. 'Make yourself comfortable,' she said. Kit threw herself at a chair. What a lot of energy she had – but then, just as suddenly, it would seem to drain out of her.

'I went to Walsingham,' Emma said. 'To pray about Felix. Wasn't that odd of me?'

'Did you go to the wells?'

'No, just to the shrine.'

'There's one well, you know, the round one – I used to know a girl who believed that if you drank the water you'd have a secret wish come true within a year and a day.'

'A secret wish?' Emma said. 'Secret from the rest of the world, or secret from yourself, I wonder.'

Kit smiled. 'That's the trouble, isn't it? It's like – didn't somebody say there's no such thing as unanswered prayers? All prayers are answered, but not in the way that you notice.'

Emma filled the teapot and brought in plates. She had managed to mash the shop cake, somehow, in getting it out of its packet. She had always described herself as a free-thinker in matters of nutrition. Her house guests were fed at uncertain intervals, at unorthodox hours and on strange combinations of food.

I wonder, Kit thought now, how much of that was because of Felix; because she never knew when he'd turn up, and perhaps sometimes she'd cook him a meal and he'd say, no, I'm expected home, and then hours later she'd heat it up for herself . . .

'Cake that bad?' Emma inquired.

'The cake? No, it's fine.' Kit cultivated a hedge of yellow

crumbs at the side of her plate. 'Emma, can I ask you something? Tell me to mind my own business if you like. Only I try, you know, to fit the past together these days. I was thinking about you and Felix. I wondered if you ever talked about him leaving Ginny, and moving in with you.'

'Oh, there was a lot of talk. There always is in these affairs.' Emma ran her hand back through her hair. 'I knew him before, you know, before he took up with Ginny. We used to hang around together, when we were sixteen, seventeen, and then when I was away doing my training he'd come to London to see me. I suppose I had my chance then. But I told him to push off. He used to get on my nerves. His waistcoats, mainly. Yellow waistcoats. So it was my own fault, wasn't it?'

'But later he didn't get on your nerves, did he?'

'No, I learned to put up with him. He persisted. But Felix had children, remember.'

'Perhaps he shouldn't have done.'

'Oh, Ginny was never one to avail herself of my devices. The babies were born before we got together again. Or at least, before we got together again in any way that seemed likely to last. Yes, of course, we should have married in the first place, I see that now . . . but it was done, it was done. He wouldn't have wanted to leave Daniel and the little girl.'

'You could have had his children. I would have liked it if you'd had children, Emma. There'd have been more of us.'

'But then perhaps there wouldn't have been any Daniel.'

'Well, I don't know . . . I think I would trade Daniel for cousins. They wouldn't have been like cousins, they'd have been like brothers and sisters.'

'You mustn't be greedy, Kit,' Emma said. 'The truth is, Felix wouldn't have left Ginny, even if there'd been no children. Ginny's not the sort of woman that men leave. And what we had was enough, Felix and me. And what you have is enough.'

'I suppose so,' Kit said.

A ray of grace shone through Emma, from some long-ago Sunday-school afternoon. She said it again, gently: 'You mustn't be greedy, Kit.'

Emma had tried to stop Ralph's children calling her 'Aunt'. What you are called you become, she said; she did not want to become something out of P. G. Wodehouse. She had tried to make their lives easier for them, but it was not easy being Ralph's children.

His standards were high, but different from other people's. When they were small the children had played with their friends from the row of council houses that straggled up the lane beyond the church, a quarter of a mile from the Red House. Ralph's children had better manners, Emma thought; but the council-house children were better dressed.

It was lucky that the young Eldreds had schoolmates in similar plights, or they would have thought themselves hard done-by. Kit, for instance, had a friend whose father wouldn't let a television set in the house. Robin knew a boy whose mother knitted his trousers to her own design. Norfolk breeds such people; huddling indoors out of the wind, they give birth to strange notions.

Emma had been a refuge for the children once; they still liked to be at her house, even if she could not assemble a sandwich without the filling dropping out. She thoroughly understood her practical value to them. She provided money for heart's desires – for vital clothes and sudden causes, and treats that Ralph disdained. Poor Ralph, she thought. He made them all have music lessons, but they were neither musical nor grateful. Robin had said last year, 'Dad's supposed to be good with young people, but it's other young people he's good with. Not us.'

Emma and Kit finished their tea, drove the three miles to the Red House. As they pulled up, Kit said, 'Is Dad still on Julian's back – about doing a year for the Trust?'

'I think he's given up on it. Julian wouldn't do in London, would he? He'd be back within days.' Emma leaned across to kiss her niece. 'I'm not coming in. The partners are going to the King's Arms tonight, we're going to paint the town red.'

'Have a good time.' Kit put her head in at the car window. 'Maybe I'll do it, instead. Do a year . . . it wouldn't hurt. Or would it?'

Emma was surprised. 'I thought you were doing post-grad? I thought it was all fixed?'

Kit shook her head. Her face was placid, almost sad. 'Nothing's fixed. I had this idea – I wrote home to Dad – I said I didn't want to be in London . . . but I suppose I could face it, if it were for the Trust, if I could be any use there.' She looked away. 'I don't know what to think, though. I've lost my . . . no, I don't know what I've lost.'

Your virginity? Emma wondered. The thought must have shown on her face. 'It's not Daniel,' Kit said. 'I wouldn't stay around here for Daniel. Though if I needed an excuse, I suppose he could be one.'

Emma drove away. The door of the house was thrown open and Julian came out, pretending to peer into the bushes, and calling 'Come in for your dinner, kitty kitty kitty.'

Rebecca, behind him, said, 'Kate of Kate Hall.'

Her brother looked well, Kit thought at once, he looked happy. He straightened up to his impressive height, put his arms around her and hugged her. Behind him was his red-haired girlfriend, Sandra Glasse.

Kit found Daniel Palmer in the kitchen with the rest of the family. All of them were watching carefully, to assess how pleased she was to see him.

'Hello,' Kit said. 'I didn't expect you, where's your car?'

'I put it under cover.' Daniel did not know his status with Kit; did not know her mood; wondered what the family thought his status was. 'Welcome home,' he said. He picked up a strand of Kit's hair and touched the end of it to his lips.

'He's got a new car, you see,' Julian said. 'He's afraid rain will fall on it.'

'It's my Morgan,' Daniel said. Amazed delight showed on his face. Kit retrieved her hair and tucked it back, among those strands romance had not distinguished. 'Hand-built,' Daniel said. 'I've been waiting four years for it.'

'Goodness,' Kit said. She wondered how desire could last so long.

Ralph said, 'I'd be afraid to drive it, I think.'

Becky said, 'It pretends to be old, but it's not.'

'Where's Robin?'

Ralph said, 'He's playing in it.'

Daniel displayed the car's keys, holding them as if diamonds trickled from his fingers. 'Don't worry. He won't get far.'

Sandra Glasse had not spoken at all. She did not seem to know what the others were talking about. She had just arrived, Kit saw: she had a paper bag in her hand, which she cradled against her old jersey. 'Oh, Mrs Eldred,' she said, 'I've brought you some hen's eggs.'

Daniel, who had not met Sandra before, looked around at her with a quizzical smile. It seemed to him she must have dropped in from another world.

They had decided to eat in the kitchen as usual, because the evenings were cold and the central heating was playing up again. Earlier Ralph had met Anna dragging into the boiler room with a scuttle of coal. 'Anna,' he had said, 'with two sons in the house, I don't expect to see you —'

'This effort is voluntary,' Anna said. 'I'm doing it to warm myself up.'

By the time they had fought a bout with the boiler, they were both warm. 'The poor desperate thing,' Ralph said. 'I suppose it would be a mercy to knock it out and send it wherever boilers go to die. Still, I can't see us changing over to oil. Not this year. Besides, with oil, it's so political, the prices shoot up, they hold you to ransom.'

'Daniel explained to me once,' Anna said, 'that when the price of one sort of fuel goes up, the price of all the others goes up soon after.'

'But the installation . . .' Ralph said. 'Honestly, the bills just at the moment . . . the telephone bill alone.'

'Yes,' Anna said. 'Yet when anyone comes by and says "Can I use your phone?" you say, "Of course, go ahead," and when they offer to pay for the call you say, "No, I won't hear of it." You remember that volunteer – Abigail, was it? – the one who said could she phone her boyfriend? And it turned out he'd gone to be a jackaroo for a year?'

'An extreme case. Anyway, it stopped her fretting.'

'People should have less expensive emotions,' Anna said. 'They should have them when it's cheap-rate.' Then she said, 'By the way – while we've got a private moment – what do you think of Daniel these days?'

He was all right really, was Ralph's opinion. He had always felt comfortable with Felix's son. Daniel wore the same clothes as he did – corduroy trousers, old tweed jackets, Fair Isle and lambswool from September through to May. Only recently had he become aware that Daniel's clothes were not, like his, organic developments. Daniel went to London to get them at vast expense, it seemed. They looked old because they were made that way. Ralph wore his clothes because they were what was in the wardrobe. Daniel wore them for another reason – to become someone. To become a country gentleman, Robin said; it was a pose.

Robin knew these things. Still, he was enthusiastic about the two-seater, the Morgan, could hardly be dragged inside to eat. Later Ralph went out too, to pass a hand over its gleaming body and murmur its praises. Daniel was like a child at Christmas, beside himself with glee; it would have been churlish not to admire. But he felt uneasy about the car and what it might mean. Modern mechanics purred beneath its bonnet; as Rebecca said, it purported to be what it was not.

All the same, he thought, if Daniel was Kit's choice, you wouldn't find him raising objections. Daniel would look after her. There was nothing fake about his bank balance, and the architects of the county were coming men. He could afford the car and he could afford Kit. He would design them a house, no doubt, and build it on a prime site, and Kit would have a cleaning lady and hot water whenever she wanted it, and . . .

An awful spasm of grief took hold of Ralph; he stood in the outhouse with Daniel and Robin, an old mac around his shoulders, rain and blue evening air gusting in at the door, and felt grief take him by the windpipe, grief shake him like a mugger. He turned away; no one must see his face.

This happened sometimes. More, lately. And trying to separate himself from the emotion, to pull away from it, he wondered: why is this? He went back into the house. In the kitchen, Sandra was washing up; Becky was drying; Anna was decanting the leftovers into boxes for the fridge. A usual kind of family: 1980, and all's well.

It was a year now since Julian had met Sandra Glasse.

It was a Sunday in April; Julian could not mistake the date, because the Scouts in North Walsham had been holding their St

George's Day parade. And what was he doing in North Walsham? He had wanted to get out of the house. There were some particularly nasty Visitors, Sad Cases. Robin had the excuse of some sporting fixture or other; he always had a means of escape.

His mother, who was sensitive about the Visitors, had seen Julian's plight. 'Would you go to North Walsham for me? I have a bundle of clothes for the church jumble sale, which includes some things of your father's that I particularly wish to see the back of. If you could just drop them in at this address I'll give you — leave them in the garage if they're out — then you could have the car for the afternoon. How would that be?'

Nothing doing in North Walsham; nothing doing, in a little market town on a Sunday afternoon. Only the Scouts marching down the street with their band, and a gang of bike boys jeering at them. He parked the car, delivered the bundle to a house near the church, walked up the empty street in fitful sunshine. He stopped to stare for no good reason into the window of Boots the Chemist. There was a razzmatazz of vitamin supplements and glucose tablets, and a come-and-get-'em pyramid of Kodak films, and an alluring display of hot-water bottles, for pessimists who might be buying them in for the summer ahead.

The bike boys had gathered around the Market Cross, their machines at rest, and they in their leather jackets pushing and shoving about its venerable dome. Julian always liked to see the Market Cross, but he shied away from approaching them. He was not afraid — or he did not want to think so; but like the Scouts he would have been an incitement to them. He was tidily dressed, like a good schoolboy at weekend, in a loose cream cotton shirt and well-ironed denims — no one could stop his mother pressing clothes. His hair was the colour called dishwater-blond; still, it was too blond, and conspicuously shiny and clean. He knew his own features: his unformed face, his large unclouded blue eyes. He knew what they represented – provoking innocence. It did not seem to matter that he was physically stronger than most people. Strength's not much good without permission to use it.

The boys leaning on the columns of the Market Cross had leather jackets with studs and hair shaved off to stubble. The girls with them had long metal earrings and aggrieved faces. They sprawled against the machines or pawed at the boys' jackets, keeping up a braying cackling conversation of sorts. One girl hitched up her thin skirt and threw a leg over one of the bikes; she slithered across the saddle and rode it in seesaw movements, in a mimicry of copulation.

Another girl stood slightly apart from the group. She was with them, but didn't seem to belong to them at all. She had a shaggy head of thick, dark red hair; he could hardly see her face or shape, and it was the oddity of her that made him give her a second look. She wore a black-and-white tweed jacket that was several sizes too big; it was well-worn, and the kind of thing that a settled Norfolk matron of fifty might call 'my old gardening coat'. No pretence at fashion in it, or even anti-fashion. She had lace-up school shoes: also not a rebel's possessions. Someone spoke to her, and she shook her red head violently, and started across the road, cantering off, like an animal, in the direction of the church.

Julian turned and put the car keys in his pocket. He crossed the road too, followed her into the church grounds. She stood beneath the broken, collapsed tower, whose craggy top overbore the streets, the Market Cross, the bike boys. Seeing him, she seemed to shake herself inside the vast stiff jacket, and trotted further off, to the far side of the churchyard. There she sat down on a bench (put there by the Old Folks' Welfare Committee) and waited for him to catch her up.

At first he hardly dared sit down beside her, in case she took fright and hurtled off again. Her animal quality seemed pronounced, and he wished he had something to offer, a sugar lump or even a piece of bread, to show that he meant well. As if reading his mind, she reached into the jacket and took out an apple, then a second. She offered one to him, holding it out at arm's length, without a smile.

'Do you always carry your supplies with you?' he asked.

She said, 'Yes, certainly.'

He tossed his head back towards the market-place. 'Do you know that lot?'

'Not really.'

'I thought you were with them.'

'I picked up with them this morning. I'd nothing else to do. I went to Cromer with them. Nobody had any money. We came on here. They fetched me.'

He took the apple and sat down on the bench beside her. She wiped the fruit on the sleeve of her jacket and bit into it. She chewed gloomily, reflectively, eyes on gravestones and the church's ancient walls.

'Are you going back with them?'

'No.' She was angry. 'They're senseless.'

'Where do you live?'

'In the Burnhams. You know it round there?'

'You're a fair way from home.'

'You can get a fair way when you go on the motor bikes, that's one thing about them. Still, I don't care for it. I ought to be getting back.' She threw her apple core on the ground, but didn't move, just huddled into her jacket. It began to drizzle. 'I'll take shelter in the church,' she said.

Later, it seemed to him that Sandra knew all the county's churches, great and small. She treated them as other people treated bus shelters and waiting rooms. He had to stride to keep up with her, as she bolted for the porch. 'If you're not going to eat your apple,' she said, 'I'll have it back, I might need it later.'

He said, 'I could take you home.'

'Have you got a car?'

'Yes.'

'You're young to have a car.'

'It's my mother's car. I don't mind taking you. You'll never get back any other way, and this rain's setting in.'

'All right,' she said. They stood in the church porch for a minute and watched the rain fall. 'Sanctuary,' she said, unexpectedly.

'Do you know about this church?' Julian looked sideways at her, into her face. Such pale eyes. 'When they were building it, it was the Peasants' Revolt. There was a battle near here. It was the last battle, I think. Some of the rebels came in here begging sanctuary, but the church wasn't finished, so it didn't count. The Bishop of Norwich came after them and killed them all.'

The girl blinked at him. 'I never heard that,' she said.

He loathed himself, spouting semi-facts. Why had he done it? He laughed and said, 'Didn't they tell you about it at school?' He loathed himself more. What had made him go on about the Peasants' Revolt, for God's sake? She unnerved him, that was it. She had not told him her name. Her sandy-gilt lashes drooped on to her cheek.

'I don't recall anything about it,' she said. But then, very kindly, 'I'm always glad to know anything about old places, so if you've anything to tell me you needn't be afraid I won't like it.'

It seemed she expected a long acquaintance. The rain slackened a little. Julian took her jacket by its bulky sleeve and hurried her to the car. The bike boys had scattered. She was his responsibility.

★

A fine drizzle hit the windscreen. The sea, on their right as they drove, was obliterated by a rising mist. The Sheringham caravan sites loomed out of it, and the wind plucked at the blossom on the cherry trees in the bungalow gardens. The trees looked as if they had been left outside by mistake, or transported from some softer country.

Between Cley and Weybourne, the heathland melted invisibly into the marshes. Bird-watchers, hung about like pedlars with the tools of their trade, strode towards the invisible sea. There were sheep in the fields; among their ambling forms they saw the necks of resting swans, as hard and clear as marble, startlingly white in the thick air. By the roadside, signs – crudely chalked blackboards, or painted boards – advertised FRESH SEA BAIT, SHRIMPS, COCKLES, FRESH CRABS, DRESSED CRABS, KIPPERS. The tourist season was beginning.

They drove in what seemed to be a companionable silence. At Blakeney – the salt marshes a nebulous blend of earth, sea, air – Sandra turned in her seat. 'I'm sorry if I was angry back there. I'm not usually angry.'

What Julian saw, from the tail of his eye, was a face set on placid lines; a face with a translucent pallor, and those pale eyes. She seemed strong, composed; she held her white hands on her lap, the one reposing confidingly in the other.

'What did the bikers say to you, to make you run off like that?'

Sandra thought, then said, 'They criticized my garment.'

After a moment, they both yelled with laughter, the noise filling the shabby body of Anna's car. A gust of wind, blowing inland, peppered the rain against the glass.

'Well, I admit . . .' Julian said. 'Why do you wear it?'

'We got it donated,' Sandra said. 'I can't afford clothes like they've got. It's funny, I always think – when you've got a bit of money you can afford cheap clothes, you can throw them away when they fall apart. But if you're poor your clothes go on for ever. You get given things the Queen would be proud to wear.'

'Who was it gave it you?'

'Some church. My mum has her contacts. She used to clean for a churchwarden's wife. So we get remembered when it's jumble sales.' She paused. 'It's just our size she forgets.'

They began to laugh again. The windscreen wipers swished; ahead of them, towards Wells, the horizon had the pearl sheen of brighter weather. 'I dare say it'll outlast me, this old jacket,' Sandra said. 'I once ran through a hedge in it, and it didn't flinch.'

By the time they reached Holkham, the mist was clearing. Flashes of light struck from the dwarves' windows of flint cottages, little houses tumbling towards the coast; flint sparkled like gemstones in the wall of a round-towered church. 'Turn off here,' Sandra said, directing him towards the sea. They turned between high hedgerows, leaving behind a wide view of windmills and the red roofs of distant barns. The road narrowed. 'I live down this track,' Sandra said. 'Do you want to come in? You could have a cup of tea.'

The car bumped down an incline. 'My mother calls this "one of the foremost hills in Norfolk",' Sandra said. 'OK – stop here.'

They came to a halt in front of a huddle of low buildings, the doors facing inwards, out of the wind. There was a pear tree on a sheltered wall, geese on a pond, a vegetable plot screened off by an amateur windbreak. There were some rotting hen-houses, an old cartwheel leaning on a fence, and by the front door a wheelbarrow filled with something shrouded in polythene. They got out of the car. A woman came to the door. 'That's my mother,' Sandra said.

Mrs Glasse seemed taller than Sandra, not very old. She wore patched jeans and two shapeless pullovers, the one underneath longer than the one on top. She had red hair too, longer than her daughter's, scooped up with pins. Julian saw that bits of it straggled down her back as she turned to lead the way inside. For the first time, he wondered how his own mother managed to keep her hair fixed in its dark cloudy shapes, arrested in its whirls and coils. There must be an art to it.

Mrs Glasse had been working outside. Her muddy gumboots stood by the door. There was a wide lobby, full of swirling air – peg rugs on the floor, an accumulation of dark furniture.

'You're not one of the bike boys,' Mrs Glasse said. 'Come through, I've got the kettle on.'

He followed her to the kitchen. It was a big room, light, square, tiled underfoot. Two hard chairs stood by an old-fashioned range, in front of which some clothes were drying. There was a smell of burning wood and wet wool. Mrs Glasse hoisted the clothes away, and dragged up a third chair, manipulating it with an agile foot in a fisherman's sock. 'Where d'you find him, Sandra?'

Expecting no answer, she gave him a mug of tea, the sugar already stirred into it. Julian could not think of anything to say. Mrs Glasse did not make small-talk, or ask again where her daughter had been. He sat facing the back of the house, watching the light fade. Through an arched doorway, down steps, he caught a glimpse of a small dairy, with its deep stone shelves and recessed windows. Feeling the draught, Mrs Glasse leapt up and closed the door. He snapped his gaze away. He had wanted to step into the dairy, and run a hand over the icy, ecclesiastical curves of the walls.

As he left the house and drove away, he noticed a glasshouse, its panes shattered; a gate, off its hinges. He felt like stopping the car, going back, offering his services. But then he thought, you can't ask people to rely on you, if you're going away at the end of the summer. Between now and October I couldn't make much of an impression on that place. It would only break my heart.

After this, Julian did not see Sandra for some weeks. But in June, driving back from a friend's house in Hunstanton on a bright windy day, he saw by the roadside two women selling vegetables from a trestle table. He knew them at once, with their white faces and long flapping scarves. He pulled over and climbed out of the car. 'Hello there, Julian,' Mrs Glasse said. She had a bag of money slung about her waist, like a market trader. Sandra pulled her woollen hat further over her brows, and smiled shyly at him.

'We'll have strawberries shortly,' Mrs Glasse said. 'That fetches 'em.'

'Is there a lot of trade?'

'Passing trade,' Mrs Glasse said. 'Golfers on their way home, full of golf courses this place is.' The wind ripped the words out of her mouth. 'In high season we get the self-caterings. I do vegetables, peeled and quartered, slice the carrots, whatever, put them in polythene bags, if they don't sell we have to eat them. I do samphire, not that the self-caterings know what that is. We make bread when we've got the oven going, when we're in the mood. I'm learning from a book to make bread into patterns. I can do plaited loaves, wheatsheafs, prehistoric monsters, frogs and armadillos. The armadillos get a lot of admiration – but all you do is make a monster, and squash it, and bake the top in points.'

'It must be hard work,' Julian said.

'Labour-intensive,' Sandra said. 'Of me.'

'We get bird-watchers, I make them sandwiches. We get that lot going to Brancaster and Burnham Thorpe, studying the haunts of Lord Nelson.'

'Early haunts,' Sandra said. 'Birthplace.'

'We do goats' milk, duck eggs. Sandra pushes it all up in the wheelbarrow. This table's a bugger, though. We have to carry it up between us.'

'Up the foremost hill,' Sandra said. 'We tried putting it on the barrow but it barged our legs.'

'Couldn't you leave it up here?' Julian said. He looked around. 'By the wall?'

'Self-caterings steal it,' Mrs Glasse said. She clapped her hands together, to warm them, hopped from foot to foot. 'Summer coming on,' she observed.

'I'm sure I could fix up something,' Julian said. 'I could drive a post in behind that wall, nobody would see it, I could chain the table to it. Wrap a chain around the legs and get a padlock.'

'We never thought of that, did we?' Sandra said to her mother. 'Well, we did actually, but we're busy, we didn't get round to it yet. It'd have to be weather-proofed, though. We couldn't have our table rotting.'

'Perhaps Julian could build it a house,' Mrs Glasse said. 'Seems cruel to leave it out in the open air, chained up like something dangerous.'

The two women exchanged a glance. They laughed; comfortably enough. Julian felt almost comforted.

The following day, Julian went back to the Glasses' farm. The women were very busy; Mrs Glasse sitting by the stove, knitting in an effortful fury, and Sandra, after she had let him in, returning to her task of stuffing dozens of sisal doormats into black plastic bin-liners.

'For the market at Hunstanton,' Mrs Glasse said. 'We're going tomorrow, we have a stall. Doormats do well, because people live amid such a quantity of mud. And basketwork of all types.'

'Where do you get the doormats?' Julian asked.

'I buy them cheap from a fool.'

'Baskets we make ourselves,' Sandra said. 'She taught me. We do it in the winter when the weather keeps us in.'

'How do you get to Hunstanton?'

Mrs Glasse rolled her eyes. 'He do ask questions,' she said.

'Do you like her verb?' Sandra asked. 'She does it for the tourists.'

'I only thought, with all your stuff –'

'We have a vehicle,' Mrs Glasse said. 'Of sorts. We try not to take it out more than once a week because of the summonses.'

'She got done for no tax,' Sandra said.

'We have to hide the bloody thing,' Mrs Glasse said. 'The police come down from time to time, sniffing, seeing what they can do us for. We used to have a dog, Billy, they didn't care for him, weren't so keen then. But he died.'

'You should get another dog,' Julian said, 'if that's what keeps you safe. I'm sure I could get you a dog.'

'No,' Mrs Glasse said. He was sitting facing her, and he saw that her large light eyes filled with tears. She was pretty, he thought, might have been pretty, must have been. As if angry with herself, she gave the weighty knitting a push and watched it slither off her lap. 'Billy wanted meat,' she said. 'I used to feel sorry for him, you can't expect a dog to get by on carrot and turnip.' She stood up. 'That's enough doormats,' she said. 'We'll bag up the baskets later on, we'll just have a sit now and a cup of tea.'

Julian said, 'I'll come with you when you do the market. Do you have to take the table? I'll help you load and unload.'

'You needn't,' Sandra said. 'We've always managed.'

'I can do anything you want,' Julian said. 'I can patch up the roof if you've got a ladder, you've got some tiles off. I can do carpentry. I could put you on some new wallpaper if you want. I could lift your potatoes for you.'

Mrs Glasse said, 'Sit down, boy. There's no need to do anything.'

Julian sat down and drank his tea. He could never remember a time when he had been commanded to do nothing – when it had been enjoined on him.

That summer, it seemed to Ralph, Sandra became a fixture in his house. She was to be found in the kitchen, occupying the rocking chair, her hands folded together, her legs tucked beneath the chair, her ankles crossed. He liked to talk to her if he found her sitting there. She had her wits about her, he told Anna, despite her quaint way of talking; she had a native clarity of mind which the educative process had not succeeded in clouding. School had been an interruption to Sandra's life. She had left as soon as she could. 'I didn't see the point of it,' she told Ralph. 'It was such a long way, it took hours getting there. It used to be dark by the time I got home.'

Sandra never turned up empty-handed. She brought perhaps a modest present of a lettuce, or some fresh bread; once, when they had not baked, a can of peaches from their store cupboard.

Anna was touched, then exasperated. 'Sandra,' she said, 'you don't have to bring us presents. You're welcome to come here and eat every day and stay as long as you like, nobody who comes here has ever had to pay for their keep.' No one else has ever offered, she thought.

Sometimes Sandra brought a cake; but they baked cakes only as a last resort, when they had nothing else to take to market. They only had to get their fingers amid the eggy stretch and cascading currants, to start cursing and swearing; they were fair set, Sandra said, to slap each other with their wooden spoons. Mrs Glasse's cakes had something sad and flat about them, a melancholy Fenlands quality. Sandra's cakes rose, but in a violent, volcanic way: then cracked on top. How two cakes containing opposite faults could come out of an oven at the same (albeit unreliable) temperature was, Sandra said, one of the mysteries of East Anglia.

But despite their appearance, the cakes sold well enough. People like to buy the fruits of other people's labour; they like to put the small coin into the very hand that has toiled. Julian thought that it was not the wares that drew the customers, but the women's full, grey, mesmeric eyes.

That summer he spent market days at Hunstanton, behind the Glasses' stall; flapping canvas divided him from neighbouring stalls, from the shiny acrylic clothing, the check workshirts, the nylon leopard-skin car-seat covers and rubber mats, the cheap lace tablecloths, the bright plastic kitchen gadgets, the inflatable toys for the beach. He felt himself grow an inch taller, his hair tousled, his face sunburned, a canvas bag of change thrown across his body in ammunition-belt style. As summer ended the sea turned to the colour of mud, and soon came the wind that cut through the clothes, cut to the bone, propelling the shoppers inland towards the teashops and the amusement arcades.

Ralph said to him: 'Look, I know you're old enough to make up your own mind, but don't get too involved, will you? Remember you're off to university in October. You've worked hard for it, I don't want you to be upset by anything, to have any, you know, regrets, or things pulling you back.'

Julian went over to the Glasses' farm most days. He oversaw the vegetable plots, sawed logs and mended fences. He thought about reglazing the greenhouse, but did not get around to it before it was autumn, and he had to go away.

Ralph worried. Possibly Anna worried, too; but he did not ask her to talk about it. He remembered Julian as a little boy at his first school, unable to tie his shoelaces or learn his times tables or do up his tie. Tears had been shed, about the tie. Julian did not mind that his mum or dad put it on for him, every morning; but there would be PE lessons, and he would have to take it off. Then he would not be able to put it back, he sobbed. And this was the problem: he would have to scramble it into some knot of his own devising, he could not manage the knot that society required; he would have to stretch and mangle it and treat it like a piece of string. Then, he wailed each morning, they would all know he was a spastic.

'You're not a spastic,' Ralph said. 'Is that what they say? It's very naughty of them to call you that.' Ralph felt, when he placed the length of cloth around his child's neck each day, that he was snaring him in a noose.

Then one tear-stained Wednesday afternoon, Kit had taken the situation in hand. She had re-formed the tangled mess which Julian had created, into its approved shape; then simply loosened it, eased it from beneath his collar, and lifted it over his head still knotted. She hung it on the end of his bed. 'There,' she had said. 'Now, in the morning, you see, just put it over your head.'

'Oh yes.' Julian's face lit up. 'Then all I have to do is –'

'Just pull the knot up,' Kit said. 'Here you go.' She fastened his fingers around the short end of the tie. 'Gentle, now – not too tight. That's it. Lovely. Just you wait and see. They'll all be copying you soon.'

Years later, Julian remembered Kit's good idea with a pathetic gratitude. Even now when he was grown up, he said, no one had ever taught him anything so useful. Ralph wished he had thought of it.

He had not known how to help Julian; ordinary patience did not seem to be enough. He was slow to learn to read, slow to tell the time; when he tried to learn to write he seemed to be using a foreign alphabet. Even when he had mastered the letter shapes his progress was slow. He was always stopping to rub out what he had written and start again. His collection of erasers was something he prized. Robin sneaked to his mother that he had names for each one: Mouse and Cat and Mother Bear. Julian fell asleep over his reading books, exhausted by the effort of trying to comprehend them.

They took him for an eye test but his sight was perfect. Anna thought of him as a baby: his eyes always on their way from his mother's face to somewhere else.

Julian had a long memory, longer than seemed possible. One day when he was six he said, where did the cat go, Emma?

'I haven't got a cat,' Emma said.

'But you had, you had Freddie.'

He described the ancient tabby, vast and slow like a sofa on the move, its lop ear, its tail without a tip. Emma was astonished. Freddie had died long ago, before Julian could walk or talk. It was a prodigious feat of memory, truly extraordinary: Emma reported it to Anna and Ralph. Anna said, 'He must have heard him described. I'm sure we've often talked about Freddie.'

Kit was listening. 'Julian does have lots of memories,' she said. 'And so do I. We can remember from before we were born.'

'Don't be silly,' Anna said. 'You know better. No one can do that.'

They plucked Julian out of the village school, saying that they had got him a place in a prep, weathering the scepticism of the headmistress. They kept him at home for a term, feeling guilty about it, and tried to teach him themselves. Mostly he played with bricks, building houses then knocking them down. But he started to look at books, just for the pictures. His fright diminished. Imperceptibly, very slowly and cautiously, he began to read.

The problems were not over; at least, his new teachers did not think so. Hard not to nag such a child, at home and at school. Julian was unpunctual, dreamy, sweetly polite but deeply uncaring. His conversation was intelligent but elliptical. He was seldom on time for anything; he did not seem to see the point of punctuality. Even when he reached his teens, he never wore a watch. 'He's a natural animal,' Kit said. 'He goes by the sun.'

Julian was wary of surfaces, it seemed. When he drew a house he began with its contents. Pots and pans came first, objects in cupboards. Then beds and chairs; only then, walls and doors and windows. When he drew a tree he drew not just the trunk and leaves and branches but the roots, running deep under the soil, beyond the range of normal vision.

By the time he reached his teens Julian had adapted to the world, learned to fit in. Sporadically attentive, he passed just enough exams, with just the grades he needed; and passed them doggedly, until the prospect of university loomed – if that was what he wanted. Ralph tried to interest him in geology, think-ing that the strenuous, outdoor aspect of it might appeal. But Julian associated the subject with the wrapped, labelled specimens which Ralph still kept in boxes in the attics. He seemed to have a peculiar horror of them: their broken traces, their dead-and-gone lives. Then Rebecca began to have her nightmares about the fossils. 'You might get rid of them, give them to a museum,' Anna suggested. 'You never look at them.'

True, he thought. I never do. He went up there one weekend, spent a bit of time unwrapping them, labelling them in his mind. There was the devil's toenail, fresh and horrible and impressive as ever, lying cold in his palm and smelling of the sea. Phylum: Mollusca. Class: Pelecypoda. Order: Pterioda. Family: Gryphaeidae. Genus: *Gryphaea*. Species: *arcuata*. Old Nick's remnant ... he knew people, or his father had known people, who maintained that all fossils were planted in the rocks by Satan, to tempt scholars into scientific hypotheses, which led them from the knowledge of God.

He put *arcuata* into his pocket and, downstairs, transferred it to the drawer of his desk. Why not keep it to hand? It was his trophy, taken in the battle for reason.

As soon as he arrived at his university, Julian wrote a long letter to Sandra Glasse. He received a picture postcard two weeks later, showing countryside views, clouds and church towers. He wrote again, asking her to visit him. She didn't answer. He thought that probably she did not have the money for a train ticket; but if he sent the money, would she answer even then? Perhaps his letters were not arriving: perhaps the postman couldn't be bothered to turn down the track.

He wrote to his father: would he consider driving over to the farm to see if everything was all right? His father wrote back in surprise, to say that of course everything was all right; Sandra had been over a couple of times, turned up unexpectedly, hitched lifts, coast road to Fakenham, Fakenham to Bawdeswell, then walked to the house. He didn't like her hitching lifts, in fact he was very upset, but she wouldn't be told. Julian should write to her on that topic. He shouldn't expect much by way of reply, she said she wasn't used to writing letters.

Just before Christmas Julian wrote another letter, to his head of department. Then he packed his bags and took the train to Norwich; then hitched lifts and, changing his suitcase from hand to hand, walked the last few miles from the main road to the Red House. There he had stayed, ever since.

When he was not at the market, or working on the Glasses' small-holding, he was underneath his new car; his old car that is, the one Emma had given him the money to buy. He coaxed it along; it got him to the coast and back. His new skills were undeniably useful; Anna's car was now a barely coherent assemblage of rattles and squeaks, and the Citroën caused oily boys at garages to titter and roll their eyes and cast their rags to the ground.

Then there was the Glasses' Morris Traveller to be rescued from its decrepitude and illegality. He told Ralph about the tax and insurance problem; Ralph immediately handed over some cash that had been earmarked for a new vacuum cleaner and some school clothes for Rebecca. Julian promised to mend the old Hoover; it had value as a technological curiosity, Ralph said, in a year or two they might be able to take it to London and flog it to the Science Museum. Rebecca did not really need new clothes – she would, on the whole, fit into her old ones. With school uniform, it is often heartening if you look a little different from the other girls.

Julian gave the money to Mrs Glasse. No question of paying it back, he said, it wasn't like that. 'I just don't want to think about you being pulled up,' he said, 'or about the police coming round when I'm not here.'

'They'll still come if they want,' Mrs Glasse said. 'You'd be surprised how many offences there are, that a person can commit just without thinking about it. You know, I don't want to take your money. But I can see that you want to give it.'

Even now they were legal, she would only take the car out on market days, she said. There was the problem of money for petrol. 'You can't knit petrol,' she said. 'And they won't let you barter for it.'

He did not tell Sandra about his sister's school uniform, or about the row his parents had when the story came out. Privately, he agreed with his father; it was Anna's fault, it was the fault of her habit of saving bits of money in pots and jars around the house, like some old granny in a cottage. It was too tempting for other people, when they had a prior need.

He did not tell Sandra because he knew she would think the
' row was ridiculous. She thought his family was rich; she said so.

'Oh, come on,' Julian said. 'There's four of us and none of us has earned anything yet. My mum's a teacher but she had an illness and she hasn't been able to work for years. My dad works for a charity, he doesn't draw a big stipend, he just draws enough to keep us solvent.'

'There you are,' Sandra said. 'Stipend. Solvent. Of course, we're mostly solvent, because we never buy anything if we can help it. Money doesn't enter into our calculations. I learned it in geography, it's the only thing I recall. We're a subsistence economy.'

'I think you're proud of being poor,' Julian said.

'No, we're not proud. We just don't think about it. We just go along.'

'You could get benefits,' Julian said. 'Other people do it.'

'Oh, we know all about that. My mum's been to offices appealing for benefits. Sometimes you get things, other times you don't. The trouble is, they keep you sitting in a waiting room for hours when you could be out trying to earn something. You get coughs and colds from the other people. Last time my mum went they asked her if she had a man friend. She said, better eat turnips all winter than talk to bureaucrats of romance.'

After Julian's own household, constantly full of Visitors and their noisy upsets, the silence and peace of the Glasses' farm was like a convalescence. Only one thing had changed: during his term away, somebody had given them a black-and-white television set. They watched all the soap operas, and discussed them in terms of gentle surprise, as if the characters were people they knew. They explained the characters to him, and he sat with them and watched, predicting the plot developments out loud, as they did. It was something new for him. There was a television set at home, but it was kept in the cold back sitting room, like an impoverished relative whom it was best not to encourage.

Also, they had discovered a big enthusiasm for story-books. When Sandra had been over at the house one day Anna had taken her into Dereham to help with the weekly shopping, and at the secondhand bookstall Sandra had bought a book called *Middlemarch*, with the back off, priced 20p. They called this book 'the book we're reading', and talked about Dorothea all the time, with the same mild interest, the same mild censoriousness. 'That's it,' Mrs Glasse said. 'When you're young you just don't know what you want in life. You've messed everything up before you find out.'

'The die is cast,' said Sandra.

Julian was confused by them. He was only a geographer; that, at least, had been his subject before he ran away. People from other faculties claimed that geography was a subject studied by slightly dim, marginal students, who enjoyed superfluous good health. It might be true: among those few people in his year with whom he had casual conversation, three or four said they were going to be schoolteachers, teach geography and games. He could not imagine teaching children anything – least of all, to kick footballs about or swing from ropes. If he was going to be healthy and stupid, he could do that at home.

So he reasoned. It didn't seem to convince his mother. His father didn't ask him any questions; strangely, though, this seemed to make him like his mother more and his father less. He's not bothered about me, he said to Robin. He can't get me to be a Good Soul, and I'm not enough of a Sad Case. He's only worried about those spotty kids with carrier bags.

Not yet, you're not enough of a Sad Case, Robin said.

One day in February, he went to bed with Sandra, upstairs in her large brass bed. Mrs Glasse, downstairs, carried on knitting. Sandra bled all over the sheets.

'He's drifting – that's all.' Anna said. 'When I ask him what he wants to do with his life, he changes the subject.'

Ralph said, 'He's always been like that. Anyway – is there any point in knowing what you want to do with your life? There are so many things that can go wrong.'

Anna's voice was strained. 'So you just drift with the tide?'

'Remember when he was little,' Ralph said. 'We thought he would never learn to read, never do anything. But we cured him just by letting him be. Those few weeks of peace cured him. If we'd have left him at school, with ignorant infant teachers bawling at him, he'd never have made anything. As it is, he got to university –'

'And passed up his chance,' Anna said. 'And what will happen to him if he gets tied up with Sandra?'

'He could do worse.'

'I'm aware,' Anna said, 'that Sandra is a charity case of yours.'

Ralph said gently; 'I hope we can be charitable. Now that the need exists.'

'Hasn't it always?'

'I mean, in our own family.'

'I suppose I'm not charitable,' Anna said.

Ralph didn't answer. But he thought, I will never be party to bullying and hectoring my children as my father bullied and hectored me.

Julian explained to Sandra and to Mrs Glasse what he had not felt able to explain at home. As he talked, he remembered the place in which he had been stranded, this Midlands place, where mean slivers of sky showed between tower blocks. 'Homesick,' Sandra said. 'Wouldn't you get over it in time?'

She was not vain; it did not seem to enter her head that – partly, anyway – he might have come back for her.

'You don't know anything about it, Sandra,' Mrs Glasse said. 'You've never been away. It's like an illness, that's why it's called homesickness. People don't realize. Are they blaming you, your mum and dad?'

'I couldn't give a reason like homesickness,' Julian said. 'They'd think it was feeble. They weren't that old when they went to South Africa.'

'Did they?' Sandra said. 'I didn't know that.'

'Some people just aren't cut out for travelling,' Mrs Glasse said.

Ralph said to Anna, 'You are right, of course. About Julian. I apologize.' She stared at the spectacle: this sudden attack of public humility. 'I probably ought to find out more about the whole thing,' he said. 'I think, after Easter, I'll go over and see Mrs Glasse.'

SIX

The week after Easter the winds were so violent that they seemed likely to tear up small trees by the roots. There was never a moment, day or night, when the world was quiet.

Mrs Glasse had no telephone, so Ralph couldn't contact her to arrange a time to meet. 'Should I drive over with you?' Anna said.

'No. It would look like a deputation. As if we'd come to complain about her.'

'You wonder what sort of woman she can be,' Anna said. 'Strange life they lead.'

His car joined the coast road at Wells. The sky was patchy, clouds moving fast, rushing above him as he skirted the dusky red walls of Holkham Hall: parting now and then to reveal a pacific blue. The sea was not visible at once; but as the road turned he saw on the broken line of the horizon a strip of grey, indefinite, opaque.

It was ten o'clock when he rattled down the stony incline to the Glasses' house. The door opened before he had switched off the engine. Mrs Glasse stood waiting in the doorway.

His first thought: how young she is, she can't be more than thirty-five, thirty-six. She was pale, straight-backed, red-haired: the hair a deeper red than her daughter's, long and fine. The wind ripped at his clothes as he stepped out of the car, billowing out his jacket like a cloak. 'This weather!' Mrs Glasse said. She smiled at him. 'Hello, Julian's dad.'

It was a low house, old; its bones protested, creaked under the onslaught of the weather. He heard its various sounds, as she stood hesitating inside the door; he thought, it is a house like a ship, everything in movement, a ship breasting a storm. 'On your left there,' Mrs Glasse said. 'Go in the parlour. There's a fire lit, and the kettle's on.'

'You might have been expecting me,' he said.

He sat by the fire, in a Windsor chair, waiting for her to bring them tea. The wind dropped; it was as if a noisy lout had left the room. In the sudden silence he heard the mantel clock ticking. She returned. Handed him a mug. 'I didn't put sugar in. Did you want it? No, I didn't think you were the sugar sort.'

'Goodness,' he said. 'What does that mean?'

She pushed her hair back. 'Sugar's for comfort,' she said.

'You think I don't need comfort?'

Mrs Glasse didn't reply. She pulled up a stool to the fire. Ralph half-rose from his chair; 'Thanks, I'm comfortable here,' she said.

'That clock up there.' Ralph shook his head. 'We had one just like it at home when I was a boy. It was my father's. His pride and joy. He wouldn't let anybody else touch it.'

'You're not going to tell me,' Mrs Glasse said drily, 'that it stopped the day he died?'

'No, not exactly. My mother threw it out.'

'That was extreme.'

'For her, yes, it was. She couldn't stand the chime.'

'Did she ever mention it? In his lifetime, I mean?'

'I shouldn't think so. She was a self-effacing woman. At least, she effaced herself before him.'

She had fine hands, Mrs Glasse; the calloused hands of a woman used to outdoor work, but still white, long-fingered. They were hands that rings might adorn, and that one did adorn: a plain red–gold wedding band, an old ring, one that might have been in a family for generations. Her skin had begun to line a little round the eyes: so many years of looking into the wind. All this he saw in the vibrant light that spilled into the room, morning light: sliding over the cream walls, turning them the colour of butter.

He said, 'We have a problem about Julian. Well, not a problem.'

'A problem, but not a problem,' Mrs Glasse said.

'We thought, Anna and I – Anna, that's my wife – that perhaps he talked to you. He doesn't talk to us.'

'Do you see a reason for that?'

'There's no reason, I hope. It's just his nature.'

'Well then,' Mrs Glasse said placidly. 'If it's his nature, what is there to be done?'

Ralph leaned forward, to engage her attention. 'You see, Julian's never been communicative. And a bit of a drifter – you could call him that. Still, we believe in letting him work things through for himself, at his own pace – we always have pursued that policy.'

'Sandra is the same,' Mrs Glasse said. 'Resistant to direction. Not that I try.'

'Yes . . . so we wondered, Anna and I, if he had said anything to you, about his plans.'

'Plans,' Mrs Glasse said: as if the word were new to her. 'He's not mentioned any. He's done a lot for me, around the place. I don't ask him, he just does it. You can't say he's not industrious. He fills his time.'

'But where's it leading?' Ralph said. 'I can't help but worry.'

There was a pause. They looked into the fire; the flames now were pale as air, the sun drawing their colour out. Only the flicker held their eyes. Tinny, grating, the clock struck the quarter hour. Ralph looked up at it in wonder. The sound seemed to tremble in the air. She laughed. 'You can have it,' she said, 'if it means so much to you.'

He shook his head. 'It's very kind. But no – on the whole I think I share my mother's opinion.'

'Was he a Norfolk man, your father?'

'Oh, yes. From Swaffham originally – but we moved to Norwich when I was a child.'

'A city boy,' Mrs Glasse said. 'Imagine. I've never moved much.'

'Did it belong in your family, this house?'

'Oh, no.' She seemed puzzled. 'Nothing like that.'

'It is a very nice house. Very peaceful. I'm not surprised Julian wants to spend his time here. The dairy, he said –'

'Yes – would you like to look around?' Ralph protested, politely. She got to her feet, put her mug down on the mantelpiece by the clock. She led him into the kitchen, where she and Sandra spent most of their leisure time, their chairs set one either side of the range; led him from there to the dairy, its chaste stone slabs, its chill. The tiles were cracked, and the turning world had stopped beneath their glaze; cows trod forever through squares of blue grass, through fields of blue blossom. She turned to him and smiled. 'Make our own butter is one thing we don't do,' she said, 'but I did have a cow, at one time. Daisy, she was called – that was original, wasn't it? I'd sell milk up at the top of the track there. It's against all the rules, so I had to stop.'

'You're very enterprising,' Ralph said.

'I have a couple of ponies in my top field now, look after them for weekenders. We didn't know anything about horses when we took them on. But they couldn't, we thought, be as complicated as people.'

'And it's worked out?'

'Yes – Sandra has her talents.' She took him back through the hall, up the low-rising stairs. There were four bedrooms, each of them square and neat, each with the same cream walls; and the furniture of dark wood, chests and tallboys, massive and claw-footed. 'All this furniture was my grandmother's,' she said. 'This is Sandra's room.'

'It's like a room in a picture book,' he said. 'Do you know what I mean? The bed.'

'Yes, Sandra made that quilt for herself, it was the first she ever made, I taught her. She's a careful worker, she's slow but she's neat enough. The trouble is, people don't want them. Or they want them, but they won't pay the price, there's months of work in a quilt, People go for something cheap, something run up on a machine. They can't tell the difference. But there is a difference, if you look.'

Downstairs she put the kettle on again. They sat in the kitchen waiting for it; 'I'm a woman who drinks a lot of tea,' she said, as if in apology.

'It occurs to me,' Ralph said, 'it must be worth a bit, this place.'

'I'd never thought about it.'

'Prices are rocketing. You'd be amazed. Would you be interested? I know a good firm of estate agents, old friend of mine but he's dead now. If you follow me.'

'Of course,' she said. 'He'd give me a price from beyond the grave?' She turned her head to him: such pale eyes.

'Actually, he has a son – Daniel, he's an architect, a nice lad, he sees a bit of my daughter Kit. He'd probably come out here for nothing, give you a rough figure, he knows the market as well as anybody. He'd be interested to see the place.'

'But then where would we live?' Mrs Glasse said.

'I thought . . . well, I don't want to intrude, of course, but I know money's a problem. You could buy yourselves a cottage, and you'd have a tidy sum left to invest, and it would give you an income.'

'I could live like a duchess,' Mrs Glasse suggested.

'Well, not quite that.'

'If I had a cottage, I might have to get rid of my ducks and hens. I wouldn't have eggs to sell. Not to mention vegetables.'

'You could get jobs. It would be more secure for you.'

'Oh, we do get jobs sometimes. In the high season. Hun-stanton, Burnham Market. We might go and waitress for a week or two. Not that we're good waitresses. We're not used to it.'

He was struck by the slow and thoughtful way in which she spoke, as if she weighed every word. Struck too by how she spoke of her daughter and herself as if they were of the same generation; as if they had one opinion between them, and what one felt, the other felt. She said, 'Sandra and me, we don't mind hard work, nobody could say that. But we prefer to keep each other company at home.'

'You're very close.'

'Aren't you close to your children?'

'I don't know. I like to think I am. But there are so many other things I have to do.'

'I think that parents ought to take care of their children, and that children ought to take care of their parents. That's the main thing, that's what comes first.'

'I've said too much,' he said. 'I didn't mean to interfere. I'm sorry.'

'No, that's all right, you can't help it. You're used to putting people's lives to rights, aren't you, and giving them advice?' She looked up, full into his face. 'God knows, nobody has ever advised me, it might have been better if they had. The thing is, me and Sandra, we manage. Hand to mouth, I know. But there's always something you can do. Sometimes we've gone out house-cleaning. And I know where the best blackberries are. At Brancaster – I could get you some this year. We get basketfuls, we bake pies, blackberry and apple, use our own apples, sell them up there on the road.' She shrugged. 'There's always something.'

'I admire you, Mrs Glasse,' Ralph said. 'You live the kind of life you believe in.'

She looked down, and blushed. 'What is it, Ralph? Don't you?'

The Easter holidays ended. Kit went back to London for her last few weeks. Robin began the term at his day school in Norwich; early mornings still so chilly, getting up in blue light to walk a mile to the crossroads and wait for the first bus. His efforts would be rewarded, his parents thought. Robin wanted a place at medical school, and would get it. Yet he seemed to have no humanitarian concerns. He marked off the seasons by a change of games kit; now, spring having arrived, he tossed his hockey stick up in the attics and packed his cricket bag. Weekends saw him bussed about the county, playing away. Sunday nights he bounced, or trailed, back: sad tales of full-length balls on the off-stump, or glory sagas that put colour in his cheeks and made him look like his father when his father was young: sixty-five off the first twenty overs, he would say, and then we accelerated, run-a-ball, finished it off just after tea with five wickets in hand. 'Do you know what Robin's talking about?' Anna would say – deriving a pale routine gratification from the child's health and simplicity, from his resemblance to the other boy she had once known.

'Good God, I was nothing like Robin,' Ralph would say. 'My father thought cricket was High Church. Do you think he'll ever do any work when he goes away? Suppose he became a heart surgeon, and he had to do a transplant, and there was a Test Match on?'

But Emma would say, speaking from experience, 'Robin will make a good doctor. Only half his mind will be on his work. That will limit the damage he can do.'

And Rebecca? She rode off on her bike, on the first day of term, to her school two or three miles away; a flouncy, sulky, pretty little girl, who had reached the stage when her family embarrassed her. Soon her embarrassment was to be compounded.

On the Monday morning, the week after term began, Julian came down to the kitchen with his car keys in his hand. 'I'll run you,' he said to her. 'Put your bike in the shed.'

Rebecca dropped her spoon into her cornflakes, spattering milk on the table. 'Suddenly so kind,' she said. 'But how will I get home, sir?'

'I'll collect you.'

'In your so-called car?'

'Yes.'

'But I don't want you to.'

'Beks, life's not just a matter of what you want.'

Rebecca sat up and looked pert. 'Yours seems to be.'

Julian was not drawn. 'Hurry up now, finish your breakfast,' he said. 'Don't argue.'

'What will my friends say when they see me turn up in that thing?' She popped her eyes and pointed, to show what her friends would do. 'They'll take the piss all week. I'll be a social outcast, a – what is it? Not a parishioner – you know what I mean.'

'A pariah,' Julian said. 'Come on now, girl.'

Rebecca saw that he was serious; about what, she didn't know. She turned to her mother, wailing. 'Mum, I don't have to go with him, do I?'

Anna was loading towels from a basket into her temperamental and aged twin-tub washing machine. 'Let Julian take you. It's kind of him. It's a nasty morning, very cold.'

Sulking, Rebecca zipped herself into her anorak and picked up her lunchbox and followed him out. 'When we get there you can stop round the corner, out of sight . . .' she was saying, as the back door slammed behind them.

When Julian got back, Ralph was on the phone to London, defusing the latest crisis at the hostel. The office door was ajar, and Julian could hear snatches of the conversation. 'What occurs to me,' Ralph was saying, 'is that she won't be able to buy much with our petty cash, with the street price what it is, so what will she do to get the rest of the money?' An anxious babbling came back down the line. In the kitchen the washing machine rocked and danced over the flagstones, in a creaking thumping gavotte.

Anna was sitting at the kitchen table. She looked up from the *Eastern Daily Press*. 'What was all that, Julian?'

Julian began to cut himself a slice of bread to make toast. 'It's been on my mind,' he said abruptly. 'That little girl in Devon, Genette Tate – do you remember, it was in the papers?'

'The child who disappeared?'

'They found her bike in a lane. She was thirteen. Some man took her away. They think she's dead.'

Ralph came in. 'Going to be one of those days,' he said. 'That child, Melanie – do you remember I mentioned her? Swallows every banned substance she can lay her hands on, ran away from her foster parents, absconded from the children's home?'

'What's new?' Anna said tiredly. 'Don't they all do that?'

'Just got her off a shoplifting charge last week. Now she's run away and taken our petty cash. Not that she'll get far on it. So I was thinking . . . could we have her here for part of the summer?'

'That's not really a question, is it?' Anna said. 'It's a command.'

'She really needs, you see, to be part of a normal family for a while.'

'And this is normal?' She rested her forehead on her hand, smiling. 'Yes, Ralph, of course we can have her, we must have her, poor little thing.'

'I heard what you were saying just now,' Ralph said to Julian. He put his hand on his son's head, lightly. 'What's sparked this off?'

'I told you. Well, I told Mum. This little girl in the West Country. I keep thinking about it.'

'But it was Devon. It's miles away.'

'Use your imagination,' Julian said. 'Crimes breed other crimes. People copy them.'

'Rebecca rides to school in a crowd. And back in a crowd. You ought to get behind them in a car, then you'd see.'

'Yes, but when she turns off the main road, she's on her own for half a mile, isn't she? It's not fair, it's not safe.' He moved his head irritably, pulling away from his father. 'So I've made up my mind. If either of you will drive her, odd days, that's OK. Otherwise I will. She's my sister. I'm not prepared to take a chance.'

Anna looked up. 'And will you be her escort for life, Julian? Thirteen-year-olds are at risk, but then so are eighteen-year-olds. So are forty-year-olds. You hear of battered grannies, don't you?'

'Anna,' Ralph said, 'there's no reason to be sarcastic. It's just, the trouble is, Julian, if everyone thought like you no one would ever let their children out of the house.'

'OK,' Julian said. 'So you think it's unreasonable? Look, let me tell you something. Ten years ago a boy vanished near Fakenham, he was eleven, he went up the road to see his friend and he never came back. The same year a girl was riding her bike along a track near Cromer – what do you think, is that close enough to home? April, she was called, and she was Rebecca's age exactly. She set off to go to her sister's house at Roughton. A man driving a tractor saw her, four hundred yards from her house, six minutes past two in the afternoon. At a quarter past two, three men who were mapping for the Ordnance Survey saw her bike in a field. There was no trace of her. She was six hundred yards from home. Nobody's seen her since.'

His face set, he waited for their protests to begin. But his father only said, barely audible, his eyes on the table: 'You've been studying these cases. Why is that?'

'I can't explain any more than I have.'

'I can't say you're wrong. It is a dangerous world, of course.'

'There'll be an argument every morning,' Anna said. 'I don't know what to say. I don't know what to say to you, Julian.'

'I'm going over to Sandra's now.' He glanced back from the doorway. Anna was gathering plates, noisily.

'Help me, please, Ralph.' Her tone was wounded, ragged. Ralph scraped his chair back. He began to clear the table slowly, with deliberation, his eyes on a plate, then a cup: anywhere, but not on Anna's face.

Two days later Ralph went back to see Mrs Glasse. His frame of mind was exhausted, distressed; he found it difficult to be in the same room with Anna.

Rebecca moaned and squalled; her social life was being ruined, she said. Julian explained patiently that he would drive her wherever she wanted to go; he would pick up her friends too, and see them all safe home. 'I don't want you on my back,' she snapped; Anna watched her without speaking, her face set and tense. Rain slashed against the windows; the air was thin, green, shivering towards summer. I must give the family a breathing space: that was the excuse Ralph made to himself.

And besides, he had been thinking of Amy Glasse. She was continually on his mind; she had established a hold over it, he felt, and he needed to see her again to break the hold, reduce her to an ordinary woman, naive, limited, down-at-heel. He remembered her in the doorway of the farmhouse, those white long-fingered hands flying up to drag back her hair. He thought of the dull gleam of her red-gold wedding ring, and of the curve of her mouth.

It was a finer day than on his last visit: a verdant dampness, a fresh breeze, the promise of a fine afternoon. The holiday caravans were beginning to take to the roads, and behind their flowered curtains, caught back coyly, you could catch glimpses of the owners and their miniaturized lives. Soon the coast road would be nose to tail with cars, each one with its freight of fractious children bawling, elbowing each other, complaining of hunger and boredom and heat.

Again, Mrs Glasse was waiting for him in the doorway. 'I heard the car,' she explained.

'Yes, it does have a distinctive note.'

He stood looking up at the sky. 'Good day to be alive.'

'Yes. When you consider the alternative.'

'I was passing,' he said. 'I thought, it's lunchtime. I wondered if I could take you out, you and Sandra.'

'Sandra's not here. She's gone cleaning out some holiday flats in Wells, getting them ready for the visitors starting.'

'Well then – just you?'

She dropped back from the doorway. 'Come in.' She glanced down at her jeans. 'I'd better have a word with my fairy godmother, hadn't I?'

'You don't need to dress up – I thought, just a pub lunch or something?'

'Give me five minutes.'

When she came back she was wearing a different pair of

jeans, faded but clean and pressed, and a white shirt open at the neck. She had let down her hair and brushed it out; it fell over her shoulders to the small of her back. The sunlight made it liquid. It was the colour of the cream sherry that his father's friends, with guilty abandon, had sipped each Christmas: 'Just half a glass for me, Mr Eldred.' He picked up a strand of it, ran it through his fingers; she stood passive, like a kindly animal. 'It reminds me of something,' he said.

'Something good?'

'Something sad.'

They drove along the coast. Past Brancaster the sea encroached on their view, its grey line fattening. They stopped at a small hotel he knew, whose windows looked out over the reedbeds and marshes. They were the first lunchers. A girl brought them a menu. 'Drink?' she asked.

'I'll have whisky,' Mrs Glasse decided. Two tumblers were fetched, set side by side by considerate fingers. A small wood fire burned in a stone hearth, sighing with its own life; its heart palely burning, but the logs at its margins charred from ash-grey to white, from wood to dust. Parrot tulips stood on a dresser; their stems drooped, and the vivid flowerheads seemed to swarm away from the vase, hurtling into the air.

'They have lobster today,' Ralph said. 'Would you like that?'

'Thank you, but I couldn't touch it,' Mrs Glasse said. 'I have an ingrained dislike of animals with shells. My husband was a crab fisherman, he worked out of Sheringham. Well, the life must have palled. I haven't seen him for sixteen years.'

'Sandra would have been – how old, two?'

She nodded. 'But he wasn't Sandra's father.' She looked up. 'Are you shocked?'

'Oh, God, Amy – it would take a lot more than that to shock me. I don't lead a sheltered life, you know.'

'When Sandra told me about you at first I thought you did. I

said to her, what does Julian's father do for a living? She said,
"He goes about doing good." I thought you were a clergyman.'

'I would have been, I suppose, if things had been a bit
different. It would have pleased my family. But I wasn't
concerned to please them, when I was a boy.'

'But you were a missionary, weren't you? It just shows how
ignorant I am – until Julian explained to me I thought all
missionaries were clergymen.'

'Oh no, you get doctors, teachers – just people who are
generally useful. We didn't go around converting people.'

'They'd been converted already, I suppose.'

'Yes, largely. But we weren't like missionaries in cartoons.
We didn't have a portable organ, and shout "Praise the Lord!"'

'I'm glad not to have to picture it.' Her smile faded. 'But
Julian told me, you know – about you being put in prison.'

Ralph nodded. 'It was nothing,' he said: writing off the
second worst thing that had ever happened to him.

'Julian's very proud of you.'

'Is he? We never talk about it.'

'No. He said you don't like to.'

'All that part of our lives, we prefer to forget it, Anna and
me. It's – we've closed the door on it.'

'Did they treat you very badly, when you were in prison?'

'No. I told you, it was nothing. If it had been very bad we
would have come home after we were released, but we didn't,
you see, we went north, we went up to Bechuanaland. We
stayed on.'

'It's a bit of a mystery. To Julian. He wonders why you
won't talk about it. He builds reasons, in his head.'

'Kit went through a phase, you know how children do – she
wanted to make us into heroes. She couldn't understand why I
didn't go on marches, join Anti-Apartheid, sit down in the road
in front of the South African Embassy.'

'And why don't you?'

'Because it's more complicated than they think, witless people parading around with their banners. I get sick of them using South Africa to make themselves feel good. Being so bloody moral about a country they've never seen, about the lives of people of whom they know nothing. Especially when there is so little morality in their own lives.'

'I didn't mean to upset you.'

Ralph shook his head. 'Sorry, I get – well, I lose my patience. I'm sure it is a mystery, to the children.'

'You've not been open with them, have you?'

'No.' He picked up his glass and drank off his whisky and asked for another.

They ate their ham and chicken and baked potatoes, and he turned the conversation, from past to the present, parents to children. He was curious about her life but he could not expect her to reveal anything, when he had been so obstinately unrevealing himself. They ordered some chocolate mousse and some coffee and another whisky, and then she said, 'Better get on with the day, I suppose.'

He drove her home. As he prepared to turn down the incline to the house a police car pushed its snout into the road. Its two occupants, carefully expressionless, turned to look at Mrs Glasse. One of them spoke to the other. Ralph waited for them to pull out. After a moment they did so, and drove away.

'It's a good thing I don't have a gun,' Amy said, 'or I'd probably have shot that pair by now. They're always grubbing about round here. They made sure they took a good look at you.'

'Is it because you had that trouble with your tax disc?'

She looked sideways at him. 'Ralph, you gave me the money. Thank you.'

'No, I – no, forget it, I wasn't trying to remind you or anything.'

'What it is, it's because we do the markets, me and Sandra. They think we're receiving. Stolen goods, I mean.'

'And are you?'

'Would I tell you if I were?'

'I would like to know.'

'For your son's sake,' Amy said, finishing his thought for him. 'Well, I can understand that. But you can put your mind at rest. Do you think I'm stupid? I know they watch me. Do you think I want to see Sandra dragged in front of a court?'

'No. I'm sorry.'

'I couldn't go to gaol. Not like you. Anna must be a very brave woman, it seems to me. I'd bash my head against the bars until they let me out or it killed me.'

'If they're harassing you, you must tell me. I can make a complaint.'

'And where would you be when the complaint came home to roost?' She smiled, to take the offence out of the words. 'Come in. I'll make us another cup of coffee.'

'Better not. I ought to get on.'

If she'd said, do come, do, it will only take five minutes, he would have agreed. He wanted to be persuaded. But she said, 'OK, I know you must be busy.' She opened the car door. 'I did like that, it was a treat for me, a change. Nobody ever takes me out.' She leaned back into the car, kissed his cheek. 'Thanks, Ralph.'

He said nothing. Drove away.

Three weeks passed, in which he sometimes returned. On each occasion, he made sure his son was somewhere else.

Ten o'clock, a blustery morning, Daniel Palmer at the back door: he did not like to turn up uninvited, but this morning he had prepared an excuse. 'Hello, Kit. So you're home for good.'

'I'm home for the summer,' she said.

'How did the finals go?'

She shrugged. He followed her into the kitchen. 'Me and Jule have just put the kettle on,' Kit said; not ungraciously, but so that Daniel would realize that no special effort was to be made on his behalf.

'How are you, Julian?' Julian nodded. Daniel began to take off his new acquisition, his riding mac; it was a complex coat, with many flaps and buckles, and pockets in unlikely places. 'Been over to Wood Dalling to look at that barn,' he said, 'you know the one? For a conversion. Get four beds out of it.'

'If you must,' Julian said.

Kit raised her eyebrows at him.

Julian said, 'They put in windows where no windows should be, and doors where no doors should be.'

'What do you expect people to do?' Kit said. 'Go in and out of the big doors, as if they were cart-horses? And live in the dark?'

'Of course, you would side with your boyfriend,' Julian said.

'He's not my boyfriend.'

'Look,' Daniel said easily, 'I take your point, but the alternative to conversion is to let the barn fall down.'

'At least that would be honest.'

'I don't understand it,' Daniel said, 'this reverence for the original. Because it's not, you see. I've looked into it, its history. The whole roof pitch was altered sometime in the 1880s. Probably that's when it began to fall down. For the last hundred years it's been patched up anyhow.'

Julian thought of this crumbling barn, of its roof: lichened, sway-backed, with its many mottled and graduated shades. 'It seems right,' he said, 'however it got that way. It's been that way as long as I've been seeing it.'

'I suppose we tend to exaggerate antiquity,' Kit said. 'Take, for instance, Daniel's coat.'

'Make sure you do it properly, then,' Julian said.

'Are you setting up as a vigilante, Julian? A barn warden?'

'Something like that.' He turned to Kit. 'I'm off to Sandra's now.'

'Where else?' Kit said.

Daniel said, when he'd gone, 'He doesn't like me much, your brother.'

'Oh, he likes you all right. He thinks you're a visually illiterate money-grubbing poseur, but he likes you. More coffee? Ginger nut?' Kit rattled the biscuit tin at him, aggressively. 'Come on, don't take it to heart. None of us likes any of us at the moment. Julian insists on taking Becky to school every day and fetching her back, because he's decided there are kidnappers about.'

'Kidnappers? What, the mafia or something?' Daniel smiled. 'After robbing Becky's pencil case, are they?'

'Nobody can talk sense into him. Becky's driven mad with it. She calls his car his "so-called car", and says she'd rather he walked her to school in those reins they put on toddlers. She keeps on at Mum and Dad to call him off but they won't. The more tantrums she throws, the more silent they go. We think, me and Robin, that they must have had a big row about something, but we can't work it out, because they never have a row, never.'

'All couples do. Surely.'

'That's what you read in magazines,' Kit said. 'But my parents are the exception to the rule. My father is so bloody saintly it would make you sick, but the trouble is it's real, it's all real. My mother has bad tempers but they're over in a minute. You can see her, you know, getting worked up – and then she has second thoughts, and then she's saintly too.'

'Well – how can you live up to it?' Daniel said.

'Precisely. That is what I ask myself.'

'Is that why you're so depressed?'

'Am I? I suppose I am.'

'You haven't made any plans yet? About going away?'

'No.' She put down her coffee mug. 'I'm getting like Julian,' she said. '*Mañana*. Couldn't give a toss.'

'It would suit me if you stayed around,' Daniel said. 'But you know that, Kit.'

He waited for some cross-patch response: I'm not here to suit you, am I? Instead she said, 'Suppose – well, I've sent off for forms – suppose I went to Africa?'

'Like your parents?'

'Yes, but I wouldn't go for a church group.'

'Too many strings attached?'

'Yes. And also I don't believe in anything.'

'I see. You pretend, do you?'

She pushed her hair back, restless and bothered. 'It doesn't arise. I'd not like to hurt people.'

'You don't feel you should stand up and be counted?'

'What – in the cause of atheism? Not much of a cause, is it? Better be a barn warden. It means more.'

'Yes, I see that. But you'd go as a volunteer, would you?'

'I could offer. They might not want me. I think they only want qualified people, engineers and well-diggers and so on. I could teach English, perhaps.'

'You've never mentioned this before.'

'No.' She looked at him balefully. 'I don't mention every thought in my head.'

'Have you talked to your parents?'

'I've talked to nobody, except you. Oh, and Robin, I did mention it to Robin, but he was practising his forward defensive in front of the wardrobe mirror, and I don't think he heard me.'

Daniel smiled, flicked a hand at his head. 'He's out of it, Robin.'

'Still, you can try your thoughts on him. Voice them. Feel

them on the air. See if they sound too unreasonable before you present them to the rest of the human race.'

'To me it doesn't seem unreasonable, though naturally I . . . from the purely selfish point of view . . . the thing is, why do you want to go?'

'Because I dream about it,' Kit said. 'Most nights, now. Sorry if that sounds stupid. But there's really no other reason I can give.'

He frowned. 'Good or bad dreams?'

'Neither. They have atmosphere. They don't have events. You know that kind?'

'Not really,' Daniel lied. 'I seldom remember my dreams.'

'Oh, bloody men!' Kit said. 'I think they're a lower form of life. They exist in an eternal present, like dogs and cats.'

'Look, I think I ought to get on.' Daniel moved to the edge of his chair and began to do something with one of his flaps and buckles.

'Of course,' Kit said. 'Don't pause for ostentatious consultation of your Cartier. Good God, a woman may be about to speak of her feelings! Gosh, it must be late! Better run!'

Daniel smiled: meekly, sheepishly. Bowed a little, at the kitchen door. 'May I call again, Miss Katherine?'

Kit shook her hair, made a low growling noise. Daniel clicked the door shut as he went. Kit sat back in her chair, her arms around herself. She found she had tears in her eyes. She did not understand this.

Kit had been at home for many days now. It had been the usual arrangement – Emma collected her at the station at Norwich. It was a way of easing herself back into the family, her tea with Emma. But Emma seemed preoccupied and in low spirits. 'What's the matter?' Kit asked. She misses Felix, she thought; she must be lonely.

When she walked into the Red House, the atmosphere hit her at once. 'Hit' was the wrong word; seeped into her, that was more like it. It was a cold fog of dismay; her first impression was that something was happening, slowly and stupidly, which the people concerned could not comprehend.

It sapped her strength, whatever it was; she was tired, desperately tired. She had left London healthy enough, only dogged by that usual feeling of anti-climax the end of exams brings. After this, you think, after my papers are over, I will do, and I will do . . . and then you don't. You are a shell, enclosing outworn effort. You expect a sense of freedom, and yet you feel trapped in the same old body, the same drab routines; you expect exhilaration, and you only feel a kind of habitual dullness, a let-down, a perverse longing for the days when you read and made notes and sat up all night.

But now, she had gone beyond this disappointed state. A new exhaustion made her shake at any effort, mental or physical. She discovered the curious, unsung, regressive pleasure of going to bed while it is still light. She moved her bed, so that it faced the window. She found herself two extra pillows, and composed herself against them. Eyes open, she watched the sky rush past, and the birds wheel and swoop.

Anna brought her food on trays: a boiled egg, an orange carefully peeled and divided, thin cinnamon biscuits warm from the oven. 'Don't,' Kit said. 'Don't bother. Really.' It was a strange comfort to her to go past the point of hunger; she had never been a thin girl, particularly, so she knew she wasn't going to waste away.

But it pleased her to push her situation to extremes. She fantasized that she was dying. She was old, very feeble, very weak. Her life was draining from her. But she had *lived*. She had no regrets, her will was made, and nothing was left undone. She was dying in the odour of sanctity. And indeed she was more and more tired, as if a lifetime's fatigue had banked up behind her eyes ... perhaps, she thought, I have glandular fever, some special disease suited to my time of life ...

She slept then, only to be roused by the sounds of the house below as it woke up for the evening: the shrilling of the telephone, the crunch and scrape as the family cars ground home, the slamming of doors and clattering of pans for dinner, the hard stony shower of coal going into the range; and Robin's feet stampeding upstairs to the next floor, Julian after him, sometimes Sandra Glasse's high clear voice from the kitchen: 'Shall I scrape the carrots, Anna?'

Home life. Sandra had been the first person she saw when her aunt dropped her at the gate. The girl was by the side of the house, with a laundry basket. As Kit stepped out of the car she saw Sandra stretch up to peg on the washing line the white nightdress – chaste, elaborately pin-tucked – which Daniel had given her as a present the previous Christmas. Sandra's cheeks were flushed from exertion and the wind. She looked very pretty. 'Your mother lent it,' she said. 'I stayed over. I hope you don't mind. I'll iron it and it will be just as nice as you left it. I'm a good ironer.'

Kit's brows had drawn together. 'Have it, if you want,' she said. 'Another bit of Daniel's ersatz tat.'

She'd hauled her bags into the house, and then sat in the kitchen for an hour, brushing off Sandra's attempts to look after her, to scramble some eggs, to drag luggage upstairs; not even making tea for herself, or going to the lavatory, or washing the metropolitan grime off her face. She seemed unable to do anything to bridge this gap between her former life and the life that was to come.

Then the days passed; she felt ill, a vague, nameless malaise. A white space seemed to grow around her, a vacancy. She felt that it was she who should be able to diagnose and treat the unease in the house, the sudden deficit of happiness, its draining away.

In time, as she knew he would, her father made occasion for a talk. He wanted a talk; she had nothing to say. But she had to decide soon whether she would go back to London to work for the Trust. Live in the hostel: get on democratically with all sections of society: not use expressions like 'ersatz tat'. Not make judgements on people.

'I don't want to push you,' her father said. 'We've given Julian leeway – I don't want you to think that we're discriminating against you. But you see, I have a list of applications from people who want a job, they want the experience before they do social-work courses –'

'Yes,' Kit said. 'I'm being selfish.' She combed her fingers through her long hair. He remembered Emma doing that, years ago, in Norwich. 'You see, Dad, up to a point it's easy. You go to school. You go to university. You don't have any thoughts, from day to day. You just do what's expected of you. Then somebody asks you to make a choice and you find yourself . . . slowly . . . grinding . . . to a halt. That's how I am.' She started to plait her hair now, loosely winding, looping. 'I'm a mechanism winding down.'

'A life crisis,' Ralph said.

'Yes, I should have known there'd be some jargon for it.'

'I'm sorry. But that's what it is.'

'Have you ever had one?'

'Oh, several, I'd say. The first when I was seventeen or so . . .'

'When you had the row with Granny and Grandad.'

'Yes . . . well, you know all about that. For months after it I felt as if I were walking around in fog. It was a kind of depression, suffocation – very disabling, because all the time I wasn't taking decisions for myself other people were taking them for me. That's how I ended up in teaching, for which, God knows, by temperament I am not suited.'

'Aren't you? I'd have thought you'd have been a good teacher.'

'No . . . Teachers need all sorts of large certainties.'

She looked at him in arrogant disbelief. 'And you don't have them?'

'Good God, do you think of me as a person who would have?'

'It's the impression you've given. I mean, you seem to believe in your work, for instance. And in, well, family life, and God, and the Labour Party by and large – the whole package, really.'

'The package.' He thought about it. 'I'd not deny that my own father believed in a package. But I dare hope his package seems more stupid than mine?'

She smiled. 'Yes, to be a creationist and to have family rows about Darwinism . . . yes, it does seem stupid. Victorian.'

'So it seemed to me. Even then. But we've always been behind the times in Norfolk.'

'You should have stood up to them,' she said.

'Not that easy, Kit. There were penalties they could impose. People bullied other people, in those days.'

It was his oblique way of telling her that she had nothing to fear; not from him, anyway. 'You must rest,' he said. 'Then when you have rested, think. And then you will know how you want to go on with your life.'

She didn't mention Africa, this idea she had. Better not; she was afraid of touching some well-spring of unhappiness. One night lately, walking the house in the small hours, she had found Robin alone in the cold back sitting room where the television skulked.

'Test Match highlights,' he explained. 'Just finished. I was off to bed. Want a coffee?'

She nodded; sat down on a chair, picked at its upholstery,

said, 'Do you know, in any other family this chair would be put out for the dustmen to take.'

'I'd never noticed it,' Robin said.

'You're just like your father. Don't you ever see how shabby we are? How poor?'

'We're not poor.' Robin was indignant. 'Mrs Glasse and Sandra, they're poor. Beks was laughing at Sandra because she said, "Do you like my skirt, I got it in a charity shop."'

'Beks is a brat. She knows nothing. When you're that age you think you're sensitive – well, I did, I remember. But you're about as sensitive as a bouncer in a nightclub.'

'What would you know about nightclubs?'

'As much as a child of two saints should know.' She looked up. 'What about that coffee?'

When Robin brought it back – modern coffee, grey and tepid and sugarless – she asked him, 'But do you know what I mean? Mum works so hard to keep the house going, with that furnace to be fed, and that demented twin-tub, and that antique Hoover. All Dad does is bring home hulking great hall-stands from Yarmouth, and then beam on us like Jehovah and think he's done his duty by us. Don't you ever wonder why we have to be good all the time, why we have to have such tender consciences, why we have to have these Visitors every summer?'

'We'll be getting some new Visitors soon,' Robin said. 'Morlocks, Yahoos, slags and tarts.'

'Why can't we be normal, and self-absorbed, and acquisitive?'

Robin's eyes were fixed on the blank television screen. 'Haynes 184,' he said thoughtfully. 'Hit out to all parts of the ground. Viv Richards 145. God help England. I don't know, Kit. If you want to be acquisitive, why don't you marry Daniel?'

'He hasn't asked me, and I don't want to get married. Anyway, it's not a career. What do you think this is, the era of W. G. Grace?'

'I wish it were.' Robin sighed. 'So . . . what are you going to do then? Slope about getting on everybody's nerves?'

'Do I do that?'

'No, but fuck it – there's Julian living out his rustic fantasies, and Becky with a mental age of seven, and nobody but me with any sense of purpose these days.'

'Oh, sure,' Kit said. 'Jack the Lad, aren't you? On with the hockey pads. On with the cricket pads. Why don't you take up schoolboy boxing and then you can get a padded helmet too? With that on you'd be totally impervious to life.'

They sat in silence, Robin slumped on the sofa, Kit curled into the chair, her legs drawn up into the skirt of her chain-store nightdress, which was too tight under the arms, and neither short nor long. 'All these questions, Robin. I've never had a sensible discussion with you before.'

'And you aren't now.'

'But you do have thoughts?'

'Yes.'

'Such as?'

'Such as why are we so miserable these days? Creeping around Julian and his obsessions.'

'You'd think Dad would laugh him out of it.'

'He doesn't seem disposed to laugh.' Robin turned his head back to the TV screen. 'West Indies 518.' He looked glum. 'Only rain can save us now. What was that you were saying the other day, about going to Africa?'

'Yes. I mean it.'

'Do you want to do what they did, is that it?'

'Perhaps.'

'Why, do you admire it?'

'How can I? I have no information, do I? I don't have a basis, to admire or not admire. Oh, I know about them going to prison – but even Emma won't say much, and so you wonder what really happened and whether they . . .'

'Were tortured,' Robin said.

She gazed at her brother. 'I've never been able to say it.'

'It is hard to say. I've practised.'

'But then again I ask myself, why were they there in the first place? It was only a kind of colonialism. I put that to Dad once, but he said, we did what seemed right at the time. And I know he is good, he is practical, he does help people now and I expect he helped them then. But what use would I be?'

'If you go off to some place in Africa,' Robin said, 'it won't be to do something for the country, it will be to do something for yourself.'

'Do you know what frustrates me?' she said. 'That I was born there, in Bechuanaland – Botswana, it is now – but I don't have any memories.'

When she thought of Africa she thought of a clean place, full of light and air, the sun so hot that everything was sterilized, scoured clean by its glare. When she saw the pitiful babies on the famine posters it damaged the image she held inside. She did not know what to think when she saw the pictures from South Africa: glum men in suit jackets and woollen hats, trudging by railway tracks, and smoke blowing into a granite sky.

'I do remember one thing,' she said. 'No, two things really. The first thing I remember is the feeling of heat.'

'Hardly strange,' Robin said.

'Yes, it seems obvious – but do you think that your body has memories that your mind doesn't have access to?' She thought, heat seemed knitted into me; it was as if the sun were moulded into my flesh. 'Even now, I'm surprised if I'm cold. It seems unnatural, it doesn't seem right.' She paused, looking up at him to see if he was following her. 'There is another thing, a little thing – we had a nurse, I asked Mum and she said her name was

Felicia. She used to carry me on her back. I remember my cheek pressed between her shoulder-blades, the feel of it, the heat of her skin through her dress. Isn't that funny? I must have been very small. And then I remember Julian – I must have been older then, and I must have been in my cot or somewhere – I remember seeing Julian on her back, being carried the same way, with his head turned sideways, and fat legs dangling down. And knowing exactly what he felt – your head skewed against her spine, the bone at your . . .' she hesitated, 'your temple, I suppose, though you didn't have such words, that feeling of each separate bone in her spine, and skin against hot skin, just this layer of cotton between.'

'That's odd,' Robin said.

'Yes.'

'I mean – because Julian wasn't born in Africa.'

'Surely,' Kit said. 'Because I saw him.'

'No. You can't have. Add it up. Count on your fingers. Julian was born after they came home.'

'Who then? Who do I remember?'

A silence. They turned it over in their minds. Kit thought, I do remember Felicia: her skin smelled of onions and harsh soap. Robin said, 'Perhaps you remember wrong. You were a baby yourself. Perhaps you think you remember, but you've made it up.'

She shook her head. 'No, I'm not wrong. Could it have been a neighbour's child? That must have been it. But what neighbours? I've asked them, you know, what was it like? They've always said, it was very remote, there was only us.'

'Insofar as they've said anything.' Robin yawned, threw out his arms; but she had his attention, he was listening to her now, and this was an act, which said, I wish to distract myself from the thought in my head. 'Don't you think it must have been Felicia's child?' he asked. 'Her own baby?'

'No,' she said. 'Not Felicia's child, a white child. It was Julian. Surely?'

Again, a silence. Then Robin got up and went to the kitchen and made more coffee for them, and brought it back, cool and comfortless as the first mug had been, put it into Kit's hands. Kit said, 'Do you remember Joan? That woman who cut her wrists in the kitchen?'

'No. When was that?'

'You'd be six, maybe seven.'

'There, you see,' Robin said cautiously. 'I ought to remember. Memory's odd, it doesn't work like it should. It's unreliable.'

'I think they kept it from you,' Kit said. 'You'd be out playing somewhere.'

'What happened?'

'I bandaged her up. Then she disappeared – took her things and went. I often wondered where she ended up.'

'Dad probably knows.'

'Yes.' Kit sighed. 'We labour in his shadow. At least, that's what I was telling Daniel. Or something of that sort.'

They sat on until it was three o'clock and they were stiff with cold, Kit sunk into her own thoughts, and Robin into his; then without a word they stirred, stretched, rose from their chairs. At the top of the stairs, Kit said, 'Robin, another area of mystery is this. The heart complaint. Mum's heart complaint that she's supposed to have. I used to wonder why, if she had heart trouble, she never seemed ill. But do you think it might have been the other kind of heart complaint? Like when people say "she has a broken heart"?'

Robin shivered, not from cold. 'Surely, not that bad?'

'No.' Kit's face was sombre. 'But of that order.'

Robin kissed his sister on the cheek. They parted without a word, crept into cold beds, slept at once.

★

Afternoon: on the beach at Brancaster, Ralph stretched out a hand to Amy Glasse, as if without his help she could not stand in the wind. 'I used to bring Billy here,' she called. 'Billy, my dog.' Stones and pebbles flew from under their feet.

It was high summer now. The sky was an inverted lapis bowl. Away from the sea, below the dunes and marram grass, a few families huddled behind wind-breaks. Family dogs trembled by them, constrained by habit of obedience, quivering with a passion for the stones and air and waves. 'Imagine when the seas were warm.' Ralph pulled her to his side. 'There were tropical reefs. But in those days, there were no people to enjoy the sun.'

On the beach at Cromer they have found the bones of bison, the antlers of wild deer, the skeletal remains of wild horses. There were elephants at East Runton, bears at Overstrand; there were wild boars living at West Runton. Think of this, he tells her, as you watch the caravans roaming over the hills, as you catch the reek of onions from the sea-front hot-dog stalls.

'I found something as a boy,' he said. She pressed close to his side to catch his words. 'A fossil. *Gryphaea*.'

'What's that?'

He traced the curve into her palm. He did not tell her what the balaclava man had called it; didn't want the devil to come between them.

'A shell. Very old?' Pale eyes looked into his. 'Will we find one today?'

'It wasn't here – it was near Whitby. I never found anything as good again.'

'It's luck,' she said.

She put her hand in his. He felt her loose wedding ring snag against his palm. His son had made a kite and flown it that weekend on the heath near Holt; the kite was called 'The

Sandra Glasse'. But Sandra was a child, and trifles amused her, and you cannot give a woman wood and canvas and the slight prospect of rising above the weather. Amy belonged to this coast; its jewels are jasper, moss agate, chalcedony. She should have jet from striped cliffs, to make a mourning ring for the life that was. And amber, next March; it is washed ashore, it waits for the lucky, it is tangled with the seaweed thrown up by the spring gales.

'Enough,' she said. She wrapped her arms about herself, a parody of the athlete in pain. 'I've walked far enough.' He held her upright, gathering her hair into one hand and holding it away from her face, sweeping it back into an unravelling topknot. He fitted her arm into his. They turned, and the wind was against them. It was a warm wind, and peppered their skin with sand. Through narrowed eyes they could see the sand swirling before them, like smoke. Sometimes they had to stop, and shield their faces. The sand blew into their mouths, between their teeth. It was like biting on diamonds.

He drove her home. They stopped at a store and bought peaches. They sat together in the kitchen. Amy Glasse took a sharp knife from the dresser and brought it to the table. She gave the knife to Ralph. He took one of the peaches and cut into it. It was a yellow-fleshed peach, its skin as rough as a cat's tongue, and its ripeness spread out from the stone like a bloody graze.

Later still they went upstairs and lay in the double bed, under a quilt – the second – that Sandra Glasse had made. Amy put her long white arms around him and locked his body into hers. It was as if there were a key and she had found it: a code, and she had broken it. Afterwards she cried for a moment, almost without a sound, her head turned into the pillow. He did not know what he felt: not guilt, not yet. Love, certainly; yes, he felt that. Her hair spread over her shoulders like a fan of feathers; her spine seemed dipped into her flesh, like a shallow channel scraped through wax.

That afternoon, Kit was at her aunt's house in Foulsham. They sat together in the kitchen, the half-door open to admit the sunshine, elbows propped on the table and a pot of tea cooling between them. 'So what are you asking me?' Emma said. 'About Daniel?'

'For your advice.'

'Kit! Come on now! You know I never give advice!'

'Make an exception.' Kit looked at the table top. Absently she scraped at it: delicately, with her fingernail. 'Emma, what is this disgusting thing? It looks like the remnant of a squashed baked bean.'

'Quite likely.' Emma grinned. 'You know they say every cloud has a silver lining, and the only good thing about losing Felix is that I no longer have to concoct a delicious little *dîner à deux* every time we fall out of bed. Baked beans are very nutritious, let me tell you.' The light faded in her face; Kit watched her eyes fade, sharp blue to grey. 'One thing about Felix, though, was how he was made happy with strong drink. Two big gins with a waft of vermouth and he'd be off back to Blakeney to dine *à deux* with Ginny, and some appetite still left. You know, Kit, they write all sorts of rubbish about people having affairs. Their tortured souls, and so on. But how is a man to eat two dinners? That's the question they should look into.'

Kit's hand lay on the table: large, white, capable. She wanted to place it over her aunt's, but taste restrained her. Emma fitted her knuckles into her eye-sockets, and ground them around, carefully. 'Sorry, sweetheart. All I can say about Daniel is this – ask yourself, how will you feel if he goes off and marries someone like Ginny?'

Kit paused. 'OK, I think.'

'Then that's not the real question, is it?'

She shook her head. 'It's home, you know. And me, me myself. I'm asking you for information, Emma.'

Emma looked up. 'For information or knowledge?'

'Are they different?'

Emma didn't reply.

SEVEN

At midnight the train stopped. Anna raised herself on one elbow, then scrambled from the top berth, reaching out with her bare toes for a foothold. She swung herself to the floor, pulled down her nightdress, and put her head out of the window. A man was walking by the side of the track. She could not see him, but she could hear the crunch of his boots. She could see the tip of his lighted cigarette, bobbing and dipping with each step.

Ralph said, 'What time is it?' He eased himself from the lower berth, put out his head in turn. A moonless night. Not a breath of wind. Useless to ask, why have we stopped, when will we go again? Best just to wait. They had crossed the border. They were in Bechuanaland, moving north through the night. Not moving now: becalmed. They had been late at Mafeking, late at Lobatsi; 'I'll give you a bed,' the conductor had told them. 'You can try sleeping two hours, three. You'll reach your station before dawn.' He brought two flat pillows and two railway blankets, and four sheets that were as white and crisp as paper.

'There must be a village.' Ralph had picked out the glow of a fire, far to their left. If there had been a wind, it might have brought voices to them. Closer at hand, a baby was crying, ignored, from some outlying hut: Anna heard the thin insistent wail.

She climbed back to her bed. She had wanted the top berth because she felt there was more air, with no other body stacked above hers. It was December now, midsummer; sunset brought some relief from the heat, but it was best if you kept moving. Ralph passed up their bottle of water. It was tepid and stale. She closed her eyes, and disposed her body carefully so that no part of it touched any other part. But the berth was narrow; she folded her hands across her ribs, till the heat and weight of them became unbearable.

The night settled about her like a black quilt. Lucy Moyo had packed a bag for her in Elim, and handed it to her at the prison gate; her cotton nightdress had been starched and smelled of the iron, but now it was a sodden rag. The sheets the guard had given them were rucked damply beneath her hips. Her hair stuck to her neck; she put her arms by her sides again, looked up at the roof of the train. It was a metal coffin-lid, a coffin in the air. Hands folded, she made a decorous corpse.

She imagined her voice, floating down to earth. 'I think I am pregnant, Ralph.'

What then? What if she said it? What would they do? Lurch from the train at some desert halt, and begin to navigate their passage back to civilization? How would they do it? The South Africans might not let them back over the border. They had been given the choice: take the plane home, or the train north.

She thought of herself decanted into the winter at East Dereham, her trunks bumping up the stairs of her parents' house for storage in the attics; she imagined rubbing together her blue hands, while she tried to explain their situation. *You've been in prison, Anna? A daughter of ours, in gaol?* And they would have no place in the world, no future mapped out for them; they would be like fish hauled out of the water, gasping in a strange element, writhing on the hooks of expectation unfulfilled.

No, she thought. My lips are sealed.

She dozed. The train began to move. It carried her onwards, into a world of dust.

★

The Security Branch had come for them before dawn: parking their vehicles outside the compound, and knocking politely, persistently, on the front door of the Mission House until Ralph admitted them. 'Will you get dressed, Mrs Eldred, please? And pack a bag?'

They began another search. They emptied the contents of the wastepaper baskets into bags to take away, and noted the titles of the books on the shelves. They went through the out-tray and read the addresses on the envelopes waiting for the mail. 'Who is Dr Eldred, please?'

'My sister,' Ralph said.

The letter was laid down again. It would go all the way to Norwich, greased by a policeman's fingertips.

When one of the men approached the filing cabinet, Ralph and Anna exchanged a glance. One impatient pull . . . they waited for the top drawer to sail from its runners and break the policeman's toes. But these officers were circumspect, almost reverential. 'We give a receipt for anything we take away,' one explained. The drawer remained anchored, innocuous. The policemen went about their work quietly, as if not to injure or alarm the incriminating evidence. The mission staff – Rosinah, Dearie, Clara the washerwoman, Jakob and his boy assistant – had been brought from their beds to stand in a line outside the back door. Their quarters were being searched. With the same creepy-fingered care? Ralph doubted that. 'Let me speak to them,' he said. 'Just to reassure them.'

'That won't be necessary, Mr Eldred,' said the officer in charge. 'My men will do all the reassuring that is needed.'

'Mrs Eldred?' They had brought a female officer; she touched Anna's arm. 'I must come with you while you get your things together.'

'Things?' Anna said.

'For a time away from home,' the young woman said.

'Where do you think you are taking me?'

'You have to . . .' The girl looked aside. She had a tender skin, a North European skin, and blushed easily; she was not hardened to her trade. 'To prison, Mrs Eldred.'

'To prison.' Anna digested it. The pause made her sound cool. 'To prison for how long? And why? On what charge?'

The female officer glanced at her superior. She didn't know the answer. An expression of impatience crossed the man's face. 'Just take her,' he said.

In the bedroom Anna pulled drawers open, aimless and distracted. She could not stop her hands from trembling. The female officer sat on the bed. 'You hurry up now,' she said, not unkindly. 'Bring your nightie. Bring soap and your toothbrush. And your sanitary protection if you think you might need it.'

When her bag was packed the woman stood up and took it from her. She ushered her back to the sitting room. The double doors to the front stoep stood wide open. The two officers had gone, and taken Ralph with them.

It was only then that Anna understood that she and Ralph would be separated. She broke away. The woman officer leapt after her, catching at her arm. A man standing outside on the steps slammed the wire door of the stoep back into her face. She heard a car drive away. She put her fingers against the netting of the stoep, as if to force them through.

There was an iron bedstead and a stained mattress; traces of vomit, menstrual blood. She had to force herself to sit down on it, but she thought it was a good sign that they had not given her sheets and blankets. Perhaps they would ask some questions, and release her before the day was out. Dawn came, her first dawn in prison. She listened to the morning sounds, still and attentive: her hands in her lap, her spine sagging slightly. They had taken away her watch, but she estimated that it was about seven o'clock when the door was unlocked. A wardress brought in a tin tray, and put it down on the metal locker by the bed. She went out again without speaking. The key turned in the lock. She heard the stout shoes squeak away.

Left alone again, she investigated the tray. There was a bowl of mealie-porridge. The spoon seemed encrusted with the remains of other, long-ago breakfasts. Quelling her revulsion she brought a spoonful of the food to her mouth, but before she tasted it she gagged, and a wash of nausea lapped over her. It ebbed, left her shivering and light-headed. She dropped the spoon into the porridge and put the bowl back on the tray.

There was a beaker of coffee; it was no longer hot, but she held it between her hands for comfort. She took a sip; it tasted of nothing. Comfort receded.

The third item on the tray was a cob of brown bread. She broke some off and put it into her mouth. It stuck there, un-negotiable, like a stone. Last night at Flower Street, she had complained it was too hot to eat. She had meant to get up early, boil an egg pre-dawn.

Some time later – perhaps an hour – the unspeaking wardress returned. She brought a water jug with a cover, and stood holding it while she waited for Anna to move the tray. In her other hand was a bucket. She put it down by the bed. 'Is that what I must use?' Anna said; looking up, without belligerence, wanting nothing but to learn the rules.

The wardress indicated the tray. 'You don't want that?' She picked it up without waiting for an answer.

'Can I have my bag?' Anna said. 'Can I have my watch?'

The door clicked shut. The key grated. She was alone again. Her hands returned to her lap. She examined the crack in the cell's wall. From the base it ran a meandering course, to a height of four feet. Then other cracks seemed to spring from it, creeping wide of their source. It was like the delta of some great river. Anna took her handkerchief from her pocket and dabbed its corner into the water jug. She laid the damp linen first against one eyelid, then against the other. Don't cry, don't cry, she said to herself. Let this be in place of tears.

At intervals, the spy-hole in the door would flick open. She would raise her face to it: let them see that I have nothing to hide, she thought, not even a covert expression. She wondered if they came to stare at her on the hour; she began to count. She thought, by the heat in the cell and what she could see of the sunlight, that it might be midday when the door opened again.

A different wardress. '*Kom.*'

'Where?'

'Fingerprints.'

They took her along the corridor to a room furnished only with a table and two chairs. A second wardress took her flinching hand, straightened her fingers and pressed them into the pad of black grease. On the waiting paper, she saw loops, whirls, smudges like ape-prints. It was hard to believe they belonged to her.

They let her wash her hands then, but she could not get the slime from under her fingernails.

When she came out into the corridor, an African woman in a prison dress was kneeling, scrubbing brush in hand, a scum of soapy water widening around her in a pool. She was singing a hymn, her voice strong, unwavering. When she saw Anna she stopped singing. She sat back on her haunches to watch her pass. Anna looked down into her face; then over her shoulder, to see the woman bend her back again. The soles of her bare feet were a greyish-white, hard as hooves. The hymn followed her as they swung open the cell door:

'How dearly God must love us,
And this poor world of ours,
To spread blue skies above us,
And deck the earth with flowers.'

When the light began to fail, they tossed two blankets into the cell, and brought in her bag. She had packed her hairbrush and a comb but she had no mirror. She could not think why it seemed so important to see her own face. She said to the wardress, 'You haven't got a mirror in your pocket, have you? That I could borrow just for a minute?'

'What do you think, that I'm a beauty queen?' the woman said. She laughed at her own joke. 'It's against the rules,' she said. 'You might hurt yourself, you see? Try and sleep now.'

Early in the afternoon there had been another tin tray, with a bowl of broth this time. She had stirred the ingredients without much hope, disturbing cabbage and root vegetables and what might be scraps of meat. Globules of fat lay on the surface, and when she brought the spoon to her mouth the morning's reaction repeated itself, and she thought she would vomit. The last meal of the day had been another beaker of weak coffee and a hunk of bread. She regretted now that she had let them take away the bread untasted. She was so hungry that her stomach seemed to be folding in on itself, curling into a hollowness above her navel. 'Can you help me?' she said to the wardress. 'I couldn't eat earlier, I was feeling sick. Can I have some bread?'

The woman hesitated. 'I'll see,' she said.

She went out, banging the door, rattling her keys. An electric light flicked on overhead, taking Anna by surprise. Anna waited, unmoving, under its glare.

She'll not come back, she thought. But after some time the woman did return, with bread on a plate and a smear of margarine.

'I can't let you have a knife,' she said. 'You'll have to do the best you can.'

Anna took the plate. 'I'm grateful.'

Then the woman took an apple out of her pocket. 'Don't tell anybody.' She put it down on the metal locker.

Anna said, 'Do you know what is going to happen to me? Can you tell me where my husband is?'

'Don't take advantage,' the wardress said.

'I want to write a letter. I have things to do. I work at a mission you see, in Elim, Flower Street, and there are things I have to take care of. I have to give instructions, or nothing will be done.'

'I dare say they got on all right before you came,' the woman said.

'I ought to be given access to a lawyer.'

'You must take that up with the colonel.'

'When can I see him?'

'In time.'

It was the least hopeful sentence she had heard that day. When the wardress had gone she broke open the cob of bread and tore out the middle, wiping it into the margarine and forcing it into her mouth. She held the apple for a long time before she ate it, running her fingers over its shape, admiring its innocence, its cleanness. She ate it in mouse-like nibbles, and wrapped the core carefully in her handkerchief, so that tomorrow morning she would at least be able to taste the juice on her tongue. She held off using the bucket for as long as she could, but in the end she had to squat over it, the metal rim cold against her thighs. She felt debased by the dribble of urine that would be her companion all night, and would be there for her when she woke in the morning.

They did not take her to see the colonel the next day, but the wardress who had given her the apple brought in a pillow, a pillow case and a pair of sheets. At least one more night then, Anna thought.

'Did you eat your breakfast this morning?' the woman asked.

'No, I couldn't.'

'You ought to try.'

'Will you get me another apple? I'd be so grateful.'

'Yes, I dare say you would.'

'Do you think they would let me have something to read?'

'That's for the colonel to decide. I couldn't decide that.'

'Would it be possible for someone to go to my house and get me a change of clothes?'

She knew the answer: the colonel will decide. But this is what prison life must be, she thought: a series of endless requests, some great, some small, repeated and repeated, until one day – in the face of all expectation – one of them, great or small, is granted. Can you arrange for me to send a message to my husband? Can I have a bowl of hot water, I cannot get the fingerprint ink from under my nails? Can I have a newspaper, can I have a mirror? Can you assure me that God loves me and that I am his child?

The next day, after the mealie-porridge but before the broth, another wardress came in. 'You want to comb your hair, Mrs Eldred? The colonel is waiting to see you in his office.'

She jumped up from her bed. 'Never mind my hair.'

The woman stood back to let her pass out of the cell. To her surprise, two more wardresses were stationed outside the door, and they trod a pace behind her along the corridor. They treat me as if I'm dangerous, she thought. Perhaps I am.

The colonel was a man of fifty, with pepper-and-salt hair shorn above his ears. The regulation belly strained at his uniform belt, but the rest of him was hard and fit looking. He motioned her to a chair. A ceiling fan creaked over her head; she lifted her face to it. Round and round it churned, the same stagnant air.

'I must apologize for not seeing you sooner, Mrs Eldred. There were some incidents in the men's prison that have been taking up my time.'

'What incidents?'

'Nothing that should bother you.'

'Is my husband in there, in the men's prison?'

'You'll have news of Mr Eldred very soon – in fact, you'll be seeing him soon, all we want is that you talk to us a little bit.' The colonel sat down opposite her. 'You've been to political meetings, Mrs Eldred?'

'No. Never.'

'You've been to protest meetings? About the bus boycott, for example?'

'Yes.'

'So, isn't that the same thing?'

'I didn't think so, at the time.'

'We have photographs of you at these meetings. We know you have held political meetings at your house.'

'Never.'

'You have had people from the ANC at your house. Agitators.'

'It's not illegal to have visitors.'

'So what were you doing, Mrs Eldred, if you weren't having a political meeting? Just having tea and cake, were you? Perhaps reading the Bible together?'

Anna didn't answer.

'We have the names of everyone who has visited you.'

'Yes. I know you have your spies everywhere.'

'It's necessary,' the colonel said. 'Believe me, Mrs Eldred. We have to keep control.'

Anna pushed her hair back, smoothing it with her hand. It

felt lank and greasy; the cell was an oven by mid-morning, and she was not given enough water to wash properly. 'Can I ask you a question, Colonel? Just one? All I want to know is if any of the mission staff are on your payroll. Has anyone been informing against us?'

'If you were innocent, Mrs Eldred, you wouldn't have to ask me that question.'

'Oh, I'm innocent, Colonel.' She felt colour rise in her face. She was not afraid. Since they had brought her to the prison she had felt every emotion, but not fear. 'I am perfectly innocent, and so is my husband, and I am quite sure that the mission society who sent us out here have been informed of what has happened, and that they will be making representations to your government on our behalf.'

'I'm sure that is so,' the colonel said, 'and I am sure their representations will be listened to with the greatest of respect.' He ran a hand over his bristly head. 'But you must understand, Mrs Eldred, that my government takes exception to people such as yourself coming out here to tell us how to run our country, coming out here in the guise of mission workers and then turning political and interfering in affairs that you don't understand.'

'I do understand,' Anna said. 'You can't expect that line to succeed with me. I've seen everything, with my own eyes.'

'With respect, Mrs Eldred, you have seen nothing and you know nothing. When you've been here twenty, thirty years, tell me then.' The colonel looked up at the ceiling, as if self-control reposed there. When he spoke again it was in a flat voice, with his former quite meaningless courtesy. 'Can I offer you a cigarette, Mrs Eldred?'

'No, thank you.'

'You don't mind if I smoke myself?'

'Feel free.'

'Do you have any complaints, Mrs Eldred?'

She looked at him wonderingly. 'If I began on my complaints . . .'

'About your treatment, I mean.'

'Could I be allowed some fresh air?'

'I'm afraid there is nowhere suitable for you to take exercise.'

'I can hear other women outside. I can hear their voices.' And laughter. Songs.

'That will be from the courtyard. The blacks go out there to do their washing.'

'I expect I shall need to do washing.'

'It will be done for you, Mrs Eldred.'

'I should like a change of clothes from home, and some books. Is that possible?'

'I will send someone to see about your clothes.'

Relief washed over her; she had not thought about it until now, but for the first time it occurred to her that they might put her into a prison dress. 'And the books?'

'You can have a Bible for now. Will that do?'

'Thank you.'

He inclined his head. 'You're a well-mannered woman, Mrs Eldred. I'd like to see you keep it that way.'

'I hope I can, Colonel.' Whatever you say, she thought, I shall have the last word. 'Could I have the light on for longer, so that I can read? I couldn't sleep last night. I never can sleep much before midnight.'

The colonel hesitated. 'For one hour, perhaps. Till nine o'clock.'

She had gained a piece of information. She had a sense of petty triumph.

'Can I have my watch back?'

'Yes, that is possible. I didn't know it had been taken away.'

'And this bucket, this so-called sanitary bucket – it's disgusting. When they brought me down the corridor I saw some buckets standing in a corner, a kind with lids. Can I have one of those?'

The colonel looked stricken. He flung himself from his chair, and chopped the wardress to pieces in blunt Afrikaans. The wardress shrugged, talked back; then became abject. 'Mrs Eldred,' he said, turning to her, 'we owe you an apology. I do not know how this can have happened. You've been given a native-type bucket. All coloured and white prisoners are automatically allocated buckets with lids, that is the rule. Your bucket will be changed immediately.'

Anna stared at him. The colonel had the last word after all.

That night, her legs began to ache; sleep was fitful, but before dawn she plunged into a dreamless stupor. When she woke she was shivering, and her scalp was sore: a vast headache lay behind it. She felt it was difficult to breathe, let alone eat. She had wrapped herself in her blanket, but it didn't help.

They came for her at nine.

'The colonel again?'

'Ag, Mrs Eldred, he must be in love with you.'

He was pacing his office; stopped pacing when he saw her. 'Good morning, Mrs Eldred, please sit down.' He looked at her closely. 'So it's a hunger strike?'

'No, it's not a hunger strike. I just prefer not to eat.'

'You don't like the food you are given?'

'How could anyone like it? It's not fit for pigs.'

'So if we were to supplement your diet, you would eat?'

Anna didn't answer. She didn't want to give him the satisfaction; didn't want to allow herself the temptation. Since that first time, there had been no apple. The skin on the back of her hands seemed greyish, as if the colour of her blood had altered.

'Come, Mrs Eldred,' the colonel said. 'What would you like? Some fruit?'

She didn't speak. The headache had gone now, but its ghost remained, and the back of her neck was stiff.

'I'd like to go home,' she said in a low voice. 'I'd like to see my husband. I'd like to know why you are keeping me here.'

'In good time,' the colonel said. 'You must understand that whatever you decide, we have to send in the prison rations. That's the rule.'

She nodded, head bowing painfully on the stem of her neck. He seemed to have made up his mind that she was on a hunger strike, even though she had denied it. Well, let him think so. Let it be so. The black woman who scrubbed the corridor, who would supplement her diet? She imagined her own body: saw herself fading, growing meeker, thinner, thinner . . . For the first time fear touched her. I am not made for this, she thought. Emma, now . . . Emma could bear it. Bear it? It would be an ornament to Emma. And yet, the fear was almost a relief to her. So I am human, she thought. If I had been in prison, and not afraid, how would I have lived the rest of my life? How could I be allowed the luxury of everyday, ordinary fears, if I were not afraid now? She said, 'Colonel, for pity's sake, tell me what you have done with my husband. All I want is to know that he is safe.'

'We should be able to arrange for you to see him.'

'When? Today?'

The colonel exhaled gustily. 'Have patience, Mrs Eldred.' She saw him struggle to quell his exasperation with her. 'Look, Mrs Eldred, I'm sorry if you think you've been treated badly, but the fact is that we are not used to prisoners like you. This situation is unprecedented for me. And for the staff, it is unprecedented for them. That is why we had the mistake about the buckets, and maybe – maybe we have committed other mistakes. No one wants to keep you here for any longer than necessary.'

'But why are you keeping me at all? You've hardly asked me any questions.'

'No one wants to harass you, Mrs Eldred. What you've done, you've done.'

'Are you asking my husband questions?'

The colonel shook his head. 'Not in the way you mean, Mrs Eldred. Why should you think such things? No one has hurt you, have they?'

'No.'

'Just so – no one has hurt your husband either.'

'I don't believe you.'

'What can I do then? Except to assure you that you are here as much for your own protection as anything else?'

'Protection from whom?'

The colonel looked weary. 'From yourself.'

'You haven't brought any charge. I don't think there's any charge you can bring. Why don't you let me go?'

'That is not possible, I'm afraid.'

'Why isn't it?'

Keep asking questions, questions: just once you might get an answer.

'I am waiting on a higher authority, Mrs Eldred.'

'Are you, Colonel? Waiting for your God to speak?'

'No.' He half-smiled. 'A telephone call from Pretoria will do for me.'

'And when do you expect that?'

He shifted in his chair, ground out his cigarette in the ashtray. 'I no longer *expect*, Mrs Eldred. I've learned patience. May I commend it to you?'

She looked up into his face. 'We might grow old together, Colonel, you and I.'

That evening, unprecedentedly, they brought her a bowl of hot water and a clean dry towel. Until now she had been allowed to wash only once a day. They brought some fruit and a bar of chocolate. 'Not all at once or you'll be ill,' the wardress said. Her face showed her disapproval of this special treatment.

Anna unwrapped the chocolate and inhaled its fragrance, its deep cheap sweetness: sugar and oil. She despised herself. The colonel saw through me, she thought, he knew I was weak. The emulsion slid over her tongue, into her bloodstream. Her heart raced. She sat back on her bed, drawing up her feet. I shall always hate myself, she thought, I shall never forgive myself for this, I shall suffer for it hereafter. She flicked her tongue around her teeth, like a cat cleaning its whiskers: collecting the last taste. Took her pulse, one thumb fitted into the fine skin of her wrist. Its speed alarmed her. But I am alive, she thought.

Then she thought, but perhaps this is only a trick. Perhaps tomorrow they will bring back the porridge and the encrusted spoon, and the native bucket. And I shall not be able to bear it.

Next day they told her that she had a visitor. 'A kaffir,' the wardress said, turning down the corners of her mouth. 'The colonel has given permission.'

Lucy Moyo was seated in the room where the fingerprints were taken. Her handbag rested on her vast knees. She wore one of her ensembles: a plum-coloured dress, a pink petal hat to tone with it. Her handkerchief was folded and secured under the band of her wristwatch. She smelled of lily of the valley.

Anna flew towards her, her arms outstretched. But Lucy Moyo took her by the shoulders and held her off, in a brutal grip. 'Brace up, brace up now, Mrs Eldred.' Her voice was fierce. 'Do not let these people see you cry.'

Tears flooded Anna's face. Letting go of her for a moment, Lucy twitched her handkerchief from under her watch-strap. She took Anna by one shoulder and began to dab and scrub at her face, just as if she were one of the nursery children who had taken a tumble into the dust. Anna's tears continued to flow, and Lucy to wipe them away, all the time talking to her in the same tone, brisk and firm and no-nonsense, as if she knew that sympathy and tenderness would break her spirit.

'Mrs Eldred, listen to me. Everything is in hand, everyone has been informed. We have telegraphed to London – Father Alfred has done it, that man is not such a fool as he sometimes appears. The High Commissioner is sending someone from Cape Town. Everyone is praying, Mrs Eldred. Do you hear me?'

'Yes, yes, I understand – Lucy, have you seen my husband? Is there any news?'

'Father Alfred has seen him. He is well and in good spirits and saying not to worry. At the mission we are all well, we are all in good spirits, the monthly accounts are done, the wages are paid, you must have no fear, everything is in good order.'

'Five minutes,' the wardress said. Her face was set into a grimace of distaste. She held out her arm, showing her watch, as if Lucy might not understand.

Lucy looked at her hard. 'Are you a Christian woman?' she asked. She let Anna go. She fell against the table, limp as a rag doll. Lucy opened her handbag. 'They said one book, no more. I have brought you this. I know this book is dear to you because you have brought it from your home in England, and as you once told me, given to you by your mother.' Lucy put into Anna's hand her copy of *The Sun-Drenched Veld*. She kissed Anna on both cheeks, shook off the wardress's arm, and sailed from the room, her bag over her wrist. She left her perfume behind her, lying heavy on the air.

Back in her cell Anna sat with the book on her knees. She heard her mother's voice: 'One of the *Windows on the World* series, Anna.' She flicked through the pages. 'There is no fruit more refreshing than the golden pulp of paw-paw . . . natives often reverence their ancestors . . . Today ostrich-keepers look back with wistful eyes at those days when fashion favoured their wares.' She closed the book, and stared at the purple-blue mountains on the cover. The hills of heaven, she thought. Another night gathered in the corners of the room.

Lucy's visit seemed to Anna to indicate that release might be at hand. Don't raise your hopes, she said to herself; but she hardly slept.

In the morning she made no attempt to eat. She had developed a disgust for the tepid water in its metal jug, and had to make an effort of will – tip her head back, hold her throat open – to pour it into herself. She was thirsty all the time, and once again shaky and cold, her nerves taut.

She wanted peace from her own thoughts, from their relentless, spinning nature. She realized that not once since she had been in prison had she prayed. It had not crossed her mind to do it. She looked into her heart, on this sixth morning of her imprisonment, and found a void where the faith should be.

At ten o'clock the cell door was unlocked and the colonel came in. 'How are you today, Mrs Eldred?'

'I want a bath,' she said instantly. 'I want news of my husband. I want you to let me go.'

The colonel held up his hand: peace, peace. 'Mrs Eldred, your husband is here. I have come to escort you to my office, where you will find both Mr Eldred and a representative of the High Commissioner. Will that do for you, for now?'

Ralph rose from his chair when he saw her, his face dismayed. 'Anna! Good God, what has happened?'

For a moment she thought she might faint. She saw that Ralph's face was puffy and bruised, his lip was cut. Her stomach tightened and churned; a spasm of physical and moral disgust shook her, and she felt suddenly raw, as if her skin had been peeled; I can't bear it, she thought. She loved him, he was her child, and it made her light-headed with rage to think that he had suffered a moment's pain, and from these swine . . . The room swam and shivered, the ceiling fan churned the air, the colonel put his hand under her elbow, and a stranger wedged into the corner of the office bobbed up from his chair and said, 'Cooper from Cape Town.'

She found herself sitting. She grasped Cooper's damp, extended hand, not seeming to realize what it was for. 'She's been a silly girl,' the colonel said. 'Refusing food.'

'And you let her?' Ralph said.

'What would you have preferred, Mr Eldred, did you want me to force-feed her?'

'It would be better if you sat down, Mr Eldred,' Cooper from Cape Town said, 'so that we can conduct our business in a seemly and civilized manner.'

'We're in the wrong country for that,' Ralph said.

But he did sit; took Anna's hand and touched her dry lips with his.

'May I begin?' Cooper said. Too young a man, ill at ease, sweating inside his businessman's suit. He cleared his throat. 'To be frank, this is turning into something of an embarrassment.'

Ralph leapt from his chair again. 'Embarrassment? We are taken away in the middle of the night and detained without charge, I am threatened with violence and my wife is starved, the mission staff are terrorized, and you call it an embarrassment?'

'Mr Eldred, you are not helping your case,' Cooper said. 'Of course you are aggrieved, but as Her Majesty's representative my duty is to extract you from the unfortunate situation in which you have placed yourself, and to do this without damage to the relations of our two governments.'

'What do you mean?' Anna swooped forward to the edge of her chair. 'What do you mean, the situation in which we have placed ourselves?'

'Please, Mrs Eldred,' the colonel said mildly. 'Listen to the man. He's come a long way to talk to you.'

'Thank you, Colonel,' Cooper said. 'Now, the situation roughly speaking is this; you can as I understand it be released almost immediately, but there are certain conditions with which you must comply.' Cooper took out his handkerchief and swabbed his forehead. His no-colour eyes travelled from side to side.

'I think it would be easier for you,' the colonel said, 'if I left you alone with your nationals.'

'Properly speaking,' Cooper said, 'that is what should occur.'

The colonel smiled slightly. 'You are not afraid of Mr Eldred?' Cooper didn't reply. 'If I hear the sound of your skull being pounded on the floor, Mr Cooper, I shall come right away to your relief. Depend upon it.'

The colonel went out, closing the door on them. There was a moment's silence. 'It will be easiest if you resign,' Cooper said.

'Never,' Ralph said. 'Let them throw me out, if that's what they want. I'm not going to do anything to make their lives easier.'

'We have been in constant touch with your employers in Clerkenwell. Your mission society.'

'So they know exactly what's happened?'

'They do, and they are less than delighted. With you, I mean, Mr Eldred. I am assured they have forsworn any political involvement, any whatever.'

'It's easy,' Anna said. 'From Clerkenwell.'

'There is a suggestion . . .' the man hesitated. 'That is, I am empowered to put to you a suggestion –'

'Yes?'

'That it would, as it were, save face —'

'For whom?'

'— for all concerned . . . if you were to leave voluntarily rather than be deported . . .'

'We've been through this,' Ralph said.

'. . . but without altogether quitting, as it were, your field of mission endeavour.'

'Do you speak English, Mr Cooper?' Anna asked.

The man swallowed. 'Do I understand that you have no wish to return to the United Kingdom as of this time?'

'No wish,' Ralph said. 'No intention.'

'Mrs Eldred?'

'I want to go home to Flower Street,' Anna said. 'That's what I want.'

'You know that is impossible.' A note of scolding entered the official's voice. 'The South African government will no longer have you on its territory. But I am directed to put to you, on behalf of your mission society, a proposal that you should take up a post, possibly a temporary one, in Bechuanaland, in the Bechuanaland Protectorate.'

'Clerkenwell is proposing this?'

'I am only the intermediary.'

'What do you mean by temporary?'

'They mean three months, probably,' Anna said. 'Until the fuss dies down and the newspapers have forgotten about us and they can sneak us back into England and then sack us.'

'Oh, I hardly think —' Cooper began.

'Shut up, Cooper,' Ralph said. 'No one is interested in what you think.'

A silence. They seemed to have reached an impasse. 'My husband means,' Anna said, leaning forward, 'that it would be better if you just gave us the facts. Where is this post they're offering?'

'It is at a place called Mosadinyana. Remote, I understand.'

'That makes sense,' Ralph said. 'Get us well out of the way.'

Anna put her hand on his arm. 'Let's listen to him.'

'As I understand it,' Cooper said, 'the couple who ran the mission station have been repatriated on medical grounds. It is not a place of any size. There is a small school, I am told.' He looked at Anna. 'There is a requirement for one teacher –'

'And what would I do?' Ralph said.

'Administer, Mr Eldred. You would administer.'

'I've never heard of this place,' Anna said.

'Your Society describe it to me as a toehold,' Cooper said. 'A toehold in the desert.' He seemed pleased with the phrase. 'There is the possibility that in the years to come it may grow into something larger.'

'A foothold,' Ralph said.

'Is it on the railway line?'

'Not exactly,' Cooper said.

'What is there besides the school?'

'There might be a trading store,' Cooper said, frowning. 'I could look into that.'

'If I went up there,' Ralph said, 'do you think there is any possibility that at a later date I might be able to return to Elim?'

Cooper favoured them with a thin smile. 'Not unless there is a change of government, Mr Eldred.'

'You are putting us in a very difficult position,' Anna said. 'You are asking us to go up-country, to a place we know nothing about –'

'I am required to encourage you to regard it as temporary,' Cooper said. 'I am required to assure you that should the posting prove unsuitable you can be replaced. Really, Mrs Eldred, there is nothing to fear. The South African government –' he hesitated – 'that is, it has been indicated to me – the South African government would have no objection to your travelling through their territory to take up this post. But should you refuse the opportunity, they have reserved two seats on a flight to London departing tomorrow.'

Ralph and Anna looked at each other. 'Tomorrow,' Anna said. 'That's ludicrous. We couldn't possibly leave at that sort of notice. We have to put everything in order at Flower Street, it will take a month at least to hand over to someone else.'

'I'm afraid you don't grasp the situation, Mrs Eldred. You can never return to Elim, as I imagined I had made adequately clear. After all, there is no one who could give a guarantee as to your conduct.'

'You make us sound like schoolchildren,' Ralph said.

'You are little more, Mr Eldred.' The man closed his eyes. 'Little more.'

Ralph took Anna's hand. 'We must decide.'

'Yes.'

'Anna, you look ill. Perhaps to go home would be best.'

'I'm not ill.'

'I can't risk you. I love you, Anna.' Cooper looked away in distress.

'If we go home now we will have failed.'

'Oh God,' Ralph said. 'I wish we had never seen this bloody country. I wish we'd gone to Dar.'

'No,' Anna said. 'I wouldn't have missed Elim, Ralph.' It will always be the place where we grew up, she thought. I shall never forget Flower Street. She looked up at Cooper. 'All right, we'll go.'

'I congratulate you on a brave decision.' Cooper put his hand out. Ralph ignored it.

In the small hours, the train set them down on an empty platform. Their two bags – their trunks would be packed for them, and sent on later – were placed at their feet; then the train gathered itself for the next haul, and steamed away up the line.

The darkness was total. They heard footsteps approach, shockingly loud. A railway employee called out a curt greeting in Afrikaans. Anna answered him. 'We are late. There's no one to meet us, where can we stay?'

The railway employee was a man of few words. 'He says there's only the waiting room. And it's here behind us. And he says that everyone knows the train is late. Everyone concerned.'

'They won't abandon us,' Ralph said. The footsteps retreated.

The waiting room had a cement floor and two wooden benches. It seemed to offer no more comfort than the platform, so they took up their station on the single bench outside. Though it was midsummer, the starlight was cold. They leaned together, their heads touching. 'We're nowhere now,' Anna whispered.

Ralph said, 'We are in the heart of Africa.'

'Yes. Nowhere.'

She lay down on the bench, her head on his knees, a cardigan draped over her. His head drooping, he dozed.

Ralph woke to a touch on his shoulder. A torch beam flashed into his face. As soon as he looked up the torch was switched off. An African voice, a man's, said, 'Mr Eldred, sir. Come, baas, come, madam.'

Hands reached for their bags. Anna stood up, stiff from sleep, disoriented, chilled. Beyond the station compound they saw the lights of a truck. 'This is yours?' Ralph asked.

'No, baas.' A silence. Ralph thought, how can I stop them calling me that? I never want to hear that word again. The man said, 'It is mine and my brother's truck, and his brother's also. Mrs Pilane, the clinic nurse, has asked me to lift you to the mission.'

'Thank you,' Ralph said. 'The train is very late. We thought no one was coming.'

'I was coming,' the man said calmly.

As they approached the truck, they saw by torchlight a half-dozen figures rise from the ground, draped in blankets. No one spoke. One by one, the half-dozen climbed into the back of the truck, handing up to each other parcels and sacks. 'Who are these?' Ralph said.

The man replied, 'They are people who are travelling.'

Ralph pushed Anna into the cab of the truck and scrambled in beside her. 'Do you work for the mission?' Ralph asked.

'No. There is only Salome. And there is Enock.'

The man did not enlarge on this. He kept his own name to himself, a private possession. They drove on in silence. The track was rough, and stones clattered away from their wheels; ruts jolted their spines. Small branches brushed the sides of the truck with a metallic click-click-click. Sometimes branches lashed across the windscreen; the glass protected them, but instinct made them duck. Anna leaned against Ralph, her head on his shoulder. The metal shell filled with their quiet, ragged breathing.

Almost imperceptibly, the sky began to lighten. The road became less bumpy. 'We are arriving,' the driver said. The village of Mosadinyana took shape about them: the cattle kraals of plaited thorns, the shaggy thatched roofs of the rondavels, the mud walls which enclosed each yard. The driver pulled up. There was a moment's stillness; Anna looked at the walls; a pattern was set into them, striped and zigzagged, ochre and dun. The travellers melted away, wrapping their blankets more tightly around them; the women balanced their parcels on their head.

The sun was almost up now, but the pale light could have been dawn or dusk. Anna looked up beyond the village. Her vision filled with low brown hills, an interminable range of hills: like the mountains of the moon. Around the borehole, donkeys bent their necks and plucked at the scrubby ground.

They jolted up to the Mission House a few minutes later. The driver dismounted to take down their bags. 'You may give me three shillings,' he said.

'Gladly,' Ralph said. 'I am very grateful to you.'

Money changed hands. The Mission House was a low building, its walls gleaming white in the half-light. There was a candle burning on a table on the front stoep. As they watched, it was extinguished. The sun burst over the hills, born fully armed: a great disc of searing gold.

They found inside the house the sticks of furniture left behind by their predecessors, Mr and Mrs Instow. There were dusty, sagging armchairs, the upholstery worn by long use to an indeterminate shiny grey. There were some scarred tables, a couple of bookcases, indecently empty: a solitary picture on the wall, of Highland cattle splashing through a stream. Their bedroom was furnished with a bulky dressing-table with a spotted mirror, and with wardrobes whose doors creaked and swung open when anyone entered the room, disclosing their dark interiors. Their ancient mothball reek lay on the air.

At once, their new routine began. There were new problems, new dilemmas, both human and ethical. There was no time for reflection, no period of induction. It was a month before a letter from Clerkenwell came. It was not an accusing letter, but it was huffy and vague. It wished them success in their new post. 'Cooper said it would be temporary,' Ralph said. 'But here they say nothing about moving us on. Still –' His eyes rested on his wife. Her pregnancy showed now, more evident because she was thin.

'Better the devil you know,' Anna said. 'The thought of packing my bags again – it's too much.' She came over to him and put her hand on his head, stroked his curly hair. 'It's all right. We'll get used to it.' And that would not be difficult, she thought. There were routine panics: a scorpion in the kitchen, a thorn under a nail. Otherwise, every day was the same.

Enock, a man with no family, dug the garden and raked it: he was aimless, erratic, prone to disappearances. Salome, in the kitchen, presided over their monotonous diet: stringy meat and mealie-pap, small bitter oranges from their own trees. After breakfast each day she washed the clothes and polished the red cement floors. Salome was shapeless, like most of the women who had passed their youth. She wore a lilac overall which she had been given by Mr and Mrs Instow: of whom she seldom spoke. She wore gaping bedroom slippers and a woollen hat; each morning by six o'clock she was in the kitchen, stoking up the cooking range, putting the kettle on the hob.

A second month passed, and already their memories were fading. Their time in Flower Street seemed to be an episode in other people's lives. What has happened to Koos, Anna sometimes wondered, did the police take him? What has happened to Dearie and Rosinah? Was there an informer? If so, who was it? Her mind recoiled from this topic. Even the better memories were soured. She could not think of Flower Street without knowing that they had been betrayed.

Each morning by eight Anna was in the little schoolroom. She had a floating and variable number of pupils: some tots who could barely grip a pencil, some big bold girls who sat knitting and gossiping at the back. Anna did not try to stop them; she had no doubt they needed whatever it was they were knitting. The boys would go off for weeks at a time, herding cattle. Months on the battered schoolroom benches; then months on the trail.

Her aim was not high: just that they should be able to count, add up, subtract, and not be cheated when they went to the store with small coins. They should be able to write their names and read from primers meant for children in English suburbs: children with lawns to play on, and pet dogs, and strawberry jam for tea. There were no lawns here, for each blade of vegetation had to pit itself against God to survive. There was mealie-porridge for tea, and for breakfast and dinner too. And if they saw a dog, her pupils threw stones at it.

They were incurious, apathetic children; impossible to know whether or not they took in what she was trying to teach them. They were, she guessed, often hungry: not with the sharp hunger that goads the mind and makes the hand shake, but with a chronic hunger, grumbling and unappeasable. There was no starvation at this date: not in the village, not in the country. There was, rather, a malnourishment which bred lethargy, which bred an unfitness for any effort beyond the minimum. The Afrikaner farmers had the best land; they sweated it and made it pay. The desert produced thorn bushes and scrub, and in spring, after rain had fallen, a sudden, shocking carpet of strange flowers.

By eleven each day, the sun high in the sky, her pupils slept, nodding and slumping at their benches. Her voice dried in her throat. By one o'clock school was over. The children pressed around her. 'Goodbye, and go well,' she would say, in her awkward, minimal Setswana.

'Stay well, madam,' they would say. And enclose her. Their hot bodies to hers. Hands patting. She felt herself shrink inside.

Why? Her own reaction disgusted her. The village men were meagre, spiritless and skinny. The women were great tubes of fat, blown out with carbohydrates. They carried vacant-faced infants, strapped tightly to their backs. Too many babies died. The clinic nurse Mrs Pilane could not cure measles. When the women spoke, they seemed to shout and sneer. Their voices were harsh, monotonous, somehow triumphal. God help me, Anna thought: but I don't like them, perhaps I fear them. These feelings were a violation of everything she expected from herself, of all her principles and habits of mind.

News came patchily from the outside world; the mail arrived twice a week, and a newspaper sometimes. Bechuanaland, the obscure protectorate, was making news itself. Seretse Khama had returned home, the young tribal leader with his white wife; ten years earlier, a bar student alone in London, he had chosen for himself this trim lady-like blonde, to the fury and dismay of his relatives and of the South African government. 'MARRIAGE THAT ROCKS AFRICA' the *Daily Mail* had bellowed. For a few weeks the world had turned its eyes on the protectorate. Frozen out, banned by the British from his own country, the chief had now returned, to the ululations of tribeswomen and the pop of flashbulbs. Ralph said, 'In the news again, think of it. James and Emma and our parents, reading about us in Norwich. It makes you feel we live in a real place, after all.'

They had been in the newspapers themselves, of course. Emma had sent the cuttings. Their story had run for a day or two, then been dropped as soon as they were let out of gaol. The papers had used photographs from their wedding; it seemed no one had been able to find any other pictures of them. In their strange ritual garments they stared into the lens, startled and shy; they looked like children, playing at weddings to pass a rainy day.

News came from Cape Town, too. The archbishop was dead. It was the government that had killed him in the end, Ralph believed. Another apartheid measure had been proposed, with a clause giving the government the power to exclude Africans from churches in white areas; and this brought the old man to his sticking point.

The archbishop drafted a letter: if this becomes law, his letter said, the church and its clergy and its people will be unable to obey it.

The battle-lines were drawn at last. Late at night, the archbishop's secretary came into his study, bringing the final version of the letter for his signature. The old man lay on the carpet. He had fallen by his desk, and his heart had stopped.

Receiving this news, Ralph felt more alone.

Within a week or two of their arrival it became clear that the mission did not provide a job for two people. And Mosadinyana would never grow, as Cooper had purported. The mission was a fossil, a relic; its time was past, and the focus of effort and activity had moved elsewhere. Ralph imagined their lives and careers filed away, in Clerkenwell's dustiest, lowest drawer.

He was angry. 'It is so stupid. They are treating us as if we have committed some horrible crime, as if we are disgraced. But the truth is that there are people in England who would not only sympathize with us but applaud us.'

'We're not heroes,' Anna said. 'We didn't do anything really. We just got in the way. We were an inconvenience.'

'At least that's something to be.'

Clerkenwell sent their small salary every month. There was nothing to spend it on.

'There's one thing to be grateful for,' Ralph said. 'When the baby's born, I can take over the teaching and you need do nothing. We can get a nurse from the village, Salome will find someone for us. Then if we have broken nights, you can get some rest during the day.'

The thought of the baby made him proud, worried, indefinably sad. That it would be born here, in Mosadinyana, in the heart of Africa. Anna's body was swollen, but her face was gaunt, and her arms were stick-thin. In those few days in prison the flesh had simply peeled away from her frame; her bones seemed larger now, and her wide-open eyes made her look sad and frail.

When they stepped out of their front door, in the morning or at evening, the go-away birds wheeled overhead, mocking and barracking, swooping and squawking their single, unvaried message; the only words which nature had given them. They were insistent companions, like someone you pick up with on a journey: someone who claims better knowledge of the terrain, who tries to persuade you to vary your planned route.

Ralph drove Anna to the Lutheran mission hospital, over roads that shook the bones and viscera. The doctor was an elderly Dutchman, worn and faded by the sun; he received her with kindly concern. All would be well, he assured her, passing his hand over the mound of her belly. There was no need for her to think of travelling down the railway line when her time came; he had delivered a hundred babies, and he had plenty of experience if anything, God forbid, should go wrong. He saw, he said, that she was a sensible young woman, stronger than she looked; and after the event, all she would need would be the most simple precautions of hygiene, the common-sense measures any mother would take. 'Think what your baby will have,' he said. 'God's blessed sun, almost every day of the year. Quiet nights under the stars and moon.'

Anna looked up at his outbreak of lyricism, half-raising herself on the examination couch. Had he been drinking? He laid a hand on her forehead, easing her back. 'Mrs Eldred,' he said, 'I have heard of your troubles in the Republic. You and your husband, you are young people who deserve the happiness that will come to you. It will be a pleasure and an honour to me to put your first child safe in your arms.'

Each night, by the light of lamps and candles, they sat over their Setswana grammars. Outside, the darkness rustled and croaked; inside, the only sound was a moth's wingbeat. And yet they were not alone; there was a settlement out there, lightless, invisible, ragged night-breathing its only sound. In the first week, a parade of blanket-wrapped men and women had come to the door, asking for work. Anna was bewildered. She did not know how to turn them away, and it seemed there was no end to them. Ralph and Anna had made little progress in the language; when they tried to speak, people grinned at them. 'You may take on anyone you need to help you,' Anna told Salome. 'But not people we don't need, not people who will just sit around doing nothing. Because it is not fair to choose some and not the others, to pay some and not the others. But Salome, listen, anyone who is hungry, you never, never turn them away.'

Did she turn them away? Anna was afraid that she did – on a whim, or according to the dictates of her own judgement. They had to acknowledge that her judgement might be sounder than theirs. She was their mediatrix, their mainstay. Her English was hybrid, sometimes sliding into Afrikaans. Once she did speak memorably, her hands folded together, her eyes resting unseeingly on something through the window, in the dusty yard: spoke with rhythm and fluency, with perfect confidence that she would be understood. 'In the days of our grandmothers, madam, there were many women to divide the task of carrying the water and grinding the millet and sweeping the house. Now there is only one woman. She must work all day in the heat of the sun until she drops.'

'An exaggeration,' Anna said, 'but, you see, she was speaking of the advantages of polygamy.'

'What will you think of next?' Ralph said.

'I think we have denatured these people,' Anna said. 'Everything old is condemned, everything of their own. Everything new and imported is held up to them as better.'

'Soap and civilization,' Ralph said. 'That was the idea. Oh, and God.'

'Oh, and God,' Anna said. 'I begin to wonder what Christianity has to offer to women. Besides a series of insults, that is.'

There were quarters on the mission compound for three servants. Two of these whitewashed rooms were already claimed, one by Salome, one by the gardener Enock. But the people Anna could not employ did not go away. The other hut was soon taken by a large family of mother and children whose origin no one knew; other families camped out in the vicinity, built themselves lean-tos even frailer than the shacks on the outskirts of Elim. They were hanging around, it seemed, in expectation; you could not say in hope, for nothing so lively as hope could ever be discerned in the expressions of these visitors of theirs. That was what Ralph called them: our visitors. Their faces showed, rather, an awesome patience, a faith; a faith that one day the beatitudes would be fulfilled, and the meek and the poor in spirit would come into their kingdom. Or into a job, at least. One day Anna would wake up, and find her ambitions quite different; she would need as many servants as Blenheim, or Buckingham Palace on a garden-party day.

Anna wrote home, in cautious terms, about her condition. Her mother's reply came, two months on: 'Last week you were in the minds of our whole congregation. Everyone keeps you in their prayers and thoughts. The people around you, though primitive, are no doubt very kind.'

The cooler weather brought relief. She breathed more easily then, above the arch of her ribs. Only one thing had sickened her, and its season had been brief: the guava tree, riotously fertile, diffusing through the air the scent of eau-de-cologne slapped on to decaying flesh.

Anna said, 'Ralph, in my grandmother's generation . . .' Her voice tailed off. She hadn't meant to sound so biblical; she must

215

be catching it from Salome. She began again. 'In our family, some years back . . . there were twins.' She waited. He looked up. She glanced away from the shock on his face. 'The doctor can't be sure, of course, but he says to keep the possibility in mind. He thinks it will be all right.'

'Thinking's not enough,' Ralph said. He put his head in his hands. 'Oh God, if we were in Elim now . . . If you could get to Jo'burg or Pretoria there would be no problems, every facility would be there for us. We should go south, Anna. Surely they wouldn't refuse us? It's your first child, you've not been well . . . Surely they'd make a gesture, a humanitarian gesture?'

'No, they wouldn't,' Anna said. 'If we turned up in Jo'burg or Pretoria they'd put us back in gaol.'

'Me, perhaps – not you, surely?'

'Why not? They put me in gaol before.' Anna shook her head. 'Forget it, Ralph. I don't want to set foot on that soil. I don't want that kind of compassion.'

Three weeks before the birth she did go south, but only to Lobatsi, a small town on the railway line. She had booked herself in at the Athlone Hospital; if something went wrong, she and the babies had a better chance here than they would have up-country. She believed in the twins, they were no longer a subject for conjecture; she imagined she could feel the two new hearts beating below her own. While she waited to be proved correct, she passed her days sitting at her window in the Lobatsi Hotel, watching the populace pushing into the Indian trading stores, wanting buckets and sacks of sugar and sewing cotton and beer. Men who had called at the butchers dragged up the dusty road, carrying sticky parcels from which grey intestines flopped. Women sat on the hotel steps and sold knitted hats; when evening came their daughters sat there and sold their bodies, elbowing each other and shrieking while they waited for trade, passing from hand to hand a cigarette, a plastic comb, a mirror encrusted with glass jewels.

The weather was cool, blue and still, the mornings sharp with frost. There were few white faces in the street. She listened every day for the call of the train, from the track beyond the eucalyptus trees; she saw the procession that trailed to the station, women hauling sacks of onions and laden with boxes and bags, and boys with oranges running to sell them to the travellers. When the train drew in, the passengers mobbed it, swinging from its sides and swaying from it, as if it were a steer that must be wrestled to earth. Sometimes it seemed to her that the whole country was on the move; yet she became stiller, heavier, more acquiescent to the strangeness and the pain that lay ahead.

In the depth of winter, and before dawn, her babies were born. Her own Dutch doctor had intended to be there with her, but he had been delayed, impeded somehow – broken axle, perhaps, or sudden minor epidemic – and she felt some protection had been withdrawn. She heard strange voices in the corridors, and the moans of another woman in labour; and this sound seemed to come to her now from her left, now from her right, now from the hospital gardens beyond her window and once perhaps from her own throat. When her daughter was born she held out her arms for the child, but when her son was born she had become an object, leaden with fatigue, her arms no longer hers to command. She heard him cry, and turned her head with difficulty, very slowly, to see him in a nurse's hands, his body transfixed by a shaft of early light. Ralph stood by her bed, and held her hand as if it were a stone. They had already chosen a girl's name, Katherine. 'The boy after your father,' Anna whispered. 'Because it will heal . . . because it will heal . . .'

Because it will heal all wounds. She left him suddenly, hurtling into sleep like an unstrung climber from a cliff face.

The doctor took Ralph by the arm and led him from the room. His heart felt small, very heavy, a pebble in his chest, contracted with shock and fear at the sight of the bloody streaked beings his wife's body had produced. Later that day, after he had slept for a couple of hours, he went to see the babies again. He saw that there was no reason to be afraid. The twins were small, but healthy. They had curls of black hair, and eyes of black-grey: hard but melting, like the eyes of puppies.

The months that followed were months of a lulling calm, shot through by the small emergencies of infant illness and ill-temper, by the vagaries of life in the wasteland; and these months, when Ralph and Anna looked back on their time in the protectorate, would seem like years. They were years of air so dry it seemed to burn the lungs; years of thorn and scrub, of a fine dust that covers every surface. The country's spectrum was narrow: rose-red, through brick, through lion-colour, to stone. In summer, under the sun's unclosing eye, the landscape seemed flattened, two-dimensional, as if it were always noon. Mosquitoes whined in the darkness, plunging unseen at swollen ankle veins, and ticks bit and clung and swelled fat with blood, engorged like blue-grey peas. About the place early one morning, inhaling a hot dawn mist, Ralph saw baboons in the garden, stripping the fig tree, handling the wormy fruit with murmurs of apprecia-tion. Still as death, he watched them from the back stoep; it was as if he were watching someone else's dream, or the re-enact-ment of a myth. It puzzled him; he could not say what myth it was.

In summer the sky was violet, sullen; when storms came, the downpour whipped garden snakes from their heat-trances. Green mamba, boomslang, spitting cobra: after the rains, the ground seethed like a living carpet. Six legs, eight legs, no legs: everything moved.

Salome found a woman called Felicia, to be the children's nanny. Felicia must have her own home; the mother and children who had taken over the third servants' hut moved out, and Felicia moved in. She would have a bed in the twins' room, but she must have privacy, a place for her possessions; and I, Anna thought, wish sometimes to be alone in my house. The displaced family built themselves a lean-to. They seemed to accept the situation. Still they waited, week after week, to be called to Anna's service.

Felicia was a tall erect woman with a smooth face and thin, almost Hamitic features. She was twenty-three years old, she said, was a mission girl herself, and had two children, who stayed with their grandmother in Kanye, in another part of the country. It was Matthew she liked best to carry on her back, but – as if in compensation – she placed on Katherine's wrist a bracelet of tiny blue beads. When the babies were tiny, she wafted the cattle-flies from their faces, and soothed one while Anna fed the other; when they grew she taught them to sit up and clap their hands and sing a song. She was scrupulous and clean, diligent and polite, but she spoke when she was spoken to, and then just barely. Her thoughts, she reserved to herself.

In winter there were porcupine quills on the paths, and the nights were as sharp as the blade of a knife. The waterless months brought wild animals to the edge of settlements, and once again the baboons crept down at dawn, shadowing the compound families, waiting to seize a porridge-pot left unwatched. Once, early in the morning and from a distance, Anna saw a leopard, an area of clouded darkness covering his chest. The darkness was fresh blood, she supposed; she imagined how the sun would dry it, and the spotted fur stiffen into points.

Anna spoke now in an arbitrary blend of English, Setswana, Afrikaans – any language which served. She loved her children with an intemperate blend of fear and desire; fear of insects and snakes, desire for their essence, for their shackled twin souls to be made free. She placed the brother beside the sister, watched them creep together, entwine limbs; she wished for them to grow and speak, to separate, to announce themselves as persons. An only child, she envied them and found them strange. When she prayed, which was almost never, it was only for Ralph: God preserve his innocence, and protect him from the consequences of it. She felt it was a dangerous thing, his bewilderment in the face of human wickedness; she felt that it left them exposed. She had been told as a child that you could not strike bargains with God, but she had never understood why not; surely God, if he had once been Man, would retain a human desire for advantage? Where simple strength is required, she bargained, let Ralph provide it; but where there are complexities, give them to me. Alone in her schoolroom and her house, below the tropic of Capricorn, she saw her path in life tangled, choked, thorny, like one of the cut-lines that ran through the bush and melted away into the desert.

Later, of course, she wondered at herself; how could she not have seen the road ahead? Even in the early days – before the wisdom conferred by the event – any trouble, any possible trouble, seemed to settle around the sullen, fugitive form of Enock, the man who was nominally in charge of the garden.

Enock, like them, was a refugee from the south. So they understood; asked where he came from, he nodded his head indifferently towards the border, and said, 'Over that side.' Ralph tried to talk to him: look, whatever you've done there, whatever happened, it doesn't matter, that was there and this is a different country. Ralph suspected that Enock had been in prison, for some petty criminality rather than for some offence against the race laws; though they make sure you can't distinguish, he said, between a criminal act and an act of protest, and God knows, he said, if a man like Enock were to cheat or steal, should we make a judgement? Who can say what I would do, in his shoes, in the shoes of a black man in South Africa today?

But then Ralph would come back, from another dragging, weary quarter hour with Enock, and say, well, we never get anywhere. I'm just a white man to him.

Anna nodded. 'And isn't he just a black man to you?'

'I try not to think like that.'

'How can you not? You have to make him into something. A victim. Or a hero. One or the other.'

'Yes. Perhaps you're right.'

'But it's not like that. He's just an individual.' She considered. 'And I think as an individual he's a waste of time.'

Ralph shook his head; he wouldn't have it. 'We can't know what his life has been. How can you know? You are talking to him and he walks away.'

'And yet he understands you. He understands what you say.'

'Oh yes, that's not his problem. He reminds me of Clara sometimes – do you remember how she would freeze you out? I used to wonder if something so terrible had happened to her that she just couldn't bring herself to speak about it – she seemed numb. And Enock's like that. Oh well,' Ralph said. 'If I think I can help him, I must be patient and persist.'

Enock was about thirty years old, a handsome and composed man, with the same thin features as Felicia, an even, impassive face. He wore tattered khaki shorts and the cast-off jacket of a European-style suit. Ralph wondered about the original owner – who would have bought such a thing? The jacket was tan, and it was tight under his arms, and shiny from wear. Sometimes, when he went about his tasks, he would take it off and hang it on the branch of a tree. One day, the puppy took it down and worried it; Anna dragged it from his jaws in a state not too far from the original, but she felt that this was one more grievance for the gardener to chalk up on his soul.

This dog of theirs; *your* dog, she said to Ralph, when it ate books and dragged blankets outside into the dust. Ralph had brought the puppy home from a trip to Palapye, a settlement on the railway line; he had climbed out of the truck dazzled by the sun, thirsty, weary, coated in dust, and put into her hands a baffling fur bundle, an indecipherable animal like a tiny bear, with boot-button eyes and a dense, lemon-coloured coat. 'Whatever is it?' she had said, alarmed, and Ralph had said, reassuringly, just a dog. The McPhersons gave him to me; they said, this is what you need, a dog about the place.

'What a strange thought for them to have,' Anna said. 'Don't they think two babies are enough?'

'The babies don't bark,' Ralph said. 'That's what he's for, a watchdog, not a pet.'

'I suppose he can be both.'

'When I was a child I was never allowed to have a dog.'

'Nor me,' Anna said. 'I had a goldfish once, but it died. Just as well. I always thought that my papa would usher some customers through from the shop, and tell them he could get two fillets out of it.'

'So,' Ralph said. 'So, you see, the twins, they'll have a dog, and we didn't have.'

'What is it, anyway, what breed?'

'The McPhersons claim its mother is a pure-bred Alsatian, and they did – Anna, give me another glass of water – they did show her to me, and she looked authentic – but then they say his father is a yellow labrador, also of good pedigree. I can't believe that. I think his mum climbed out of the compound and took potluck.'

That was what they called the dog: Potluck. Potluck, as

young things do, passed through a phase of great beauty. His button eyes grew large and lustrous, and his lemon fur turned to the colour of butterscotch. His temperament was mild, and when the twins were fractious and unrewarding Anna would pick him up and kiss the velvet, benign space between his ears. Even Salome and Felicia, who did not see the point of dogs, would sometimes take time to speak to him, and caress him in a gingerly way.

At the age of eight months Potluck grew ugly. His head was huge, his muzzle blunt, his ears pointed different ways; he developed brusque, selective barking, like an old colonel suddenly moved to write to the papers. Almost grown now, he shambled around the mission compound, winning friends and giving offence. 'It is a horrible, English trait,' Ralph said, 'to despise people who are afraid of dogs.'

'Enock's not afraid,' Anna said. 'He just affects to be.'

'I like to think well of Enock,' Ralph said, 'and in fact I make it my policy, but it has to be said that he's becoming a bloody nuisance.'

It was Salome who had begun the complaints. 'He has stolen from me,' she said. 'My straw hat.'

'Do you think so?' Anna said. 'What would Enock do with your straw hat?'

'Sell it,' Salome said. Anna almost asked, sarcastically, and what do you think it would be worth? She checked herself. These people negotiate in pennies, rather than shillings, so perhaps it's true, perhaps Enock has sold her hat.

She said to Ralph, 'Salome is always complaining about Enock, and now she says he's raiding her wardrobe.'

'Then I must have a word with him. We can't have Salome upset. Do you think she's telling the truth?

Anna frowned. 'Hard to know. She has a preoccupation with clothes at the moment. She thinks she should be given dresses, cast-offs. But I have a difficulty here, because I can't manufacture cast-offs, no one can. I could make her a dress, that would be no problem, but it wouldn't be the same, it's *my* clothes she wants.'

'Nothing of yours would fit her,' Ralph said. 'Even if you wore your clothes out, which you don't.'

'I gave a skirt to Felicia – that one I made in Elim, out of the roll Mr Ahmed gave me. That grey-green paisley skirt, do you remember?'

'Yes,' Ralph said, lying.

'I was pleased with that skirt, it was the nicest thing I'd ever made for myself. Now I'm an inch too big for it, so I thought I'd give it to Felicia, she's so smart and neat.' Anna smiled. 'She doesn't like it much. She thinks it's drab. Still, I like to see her wearing it. It hangs well.'

'So Salome is jealous?'

'More than that. Jealous and aggrieved.'

'Perhaps Mrs Instow used to give her clothes. The best Paris labels.'

They laughed. In the back of a drawer, they had found a photograph of the Instows, the kind of fading snap that people describe as 'taken with my old Box Brownie'. A little, huddled, sexless couple they were, false teeth bared in haunted smiles. Where were they now? The mission society's pension arrangements were not generous. A bed-sitting room and kitchenette, Ralph thought, somewhere like Leamington Spa. God save us. Sometimes now his thoughts turned to what he would do when they left Mosadinyana. His father would be seventy in three years' time, and his mother's letters hinted that the work of the Trust was getting too much for him. The Trust had grown a good deal, from its original local foundation; and Uncle James, still toiling among the London derelicts, was approaching what would normally be thought of as retirement age. I should be putting my mind to taking over from them, Ralph thought, going home and finding us a house and beginning the next phase in life. I can face them now, he thought, my mother and father, because I have done and seen things they have never dreamed of. And I have children of my own, now.

Anna seemed disinclined to speculate about the future. She had too many petty day-to-day concerns. A kind of kitchen war had broken out. Someone had taken a whole sack of sugar, just brought in from the store; it must be Salome, Anna thought, because sugar was one of her perquisites, she took it for granted that no one would prevent her from carrying it away by the pound, under her apron. 'But a whole sack, Salome,' Anna said, turning on her disappointed eyes. 'So that I go to the pantry and there is none – none – not a spoonful for Felicia's tea.'

Salome said nothing, but a peevish expression crossed her face. Later that day she began her ritual complaints about Enock. 'He is not doing his work properly. Always at a beer-drink when he says he is going to a funeral.'

Beer-drink, Anna said under her breath; yes indeed, there are plenty of beer-drinks, with beer brewed by you, madam, brewed with my sugar. Later that day, Salome came back for another attack: 'All my vegetables I have planted, they are dying and dead.'

Anna considered. There was some truth in this. What she did not like about Enock was his attitude to the poor things that tried to grow in the earth. It seemed to her that he had chosen his trade specially so that he could be destructive. When things grew, he cut them down. You might call it pruning, she supposed, but he liked to cut until you could see plant-blood; she felt for the stunted, cropped-back plants, and remembered how when she had been a small child her mother had in the name of hygiene pared her nails to the quick; five years old, she saw her little fingers, sore and blunt and red, turning the pages of her first reading book. And again and again her mother had done it, and so did Enock, and you could not argue, for they thought it was a thing they were morally obliged to do. What flourished, Enock left unwatered. He killed with his sharp blades, and he killed by neglect.

'Ralph will take over looking after the vegetables,' Anna said. 'And I will look after them too when the babies are bigger.'

Salome looked shocked. 'No, madam,' she said. And for the first time referred to precedent: Mr and Mrs Instow would never have done such a thing.

Ralph said, 'They're against Enock because he is an outsider.'

'He is not an outsider,' Anna said. 'He has plenty of friends.'

'Where?'

'I don't know. Somewhere. On the railway line. He's always sneaking off, you know that. Salome says we should give his job to one of the visitors.'

'Give him another chance,' Ralph said. 'Please, Anna? There must be some story that he's not telling us. There must be some reason he's like he is.'

Must there? Anna had the feeling a row was building up.

The next thing to occur was the loss of most of Ralph's clothes. Ralph had gone to Palapye for the day, and she must have been in the schoolroom when it happened; classes were over, but she was making a coloured chart for the wall, a coloured chart with the nine-times table. The babies had been put down for their afternoon sleep, and Felicia took her own siesta beside them. Anna finished her work, put away the scissors and the big paste-pot; closed the schoolroom door behind her, shutting in its heat; trailed into the house, washed her hands and face, and made for her own bedroom, hoping to rest for an hour. The wardrobe door gaped as usual, but the camphor-scented interior was nothing but an area of darkness.

Enock's disappearance could not be entirely coincidental. Odd items had gone missing before; Ralph's wardrobe was not so extensive that she did not notice the loss. She would not have minded so much if Enock himself had seemed to profit from either the theft or the sale. But he still wore the tight tan jacket, sweat stained: the same ragged shirts and broken shoes.

'This time he's gone too far,' she said. What bothered her was the thought of Enock in the house, pawing their few possessions. She imagined herself confronting him, and could see already the arrogance of his expression, his superiority; at the back of her mind she heard Ralph saying, well, perhaps he is entitled to his expression, perhaps he is indeed superior to us, but she did not believe it, she thought Enock was just one of those people you find everywhere in the world and in all cultures, one of those people who spread disaffection and unease, who sneer at the best efforts of other people and who make them restless and unhappy and filled with self-doubt.

'Let it go,' Ralph said. 'We've no proof it was him. Where was Potluck, anyway?'

'Asleep under a bush. Besides, he knows Enock, doesn't he? I've had to teach him to leave Enock alone.'

'It could have been one of the visitors. Anyone could have come in.'

'Don't be simple-minded,' she said. 'It's Enock, he has his trading routes, everybody tells me about it. He takes things and puts them on the train and his pals take them off in Francistown.'

Ralph looked miserable. 'We'll have to start locking the doors, I suppose.'

Anna thought of Elim: the great bunch of keys that Lucy Moyo had put into her hand on her first day at Flower Street.

'Yes, we will,' she said. 'And I'll have to start locking the larder and counting the supplies and giving things out only when they're asked for. Goddammit, Ralph, are we going to let ourselves be robbed blind?'

'It hardly matters,' Ralph said. 'My clothes weren't that good.'

Then, two days later, Felicia came crying that her skirt had gone, her best skirt, the one that madam had given her. She looked dangerous; she wanted to make an issue out of it.

Anna thought: oh, the bare-faced cheek of the man! She had done as Ralph told her, she had said nothing, but now she was not going to consult Ralph, she was going to sack Enock that afternoon and be done with him. Her patience was at an end. Felicia had been a good girl, she was careful with the babies, it was against their interests to have her upset.

She called to Enock from the back stoep. He sauntered towards her with his corner-boy's gait. Salome stood by, swollen with self-righteousness.

Anna looked out over her parched, devastated garden: 'Enock, what has happened to Felicia's skirt?'

Enock's lip curled. 'Ask that woman,' he said, barely indicating Salome with his eyes.

'You skelm,' Salome said, furious. 'God will strike you.'

'Don't be stupid,' Anna said. 'Salome does not steal.'

'Sugar,' Enock suggested.

Anna conceded it. 'Maybe.' Her eyes travelled sideways to Salome. 'I don't mind sugar, or anything within reason. But it is you who steal clothes and sell them, Enock. It is a bad thing to steal from my husband, bad enough, but it is worse to steal a skirt from Felicia, who is poorer than you are.'

'I did not see this skirt,' Enock said.

'Rubbish,' Anna said. 'That's rubbish, Enock, and you know it.'

And into the sentence she put contempt; what she meant to say was, Enock, I don't hate you, I just despise you, you're in my way and I want to clear you out, and get something better.

228

The man looked straight at her, into her face. Their eyes locked. She tried to face him down, and was determined to do it. The moment drew itself out. A voice inside her said, it is ridiculous, that you should engage in a battle of wills – you who have everything, you who have an education, a husband, twin babies, you who have God's love – with this poor wanderer, this gardener, this man with no home. A further voice said, it is ridiculous in itself, this battle of the gaze, perhaps it is some convention that we have in Europe, yet how does he know of it? Perhaps all people know it, perhaps animals even. And perhaps, thought Anna, it is one of the battles that I am equipped to fight.

So it proved. Enock, his mouth moving around words unspoken, dropped his gaze and turned, his head down, and moved hunch-shouldered towards his own quarters.

There was a silence. Anna looked down at her dusty sandals, as if her eyes were worn out from the effort. Salome spoke, taking her own time, and her voice had a sick gladness in it. 'Oh, Mrs Eldred, oh, madam. You know it is a thing you must not say, you must not say to a person, you are rubbish.'

'What?' Anna said. She looked up again. 'I didn't say that. I didn't say he was rubbish. I said his excuses were rubbish.'

'It is the same,' Salome said complacently.

Anna felt a quiver of doubt inside. There were, she knew, these forbidden phrases in every language; phrases that seemed harmless in themselves, but contained some deadly insult. Uncertainly, she asked, 'I've said something bad?'

Salome nodded. 'Enock will go away now,' she said.

'Good,' Anna said. 'That is what I want. I don't like to sack him, you understand? But if he goes because I have spoken the truth, I can hardly be responsible for that. We can have another gardener now. One of the people who lives in the huts may come.' She heard her strange, stilted speech, but didn't regard it. That was how she talked these days.

That morning would always stay in her mind. It was many months since rain had fallen. There were bush fires on the hills, ringing the village and the settlements near by. They smouldered, sometimes flared: at night you could see them moving slowly, like an affliction in the blood.

It was just as Salome had predicted; Enock was gone by nightfall. His room had been cleared, and there was nothing left of him but his distinctive footprints dragged through the dust. Anna found them next morning on the cement steps of the back stoep, outside the kitchen. Perhaps he had come to make amends, to plead his case? If so he had thought better of it, and turned away, and vanished into the bush. By afternoon they had engaged another gardener from among the visitors, and the whitewashed room was occupied. Enock had taken the curtains with him, and Anna sat down at her sewing machine to make another pair.

She brooded while she worked: so much unpleasantness, over so little. She was reluctant to have perpetrated even the smallest injustice, though she tended to be practical in these matters; to be brisk about other people's squabbles, as schoolteachers are. Nothing would ever be taught or learned, if you stopped the lesson every two minutes, to hold a court of inquiry: *Madam, madam, Moses is stealing my pencil, Tebogo is sitting in my chair, Effat is hitting me and calling me a cat.* It seemed to her that this was a case of the schoolroom kind. Perhaps Salome had taken the skirt, out of spite. It was possible. And Salome herself had been claiming for the past month or more that she had seen the gardener leaving Felicia's room in the early morning. Would Enock steal from his mistress?

Yes, quite likely, Ralph said, when she put it to him. He seemed to have grown tired suddenly. Or tired of this situation, anyway. 'You were right,' he said. 'We should have sacked

Enock long ago. Anyway, he's out of our hair now. Not that you have much,' he said to his son. He lifted Matthew above his head. 'Up to the roof,' he said. 'Up to the roof and up to the moon. What a big strong boy! But when will you get a head of hair like your sister?'

Kit watched from her cot, a finger in her mouth, her face dubious. 'Up to the moon,' Ralph said. 'Up to the moon, baby. And down again.'

Next day Salome said, 'Storms tonight, madam. The weather is coming up.'

It was August now, and not warm; there were clouds blowing over the hills. 'Good,' Anna said. 'We need the rain.'

Let it be a good storm, she thought, one that fills the water tanks. I don't mind tomorrow's cold and the damp, even tomorrow's snakes, as long as we have water to see us through the winter.

Early in the afternoon, just after school was over, Potluck came in from the garden – plodding, poor dog, as if his feet were lead. It was not like him; usually he bounded and bounced. 'What is it, Potluck?' He staggered towards Anna, falling against her legs. 'What's the matter, chicken?' His great butter-coloured head drooped, nuzzling her shin. Then suddenly his body contorted. He seemed to shiver all over, in a violent spasm or fit; then his ribs arched, and he began to vomit.

Anna watched him, stepping back in shock, calling out to Ralph to come and see; but Ralph was not in the house. Potluck's body seemed to shrink, as if his bones were contracted by his efforts. And yet there was no effort, because a stinking liquid seemed to flow from him as if a tap had been turned on inside. Yellow-green, viscous, the fluid pooled about his feet, washed across the carpet, widened about the room. Its stench rose up; it hit Anna like a fist. She herself gagged; it was like

231

nothing she had smelled before, a hellish compound of rotting plant-life and burnt rubber, a smell of panic and morbidity and flesh revolted against itself. On and on it went, a ceaseless flow. She had heard of cancers, of malignities that are so foul that even the most Christian of nurses must enter the rooms with masks. Was that what she was inhaling now? She wanted to turn and run, skitter down the steps of the front stoep and out into the air. But pity for the creature gripped her; it held her to the spot. She saw the dog's ribs heave, saw his eyes turn up into his skull; hand over her mouth, she saw his whipped crouch, his buckling joints. Potluck fell, lurching stiffly on to his side; but still that revolting fluid pumped on, and on. How could his body contain so much? She moaned his name; oh, Potluck, my little dog, what has happened to you? She crouched beside him and put her hands on him. His fur was wet, and a thousand pulses seemed to jump at her through his side.

But as she touched him, the flow stopped. The feculent pool ceased to grow. With a final expulsive effort the dog heaved his body clear of the floor, like an animal galvanized in an experiment. He dropped back, thudding against the floorboards. He drew a great breath, shuddering as a human being might. His whole body twitched, and his lips curled back from his teeth. He closed his eyes.

But Potluck was not dead. When she put her hand on his head, his tail moved, once. It beat the floor, spreading the hideous efflux to her skirt. She looked up, saw Ralph in the doorway, staring down at them. 'Poisoned?' he whispered.

They said nothing further. They were afraid to speak. They picked up the dog and carried him to the veranda next to their bedroom; they sponged the filth from his coat, wrapped him in blankets, and dabbed water on to his dry muzzle, hoping he would lick. Anna sat by him while Ralph dragged the ruined carpet into the air, and threw buckets of water and disinfectant on to the floor, and swept out the froth and scum.

232

When he finished, and returned to Anna, Potluck was licking water from her fingers. His eyes were still closed, and the orbs danced and jerked under his lids. 'I think he's saved himself,' Ralph said. 'God knows what it was, but no doubt if it had been in his system another hour it would have killed him.'

Potluck is a big dog, Anna thought. The poison for a dog would kill a child, kill two babies. A horrible rush of fear swept over her, left her nauseous, weak, clinging to the windowsill. 'What can it have been?' Her voice shook. 'What can he have eaten?'

'Something left for him,' Ralph said. 'Bait.' He dropped his head. 'I'm sorry, Anna. Enock's final act of spite, I think. He never liked Potluck and he knew that we loved him, I have seen his lip curl when he has heard me talk to him. You were quite right about the man, I should have listened, you were completely right and I was completely wrong.' He held out his hand. She took it. 'Anyway, he's failed.' He stooped, patted the animal's side. He looked vindicated, as if good had won out. As if it had prevailed. As if it always would.

For the rest of the day Anna checked Potluck at intervals, first every ten minutes, then every half-hour, then on the hour; keeping a fearful vigil, as she had for the twins in their first months. She would have brought him to a more convenient place, but he was an outdoor dog, and did not understand carpets and furniture; to lie on the stoep was as much as he could tolerate. By dusk he had heaved himself from his side into a more alert position, and his strange swivel-mounted ears had begun to move in accordance with the sounds of the household and the compound. But he was half-hearted about his vigilance, and when he tried a bark he had to ponder it; the sound was muffled, and afterwards he looked bemused and exhausted. 'Never mind, Potluck,' Anna said, rubbing his head. 'You're off-duty tonight.'

'He'll be all right now, won't he?' Ralph said. 'I would have cried, I think, if we'd lost Potluck. I love him for his simple and greedy character.'

'He's like the twins,' Anna said. 'That is their character, exactly.'

He took Anna in his arms, pressing her head against his shoulder, feeling her shiver from the stresses of the day. He stroked her back, murmuring meaningless, reassuring words, pet-names; but he was shot through by self-doubt, shaken inside by it. This business with the gardener, it had bothered him, disturbed him a good deal. Anna would say, oh, of course there are injustices, there are miscalculations: they all even out. But he did not believe that. He did not say so to his wife, but he thought her attitude faintly repulsive; it is fatalistic, he thought, it releases us from the responsibility which we should properly take. We should do our best, he felt, always our best – consult our consciences, consult our capabilities, then, whenever we can, push out against unjust circumstance.

Enock was a crook, a petty criminal, perhaps accused of the one crime he didn't commit; all acts of injustice are magnified in the victim's eyes. The error may be irretrievable, Ralph thought; we have made a choice about him, perhaps the wrong one, but what can we do now? The situation could not stand still. We had to choose.

Lying awake sometimes, listening to the sounds of the bush, he brooded on the larger thoughts that routine keeps at bay. This I could do, or that . . . Each action contains its opposite. Each action contains the shadow-trace of the choice not made, the seeds of infinite variation. Each choice, once made, trips contingencies, alternatives; each choice breeds its own universe. If in the course of his life he had done one thing differently, one tiny thing, perhaps he would not be where he is now; his frail wife in his arms, his twins on the knee of their dark nanny, his convalescent dog at his feet, ribs heaving with delight at mere survival. Everything in the universe declines to chaos and waste; he knows this, he is not so poor a scientist. But he believes that his choices have been the right ones, that this is where he wishes to be; believes it simply, as he believed in Bible stories when he was a child. If his choices have led to this, have brought him to this moment, they have an intrinsic rightness; as for those other worlds, the alternative universes, he will not inquire. And surely, in the end, he says, my will is free? The world is not as Anna says. There is no dispensation that guarantees or provides for an evening-up of the score. If we are not to be mere animals, or babies, we must always choose, and choose to do good. In choosing evil we collude with the principle of decay, we become mere vehicles of chaos, we become subject to the laws of a universe which tends back towards dissolution, the universe the devil owns. In choosing to do good we show we have free will, that we are God-designed creatures who stand against all such laws.

So I will be good, Ralph thought. That is all I have to do.

The storm broke that night, around nine o'clock. Ralph and Anna had lit a fire in the twins' room, and left them, warm and drowsy, under Felicia's eye. The twins did not wake much at night now, and Anna was happy to attend to them when they did; so usually the nanny would have been back in her own quarters. But the rain was heavy, unrelenting, cold like frozen metal and falling like metal rods. On her haunches before the fire, Felicia rubbed her shins and indicated that she would stay; and her own bedstead, with its two plump pillows and crocheted blanket, was more inviting than the battering wind outside.

The world was full of noise, you had to raise your voice against it; the metal rain drummed the roof, and the wind moaned. Anna stood at the window, watching sheet lightning illuminate the garden, the fig tree, the mutilated fig tree that was part of Enock's legacy. It lit up the straggling boundary fence of the mission compound, the shacks of their visitors – lighting them as they had never been lit before, because there were people in those shacks who could not afford candles. The inhabitants would be awash in brown water and mud, their roofs carried off perhaps, their cooking fires dowsed, their cardboard suitcases spoiled and their bundles and blankets and Sunday clothes now sodden. Tomorrow, she thought, we will tackle everything. Nothing can be done tonight, nothing can be done while this rain is still falling. She shivered. Ralph put into her hand a glass half-full of Cape brandy. She stood sipping it, still at the window; behind her the paraffin lamp guttered and flared. The coarse spirit warmed her. 'Fetch Potluck,' she said to Ralph. 'Carry him in. We could put him by the fire, it would do him good, I know he doesn't like to be inside but he might like the fire. Besides, if the wind veers round, that stoep will be awash within a minute.'

Ralph went out, a torch in his hand, down the passage to the back of the house. No respite; still the wind howled, the rain slashed in its rhythm against roof and wall and window. He heard the dog lift his head and whimper. Ralph clicked his tongue at him. 'Come on, Potluck.'

Potluck tried to get to his feet, his paws scraping on the polished floor. But the effort was beyond him; he fell back and lay miserably on his side. Ralph put down his torch, squatted by him, heaved him into his arms; his legs thrust out stiffly, Potluck grunted, half in indignation and half in relief.

It was dark in the house's central corridor, and Ralph guided himself by letting his shoulder brush the wall; he was on his way back to the sitting room, to Anna standing by the fire with her brandy. Now Potluck kicked his legs, as if he would like to make efforts for himself – so outside the kitchen Ralph lowered him gently on to his feet. Wagging his tail feebly, the dog crawled away under the kitchen table. 'Come to the fire,' Ralph said to him. 'Come on with me, Potluck.'

From outside the back door, Ralph heard a little noise, a scrape, a cry. It was a woman's voice, very small: *Baas, let us in.* He thought, it is our visitors, the poor people in their shacks; they are panic-stricken, their houses are carried off, they want shelter. The thought crossed his mind: your dog has been poisoned today, there is a man with a grudge against you, you are not entirely safe. Then he heard the voice again, little and pleading: baas, we are washed away, we are frightened, let us in.

And so, without more thought, he made his choice; he turned the key, stepped back, and drew the stiff bolt. As he swung open the broad, heavy back door, he felt it pushed, smashed back into his face; and he was not then surprised that Enock stood there, his face mild, curious, composed. Enock reached inside his jacket. As calmly as a man takes out his wallet – as calmly as a man in a grocer's shop, offering to pay – Enock took from inside his coat a small hatchet.

At once, Ralph smashed it from his hand. He had time to think, and he thought at once of his superior strength; so many years of full-cream milk, of lean beef, of muscle-building protein, and beneath his hand this poor felon, whose cloth jacket tore under his hand, ripping at the seam. Enock slid along the wall, his hands thrown up in front of his face.

Ralph smashed his fist into the man's jaw. He felt the intricate resistance of tooth and bone, felt pain in his own hand; and as he closed in on the man to throttle him he felt the slithering resistance of his sinews, of his stringy muscles and green bones. He had ripped away not just the jacket but the familiar sweat-soaked third-hand shirt, and he pushed against the wall clammy hairless flesh, pounding his fist above the man's heart as if that would stop it, adding this rhythm, thump, thump, to the drumming of the rain. He wanted nothing but death, nothing but to feel Enock wilt and stagger, droop, retch, fall, and then his feet would do the rest; and already in a kind of red-out of thought, a bloody dream, he saw his booted foot kicking in the delicate skull, splintering bone, scattering teeth, thudding and rebounding, thudding and rebounding like a machine, until the creature was dead.

He saw this in his mind; yet at the same time sensed movement in the darkness behind him. He heard the dog stir, try to get to his feet, fall back. Then a dull blow, very hard, between his shoulder-blades. He believed he had been hit with some huge, blunt object, like a fence pole. His mind filled with a picture of damage, of a huge bruise like a black sun. He turned around on this presence behind him, moving more slowly than before, and put the palm of his hand against a looming face, and shoved it away. It was a stranger's face, and though later he would think and think about it he would never be able to identify it. He also wondered, later, at how long it had taken him to realize that he was bleeding. The dull blow was a knife-wound, a wound between his ribs; and as his blood began to flow, he fell against the kitchen wall.

The next moments were lost, would always be lost. He had a vague consciousness of his own heart, an organ he had given no thought before. Unregarded, unpraised, heart beats and beats: but heart jibs now.

He lay down, passively, curiously tired. He was waiting to die. Let me die, his mind said, dying is not too bad. It is too much trouble to stay alive. I am warm now. This easy emission of blood is to be desired; flow on, and on. I am warm now, and soon I will be safe.

When the stranger entered the room where she stood by the

238

fireplace, her drink in her hand, Anna did not scream, because she found she had no voice; she knew the essence of fear, which is like a kind of orgasm, and she was numb and white and still as she listened to the man's demand for money, as she took the keys from the top drawer of the sideboard, opened up the mission cash-box and gave him what was inside. Without looking at them, the man thrust the notes into his pockets with his free hand. He spilled some coins; he did not seem to care about them, and yet those coins too were money, a lot of money. She watched them roll away, under the furniture. The man kept his eyes on her face. So, she thought, have they come here to kill us?

She saw a torn shape creep into the room. 'Enock!' she said. The strange man closed in on her, took her by the arm. But rage made her strong enough to tear her arm from his grip – to pick up the bottle of brandy from which Ralph had poured her drink, to smash it against the sideboard, that ghastly piece of furniture the Instows had so loved. Let them turn it on me, she thought, let them take it out of my hand, let them blind me, but let me blind them first.

A moment later she was alone. They had gone. The alcohol fumes rose into the room. Shattered glass lay about her feet. The neck of the bottle was sealed in her palm, as if it were fused to the bone. She was alone, the storm still battering the house; within her was a small dangerous silence, like a chip of ice in her heart.

She must move from the spot, and find out what hideous thing had occurred; the splintered bottle in one hand, the lamp held high in the other. She must walk from the room to the kitchen, see her husband slumped in death's narcotic embrace; she must walk from the kitchen to the room where her children were left sleeping. In that room she will receive her own death-blow; the one that will leave no mark on her skin, but will peel and scalp her, part the flesh of joy from the bone of grief. Let her move from this room, and she will be impaled to suffer slowly, to suffer as much when she is a woman of eighty as she will suffer now – a little pale English girl with black hair, footsteps pattering down a black corridor, running into an abandoned, empty room.

Dawn came late. Felicia had gone, and taken everything from her hut, all her possessions; she had packed and flitted, in an orderly and premeditated way. There was blood on the kitchen walls, and less noticeable blood, dark and slippery, on the red cement floors. Ralph, white as a bandage, lay cocooned in other bandages. The light was splintered, refracted, full of water; the grass moved, the bush moved, the earth seemed to shiver and shift.

Anna walked, tottering, between Salome and an Englishman who appeared to be an official, perhaps a kind of policeman. Everything will be done, she was told; for, Mrs Eldred, this is unprecedented, we have never before in the history of this country recorded the abduction of a white child, of two white babies, and from their family's compound at night – no, Mrs Eldred, there has been nothing like it.

She thought, because there is no precedent, they wish to believe it cannot be true. They wish me to say that, finding myself alone, finding this shattered bottle welded to my palm, I ventured out, saw my husband half-dead on the floor, saw by the light of my lamp the blood on the walls; that I proceeded then into my children's room, saw that their nurse was gone, saw the doors open, saw all the doors of the house open, saw the wind and rain flying in – saw my children's beds empty, but no: no, there I was mistaken, for there is no precedent for it, it has never been heard of, such monstrosities cannot be entertained. I was mistaken when I thought my twins were gone; my son Matthew, my daughter Kit. They were safe all the time, dear policeman. My husband's life-blood had to be washed from the walls, and I am the woman who did it; but no, in this matter of my twin children, I was mistaken. I must be. You cannot bear it, otherwise, your official burden is too great. For if they are really missing, you must track them now, in the fractured light of the day after the storm: the country awash, the mud sliding, the fords in flood . . . Anna broke away from them, from the supporting restraining hands, and walked alone in the gardens, red mud caking her bare legs, her arms wrapped across her chest, walking, walking, while living creatures scattered from her feet.

It was nine o'clock that morning when Anna found her daughter. The party on the stoep saw her stumble towards them, holding in her arms what they believed to be a baby's corpse. They saw her approach them through a shivering silver light: like a woman breaking through sheets of glass, like a woman ploughing through mirrors. One child in her arms, but only one: plucked from the snake-seething ditch, plucked from muddy-brown water, blood-caked, rigid, frozen. Hands reached out again – to pull into the circle of humanity the bereft woman, the tiny carcass.

'Oh, Mrs Eldred,' Salome moaned. 'That God in all his goodness should send this trouble to you.'

But then the child began to utter: not to cry, but to make a jarring, convulsive, sucking sound, louder and louder with each breath, as if her tiny ribcage were an uncoiling spring.

EIGHT

After a month Ralph wrote to his Uncle James:

There is no news. If in two weeks there is still no news we are to return to England. After all, they say, they can carry on the search without us – and they will carry it on, and thoroughly, I have confidence in that, if in nothing else. Still, I dread the thought of leaving here, because the day we leave we will be admitting to ourselves that there is no hope.

I am much better than when I wrote last. I was 'lucky', the doctor said. I'm afraid I laughed in his face. Anna and I, we dislike being in different rooms now, and we never let Kit out of our sight. The same doctor who told me I was lucky said that this was a shock reaction and it would wear off, and that we must expect to find in ourselves certain oddities of behaviour, jump at any noise, suffer nightmares and so on. I don't suffer nightmares, because I don't sleep.

I feel I am living in an alien world now. I know that is one of those phrases that your brain reaches for when it's tired, but I can't think of any other way to express it. To be more exact I feel that I am suspended, that I am like someone hanged, that the ground has been dug out from under me, or my support kicked away. This woman, Felicia, the children's nanny, how could she do it? There is no doubt that it was planned. I must have told you in my earlier letter that Felicia had packed her clothes – everything in her room was gone. The two men brought a truck – the police found the tyre tracks. And Felicia stayed in the house that night, whereas for some months she had been in the habit of going back to her own room as soon as the

242

twins were settled. I thought it was the storm that made her want to stay by the fire — but she was staying for another purpose. If I had not let the men in, she would have let them in. I suppose that might be some comfort to me. But then, it isn't. There is no comfort. I am the one who opened the door to them. They said they wanted shelter. I decided to do a good action, and by it my life has been split open and destroyed.

James, can you please explain to my mother and father and to Emma what we think has happened – I mean, can you explain to them that it is not likely Matthew has been taken for ransom? I can't write it in a letter. Besides, people in England wouldn't believe that crimes of such a nature occur. I would not have believed it myself, but when we were in Elim our doctor, Koos, told me one day about medicine murders. So when I asked the police why anyone would take my boy – and they told me – I knew I should believe them. They don't know how many children are stolen in a year and sold to the witch doctors. Sometimes children, older children, wander into the bush. The disappearance is not reported because there is no one to report it to. These children never come back. Perhaps animals kill them, or they starve. That is possible, of course.

Anna believes that Matthew may still be alive, and that is what she fears most. She says 'If he is dead, he is not suffering now.' But she is not sure. There is not a moment when we can be sure of anything.

There is of course a hope, a possibility, that the police will arrest these people. After all, we can identify Felicia and Enock, though I could not swear to recognize the man who stabbed me. If they are caught, perhaps they will tell us what happened to Matthew, but I am given every reason to doubt it. When these cases come to court no one will ever give evidence. They are too afraid of the witch doctors, I am told. If they are caught, they will probably be hanged. That matters nothing to me, one way or the other. I have no feelings about it. I would only want them to speak – so that I can know, so that we can know our little boy is dead, so that we can mourn for him. It is hard to mourn when there is no body to bury. I think – I try to imagine – how many people have said that in the history of the world. But most of them have entertained some hope, I suppose, whereas we must accept that there probably never will be a funeral. In these cases the police never find an identifiable victim. One man said to me, 'Sometimes we find traces.' I asked him what he meant by traces, and he said, 'Substances, in bottles and jars.'

Why was Kit spared? They wanted the boy, that's clear. They could have taken and killed her too, but perhaps there would have been no money in it for them. It seems a strange impulse of grace, to lay a baby down in a ditch, with a storm raging. She could have drowned in that ditch, or have died of cold before we found her, or have been savaged by an animal. It seems to me that she has been selected for life, and her brother for death. I shall always have to think about this. And I do not think the years that pass will make it easier to understand. Do you?

Kit is a strong child. She cries a lot now – for her brother, we suppose – but she is too little for us to explain anything to her. It is a blessing, in a way – you see that I am looking very hard for blessings, James. She will never remember what has happened. We mean never to tell her. Because how, in God's name, would we begin? I want you to impress this, to impress this very strongly, on my mother and father and on Emma, that as Kit grows up she must be protected from knowledge of this horrible thing. If she learns about it, it will contaminate her life.

I wish we had never left England. I do not believe that any good we have done here can compensate for a hundredth part of what we have suffered, and for what we will suffer as our lives go on. It seems to me impossible that we will ever lead lives like other people, or that anything ordinary and normal and safe will ever be within our reach again.

Don't advise me to pray, because I don't feel that prayers meet the case. I wonder about the nature of what I have been praying to. Before now I have looked at the world and I have seen no compelling evidence of the goodness of God, but I chose to believe in it, because I thought it was more constructive to do so. I thought that not to believe in it was a vote for chaos. I thought there was order in the world, at least — a kind of progress, a meaning, a pattern. But where is the pattern now? We've tried blaming ourselves, but we are not very convincing at it. If I had dealt earlier with this man Enock, if Anna had not insulted him . . . if I had not opened the door. I accept that I made choices and they were wrong, but then I think, too, that our lives have been ruined by malign chance. I do not see any pattern here, any sense, any reason why this had to happen.

James, in his office in the hostel in the East End, turned over the letter. On its back he wrote, 'If it is chance, can it be malign? If it is malign, can it be chance?'

From beyond the flimsy partition he heard the broken and shabby men in his care, going about their evening routine. He heard the thump and scrape of furniture, the clink of spoon against tin mug. He heard the reiterated wild shout of a frequent customer of his, a tramp with pre-senile dementia: 'Tommy didn't do it. Tommy didn't do it, Tommy didn't . . . he never.'

Tommy didn't do it, he thought. No, no, he pushes off the blame, he places it elsewhere. And Enock didn't do it? God did it. Ralph will think so, anyway. How not – if God made us, if God made us as we are, if he is all powerful, all knowing – could he not have stretched out his arm? In Ralph's mind, God works through Enock now, just as once God worked through Hitler. He will think it is God that plunged the knife into his back and took his child and cut him into pieces, dissected his child alive.

A wash of bile and saliva rose into James' mouth. He struggled not to vomit. He rose from his chair, gripping the arms. Let no one come in; he cannot face them, cannot meet human eyes.

Animals are better than we are, he thought; they do what they must. Pounce, tear, suck the blood; it is their nature, God has made them so and given them no choice.

He moved heavily across the room to the small window, which was barred against thieves. He looked out at an East End evening: waste paper scudding in autumn gutters, and cabbage leaves from some street market, white veins shining in the dusk. Early darkness: months ahead of rain and fog, slush and thaw. God had to permit his creations to do evil; it was the penalty of giving them a choice. Animals have no choice; it is why they are different from us. If we could not choose to do evil, we would not be human. I will tell him this, he thought, tell his poor wife. I will not say what I have often thought: that animals, who have no choice and so commit no crime, may have a guarantee of heaven, but that we, who are God's apes, may be shut out for eternity in the cold and the dark.

From beyond the office door the banging and clattering grew louder. He heard cursing. No doubt there was a fight about to break out; perhaps one of the old men had fallen over, or pulled out a knife. James turned from the window, caught sight of himself in a square of dusty mirror that hung on the opposite wall; saw a spare and desiccated old man, worn by humility, sucked dry by the constant effort of belief. He spoke aloud for a moment, as if Ralph and his wife were in the room with him. 'Anna, there is nothing, there is nothing worse, there is nothing so burdensome ... there is nothing so appallingly hard ... as the business of being human ...' His voice died in his throat. I should take that mirror down, he thought, I have often meant to do it, glass is a danger in a place like this.

When Ralph and Anna returned to England they began at once upon the business of finding a house. Practical considerations would not go away; there were decisions to make. Anna had talked only briefly, grudgingly, about her missing child. What was the point of talking? she asked. No one could share her feelings. No one could enter into them.

'Anna, don't injure yourself more,' James said. 'There is a thing people do – when they have been hurt, they hurt themselves again, they compound the damage. Don't become bitter. That's all I ask.'

'It's a great deal to ask,' Ralph said.

'Next, James,' Anna said, 'you'll be asking me to forgive.' A kind of hard jauntiness had entered her voice; it was her usual tone now.

'No, I wouldn't ask that. Not yet.'

'Good,' Anna said. 'I am not up to the effort.'

'If you could think,' James said, 'that there are some things that God does not control or will, then you could ask God for comfort . . . but it's very difficult, Anna.'

'It's impossible,' she said. 'I asked God for comfort when I came home to Elim every night, and saw these beaten people waiting for me on the stoep – but God kept very quiet, James. God did nothing. It was up to me to do something, but I acted within constraints – I tried to be good, you see, I felt the love of God biting into my wrists like a pair of handcuffs. So what did I offer these people? Bandages and platitudes. Suppose my training had been different? I might have stepped on the train to Cape Town with a revolver in my bag, I might have shot Dr Verwoerd – then I might have done some good in the world. Now, James – when I had in the room with me the man who was going to kill my child – when I had in my hand a broken bottle, suppose I had drawn the edges across his eyes? Suppose I had sliced his eyes to ribbons, suppose I had severed his veins and made him bleed to death? Then I would have done some good in the world.'

'Anna –' he said.

247

She saw the fear in his face. 'Don't worry,' she said. 'You leave me alone, James, and I'll leave you alone. You don't come at me with your theology, and I won't stop Ralph doing his job. It was planned that he should take over the Trust, yes? So there's no reason to change the plan. It doesn't matter what I think, inside myself. Nobody could imagine or know what I think, inside myself. But I promise you I won't stand up in church and bawl out that it's all a sham. We're professional Christians, aren't we, Ralph and me? That's how we make our living. Why should we be poor, when every hypocrite is rich?'

No one had seen her cry, not once; not from the beginning. Emma knew right away, when she met them at the airport: 'Anna is too angry to cry. She is almost too angry to breathe.'

They found a house quite easily. Emma's friend Felix drove them through the country lanes, away from the bustle of Norwich: which seemed to them, after their time in the wilderness, like some vast metropolis. Felix stopped his car under a tree by a red-brick, rambling, ill-proportioned house: 'It needs work,' he said. 'But it will accommodate both your office and your family.'

He looked over his shoulder at Anna, in the back seat. No point trying to avoid the word. Anna was expecting another baby. Everyone said it was the best thing that could have happened.

They went inside. 'The drawing room,' Felix said.

They moved into the light of the long windows. Anna noticed how they were liberally bespattered with mud; Ralph noticed the panelled shutters of old pine. He admired the wide staircase, the lofty ceilings; she breathed the house's air, the compound of strange moulds and the trapped smoke of long-dead fires. 'We must have it,' he said. Anna shook her head. But then she felt — or thought she felt — the child move inside her.

She registered its claims. She thought of having more children, many children, to fill the aching void of grief.

They moved into the house three months before Julian's birth; two months after the birth, Ralph's father died. It was a shock, because he had seemed a fit man; but last year's news from abroad, the news carried in Ralph's first incomprehensible and distressing letter, had dealt him a terrible blow. The whole business perplexed and maddened him; he was used to taking control of life, but now here was a problem without a solution, the theft of a child he had not seen in a country he could not imagine. When his son came home he seemed unable to speak to him, barely able to be in the same room. James said, 'To some people, great grief is an indecency. They cannot look at it. They blame the bereaved.'

Matthew became, more than ever, subject to sudden outbursts of temper, to seizures of indignation about the state of the world. The sight of Julian – his second grandson – made him want his first; it made him rage with disbelief and dismay. 'Why did you go?' he said to Ralph one day. 'You didn't need to go. The missions must be staffed, but you needn't have gone, you shouldn't have gone, there were plenty more experienced people to go. Pride made you do it, I think – pride, and being above yourself, knowing better than other people. That's always been your fault, boy.'

Ralph said, 'You want to know why I went to Africa? I'll tell you. I went to get away from you.'

The day after the quarrel, Matthew suffered a stroke. Ralph never spoke to him again – or rather, he spoke, but the old man gave no sign of hearing or comprehending, though somehow Ralph believed he did both. Ralph whispered to him: forgive me, for the things I have done that hurt you, and for the things that hurt you that I didn't know I had done.

By his father's deathbed he felt himself begin to grow up. He said, after all, my father was not so old himself in the days when he treated me so badly. He was still learning the world, he felt responsibility heavy on his back. It is hard to be a father; no doubt he was not malicious, no doubt he did the best he could. 'Please forgive me, because I forgive you,' he whispered. His father died after three days, the pardon ungranted.

What to do now, with ordinary grief, ordinary guilt? All emotions seem attenuated in the wake of the one great disaster. 'Nothing can hurt you worse,' Ralph's mother said. 'Nothing can hurt you worse than you have been hurt already. I don't expect you to cry for him, Ralphie. Let's just get him buried.'

After this, Dorcas moved in with them, a carpet-slippered presence in the draughty hall of their new house.

It's not so easy to return from Africa, even when circumstances are favourable and the return is planned. Hostilities against the cockroach and the ant cease only gradually. A mark on the wall converts itself into a crawling tick, and there is effort and vigilance all the time – it is hard to sit in the fitful English sunshine, in the heat without threat, harmless insects brushing your bare arms. It was more than a year before Anna could bring herself to leave a plate or a cup on a table; after it had been used, she would snatch it away and wash it, to thwart the advancing carpet of crawling greed. 'Poor Anna,' people said. 'She's always on the go. She'll wear herself out, that girl.' The words used about her, the trite kindnesses, had a sting of their own. There had been a tragedy in her life, and no one here had the terms for it. In winter the weight of her clothes oppressed her; wool and shoe-leather chafed and cramped and squeezed.

And how England looks like itself! After the white light, the sun that bleaches out colour and destroys perspective, here are the discrete, exclusive Old Master tints, sienna, burnt umber, indigo: the dense conifers in shadowed ranks, the tan flash of stripped bark, the flush on the trunk of silver birch at sunset; breath on the raw air, and owls calling at dead of night. Another spring will come, and summer: green layered on green, the mossy wall, the lichened fence: and drowsing horses beneath an elm, flanks fly-buzzed, necks bowed, dreaming of George Stubbs.

So now, where should they begin? How should they coordinate their slow crawl back from the desert? What should they say? What could they tell people? Who was entitled to the whole story, and who could be kept at a distance with a half-truth?

Anna's parents knew the facts – knew the probabilities, that is – but they settled for not talking about them. They pretended that they were sparing their daughter's feelings, but really they were sparing their own. Nothing in their lives had prepared them for catastrophe. They worshipped routine; *events* were dubious matters, and often in bad taste. It was a form of showing off, to have things happen to you. 'Of course, it's terrible, a horrible thing, dreadful,' Mrs Martin said, 'but although I don't say so, of course, I blame him for taking her there in the first place. He could have had a nice job with his father, there was no need to trail half-way across the globe.'

The Martins had spent much of their lives beating the drum for the Christian faith, getting up jumble sales and flower shows so that the dark races could have the benefit of the company of brisk young Englishmen who were familiar with the Psalms and (among other Books) the Book of Job. But they did not expect to have one of these young Englishmen in their back parlour behind the shop, frozen and speechless with misery. They did not expect the Book of Job to have any practical application.

And friends of the families – what to tell them? They

flinched from detail, and Ralph flinched more than Anna. He thought, if we tell them what we think has happened, we will pander to their filthy prejudices, we will seem to traduce a whole nation: savages, they will say.

It was possible to say, 'We lost our son.' That covered everything. Few people inquired further. Rather, they would shy away, as if the bereaved might break down in front of them, lie on the floor and howl. It was surprising how vague people were, even the people who claimed they had been praying for them every Sunday. I thought the young Eldreds had two children, people would say, didn't I hear from somewhere that they had twins? Unease would cross their faces; was there some story about it, an accident perhaps, or was it just that the child succumbed to a tropical fever? Ralph had feared intrusive questions, but instead there was an indifference that he felt as an insult. He made a discovery, common to those who expatriate themselves and then return: that when he and Anna went abroad they had ceased to be regarded as real people. Out of sight, out of mind. Nobody, even the most generous donor to mission appeals, wanted to hear anything about Africa.

In the early years after their return, huge areas of reference were excluded by their family, their close friends. They were surrounded by acres laid waste, acres of silence. Slowly, cautiously, normality tiptoed back; the family no longer censored themselves, guarding conversation from all mention of Africa. After a while they ceased to flinch when a picture of a lost child appeared in the newspapers. Finally the dimensions of the tragedy shrunk; there was a little barbed area in which no one trod, in which the secret was sequestered and locked away. Was it less potent, confined? No: it was more potent, Ralph felt. He dreamt of scrubbing blood away, scrubbing his own blood off a cement floor; but the stain always returned, like the blood in Bluebeard's room. He understood, then, what the fairy-tale means; blood is never wiped out. No bad action goes away. Evil is energy, and perpetuates itself; only its form changes.

Over the next few years Ralph made himself busy, burying the past under a weight of daily preoccupation. Anna watched him change, cultivate a sort of shallow and effortless bonhomie – beneath which, she imagined, his real thoughts teemed on, guilty and seething and defrauded. In daily life he became an exacting, demanding man, who gave her only glimpses of the gentleness of those early years; she had to look at his sons, as they grew up, to see the kind of man Ralph had once been. She had realized very early, when they lived in Elim, that his kindness had a detachment about it, that his care for people was studied and willed; now it became a hard-driving virtue, combative.

During the 1970s the Trust became one of the better-funded small charities, and attracted a member of the royal family as patron. Ralph was contemptuous of the young man, but he would put up with anyone's company to further his aims. He must see progress everywhere; he must see improvement. All day there must be action, or the simulation of it; letters in every direction, telephone calls, driving about the county and up and down to London; there must be advertising and exhortation, press campaigns and fund-raising drives. He took charge of policy, of the broader picture, engaged the services of a freelance public-relations expert; he rebuilt the hostel, updated its aims and methods. He granted an interview to the *Guardian* and one to *New Society* and was sometimes called into television studios to engage in futile scraps with those who thought differently about drugs, housing policy, education. At the hostel he was available to oversee the minutest detail, the supply of paper-clips and pillow cases; he spent a lot of time sitting with the sullen, inarticulate, unlikeable children who found themselves in his care. In Norfolk, too, he became well-known as one of those men who you telephone if you want something done; sometimes the novelty of his ideas outraged the *Eastern Daily Press*. The power of his will, he seemed to think, could pull the world into a better shape. Underneath, Anna thought, he must know it is all an illusion. A futility.

For a year or so after their return from Bechuanaland, she fought to keep her hold on the past, on every detail of it. She had been afraid to forget anything; to forget seemed a betrayal of her child who might – it was possible – still be alive. She rehearsed constantly in her mind the incidents of their life at Mosadinyana: from their arrival on the station platform under the stars, to their final exit, bags packed for them by commiserating strangers. But though the pain remained fresh, specific memories staled and faded; they receded from her, the little events of this day and that. The one night remained in her mind, indelible – the thunder snarling overhead, the hammering of the rain on the roof, Ralph's blood coating her hands to the wrist. But after two years, three, her inner narrative slipped, became disjointed. What remained as memories were a series of pictures, some hard and sharp, some merely cross-hatched blurs of light and sound.

On the day Julian was born, Anna had no interest in resisting pain, or behaving well, or making the process pleasant for those who attended her. When a medical fist squashed a mask on to her face, she gulped oblivion; and she would not allow herself to come back. She wanted the gas and not the air; oblivion informed her, it was what she craved. When Julian was first placed in her arms – a neat, clean, pink little baby, held by the unfeeling hands of nurses, scrubbed and sanitized before they gave him to her – she felt a certain flinching, a pull away from him; she hated to place any burden of expectation on this fragile scrap of being wrapped in a shawl. She saw the tight folds of his lashless eyes, his sea-sponge mouth, forming and re-forming, the stiff mottled fingers that thrust through the cobweb knitting of the shawl: she tried to pretend she had no other son, that she was seeing a son for the first time. Julian had fair curls and soft eyes; he lay in his father's arms and trusted him. He did not remind her unnecessarily of her sharp, small, dark child, his fragile skull still showing when she lost him, the pulses visible, beating beneath that fluttering baby skin.

Ralph's mother Dorcas was a friend to her, in those early years; a close-mouthed, uncommunicative old woman, but always there, always attentive, always to be relied on. Anna shrank from her sister-in-law at first; bossy young GP, driving over from Norwich every other Saturday, full of specious knowledge, worldliness, vitality. She shrank from the world, indeed; there were days when she wouldn't go out of the house, couldn't go out, when a word from a stranger would make her blush and shake, when she could not bear to lift her head to meet another person's eyes.

Sometimes she woke with her right hand contracted, clenched, as if she were still holding the neck of the bottle she had broken against the Instows' sideboard. For a year and a half she kept Julian's cot in her room, and only when Robin was born, and she had something frailer to concern her, did she cease to wake and check his breathing many times during the night. When Kit went to school, she could hardly be persuaded from the school gate.

Of course, people noticed her behaviour. They said, Anna, you're a trained teacher, you've got your mother-in-law to look after the children for you, why don't you go back to work? You need an interest, it would take you out of yourself. They wondered why she was seen so seldom, outside her own house; why she did not take what her mother called 'an active interest in charity work'.

After a year or two of this – the searing gaffs of other

255

people's demands – Ralph's sister Emma took her aside and spoke to her, just in time to save her life. She saved it by small, usual words, trite in themselves, but very important if you were dying.

'Anna,' she had said, 'you don't seem well to me, you seem out of breath, shall I listen to your chest? I wouldn't treat my own family, of course – but I could just tell you if there was anything obviously wrong.'

'It's nothing,' Anna said, 'it's the cold weather, you know, it puts me out of breath – besides, I've always been like it.'

'Have you?' Emma said, interested.

'Oh yes . . . I'm strong enough, in myself, but I could never run much. Even when I was little. Don't you notice me, when I dash upstairs?'

'No, what do you do?'

'My heart pounds.' She frowned. 'I've always been like it. I told you. It was easier when we went to Africa. There were no stairs.'

'I never realized,' Emma said. 'What an idiot I am.'

She was able to tell Ralph, after investigations, that Anna had a slight defect in a heart valve: nothing that required surgery, nothing that was going to kill her, nothing that would ever give her more than the minor inconvenience she had suffered all her life, and which she had never thought to speak of. 'It's common enough,' Emma said, trying to create the proper balance between reassurance and alarm. 'But you must give her a quiet time, Ralph. She has enough with the house and the babies, you mustn't let anyone try to prod her and pester her into supporting amateur dramatics and doing these damn flower festivals and calling on old gossips who are fitter than she is. You must protect her, you see. When people want her to do something, you can sit back in your chair, and frown, and say, well now, my wife, didn't you know she is not precisely well?'

Not precisely well. Ralph wondered if it was fear that impeded Anna's breathing, fear that stuck in her throat.

'It's difficult,' Emma said, 'to disentangle the causes and effects. Certainly, Anna has anxiety attacks. I've seen them, I've seen it happen. It's not surprising at all that she has them, when you think what she's gone through. After some great upset in your life you may think you're coping, in your mind – you may feel you're on top of life. Very well – the mind has strategies. But the body needs different ones. It has a memory of its own.'

'But this defect, in her heart, the valve – that's not to do with anxiety attacks, it's something in itself, you're saying?'

Emma hesitated. 'Yes, it's something in itself – something and nothing. But Ralph, people are very ignorant and cruel, and they won't accept mental suffering as an excuse to avoid anything. They say, "Pull yourself together." I am afraid I couldn't bear to hear anyone say that to Anna – and we are not far off the day when they will. But – trust me, I know what people are like – they'll respect a heart complaint. A heart complaint is very respectable, very respectable indeed.'

Ralph said, 'Sometimes I feel panic too. And a . . .' he put his hand to his throat, 'something here, a heaviness, it won't move. Still, I . . . I keep going.'

'That's what men do,' Emma said. 'Keep going. Often at the expense, don't you think, of the people around them?' They shout at the news on the television, she thought, and call politicians fools – that's a release for them. They lose their temper and hit people, and are admired for doing it. They sit on committees, or enforce laws. Whatever is wrong inside them they project to the outside, they find somebody out there to stick the blame on. But women – women turn inwards. 'Men make decisions,' she said, 'and women fall ill.'

'That seems a gross simplification.'

257

'Of course it is,' Emma said. 'Of course it is. But you can help your wife now, can't you? Why do you want precision reasoning? I've given you something, Ralph – won't it do?'

'Thank you, Emma,' he said. 'You may have saved her life.'

'Oh, she wouldn't die of it –' Emma began; but then she stopped because she saw the extent of his fear. Impenetrable, delicate, dry-eyed Anna: she had been near that cutting edge? 'Oh, Ralph,' his sister said. 'I didn't know. I'd have come up with something before. Doesn't she want to *live*, for the children she has?'

'It is the one we don't have that dominates our life,' Ralph said. 'It's what is missing that shapes everything we do. Sometimes she smiles, but have you noticed, Emma, she never laughs. She is crippled inside. She has no joy.'

'Joy,' Emma said. She smiled her twisted smile. 'A word to be kept for Christmas carols, don't you think, Ralph? Don't expect joy. Survival, that's all – survival should be the ambition.'

There was some surprise when – after Kit, Julian, Robin – Anna Eldred became pregnant for a fourth time. People said, Anna, I thought you'd stopped; three is enough in this day and age, and I heard you had heart trouble. Yes, I've got heart trouble, Anna said. Yes, I've stopped now. The world had moved on by the time Rebecca was born. There were people who knew nothing of what had happened to them in Bechuanaland, and people who had known but had contrived to forget. There came a time when she didn't think, every minute, about her stolen child.

But the grief waited in the thickets of daily life, in unoccupied hours, ready to bludgeon her again, to drag her down: drag her under like a woman drowned, a woman sewn in a sack.

One day Dorcas had a fall in the kitchen, broke her wrist. They took her in to hospital, to casualty, but it was a Friday night, and they had to wait, and the wait and the pain and the other clients distressed Dorcas beyond bearing. There were young men with springing scalp wounds, blood leaking and pumping out of them as if blood were as cheap as water; there was a woman brought in after a road accident, dumped in a wheelchair waiting for attention. One eyelid was cut, puffing and oozing; she had lost one high-heeled shoe, and in the twenty minutes she waited for attention she never stopped sobbing and asking for her husband.

In time Dorcas was led away, curtained off, her arm manipulated; she was wheeled through cold corridors to X-ray. The hospital offered a bed. 'No,' Anna said, 'this place has frightened her, I'll take her home.' The doctor seemed relieved. 'Call your GP in the morning,' he said.

'Keep her wrapped up,' their GP advised, 'keep her in bed, don't let her get worked up about things.' When Emma came to see her late that afternoon she was dismayed by the old woman's low spirits; she seemed in pain, could not rest, would not eat. 'You know what I think?' Emma said. 'I think she's had enough.'

When a chest infection developed their GP arranged for Dorcas to go back into hospital. But because she fretted, and still would not eat, the hospital sent her home. She insisted that Ralph stay by her, then; she began to hold his hand tightly with her good hand, and to talk to him, talk with a grim fluency, about her girlhood, her courtship, her marriage, her husband. It was as if, on what she acknowledged to be her deathbed, she was giving birth to a new version of her life.

'You thought he didn't believe in science, didn't you, Ralph?' Her face was very small against the pillows. 'But he broke my spirit, scientifically. I wasn't always the carpet under his feet, I wasn't born like that. No, I had a life, when I was a young girl – my family weren't so strict. I used to go to dances.'

'Mum, don't cry,' Ralph said.

'Let her,' Emma said. 'Crying does no harm. It might ease her chest.'

'That Palmer boy, young Felix – that friend of yours, Emma – I knew his father. He was a good dancer, very light on his feet. And a gentleman. He'd buy me ginger-beer.'

Emma sat on the bed. She lifted her mother's hand and rubbed it between her own. 'Was he sweet on you, Mum?'

'Oh yes.' Dorcas smiled, painfully. She seemed to sleep for a moment. But then she continued quite smoothly, just where she had left off. 'The thing was though, your father came along, and I thought he was more of a man, really. His father was a lay preacher,' she said, as if they hadn't known it, 'and he had a fine voice.'

'Ah,' Emma said. 'So you gave up Mr Palmer?'

'Yes,' Dorcas said, 'I did, I did give him up, I told him he should look elsewhere. He was a snappy dresser, you know, I'll say that much for him – and oh, could he make you laugh! Still, that's not life, is it ... laughing, that's not life. He married a bottle-blonde from Cromer, went into the building trade, he did well I always heard, that's how little Felix got his airs and graces. Your father was a serious man. We never went to a dance.'

'Mum, you're tired,' Ralph said. 'Why don't you have a sleep now?'

'Don't try to shut her up, or I'll never forgive you,' Emma said mildly. 'This is my mother, and –' she turned to him, and whispered – 'and I've got to my present age without ever hearing her say anything of interest. So don't you try to stop her now.'

Dorcas looked up. 'You see, I always had to please him, Ralph. I was a good girl and went to church, but six months after I was married I gave up fearing God and started fearing

260

your father. I mean that, you know. I don't mean it as a blasphemy. He always seemed to me like a person from another age. Abraham. A patriarch. He wasn't fair to you, Ralph, and the worst thing, you know – he made me take part in it. Oh, you hated me then. That night when I came into your room and said to you, you have to fall in with him, Ralph, or you'll see your sister suffer for it.' She closed her eyes. 'He knew you loved your sister.'

Emma said, 'What does she mean?'

'Nothing,' Ralph said.

'What is it? Come on, Ralph! If you won't tell me, she will.'

Ralph glanced at Dorcas; she seemed to be sleeping, but he had a feeling she was listening still. He reached out for his sister's arm. 'Emma, come with me, come, let's get out a bit, let's go and walk, or let's make tea, do something, go and sit by ourselves . . . this is such old ground, I didn't think I'd ever have to go over it.'

Emma seemed stunned. 'But Ralph, why didn't you tell me? All these years have gone by, events making no sense or partial sense . . . I used to say to you, why did you let him bully you?'

'Yes, you did.'

'How did you bear it?'

'There was no alternative.'

'I thought you were spineless. Weak.' Emma looked very young, as if layers had peeled away. 'He'd have done it, you know – he'd have kept me at home to punish you. With most fathers it would have been bluster, but with him – no, he meant every word he said.' She shook her head. 'Imagine – it would have been a better revenge than anything he could have done to you directly. If you'd have insisted on your path in life, I'd have been turned off mine. And think of the hook of guilt it would have put into your flesh.'

'Yes.' He remembered a thorn that had once, at Mosadinyana, embedded itself in the pad of his middle finger, and made his arm numb to the elbow: an intricate thorn, like a medieval battle-weapon, designed by man to do its worst. 'But she, Mum – she's no saint. She colluded with him.'

'She was frightened, Ralph.'

'Can't you overcome fear?'

'You ask too much of people,' Emma said sadly.

They did not speak for a while. Then Ralph asked, 'Will she live?'

His sister said, with professional accuracy, 'She'll die the day after tomorrow.'

It is a pity that she cannot, with similar accuracy, put a term to the after-life of the missing child. It would be possible, if one were harsh, to regard this lost child not as an innocent, but as a malign half-presence, a destroyer, a consumer of hope. Katherine grows up; they search her face for signs of what her brother would have been. As babies, they were not much alike. So no consolation there; but no further suffering, either. Except you cannot help but mark out the course of the shadow-life . . . he would be six years old, he would be seven years old, he would be seventeen. He has all we lack, he is everything we are not; we have our gross appetites, but he is the opposite of flesh. Somewhere in Africa the little heart rots, the bird-bones crumble or – alternatively – the traces dry in their jar; their child becomes a bush-ghost, powder on the wind.

Norfolk, 1980: midsummer. Cyclists take to the road, with flapping shirts and fluorescent saddle-bags. Women in loud print dresses, their cardigans over their arms, pad downhill in seaside streets, with wide feet like the feet of waders. There are fathers in cars, lost in country lanes: irate metropolitan faces behind glass, and wives tearfully slapping at maps that won't fold.

There are poppies in the verges – indecent splashes, as if blood were welling up beneath the landscape. In every vegetable garden in the county, cabbage-whites hover dangerously over the brassicas. Those hedges that remain are towering walls, walls of deep green; lemonade bottles perch in them, chucked out from passing cars. Small animals are smashed into the tarmac of the A149 – so flattened, so thoroughly dead, that they look like animals in cartoons, who will instantly spring back into their old shape.

Sandra and Amy Glasse are selling samphire, cauliflower, lettuces, beans and new potatoes. They are selling large fleshy tomatoes, because last winter Julian reglazed their greenhouse. Ralph is now in love with Mrs Glasse, and sees her once a week, twice a week, three times if he can contrive it. Contriving is hard and goes against his nature; but when has his nature ever been what it should be?

Summer visitors came to Ralph's house, children from the hostel. Ralph's own children treated them with the usual distant tolerance. Kit had not resolved her future; she drifted around the house, and bickered with Daniel, who found himself in the neighbourhood every other day.

The Visitors exhibited their customary bewilderment. They had grown up in cities, and spent a lot of their lives standing about in the street. Here, there was no street worth standing in – just a lane, its high verges choked with thistle and fern, cow-parsley and rose-bay willow herb. They did not go out of the house much, because they did not like to walk anywhere or ride bicycles. Sometimes they begged lifts to Reepham, the nearest market town. They would swagger across the market square, then lean on the railings outside the Old Brewery, looking hopeless; stare into the butcher's window, to see if the lamb chops were doing anything exciting; shove and barge into the post office, which sold stationery and newspapers and picture postcards of Norwich, and there shoplift packets of paper doilies, and marble-swirl pencils with erasers on the end. Then they would vandalize a few hanging baskets, and beg a lift back to the house again.

'If this goes on,' Kit said to Robin, 'the people in Reepham will start complaining. They'll get up a petition.'

'They'll get up a mob, I should think.' Robin lurched unsteadily across the kitchen, pulling his forelock and pretending to be a vampire's manservant. 'My lord, the villagers are advancing, armed with staves.'

'No, seriously,' Kit said. 'The Visitors seem worse than ever this year.'

'It's you that's changing. Getting old and mean.'

'And where's Julian? He's no help. He's always over at Sandra's house, you'd think he'd decided to leave home. When he's here he doesn't speak.'

'Well, he's gone mad, hasn't he?' Robin said. 'Round the twist. I thought we'd established that. What I want to know is, how is he going to keep a grip on Becky now it's the school holidays? He can't be over there screwing Sandra and here guarding his little sister, not both at the same time.'

'No,' Kit said. 'Think how he must be torn.'

'Very odd, our family.'

'I said that. A few weeks ago. You seemed to disagree. You seemed to think they were normal.'

'I've changed my mind.'

'A man's privilege.'

'But Kit – can you make sense of it? Don't watch television, it contaminates your brain. Don't hang around with smart kids with money, or you might contract that fearful disease materialism. So what do we get instead, for entertainment and company? Child prostitutes from Brixton. Heroin addicts. Thieves.'

'We're supposed to be proof against it,' Kit said. 'We've been so well brought up that they're not going to influence us, or do us any harm.'

'That's the theory,' Robin said.

'It works, doesn't it? I don't see you shooting up, or selling your body.'

'True,' Robin said guardedly. 'But Kit, isn't it time you got away? Once I go off to medical school you won't catch me hanging around here in summer. Not if summers are like this one. All this snapping and snarling, and creeping about.'

'Yes.' Kit turned away. She had been thinking a lot, since her midnight conversation with Robin, and she was uncomfortable with her thoughts. She didn't want to risk having them exposed. 'Anyway,' she said, changing the subject. 'Anyway. The Visitors will have gone soon. All except this Melanie.'

'Oh yes, Melanie – when does she get here?'

'Tomorrow, I think.'

'Kit,' Ralph said, as the family sat down to eat, 'do you have any nail-polish remover?'

'Why, Dad, do you want to do yourself a re-varnish?'

'Christ,' Robin said. 'Dad's a transvestite. He's got a secret life.'

'Don't worry,' Kit said. 'There's probably a self-help group we can join.'

'Yes,' Robin said. 'Ask Dad. He'll know.'

'For goodness sake,' Anna said. 'Listen to your father and stop being so slick.'

'Ah,' Kit said. 'Mum doesn't like the thought that he's got a secret life.'

'My problem is this,' Ralph said. 'Melanie. She might inhale it.'

'Dad, look.' Kit held up her hands, 'I am a stranger to the manicurist's art.'

'Oh, good,' her father said.

'Not very observant, are you?' Robin put his chin on his hand and watched his father.

'I'm not,' Ralph said. 'It's a fault of mine.'

'People are just problems to you,' Kit said. 'Problems on two legs. That's why you don't notice things.'

'Well, I – you may be right, but in my line of work – if you think about it – I don't meet people without problems.'

'That's not my point,' Kit said. 'My point is that you don't see – what's her name, Melanie – you see "persistent absconder, multiple addictions" – whatever the jargon is at the time.'

'Do I? Well, I yield to you in charity, you are my superior. The problem is that the nature of what I do is so contentious, so risky – wading into children's lives and trying to put them right – that I'm always glad if I can identify a pattern of behaviour. And there are such patterns, you see.'

'Everyone is unique,' Kit said. 'Surely.'

'I used to think so. But then I see how they – my clients – behave or react in the same way as others who have gone before – or, let's say, they have a small range of possible reactions.'

'Don't they have free will?'

Ralph looked at his daughter appraisingly, as if to judge her seriousness. 'I used to think that was the single question,' he said. 'I used to think, of course they have free will. But then after a few years I saw these patterns repeat themselves, as if people were born into them. I read case files all the time, and sometimes, quite often really, I get one client's story mixed up with another. People use certain drugs, perhaps, or drink, or whatever – they are as they are, and that is much as their parents were – they beat their children or neglect them, they go into prison and come out and go in again, and you feel that you could write the next page in the file, you know what their future is going to be, and their children's future too. Nine times out of ten you'd be right. It depresses me, how seldom people do the unexpected. They start off down a path and they stick to it.'

'In my opinion,' Robin said, 'stupidity has a lot to do with it. I know people can't help being thick, but if they're so thick that they can't control their lives properly I don't see how it matters if they have free will or not. That's just theory. In practice they don't have choices.'

Rebecca kicked her brother's shin, under the table. 'I asked you half an hour ago to pass the sweetcorn.'

'Shut up, Becky,' Kit said. 'But Robin, you can be quite bright and not have choices. Take love, for instance.'

Anna sat back in her chair, putting her fork down. 'Take love?' she said.

'Sorry,' Kit said, 'I know I'm contradicting what I said earlier, but I do see your point, Dad. Love, you know, it's a chemical thing. When people say they're in love it's just a set of physical reactions, there are all these substances whizzing around your brain, and hormones making you obsessed –'

'Very scientific,' Robin said.

'– and that's why although everybody thinks that nobody in the world has ever felt like they do, they all listen to these schmaltzy songs and write poems and feel at one with the universe. They're all going through the same process. We're programmed for it.'

'You may be right,' Ralph said. 'Are you in love, Kit?'

'No. I'm sure that if I were, I wouldn't talk about it with such a lack of respect.'

'You'd be like everyone else,' Robin said. 'You'd think you were unique.'

Kit made coffee. As if on cue, Daniel came to the front door. 'How are you, young man?' Ralph said. He liked Daniel, he had decided, because he seemed to have evolved; in the present casual optimist, in his new stiff tweeds, you could seem to see his grandfather, the snappy dresser so slick on the dance floor and free with ginger-beer.

'I came to thank Julian,' Daniel said. 'Shame he's not here. Peace is much better than war, isn't it? Oh,' he looked around, 'don't you know what I've been up to?'

'Barn conversions?' Ralph suggested. 'That's the usual bone of contention, isn't it?'

'Not any more. You know Julian's girlfriend? I've been over to their farm. Mrs Glasse has this outbuilding that Julian wants to demolish because it's falling down anyway. Mrs Glasse was very mysterious about it and made objections, she said, "I use it to keep buckets in." Anyway, when I had a look at it, I came in and told her what I would pay for the roof-tiles, which are beautiful, absolutely beautiful – and she said, quick, Sandra, let's all go and lean on the bugger, it can't come down soon enough for me. I said, "What about the buckets?" and she said, "They can be rehoused. Or get foster-homes. Ralph knows all about it. He'll get them a social worker if I ask him."'

'Oh,' Kit said, 'so you're best mates now, you and Jule?'

'He still says I'm a vandal, but I think he's glad to find a way of reducing the damage. By the way,' he said to Anna, 'have you met Sandra's mother? She'd interest you.'

'In what respect?'

'She's not what I expected – quite a clever woman, I'd think, very sharp, very, what's the word, droll – but just absolutely content to stay on her patch. No wider ambitions, none at all.'

'You mean she's like me?' Anna said.

'Oh no – I didn't mean that.'

'You needn't blush. She sounds an admirable type.'

'She's so young,' Daniel said. 'Of course, you know her, Ralph. I was amazed, she's so attractive – I mean, Sandra's not much to look at – don't mention to Jule I said so – but Mrs Glasse is quite stunning, in her way.'

'Did you tell her so?' Anna said.

'God, no,' Daniel said. 'Mrs Glasse? I wouldn't dare.'

'I don't see why not. She leads a solitary life, from what I hear. She probably goes short of compliments.'

There was a fine disgust in Anna's voice. Ralph's pulse-rate rose when he heard it. Daniel looked covertly at Kit, to see if he had made her jealous. But Kit only smiled her placid smile.

It was a chilly evening, for August. Daniel's pullover had a suggestion of cashmere, a certain Burlington Arcade air about it. Ralph was wearing an army-style sweater, with fabric elbow and shoulder patches, which Rebecca had given him last Christmas. Ralph disliked it, because it was shoddy, militaristic and already fraying; but Becky had saved up for it, and thought it dashing, so he wore it to please her. Daniel seemed to be eyeing it – not covetously, Ralph thought. 'How's your car running, Daniel?' he asked. He lunged into the conversation as if at a runaway horse, trying to catch it and lead it away from Amy Glasse.

Ten o'clock – Daniel on his way home, Kit washing up – he went out to attend to the boiler. This brute occupied its own hot little room – in the depth of winter, it was a popular meeting place for the family. The air was dry, calcified, osseous. He would have let it go out in the summer, except that it supplied the family's hot water too. When the children were babies it had seemed quite natural to dunk them in and out of each other's bath water; when they were older, he had expected them to exercise economy. One Easter holiday long ago, Kit had a friend to stay. 'You can have first bath,' Kit had said, 'but leave me your water.' Her friend had stared at her. It's like the middle ages here, she'd said. And telephoned her parents to be collected next day.

All these thoughts were running through Ralph's mind – to block out certain other thoughts – as he drove the scuttle vengefully at the coal, felt the coal rattle in, felt the dust fly up and sully his cuffs. He straightened up, and Julian was there, in the doorway, leaning against it.

'What do you think you're doing?' Julian said.

'The boiler,' Ralph said.

'Don't be funny. It's not funny,' Julian said. 'I've just come from Sandra's. I've been covering up for you so far, but why should I go on doing it? Why should I? You're going to wreck up everything for me and Sandra, and that's only the beginning of the damage you're going to do.'

Ralph said, 'This is neither the time nor the place, is it?'

Julian leaned forward and took a handful of his father's sweater, somewhere around the shoulder patch. He shifted his grip, seemed uncertain whether he had his father or not. 'Look, what the hell are you doing?' he said.

Ralph said, 'Give me an inch of space, Julian. What am I doing? I don't know.'

Melanie, their Visitor from London, arrived next day. The children always hung around to see a new arrival, but they were disappointed by this one. She was wearing an ordinary pair of jeans, black lace-up boots with domed toe-caps, and a leopard-skin print T-shirt with a hole in it. 'Very conventional,' Kit said. 'Almost Sloane Square.'

'Boring,' Rebecca agreed.

Melanie had a nylon hold-all, but it seemed to be empty. 'What's happened to her clothes?' Anna said.

'She burned them,' Ralph said shortly. It was clear that he didn't mean to enlarge on this.

Anna sighed. 'We'll have to get her kitted out, then. That will be a battle.'

She took Melanie upstairs to settle her in her room. 'Have you got any tablets, my dear?' Anna said. 'Anything you shouldn't have? Needles?'

Melanie shook her cropped orange head. Anna felt that she was lying, but balked at a body-search. The girl slumped down on the bed and stared hard at the wall. She was here against her wishes and she meant to make this clear. Anna looked out of the window, over the fields. Fields, fields on every hand, all choked with snares for the urban young. To Melanie – who had broken out, sooner or later, from everywhere she had ever lived – it must feel like a Siberian labour camp. The permafrost on every side; searchlights and razor wire. As if catching her thought, the girl said, 'Is there bulls?'

'In the fields? No, not usually. We don't have that kind of farming. In the fields we grow things.'

'What, like bloody grass?' the girl said.

'Oh, sweetheart,' Anna said. 'Don't swear at me. It won't make you any happier.'

'But it does,' Melanie said balefully.

Anna went downstairs, and checked that anything Melanie might inhale or swallow was locked away. Not many women have to padlock their oven-cleaner, Anna thought. They had tried to exclude from the house any substance with a potential for abuse, but you could never be sure; a boy who'd stayed last year had a predilection for a certain brand of suede-cleaner, and had ransacked the kitchen cupboards and her dressing-table drawers on the off-chance that she might have some lying about. Again, these children were given to what are known as 'suicidal gestures' – drinking bleach, for instance. Some of their experiments were so unlikely that it was only later, when they got out of hospital, that you could find out from them whether they'd been in search of euphoria or oblivion – a temporary exit, or a permanent one.

'Ralph,' Anna said. 'I'm afraid Melanie is a Sad Case, a very sad one indeed. You're not going to leave me with her this afternoon, are you?'

'I have to go out,' Ralph said, 'for three hours.'

'Can't you cancel? I don't think I can be responsible.'

Ralph wavered. 'I'm expected,' he said. He thought, how easy it is to lie. 'Robin's locked the bikes away. She'll not run off, I don't think. Nowhere to run to. She seems dazed, doesn't she? It's odd, because she was all right at Norwich station when the volunteer handed her over. But then as soon as we got out of town she seemed to go rigid. In the end she shut her eyes and wouldn't look out of the window.'

'I'm not worried about her running away,' Anna said. 'I'm worried about what she might do if she stays here.'

'We've had worse than Melanie.'

'I know – but Ralph, I know we've done this for years, had these poor things here in summer, but I'm beginning to wonder if it's fair on them – they hate it so much. And we hate it, too.'

'We've had this out before,' Ralph said. 'And I really do believe it does some good. They get good food, they get at least a bit of fresh air, they see something different from what they've seen all their lives – and there are people around who are willing to spend time with them and sit and listen if they want to talk.'

'Let's hope she doesn't want to talk this afternoon, then. Because you've gone and fixed some meeting, which will probably go on into the evening.'

'No. I'll be back for five. I promise.' He was already on his way out of the back door. I have to see Amy, he was thinking, *I have to*. He felt nauseous at the lies he was telling, at the thought of his duties neglected; felt almost sick enough to turn back. But *I promised I'd see Amy, I have to*. He drove away, cherishing the comforting belief that he was under a compulsion.

Anna was annoyed with herself; she hadn't meant to get involved in a debate about the philosophy of Visitors, she'd really meant to get a phone number from him, so that if there was any crisis with Melanie she could get him out of his meeting. She went into his office. His diary was in its usual place, top right-hand drawer. From his pewter frame Matthew Eldred frowned at her, hand on his watch-chain; Uncle James, in his tropical kit, squinted into the sun. And Ralph was there, too; Ralph on the stoep at Flower Street, one hand in his pocket, leaning against the wall. It was the only photograph they displayed, of their life in Africa. It was there because Rebecca, a couple of years ago, had begged to see some; she had taken a fancy to this, saying, 'Oh, Dad, weren't you handsome, you're not a bit like you are now.' Ralph had decided the picture should go on his bureau, to remind him of his present imperfections. It was a photograph devoid of associations; he did not remember it being taken. He saw a smiling, insouciant boy, a lounger with curly hair; a broad-shouldered boy, who looked – if only momentarily – at ease with the world.

Anna took out the diary, found the week, page, day.

'9 a.m.: Meet Red Cross about Home-from-Hospital scheme. DON'T FORGET – ring the bishop.

11 a.m.: Collect Melanie Burgess from station.'

Then nothing. So he had left the afternoon free, and something had come up at the last minute. Why didn't he say so? Anna put the diary back in the drawer. She thought no more about it.

Ralph left Amy's house at half-past four. As he reached the top of the track he saw a police car, apparently waiting for him. He stopped the engine and waited in his turn. He recognized the officer who got out first; it was one of the men he had seen previously at the same spot, one of those who, Amy said, were always watching the house.

Ralph wound his window down. 'What do you want?'

'Could I have your name, sir?'

'Eldred, Ralph Eldred.'

'And your address?'

He gave it.

'Is this your car?'

'Yes. Unfortunately.'

'Can you tell me the registration number?'

He told it.

'Would you have your driving licence on you?'

He took it out of his pocket. The policeman looked at it, handed it back; clean, not a penalty point, nothing to be done there. 'We've seen you round here before.'

'Yes. I've seen you.'

'Been calling at the farm down there?'

'Yes.'

'Reason for visiting, have you?'

'No,' Ralph said. 'I just drive about Norfolk at random, calling at farmhouses whenever I feel like it.' He swung open his door and stepped out. 'What is it you want? To look in the boot, is that it?' He walked around and unlocked it. 'OK. There you go. Get on with it.'

The officer didn't know what he wanted, really; but he ferreted about in the boot of the Citroën, found a pair of wellingtons, a jack, a tool box, a bundle of old newspapers. 'All right?' Ralph said. 'It doesn't make much sense, this, does it? If you think I'm supplying stolen goods to the people down there, why didn't you search the car on the way down?'

'We might just go and check out the farm, now,' said the other constable, who was leaning against the police car.

'You are harassing Mrs Glasse,' Ralph said. 'You know perfectly well that all her market-trading is legal and above-board, but you like the thought of tormenting two women who can't torment you back. But I can, and I will, because I know the procedure for making a complaint against the police, and I know when to make one and I know how to make it stick.'

'Had many dealings with the law, have you?'

'God's my witness,' Ralph said, 'I don't know how you blokes keep your front teeth. Finished with me, have you?'

'Oh yes, sir. We've got your name and address.'

'Oh no, sir, you mean.' Ralph got back into his car, slammed the door, spoke through the window. 'Right, so we'll be seeing each other again, will we?'

'Look forward to it,' one of the policemen said.

At the Red House next morning, Melanie did not appear for her breakfast. 'Leave her,' Ralph said. 'Let her get some rest.' He sat at the breakfast table, trying to argue sensitivity into his younger daughter. 'Be kind to Melanie,' he said.

'Why?' Rebecca asked.

Ralph looked at her in exasperation. 'Because it might achieve something. And the opposite won't.'

'Melanie,' Rebecca said, 'is filthy and foul.'

'Perhaps,' Ralph said. 'Maybe. But how will she get any better unless people treat her kindly? And you must ask yourself, before you start, if any of it is her fault. Melanie has what we call a personality disorder.'

'Oh, come off it,' Robin said. 'She can't have. She hasn't got a personality. She just sits there with her mouth half-open, staring at her boots.'

'If that were true,' Ralph said, 'there wouldn't be a problem. But I'm afraid she's not really like that. Come on, Robin, I don't expect much of your sister, but you ought to have some sense at your age. Melanie has barely been under this roof for twenty-four hours, you can't know anything about her. Don't tease her and don't provoke her, because she can be violent.'

'Oh, we won't stand for violence,' Kit said. 'Robin will bring her to the ground with a flying tackle.'

'You don't understand,' Ralph said mildly. 'The violence would be against herself.' He paused. 'When she comes downstairs, look carefully at her arms, the inside of her arms. You'll see she has old scars there.'

'She cut herself,' Anna said. 'Did she use a razor blade? Or something else?'

'You noticed, did you?'

'Of course I noticed,' Anna said, annoyed. 'Do you think I'm as heedless as the children?'

'I'm sorry,' Ralph said.

'So you should be. You went out and left me with her yesterday afternoon, and you warned me about things she might sniff or inhale but you didn't warn me about knives and scissors. When I noticed her arms I had to slide away, and then run around the house hiding anything sharp.'

'You're right,' Ralph said, 'I should have warned you, but it was a long time ago she did the cutting, she seems to have other means now of relieving the stress. She was bullied at school, that's where it started, and so she played truant and then she got in with a gang of older girls, and they took her shoplifting.'

'The usual story,' Robin said.

'True,' Ralph said. 'But with one piquant variation. She was taken into care, and after three months she was allowed back home. Her parents had sold her record player and her records, and they'd given away the toys she'd had as a baby, and her clothes. Anything they couldn't sell or give away they'd just put out with the rubbish. Maybe the social workers hadn't done their job properly, or maybe the family hadn't listened, maybe they didn't take in what they were told, because it was quite obvious that they never expected to see her again.'

The children were quiet. 'So what did she do?' Robin said in the end; his tone respectful now.

'There's some waste ground near her family's council flat — she found some of her clothes there. In a black dustbin bag, she told me. She went around for a bit trying to find out who they'd sold her things to, and knocking at their doors trying to persuade them to give them back, but naturally as they'd parted with cash they thought they had a good title, as the lawyers would say. After that I don't know what happened, it's a blank, she won't tell anybody. She turned up in London about ten days later. She hadn't a penny on her when they brought her to the hostel. She had the dustbin bag, though.' He sighed. 'We bought her some clothes, but she wouldn't wear them. She wanted the originals, I suppose. She went out at the back and had a bonfire.'

Kit had stopped eating. 'It seems a terrible thing,' she said. 'That a child could be worth so little to its parents.'

'What do you expect?' Anna pushed her plate away. 'We live in a world where children are aborted every day.'

'Hush,' Ralph said. He did not want Rebecca to start asking questions. Or anybody to start asking questions, really. He had not seen Julian since their confrontation two nights ago. His son had gone back to the coast and not returned. He, Ralph, wanted so badly to see Amy Glasse that it was like a physical pain. He didn't want to drive to the farmhouse and run into Julian again, but what could he do? I am going to have to speak, he thought, tell Anna — or break this off — break it off now, because it's already too serious — how could it not be? All these years I have never looked at another woman, never thought of one, my life in that direction was closed, there was no other woman in my calculations.

If only Julian would come home, he thought. Then I should make some excuse, get into the car, drive.

He looked up. Melanie was standing in the kitchen doorway, staring at them. 'Come on, my dear,' Anna said. 'There's plenty of food left. Pull up a chair.'

Melanie recoiled: as if she had been asked to sit down with tribesmen, and dine on sheep's eyes. For another minute she studied them, poised as if for flight; then her big boots pounded up the stairs again, and her bedroom door slammed.

Summer heat had built up. White sky and a smear of sun. No wind. Heaven and earth met imperceptibly in a straw-coloured haze, and the outlines of trees were indistinct. Through this thick summer soup Julian and Sandra walked together by the footpaths, tacking inland. There was thunder in the air.

'You can come and live with us, if you want,' Sandra said. 'My mum would be glad to have you. And then – though you'd have to see Ralph – you wouldn't have to go home and face Anna.'

'My father,' Julian says, 'actually believes that you don't know what's going on.'

'There he's wrong. The first thing I noticed, he was always there when he thought I was away.' Sandra raised her hands, and tucked her red hair modestly behind her ears. 'He doesn't see me, so he thinks I don't see him. But I do see him – because you know my habit of coming home across country.'

'Through hedges and ditches.'

'If need be.' Sandra stopped, and looked directly at him. 'I brought this on you, Jule. If I'd never come to your house, this would never have happened.'

'But you did,' Julian said. 'You did come. So what's the use of talking like that?'

'I don't know. It's no use. But it's a point of interest, isn't it? If you hadn't come to North Walsham that day, when I'd gone out with the motor bikes. Or if it had rained before, five minutes before, you'd never have seen me. You'd have turned up your coat collar and gone striding off back to your car, and I'd have taken shelter in the church. And your dad would be at home with your mum, and everybody would have been happy.'

'No, not happy,' Julian said. 'That's not how I'd describe us.'

They were heading towards Burnham Market. But before they reached the village she said, 'Come in this church.'

'Why? It's not raining.'

'No, but there's a thing in it I look at. I want to show you.'

An iron gate in a grassy bank, a round tower; their shadows went faintly before them over the shorn grass. Inside, an uneven floor, cream-coloured stone; silence, except for the distant hum of some agricultural machine. Light streamed in through windows of clear glass. 'The old windows blew out in the war,' Sandra said. 'So my grandmother told me.'

'I didn't know you had a grandmother.'

'I called her my grandmother. She lived at Docking.'

'But who was she really?'

Sandra shrugged. 'My mother, she never talks about her life. I don't know who my dad was, so I'm not likely to know much about my grandmother, am I?'

The chill of the floor struck through his thin rope-soled shoes. He looked around. A square, massive ancient font, of the kind he had been dipped in, he supposed; he found it easy not to examine it. But there was something here worth attention; he saw a wine-glass pulpit, delicate and frail. 'Is this it?' he asked Sandra.

He stood before the pulpit: I should not touch it, what if

everyone touched, it would dissolve. He made himself an exception: his fingertip grazed the outlines of church fathers in their mitres and cardinals' hats, their quills inscribing scrolls: deep green and crimson scratched and flaking away to show the wood beneath, so that the faces were half of paint-flake, half of the wood's grain. On the walls he could pick out the curve of a halo, a line of colour faint as thought; he would not have seen it if Sandra had not traced it for him with her finger.

Then she touched his arm. 'But look, Julian. Come here. This is what I want to show you.'

She led him away from the pulpit to the south aisle, turned him with his back to the altar. She pointed to the flags at their feet, and to one stone, grey-black, mottled, scarred: yet each letter perfectly incised and clear. 'This one,' she said.

> In Memory of Mrs Theaophila
> Thurlow, Daughter of the
> Reverd Mr Thos Thurlow
> Rector of the Worthams in
> Suffolk, descended of the
> Thurlows of Burnham ulpe
> She departed this life 18th of
> Iune 1723 aged 24 yeares.
> And Frances Hibgame her Niece,
> Daughter of Iohn and Catherine
> Hibgame of Burnham Norton, who
> died 19th of Decemr 1736 aged
> 10 yeares, 5 months, 2 weekes and 1 day.

They stood for a moment without speaking. Then Sandra touched his arm. 'They say that people in those days didn't love their children, but it can't be true, Julian, can it?'

'No.' He dropped his head. 'Of course they must have loved her. Because they counted up every day.'

Again, silence. Sandra said. 'Listen, this thing about Becky –

you must stop. It's cruel, you see. It's cruel to your mother and father.'

'Cruel to *them*?'

Unwanted knowledge lay inside her like a stone. 'Just let it go,' she said. 'Let her grow up, will you? You talk about them being unhappy, but can't you see? What you're doing, it's like putting a knife in them.'

'Why? You mean, because I say they can't look after her?'

'Yes, just for that reason.'

'I'm frightened for her,' Julian said. 'Such evil things happen.'

'I know. I know you're frightened. But let it go now, will you?'

They walked away down the aisle to the back of the church, and again their shadows moved before them, merging and melting, their limbs like those of giant animals, their shapes outlandish; but soft, very soft, shades reflected, shadows seen through glass. The machine in the distance had cut its engine; the thunder in the air had killed the bird song, the insect hum. They touched hands as they came out of the porch – just the back of their hands brushing against each other. Sandra did not dare look into Julian's face; he did not look at her. In the distance, imaginary no doubt, the undisturbed pulse of the sea.

NINE

Julian telephoned home from a call-box in a pub on the coast road. 'Mum, is everything all right at home?'

'Where are you?'

'In the Ship,' he said, confusing her.

'When can we expect to set eyes on you?'

A pause. 'In a day or two.'

'Robin seems to think you've moved out for good.'

'He's no reason to think that.'

'Julian, is there some problem over there?'

Another pause. 'We'll have to have a talk sometime. But not just ... not just yet. Till I know what's happening here. But look, don't worry. It's just that I can't come home at the moment.'

'Julian,' she said, 'if you are trying to reassure me, stop now. All you are achieving is to alarm me wildly.'

'Mum, don't tell Dad I called, OK?'

'Why ever not?'

'I only wanted to know if you were all right.'

'Julian . . .'

No answer. The line went dead. I'll drive over, she thought, see what's what. It occurred to her that she wasn't entirely certain where Mrs Glasse lived. Still, she could find it, it wasn't beyond her capacities . . . but then, she thought, there's Melanie, and it's getting urgent to find some clothes for her, I ought to take her shopping; and even if I put it off for another day, I can't leave Kit at home with her while I go chasing after Julian, it's not fair. What does it matter if he doesn't come home for a few days? It's not like him to make mysteries, but perhaps it's something to do with Sandra's mother, family business, something he doesn't want to talk about. Not trouble with the police again, surely? Another thing went through her mind, that goes through the mind of every woman with a grown-up son on the loose: could Sandra be pregnant? Probably I'm being melodramatic. I wonder . . . would Ralph have time to drive over? She looked at her watch. I'll catch him at Mrs Gartree's, she thought.

Mrs Gartree was an old woman, very deaf and vague. She had been a friend of Ralph's parents, and a great churchgoer in her prime, and Ralph had taken it upon himself to call on her once a month. Mrs Gartree liked to discuss parish politics in her strident bellow, and was assiduous in filling out forms for obscure state benefits to which someone had told her she might be entitled. She had a fortune in the bank, Ralph said, but he helped her with the forms all the same; she had few pleasures left in life, he said, just this one and planning her funeral.

Mrs Gartree's voice: indignant, very loud. 'My telephone flashed at me. Who are you? What do you want?'

'It's Anna. ANNA. ANNA ELDRED. Ralph's wife.'

'Oh yes.' Mrs Gartree sounded mollified.

'Is he there?'

Mrs Gartree dwindled into vagueness. 'Oh, I don't think so.'

'Has he left?'

'What?'

'Have I missed him? Has he been and gone?'

'Missed him? Oh, I'm sure I would,' Mrs Gartree said skittishly. 'But he was here last week. I think so. Within the month.'

'But today?' I should have known better than to get into this, Anna thought. 'Today – he said he was going to call on you.'

'No,' Mrs Gartree said. 'You called me. I haven't spoken to Ralph. No, not for many a moon.'

Anna turned up her eyes. 'OK, Mrs Gartree. Sorry to have bothered you.'

'I wouldn't, except I'm deaf,' Mrs Gartree said.

'Goodbye,' Anna said.

'Toodle-oo,' said Mrs Gartree.

Anna went into Ralph's office and found his diary. He really is beginning to move in mysterious ways, she thought. In the afternoon, at two o'clock, he was due for another meeting in Norwich about the Home-from-Hospitals scheme. The Trust was funding a project to create networks of helpers for the old and chronically sick; discharged from hospital to isolated cottages, or to homes in villages with no shop or chemist, they needed failure-proof rotas of visitors if they were to be kept free from anxiety, hypothermia and the risk of falls.

She flicked through Ralph's address book; the Norwich number came to hand. 'Pat? It's Anna. Ralph's wife.'

'Oh, yes. How are you, Mrs Eldred?'

'Look, when Ralph arrives for your meeting, would you ask him to ring home? I'd like a quick word.'

There was a silence. 'Just a minute.' A pause. Then 'Mrs Eldred? I think there must be a mix-up. We haven't got a meeting today.'

'Are you sure?'

'No – yes, I mean – I've just checked my diary.'

'I'm sorry,' Anna said. 'I must have got the dates confused.'

'That's OK.' The woman sounded relieved. 'For a minute I thought I'd made some awful mistake. I'd hate to make a mistake about a meeting with Mr Eldred, he's always got so much to do.'

'Yes, hasn't he?' Anna said. She put the phone down. Well now, she thought. But she did not like what she thought. Mrs

Gartree could be discounted, as a witness; but it was strange that Pat Appleyard wasn't expecting him. It was agreed between them that he would always leave his diary for her, and update it each evening, in case there was an emergency at the hostel, in case she needed to contact him; and he had always stuck to that diary, he was known to be reliable and punctual and to save his severest strictures for people who were not.

I am not quite an innocent, Anna thought. I have read a novel or two, in my time. A disappearing husband – unless he's a drunk or a criminal – means another woman; yet there's something farcical about it, isn't there, if a disappearing husband covers his tracks so badly, or doesn't try to cover them at all? But no doubt, if Ralph took to lying, he wouldn't be very proficient at it. Not at first. As far as she knew, he'd had no practice.

Anna sat down in the hard chair at Ralph's desk. Her mind moved slowly, cautiously. Opportunity? He had plenty. He met hundreds of people in the course of his year, clients, social workers, journalists. Routine to fetter him? He had none; each week was different, and the diary was all that constrained him.

Anna tried to smile – as if there were someone in the room to see her effort. You are being ridiculous, she thought. Yes, he meets women, but so he has done for years; he meets women, but if he were interested in one of them, who in particular would it be? No answer suggested itself. I would have imagined, she thought, that though you cannot know people, not really, I would have imagined that I did know Ralph.

She felt very cold, and went upstairs to fetch a cardigan.

The day must continue, though the cardigan somehow failed to warm her. She said to Kit, 'Are you doing anything this afternoon?' Silly question; when was Kit, this summer, ever doing anything? She sat around, she slept, she made herself intermittently useful. 'Because if you're not, would you come shopping for clothes with Melanie and me? I thought, you see, as you're nearer her age –'

'Sure,' Kit said. 'We've got a lot in common.'

'Where do you think we would do best?'

'Depends what she wants. If she wants another leopard-skin print T-shirt, we could try Woolworths in Dereham.'

'Such snobs, my children.'

'OK,' Kit said grudgingly, 'I'll come. What does she need?'

'She needs a coat of some sort. And some shoes to wear in the house.'

'To spare us the clatter of the boots.'

'A sweater, as well, in case it turns cold.' She pulled her cardigan around her. 'And another pair of jeans, perhaps, and a couple of shirts or T-shirts. And underwear, I feel sure – I've not inspected, I don't feel up to it.'

'She doesn't wear any,' Kit said.

'Who says so?'

'Robin.' Kit sighed satirically. 'He's of an age to notice. Well then . . . we could go to Norwich, and catch up with Dad after his meeting. We could make him take us out, for tea and iced buns, so Melanie can see us behaving like a family in a picture-book. We could have anchovy toast, and dote on each other.'

'No,' Anna said. 'Not Norwich. I tell you what we'll do – it's a nice day, let's go to the seaside. Get some fresh air. We'll go to Cromer. She might like it.'

'She'll be crying for candy-floss, and to ride on the donkeys, I suppose,' Kit said. 'Honestly, you do have a strange idea of what constitutes a treat for a person like Melanie.'

'You know what your father said. Try to be kind.'

Anna went upstairs. She stood outside the closed door for a moment, gathering herself. Then she tapped on it. No answer. Softly she turned the handle. 'Melanie?'

The curtains were drawn, and the room was dark and close and tainted; no one, so far, had seen Melanie wash. She had hauled her mattress on to the floor, and heaped the sheets and blankets and pillows into the middle of it. At first Anna thought that the bed was empty, and Melanie had somehow escaped; but then there was a slight movement at the centre of the heap, and the girl stuck her head out. 'Do you prefer to sleep on the floor?' Anna asked.

Melanie stood up amid the wreckage. Sheets fell away from her body. She was wearing a pink T-shirt that belonged to Becky. It was painfully tight under her arms, and rode up to show the frail rack of her ribs. 'Where did you get that?' Anna asked. She wondered if it had been on the washing line, but thought not. 'You shouldn't go into Becky's room without telling her, you know. She won't like it.'

'She won't like it,' the girl mocked, aping her tone.

'You're welcome to borrow anything. Anything you like. But you should ask.'

'Why?'

Because, Anna thought. Because . . . for a thousand reasons. Because it is what civilized people do. She heard the flat anthropologist's tone of the question: why? Passing no judgement: just, why?

'Besides, you're a big girl, Melanie, Becky's things won't fit you. Would you like Kit to lend you something?'

'Borrow. Lend,' the girl said. 'Snobby cows.'

'I was thinking we'd go out.' Anna tried to make her tone easy. 'Go to the seaside.'

'For kids,' Melanie said.

'Yes, but a shopping trip. To get you some clothes.'

'I had clothes.'

'Yes, but you burned them.'

'Before that. My own clothes.'

'I know you did. Don't pick your fingers like that.' Melanie's finger-ends were raw: the skin peeling, the nailbeds inflamed. She constantly tore at them, tormenting each one with her other nails and her teeth; it was a habit she had picked up in her amphetamine phase, it was something that these children did. And it hurt; Anna remembered – memory like a needle under the skin – her own fingernails, cropped to the quick. And then a picture flashed into her mind of Enock standing in the compound with a scythe in his hand, wasted nature at his feet: the torn-out blossom that would only have annoyed him, anyway, for a few hours before the sun killed it.

'What's the matter with you?' the girl said. Anna looked up and met her eyes. What she saw shocked her; almost evidence of humanity.

'It's nothing,' she said.

But the girl persisted, her tone cold. 'Did you think about something you shouldn't have?'

'Yes.'

'What sort of thing?'

'I can't say.'

'I can't say.' Again the imitation, cruel and strangely exact. 'A bad thing, was it?'

'Yes . . . if you like.'

'How bad?' The girl's face was intent: for once, she was asking a proper question. She needed evidence of iniquity, Anna thought, of fallibility at least. How not? She needed comparisons and juxtapositions, if she were ever to find her own place in the scale of things. 'Like killing somebody?' Melanie inquired.

'Yes.'

'Have you ever killed somebody?'

'What a question! I'd be in gaol.'

'Have you ever been in gaol?'

'Yes.' The answer surprised Anna. 'I have.'

'For nicking things?'

'No. Not that.'

'You'd have no need, would you? You've got everything.'

'You may think so.'

'You've got a house,' Melanie said.

'Yes, that's true.'

'I haven't got a house. I've been in homes.'

Anna's face softened. 'Yes . . . they shouldn't call them that, should they? Homes. Look, Melanie, your mum and dad . . . how long is it since you saw them now?'

At this question, Melanie's eyes dulled; but behind her locked-and-barred expression Anna sensed a small movement of mind, the dawn of a precarious desire for cooperation: saw the mind moving, vaguely, around the months and years. Perhaps she was trying to come to terms with an alien chronology, the dates of court orders and social inquiry reports. 'I've forgot them,' she said.

'No. You can't have.'

'I can. I have.'

'So, now . . . what about this day out we're going to have?' She smiled with a professional brightness. She had learned from Ralph, to talk in this way: to presume assent to any initiative, to state always the positive, never to consider the possibility of no for an answer.

'Are we? Us? Going out?' Melanie's eyes were like two big grey pebbles; she rocked back on her heels, as if Anna might try to haul her by force into the open air.

'Yes. Why not?'

'I like it here.'

'You do? That's something.'

Melanie saw that she had lost an inch of ground. 'And these clothes, I like these clothes, I don't want any others.'

'I'm sure you know why that is quite unreasonable,' Anna

said. 'You're clearly not without intelligence.' Ralph's tone was less evident; she was cool, at the end of her patience. 'You know perfectly well that you can't spend the rest of your life wearing a T-shirt that belongs to a child two or three years younger than yourself, so it's only a matter of when you get new clothes, isn't it, not whether?'

They surveyed each other: level ground. Anna calculated that Melanie might hit her: it would not be unprecedented, in a Visitor. She weighed the prospect: the pale stringy arms below the tight sleeves, arms laced with cuts, and the torn hands, the right middle finger with its cheap heart-shaped ring. She knew that she should step back a few inches, beyond Melanie's reach. The girl's arms hung at her sides, and Anna – who had seen men fight – imagined that she might jerk one fist up, straight-armed, to catch the point of her jaw. But I will not step back, she thought. I will not give way. Melanie whispered, 'Tell me what you thought.'

'What do you mean, what I thought?

'Before. When you thought about killing somebody.'

'What will you do, if I tell you?'

'Come with you. Get clothes.'

'No, you'll break your promise.'

'I won't. I'll come. But tell me.'

'All right.' Their eyes locked: Anna thought, I'll tell you something you don't know. 'I had another child once,' she said. 'A boy. A baby. He was taken from my house and murdered.'

The girl nodded. Her eyes slid away. Stayed on the floor: on the heap of crumpled bedding. 'That was hard,' she whispered.

And it was that – the very poverty of her response, the laughable poverty of her vocabulary – that made Anna speak again. 'Hard. Yes. Extremely hard. You ask me what I was thinking about – I'll tell you, Melanie, why not? I was thinking about the man who did it. About how I would kill him, if I had him.'

Melanie watched her. 'And how would you?'

'I don't know. I think about it, but I can't choose. You see, there are so many ways.'

The girl dropped her head again, and for the first time Anna saw it as a frail, living thing; half-destroyed, bruised, but a blossom on the stem of her thin neck. Her skin was white and fine, her hair, no doubt, had a colour of its own, and only parts of her body were cut and marked. She is retrievable, she thought: possibly, in some small way. But I should not have said what I did, I should have found some way to lie; I should have tried to retrieve her, but not by that method.

She moved to the door. 'You made a promise,' she said. She held the door open. 'Come on now, Melanie, you drove a bargain and you got more than you asked for. You made a promise that you'd come and buy some clothes.'

Melanie nodded. Again, there was no expression on her face now: no reaction to what she had been told. She will suppose it is a dream, Anna thought; she lives from moment to moment, perhaps, her memory constantly erased. Behind her, the big boots descended the stairs. In the strong sunlight that shone through the kitchen window, she observed the girl's flawed, bluish face, and put up her hand to touch her jaw. 'Do you not sleep, Melanie?'

'No. Cough keeps waking me.'

'Keep off the glue, and your cough will clear up,' Anna said briskly.

Anna lapsed into silence as she drove; Melanie was silent anyway. When they arrived in Cromer she lifted her feet in the big black boots and locked her arms around her knees, wrapping herself into a knot in the back seat. She didn't want to see the sunlight on the cold North Sea, or hear the ice-cream van chimes and the gulls' cries. Kit saw the birds' bodies floating and skimming, mirrored in the high windows of the old sea-front hotels: skimming the turrets and dormers and gables of the red-brick houses, wheeling inland to swoop and cry among the pines. The gulls leave an after-image, on the ear and eye, and the waves have the sound of a laboured breath; trippers tramp over mastodon bones, and plaice is fried in cafés with plastic tables.

Melanie shut her eyes tight; she wasn't getting out of the car. Anna seemed to have run out of energy to coax her.

'You know you need clothes,' she said feebly.

'I've got clothes,' Melanie said. 'I told you.'

Kit said, 'You've got what you stand up in, and some of that stolen. Come on, you silly bitch! What you're wearing has to be washed, for our sake if not for yours.'

'Why?'

'Because,' Kit said mildly, 'if you start to smell any more we'll make you go and live in one of the bike sheds.'

Surprisingly, this seemed to have an effect on Melanie. She unwrapped her body like a stiff uncurling fist, and tumbled from the car. Kit, having warned her about the sea breezes, had brought along a spare jacket of her own. She tried to put it around the child's shoulders. Melanie bellowed, 'Get off me. *Murdering* pig.'

'Not quite,' Kit said. 'Not yet, but don't try me, honeybunch, I'm bigger than you and if I wallop you round the head you'll know about it.'

Anna shivered. She had abdicated to Kit now, lost control: she was terrified by the thought of what she had said to Melanie, the ease with which it might seep from that pale inarticulate mouth.

Kit took Melanie by the arm. What a formidable wardress she would be, Anna thought; very strong and very sure, with that hand that sinks into the tender female flesh above the elbow joint. She felt that bruises might blossom out again, on her own flesh. She asked herself, have I something for which I must forgive Kit? Have I forgiven her for living?

They headed off into the town. Kit released her prisoner, and strode out smiling equably. Melanie slouched, sullen and furious, her green-twig arms whipped by the wind. Anna had made a move to pick up the coat, for use when Melanie changed her mind; but Kit, almost imperceptibly, shook her head at her, and Anna let it lie on the front seat of the car.

An hour later they had managed, after a fashion, to get Melanie equipped. They had to apologize for her rudeness to the people in the shops, and received commiserating smiles. 'They think she's my retarded little sister,' Kit whispered.

Melanie at least was willing to carry her own parcels. The day darkened, there was drizzle on the wind; now, while the trippers turned blue and rubbed their hands, the local women leaned into the squall in their quilted jackets and wool scarves. Anna swept her collar up to her throat, and glanced at Melanie's white arms. Norfolk may teach forethought, in a way London never does.

'Look!' Kit put a hand on her shoulder. 'Mum, look at that washing machine!' She arrested her before the electricity showroom. 'Sixteen programmes! Just think!'

Anna said, 'Yes . . . but you know, with the twin-tub still going strong –'

'Going strong?' Kit was outraged. She glanced over her shoulder, to ask Melanie – their relationship had flourished in the last half-hour – if she'd ever heard of such a thing as a twin-tub washing machine, where you hauled the sodden shirts with tongs and rubber gloves from . . . but Melanie wasn't there. Kit spun around. Her long hair flew out in the wind. 'Run,' she said. 'It's thirty seconds since I saw her, so how far can she have got?'

They gaped up and down the street. No trace, no sign. 'In a shop,' Kit said. 'Quick.'

They put their heads into the neighbouring shops, gabbling questions, apologies: 'Have you seen a young girl, short reddish hair, jeans, pink T-shirt?' The queue turning: what, your daughter is she, how old would she be? A woman behind a counter stood with her hand poised, ready to drop Norfolk shortbread into a paper bag. Blank faces. 'Sorry, my dears,' the woman said.

'We're wasting our time. Where would she go?'

'Anywhere,' Kit said. 'She doesn't know her way about, so she'd go anywhere.'

They looked into each other's faces. 'I don't want to sound like a silly film,' Kit said, 'but why don't you go that way and I'll go this way? And if you see her, grab her, don't hesitate, just hold on to her, OK?'

'Where will I meet you?'

'Here,' Kit said. 'By the washing machine. Give it ten minutes, then start walking back. I'll see you in fifteen, twenty. If we don't find her by that time we may as well give up, she'll probably have got on a bus and gone somewhere. Has she any money?'

'A fiver,' Anna said.

'Oh, right, a fiver.' Kit pounded off down the street, her head turning from side to side. Anna watched her for a moment and then skittered awkwardly in the opposite direction, high heels uncertain over the paving stones. She hadn't known it would come to this, or she'd have dressed for it.

A few minutes, and her efforts were over. She leaned against a wall. I can't run, she thought; never could. Still, she had done what her heart allowed, her ribs heaving and her chest sore, her head swivelling from side to side to see if she could catch a glimpse of Melanie's orange hair. Surely, she thought, if she tries to hitch a lift out of town, no one will give her one? She's too peculiar, she looks deranged. Unless, perhaps, they take pity on her. For people do, of course. They do the most amazing things; prisoners escape, and people give them lifts, and every runaway gets money and shelter somehow.

Fifteen minutes later, distressed, her lips almost blue, she was back with Kit before the washing-machine shop. Kit put her hands on her mother's shoulders, then under her elbows to hold her upright. 'Are you all right? I didn't say kill yourself.'

'Fine,' Anna said. 'I'm fine.' She pulled back and held her midriff, one thin hand folded protectively over the opposite wrist.

'We've lost her. I questioned bus-queues, in a melodramatic fashion. Ought we to go to the police?'

'No. She's not done anything wrong.'

'But she might. Or something might happen to her.'

Anna straightened up. Breath was coming back. 'Nobody's obliged to take their holidays with us,' she snapped.

'No, but –'

'Kit, if we get the police involved it is almost sure to land her in some sort of trouble. And what would your father say? She'd never trust us again. We should give her – I don't know – we should just stand here for a quarter of an hour. She might come back.'

'She won't be able to find her way back.' Kit rubbed her hands together, to warm them. 'OK, but we should let someone know – I don't suppose you've got Dad's number in Norwich?'

'No.'

'We can call Directory Enquiries. Get him back home. Listen, you stand here. There's a phone-box over there – Red Cross, isn't it? What's the name of the person he's meeting?'

'I don't know.'

'Never mind. I'll tell them to turn him round and send him home.'

'No, Kit.' Anna tore at her daughter's arm. She thought, if my daughter phones Pat Appleyard asking for him, that'll be twice in a day, so she'll know there's something wrong, she'll be asking questions, starting gossip ... 'Kit, he's not in Norwich.'

'Where is he then?'

'I don't know.'

'But he said he was going to Norwich! This morning!' Kit swept her hair back, then flung out her hands, exasperated. 'Robin said, bring me a *Wisden Cricket Monthly* and he said, all right, but if I can't see one, will anything else do, and Robin said no. Rebecca said, bring me something. He said, what? She said, a surprise. Dad said, OK. Robin said, you spoiled brat.'

Anna drew herself gently from her daughter's grasp and leaned back against the plate-glass window of the washing-machine shop. She covered her mouth with her hand, and a little, bitter bleat came from her; laughter?

Kit tried to pull her hand from her mouth, to claw it away, as if her mother were a baby that had eaten something it shouldn't: earth or soil or a stone. On and on it went, the little noise: the heave of the narrow ribs, the out-breath like a moan, the breath sucked in as if air were poison. Anna's ribs drew up, into a panic-stricken arch, and for a moment she was frozen, paralysed, eyes closed. Then she let out her breath – with more than a gasp, with a muffled scream heaved up from her stomach. She sucked in the air, the raw salty Norfolk air. 'I knew I should lose everything,' she said. 'I knew I should lose everything, one of these days.'

Late afternoon, someone came to the door. Anna let Kit answer it. She noticed that Kit had changed out of her jeans into a neat skirt, and had tied her hair back, as if she anticipated a sudden transition into adult affairs.

Anna sat in Ralph's study, in the old wooden swivel chair he used at his desk. It had come from Emma's surgery, this chair: given to him when it was too disreputable for the patients to see. In better times, they had joked that it was impossible to sit in it without the urge to swing around, to say, 'That sounds a very nasty cough.'

But these are worse times. Anna was exhausted by the effort of imagination chasing its own tail. I can formulate no sensible ideas about Ralph, she thought, and my head aches; Kit will never trust me again, never trust me not to break down and start screaming in the street. And the girl has gone, Melanie, and somehow I will be held responsible; screaming doesn't get me out of that one. Now with each little breath she took, the chair swayed under her, sedately. Each movement brought forth its ponderous, broken, familiar complaint.

Kit came in: two policemen followed her. She looked grave, pale, very correct. 'They've found Melanie. She made it as far as Norwich. She's in hospital, I'm afraid.'

Anna stood up. 'What's happened?'

'Mrs Eldred?' one of the policemen said.

'Yes. What's happened to her?'

'She gave us your name,' the policemen said. 'Mr Eldred's name, I should say.'

'Oh, for God's sake,' Anna said. 'Answer my question.'

'She's taken something, swallowed something maybe, that's what we've been told. Would you have any idea what it might be?'

'I told him,' Kit said. 'I've already explained how she ran off.' She turned to the policemen. 'She was fine then. I told you.'

'How is she?'

'She's comfortable.'

'Comfortable?' Anna stared at the man. 'How can she be?'

The other policemen spoke. 'The hospital won't let us interview her. She's drowsy, you understand.'

297

'Is she in any danger?'

'That's not for us to say.'

'We understand,' the first man said, 'that Mr Eldred would be *in loco parentis*.'

Anna nodded. The other policemen said, 'Mr Eldred not home from work yet?'

'He doesn't work. That is, he doesn't go out to work.'

The men looked confused. 'He's an invalid?' one suggested.

'My husband is an officer of a charitable trust. He works from home.'

'That's why we have Melanie,' Kit said. 'I tried to explain.'

'Would it be all right if we looked round, Mrs Eldred? Around your house?'

'No, I'm afraid I can't allow that.'

'They want to look in Melanie's room,' Kit said. 'In case there's something there that she might have taken, a bottle of pills or something.'

'Yes,' Anna said. 'I know what they want to do.'

'I'm sure it's fine,' Kit said uneasily, to the men.

Already, Anna thought, she is treating me as if I were of unsound mind, unable to speak up for myself. I must expect it, I suppose. 'Go and get the proper warrants,' she said. 'The papers. Then come back. And then you can search.'

At once the atmosphere changed; the men changed, their natural obstructiveness and obtuseness giving way to a sneering hostility. 'Why do you want to make it difficult?' the first man said.

'I don't want to make it difficult. I just want things done properly.'

'If the young girl dies,' the second said, 'you'll be to blame.'

'I thought there was no question of her dying. I thought she was comfortable.'

'Mum —' Kit said. Her face was shocked; she thinks I'm a new woman, Anna thought. 'Mum, look. It's just to help Melanie.'

'There's a principle,' Anna said to her daughter. 'There's a correct way. Once you depart from it, you leave yourself open.'

'It's not South Africa,' Kit said.

'Not yet,' Anna snapped.

Her daughter was silent. A policeman said, 'Well, madam, perhaps it would be better if we talked to your husband. What time are you expecting him?'

'No particular time.'

'Doesn't he keep regular hours?'

'By no means.'

Kit said, 'We usually know where to contact him, but today there seems to be some mix-up with his diary.'

'Oh yes?'

'So we don't know how to get hold of him, you see.'

'That's unlucky,' the second man said. 'We'll have to radio in. Say he can't be found.'

'I can come to the hospital,' Anna said.

'Yes, madam, but it's not you that's *in loco parentis*, is it? Well now, we have got a problem.'

None of their language, Anna thought, means what it says. It is a special dialect, charged with implication. One of the men was looking over her shoulder. He seemed to be staring at the wall. She turned to see what he was looking at. 'That picture there,' the policeman said. 'That photo. That wouldn't be Mr Eldred, would it?'

'Yes.' She picked up the photograph, defensive, startled: Ralph on the stoep at Flower Street. 'If you're thinking of putting out a wanted poster, I'm afraid it won't be much use to you. It's twenty years old, this picture – more.'

'Is it, now? It's not a bad likeness, not bad at all.' He turned to his colleague. 'Brancaster way? Down the track? The market-trader?' He turned back to Anna. 'We've had a few dealings with Mr Eldred. We've seen him coming and going from a small-holding, just off that loop of road before you get to Burnham Deepdale. I wouldn't be surprised if that's where we'll find him, madam.'

Each time he said this – 'madam' – it was like a kick or a blow with his fist. He meant it so; he was watching her face, waiting for her to flinch. 'Would *you* know a woman over that way, involved in market-trading?'

'A Mrs Glasse?' Anna's face seemed frozen. She nodded. 'Will you go over there now?'

'It might be worth a try.'

'Kit,' Anna said, 'when Rebecca comes home from her friend's, will you see that she has something to eat? Then take her over to Foulsham and ask Emma to put you both up for the night.'

'What for?'

'Because I don't want her here. OK?'

'Can I take your car?'

'No. I need it.' She turned to the men. 'I'll follow you,' Anna said to the men.

'We can't stop you, madam.'

Anna said to Kit, 'You can bike over, can't you? Just take your toothbrushes.'

'I'll leave Becky with Emma, and I'll come back.'

'No. Stay with your sister. Kit, look – do this one thing for me, please?'

Anna was brittle, exasperated; Kit knew the tone, it was familiar. But she saw how Anna's nerves were stretched – tight, tight. 'What shall I say to Emma?'

'I don't know. Must I think of everything? Aren't you old enough to help me?'

'No,' Kit said. 'Not really.'

Anna picked up her car keys from beside the photograph. She has been waiting for this, Kit thought, waiting to go out, her bag ready and to hand.

Anna followed the police car. They could have lost her, at this junction or that, but they preferred to dawdle and let her stick with them.

It was evening now. The sky was striated, precise overlays of colour working from regal purple to the palest blush. Amy Glasse woke and sat up in bed, stretching her arms and fingers, rippling her fingers through the liquid light like a stage pianist preparing to play. Ralph turned and reached for her as she slid from the bed; sleeping, he followed the heat-trail of her body across the sheets. His arm, empty, cupped the space from which she had moved.

From below, there was a monotonous thumping, a solid hammering, like the copulation of giants in a myth.

'Oh, God,' Amy said. 'We're back in the old routine.'

Ralph woke to see her shape against the window. Her long back, white in the dusk: 'Sweetheart, come back to bed.' He put out a hand for her, drowsy; didn't see why his peace should be disturbed.

'Sorry,' Amy said. 'I don't know, shall I go down, or shall I pretend I'm not here? Ralph, you're not awake, are you?' She cast around, snatched up the T-shirt she had taken off, and swabbed the area between her thighs. She looked around the room for something else to wear, then with a little laugh pulled the T-shirt over her head. She reached for her skirt. 'What shall I do? If I don't go down now they'll only come back later.'

'Who?' He had focused now, on that sound of fist on wood. 'Who is it?'

'Purvis and his mate,' she said. 'The constabulary, my dear. Sometimes I wish I lived in the city, then you'd get a choice of bastards. Not always the same old pair.'

He pushed back the covers. 'Ralph,' she said, 'don't go down. No, listen to me.' She was at the window, the curtain parted minutely. 'There's two cars here. Just get dressed, but stay up here and be quiet. If they come up say nothing – don't antagonize them.'

Buttoning her skirt, she flitted from the room. No one could crouch and hide, and listen to that destructive thump-thump-thumping; Amy couldn't do it, and neither could he. Panicking, he began to pull himself into his clothes. He must get there before her; feared violence. Once before he had imagined hitting Purvis. Once, a long time ago . . . his hand, clenched to pull in and fasten his belt, felt itself sink into belly-flesh: propel a bully towards ridicule and the stoep door, one foot in a wastepaper basket. The body has its own memories; muscle and bone, marching its own ghost-trail.

He put his shoes on, straightened up: randomly buttoned his shirt, skittered down the stairs after Amy. The front door was open: he went out into a September evening, a confrontation, the air a golden-rose; the past summer a memory, bloom of sea-lavender, scent of tourist tyres on narrow burning roads. Purvis said, 'Mr Eldred, isn't it?' Yes, it is, he said, yes, I do: what's happened, how is she?

Anna's car drew up behind the police car. It rattled to a halt. After a moment, Anna stepped out. She did not move away from the car, held the vehicle's door before her like a shield; but she took the time to let her eyes rest on everything. She raised one foot, tucked an ankle behind her, balancing it on the car's rusting door-sill. The policemen's eyes slid like snakes over Amy Glasse, her creased homemade cotton skirt and her breasts bouncing beneath the stained white cloth. 'Fuck off out of here, Purvis,' she said. 'You were here last week and into everything, so what the fuck do you want now?'

Ralph put his hand out, to take Amy's wrist. 'Calm down. It's nothing. They want me, not you.'

Amy's eyes travelled: to Purvis, to Ralph's face, to Anna still as a statue in the fading light.

I have lost track of the time, Ralph thought; I should have been home an hour ago. Anna, without a word, climbed back into the car and drove away.

When the police had given their news, and driven away in their turn – their eyes roaming around the farmyard and outbuildings – Ralph said to Amy, 'I must go right now. You understand, don't you? I have to go to Norwich and sort this out.'

'Of course you must go.' Her smile was twisted, bleak. 'Then you've your wife to face.'

'Yes. That will be later.'

'I'll not be seeing you, then?'

He didn't reply. 'We've seen it on the television,' she said. 'Me and Sandra. Men always go back to their wives.'

'I'll see you tomorrow.' He felt shaky, weak; was not sure whether he was lying or not. 'Unless I'm at the hospital, that is. There'll be all sorts of people I have to talk to – social workers, and her parents if she's really ill, and my own people, the Trust committee, because if there's any possible legal problem I like them to know about it. I'll be on the phone all day.'

'Anna, she's beautiful,' Amy said. 'Sandra didn't tell me. I had no idea. I thought she was some biddy in a print frock.'

'I can't talk about it. I haven't time. I'll be back as soon as I can.'

'I'll not count on it,' Amy said. Her voice was light and bright. She was fighting back tears. Ralph felt inside him a great rolling mass of nausea and cold, of apprehension and self-hatred.

At a phone-box on the outskirts of Fakenham, he stopped the car and rang his home. He calculated that Anna would just have arrived; if she were walking in, he thought, that would be best, that would be the best time to get her.

He let the phone ring for a long time. He checked his watch

again. She should be home by now. Where would she go, except the Red House?

As he was about to replace the receiver, he heard it picked up. 'Anna? Anna, are you there?' Silence. 'Please speak to me.' Silence. 'I'm going to Norwich,' he said. 'I have to. To the hospital. I'll call again from there. Anna, please . . .'

She had put the phone down. He got back in the car and drove away.

I would have spoken, she thought: I would have spoken, except that I could not think of a single thing, not one thing to say. She went into the kitchen and made herself some instant coffee. She drank it standing up, by the sink. Then she washed her cup. There was a long night ahead, and she would be alone. Robin was playing in a school match, he would not be back, he was staying over in King's Lynn. Julian, she supposed, was at the farm; and she had sent her daughters away. She dried her hands, folded the towel, laid it over the back of a chair.

It is in the nature of betrayal, she thought, that it not only changes the present, but that it reaches back with its dirty hands and changes the past.

She could not be still. She wandered through the rooms, then returned to the kitchen to make herself some more coffee. She sat at the table, trying to subdue her ragged breathing. She got up and went to the sink again. She saw from the kitchen clock that only half an hour had passed since she put the phone down on Ralph. You cannot pass the time like this, she thought: washing your cup and washing your cup.

Darkness had fallen. Autumn would choose a day like this, to announce its presence: stealthy feet, chilling the rooms. Ralph had lit the boiler this morning, but she had forgotten to attend to it. A major salvage operation would be needed now. She felt she did not have the strength for it. She took a blanket from the airing cupboard and walked downstairs with it gathered about her, African-style. She went into the sitting room. Did not put on the light. Chose herself a chair. She wrapped the blanket around her and pulled it almost over her head. She was swaddled now, like an ambulance casualty.

There had been times before, when she had thought they could not survive. There had been times when she had wished to erase her husband and children, her whole biography. There had not been a day, in twenty years, when she had not thought about her lost child. Sometimes on the television – they often watched the ten o'clock news together – they had seen the parents of missing children, shaking, bleating, heads sagging: making what was called an appeal, trying to wring some killer's heart. No such appeal had been open to her. They had left the corpse behind, in another country. The verdict was final. When you have suffered together as she had, she and Ralph, what lies between you can't be called romance. You can't talk about a marriage, in the normal terms people use: a happy marriage, a marriage under strain. You are not partners, but the survivors of a disaster. You see each other and remember, every day. So how can you live together?

But how can you not?

She fingered the blanket's satin-bound edge, and sat, apart from this fingering, without moving. When the room grew quite dark she put a hand out of her wrappings and switched on a lamp which stood by her on a round table. This table had a white cloth, on which Sandra Glasse had embroidered a scatter of daisies, violet and deep blue, their centres black like poppies: fantasy flowers, bouquets from an alternative world. Ralph said that every action contained its opposite. That nothing was fixed, nothing in creation; that cells made choices all the time. If we could rewind the tape of the universe, play it over again, we might find ourselves to be different: six-legged intelligent creatures, crawling on the seabed, and speaking like birds, in song. But no, she thought, perhaps that is not what Ralph says. Perhaps I have got it wrong, he would be talking to the children and I would not be listening properly, that is usually the case with me. Have I not imagined, often enough, a universe in which other choices were made? The girl, Felicia, we turned out of the house. Some instinct warned me, so that night I kept my son in my arms. Or, Ralph took no pity on the wanderers in the storm, kept the bolts drawn, the key turned in the lock. She shivered. She felt closer to that night, now, than she did to the light and air of this morning: to the sea wind and coastal showers, the truculent girl in the back seat of the car, Kit with her hair streaming about her as she ran calling for Melanie through the streets.

The telephone rang, in the next room. She did not stir. It would be Emma, perhaps, wanting to know what was happening. Or Ralph, calling from the hospital. She still had nothing to say to him, so what was the point of answering? She withdrew her hand into the safety of her blanket. An hour passed. The phone rang again. It was raining outside, and now the house was very cold. Anna thought of nothing at all. Her ideas seemed to have stopped, as if chilled and narrow conduits no longer carried blood to heart and brain.

Very late – it must have been towards midnight – she heard the doorbell. She sat listening; someone had a finger pressed on it, insistent. Ralph would have his key, so would the children. Emma? She pulled the blanket around her. She did not want to see Ralph's sister. Emma had a key for emergencies, but who was to know what she would consider an emergency? The person was knocking now, thudding at the door.

The police again? That's possible. She could not ignore the noise. She extricated herself from the blanket. Her legs felt stiff. She fumbled for the light switch in the hall. 'I'm coming,' she called. 'Don't break down the door.' Her voice sounded peculiar, precarious. She opened the door.

'Anna? Kit telephoned me from her aunt's.'

He was the last person she had expected. 'Daniel, come in from the night.' Rain blew in with him. 'What did Kit tell you?'

'About the young girl you have staying. And that the police came. That you had gone off after them to find Ralph. You did find him, I suppose.'

'So Kit knew.'

'Had an idea.'

'A shrewd one, I'll bet. And Julian would know of course, and Robin, I suppose. And you, now. The whole county, soon.'

'No, Anna, it's nothing like that.'

She began to fasten her hair up; saw herself dimly in the hall-stand mirror. 'I used to laugh at Ralph because he went on for years without knowing about Emma and your father. Now the laugh's on me, isn't it?'

'Believe me, I knew nothing,' Daniel said. 'Not until to-day. When Kit telephoned I found it hard to take in. Ralph, I mean . . . it doesn't seem possible.' He looked down at his shoes. How young he is, Anna thought. A boy.

'And Kit asked you to come here, did she?'

'She wants to come home herself, but she promised you she'd stay and look after Becky. Becky's asking all sorts of questions, but Emma can deal with that.'

Questions suitable to her time of life, Anna thought. Between us, we will have to come up with some suitable answers. 'Yes, I made Kit promise to stay at Foulsham . . . you see, I can't face anybody.' She looked up at him. 'I have to prepare myself, Daniel. I have to think out what I am going to say.'

'I don't think you should stay here on your own. Have you . . . I mean, Ralph, has he been in touch?'

'The phone's been ringing. I didn't answer it.'

'He's probably still at the hospital. Kit would like to know how the child is.'

'I don't care,' Anna said.

'Don't you?'

'No. I've had enough of all that.'

'Yes, I can understand. But you're doing yourself an injustice.'

'Oh, I'm not good, Daniel. I'm not a good woman. Not at all.'

Daniel hesitated. 'It – your standard of goodness, Anna – I think it would defeat most of us.'

'Oh, my standard, yes. But what I live up to, that's another question.'

Daniel became brisk. 'Have you eaten? No, of course not. The house seems very cold. I think I ought to try to track down Ralph. The hospital's number, do you have it? They could find him and bring him to a phone. You don't have to speak to him. I'll do it. Just to see what the situation is, what his immediate intentions are.'

'Don't bother.' She turned away. 'As for the child – I've told you, I don't want to know. Year after year he's inflicted these dreadful children upon me, awful, hopeless children –' She stopped. 'He will come home. Eventually.' She leaned against Daniel. He put an arm around her. She began to cry. 'I can't face him. I feel ashamed. It's as if it's me who's done something wrong. I won't be able to look him in the eye.'

'Then you don't need to stay here. Let me drive you over to Blakeney.'

'To Ginny's? Oh no, it's late . . . and besides . . .'

'She wouldn't ask you questions, you know.'

'Daniel, how can you believe that?'

'I'm an optimist.' he said. His face looked grim, as if he were

308

ageing in a night. 'Come back to my flat, then. Just bring what you need for now. I've got a spare bed. I'll make you comfortable.'

'Yes, take me to your flat. I want to be gone before Ralph gets here. I must be.' She moved slowly back down the hall. 'I'll be five minutes.'

As she packed her toothbrush, nightdress, a change of clothes, she remembered the policewoman, standing over her in Elim: telling her what she would need. She should have a policewoman now; directionless, enfeebled, her hands moved among her possessions. She heard Daniel downstairs, talking on the telephone. 'No, Kit, I don't think she should come there to you, she'd have to think of something to say to Becky, she can't face it . . . Just you and Emma hang on for now, can you? . . . It's very late, we're all tired, tomorrow things will be . . . Yes, to Blakeney, why not? If she still feels she must keep away from Ralph.'

They are making arrangements for me behind my back, she thought. As if I were a sick or injured person. Which I am, of course. She had an image of herself and Ralph, two sick or injured animals yoked together: dragging their burden, sometimes in circles.

In the car she began to cry. The lanes were dark, the trees dripping, puddles shining in their headlights; the half-hour journey seemed a lifetime. Holt was deserted: a few shopfronts dimly lit, the pub doors bolted. Daniel parked his car, walked around it to help her out. She needed the help; slumped against him, leaned on his arm. 'It's clearing,' he said, looking up at the sky.

'Yes.' She scrubbed at her face. Tried to smile.

Daniel unlocked his door and flooded the night world with a vast, white, hard light. She climbed a steep staircase, seeing the phantom outlines of drawing boards through a glass door. 'Up to the top,' Daniel said.

'You are being very kind to me.'

'It's nothing, Anna.'

The staircase opened into a large and lofty room, sparely furnished: the walls of exposed flint, the timbers exposed, the floor bare and waxed: its expanse broken only by two dark fringed rugs, their design geometric, their colours sombre. Flying carpets, she thought. No clutter anywhere, just those matt black machines that young men have: no windows, but skylights enclosing the weather and the night. Anna stood considering it. 'Kit never told me about this.'

'A way of being outside when you're inside. Kit hardly comes here.'

'True. I know.'

'Do you like it?'

'Very much.' A life free of complexity, she thought. 'Can you keep it warm?'

'Not easily. Can't have everything. Would you like to bathe your face?' She nodded. She sat on the sofa, and he brought her a bowl of water, some cotton-wool, and a small cream towel. He sat down next to her, as if she must be supervised. 'Lukewarm water is best,' he advised. 'If you have ice, it makes your eyes swell even more.'

'I'm sorry, Daniel,' she said.

'Nothing to be sorry for. Better to cry among friends. Look, Anna – all this, with Ralph, it's ridiculous. An aberration.'

'You think so?'

'I know it is. Just one of those things that happen in marriages.'

'The marriages of middle-aged people, you mean.'

'Look, everything is easier to face in daylight.' He ventured a smile; took from her fingertips one of the sodden balls of cotton-wool. 'In the morning you can have your choice. The greengrocer will be open, so you can have cucumber slices for your eyes. Or tea-bags, if you like. I have Earl Grey, Assam or Darjeeling.'

'Goodness. What a lot you know about female grief.'

'My mother, you see.'

'Since your father died?'

'Mainly before. Years before – always, really. We'd be alone in the house and she'd cry buckets. Horse-troughs. Oceans. So,' he said, with a soft bleakness, 'I'm used to comforting.'

She looked up. 'You mean . . . this, it would be when your father was with Emma?'

'Where else?'

'She always appeared – I don't know – so self-possessed.'

'Yes. Of course, the tea-bags helped. The cucumber slices. And the fact that she's got a nice sort of flippancy, my mother, a sort of veneer of stupidity. So you wouldn't know – why should anybody know? Emma broke my mother's heart.'

She took his hand. After a while he said, 'Brandy, that's the next thing. Can you drink brandy? It will warm your heart, Anna.'

He gave her a glass. It did warm her, stealing through to feelings, levels of comprehension, she had not known were there. 'It would be nice to get drunk,' she said. 'I don't think I ever have. I see the attraction, though.'

'The bottle's at your elbow.'

'One doesn't know . . . one doesn't know other people's histories at all.'

'No, of course not. Not the half of what goes on.'

'I feel I have been stupid.'

'You were misled. People do mislead you, don't they, they have an instinct to cover up the mess. It's how we're taught to live. I've always thought, or rather my concern is, that history shouldn't repeat itself. I've thought, I don't want to marry some poor girl who I'll end up leaving for Kit.'

Anna tried to answer him, but the effort was almost beyond her. 'I'm exhausted,' she said flatly.

'It's emotion. It is exhausting. I dare say that's why we try to get by without it.'

He helped her up. Her legs were jelly. He took her into the little spare room. 'The bed's made up. Do you want anything?'

'I'll be fine.'

He touched her cheek. 'You should know, Anna, that Kit's going to Africa. She had a letter, she says, this morning. Some volunteer project has accepted her. She wants to see the place where she was born.'

Anna shuddered.

'I know,' he said. 'Emma's put me wise.'

She looked up. 'Wise. And Kit? Has Emma put her wise?'

'That's more than I can say. In the circumstances it would be very wrong of me to make assumptions about what other people know or don't know.' He paused. 'I think, Anna – for what it's worth – that you are a very brave woman.'

She shook her head. 'My heart failed me, Daniel. I had to be rescued from myself. And my kindness has failed me, many a time. I've harboured such thoughts – I couldn't tell you, thoughts that there are no ordinary words for. Only this thing – with Ralph – I don't deserve it. I know I don't.'

He left her to put on her nightdress. She promised that if she could not sleep she would come for him. We can see the dawn together, he said. She eased herself into the narrow bed. He had put two hot-water bottles in it, one for her feet and one for her to hug to herself, burning her ribs, slapping and washing itself against her. The Red House is empty, she thought: for the first time in years. And she had not slept in such a little bed since she had been in prison.

There was another skylight above her, its glass containing the night. Oh, Daniel, she breathed, I might see the stars. She was afraid she had spoken out loud; but she was past that, too tired to have a voice at all. Her heart hammered, but then lay still: obedient creature. She turned on her back. The blankets were heavy; she pushed them back a little, to free her chest with its great weight of misery. The air was clearing, it was true; still, she was looking up through a veil of water. She saw two stars, then more. Very faint, old stars: light attenuated.

Kit woke her. She brought a tray with a glass of orange juice and a pot of coffee.

'Daniel promised me cucumber slices.' Anna said.

'You need them. You look awful.'

'What do you expect?'

'It's ten o'clock. What would you like to do?'

Anna pushed herself upright in the bed. 'What are the choices?'

'You could go home. I understand if you don't want to. Daniel had to go and see a client, there was an appointment he couldn't break. You can stay here, you're welcome, he says. You can go to Emma. She's very worried about you.'

'I seem to be homeless.'

'Not at all,' Kit said. She thought, it's everyone else who is homeless, waiting for what will occur.

'Robin will be back, you know? Maybe five or six o'clock. He won't know what's happening.'

'I can intercept him. Don't worry about that.' Kit seemed impatient. 'Worry about yourself. What do you want to do?'

'What do I want to do? With the glorious prospect that stretches before me?'

'Dad rang. Last night. Said he was calling you but you wouldn't answer. He was very upset, very concerned about you.'

'A bit late for that.'

'Melanie's going to be OK, they're pretty sure, but they're keeping her for a few days, because she still won't say what it was she took. Dad spent the night at the hospital.'

'At the hospital, did he? That was blameless, at any rate.'

Kit blushed. She looked stern, set. 'How can you?'

'What?'

'Make these weak sarcastic little jokes?'

'I don't know how I can. Do you happen to know your father's programme for the day?'

'He's got a lot of calls to make.'

'He'll want his office, then. To be at home.'

Kit sat down on the bed. The tray wobbled; she put out a hand to steady it. The coffee cooled in its pot. 'You think we've let you down, don't you?' she asked. 'By not telling you?'

Anna didn't reply. Kit said, 'We would have told you. But it was too difficult. We couldn't think of the right words.'

'Yes, I understand.' Anna sounded sad, remote, resigned. 'It explains some things, though. This summer we've had.'

Some things, Kit thought, but not that uprush of strange fear. Who knows where a crisis comes from? The world should be more predictable. 'Let me pour your coffee,' she said.

'I'd be sick,' Anna said. 'How can you ask me to eat and drink?'

'Look, you must fight for him.'

'What? Like a dog with a bone?'

'No, but you must let it be known – let it be known that –' Kit pushed her hand back through her hair.

'Oh, Kit,' Anna said. 'Don't talk about what you don't understand.'

'What will you do?'

'Go and see Ginny,' she said, unexpectedly.

Ginny's house was a low, sprawling complex of buildings –

boathouses once, no doubt – by Blakeney Quay. It had been built for Ginny and Felix by a local firm, and its additions and extensions had been crafted with reverence for the vernacular; but its most startling feature was a huge picture window of staring, blank plate-glass, which looked out over the creek to the invisible sea.

This window was one of the great acts of Ginny's life. Some women die and leave only their children as memorial; but Ginny, like some anointed saint, would have a window. It represented a moral choice, an act of courage. Some would shudder at it, though secretly they would crave the vista. Questions of taste would cow them: questions of vulgarity, even. Ginny simply said, 'Why live at Blakeney, if you don't have the view?'

Mid-morning, Ginny began to issue large drinks. When her hands were unoccupied, without a glass or a cigarette, she rubbed them nervously together, so that her rings clashed and chimed: her engagement ring with its grey solitaire, her broad yellow wedding ring, the 'eternity rings', studded with chips of sapphire and ruby, that Felix had given her at a constant rate through the years. She was never without these rings; perhaps, Anna thought, she used them from time to time to deliver a scarring blow. But Felix had never appeared scarred. She remembered his handsome, bland, betraying face.

'I've heard,' Anna said, 'of women who came home to find a note on the table. Until then, they had no inkling.'

'Had you an inkling?'

Anna smoothed her hair back. It was very smooth already. Ginny thought, she seems to be the one in charge here.

'As I see it,' Ginny said, 'you have three courses before you. When you choose which to take, you must bear in mind that this affair of his will very likely not last.' Anna raised an eyebrow. 'Oh, you know my situation,' Ginny said. 'It was different with me. Felix and Emma, they were old flames.'

'You don't have to talk about it.'

'Why else are you here?' Ginny lit another cigarette. 'Really, Anna, I don't mind. I know you're here because – well, whatever did Daniel tell you?'

'He gave me a version of your life that was different from the one I knew. I'm sorry. It is an intrusion on your privacy.'

'Bugger that,' Ginny said. 'It's a relief to talk about it. More gin?'

'Why not? Ralph's not here to see me.'

'He stopped you drinking?'

'Not exactly. It was more the weight of tradition. Our families. And his uncle, Holy James, the total abstainer. Who'd seen otherwise competent missionaries go out to the tropics and be pickled in spirits within the decade.'

'Yes, I remember James – whatever happened to him?'

'He went abroad again. Back to Africa. After, you know . . . a year or two after we came home.'

'But he was old! Wasn't he?'

'Yes.'

'And then?'

'He died.'

'Of course. Well . . .' Ginny breathed smoke. 'You see, with Ralph, you've been married all these years, and now you're in a position to renegotiate. I say it won't last, because they don't – these affairs between men of fifty, and young girls.'

'She's hardly that.'

Ginny looked hard at her. 'Comparatively.'

'Oh yes – comparatively.'

'You see, there's a pattern to it. These men of fifty – they never fall for women of their own age, you notice. It's always someone who makes them feel young.'

'How comforting to be part of a pattern,' Anna said. 'I always wanted to be.' It struck her, then, that Ginny did not know the course of her life, not in any detailed way; that if she had ever known, she had forgotten it. 'But Mrs Glasse,' she said. 'I haven't an idea of what her attractions might be. And so, I have no idea how to combat them.' She picked up her drink. 'Well now, Ginny, you said there were three courses I could take.'

'Yes. Bearing in mind that it won't last, you can negotiate with him. You can ask him to live with you and let him see her when he wants. That may prolong the agony – it did for me. Or, you can let him stay with her for the while, and sit it out – keep your home and finances intact, and prepare for a return to normal on the day he says he wants to come back.' Ginny ground her cigarette out. 'Or, of course, you can give him the push.'

Anna shook her head. 'I'm not patient, Ginny. I couldn't sit it out. What do you do, while you're sitting it out?'

Ginny reached for another cigarette, flipped it into her mouth. 'This,' she said. She flicked a nail at her glass. 'And this. Alternatively, you can count your blessings. Think of people less fortunate than yourself. Cripples.' She smiled. 'Women who work in launderettes.'

TEN

The child had been scraped up off the streets. She was drowsy and confused, her speech slurred, her eyes unfocused. Her mouth was bleeding. She hadn't a penny to her name.

She remembered jabbing a fist out at some woman who leaned over her; it was a face she didn't know, and that was enough to provoke her. Then the rocking motion of a vehicle, an interval of nothing: and a rush of light and air that hit her – like a drench of cold water – as they carried her from the ambulance into casualty. She bent her arm and laid it over her eyes, to protect herself from this brightness and cold; a nurse saw the scars on her inner arm. 'What's this?' she said. 'Silly girl!'

That was how they talked to her. As if she were two years old and yet at the same time a piece of filth off the street, something they had got on their shoes. They shook her to try to keep her awake, to make her talk. They tried to keep her eyes open. This tortured her, and she didn't know why they wanted to do it. She wanted just to slump on the hard hospital trolley, to melt into it: to give way, to give way to the covering darkness, to pull over her head the blanket of death. 'What was it?' they shouted. 'Tell us what you've taken. You silly girl! Nobody can help you if you don't help yourself.'

Their voices were very loud and hard, the edges of their words shivered and blurred; but she could hear whispers too, nurses talking behind screens. 'I never could have patience with suicides.'

Her head lolled. To buy some peace for herself she gave them the address — or an idea of the address — at first able only to describe a house set in fields, with many staircases and people, many huts and sheds and small buildings around it, so that they said, 'Some kind of camp, could it be?' and for a while there was a respite. A policewoman in uniform appeared at the end of the bed. When she saw this she tried to climb out. 'Your drip!' a nurse yelled, and another nurse and the policewoman dumped her back into the bed and held her there while they rearranged the stand and the tube they had put in her arm.

'Why don't you let us help you?' the nurse said. 'Just your name, my dear.' But there was no love in the words, no my dear about it.

'Where's my clothes?' she said.

'Why? You don't want them. You're not going anywhere, are you?'

'That T-shirt's not mine,' she said. 'That pink top, it doesn't belong to me. You had no right to take it.'

She meant to say that they had done wrong, double-wrong, taking from her what she didn't even own.

But one thought disconnected itself, unplugged itself from the next, and her words slid out through bubbles of spittle that she felt at the corner of her mouth but was too weak to wipe away. One of the nurses mopped her mouth for her, with an abrupt efficient swipe: as if she were not aware that her lips were part of a living being. Suddenly, memory flooded her; this is what it is like to be a baby. You are a collection of parts, not a person, just a set of bones in flesh, your hands grasping and your mouth sucking and gaping; you are a collection of troubles, of piss and dribble and shit.

Her mouth stretched open for air. She was sick; she was sick and sick and sick. First on the blanket, which they dragged away from her legs, then in a metal bowl which she held herself, so hard that the rim dug into her fingers. The nurses stood by approving of this, of the awful corrosive fluid that poured out, the stained water and yellow bile.

For a time after that she lay back stiffly, her arms wrapped across her body. Perhaps she slept. Then the door opened, rousing her, and Mr Eldred came in. He stood at the end of her bed without speaking, just looking at her. She looked at him back for a minute, then turned her head away. There was a crack in the plaster of the wall. She studied it. Eventually he spoke. 'Oh, Melanie,' he said. 'Whatever next?'

Sometimes she woke up and the man was there. Sometimes she slept. Sometimes she woke up and he was not there. She shouted to a nurse – her voice surprising her, issuing from her mouth like some flapping, broken-winged pigeon – and asked where he had gone, and a nurse said, 'He has more than you to attend to, Miss.'

She raised her hand, the one without the drip, and scrubbed her wrist back and forth across her forehead. She looked down at her legs, lying like dead white sticks; her body was hot and clammy, so she kicked the covers off, and then, tight-lipped, they dragged them back again. 'Look, I want to talk to you,' she shouted to a nurse, but as soon as she started to talk she began to cry, a wailing sort of crying she'd never done before, which hurt her throat and made her have to blow her nose, and made her breath stick in her throat as if it were something she'd swallowed, a bone. 'Please,' the nurse said. 'Do you think you're the only patient we have to attend to? Have some consideration for others – please!'

The thing it was necessary to say was where she'd got the T-shirt from; that she'd taken it out of a basket in the bathroom, where somebody had said dirty clothes went, but that was all the same to her, all her clothes were neither clean nor dirty but just what she wore, and it seemed to her the ones in the basket

320

were just that, clothes. When the policewoman came back, she tried to explain it to her. 'Not out of her bedroom,' she said. 'I never went in there.'

The woman frowned. 'I'm sorry, darling, I don't know what you're on about. What T-shirt is this, then?'

'Shoplifting,' a nurse breathed. 'I'll just bet you.'

'Look, just don't go on about it,' the policewoman said. 'All right? I'm sure it'll just be forgotten about, if you don't keep on.'

Behind the screens the nurse said, 'As if that were all she had to concern herself about.'

'She had a bag of clothes,' the policewoman explained. 'New ones. That'll be it. Couple of hours before she collapsed somebody saw her selling them.'

'Well, where did she get them from, you wonder? And did nobody do anything about it?'

'You see all sorts of things on the streets,' the policewoman said. 'The first thing you learn in this job is to expect no assistance from passers-by.'

Time passed; she could not guess how much. The nights were bright and full of action, full of squeaking wheels in the corridors and the squeaking of shoes as nurses ran. Days were indistinguishable. She didn't know the day of the week, not that she ever had. They put her in a side room, said, 'I should say you're privileged, Miss.' She heard diagnoses, part-diagnoses of her condition. Can't or won't eat. Can't or won't remember. Their voices were hard and bright, like knives.

She heard nurses gossiping, talking about an abortion, one that had breathed. Her own breathing became painfully tight, as if she were trying not to draw attention to herself, trying not to take up space. In the hospital there were sluices and incinerators. She lay in the ward's half-day, half-night, deciding when and how to run.

★

321

Ralph drove to Blakeney. Ginny let him in, twittering nervously and offering him a drink. 'I don't think so,' he said. 'I'd like to talk to Anna alone, I suppose that's all right with you?'

Ginny waved him towards her drawing room. The shock of the vast window: the grey day flooded in, its monochromes intermingled, the dun mud of the creek and the shiver of gulls' wings.

Anna sat with her back to the light. She was wearing a grey dress, and he noticed it because it was not hers; it was too short, too narrow, and even as he came in she was pulling at its neckline, straining it away from her white throat. Seeing him, she let her hand settle on her thigh. 'I hardly recognize you,' he said.

'We have that in common.' He understood that she had been crying. Her voice was coarsened, blurred, at her elbow was a glass of dissolving ice.

At first, she didn't speak. The moment spun itself out. Her eyes rested on his face. Then she spoke all at once, in a rush.

'Ralph, I want you to know that I don't want anything. The house, everything, you can have it. At first — last night — I didn't think that. I thought, this woman, whatever backwoods berry-picking life she's been leading, I don't want her to improve her position at my expense. But now I realize —'

'Anna, you're exhausted,' he said.

'Yes. But I think now, what's the point, what's the point of hanging on?'

'You give me up, Anna?'

'What choice have I?'

'Every choice.'

'Every choice? I don't think you will indulge me while I consider them.'

'It's not a matter of indulgence. You have every choice. Trust me.'

'You have no right to ask that, Ralph. Of all the things you could ask, you have least right to trust.'

He nodded. 'I see that. I suppose I meant, trust me for the sake of the past, not the present.'

'I shall have to go back home for a little while. A few weeks. To work out where I am going to go after that, and what's to happen about a school for Rebecca. So what I want – I want to make this agreement with you –'

'Anna, this is not what I meant.' Ralph was panic-stricken. 'You can't just – re-invent yourself like this, people don't do it. I thought we should sit and talk –'

'Too much of that,' Anna said. 'So much talk, but here we are.' Again her hand went to her throat, trying to pull the neckline of Ginny's dress away from her skin. 'I want to make this agreement. That you will come home and get your things and do it all at once. I mean that you should get yourself organized and move out. I don't want sordid to-ing and fro-ing with suitcases.'

'So that's the decision you have made?'

'That's the first decision I have made.'

Ralph looked away. 'I wish you would get back into your own clothes.'

'I didn't bring any.'

'Why did you come here?'

'Ginny's a friend.'

'Ginny is pernicious.'

'Oh – because she gave me a drink, and a dress to wear?'

'This is childish. A childish conversation.'

'True. And you, of course, are acting like a mature man.'

'You must not think,' Ralph said, 'you must not think that this was some stupid fling.'

'Oh, wasn't it? I see, I do see. Your emotions were engaged, were they? Your poor little emotions.' That first rush of energy had died out of Anna's voice; it was low, toneless now. 'Then let me congratulate you. You've found the love of your life, have you? Well, go to her then. Quick about it!'

'I don't want to go. I want you to forgive me, if you can. That's what I came here to ask you, but you didn't give me a chance.'

She shook her head. 'Ginny has been talking me through it, a woman's options. A woman in middle life, whose husband flits off to something more juicy. But I don't feel that I can consider these options, I feel that I'm not going to sit in the house, waiting and hoping. I have done it before, and I'm tired of it.'

Ralph sprung up from his chair. He wanted to cross the room to her, but he did not dare. 'I'm not asking you to wait. Or hope. Or anything. Just talk to me, let's talk it through. I wanted to explain my feelings –'

'Why should you think I might want them explained?'

'Because it is usual. In a marriage. To talk about feelings.'

'Oh yes. Perhaps. *In* a marriage.'

'Listen to me,' Ralph said. 'There is nothing to be gained by bandying words and freezing me out. I wanted to tell you what had happened, I wanted to be truthful with you – and if you can't forgive me now, which I well understand, I wanted to go away with the hope that you might forgive me – in time.'

'I'm no good at forgiving.' She looked down at her nails. 'Don't you know that? It doesn't matter if the action is to be deferred. I can't do it. The years pass and they don't make a difference. I know, you see. Because I've been betrayed before.'

'It's useless, then,' he said. 'If you will insist on seeing this as some kind of continuation or extension of what happened to us twenty years ago.'

'All my life has been a continuation of it.' She raised her eyes. 'I know you have put it behind you. You have been able to say, let us not hate, we are reasonable people. Even though what happened was not reasonable. Even though it was barbaric and foul.' She put her hand to her throat again. They had hanged Felicia.

'You were not the only person betrayed,' he said. 'I was betrayed too.'

'Not so much. After all, you opened the door to them.'

'Yes. Is it the action of a human being, to throw that in my face now?'

'There is no limit to what human beings will do. We know that, don't we? There is no depth to which human beings won't sink. And I've never claimed to be more than human. Though you would have appreciated it, if I had been.'

He looked as if the breath had been knocked out of him. Sat down on one of Ginny's fringed Dralon armchairs; on the edge. Wiped his hand across his face.

When evening came Anna and Ginny put on their coats and went to walk by the quay. The water was flat, motionless. The small boats were perched on it, like toys on a steel shelf.

'How are you now?' Anna asked her. 'About Felix?'

'You mean him dying?'

She really is faintly stupid, Anna thought. 'Yes, that's what I mean.'

'Well, you get to a stage where you don't think about it every day,' Ginny said. 'At least, so I'm told. I haven't reached it yet.'

Anna saw the bulk of the Blakeney Hotel, a ship of flint, bobbing at the quayside and showing its lights. She heard the evening complaints of cattle from the salt marshes, and the competing snicker of sheep. She said, 'I don't understand this thing about forgiveness, Ginny. You hear about these people in Ireland. Their husband's been shot, or their children blown apart. And you have some woman propped up before the cameras, saying oh, I forgive the terrorists. Why forgive them? I don't.'

'I thought you were religious,' Ginny said: her tone careful, distant.

'I'm barely a Christian. Never was.'

Somewhere in Ginny's mind a door opened, just a crack; was there not some story, long ago, about a dead child?

'Why don't we drop in to the hotel for a drink?' she said.

'A drink, for a change!' Anna said. 'Yes, why not?'

They sat in the bar for half an hour, sipping gin among pseudo-mariners. Evening light on blazer buttons: early diners tripping in to their shellfish and game. 'I could ask if they had a table,' Ginny said.

Anna shook her head. 'It would be a waste. I couldn't eat. And I hate to waste food.'

'I'll make us an egg then, shall I? A nice scrambled egg, or would you prefer it boiled?'

'Whatever,' Anna said. Widow's food, she thought; food for women alone, for their pale little appetites. Who cares if the flesh drops from their bones, if the light fades from their eyes?

Ginny said, 'Be careful, Anna. You're fifty.'

'Whatever do you mean, I'm fifty?'

'I mean you might lose everything, if you don't put up a fight.'

Anna sat eating peanuts from a glass dish, looking out at the mud flats. 'Tomorrow I must go back to the Red House,' she said. 'Everything must be faced.'

Foulsham: 'Both our parents have run away from home,' Rebecca said. 'I'll have to come and live with you, Emma.'

'Your mother telephoned, my dear. She'll be back in the morning. She wants you not to worry, she says she knows you're a grown-up sensible girl – and soon everything will be explained.' Somehow, Emma added under her breath.

'Till then Kit has to be a mother to me. And Robin has to be my father.'

'That's a very nice way to think of it,' Emma said admiringly. 'But it's really only for one night, you know. And you can stay with me if you like.'

'People who run away never go for long, do they?' Rebecca's face was bright, avid, sharp with fear. 'That girl who was here, Melanie. She used to run away all the time, Dad said. But people caught her. The police.'

She is too young for her age, Emma thought; they've kept her that way, her brothers and her capable sister, even with all the Visitors they get, even with all that's happened under that roof, each summer's tribulations: 'It's not the same when people are grown-up,' she said. 'You see, they have to make their own decisions about where to live. And sometimes it happens . . .' Emma shut her eyes tight. What must I tell her? She felt weary. Perhaps it is premature to say anything, she thought, perhaps in some way the row will blow over. She remembered Anna's voice on the telephone: obdurate, balanced on the steely edge of tears. They've been married for twenty-five years, Emma thought; can it fall apart in a night?

But what do I know about marriage?

Rebecca said, 'When Dad comes home I'm going to ask him if we can have a donkey to live in the garden. He'll say no, certainly not, but I'll keep following him round saying "Donkey, donkey, donkey", till he gets tired and says yes all right then if you must.'

'Is that how you usually get your way?'

'You have to ask,' Rebecca said. 'Don't ask and you don't get. Did you know Julian came home?'

'No. Did he? When?'

'He came like a highwayman at dead of night. Two nights ago, or three, I don't remember. He came climbing up – there's a way the boys get in, you know, like burglars?'

'I didn't know.'

'Oh, they've always done it. Kit says it's to show off and they could just as well come in by the door.'

'So didn't your mum and dad see Julian?'

'No. He stayed in Kit's room. Robin came down. They had a very serious talk.'

'Where were you?'

'I was sitting on the stairs with my ears flapping.'

'And what did you hear?'

'I don't know.' She jerked her head away, and began to cry. 'I couldn't understand,' she said. 'I had a dream, that I was on my own in the house.'

Emma said, 'It wasn't a dream, was it, Becky? You mean that's what you're afraid of.'

'Yes. Because what if they all go, what if everybody runs away? Jule's gone already. And Kit said she was going to go to Africa.'

Emma drew the child against her. 'Becky, put your arms around me. Take hold of me very tight. I'm here, aren't I? Don't I feel solid to you? Do I feel as if I'll run away? No one will leave you in the house alone.'

There was no more she could say. She was incoherent with love for the child and anger at Ralph and dismay at what had overtaken them. At the beginning of summer, she thought, never in my wildest dreams could I have imagined such a thing; but then that's perhaps the problem, my dreams have never been wild enough. I don't understand what drives people, who does? I don't understand the process by which our lives have unravelled. Why this year, and not other years? Because they are growing up, I suppose, and there had to be a turning point; Ralph met this woman, spoke to her no doubt of certain things, and after that everything must change. When a secret has been kept for twenty years, reality has been built around it, in a special way: it is a carapace, it is a safe house. When the walls have been pulled down and the secret has been let out, even to one person, then it's no good trying to rebuild the walls to the same plan – they are walls to hold in nothing. Life must change, it will, it has to.

She wondered about going to the coast to see this woman, Mrs Glasse. Pleading with her in some way. She would be laughed at, of course.

'We ought to be spared this scene,' Amy Glasse said.

'Yes.' Usual kinds of words came tumbling out of Ralph's mouth, lines that she could swear she had heard on the television. For the sake of the children I really feel . . . Ah yes, comedy half-hour, she thought.

She said, 'You look weary, my dear.'

'Yes. I seem to be on the road all the time, driving about between one place and another.' He had spent the best part of a night – by far the best part – sitting at Melanie's bedside, while she dipped in and out of the conversations that were held around her, picking and mixing as she liked. Nobody had filled in the missing hours, and so they would keep her in hospital till they were sure there was no delayed liver damage from anything she might have taken. What was most likely, given the limited means at her disposal, was that she had been inhaling some type of volatile solvent, enough to make her almost comatose when they fetched her in; but he was aware of her history, the range and type and peculiar dosages of the various means she had used to effect escape, and his greatest concern was that her broken and incoherent conversation, her apparent thought-disorder, should be seen as a possible consequence of drug abuse and not madness. He had witnessed this before, a heavy amphetamine user become agitated, hear voices, hallucinate – and then a cell, and then a prison doctor, and then the liquid cosh: and then the inquest.

Slowly he dragged his mind back, from that sorry afternoon in court to this date and place. 'For one thing,' he said, 'I feel I would have nothing to offer you. I would probably lose my job, you see. I would have to offer my resignation to the Trust's committee. They would be obliged to accept it.'

'Hypocrites then, aren't they?' she said.

'People aren't enlightened, you know, you think they move with the times but they don't. I suppose it's that they're always looking for a stick to beat you with . . . there's the press, if it got into the papers . . . you see it's all complicated by the fact that Sandra is my son's girlfriend and they would twist the whole story around – believe me, I know about the newspapers – into something that resembled incest.'

'Sandra is your son's mistress,' she said. 'Let's get it right.'

'Yes, I know that. I can't afford to damage the Trust, because if there is a scandal it affects our fund-raising, and then if we have less money it means we must disappoint people and turn them away.'

'Are you married to Anna, or the Trust?'

'I don't know what you mean, Amy.'

He did know what she meant, of course, but he was buying time, thinking time; surely, he thought, no one could accuse me of being one of those who love mankind in general but not persons in particular? Perhaps I incline in that direction, no doubt I do, but I try to correct my fault: I love Amy, who is easy to love, and I love my children and Sandra Glasse, and I love Anna, who is another proposition and a tougher one. What person could be harder to love than Melanie, and even there I try; I have made a study of love, a science. He thought, I cannot let them admit the child to a mental hospital, because Melanie is clearly, reluctantly, spitefully sane; stupid perhaps, self-destructive, but in possession of her faculties when she is not under the influence of some dubious tablets bought on the

330

street, or cleaning fluid, or lighter fuel. If she is diagnosed as schizophrenic, or labelled as psychopathic, that will be the end of her, in effect, they may as well bury her now. But I can't take her out of hospital, I can't take her back to the Red House now Anna isn't there, and if I offer to take her back to London and dump her on Richard and the staff she'll run away again in hours, we can't keep her under lock and key, we have no authority to do it.

He looked up. There was a smell of baking from the kitchen; the need of income was constant, and no crisis would make Amy alter her schedule. She said, 'I think that if you leave me, Ralph, you must give me a proper reason.' Her voice shook. She put her hands to the back of her neck, raked her fingers upwards through her long hair, then let it fall. 'You came this spring, and I was lonely. I've been on my own for many years now. Since Andrew Glasse walked out of this house when Sandra was two years old, I've never let a man over this threshold, if I could help it. You came here; and you were kind, you were very kind to me, Ralph.'

He nodded. 'I see I had no right to be. Not in that way.'

'So you must give me a reason now. Don't give me some stupid reason about how it will be in the *News of the World*. Tell me you love your wife. Tell me a reason that makes sense. Tell me you love your wife and children and you have to protect them.'

'Anna says she will never forgive me. She wants me to move out of the house.'

'That's natural for her to say.'

'But she says that as soon as it can be arranged she is moving out herself. I can go back then, she says. The children – I don't know.'

I will lose them anyway, he thought. It's not a matter of who lives where, or what custody is sought and granted; I will lose them. I have taught them to discriminate, to know what is right and wrong and choose what is right. They will value the lesson now, and not the teacher. Because what I have done is so patently, so manifestly, so obviously, wrong. And not just wrong, but stupid. 'You ask me do I love Anna,' he said. 'It's not the right question. It goes beyond that. You see, when we met, we were children. We made an alliance against the world. Then what held us together –'

'Yes. You don't have to tell that story, ever again.' Her face was composed, he thought; pale, alight with pity. 'One telling is enough for a lifetime. Don't imagine I'll forget it.' She stood behind his chair. 'Ralph, listen to me. Look at any life – from the inside, I mean, from the point of view of the person who's living it. What is it but defeats? It's just knock-backs, one after the other, isn't it? Everybody remembers the things they did wrong. But what about the thousands and thousands and thousands of things they did right? You lost a child. And every day you think about it. But think of the children you didn't lose.'

'Nobody has ever said that to me before.'

She moved away and stood before the fireplace, putting her hands flat on the mantelpiece, at either side of the stupid ticking clock. 'Just tell me. When you said you loved me, was that a lie?' The careful blankness of her profile seemed to show that she was prepared for any answer.

'No,' he said. 'No, it wasn't.'

She let out her breath. 'It's a brute of a world, Ralph. A brute, isn't it?' She moved towards him. Her eyes had never been so pale and clear. 'Take your coat, my dear. It's time you left.'

'Sandra and Julian – where are they, do you know?'

She smiled. 'Last time I saw them they were sitting in a hedge like ragamuffins, eating blackberries.'

'They must come home. To you, or to us.'

'Sandra's got the key of a flat in Wells. It's one of the places she cleans. The landlord will let them have it cheap, till next season.'

'I don't see how they can afford it. Even cheap.'

'I suppose the Lord will provide.' She smiled tightly. For a moment she reminded him of Anna. 'But of course, he won't. I'll see they get through the winter.'

She turned away, presenting her shoulder to him. Before she turned, he read the coming winter in her face. As he was leaving she called, 'Ralph! Are you sure you don't want that old clock?'

'Nowhere to put it,' he said. I am houseless, he thought; I should have carried my house on my back. 'Be seeing you, Amy.'

Another night of rain; and then, fine windy weather. On the roads there were great standing pools, shattered by sunlight. The sun struck every spark of colour from the landscape, revivifying the trees with green, dazing the driver of the early bus; even dead wood, even fence poles, quivered with their own green life.

At ten o'clock, Anna returned to the Red House. She put her key in the door: thought, could there ever be a time when I will not do this?

She remembered how she had tried to sell the place, only a couple of years ago. It was a house with no centre, she had always felt, no room from which you could command other rooms. Sound travelled in its own way; from one of the attics, you could hear the downstairs telephone quite distinctly, but from nearer rooms it couldn't be heard at all. The house had its own conduits, sight-lines. Sometimes one of the children's friends had stayed overnight, without her knowing. She didn't make a practice of searching the rooms, scouring the cupboards and landings for fugitives or stowaways; the house would have its private life, whether she agreed or not. In the morning a parent would telephone, furious or distraught. She would say, 'Your child is here to be collected. I make no charge for bed and breakfast.' And then, oblivious to the babble on the line, she would put down the phone. She had not lived her life in a way that attracted sympathy. She had made sure of that.

Already – in the course of her small absence – the house had acquired an air of neglect. The vast hall-stand had a vast cobweb on it, and just off-centre sat a small brown spider, its legs folded modestly. Dirty plates and cups were piled in the sink. The boiler was out. 'Kit, couldn't you manage?' she said, exasperated.

'Is that all that's on your mind? Housework?'

Rebecca was tearful: Robin baffled: Julian absent: Kit hostile. Kit had heard – through Daniel, no doubt – that Ralph had been to Blakeney and had tried to patch things up. She propped a hand against the kitchen wall; her eyes were snapping and fiery. 'What can a person do?' she asked. 'Except say they were wrong, and try to put it right?'

Anna gazed at her. 'You know nothing, Kit.'

'I'm not claiming worldly experience. It's a general principle I'm talking about.'

Ralph and his daughter, she thought: their terrible moral energy, their relish for the large statement. She had been pre-occupied all her life with the particular, the minute; the neat stitching of a seam, the correctness of a turn of phrase. She had thought that life was governed in that way: by details. She had learned as a child, she thought, that details were what you offered God; you couldn't hope, in any larger way, to please Him.

'Oh, Kit.' She sat down on a kitchen chair. 'Will you make me something? Some coffee, with hot milk in it?'

The light of combat died in Kit's eyes. Docile, solid, efficient, her daughter moved: table to fridge, fridge to the Rayburn. 'Why should you forgive?' Anna said.

Without looking at her, Kit said, 'Because if you don't, it will kill you.'

Anna nodded. She knew such a thing was possible. Already she was becoming lighter, skeletal; her feet scarcely seemed to touch the ground. She had not been able to eat the little egg, the widow's meal. This morning there was a dizzying lightness at her centre, a space under her heart.

'I have always thought,' she said, 'that before there is forgiveness there must be restitution.'

Kit took the pan from the heat. She poured the milk carefully into the cup. 'So what do you want him to do?'

'It's not just him. You see, Kit, I've never forgiven anybody. I've had no practice. I don't know how to do it.'

She put her hand to her mouth, as if the secret might spill out. (Are you sick? Kit said. No, no, she said.) All summer she had felt the drag of it, dragging itself towards the light. But perhaps there are no words for it; it can express itself only through symbols, through shadows. And life has always been like this: something more than it appears. In safety, there is danger. In tears, the awful slicing comic edge. In moments of kindness and laughter, the murderer's fist at the door.

And year after year, Anna thought, I have occupied this room. I have sat at this table making shopping lists and writing letters, reading my daily paper, some faculty below consciousness alert for signs of disintegration: the sighing of the pipes and dripping of gutters, the malfunctioning squeak of ancient domestic machines, the boiler's cough and the squeak of old floorboards. Coal dust and mouse droppings and vegetable peelings: gas bills and school reports: bitter wrong, and bitter duty correctly performed. Year after year I have sat in the house, windows sealed against the cold, waiting for someone. Who will not come home: who will never come home now.

Ralph went back to the Red House to collect his belongings. He would stay with Emma, he supposed. Anna said she did not want the house, but of course when she had thought about it she would want it, and it would be his responsibility to support her and the children. When he thought of the possible consequences of their separation – of rent for him and rates for her, of the severing of bank accounts and the relative poverty in which they would both live – his mind sheered off and went in some other direction, towards the contemplation of his moral insufficiency. That was easier for him; he was used to abstractions. Perhaps most people are, he thought. We indulge in guilt, shame – but faced with the practical effects of these emotions, we call in a solicitor. No wonder lawyers are never out of work.

He went up to their bedroom and packed some clothes. Anna had said she did not want sordid to-ing and fro-ing – that was the expression she had used – but of course it is impossible to crush a life into two suitcases. He tried, and then gave up, and sat on the edge of their bed, his face in his hands.

He hoped Anna would come in. She would not, of course. What would she see? Nothing to lift her spirits. You wreck your family once . . . years pass . . . you wreck it twice. He had evolved very nicely, he thought: along the only possible route.

Perhaps I should leave my clothes, and take my papers, I will need to clear out my desk . . . He was conscious of Anna, moving elsewhere in the house. Wherever he was, she wasn't; they skirted and avoided each other.

In his office, he sat down in his wooden swivel chair. He looked at his photograph, the picture taken on the stoep at Flower Street. He folded the frame, laid it face down. That would be the last thing Anna would want; he should never have taken it out, it had only made the children ask questions. Sightless, his mother and father stared down at him: sepia eyes. How his father's face had coarsened, with age; the flesh swelling, the features seeming to shrink. Would he be like that? It was possible, of course, that when the picture was taken his father was no older than he was now. And surely, he thought, I'm going his way: two inches on the waist, the reading glasses, those shirts that are too small around the collar, and get put to the back of the wardrobe. I am in no shape for a new life, he thought. But, anyway. It seems I have to have one.

Will Anna just watch me go, he wondered. Or is she waiting for me to make some gesture, some sign – but how would I know what it was? She had said she meant him to go, and he must allow her to mean what she said, he must allow her that.

Everything's gone, he thought: just pride remains.

But how terrible, perhaps the worst thing in the world: to be taken at your word.

His hand crept into the first drawer of his desk. Closed around stone: Gryphaea. He held it to his cheek, and then against his mouth. A child's life; the salt and cold. He tasted it: Phylum: Mollusca. Class: Pelecypoda. Order: Pterioda. Such confidence, he'd felt as a child, about the order of the world. Family: Gryphaeidae. Genus: *Gryphaea*. Species: *arcuata*. The past doesn't change, of course: it lies behind you, petrified, immutable. What changes it is the way you see it. Perception is everything. It turns villains into heroes and victims into collaborators. He held the object up between his fingers: took a sighting, and spun it across the room into the wastepaper basket.

Anna was in the kitchen: I will do something useful, she thought. She ran the hot tap, and rinsed the crumbs out of a dishcloth. She wrung it between her hands, flapped it out, shook it and straightened it and set it to dry, carefully squaring up the corners as it hung over the draining board.

Well . . . that was marginally useful, was it not? She remembered the night Ralph had left her: washing her cup and washing her cup. A phrase from an old letter came back to her, a letter James had written: 'There is always some emergency, God-given or otherwise.' How very odd memory is: and not an ally, on the whole. She could not see how this phrase had any application to her circumstances.

In the other room, Ralph was no doubt going about his preparations.

She walked around the kitchen table, touching the back of the chairs. She had consulted their solicitor; she had better tell Ralph about this, she supposed, as a family solicitor cannot act for both parties when those parties are not to be a family any longer.

She sat down at the table, because she felt ill.

Will he go?

Surely he will not?

But what will stop him?

She felt she had set him a test, an examination; but he was not aware of it, and so he could not hope to pass.

Ralph picked up his bags. He went out into the hall. 'Anna? I'm going now.'

After a moment she appeared. She wrapped her cardigan tight across her chest. He saw the gesture: elderly, a means of defence. 'So,' she said.

'You can phone me at Emma's.'

'Yes, of course.'

'If you want me.'

'I should tell you, Ralph, that I've been up to Norwich, to see Mr Phillips. He agrees that there are grounds, advises I stay in the house, but I told him I don't want to do that. You will have to find another solicitor – I'm sorry about that, but of course Mr Phillips can't act for us both. What I mean to do is to find a flat in Norwich for myself and Becky. Then you can come back here. Kit and Julian and Robin, they won't mind. They'll stay here with you, I suppose. The kind of mothering I've given them . . . they'll probably barely miss it.'

He looked at her for a moment, considering; put down his cases. She thought, he has put down his cases, surely he will not go now? He said, 'You are indulging yourself, aren't you?'

'Oh yes, of course. Self-indulgence is my habit.'

'I mean, you are indulging a notion of failure . . .'

'Failure? How could I be a failure?' She smiled brightly. 'I mean, haven't I kept the twin-tub in trim? Haven't I managed the boiler, all these years? And the hall-stand – oh, yes, I've come to grips with the hall-stand. Say anything, but never say the Red House has beaten me.'

He clenched his hand inside his pocket, frozen around the space where he had thought *Gryphaea* would be. Then he took his hands out of his pockets and picked up his cases.

She opened the front door for him, helpfully. Unbalanced by the bags, he stepped back to kiss her cheek. He saw that she was crying. 'You don't want this to happen,' he said.

'At least acknowledge that I know my own mind.'

The door of the Red House was an old and heavy door. When it was opened the cold morning came in: a big breezy presence, filling the hall. He hesitated on the threshold, scuffing a foot, dragging the time out.

Anna touched his arm. 'Ralph . . .'

He looked away, unwilling to influence by any expression on his face the expression on hers. He glanced up, out into the garden – if garden it could be called: over the mud and the lawn churned up by bikes and neighbours' dogs that the children

339

played with, over the pond where they'd had fish once and over the rusty swing with its sodden ropes, and over Julian's vegetable plots, and the wilderness of the dog-runs and the outbuildings beyond. Something moved – dog-height – from one of the rotting sheds. Anna said, 'What's that? What on earth is it?'

A creature moved into their view, at a distance. It came slowly over the rough ground, crawling. It was a human being: its face a mask of despair, its body half-clothed in a flapping gown, its hands and knees and feet bleeding; its strange head the colour of the sun. It progressed towards them; they saw the heaving ribs, the small transparent features, the dirt-ingrained skin.

'I must put these cases down somewhere,' Ralph said. All he could think for the moment was that they were dragging his arms out of their sockets; he did not know whether to put them inside or outside the house. He wondered which of them would move first, he or Anna, towards this jetsam, this salvage; but wondered it idly, without that spirit of competition in goodness that had animated his life. Whichever, it didn't matter . . . he put his baggage down, nowhere in particular, wedged across the threshold. 'We must take her in,' he said to Anna. 'Or she will die.'

'Yes,' Anna's face was open, astonished. They left the Red House together, stumbling over the rough grass. As they approached the child, she stopped trying to crawl. She shrank into herself, her head sunk between her shoulder-blades like some dying animal. But then, as they reached out towards her, Melanie began to breathe – painfully, slowly, deeply, sucking in the air – as if breathing were something she were learning, as if she had taken a class in it, and been taught how to get it right.

In November that year, Emma went back to Walsingham. It was seasonally cold, the light struggling against an obdurate bank of cloud. In the street she saw the pug dog and his woman; these months on, both were a little greyer, stouter, their feet and pads stepping gingerly on the cobbles.

As she walked up the flagged path of the Anglican church, Emma tried to edit her usual perception – that she was entering an extravagantly designed council house. A poor thing, but our own, she thought: noting the brick arches and brick columns, the stoup for holy water. Holy water, that's going too far – and in fact there was no need for her to go any further, no need to go inside at all.

'ALL WHOSE NAMES ARE INSCRIBED IN THIS BOOK WILL BE PRAYED FOR AT THE SHRINE.' She stood in the porch, turning the pages of the great book. Back, right back to – when? What date? When had Felix died? Her eyes ran over the columns. The pages were damp, they stuck together and revealed only a clump of months at a time, a huge aggregation of prayers. Patience was required; she started to scuff up the corners, looking for dates, for clues. But yes, here it is at last: her own handwriting.

RALPH ELDRED

ANNA ELDRED

KATHERINE ELDRED

Then the missing line; then

JULIAN ELDRED

ROBERT ELDRED

REBECCA ELDRED

Why did I think God would recognize our real names, our formal and never-used names, instead of the names we are called by? There: that's a puzzle. She reached into her bag for her pen. Her pen was a present from Felix. It was a serious and expensive object, made of gold.

Damn; not there. Her fingers probed, scraped the worn silk

lining. Perhaps a child had borrowed it. She plunged her hand into her coat pocket, and brought out a furred and leaking ballpoint, its plastic barrel cracked, its ink silted. She shook it, and tried a preliminary zigzag in a corner of the page. She shook the pen again, tapped it. If you could scribble the book over, make additions . . . But it did not seem decent to her to spoil the pages. Pray for Felix, she said to herself. Pray for Ginny. Pray for me.

She began to write. Her pen moved over the vacant line. The ballpoint marked the paper, but nothing appeared: only white marks. She shook it once, slammed it on the wooden desk. At last, like a slow cut, the ink began to bleed. Laboriously – the pen faltering, blotting – she filled in the missing line:

MATTHEW ELDRED

So that's done, she thought. She ran her finger down the page. Prayers answered; after a fashion. She hesitated, her hand in the air, then placed the defective pen beside the book. You could not know what desperate soul would come along, with no means of writing at all.

She stepped out of the porch. The air held snow. Often it promises, but doesn't perform; we're not very far from the sea. She put her hands into the pockets of her coat, and began to walk uphill to the car park. The cloud had thinned, and as she walked the sun showed itself, fuzzy and whitish-yellow, like a lamp behind a veil.

My Word is My Bo

ROGER MOORE

My Word is My Bond

A MEMOIR

WITH GARETH OWEN

COLLINS
An Imprint of HarperCollins Publishers

PHOTOGRAPHIC ACKNOWLEDGEMENTS:
Plate sections: unless credited with the photograph or in the list below,
all other photographs used in the plate sections of this book are from the
author's personal collection.
All photographs from *The Man Who Haunted Himself* are © Canal+ Image (UK) Ltd
All photographs from *The Persuaders* are © ITC Entertainment/Granada Ventures
All photographs from *The Saint* are © ITC Entertainment/Granada Ventures
All James Bond images are © Danjaq LLC and United Artists Corporation,
ALL RIGHTS RESERVED 1962-2008

UK EDITION PUBLISHED 2008 BY MICHAEL O'MARA BOOKS

FIRST COLLINS EDITION PUBLISHED 2008

Library of Congress Cataloging-in-Publication Data is available upon request.

Designed by Design 23

ISBN: 978-0-06-1673887

08 09 10 11 12 /RRD 10 9 8 7 6 5 4 3 2 1

I dedicate this book to my parents, who I miss so much;
to my darling Kristina and our ever-growing family,
Deborah, Geoffrey, Christian, Hans-Christian, Christina
and the little ones – who get bigger by the day.

This is a work of nonfiction. The events and experiences detailed herein are all true and have been faithfully rendered as I have remembered them, to the best of my ability. On occasion, I have left out names and other identifying features to preserve the privacy of certain individuals. Throughout, conversations come from my keen recollection of them, though they are not written to represent word-for-word documentation. Rather, I've retold them in a way that evokes the real feeling and meaning of what was said, in keeping with the true essence of the mood and spirit of the event.

CONTENTS

FOREWORD
Memoirs of an Aspiring Actor

For years, people have said to me 'Write your book,' and for years I said, 'No, there are too many people I'd have to write about, and even if they're dead, what I might say would be an intrusion on their privacy. And apart from that, I'm too lazy.'

Irving 'Swifty' Lazar persuaded my friend Michael Caine to write his book, and tried the same tactics with me. Unfortunately, Swifty is now dead. He had said, 'I'll get you a ghostwriter.' Well, maybe he is that ghost now; it would be nice to think so. He was a great character, miniature in stature but a giant of a human being.

In 1992, I decided to put pen to paper, or finger to keyboard, to be more accurate. I thought I'd start by relating my many childhood illnesses and operations. Illness is a theme that you'll find permeates my writing – and I'm only on the first page. I tapped away at 6,000 words or so on my laptop and then, later that year, tragedy struck. There we were, just before Christmas, at Geneva airport, having flown in from London; I stayed in the baggage area to claim the luggage, leaving my former wife, Luisa, to go through to the car with the carry-on baggage . . . which turned out to be carry *off* baggage, as it happens. Distracted for a moment, and believing that our driver had taken care of putting the small things in the back of the car, Luisa settled down happily to await my arrival with the other luggage.

Imagine our horror when we discovered that the driver had *not* put the bags in the back at all. Instead they had, we presumed, been put in the back of some other vehicle and were well on their way to make some airport thieves' Christmas a happy one. We spent the next two hours reporting our loss to the police: jewels, cash, gifts, all gone. It was much later that I realized I had also lost my precious words.

In the years since then I've resisted returning to the keyboard. No, that's not strictly true. I haven't resisted, but rather have always been kept busy with so many other things that the idea of sitting down to put finger to keyboard was not one I could entertain . . . or at least that was my excuse. However, with renewed encouragement from my darling wife Kristina, my daughter Deborah and my dear friend Leslie Bricusse, I have decided it is now indeed time to make time and stop making excuses.

When, on the eve of my eightieth birthday in October 2007, I announced that I was starting work on my story again, I was adamant that it would be a fun book with no recycled scandal, tittle-tattle or dirtdishing – the expected inclusion of which had worried me so much when I tackled my earlier version. But, dear reader, that isn't to say this will be a 'fluffy' book. I want to tell things as I saw them: relay the funny stories and recall the many wonderful characters and friends that have enriched my life. When I have nothing nice to say about a person, I'd rather not say anything at all (unless pushed to say a few words by my editor!). Why give them the publicity, I say? No, I'd far rather fill these pages with words about me. This is, after all, a book about me: a suave, modest, sophisticated, talented, modest, debonair, modest and charming individual – of whom there is much to write.

Throughout my tenure as James Bond, there were many wonderful scripts to work with, and one of my favourite lines from any Bond film came from Tom Mankiewicz, who wrote the screenplay for *The Man With the Golden Gun*. Trying to find out where the million-pounds-a-hit assassin Scaramanga is, Jimmy Bond tracks down gun-maker Lazar and aims a gun at Lazar's crotch saying, 'Speak now or for ever hold your piece.'

Fearful of losing my piece, I feel it's time for me to speak . . .

ONE

The Early Years

'I was an only child. You see, they achieved perfection first time round'

It was just after midnight on 14 October 1927, when Lily Moore (née Pope) gave birth to a twenty-three-inch-long baby boy at a maternity hospital in Jeffreys Road, Stockwell, London SW8. The baby's father, George Alfred Moore, was twenty-three and a police constable stationed at Bow Street. Of course, I'm only quoting this from hearsay. I was much too young to recall such a momentous event as my entry to this world.

I was christened Roger George Moore and we lived about a mile from the hospital, on Aldebert Terrace, London SW8. I was to be the couple's only child. You see, they achieved perfection first time round.

I don't remember what the flat on Aldebert Terrace was like, we moved before I was old enough to absorb my surroundings. However, I do remember our new home: it was a third-floor flat 200 yards away in Albert Square — number four, I think. It had two bedrooms and a living room-cum-kitchen. I remember the mantelpiece seeming so high to me; above it was a mirror and the only way I could see my reflection was to stand on the bench positioned along the opposite wall.

Life was happy in Albert Square. It's funny how little things stick in your mind: the beautiful smell of freshly cut wood from the timberyard next to our garden. To this day I can visualize the two gas brackets on either side of the mirror in the living room. There was no electricity, you see, and these were our only means of light. The china mantles gave off a low, hissing illumination. It was a comforting sound and one I associated with being home in the bosom of my family. The main source of heating was a coal fire. Oh, how this schoolboy's bare legs would be red-mottled on the shin side from sitting too close to the burning coals; especially when making toast with a long-handled fork. We'd spread beef dripping on it, oh what joy! When I was a little older, I took pleasure in helping my mother black-lead the grate. I was a very obliging child.

Illness played a great – and unwelcome – role in my early life. Mumps were soon followed by a raging sore throat, and it was decided that I should have my tonsils removed and adenoids scraped at the same time. I wasn't really too sure what this would entail, but was promised that when I woke up from the tonsillectomy I would be fed ice cream. That alone would make my stay in hospital worthwhile, I decided.

Wearing only a little surgical gown and bed socks, I was placed on a trolley, rolled down a corridor and pushed into a lift, its sliding trellis doors seeming very sinister. (I'd only ever been in a lift once before, at Gamages Department Store in Holborn, and that was a much happier occasion, when Mum took me to the toy department to meet Santa Claus.) As we descended in the hospital lift, I felt sure it was to the place where naughty children went if they couldn't go to heaven. Sunday school had obviously left its mark. I still vividly remember looking up from the operating table upon which I'd been placed, at the big, round lights glowering down at me and the people wearing green masks standing all around. A lady with a sieve filled with cotton wool gazed down into my eyes and then placed the sieve over my face. I felt suffocated by a strong foul-sweet odour, which pulled me down into a long tunnel with yellow and red rings flying at my face. The sound – which I can still hear in my imagination today – was a *boom-bam-boom-bam*, gradually getting faster and faster as I fell down into hell.

My next recollection was of the smell growing fainter and the *boom-bams* replaced by the soft murmur of nurses' voices. I was back on the ward. Then I was sick. I never did get the ice cream they had promised. I was deeply disappointed at the time, but looking on the bright side it might have been strawberry flavour, which I hate.

Aged five, I started school at Hackford Road Elementary. A fifteen-minute walk from Albert Square: turn right on Clapham Road, go to Durand Gardens, cross the main road, trot round the Gardens and there was the school – three floors high, red-brick with large tall windows and surrounded by a red-brick wall.

I don't remember being left at the gates by my mother or indeed anything about my first sight of the classroom and the other boys and girls. I do, however, recall finding myself in the boys' urinal and being forced to stand facing the dark grey wall, with a trough at the base, with my legs wide apart as some senior ruffians took turns to see whether or not they could aim between them without splashing my bare legs. English schoolboys' short trousers left plenty of room between the top of the socks and the bottom of the trousers for the exercise. I can still see my mother waiting at the school gates that first day as I exited the playground, walking with my red-raw knees wide apart thanks to the stream of bubbling warm pee that did not quite make it between them. 'Tut-tut-tut,' she said, as I recounted my first day's ordeal.

It reminds me of a sign I later saw in toilets:

> Your head may be in the air, young man,
> Your thoughts away as you enter;
> But spare a thought for the floor young man,
> And direct your stream to the centre.

One evening when we were walking home from school, I told Mum that some boys who had seen her drop me at the gates had asked, 'Was that your mum? She's a great-looking tart!' I didn't know what they meant. Mum was horrified, not at being described as great-looking – but a tart! Really!

Mum was born just after the turn of the last century in Calcutta, where her father was stationed in the army. She had two sisters – the older, Amy, and then the younger, Nelly. Then came my Uncle Jack, who eventually followed my grandfather's lead and became a regular soldier.

RSM William George Pope was the grandfather I barely knew. He was widowed when Mum was just sixteen. The loss of her mother affected Mum very badly: she said she thought she would never smile again. It was never discussed how Grandma Hannah died, families didn't talk about such things, but I suspect it was cancer. A few years later, after returning to Britain, Grandfather Pope took a second wife, whom I was to know as Aunt Ada. She gave birth to my three 'cousins': Nancy, Peter and Bob, with whom I spent many of my childhood holidays in Cliftonville, the posh end of Margate on the Kent coast. Though we were all around the same age, they insisted that I treated them with great respect and address them as Auntie Nancy, and Uncles Peter and Bob. I dutifully obliged. Grandfather Pope died in my fifth year.

My paternal grandfather was Alfred George Moore. His only son was my dad, though there were a number of sisters born after him. Sadly, like

Mum, Dad was sixteen when his mother, Jane Moore (née Cane), ended her life by placing her head in a gas oven. In those days, suicide precluded the right to a church burial. Dad, who up until that time had taught in a Sunday school, was left numb and disillusioned with organized religion. His father then married the woman whom my father believed was responsible for the suicide, an illicit affair had obviously been going on for some time, and I can only imagine how it must have destroyed my grandmother, to lead her into taking her own life.

Understandably, after this, Dad was very unhappy at home and wanted to leave as soon as possible. At the age of nineteen he saw his chance, and enlisted in the Metropolitan Police. He moved into a police section house and gained his independence from the father he had now begun to despise.

Mum, meanwhile, was working as a cashier at a restaurant in central London – Hill's on The Strand. From her window position, she would often see this attractive young PC on point duty – before the days of traffic lights busy crossings were manned by policemen. Between directing the buses and cars Dad had also noticed the fair-haired blue-eyed beauty behind her till. Being a rather smart restaurant, Hill's wasn't the sort of place Dad would have been able to pop in for an afternoon cuppa. Eventually, however, the opportunity arose and he invited her to a dance. At that point he was actually considering joining the Hong Kong police – to get further away from his unhappy memories of home – but taking Mum to the dance convinced him the grass was greener at home. They married on 11 December 1926 at the Register Office of St Giles in London.

I very rarely saw Dad in uniform, since by the time I was born he had become a plan-drawer, which meant he drew up the plans of, for example, the street on which an accident had occurred, or supplied the sketches and measurements of a crime scene. He had an office at Bow Street, where he and a fellow policeman, George Church, were the E Division plan-drawers, and he remained there until his retirement.

A lot of the time Dad could work at home and, when required, would put on his uniform and go to court to swear to the accuracy of his plans – usually when I was out at school. Working at home meant that he was able to choose his hours and during the summers, if the sun was shining, he would take me swimming and complete his drawings at night. When I was asked as a child what work I wanted to do when I grew up, I replied that I wasn't going to work – I was going to be a policeman like my father!

Having left school at thirteen, Dad never lost his thirst for learning; he always had books on mathematics to hand and he taught himself French and Italian. He was a superb athlete and gymnast, and could perform on any equipment – the rings, parallel bars – you name it. He was very strong, and had powerful fingers that could grip the fleshy underside of my arms if I misbehaved. He was musical too – he could play the banjo and the ukulele – most stringed instruments, in fact. He was also an amateur magician, a member of The Magic Circle and Institute of Magicians; he even went semi-pro at one point, appearing under the name of Haphazard the Hazy Wizard.

An accomplished amateur actor, as well as playing the lead roles Dad would often direct plays, do the make-up and build the sets. He was a real jack of all trades. I'd sometimes go along with Mum to see his shows. It was so exciting to be in the theatre or church hall and enter this world of make-believe. Early seeds were sown in my mind. I was very proud of my Dad.

Mum and Dad were a great partnership. Mum was the homemaker, Dad was the breadwinner, and I always knew that they loved each other. They didn't argue a great deal, but perhaps their secret lay in the fact that they never let the sun set on an argument – they would always make it up before they went to sleep.

★ ★ ★

I'd only been at school a few months when I contracted double bronchial pneumonia. Too ill to be moved to hospital, I was attended at home by the local GP and a District Nurse. I have a clear memory of this lady putting what she called an 'anti-flagestion' poultice on my chest. I have tried to find out what exactly an 'anti-flagestion' poultice is, but to no avail; maybe it is the confusion of a child's mind. Whatever it was called, the grey, earthy-looking mess that was spread on lint and placed on my chest and back burned like hell.

One night, after his evening visit, the doctor told my father that he would call again in the morning and that he should prepare my mother for the worst: he would be signing a death certificate. One can only imagine how the young parents of an only child felt.

They must have dozed off, however, because they later told me that they were awoken by a thin voice singing, 'Jesus wants me for a sunbeam'. A year of Sunday school had prepared me well to announce to the world that my fever had at last broken. A footnote to this tale of woe was that to pay for medical fees (this was fifteen years before the National Health Service came into being) Dad had been forced to sell his motorbike, which he did without quibble or regret.

After that, my recovery was rapid and soon I was out and about. One of the things I loved to do was go roller-skating with my mother. Mum had been a good roller skater in her younger days and always promised me that when my feet were big enough I could have her precious skates. I'd measure my feet time and again to check how they were doing. I had my own set, but hers were 'grown-up' skates, and I really wanted them. We'd skate for miles together – sometimes going from Stockwell to Battersea Park, round the bandstand and back home again.

Then there was my 'gang' – Reg from number six, Norman from number three, Almo from around the corner in Aldebert Terrace, and Sergio from number sixteen – we'd shoot our toy guns, throw stones and get into the odd scrape. We were typical kids. One favourite pastime was to filch a large potato from home and take it to the night watchman's brazier to bake. It's a shame you don't see braziers any more – or night watchmen, come to that. We had a pal who would let us put the potatoes in the fire and then we'd all sit round and tell stories while they cooked. Sometimes he'd even give us a bit of margarine to put on the baked potatoes – oh the smell, the taste! Even to this day, after all the gourmet food I've enjoyed over the years, nothing compares to the flavour of those clandestine potatoes on a cold evening.

Sometime during my seventh year we moved across the Square to number 14. Our new home was a first-floor flat consisting of my parents' bedroom, a sitting room and my bedroom, off which was the kitchen. We had our own toilet on that floor, but the bathroom was shared between us and the two floors above. What a depressing room; a deep free-standing bath and a hot-water geyser that needed a few pennies in the meter for a reasonable bath.

The kitchen sink was where the family washed. Dad had what was called a Rolls Razor – the blade was stropped by moving it back and forth in a metal box that had a strip of leather on its base. When everyone was out I would lather up and stand close to the open kitchen window, with Dad's pipe in my mouth, hoping that a passer-by would catch sight of me, an eight-year-old trying to pass as a teenager. What a poseur!

For my eighth birthday, I was given a tin toy aeroplane, with propellers that turned when I wound them up and green and red lights that flashed on the wings. I remember Dad turning the lights out at my birthday party so that we could see the lights flashing. This, however, was not my principal birthday gift. Pip had four legs and a perpetually wagging tail; he was a wire-haired terrier and was just a few months old. I was so very happy. Sadly, we had only had Pip for five weeks. One evening, as Mum walked Pip to meet me from my Cub Scout meeting on Clapham Road, poor little Pip ran into the path of a taxi. His young life was snatched away and we were all devastated. I cried all night.

My tears had hardly dried when Uncle Peter, Aunt Nelly's husband, arrived one morning with a scruffy, undernourished, mongrel – part Irish wolfhound, part Heinz 57 varieties. Peter had come across this sad creature tied up in the back garden of a house where he had been doing some work. The owners were not attached to the bedraggled mutt and had no hesitation in passing him over to Peter. The poor dog must been treated extremely cruelly for most of his young life, so much so that when we took him to the local vet, he advised having the dog put down, as he would never recover from his fear of humans. However, the vet had not taken into account my mother's fierce love for all creatures. He was named Ruff. And rough is how he seemed on our first meeting. But kind words, good food and plenty of walks turned him into the most loving, funny and adored member of our small household.

Another momentous event in my eighth year was learning the truth about Santa Claus. On Christmas Eve I always slept in the same bed as Mum and Dad so that, come the big day, we could share the joy of opening our presents together (actually, it was more a case of them seeing my joy on opening the presents). This particular year I wasn't asleep when 'Santa' came in to lay out the presents and, unbeknownst to Mum and Dad, I was watching them through the mirror on the wardrobe door as they tiptoed around, stuffing one of Dad's socks with nuts, tangerines and sweets. Next morning, they feigned surprise at seeing all the presents, but I knew . . . oh yes, I knew it was them! I wasn't the least disappointed that Santa didn't exist. On the contrary, I was thrilled that my parents would do this for me; that it wasn't someone else who gave me all these things, it was them.

Still in my eighth year, I complained to Mum that my 'wee man' was sore. I was hauled off to the doctor and had to stand with my trousers around my ankles while the offending portion of my anatomy was bounced on the end of a pencil. The decision was taken that, for hygiene's sake, I would be circumcised. That, I knew, was something they did in the Bible: I'd heard it mentioned in the morning lesson during prayers at school. The word always made the girls snigger.

Knowing I probably wouldn't get any ice cream this time either, the only appealing thing about the whole episode was that we would have to take a bus ride to Westminster Hospital. In those days the famous hospital was across the road from Westminster Abbey.

Once again I experienced what was to become a familiar routine of being dressed in a surgical gown and bed socks. Then came the oh-so-hateful sickly-sweet smell of chloroform, the tumbling down of the yellow and red rings, accompanied by rapidly increasing *boom-bams*!

Awakening in a large ward, I found myself in a bed at the very far end of what I discovered was the male, not the children's, surgical ward, next to an extremely tall window from which I could see across to Westminster Abbey. I could also hear the regular booming of the bell from the Clock Tower of the Palace of Westminster, better known as Big Ben. I had a sort of 'cradle' over my nether regions to ease the discomfort of the bedclothes coming into contact with the aftermath of the unkindest cut of all.

Having vomited for what seemed an eternity after the surgery, my body was left aching and, eventually, starving. No food that day, they said; all that was allowed was that my fevered lips were moistened occasionally with damp cotton wool. Next morning, the ward became a hive of industry: beds being made, pillows plumped up, bedpans and bottles being shunted around and then, the breakfast trolley! Tea was poured from a white enamelled jug with a blue lining, why that particular piece of information springs to mind, I have no idea. Maybe to delay the memory of the porridge? Ugh. A thin gruel-like mixture with a knob of margarine floating on the surface which, in turn, supported a blob of 'strawberry' jam. Not Mum's cooking, that's for sure.

At tea time the man in the next bed to mine told the nurse to give me one of his boiled eggs; a luxury supplied by his family. Picking the top off the egg I discovered that it was very runny, hardly boiled at all.

My nose wrinkled with disgust and I must have a let out a sigh of discontent, as it resulted in a torrent of abuse from my neighbour, who went on to tell me that I was an ungrateful little sod and to get on with it. I did. You would think that after that humiliating experience I would never ever complain about the way my eggs are cooked. Wrong! Three score and ten years later, I still complain in hotels if the eggs aren't right.

When it was time to leave the hospital, after thanking the nurses and my generous neighbour, as we boarded the bus home Mum told me that, as I had been a 'good boy', she had a surprise for me: a new pair of roller skates. I couldn't wait to try them out . . . and it was with knees wide apart, trying to protect my very tender member, that I shuffled and rolled my way around the Square before having to surrender and wait for happier and less painful times.

The one advantage I had over the other boys in my gang was a bandage on my pecker. A flash of that bandage was enough to gain much respect. There is a lot to be said for a little suffering. For the week or so that I bore my bandage, I was the leader of our gang. Whenever there was any query as to who was boss, a flash of that bandage swiftly saw me confirmed.

My 'new look' evoked quite a lot of interest in the Square too. The sister of a friend, who was some three or four years our senior, decided that she should be awarded a private screening, so to speak. This grand preview took place as we perched on a bricklayer's cart, in the alleyway at the back of our house. The cart had two big wheels, a long handle and was extremely unstable. The young lady, so excited by the sight of the object of so many people's attention, tried to sit on it; thereby upsetting the delicate balance of what should have been Cleopatra's barge on the Nile when she enjoyed her first tryst with Antony. We were deposited in the dirt, she with her knickers adrift and I with mud on my bandage, which I knew would have to be explained away.

There were others who were interested in what was kept buttoned for the most part too. I first related the following story in 1996 at a UNICEF conference on child abuse, where Her Majesty Queen Silvia of Sweden delivered the keynote speech. There is a reason for prefacing my story with this fact.

My friend Reg and I, both being cubs (cubs scouts in the US), somehow or other acquired a tent that we carried up to Wimbledon Common, which was, we thought, like being inside the railings of

Albert Square, only a million times bigger. We set up our camp and, feeling very grown-up indeed, sat inside our stronghold to decide what we would do next. Should we eat our sandwiches? Or go looking for tiddlers and frogs in the big pond? Our deliberations were interrupted by the entrance of a stranger who had the nerve to sit down, uninvited, and then start to mutter something about me having nice knees. I was not one who enjoyed that sort of compliment and so exited the tent, leaving Reg to tell him to sod off, or to come outside with me.

A few minutes later, the stranger emerged from the tent and approached the branch of the tree where I sat swinging my 'nice knees'.

'Your friend says that you have a big dicky,' he said.

'I don't know what you're talking about!' I stammered.

He moved even closer, saying something about he would show me his ... I did a backward roll off the branch, at the same time screaming, 'Reg!', who scurried out of the tent. Together we ran off to the pond, where we proceeded – as small boys will do under such circumstances – to paddle, splash around and skim a few flat stones across the water.

Some time later, bored with the pond, we took ourselves back to our tent. It was still there but our friend was not. Neither were our sandwiches! The dirty old pervert had obviously decided that if he couldn't have our bodies then he would have our grub. We trudged back to our respective homes, hungry and wiser – and hoping that the sandwiches would choke him!

I did not tell my mother about that day until I was well into my teens. Somewhere in the back of my childish mind there must have been some feeling of guilt.

When I related this tale at the UNICEF conference, somehow the facts were contorted and a story appeared in the papers saying I was 'abused as a child'. Then, later, I heard another ridiculous story that stated I was abused at the hands of my father. Both are totally unfounded and untrue – and hurtful.

★ ★ ★

Two new members joined our happy family. One was a black cat, whose name escapes me, the other was a rhesus monkey called Jimmy, which we inherited from my Aunt Nelly. Why? I don't know, but he was a welcome addition to our growing menagerie.

Dad made a large cage for Jimmy and he lived in the kitchen. Having no table manners to speak of, at mealtimes Jimmy was put in his cage but would rattle his tin mug backwards and forwards on the bars as if he were a prisoner in Sing Sing (though he had not, as far as I knew, ever seen a Jimmy Cagney movie).

In the summer, Jimmy was attached by a twenty-foot chain to a tree at the end of the garden. There was an elderly lady at number 15 who liked to have her tea in the garden, and one afternoon I heard a piercing scream. I ran out to find Jimmy hanging from a branch tugging at the lady's hair, which was white and piled up in a bun, or rather un-piling from a bun. I tried to wrestle him off her, but Jimmy was hanging on for dear life and in the end she hurled her teapot at him! Jimmy's chain was shortened by ten feet after that, and my mother bought the lady a new teapot.

In another of Jimmy's exploits, the screams came from number 13. He had climbed out of the window of our flat and entered our neighbour's second-floor bathroom. Jimmy had been playing in the garden all day and I suppose he thought he'd take advantage of the bath that our neighbour had so kindly prepared. When she entered the room, ready to bathe, she discovered Jimmy looking like a drowned rat, inspecting the muddy marks he had slopped all over the walls and floor. She screamed louder than the lady in number 15. I can't think what my mother had to give as compensation.

Although Jimmy was very happy to be with our cat and dog at home, that didn't necessarily mean he got along with any other members of the canine or feline world. Mum used to take him out for a walk on a chain and he would happily hop along the railings beside her, though the sight of a dog would make him jump on to Mum's shoulder for protection. Cats brought out the very devil in him. Reaching down from the railings or wall, he'd grab the cat's tail with a quick tug and let out a screech, as if to say, 'Gotcha!'

Summer holidays in Aunt Ada's boarding house by the sea meant that the family pets had to be boarded and kennelled – which was fine with the cat and the dog, but Jimmy developed a mistrust of humans, and on a couple of occasions, when startled, he bit Mum. The vet didn't think he could be trusted after the second time and sadly we had to arrange for Jimmy to leave us and take up quarters in Chessington Zoo. Every other week or so we'd trek down to the zoo armed with nuts and assorted fruits for him – which he would never share with his new housemates. They would sit back and respect the fact that these were part of a visit from his old family.

I missed Jimmy and his mischievous ways. I always felt I could get away with a little more mischief of my own when he was around.

I was always fairly good at school. It was rare that I'd ever be out of the top three in my class in any subject, but I was fortunate in having the gift of being able to look bright and intelligent even if my mind was elsewhere. I was the sort of kid who could dash off his homework in the morning and still have time for a game of football before school started. Taking after my Dad, art and drawing were my favourite subjects and it was generally accepted that I'd use these skills in some way when I left.

Being musically gifted himself, my father was keen to see me join in, so when his great uncle Alf gave him a violin, he decided that I should learn to play. So, off Master Moore went for lessons. After about six weeks the violin teacher told my father that he was wasting his money, my time and what was even more important – the teacher's time! The violin went back in its case and was returned to my great-great-uncle Alf. I didn't mind. I had more time to play conkers (chestnuts) or collect cigarette cards.

In those days, packets of cigarettes had cards inside from which, by collecting or swapping them, one could make up a 'set' of famous people, football stars, cricketers, film stars and motor cars, and the like. They became schoolboys' currency. We'd play card flicking in the playground too. A card would be placed at an angle against the wall then, from a few feet away, you'd flick a card at it, and whoever knocked it down won the card. Fortunes were made and lost during playtimes at primary school. Sometimes I'd sneakily paste together two cards, making them stronger for flicking and winning!

Conkers was another extremely competitive game for boys. In the autumn, we collected horse chestnuts and threaded a string through each, knotting it beneath the conker. You swung your conker against your opponent's and if you broke the other conker, yours would become a 'oner' or a 'twoer', according to the number you could beat. I once had a 'thirty-fourer': thirty-four other conkers had been destroyed by my own! There was an art to all of this, and the secrets of success were often attributed to tactics such as placing the conker in an oven and letting it heat for a while, or soaking it in vinegar.

* * *

Saturday mornings started with a trip to the 'Tuppenny Rush' to see a kid's film either at The Supershow Cinema or the Granada, both in the Wandsworth Road. We were well served with 'picture palaces', as they were so aptly called. The inside of the Astoria, Brixton, was designed to resemble a gigantic Moorish Garden. The Regal in Brixton was another favourite, and the Ritz, opposite the green in Stockwell, was where I saw my first Tarzan film. Flash Gordon, played by Buster Crabbe, was a particular favourite, and his derring-do in *Flash Gordon's Trip to Mars* or *Flash Gordon Conquers the Universe* was great stuff and greeted with mighty cheers from all us youngsters. Then there'd be a couple of western series with Ken Maynard or Tom Mix. When a Red Indian (not very PC these days, I know) bit the dust, or when Ken or Tom shot the villain, you could hear the shouts from outside the cinema. And there were the cartoons as well.

Then there were the 'birthday children'. If it was your birthday and you were a registered cinema-goer, your name was read out and up you'd go onstage, for a presentation – a free seat for next week's show and a copy of a movie magazine.

I never imagined, sitting in those cinemas, that I would one day be working on cartoon films and even be an actor up on the silver screen. It was during those wonderful trips to the Wandsworth Road that my love of cinema was established.

Mum and Dad would sometimes take me to the cinema with them too. A Jean Harlow movie was a must for my dad and in return, Mum would see Richard Dix's latest – I particularly remember *The Tunnel*. At MGM, years later, one of his twin sons, Bob Dix, was under contract at the same time as me, and we became firm friends, leading to me suggesting Bob for a part in my first Bond film, *Live and Let Die*. Mind you, he was killed in the first minute!

The 'Tuppenny Rush' left a penny over from my normal pocket money. Me and my gang – young sophisticates that we were – would go to a pie-and-mash café and have a halfpenny bowl of soup complemented by a halfpenny bread roll; dining on a marble table top. What luxury!

Occasionally, if I was needed on a Saturday morning, I helped the United Dairies milkman instead, for which I would be given the princely sum of sixpence – threepence more than my pocket money from Mum and Dad. I understood that money was tight and I'd been taught never to accept any money from a neighbour, if I'd done a good deed or run an errand for them. With this in mind, one Saturday I was collecting the milk money from an elderly lady – I think she had something like a pint and a half and the bill would have been a penny and three farthings. She gave me tuppence and told me to keep the farthing change. I declined her generous gesture and before I could say that I was not allowed to accept money from neighbours, she berated me, calling me a 'snotty little ungrateful bastard'!

★ ★ ★

Summer 1939 was almost over and that brought the end of our visits to Jimmy at the zoo. The clouds that were gathering didn't portend rain. They were clouds of war, and children and families from the cities were being evacuated to safe country areas. And so it was that, on 1 September 1939, I was to be found with a cardboard label in my buttonhole, a gas mask in a cardboard box over my shoulder, and a case packed with clean underwear and shirts and my best school uniform.

By this time I was a pupil at Battersea Grammar School. I had won a scholarship to enter this posh seat of learning, with its black-and-white striped blazers and black-and-white striped caps with a red-and-yellow falcon. Or was it an eagle? You see, I wasn't at the school long enough to know the difference. I do know that when the results of the scholarships were announced at Hackford Road we were allowed to go home early, and Mum took me to Lyons Corner House for the celebratory baked beans on toast and lemonade with real ice and a straw. I tried to drain all the lemonade without making the sucking-up noise that always brought complete hush over the restaurant, but it wasn't easy. I was also allowed to speak to Dad at Bow Street Police Station on the telephone in a red kiosk. A rare treat and a memorable day!

Special occasions were always marked with a visit to Lyons. There were Corner Houses in Coventry Street and Marble Arch, they were all equally wonderful and I imagined that kings and queens lived in places like these – with lots of servants called 'nippies', dressed in black, with white aprons, and little white caps. There'd occasionally be an orchestra too, in these white-tableclothed rooms. Oh, it really was heaven. Alas, it was followed by a miserable few months.

It must have been horrible for my parents, seeing their only son evacuated to a strange home in an unknown town, but for me it felt like the start of a big adventure. Here I was, with hundreds of other children all lined up at Victoria Station, embarking on a train ride to who knows where? There were a few tears as the train left the platform, but by the time we reached the countryside, we children were having a ball.

Neville Chamberlain's attempts to avoid war had been in vain, and so they were digging trenches in the parks. Sandbags were in evidence everywhere and Europe trembled on the brink of the Second World War. Children were being evacuated from all the major cities and my school was taken by train to Worthing on the south coast: ironically, a spot closer to Germany could not be found. I can't say I remember being scared or having time to be miserable, it was all too new for me to really absorb and process.

We were divided up and taken off in ones, twos and threes to houses that would accept these city kids for the duration. I was taken on my own to a rather smart house, with Tudor-style beams and a red-tiled roof. The owners had two sons a little older than me. We were walking down a road on my first Sunday morning – it was sunny and windows were open – and I heard the voice of the prime minister on the radio, saying that a state of war now existed between Britain and Germany. As if to punctuate that statement the air-raid sirens started to wail. What, up until then, had seemed like only a game, became a reality. The sirens were a false alarm. In fact, the only real conflict going on was in Worthing between the two boys and their new boarder.

Looking back, I can see it must have been strange for them to have an unknown eleven-year-old dropped into their lives and be told they had to get on with him, but they made it abundantly clear that I wasn't welcome, and for a suddenly very homesick young boy that's hard to take. Children can be cruel to each other in many small ways, and in fact it was their attitudes towards me that made me decide never to send my own children away to boarding school. Unfortunately their mother didn't like me much, either.

For tea one day there was a special treat, boiled eggs. I lovingly prepared my little white bread soldiers to invade the runny depth of my yolk and, having taken the first dip, was coldly reprimanded by the lady of the house. There was a lot of tutting and sniffing and I was informed that I was a common and dirty little boy. What was it with me and boiled eggs? I had no idea what was 'dirty' about sticking a piece of bread in an egg.

The family just did not take to me at all ... I had many friends who recounted their experiences to me after the war; and they seemed to have had a good time with their surrogate parents. I was just unlucky. My escape from this minor hell was achieved by yet another trip to hospital, courtesy of an outbreak of impetigo. Unattractive and highly contagious, nasty scabs appeared all over body and face. I, of course, went down with it and was placed in isolation, in a small cottage hospital. I remember my room was big with pale blue walls and a large bay window. I felt terribly lonely.

By this time, my father had sent my mother to Chester, to stay with the family of one of his police colleagues. No one knew what exactly was going to happen in those early days of the war. We had seen the rehearsal that Hitler had enjoyed with his dive-bombers in the Spanish Civil War and that was what we expected. My father had to stay on in London, at Bow Street. From my lonely room I sent Dad a pathetic card, telling him how sad I was and, fortunately, he came to my rescue. I can remember him coming into my solitary sickroom, taking a quick look around and saying, 'Come on, son, get dressed. I'm taking you up to Mum in Chester.'

Chester was brilliant. The Ryans, with whom my mother was staying, could not have made me feel more welcome. The father of the house was in charge of a railway signal box in Chester and I spent many happy hours among all the levers that changed the points and signals, sometimes even being allowed to pull them when required. In the evenings, the adults would play cards, while I would sleepily lean my head against my mother's ribs and doze. I can still hear the beating of her heart. What I wouldn't give to hear that same heart beating now. I did go to school for a short time in Chester, but I always wore my Battersea Grammar cap! We only stayed there a few months before, early in 1940, moving back to London and Albert Square. The war seemed far away, and the threats of bombing had thus far proved empty.

Then came Dunkirk: thousands and thousands of British and French troops being rescued from the beaches by gallant little boats that set out across the English Channel in the face of the Führer's might. I stood by the side of the railway at Clapham North and watched the bandaged and dishevelled troops being transported to the capital. Three hundred thousand British, French and Belgian troops were evacuated between May and June of that year. Prime Minister Churchill declared it a miracle.

The summer of 1940, after Dunkirk, was warm and sunny in Albert Square. To me it seemed one of the best summers ever; the sun shone and I was able to pursue my now favourite pastime – swimming. We had two pools to choose from: it was either a walk down to Kennington Park or a tram ride to Brockwell Park, which was my favourite. The best, however, was when Dad could take me to Ashstead Ponds, which was a train ride away but well worth it. A natural pool in a former quarry, Ashstead Ponds was situated in the middle of fields and bordered by a flower nursery. The water was cold and dark, with no hint of chlorine.

In the middle of the pool was a raft where one could lie down and take a break. Lazing on the raft one day Dad and I heard the drone of approaching aircraft and the stuttering rat-tat-tat of machine guns. The drones got louder and became a roar. There, above us, were two planes engaged in combat – a real dog-fight. They twisted and wove above us, then moved out of sight. Dad told me to swim with him to shore and to take cover before anything else happened. Not long after, the Hurricane fighter came thundering back – rolling from left to right – executing what was to become a very welcome sight: the Victory roll.

Saturday nights in Albert Square developed a ritual. Two family friends – Bert Manzoni and Dick Wilde – came for a late tea and then stayed on to play cards, either whist or something called nap. Only pennies were ever won or lost. Bert was a son of my godparents, an Italian family who had owned a café where Mum and Dad had done some of their courting. Such was their friendship that when young Roger came along, the Manzonis were asked to do the honours, despite the fact that they were Catholic and we were Church of England.

Bert must have been in his late twenties or early thirties when I knew him, but when he was six or seven he had started to develop a disease that would eventually eat all the skin and features of his face away. I don't know what the condition was called, but it was as if his face was one big running sore. He had hardly any eyelids and in winter the cold would make his eyes run incessantly. He could never go to a restaurant as unkind and ignorant people would stare. On buses or trams they would move away from him. As far as I was concerned I had never seen him any different and he was the kindest man I knew.

His best friend, Dick Wilde was a carpenter and worked at the Elephant and Castle, an area of South London not far from Stockwell, and the birthplace of Michael Caine. Dick had been born with a club foot and as a consequence had spent his entire life with a built-up boot, leaving him with an uncomfortable hobble. Dick was a communist, a real radical who firmly believed that the red flag should be flying over Buckingham Palace, and I'm sure he must have been under observation by the Intelligence Services. I don't think for a moment that he would have been involved in any act of sabotage against our country, he just talked a lot and, of course, when the USSR finally came into the war, and became an ally everything in Dick's garden was rosy.

One Saturday afternoon in September, the tea table had been cleared and the cards were about to be dealt, when we heard the not unfamiliar wail of the air-raid sirens, followed quickly by the distant drone of planes and the thumping bangs of anti-aircraft fire. Dad led us all down to the Anderson shelter that he had helped erect in the garden: heavy sheets of corrugated iron set just below the surface of the ground, with a heavy wooden door. The shelter was useless against a direct hit, but would protect you from shrapnel and save you from being buried under the rubble of the house collapsing. There were two bunk beds, on which we were all sitting when we heard the haunting whistle of a falling bomb. It seemed an eternity before there came the not too distant crump of the explosion. The war was really with us.

This was the start of the Blitz, and for the next two hours the explosions continued all around. The noise was deafening; the bombs and the anti-aircraft fire were combined with the clanging of fire engines and ambulances. From time to time the ground shook under us. After a couple of hours, there came an eerie silence. Dad opened up the shelter and the bombardment seemed to be over. Looking up, there was no more blue sky, just dark grey billowing smoke clouds drifting overhead. When the all-clear sirens were finally heard, we made our way out of the shelter, only to witness the skies flame red as hundreds of homes and warehouses blazed away. We went up to the roof and to the east we could see where the worst of the bombing had taken place. On that night over nine hundred German fighters and bombers had spread death and destruction – mainly over East London and the docks.

One family we knew well caught it badly. The Messengers lived near us and had a shelter built in their basement. During a raid their son, Bob, went back into the house – his dog following him up the stairs – when a bomb dropped on the house. The house was totally demolished and everyone in the shelter was killed. When the rescuers were working through the rubble they heard the dog whimpering and found Bob, almost unhurt, next to him. Bob and that dog became inseparable after that. He even took it to the cinema with him.

It was to continue like this for months, but after two weeks, Dad took time off from Bow Street to take Mum and me out of London, and to safety away from the bombing. Why he picked Amersham I do not know, but after a visit to the local police station he found a special constable's family who could take us in. It wasn't a particularly happy experience for Mum and me. The head of the house kept pigs and as far as I recall he looked a lot like one of them. There always seemed to be the stench of old potato peelings stewing away to feed the pigs, and the nights were made intolerable by the distant sound of the Blitz and us knowing that Dad was there in the midst of it all.

I was enrolled in the local school, Dr Challoner's Grammar School. I don't know if there ever was a Dr Challoner; I never met him. I do remember that it was a particularly cold winter and the snow that fell was the first I had seen that was not on London pavements. The surrounding hills were turned into sled runs, a great improvement on the curved pieces of tar barrels that we tied with string to our shoes and with which we attempted to ski down Aldebert Terrace.

The end of May 1941 saw our return once more to Albert Square. I don't know if we'd outstayed our welcome or whether Mum just wanted to be back home with Dad. On that journey back, it was strange to see the devastation that Hitler had wrought on a city, and it struck me that I was only seeing one city out of many that had been bombed. What evil, what slaughter. As we approached the centre of London we saw nothing but rows of terraced houses with four or five missing from the row, and empty burnt-out warehouses with their glassless windows staring unseeingly as blind men at our passing train.

We were relieved to find our flat undamaged. It was good to be home. Of course, there were things in Amersham that we missed. Ruff, who had been with us through that sojourn, would certainly miss our long walks around the woods of Chesham Bois. But we were home, and with Dad. Nothing came close to that joyous feeling.

It wasn't to last though. Herr Hitler's continued attacks on London made my parents fearful for my life once more, and that summer I was sent off by the school authorities to Bude in Cornwall. Our final destination was to be Launceston College. However, three of us London boys were selected from the gang to live with a family named Allen. The Allens were farmers – and the most delightful people you could imagine.

Before starting the autumn term at Launceston College, we spent our days on and around the farm, helping with the daily chores, and wandering off to the nearby Tamar River and bathing in crystal-clear water. The food was wonderful! Mrs Allen made the best pies, particularly blackberry and apple, with which we were able to have lashings of Cornish clotted cream. Our particular treat was to have the crust that formed on top of the cream as it was laid out in wide dishes close to the kitchen range. Oh, what gourmet days!

There was one incident, however, that has stayed with me all these years. I was in one of the barns with a couple of other boys, and we saw a swallow nesting in the rafters. In a moment of complete madness – I can think of no other reason – I threw a stone and the bird fell dead to the ground. This had such a profound effect on me that, as a consequence, I am completely opposed to any form of blood sport whatsoever where animals are injured or killed. I loathe hunting and shooting.

I can't say that I liked Launceston College either, possibly because I was expected to study hard. I wrote to my parents begging to come home, and adding that I'd happily cycle all the way back to London, as I only had sixpence and that would not buy a train ticket. I didn't actually own a bicycle in Cornwall: it was a ploy! It worked though and my ticket back to London duly arrived. I missed the blackberry and apple pies and the cream but again was joyous to be homeward bound, bombs or not.

By this time, the raids on London had ceased. Children started to trickle back, which created a problem for the school authorities: there was no Battersea Grammar now, so I was enrolled at Vauxhall Central School. Because of the wartime conditions, and with lots of children still evacuated from London, Vauxhall Central was a 'mixture' of grammar, art and technical schools. This suited me fine, as subjects such as Technical Drawing, never offered by grammar schools, were on the syllabus. We also had classes in shorthand and typing. The latter was a great favourite with the boys, due mainly to the lady who taught that particular subject: she was very well endowed in the breast department and when she demonstrated speed typing, her breasts joggled in time to her fingers. Lots of suppressed, 'Cors!' from the newly arrived pubescent boys.

As I said, I always found school pretty easy going, so in addition to doing well and managing to get through the Royal Society of Arts exams without too much bother (it has to be said, standards weren't particularly high at the time), I became a prefect and a bit of a leader at the school. Maybe it was my height: I was always taller than anyone else. There was one thing, though, that always bugged me as a youth: I had a slight weight problem. Always tall for my age, I was also 'chubby' – some even called me 'tall, fat and ugly' – which seems a little harsh.

It was at this time that I started to feel the first pangs of 'love'. The object of my adoration was a very pretty girl of about my age, with blonde curly hair and bright blue eyes. I lusted for her and sometimes would walk her home from school as she didn't live that far from me. The romance might have been permanent had I not met her mother. When I looked at her and then at her mother, I thought, 'One day she is going to look like that . . .' and that was enough to put me off.

So much for real love.

TWO

An Actor's Life for Me

'It is purple on the green below'

My friend Norman, from number 3, was a few years older than me and should have known better . . . I had 'borrowed' Dad's air rifle and air pistol – I knew it was absolutely forbidden to do so, but boys will be boys. Norman took the air rifle and I armed myself with the pistol. Before I had a chance to load my weapon with a pellet, I felt a sharp whack in my right shin; Norman had taken a pot shot at me from the end of the garden. He thought it was really funny to see me jump three feet into the air, whereas my immediate thoughts turned to explaining away the hole in my trousers. Examining them closely I discovered there was no hole – just a small blue mark on my leg, like a little tiny bruise. I rapidly replaced the guns on top of Dad's wardrobe – the hiding place I was never supposed to know about – and the rest of my day was spent with an aching, bruised leg.

That evening, Dad took us to the cinema in Brixton to see a Frank Randall comedy – I'm sure it was *Somewhere in Camp*. When the programme finished and the lights came up, I tried to stand but my right leg was having none of it. I hobbled behind my parents as we left the cinema, my leg now refusing to bend.

My mother asked what was wrong, 'Oh, I fell over in the garden,' I replied. Well that was partly true, I just omitted the bit about the rifle.

At home, as I got into bed, Mum asked me again what was wrong. There was no fooling my mum. I told her that Norman and I had planned a little target practice with Dad's guns, and I inadvertently ended up being the target.

'Don't tell Dad!' I pleaded.

She examined my leg and confirmed there was really very little to see, just a little blue-black spot. Phew, I thought, I've got away with it.

Alas, I had no such luck. The following morning, the pain in my leg was unbearable, my right knee was locked rigid. Of course, my mother had to tell Dad. I fully expected to be on the receiving end of a quick thump but instead a look of concern came over him: 'Let's get him to Westminster Hospital.'

The three of us, with me hobbling, caught the bus in South Lambeth Road and arrived at the emergency department of the newly built Westminster Hospital, now situated in Horseferry Road. I had a feeling that the doctor thought that I was exaggerating the limp when he saw me hobbling towards him, but on hearing my story he sent me, albeit reluctantly, for an X-ray. Sure enough, an inch or so below the knee, having penetrated the bone, lay a lead airgun slug.

Things started to move rather rapidly at that point. I was stripped for action, bedecked in my usual surgical gown and took another trip down the boom-bamming red and yellow tunnel, followed by the inevitable nausea and head-hanging in a basin.

I've hated guns ever since.

The next morning, heavily bandaged, with a drain in my leg and supporting myself on crutches, I was discharged into the care of my mother. I had a mild dose of lead poisoning and had to return to the hospital daily for the dressings to be changed. After the next day's dressing-change, I made my way to the bus stop to return home. The conductor gave me a helping hand on to the platform and I sat with my leg and crutches fully extended on the nearest bench seat.

'What happened, son?' asked the conductor. I paused and, swallowing rather bravely, replied, 'Jerry!'

I then expanded, caught up in one of my appalling fantasies, 'Yes, I was helping to clear rubble on a bomb site and a Messerschmitt machine-gunned us!' At the time, I took his look of disbelief for concern and just smiled bravely at him.

He must have thought I was a real twit!

Once I had recovered, my friends at the lido in Brockwell Park who, in the main, were all older than me, took me across the road from the park to a pub. Underage and never having had anything stronger than one glass of cider, I opted for a glass of mild and bitter. I drank it quickly, before the landlord had a chance to spot this rebel teenage drinker. Before I knew it, I had another pint bought for me and maybe another one after that – things were getting a little hazy and I lost count.

Knowing that I had to get home before dark, I remember sharing my concern that Dad would kill me if he smelled beer on my breath. One of my so-called 'friends' said that I should smoke a couple of cigarettes to disguise the smell. So, armed with five Player's Weights, I made my way on to the top deck of a homeward-bound bus and puffed away, coughing and spluttering the whole time – I'd never smoked before in my life. Oh what a fool! It suddenly dawned on me that the smell of cigarettes would bring down the same wrath as the smell of booze. I swayed and staggered my way up Albert Square and as I mounted the steps of our house the sirens started to wail. Saved by the bell!

Straight down to the Anderson shelter we went – Mum, Dad, Ruff and the beer-and-nicotine-smelling teenager. The shelter started reeling in front of my eyes, as I collapsed on my bunk. It was the same feeling as emerging from the red and yellow tunnel. I started to heave.

'George! Roger is sick,' said my mother.

'*Sick!*' Dad shouted. 'The bugger's drunk!' and with that I received a whack across the back – which only served to make matters worse.

Oh, the smell! The mess! The *shame*!

Fortunately the all-clear sounded and we did not have to spend the night immersed in the evidence of my intemperate ways. A good week passed before I could get back in anybody's good books.

★ ★ ★

I often blush deeply when I think of some of the stupid things that have emerged from my mouth.

Aged about fourteen, I was sitting in the Astoria Brixton on my own when two girls sitting in front of me turned around and asked if I had a light for their cigarettes. I exaggeratedly patted all my pockets and said, 'I am so sorry, I must have left it in the shop.' What the hell did that mean? I still think of it sixty-odd years later.

I used to go on a Saturday-night jaunt to the Locarno dance hall in Streatham. My shoes were shined and my hair was Brylcreemed – as advertised by another childhood favourite actor, Richard Green. I danced – or rather shuffled – around with any girl unfortunate enough to accept my invitation, to songs such as, 'Down in Idaho, where yawning canyons meet the Sun', or 'In the Mood'. Not that many of the girls were 'in the mood' after I'd stamped on their toes.

One night – I guess I was pushing sixteen – I was attracted to a rather well-developed blonde and, to my surprise, she accepted my invitation to dance. There was certainly a *frisson* between us. We arranged to meet the following Saturday. (The trick was always to arrange to meet *inside* the dancehall: girls were an expensive habit, so I was always delighted to get away without having to pay two entrance fees.) Anyway, come the following Saturday we met once more and after the last waltz she agreed that I could walk her home.

Her hand was rather warm in mine and she returned my fervent squeezes. With my knees shaking I pulled her into a shop doorway and we kissed! It seemed that the earth had stopped turning. As I leant forward for a repeat she asked me how old I was. Oh dear!

'Oh, er . . . I'm going to be um, er … nineteen next birthday.' I spluttered.

That seemed to please her and as I moved again towards her parted lips we were suddenly bathed in torchlight: it was the Old Bill.

'Hello, hello,' said the policeman. 'Can I see your identity cards please?'

Lovely-Lips produced hers and, as I fumbled in my jacket pockets for mine, the constable enquired as to my age.

'Se . . . sev . . . eighteen . . . sir,' I mumbled.

'Ah! Well then. Where's your exemption card?' he asked.

Damn it! He'd called my bluff.

An exemption card was issued to people beyond the obligatory call-up age of eighteen to prove they had a valid reason not to be in the armed forces. I smiled awkwardly and having found my identity card, handed it to him hoping he would – being a red-blooded male like myself, fond of a kiss and a cuddle – take it surreptitiously and not reveal my little deception to Lovely-Lips.

He shone his torch straight into my eyes, 'Sixteen?' he said. 'Well, Sonny, it is getting late you know.'

I knew it was getting late! Too damned late for the Lovely-Lips to remain inviting! Though they did part one more time for me, only to utter the words, 'I don't fool around with kids!'

My first real love melted into the cool night air and I made my way homewards. So near, and yet so far.

On another outing to the Locarno I really thought my luck was in: a winning hand at last. A most attractive brunette had shared a few dances with me and agreed that I should walk her to the bus stop. We walked as far as Streatham Common and found ourselves seated on a bench – not too close to the road or any illumination. Lots of heavy breathing, fumbling and passionate kisses ensued.

'Come home with me!' she murmured.

I took a deep breath. 'What about your parents?' I asked.

'I'm alone,' she said. 'My husband's in India, in the artillery.'

It's strange how two small words can extinguish desire. Those words for me were 'husband' and 'artillery'. Not only was she married, her husband was in the Army and – knowing my luck in love matters – was likely to be a hulking great brute who was sitting at home waiting to surprise her.

I made my excuses and returned home.

Just prior to all these sexual shenanigans, I had designed a number of patriotic posters as an exercise for art class, along with a few cartoons – liberally influenced by the Disney cartoons I loved. Dad was quite proud of my artistic efforts and showed them to his co-plan-drawer George Church, who in turn showed them to some people he knew in the animated film business. As a result I was invited, with my father, to Publicity Picture Productions (PPP) in Soho. The outcome? I left Vauxhall Central and was engaged as a fifteen-and-a-half-year-old trainee animator.

Before I could start work, PPP enrolled me in the technicians union, the Association of Cinema Technicians (ACTT), which stood me in great stead later in my career when I wanted to direct.

How proud I was at the end of the first week's work to present my buff wage envelope to Mum. My salary was three pounds and ten shillings per week: I had started paying my way. Mum then gave me thirty shillings back, from which I had to pay my bus fare and buy a spam or cheese roll each day for lunch.

All these years on, I still remember my route in to work: first it was the 58 bus from South Lambeth Road to Regent Street – at the corner of Great Marlborough Street – then I walked past the Palladium Stage Door, the Magistrates' Court and on to Poland Street. I took a sharp right, followed by the first left, and there was D'Arblay Street. Marshall Street swimming baths was around the corner, so at lunch times I could keep fit and have fun – much better than school.

I had a wide variety of tasks at PPP, including tracing pencil drawings on to celluloid sheets, and then reversing the cells to fill in between the lines with various paints. I also did a little title and advertising lettering work, which meant painting white letters on black, which were then superimposed over pictures for cinema advertising. I also learnt how to edit film, which taught me a lot about timing, which again proved invaluable when I began directing years later.

Another of my duties was to carry cans of training films from our offices to the headquarters of AK1, Army Kinematography in Curzon Street, an imposing building that was windowless for the first three floors and heavily sandbagged from street level to protect its inhabitants from foreign intelligence, and hopefully anything but a direct hit from the Luftwaffe. It was here that I first met a man who was to become one of my closest friends in later years, although there was no friendship between us at the time. He was Lt-Col. David Niven, our technical adviser. We were all hugely impressed when he came into the office, looking dashing and handsome in his uniform. Of course, when we met later, on some film set or other, he didn't remember meeting the office junior at PPP. But I remembered him.

My other important tasks at PPP included running next door to purchase rolls and buns from 'Davies the Dairy' to accompany the mugs of tea that I also prepared in my basement office. It was a busy life for a future Walt Disney.

★ ★ ★

On 6 June 1944 I arrived in D'Arblay Street to find a crowd of my colleagues out in the street. It was a sunny morning and windows were open, from which we could hear radios announcing that the Allies had landed on the northern coast of France. D-Day had arrived. A week after the allied landings in Northern France, we were introduced to another diabolical weapon from the Third Reich. It was known as the V1, buzz bomb or doodlebug, an unmanned jet-propelled plane carrying a heavy payload of explosives. When the engine cut out, somewhere over London, the messenger of death would drop to the vertical and howl its way to earth.

At the PPP offices we drew up a rota system and took turns to roof-spot and sound the alarm for employees to take cover. This became the practice at offices all over London and when the air-raid sirens began to wail, we'd take our positions, armed with our warning whistle. D'Arblay Street is just south of Oxford Street and our 'nearest hit' occurred on my watch. I saw it quite distinctly from my vantage point, and as the engine cut out and the doodlebug started its downward descent, I shot down the stairs like a bolt of blue lightning, blowing my whistle all the way. Fortunately for us it rolled the other way and fell just north of Oxford Street.

The next few months changed many things in my life. First, there was the tremendous sadness and grief we all felt at the news that on 3 August, my beloved Uncle Jack, Mum's younger brother, had died in action. He had served in North Africa at El Alamein and then was part of the allied landings in Italy. As a sergeant in the Royal Engineers, Jack was attached to the 51st Highland Division and when he was transferred to the 6th Armoured Brigade at Arezzo, he was ordered to clear landmines during the battle of Monte Cassino. He was killed when a mine exploded.

I had never before felt such grief and anger. Yes, I had lived through the war and seen great destruction and people lose loved ones, but somehow I'd always felt slightly removed. Until that day. That day was the day it all came home to me and the day I realized just how cruel, and how needless, war can be.

Then things took a turn for the worse at work. One of my extra new duties was to collect cans of rushes (processed film) from laboratories in North London and deliver them by taxi – as the film was volatile nitrate I wasn't allowed on buses or the tube – to D'Arblay Street by 9 a.m. It meant an early start. I was late on a couple of occasions and once, just once, completely forgot to pick them up at all. That was it! There was no second chance at PPP. The young Walt Disney was out on his ear.

I looked on the bright side. The sun was shining and I had friends at the lido in Brockwell Park who'd be only too happy for me to join them for a swim, and finding another job would be easy, wouldn't it?

★ ★ ★

As I said, many of my swimming companions were older than me. A few had been invalided out of military service and were now earning money doing 'extra' work on films. One day they let me tag along to the office of Archie Woof above a shop opposite the Garrick Theatre on Charing Cross Road. There was a waiting room where eager aspiring extras gathered each day, and Archie would pop his head out of a hatch in the wall of an adjoining office. He'd look around and then point to various individuals saying, 'Right. You and you – seven o'clock tomorrow at Elstree. You and you – six-thirty at Denham.' After two days of turning up at his office, I became one of the 'yous' and had to be at Denham studios bright and early the next morning for *Caesar and Cleopatra*. That was all I knew about my new job.

The early train to Denham, packed with would-be Roman soldiers and citizens, was quite an experience. Those who were old hands at the game were already working out who was going to be in which poker school. I got off at Denham station, but had no idea where the studio was so I just followed the crowd. Ten minutes later I found myself outside the great Sir Alexander Korda's grand studio gates, which had 'London Film Productions' emblazoned across the front.

On our arrival, a third assistant director told us what we were to be – soldier, centurion, citizen etc. – and directed us to the respective costume tents. Kitted out in my red toga and sandals, I followed the other extras to breakfast: Rome did not move on empty stomachs. As I digested my bacon roll I discovered that the lovely Vivien Leigh was playing Cleopatra and Claude Rains, Caesar. Of course, I knew them both from my many cinema outings. This is going to be fun, I thought.

The third assistant told me to stand with a group of legionnaires. I spent the rest of the morning there watching my hero Stewart Granger saying something like, 'It is purple on the green below,' before diving into a water tank, which was meant to be either the river Nile or the Tiber.

I was recalled the next day, and the next, and the next. At thirty shillings a day, plus a good meal or two, it wasn't bad for an out-of-work animator. On the fourth or fifth day, as I was leaving with my lido mates, an assistant told me that the co-director wanted to see me. Oh no! Was I going to be fired?

It was just the opposite. A large jolly Irishman by the name of Brian Desmond Hurst (later known as The Empress of Ireland) was directing the film with Gabriel Pascal, and wanted to know how I came to be working in the crowd. I gave him a quick rundown on my career, such as it was, to date and he asked if I had considered becoming an actor. Was I interested? Of course I was. I had been practising saying, 'It is purple on the green below,' every night when I went to bed, and thought I could do it almost as well as Mr Granger himself.

Having established my initial interest, Mr Hurst asked to meet my parents and before I knew it he was talking about me going to the Royal Academy of Dramatic Art (RADA). That night, disgorged from the tube at the Oval, my feet hardly touched the pavement as I raced to Albert Square. I think I was only halfway across the Square when I started shouting, 'Mum! Mum! I'm going to be Stewart Granger!'

A couple of days later, Dad met with Mr Hurst, who said he thought I had good potential, and if my parents could support me and I could take the entrance test for the Academy, then he would take care of the fees. Dad was thrilled. Being an enthusiastic amateur actor himself, he felt he might now be able to live out some of his dreams through me. For my part, from the moment Brian Desmond Hurst made the offer, I wanted to be a star. It never occurred to me that I might just be a jobbing actor. What was the point in that? So, with the confidence of youth, I began to pursue my new dream.

With Mr Hurst's guidance and help, I started swotting up on a couple of pieces for my RADA audition. I elected to do a monologue from *The Silver Box* by John Galsworthy and an extract from *The Revenge* by Tennyson.

While I waited for the audition day to come round, Archie Woof sent me out on a few other 'extras' jobs. One was on Hazel Court's first big film, *Gaiety George*, and another was – oh thrill of thrills! – as a sailor sitting in a railway carriage opposite the lovely Deborah Kerr in *Perfect Strangers*. All this was very useful in helping me to think of myself as actor material – not that I've been guilty of that in later life!

I walked on to the stage of the small theatre at the Gower Street headquarters of the academy (RADA had been bombed out of its main building) with shaking knees and just about managed to deliver my offering without 'drying'.

As I stood on the stage, I knew at that moment that all I'd ever wanted to be was an actor. I'd found my true vocation.

I passed the audition and joined three other boys and sixteen girls to become part of the new term's intake. Sixteen to three! I might not have learned a great deal about acting, but I did figure out quite a bit about girls.

At RADA I learnt all aspects of voice production and diction. They taught me to talk 'properly' without a South London accent, the art of mime, fencing, ballet (I wasn't too keen on that), and something called 'basic movement', which consisted of wearing swimming shorts and bending and stretching whilst swinging my arms . . .

Occasionally, we had a guest personality come along to RADA to discuss their life and experiences in the theatre. We students were all gathered for what were generally very informative and interesting talks. I recall one in particular – Dame Flora Robson. She was both a splendid actress and a very warm human being.

At the end of her fascinating address, in which she talked of the many great actors and directors with whom she had shared the stage and screen, she invited questions from the students. One dim young thing raised her hand.

'Dame Flora, why is it on screen you are quite ugly and yet you don't look half bad today?' There was a pause. Silence befell our ranks. How could anyone ask such a stupid question of one of the world's finest actors?

Dame Flora gazed down at the girl with a beatific smile. 'If you are ever fortunate enough to get a job in the cinema,' she said, 'you'll find there is such a thing as make-up and lighting.'

There were no more questions!

Our class performed three plays in the first term. I was an extremely young Professor Higgins in *Pygmalion*. I shudder to think what I was like. Then I played the King in a few scenes from *Henry V*, followed by a dashing Darcy in *Pride and Prejudice*, with Lois Maxwell as Elizabeth. Lois, of course, was to be cast as Miss Moneypenny in the first Bond film, and I enjoyed working with her on the seven I made, as well as on *The Saint*.

Also in my year was Tony Doonan, son of comedian George Doonan, and brother of the then rising star Patric Doonan (who, sadly, committed suicide aged thirty-three). So too was Yootha Joyce, who went on to great fame as the long-suffering Mildred Roper in *Man About the House* and *George and Mildred*.

The next term's intake included a beautiful blonde with the exotic name of Doorn van Steyn. She was known as an ice-skater at that time. We became, as they say, an item.

★ ★ ★

From time-to-time Brian Desmond Hurst would call to enquire as to my progress at RADA, and occasionally invite me to join him and a couple of friends to see a play. By now I had realized Brian was gay; although in those days the word 'gay' had quite a different meaning. Brian would let his friends know that I was 'not that way inclined', and when Doorn came on the scene that confirmed it for all of us.

I had what I considered to be quite a narrow escape on one occasion – I did think a lot of myself! – and delivered another of those immortal lines of acute embarrassment. Brian had asked me to stop by his home in Kinnerton Street, Belgravia, one evening after I got out of RADA. He said there were a few people that I should meet. I don't know whether this was a test to see if I had any gay tendencies, but I found myself seated on one of those Knole settees – with high sides and a cord tying the sides to the ends – between Godfrey Winn, a well-known writer, and playwright Terence Rattigan.

Godfrey was twittering away, rather suggestively, about how, when he was my age, he too was the most beautiful man in London.

At which point I interrupted. 'I am not queer, you know!' I said in the deepest voice I could muster.

There was a silent moment as Godfrey stroked his balding head. Mr Rattigan started to say something, but before I heard what it was, I quickly repeated that I was 'not one of those', and excused myself on the pretext of needing a drink.

A few minutes later, I saw Brian with a great grin on his face. He had witnessed my obvious moment of panic and I think he enjoyed it in a sadistic sort of way. I don't mean to sound homophobic. I'm not. But back then I was – as they say – a red-blooded male eager to prove my manhood. I'd rather hoped to receive such adulation from members of the *opposite* sex!

Doorn was actually a London girl, having been born Lucy Woodard in Streatham some five years before me. She was a skilled ice-skater and had already appeared in a few films, as well as in ice shows and stage shows. When we were courting I had to learn to ice-skate to be near her.

Doorn shared a house in Streatham with two Welsh friends, Betty and Lee Newman, who had both been champion ballroom dancers. By this time they were both doing extra work in films, and in fact Lee was a stand-in for the great romantic hero Michael Wilding. The house, more of a cottage really, stood in its own grounds and was very secluded. Although I lived at home with Mum and Dad, I often stayed there overnight, giving Mum the less-than-perfect excuse: 'I slept on the couch, Mum. The last bus had gone!' in a naïve attempt to make her believe her boy was still a young innocent.

Like most students, we were pretty broke all the time, but there was always someone in the gang who was willing to share whatever they had, and the few of our friends who did have money were generous with it, buying meals and drinks, and so on. A group of six of us used to go to a Chinese restaurant on Gerrard Street – long before it became Chinatown. We'd each order a dish for sixpence, and then share them all. That was living high off the hog.

There was a little café next to Goodge Street station where we'd all go after classes. Out of concern for the other customers, the management would put us students on our own in a room above the shop, where we'd push tables together for a makeshift stage and put on an impromptu show. Then there was Lyons Corner House, where several of us used to go to take advantage of the buffet. You could eat as much as you wanted for one shilling and sixpence – and we did!

On one outing to the Lyons in Coventry Street, a couple of male friends and I were approached by a middle-aged man who asked if he might sit with us, and offered to supply us with some more wine. Why not? As we left, he suggested a drink at Murphy's Irish bar in Piccadilly. We had a fair inkling what his game was: dare I say, we were good-looking lads.

'OK,' we said. 'We'd like gin and tonics.'

As he went to order, we walked straight out of the other entrance on Shaftesbury Avenue, leaving him standing with four rather expensive drinks. Naughty, I know.

One larger-than-life character in Doorn's class with whom I became great friends was Dickie Lupino. He was the nephew of a famous English actor, Lupino Lane, and the cousin of Hollywood star Ida Lupino, so he knew a little about the business. One of his great talents was scrounging. We used to send Dickie upstairs on buses where he'd ask passengers to sell him a cigarette. Everyone he asked just gave him one, never taking any money in return.

In those final days of the war, you could only buy cigarettes from a tobacconist who knew you. Some of the things I smoked were really quite disgusting, including one type that made you lose your voice (I only had three lines in the play I was in at the time so it didn't bother me too much). Another brand I smoked was Joystick, which were rather long, so I'd cut them in half. Then there were the 'specials' – mixed packets – two Turkish, two horse dung, two Virginian and, if you were lucky, a black-papered Balkan Sobranie. So we were always very grateful to Dickie when he'd come downstairs from the top deck and share out his horde of scrounged smokes.

In my second term at RADA I was allowed to work in the Arts Theatre Club in a production of *Circle of Chalk*. I wasn't nervous for my world premiere in front of a paying audience. I simply took a deep breath and got on with it. It was a job, after all. This strategy worked a treat – and has done ever since. My mother came to the first performance, but was upset that she'd missed me. She didn't miss me, she just didn't see me under the bloody great helmet I was wearing, along with most of the other members of the cast.

One of the beauties of working in the professional theatre, I decided, was that, unlike at RADA, we did not have Sir Kenneth Barnes – RADA's founder and principal – grumbling and shouting, 'I can't hear him!' from the principal's box at the back of the stalls. Sir Kenneth – or 'Granny' Barnes as we students called him – always wanted to nurture 'ladies and gentlemen'. He was a bit of a snob, if truth be told, which was admirably demonstrated when, after a year in the army during my national service, I had just received my commission and, on leave one day, popped my head into RADA to say hello to Morecambe, the commissionaire. As we stood chatting, Granny Barnes emerged from his office.

'Ah! Young Moore. Commissioned, eh? Well done. What regiment?' he asked.

'No regiment, Sir Kenneth,' I replied. 'Royal Army Service Corps.'

He sniffed, stared as me for a moment as though I'd entered his hall with something unsavoury on my shoes, turned on his heel and muttered, 'Um, yes, well. Well done.' That was it.

In April 1945 I was offered a second job at the Arts Theatre Club, in *The Italian Straw Hat*. There I was, singing and dancing as a guest at the wedding of 'dear little Helen to Mr Fadinard', wearing an oversized top hat that fell down over my ears. My mother came to see me, but again she didn't recognize me in all my finery. I was obviously a convincing actor, and was getting seven quid a week too. Things were definitely on the up.

On 9 May 1945 came the end of the war in Europe. VE Day. What a night that was! Tony Doonan, who was appearing at the Arts Theatre with me, joined Doorn, me and a mad group of RADA students to sing and dance with the crowds in Leicester Square, Piccadilly and down to

Trafalgar Square – where we ended up between the paws of the lion on the right of the base of Nelson's Column. Somewhere along the way we had collected a sign from a pub called, appropriately enough, the Red Lion. It was a night of complete madness and overwhelming joy: the bombing would be no more and our brave lads would soon be returning home. People were dancing and kissing like never before, as I think Doorn and I did. I say *think* as although it was a night to remember, I can't remember everything about it!

My days at RADA, Granny Barnes notwithstanding, were very happy indeed. Everyone in my year was dedicated and, in the main, talented. New productions were greeted with great enthusiasm and we all threw ourselves into every rehearsal. As at school, I rather sailed through my work at RADA. Having been out to work already, I had an advantage over some of the other students, even though most were actually older than me. I felt more adult than them – I'd seen more of the real world. I can't say I excelled as a drama student, but then how does one measure an actor's success? Awards? Medals? They are great to win, but they're no guarantee of success, after all.

So, at the end of the first year, with my eighteenth birthday and the prospect of national service looming, I decided to leave RADA. I was determined to get some more acting experience under my belt – paid acting experience, that is.

THREE

You're in the Army Now

'Hands off your cocks and on with your socks!'

I had heard that theatre director Norman Marshall was about to stage a season of George Bernard Shaw plays, including *Androcles and the Lion* and the potboiler, *Passion, Poison and Petrifaction*, at the Arts Theatre in Cambridge. Having decided that I really wanted to learn my trade through practical experience rather than training, I went for the audition and was subsequently cast as a 'supporting player'.

I found digs in Trumpington Street with another mate from drama school days, Patrick Young. This was my first time living away from home since wartime evacuation. Oh, how very different life was now I was no longer that snotty-nosed boy who relied on charity in someone else's home.

Patrick and I were in 'self-catering' accommodation, thanks to the addition of a little hotplate in the corner of our room. We could eat what we wanted and we weren't answerable to any matriarchs. Not only did we eat, we drank – both of us developed a taste for the odd glass of mild & bitter and cider. After our lavish dinners – which usually came out of a tin – we amused ourselves by filling condoms with water and hanging them on string outside the window, bouncing them on the heads of passers-by . . .

Our production attracted the attention of the Cambridge University undergraduates, or rather those with a leaning towards the art of Thespis. One day I found myself invited for tea by one of my most ardent fans, to his rooms at Magdalene College. He insisted on referring to me as '*dharling* dear boy', which, you'd think, might have given me an inkling as to the purpose of his invitation. Anyhow, before the first cup of tea was poured he dived at me, causing me to fly backwards over his settee. Startled, I scrambled up off the floor but before I could politely make my excuses and leave, Lothario flew full pelt towards me. I ran for my life and, thankfully, found I could run faster than him. I ran all the way back to my digs at full power and fell through the door, bright red and gasping for breath.

'What happened to you?' Patrick asked.

I began relating the story of how my biggest fan had invited me for tea, and Patrick roared with laughter, asking how on earth I hadn't realized. Oh, I was so naive back then. We left for the evening performance at the theatre and I prayed I wouldn't see Lothario in the front stalls. I was back in a Roman toga – but this time ensured it was a longer one than the others in the cast to avoid any further undue attention.

In rep, you appeared in one play for one week, moving on to a new play the following week. But when we started rehearsals for our next production I was feeling really rotten and unable to concentrate. What's more, I was passing extremely dark water. A quick trip to the doctor confirmed that I had yellow jaundice. He said that I had to stop working and go home to London to rest and recover. That was the end of my career in rep, for now – but not before I had to have my Army medical prior to call-up. After passing what resembled a draught Guinness into the army doctor's proffered receptacle – I was duly passed A1-fit.

Some doctor!

A few weeks later, recovered and full of glucose, I bid my family goodbye, shared some tearful kisses with Doorn and presented my train pass to the guard at Paddington railway station. From there, I was shunted off to Bury St Edmunds to start six weeks' basic training with the 'Beds and Herts' Regiment.

There, thirty of us spotty, gawky youths shared a Nissen hut, the centre of which was dominated by a wood-burning stove – our only source of heating. Against the walls were our bunks. Coins were tossed for 'top or bottom' and thank the Lord I chose heads and got the top.

After dropping off a few belongings in our new home, my platoon all made an effort to keep in-step as we shuffled off to the stores. There we were issued with uniforms and equipment – boots, mess tins, knife, fork and spoon. I noted how various sergeants and corporals tried to be very helpful and solicitous as we returned to our hut bearing the quartermaster's gifts.

'Right, lad! Let's see where we can take that oversized jacket in a bit for you, and get a nice crease into those strides and have you shining like a nice little soldjah. OK, lad?'

Such generosity I thought. Yes, and it came at a price – my first week's thirty bob!

Come the morning, I realized how lucky I was to have won the toss for the top bunk. My homesick downstairs neighbour had heard, incorrectly, that if you were a bed-wetter you would get an instant discharge. The floor was covered in a sea of pee. Being careful not to wet my socks, in which I had slept to keep warm, I leapt twenty feet across the wet floor when a sergeant major barged in, shouting what was going to become a very familiar rallying call:

'Right now! Hands off your cocks and on with your socks! Wakey, wakey, you dozy bastards! I'll make soldjas out of you lot! Outside on the double and do your ablutions! And another thing: stand *very* close to the razor cos I do not want to see any bum-fluff when you lot get on parade.'

I shivered in the cold November air carrying out my ablutions – with nothing but cold water to wash and shave in – combed what the army barber had left of my hair and threw my uniform on. It fitted quite well compared to others I saw. Then we grabbed our mess tins, knives, forks and spoons before vaguely forming three ranks to march off to our first army breakfast. I remember thinking if an army marches on its stomach then we were going to march to bloody Scotland and back on the abundance of porridge, eggs (fried and more than a little congealed), bacon, baked beans, fried potato, toast and hot steaming tea that was served up.

Basic training consisted of learning how to march, shoot a rifle, assemble a Bren gun, drill, order arms followed by sloping arms, to fall in and fall out, attend pay parade, go to the NAAFI (Navy, Army and Airforce Institutes) or the Sally Bash (Salvation Army Canteen), polish boots, press uniforms and salute. In any spare time we were encouraged to write letters home to our loved ones. There were usually two types of loved ones, of course:

> '*Dear Mum and Dad,*
> *I am fine, hope you are too,*
> *your loving son, Roger.*'

Or:

> '*Darling Doornikins,*
> *I cannot wait for a weekend's leave.*
> *I love you and miss you,*
> *many kisses.*
> *Yours always, Roger.*'

As the six long weeks of basic training drew to a close, there was talk about which regiment or corps we would be posted to.

'I Corps for you, lad!' my platoon sergeant told me. What the hell was 'I Corps'? Did he mean 'Eye Corps', I wondered – some remote branch of the Medical Corps? It turned out that he was actually recommending me for the Intelligence Corps, but when he found out I had no idea what he was talking about he never mentioned I Corps again!

For a while it seemed they didn't quite know what to do with me. One minute I was in my hut with twenty-nine other recruits, the next I was there virtually alone, everyone else having been posted away. So, they put me to work drawing recruitment posters for a few weeks until, eventually I was told to report to WOSBY – the War Office Selection Board – where I was to be assessed for possible officer training. At a big house somewhere in the south of England I underwent four days of tests: how to command, how to get ten men across a river, how not to eat peas off a knife, that kind of thing. There was fun to be had though, and a very nice girl from the ATS (Auxilliary Territorial Service) to have fun with! In fact, I've always wondered whether the problem of getting her in and out of the barracks without getting caught was one of the WOSBY tests . . .

After my assessment I was given a few days' leave, while they obviously thought over the results. I dashed down to London to spend time with my darling Doorn, and enjoy some of Mum's home cooking – another thing I'd greatly missed.

Those days flew by and before I knew it I was in Wrotham, Kent for 'pre-OCTU' (Officers Training Unit). I was let loose on rifle ranges and there was more 'leading ten men across rivers' and 'charging down hills with bayonets drawn'. I was taught more drilling, how to drive a three-ton Bedford lorry and how to ride a motorcycle. It seemed odd to me that the military simply assumed we could handle things like motorbikes. There wasn't much instruction before we were sent off careering round the camp to see if we could keep our balance, and then straight out on to the main road. One morning I was going down a very steep hill in Dartford when a policeman stepped out in front of the bike and raised his hand for me to stop. I had no hope of stopping in time, so turned sharp right and went straight into Woolworth's on the high street!

One thing I'm eternally grateful to pre-OCTU for, though, are the many useful Dutch swear words I learned, thanks to sharing a hut with twenty or so Dutch officer cadets.

Having been deemed proficient in all of the above, I was next ordered to Buller Barracks, Aldershot for 'Basic OCTU'. More strange terminology, but I was at least advancing from 'Pre' to 'Basic' in something. I was now announced as an officer cadet in the Royal Army Service Corp and commenced training in 'transport and supplies'. There was yet more drilling: 'To the front Salute!' . . . 'Up-two-three, down-two-three!' Aldershot was made more bearable as weekend leave was fairly easy to come by and London was just up the railway line, along with my darling Doorn.

After passing-out of Buller and 'Basic OCTU' training, I was given a few days' leave, which I managed to turn to my career-advantage. Doorn's housemate in Streatham, Lee Newman, was standing in for Michael Wilding, who was starring in the film *Piccadilly Incident* with Anna Neagle. As it was a wartime romance there were plenty of scenes featuring service personnel and, I was told, if you had your own uniform, you were a dead-cert for a part.

Officer Cadet Moore certainly had his own uniform!

I took an early-morning train to Welwyn Garden City and reported to the studios. An assistant director told me that my uniform 'looked authentic', which was gratifying to know, and that I was to wait while they decided what I should do. I duly waited, clutching a welcome mug of tea, when I suddenly had the feeling that I was being stared at. The assistant then told me that 'Mister Herbert Wilcox' – the director and husband of the leading lady, Miss Neagle – wanted to talk to me.

Mr Wilcox asked if I really was in the army, as his wife was curious. I confirmed that I was, and also that I had been at RADA and had done a couple of plays in Cambridge. This seemed to intrigue the great man. He told me to sit at a table with Michael Wilding and 'laugh at what he might say'. Before they even called action I started laughing, and I did it all day long. Many years later, when we were both at MGM, Michael Wilding told me he thought I'd been very kind to him by laughing at his jokes, as it had relaxed him enormously. What praise!

At the end of the day, Mr Wilcox suggested that when I came out of the army I was to get in touch with him.

Dissolve – as they say in the movies – to a few years later. Doorn had a small part in another Wilcox/Neagle film, *Maytime in Mayfair*, which was shooting at Borehamwood Studios. I had left the army by this time and had been trying, unsuccessfully, to reach Herbert Wilcox through his casting agent, Pat Smith. Here was my chance! I went out to the studio to have lunch with Doorn, keeping my eyes peeled for the great director. When I popped into the restaurant toilet, there standing next to me was the man himself. It was an opportunity I couldn't let pass.

'Ahem!' I cleared my throat. 'Mister Wilcox, I er, have been trying to . . .' Before I could finish the sentence, Wilcox hastily buttoned his flies and beat a retreat, convinced that a young man was trying to pick him up in the loo.

And the moral of this story? Never accost anyone in a toilet.

Michael Caine once told me that John Wayne had advised him never to wear suede shoes. Apparently Wayne once did and was standing in a pissoir when someone next to him looked over and said, 'My God! It's John Wayne!' and, as he turned to face the Duke, peed all over his suedes.

Once I had finished my Aldershot training, I was told that those of us that were 'still considered officer material' were going to be posted to Mons Barracks, just down the road. I was placed under the eagle eyes of RSM Tubby Brittain of the Coldstream Guards: six-foot-three and a voice that could shatter plate glass twenty miles away.

'PAAARADE! WILL ADVANCE IN REVIEW ORDER, SEVENTEEN PACES BY THE CENTRE, QUICKKKK . . . WAIT FOR IT! WAIT FOR IT! QUIIICK MARCH!!'

We were all from different regiments and corps but he, from a hundred yards away, could tell who you were by your cap badge.

'THAT DOZY IDLE BLOODY SERVICE CORPS CADET! WAKE YOUR IDEAS UP!'

I still dream about that voice. I sometimes wonder if my grandfather, RSM Pope, had terrified his men during the First World War as RSM Brittain terrified me.

While at 'Final OCTU' (that, in army language, came after 'Pre' and 'Basic OCTU') I had my service dress uniform made for me at Austin Reed in Regent Street. Pips were sewn on my battle dress, but had to be covered from view by a white band – as were the badges on my cap – until I had officially graduated. I was told that we were all allowed to wear the standard officer's raincoat, which had no rank showing, over our uniforms if required. Outside barracks we all took off the white bands and, to all intents and purposes, looked like proper officers. This was useful in soliciting salutes from other ranks; mind you it was probably only me that did that — forever the poseur.

Newly commissioned, I was shipped off to Germany to be part of the British Army on the Rhine. My first posting was to a supply depot in Schleswig-Holstein. Green as grass, I was given command of the whole depot, responsible for about fifty other ranks and NCOs. I may have been green, but luckily I did have a wonderful staff sergeant who had all the savvy of an old hand at the job. Everything ran smoothly enough.

Schleswig was an RAF provost town, so any disciplinary charge against my men was always handed down from the RAF. As most of the charges were for little things like not having badges on or leaving buttons undone, I would ask 'Staff' what I should do with those who misbehaved, to which he'd reply, 'As you feel fit.' So I fitted them into the out tray and left it at that! I never was one for too much discipline. That was fine until the RAF provost marshal called and wanted to know what the hell I was up to, letting everyone off all the time. Thank heavens he had a sense of humour and the matter was settled in the local officers' club with me agreeing that on my next supply trip to Denmark, I'd come back with fresh eggs, butter and all sorts of other goodies for him.

Shortly after that, I had a leave due and I raced as fast as I could into the arms of my loved one. It was then that Doorn and I decided to get married. Too young at nineteen? Maybe. But I felt very mature and then of course there was the marriage allowance — much welcome extra income. I've always been practical.

We were married on my first leave home from Germany, on 9 December 1946 at Wandsworth Town Hall. It wasn't a big affair. Doorn's sister, Fleur was a witness, as was my Dad, and there were only a few members of each family present. The thing I remember most was how cold it was — absolutely bitter.

A couple of months later I was moved from my cushy billet in Schleswig to a Main Supply Depot in Neumünster, some sixty miles away. There, I was promoted to Chief Stores Officer. I involved myself with 'welfare work' for the troops in the form of staging 'Double or Quits' gambling shows and quizzes around the various units. It was when I was returning from one of these evenings that the jeep I was riding in had an altercation with a tree. The tree won. I hasten to add that I was not driving.

Concussed, I only became aware of the accident a few days later when I found myself at the Royal Army Medical Corps base in Schleswig. My split head and chin were stitched up. However, the few weeks I spent recuperating made me realize I wasn't cut out for Stores – or the army. I longed to get back on the stage and decided to attempt to get a transfer to the Combined Services Entertainment Unit (CSEU). As we hadn't had time for a proper honeymoon, Doorn came over for a few weeks to help in my recuperation, only to find me back in hospital yet again with acute appendicitis!

But I'd made up my mind and so it was that, discharged from hospital once again and after a brief stint with No. 4 Training Brigade in Lippstadt, I found myself on the telephone to the CO in charge of the CSEU, Lieutenant-Colonel Sanders 'Bunny' Warren. In civvy street, Bunny was an actor, someone I'd known for a while. His pre-war career had included a stint as the 'Red Shadow' in a touring version of *The Desert Song*. He said he'd see what he could do for me.

To my relief, Bunny effected my transfer to the CSEU almost immediately, and I reported to the unit's headquarters in Hamburg, opposite the Hauptbahnhof, in what I believe was then the Stadt Opera Haus and is now the renovated Deutsches Schauspielhaus. I found myself back with half the people I'd known in my RADA days – Sergeant Bryan Forbes, Joey Baker, Basil Hoskins, playwright David Turner, Charles Houston and comics like George and Jimmy Page.

Members of the CSEU lived a few hundred yards away in the Hotel Kronprinz – what a change from what I called the 'army proper' – there wasn't much discipline and there was no dreaded marching or drilling. In fact, the only formal affair was 'Pay Parade' and that was the first task that I was set by the adjutant, Captain George Fitches.

I sat behind a desk with a company sergeant major beside me and as the men and women came in presenting their pay-books, I handed them their allowances in BAFF's – British Forces money. They were then, I was told, to throw up an arm in salute, about turn, and depart. The first in was a very pretty ATS girl – an ex-dancer I believe – who smiled at me. I was just about to smile back when my eardrums nearly burst.

'Do not smile at the officer on pay PAARADE!' screamed the sergeant major.

She never smiled at me again.

For some reason, I was promoted to Acting Captain and was put in charge of routing CSEU shows around Germany, Austria and Italy. I remember the first time I saw Austria was when we were bringing a convoy of trucks from Padua in Italy through to Hamburg. As we drove over the Dolomites I saw this most beautiful country laid out before me – a picture postcard of mountains, green forests and pale blue lakes. One stop on our tour was at a tiny village called Krumpendorf, near Klagenfurt on the Wöthersee. To us, this was paradise: we were in the army, acting, getting paid and had all this luxury before us.

I can't remember how many theatres we had to entertain in on this tour, but it was a lot. The casts of our plays and revues were made up of both civilians and members of the armed forces. They all had to be transported to the venues by thirty-seater Bedford buses, whereas our instruments and sets were loaded on to Bedford three-tonners. It was quite the military operation.

One of our touring acts was Robin Richmond, who was billed as 'Robin Richmond – the only man to have his organ transported by a three-tonner.'

Another of my tasks was to meet and greet civilian acts coming in from England. Could life get any better? I wondered.

Once, I had to drive to Altona Station and escort the much-revered Ivy Benson and her 'all girls band' to the Hauptbahnhof, just across the road from our HQ, and on to the Bocaccio Hotel where civilians such as they stayed. On another occasion I was charged with greeting the knockout-gorgeous Kay Kendall. At that time, she'd only made a couple of movies in the UK so hadn't quite reached the dizzy heights she was destined for, albeit tragically cut short by leukaemia. My buttons and shoes were shining so brightly that she nicknamed me The Duchess. This in turn aroused the interest, as it were, of another civvy entertainer who'd arrived at the same time, Frankie Howerd. He 'OOHED' and 'AAHED' all the time at me, but ended up disappointed on discovering that I was far more interested in Kay and the Ivy Benson lot! Both Kay and Frankie remained good friends of mine until they died.

There was very little saluting in the CSEU, unless of course we were out in public and then some decorum of military discipline had to be shown! Otherwise, it was usually a case of us throwing our arms around one another and hugging warmly. Bryan Forbes did this once in front of the adjutant – he was 'army proper' – and he gave Bryan a bollocking. And me? He said I would be reported to the colonel for disrespecting army protocol. In the event, I was reported to Lt-Colonel 'Bunny' Warren. He merely smiled.

Three months before my release from the army, Colonel Warren suggested that I might like to tour in a play. It was not customary for an officer to act, but Acting-Captain Moore readily agreed to play the juvenile lead in *The Shop at Sly Corner* – very much shades of 'Anyone for tennis?' We had great fun playing in Hamburg, Celle, Hanover, Cologne, Lübeck, Bremen and then Trieste in Italy. It was in Trieste that our company manager ran into some old friends from Cairo and proceeded to have a glorious – for want of a better word – piss-up. Nothing wrong with that, you say; except, that night he had to appear on stage! He was playing the police inspector investigating the murder, and arrives on stage at the beginning of Act Three.

I had seen him during the interval, between the first and second acts, and suggested that he should be plied with strong coffee in an attempt to help sober him up. The curtain went up on the third act and the inspector made his entrance; he swayed – trying to take in his exact location – but not a word came out of his mouth.

'You're a police inspector?' I said.

He gazed at me and gave a nod.

'You have come to make enquiries into the death of . . .?' I frantically tried to feed him his line.

Another pause and a nod.

'And you remember me from Oxford, right?'

'Hummm . . . er!' He continued to sway and I continued to paraphrase his scripted questions and answers.

When the curtain went down, he exploded at me: 'You effing bastard, you trod on all my lines!'

'You are pissed,' I countered.

He stormed off stage and emerged from his dressing room wearing his battledress jacket. He tore his CSM crown off the sleeve, and at the same time shouted: 'You can tell bloody Bunny effing Warren that he can shove this up his arse!'

Needless to say, the next morning he was the proud possessor of a gigantic hangover and had completely forgotten about the events of the night before. Just as well really.

Towards the end of 1947, and nearing the very end of my three years in the army, I heard that I had been accepted to test for a film at

Pinewood called *The Blue Lagoon*. It was to star Jean Simmons and they were looking for the boy. Bunny Warren agreed that I should have a week's leave to go to London. So, off to Cuxhaven I went, catching a ride on a ship to Hull, from where I took the train to London. Two days later – clad in my uniform, as my civvy clothes had by now become too small – I reported to Pinewood. Little did I know then how important this corner of Buckinghamshire was to become for me.

I was greeted by a man who later became my agent, Dennis van Thal – then an executive of the Rank Organization. He introduced me to the famous film-making partners Frank Launder and Sidney Gilliat, the producer and director of the film. Two other young men were testing that day, along with three girls. As the female lead was already taken by Jean Simmons, the girls were aware they weren't going to be in the film but Launder and Gilliat wanted to have some footage of them for consideration in future projects. The young lady I tested with was a sixteen-year-old Claire Bloom. One of the other two men was a chap called Larry Skikne – he changed his name to Laurence Harvey and went on to great success as well as becoming a very good friend.

Clad only in a loin cloth, and painted from head to toe with a healthy tan, I endeavoured to hold my stomach in for the length of the test. Afterwards, I went to lunch with the girls whilst the other young men made their way home. Generous to a fault, and from my humble army pay, I picked up the bill.

Dennis van Thal asked me to invite Claire Bloom to the bar after the test was over, as he had a couple of producers he wanted her to meet. Her career took off, and she never looked back.

After spending my few remaining days with Doorn, I returned to Hamburg and waited for news from Pinewood. When the news came, it was bad – I had not got the part! It went to Donald Houston instead. However, I did get a cheque from Dennis for ten guineas – for 'out-of-pocket expenses'. Manna from heaven.

Meanwhile, the curtain came down on the last night of *Shop at Sly Corner*. Having removed my make-up and packed my bags, I bid farewell to my chums in CSEU and left my cushy job as Acting-Captain Moore w/s Lieutenant for the harsh reality of being a twenty-one-year-old, married, out-of-work actor.

FOUR

Civvy Street

'You're not that good, so smile a lot when you come on!'

Before being officially discharged from national service everyone was issued with a demob suit, or a sports jacket and trousers. We were then set free to make our own way in life. At least I was making my way with a suit that fitted!

Doorn and I made our first home together in a room on the first floor of her sister's house in Streatham. It was very pleasant and looked out on to the garden. The bathroom was just outside our door too. In the corner of our meagre room we had a two-burner electric hotplate, from which our daily menu was served – usually coming out of a frying pan. I used my mother-in-law's stabs at oil paintings to protect the wall from splashing grease. The artworks had to have the dripping scraped off in the event of an in-law visit!

Doorn had a small son from a previous relationship – Shaun – who lived in Southport with Doorn's mother and father. It would have certainly been a little cramped if he had been with us. We would visit them in Southport from time to time, and they came down to us occasionally, but I didn't get to know Shaun that well – although we are still in touch now.

Money was tight, of course. There wasn't much work around. After the security of three years of army life I suddenly had to start again and find my feet in the theatre. I auditioned for several parts but didn't seem to 'fit' in any of the roles. Before call-up I had acquired an agent, a tall, English gentleman called Gordon Harboard. Gordon suggested I attend auditions in uniform, which was just as well as it was the only decent suit I had. But I was always too big, too young or just out of character for the parts I went up for. Luckily, Gordon's wife, Eleanor, who kept the books, was a soft touch for a couple of quid advance when a job was in the offing.

I called Brian Desmond Hurst to say that I was now one of the great unemployed. He said that I would have a job on his next film, *Trottie*

True, but that was a few months away. Both Brian and Launder & Gilliat had suggested I could be contract material for the Rank Film Organization, based out of Pinewood. However at this point, following some expensive flops, Rank was trying to cut costs and started reducing the number of players under contract, with only the big stars such as Dirk Bogarde and Kenneth More surviving.

Dashed again.

Gordon suggested I should meet Jimmy Grant Anderson who ran the Intimate Theatre in Palmers Green, North London, which had a reputation as a very good repertory company. The meeting went well and soon after I was engaged, earning the princely sum of ten pounds a week. A pound went to Gordon in commission, and I repaid Eleanor two, but I still felt flushed with money and pride. So much so that I treated myself to a pack of Passing Cloud cigarettes, which cost a penny more than brands such as Players. I sat on the top of the bus on my way home and made a great show of tearing the cellophane and selecting one of the oval-shaped symbols of newly acquired wealth. Ever the poseur.

Weekly rep was the training ground for most English actors. The routines were the same all over the country. Monday night was always the first night of the play being performed that week; then on Tuesday morning we'd have a read-through of the following week's play. Tuesday afternoons were spent 'blocking' (learning) the first act of that new play and that night we had the second performance of the current play. On Wednesday morning we'd block the second act of the new play, and in the afternoon we'd block the third. Thursday usually saw a matinée in the afternoon, so we'd have just the morning to rehearse the next week's play. Friday and Saturday saw more rehearsals, but Sunday was free!

On the following Monday morning we'd run through the new play again, with a dress rehearsal in the afternoon, before curtain-up on the new play that night.

It sounds a complicated routine, but I assure you it is one easily fallen into. I'd find myself learning lines in every spare moment – on the tops of buses, on underground trains or at home. As most of my rep jobs were around London, I was able to live at home with Doorn. I'd sit on the bus with a copy of the play in my left hand, as my right hand slid down the page with each line committed to memory. This was also a good way of showing, to the casual observer, that they were in the presence of a 'Working Actor'!

The other method of showing that one was a member of one of the two oldest professions, was to wear dark sunglasses even on the darkest of days. Many still do.

My first play at the Intimate was Noël Coward's *Easy Virtue*, with Noele Gordon as the leading lady. I remember during rehearsals, Jimmy Grant Anderson said to me, 'You're not that good, so smile a lot when you come on!' Dad's sisters didn't live far from Palmers Green and one night Aunts Lily and Isabel came to witness one of my 'smiling a lot' performances. I made my first entrance and heard a loud female voice exclaim, 'My God, he's got George's ears!' I managed to get my first line out without collapsing with laughter, but my cheeks were so red that I swear they shone like traffic lights through my make-up.

As most of my meals consisted of baked beans on toast I, unfortunately, suffered a great deal with wind. One night I made my entrance upstage-left and briskly walked downstage-right to warm my hands at the fireplace saying as I moved, 'My word, Mother, it is freezing outside.' As I squatted on my haunches in front of the fire a 'brrrp brrrmp' escaped and, in less than a second, the young female assistant stage manager's face popped into my line of vision behind the fireplace. 'You'll sweep the bleeding stage tonight!' she hissed, a comment that was heard by the first three rows in the audience, who – I have to admit – shared in my mirth.

That September, good to his word, Brian Desmond Hurst engaged me to appear in *Trottie True*. It wasn't much of a part, to tell the truth. I was a 'Stage Door Johnny' at the Gaiety Theatre where 'Trottie True', played by Jean Kent, was appearing. I never had more than an 'I say!' or a 'Gosh! By Jove!' but over two months it was about thirty days' work at six guineas a day.

There were another twenty-nine Stage Door Johnnies, and we were all crushed into a large dressing room at Denham Studios. Among them were a couple of my army companions, Patrick Cargill, and Peter Dunlop, who went on to become a very successful agent. Then there was a tall, dignified chap who informed me that if I had been in the services with him I would have stood to attention. We did go on to become firm friends, but I never stood to attention. He was Christopher Lee.

Christmas was pretty lean that year. Like me, Doorn hadn't had a great deal of work, but we got by and I was optimistic that success was just over the horizon. It wasn't an easy life by any means – but whose was, back then?

A job with BBC television came up early the following year. In those days there were only two stages at the corporation's headquarters at Alexandra Palace, and rehearsals took place in church halls and basements all over London. The first play I was in was a little known late-Victorian melodrama by Patrick Hamilton, *The Governess*. The story centred around the kidnapping of a young girl from a well-to-do family, and the ensuing conflict between her father and the police inspector assigned to investigate the case. I played the girl's brother and I have always been puzzled about my first line in the piece: I came into the family living room and exclaimed, 'I say, Mother! What is going forward here?'

Other plays came my way, both for television and at the Intimate and the Q Theatre in Kew, and it was there that a photographer friend of Doorn's suggested I might do some photographic modelling to swell the family coffers. I was duly introduced to a lady named Pat Larthe. She ran a modelling agency from an office at Cambridge Circus. In that very same building was an agent called Miriam Warner who specialized in booking actors for rep companies. Legend has it that two actors appeared in her office, holding hands. She said that she was only doing single bookings, to which they replied, 'We only ever work together!'

She fixed them with a firm gaze. 'Anyway,' she said. 'I don't engage queers.'

'Well! Be like that,' the boys countered. 'But you should know that Jesus was a queer!'

'Well Jesus wasn't on my books,' snapped Miss Warner. 'So piss off!'

Although I wasn't very keen on the idea at first, over the next couple of years I secured lots of photographic work – illustrations for women's magazines in the main. I was always the romantic hero in the 'true-love' stories, as well as featuring as the illustration of The Doctor in *Woman's Own* magazine. I was even the model for the illustrations of David Niven that appeared when one of the magazines bought the rights to publish extracts from his autobiography *Around the Rugged Rocks*. Then there were the dreaded knitting patterns – for which in later years Michael Caine dubbed me 'The Big Knit'. However, I learned never to knock a knitting pattern: they kept the wolf from the door and I was able to do more rep.

In between rep work, I also stage-managed at the BBC headquarters at Alexandra Palace for a variety-type series that ran on Thursday evenings. I remember one of our guests on the show was a very young singer, Julie Andrews, and from Jamaica we brought over the very first steel band, led by Boscoe Holder – whose brother Geoffrey later appeared with me in my very first Bond film. It was certainly an innovative show and became the forerunner for the big budget 'variety shows' that became so popular in the schedules.

Meanwhile, Doorn was keeping herself busy with ice shows, both in the UK and around Europe. With all the touring and auditioning we were doing to further our careers there were quite long periods when we hardly saw each other, and Doorn was becoming frustrated at my seeming lack of success. On her return from one trip to Portugal I managed to scrape up enough cash for a taxi and picked her up from Victoria Station. However what should have been a happy reunion declined into a furious row as Doorn told me in no uncertain terms what she thought of my acting ability. 'You'll never be an actor,' she said. 'Your face is too weak, your jaw's too big and your mouth's too small!'

As luck would have it, shortly after this I was offered a tour of *Miss Mabel,* a play by R. C. Sherriff. A delightful elderly actress, Mary Jerrold, played the title role. She was regarded as very much of the 'old school'. I remember her woefully telling me how much things had changed with the advent of television. She had appeared in a couple of plays on the box and one day was riding on a London bus when, 'A man leaned over and *actually patted my knee*, at the same time saying, "Very good, Molly, the wife and I enjoyed you very much!" I was shocked I can tell you, they do feel that they know you because you have been in their living rooms.'

I shared a dressing room with Arthur Lowe who later achieved great popularity as Captain Mainwaring in *Dad's Army*. His wife Joan was the stage manager. It was a happy tour, despite some of the awful digs I had to endure. The worst digs were in Bath, where Charles, another member of the cast, and I found ourselves staying. What's more, when we got there we discovered we had to share a room on the top floor. I hated sharing but there was no alternative and anyway Charles was a good egg. The ceiling sloped down to a wall against which was his bed, and mine was against the dividing wall to the next room. There was no bathroom in the house and the toilet was on the ground floor – four storeys down! We had floral chamber pots under each bed in case we felt it too far. It often was.

The supper served in our room that first night was OK – sausages and mash, watery cabbage and some sort of sponge pudding with watery custard. We had not as yet met the landlady, as our needs had been taken care of by an old crone referred to as 'Aunty'. I think she was a sister or cousin, or maybe she had just fallen on hard times and ended up slaving for the Missus. During the night I heard a scratching noise coming from the wall by my bed.

'Charley, are you awake?' I hissed.

'I am now, you silly sod!'

'Can you hear that scratching, banging sound?'

'It's probably mice . . . or rats,' he replied. I thought no more of it, and dropped off back to sleep.

The next morning I decided to investigate what, or who, was in the next room. It turned out to be Mademoiselle Fifi, the star of the nude revue that was playing in the theatre opposite ours. Her bed, I also discovered, was in very close proximity to my wall and she had been sharing it – as indeed she was to do for most of the week – with a rather athletic boyfriend.

On the Friday of that week, before turning in for the night, I had to make my usual four-storey trip down to the loo. I opened the door quickly, as any man on a mission would do, and there seated, with a pair of woollen knickers around her ankles and a fag hanging from her mouth as she read a paperback, was Mademoiselle Fifi. She glanced up and very unconcernedly I thought, said in a broad north country accent, 'Shut t'door on way out, lad!'

Ooh-la bloody la! Charles choked when I told him, and was all for going down there himself.

On the Saturday night Aunty presented us with the bill, at the same time as our sausages. We had decided in advance that there was no way we were going to pay the price asked, as sharing had not been an option when we booked. I told Aunty that we giving her a pound less. She sniffed very loudly. 'I'll call the Missus,' she clucked and with that sped from the room.

Ten minutes passed before the door opened again. There was the Missus! Broad-beamed, her arms folded across her ample bosom. 'Either you pay up or I shall go to the police station and fetch my son!' she growled.

I just couldn't resist retorting, 'Madam, they will not release him from prison over a paltry matter like this.'

The Missus's ample bosom expanded and I thought fire would soon spurt from her flared nostrils, 'We'll see, we'll see! Come along, Aunty,' she sniffed very loudly and they exited, slamming the door for good measure. We waited an hour, no policeman, or prisoner, appeared.

The next morning, after a breakfast served by Aunty in clench-mouthed silence, we placed the money we thought more than appropriate on the breakfast table. As a parting shot, we put the previous night's sausages and the contents of the teapot in the chamber pots and left them under the beds. Thinking about it, we should have purchased a kipper the day before and nailed it under the table. This always served as a warning to the next occupants that there was something fishy about the digs. That, dear reader, is an old theatrical custom.

On my way back from the tour I gathered there were to be auditions with H. M. Tennants – the biggest theatrical concern in the UK at that time. There were two imminent productions, one being André Roussin's *The Little Hut* and the other being an American production of *Mister Roberts*, an adaptation of a novel by Thomas Heggen.

I was summoned to the Lyric Theatre in Shaftesbury Avenue for the first audition. As required, I exhibited my 'magnificent' pectoral muscles and was then asked to read some dialogue. Peter Brooke, the director, must have thought either my pecs were suitable or the reading was OK, as I was engaged to be understudy to Geoffrey Toone, who was playing the 'native' on the desert island, and second understudy for David Tomlinson. I also secured a little extra money by becoming Geoffrey Toone's dresser for matinée performances, which entailed covering him from head to toe in brown greasepaint for his role. Success!

I then turned my attention to auditioning for *Mister Roberts*, which was going on at the Coliseum in St Martin's Lane. It seemed that as both productions had the same management, I would be able to appear as a bit part player in *Mister Roberts* while also understudying on *The Little Hut*. If one of the principals in *The Little Hut* fell by the wayside I could dash over from the Coliseum and wouldn't be missed. It was what was called 'riding the Tennant bicycle'.

At the Coliseum, the director, Joshua Logan, was a giant of a man – so full of energy, which he conveyed so well to his cast members: Hollywood star Tyrone Power as Mister Roberts, Jackie Cooper as Ensign Pulver, Russell Collins as the ship's doctor and George Matthews as the sadistic captain. After exhibiting my pecs once again, I was cast as a member of the ship's crew, along with about twenty actors plus another thirty or so stuntmen, bodybuilders and the like.

In rehearsals, I ran around like a blue-arsed-fly between the two shows: all for fifteen quid a week, but then again I really was a Working Actor.

The set on *Mister Roberts* was enormous and was built on a 'revolve'. In one scene it was a cross-section of a ship, with the Captain's bridge and the deck where all the crew action took place – a hive of activity with cranes and swinging nets carrying the supplies that, in the story, were being distributed to warships in the Pacific fleet. Then, during a semi-blackout, the stage revolved and transformed itself into the interior of either Mister Roberts's or the captain's cabin.

We were rehearsing a scenery change one morning where the stage revolved. As the lights went up, the audience were supposed to see the crew assembled on deck in their white uniforms, standing absolutely, perfectly still. Everyone had to remain rigid in the semi-darkness. Suddenly, out of the darkness came one of our bodybuilders, shivering as if he were in a giant refrigerator.

'Hold it, Hold it!' boomed Josh Logan. 'What's your name?'

The shiverer realized that it was he who was being addressed,

'Arfur, Arfur Mason . . . sir!'

'OK, Arfur, what the fuck do you think you're doing?'

Arthur stopped shivering long enough to say that he was following the director's instructions: 'Sir, you said we should *freeze* when the stage turned, so I was fucking freezing.'

The second act started with Mister Roberts hearing a complaint from a shore patrolman, who is describing the murder and mayhem that has taken place on shore, while a net full with half a dozen drunken sailors is being lowered on to the deck. Arfur Mason had decided to build his part up a bit, and instead of being inside the net he perched himself on top and leapt the last couple of feet to the deck, saluting as he landed and said, 'G'Night, Mister Roberts!' in the worst cockney-American you can possibly imagine.

Leslie Crawford, who became my stuntman and double in later years, was also in the net. One night he and the others decided to tie Arfur's laces to the net, resulting in Arfur leaping to the stage with his feet still attached to the net while his nose spread blood and snot on the deck and all over Tyrone Power's feet. I don't think Ty was terribly amused.

In the story, Mister Roberts blackmails the captain into giving the crew liberty. As the announcement of their new found freedom is made over the ship's speaker system the crew all burst into song with a lusty rendition of, 'Roll Me Over in the Clover'. All the crew had to assemble on the stage right, behind the set of the captain's cabin, and under the baton of Jackie Cooper, burst forth into song.

A complaint was lodged that as the crew assembled they made far too much noise with their size-eleven boots. 'Everyone must come in stockinged feet,' was the order. Some joker, meanwhile, thought that scattering drawing pins would be a jolly good wheeze. Tyrone Power and George Matthews did not agree! All they could hear, as the crew stumbled over one another in the dark, was a series of, 'Fucking hell!', 'Oh! Bollocks to this for a lark!' and 'Oh, shit!' The management were not impressed and some crew were fired on the spot.

Another memorable trick they pulled was one Guy Fawkes night, when a group of them took a large box of fireworks, thunder flashes, Roman candles and the like, and threw the lighted box through the wardrobe mistress's door at the top of the theatre. The explosion nearly took the roof off the Coliseum, and scared the poor wardrobe mistress half to death. More were fired.

Mister Roberts ran for six months or so but closed when Tyrone Power's studio called him back to Hollywood.

Meanwhile, over at the Lyric, everything had gone well and I had not been required to be there except for rehearsals a few times a week. After the closing night of *Mister Roberts*, I took up full-time residence on the third floor of the Lyric and waited for someone to break a leg or catch pneumonia. To pass the waiting hours we understudies played cards, made tea and took trips over to The Nosh Bar – a deli across the road from our stage door, which made delicious salt-beef sandwiches on rye.

Across the road from my third-floor window I could see into the room of a 'lady of the night' – and/or of the afternoon, as it happened. We used to time how long it took for a raincoat-clad gentleman to negotiate the three flights of stairs, take care of his lustful desires, leave some dosh on the mantelpiece and exit very furtively on to Great Windmill Street. Seven minutes was the quickest. The lady in question was a jolly sort. She knew that we were observing her as she plied her trade and when she was in a good mood, she would open the curtains a little wider and throw us a wink!

The stage door of the Lyric was adjacent to the entrance of the famous Windmill Theatre, which in the forties and fifties was the home of near-nude entertainment, made possible on the understanding that the 'models' on show did not move. The main movement in there in fact came from the horny men who scrambled over their seats to get to the front row. Kenneth More, who was to be my best man at my third wedding, actually started work at the Windmill, screwing down the seats that were tipped over by the oh-so-eager customers.

Many top comedians started their careers there: Jimmy Edwards, Tony Hancock, Harry Secombe, Peter Sellers, Barry Cryer and the ever-youthful multi-talented Bruce Forsythe. Bruce loved to come into the Lyric to chat to David Tomlinson and the feeling was mutual. In fact sometimes David would take me with him to have a cup of tea with Bruce ... and occasionally some of the young ladies, who were by then, I hasten to add, at least partially dressed.

The cast of *The Little Hut* was led by Robert Morley; Joan Tetzel was the leading lady, David Tomlinson was the love interest and Geoffrey Toone was the stranger on the island. I had many opportunities to step in for Geoffrey, but being second understudy to David it hardly seemed likely that I would ever have to go on for him. But one fateful Wednesday lunch time, I strolled casually into the theatre, knowing Geoffrey was in already, to be greeted by a slightly hysterical company manager who said that I was late and understudy number one was off. He added that I should have been in make-up 'half an hour ago'.

Sweating and panting, I slapped greasepaint on my face and, still pulling on my dinner trousers, I sped to the stage just in time for curtain-up. I knew all the words – everybody's words in fact – but I was not too sure of the moves. Robert Morley was brilliant, he flicked his eyes at me indicating the direction I should take and somehow or other I got through the matinée performance unscathed.

Coming offstage I bumped into Binkie Beaumont – the Big Boss of H. M. Tennants. 'You were very good this afternoon, dear boy,' he said. 'Very good.'

'Oh, thank you, sir.' I replied. 'Don't you think I deserve a rise?'

Mr Beaumont stared at me for a moment. 'You're married, aren't you?' he asked.

I nodded. 'Yes, sir. I am.'

'Well, dear boy, you are very lucky to be working at all!'

Ouch!

A month later I handed in my notice. I knew I wasn't going to get anywhere in his company. As my career seemed at a semi-standstill, I decided I needed to find myself a new agent, and by chance, one afternoon I was introduced to Kenneth Harper. It was Kenneth who got me a spit and a cough in a film called *One Wild Oat*. Also spitting and coughing in that film was a very young Audrey Hepburn – she actually did get a mention in the credits though. As for me? Well I didn't even get a used Kleenex, but in Audrey I did find a friend and colleague whom I will never forget.

The situation at home was also in turmoil. Doorn and I spent less and less time together and her conviction that I'd never make it as an actor was disheartening. I wanted a divorce. At first Doorn disagreed and, in that painful way of all broken marriages, ours descended into bitter recrimination, culminating in a very heated argument one evening after a performance of *The Little Hut*. As I left by the stage door, followed by Robert Morley and David Tomlinson, Doorn was waiting outside. She was clearly looking for a row, which, much to Robert and David's glee, she got.

We both knew it was over, and eventually she agreed to a divorce.

The divorce laws at the time dictated that the easiest way to gain said divorce was to establish that one of the partnership had committed adultery. In order to do so half of London's hotel rooms were occupied by spouses camped for the night with a man or woman they had never met before. And so it was that I found myself in a room in a hotel in Russell Square with a kind lady who had offered to help. When the maid entered the room the next morning we were sitting in bed – ah-ha! the evidence! – it really was quite ridiculous to think of it now. That obliging lady was not Dorothy Squires, as people have often conjectured in later years, but I did meet Dot shortly after this fateful night.

And a new story, as they say, was about to begin.

★ ★ ★

Betty and Lee Newman – my Welsh friends from Doorn's cottage in Streatham – had by this time been invited by singing superstar Dorothy Squires to live in the guest house above her garage at St Mary's Mount in Bexley, Kent. Dorothy – simply 'Dot' or 'Squires' to me – lived in the main house with her sister Renée, Renée's husband Dai, and their father Arch. They were all very Welsh, 'from the valleys, look-you'.

Dot had achieved huge success in the 1940s and into the early 1950s as one of the UK's most popular singing stars. Along with her songwriter and band leader, Billy Reid, she topped theatre bills all over the country. She was, quite frankly, the equivalent of superstars of today such as Barbra Streisand, whose concerts sell out faster than they can take bookings.

Dot had masses of friends, mainly in the variety and music business, and it was very rare to visit her house at weekends without a roster of famous guests – such as Frankie Howerd, Jess Conrad, Hylda Baker, Petula Clarke, Diana Dors and many others – being in attendance. It was often a very starry cast.

One day, Renée and Betty called me to extend an invitation, from Dorothy, to join them on one of these weekends. The people I met there were fascinating – entirely different from my friends in rep and West End theatre. The old saying that 'there's no business like show business' couldn't be truer than when it came to Dot. I was now mingling with top musicians, comics and agents in the most glorious of surroundings.

Further weekend invitations followed and I soon found myself drawn into this exciting new world . . . and into Dot's. Apart from being highly social, Dot was very attractive and hugely generous to her friends and family. She was twelve years older than me and I was naturally flattered by the attention and interest this amazing woman showed in me. We became lovers.

When Dot was not performing, she – with me tagging along if I wasn't working – would immerse herself in a round of visiting music publishers' offices looking for new songs, or visit variety theatres to see her peers; she particularly enjoyed the thrill of visiting the London Palladium with headliners such as Johnny Ray, Frankie Lane, Judy Garland and Winifred Atwell. Or perhaps we'd go to the Victoria Palace to see The Crazy Gang, with their wonderful comedy shows.

After the curtains came down in the many variety theatres that were then dotted around London, the 'starring acts' would converge on Olivelli's, a real show-biz Italian restaurant in Store Street where, at some point, each of them would stand and entertain their fellow diners. It was a world I'd not been privy to before, but with Squires I now found myself in the very centre of it.

Summer weekends at the Mount attracted an even larger variety of guests, mostly because of the huge pool they could take a dip in. Dot's father, Arch – or Pop as he was called – had his eyes out on stalks when he caught sight of Diana Dors' and Jackie Collins' bikini-clad bodies.

I remember one weekend a lady named Koringa came to the Mount. She worked with snakes – hypnotizing pythons and the like. Frankie Howerd took a great exception to her, for some reason, and was sitting very petulantly on a settee in the drawing room, glowering at her. Squires stretched her hand out to ruffle Frankie's hair and said, 'Ooh, don't let her upset you, Francis dear!' As she withdrew her bejewelled hand, to our horror we saw she had his wig attached to a bloody great diamond ring. In a flash she slapped her hand back on Frankie's pate and managed to unsnag the ring. To everyone's relief Frankie remained unaware of the exposure of his ill-kept secret.

Squires told me that she had once shared digs with Koringa, in the north of England, where their landlady had a cat called Tibby. All week the poor landlady stood outside calling for Tibby, who had gone missing as soon as the new lodgers had arrived. Squires said she could see the lump in the python's throat gradually diminishing and working its way through the reptile's body!

Poor Tibby.

Among Dot's many musical friends, and a regular visitor to the Mount, was Norman Newell. He wrote tens of hit songs including, 'Portrait of My Love', 'This Is My Life', 'More', and 'The Importance of Your Love' – which was the English version of 'C'est La Rose'. Norman was also the head of EMI's Columbia recording company and produced countless hit records with Shirley Bassey, Vera Lynn, Russ Conway, Petula Clark, Judy Garland and Bette Midler among others. One weekend Norman brought Petula Clark with him – she was then still in her teens – and I have fond memories of Pet sitting on elderly actor Charles Coburn's knee, as he sang 'It's a long, long way from May to December', though clearly not as long as it took for him to move his hand from her knee to the hem of her skirt, much to her disapproval!

Dot owned a theatre in her home town of Llanelli, South Wales, and when she wasn't touring she'd often take the train down there to check on everything. My fascination with the world of variety was so great that one year, when Dot was on a music-hall tour around Wales, I decided to have a go at some stand-up comedy myself. Ever the joker, I'd always had a yearning to try it out, and I opened one miserable rainy night in Pontypridd as a comedian-cum-compere. I'd do a bit of patter then introduce the next acts. The audience didn't look inviting. The few people that were there were all wearing raincoats and looking very glum. The steam from the raincoats rose into the air. A few comedian friends had told me that laughter builds: once you've got the audience laughing, they'll go on laughing. In my case, silence built. And went on building. Worse still, in my increasing nervousness I kept forgetting the names of the next acts.

That week in Pontypridd was the beginning – and end – of my variety career.

I discovered there was a very important maxim among music-hall people: never tell the truth as to how much money's been taken at the box office. During one of the noisy Sunday lunches at the Mount one of the guests enquired, 'What did you take at Llanelli last week, Dot?'

'Oh, it was quite a good week,' I piped up, like a fool. 'Eleven thousand, four hund –'

Whack! Dot's stiletto-clad foot cracked me in the shin, 'It was bloody smashin,' she answered. 'Thirteen thousand, eight hundred!'

A little later in the afternoon, after the pain in my shin had subsided, I asked Dot what that was all about. 'Never tell the buggers the truth – they'll only reckon you're bending the truth, anyway!'

Confusing, but true to this day, I've found.

★ ★ ★

No matter how many times we had seen the New York skyline at the cinema, I don't think either of us was quite prepared for our first glimpse of it from the car transporting us from Idlewild Airport, as Kennedy Airport was called back in 1953. We had arrived from London on a BOAC flight, Dot hoping to make a hit of her latest recording, 'I'm Walking Behind You', and me just hoping to find some work in American TV. I was lucky, very lucky in fact. I had an introduction to MCA, one of the biggest US agencies in TV, movies and theatre. They asked to see my passport – this was in the days when passports documented one's occupation. Mine said 'Actor-Manager'. The 'manager' part was due to me helping look after Squires.

'That's not a problem then,' they said. 'You're an actor-manager. You can get a work permit easily.'

Dot and I settled into a small apartment in Manhattan and I set about looking for work. The permit came my way, and I was put up for *Robert Montgomery Presents*. The television drama series was produced by NBC from 1950 until 1957. Each ninety-minute live episode was introduced, hosted and produced by the film actor Robert Montgomery: his presence lent a degree of respectability to the new medium of television and he was able to persuade many of his Hollywood contemporaries to appear. I appeared in two.

One of the peculiarities about American commercial TV, not present in UK at that point, was product placement and sponsorship. In this case, Lucky Strike cigarettes. So each episode kicked off with, 'Robert Montgomery presents your Lucky Strike Theatre . . .'

In my first episode, *World by the Tail*, with Phyllis Kirk and Diana Lynn, I played a UN French diplomat, complete with French accent. One of Diana's lines was: 'On the last date I had with a UN diplomat, he came riding down 5th Avenue on a camel.'

This went unnoticed until the day of transmission – and then it was panic stations. You see, 'Camel' was a competing brand of cigarette and we couldn't possibly mention them! A hasty re-write was called.

My second episode – a month later – was *The Wind Cannot Read*. Thirty years later, on the set of my last Bond film *A View To A Kill*, I was chatting to Christopher Walken about how I got started in America and he mentioned he had started out as a child actor in live TV; and we both then realized that, aged about ten, he had appeared in *The Wind Cannot Read* with me. (Curiously, Dirk Bogarde made a feature film of the same name at Pinewood in the late 1950s and it was forever dubbed *The Illiterate Fart*.)

Anyhow, the tag line to all this is that MCA received a telephone call from a producer named Albert McCleery. He asked if the French actor he'd seen in the episode about the UN could speak with an English accent. MCA had made an anthology series (in which the leading lady plays a series of different characters) with Sarah Churchill starring, and now she was about to play Sarah Bernhardt. They wanted a Frenchman who could speak with an English accent to play her fiancé – as she couldn't speak with a French accent and didn't want to be shown up!

It was all quite preposterous.

However, meeting Albert certainly proved fruitful for me. He produced and directed many episodes of *Matinée Theatre* in Hollywood and later hired me. These long-forgotten live TV plays involved five days of rehearsing. On the day of transmission we all had to arrive at the studio for 5 a.m. We'd then have a dress rehearsal, followed by a 'polishing rehearsal', before live transmission at 12 noon, or 3 p.m. in New York. There was no room for mistakes.

In one episode I played a ninety-year-old Scottish man, and then had to switch to him – in a sort of flashback – as a thirty-year-old. I played the old man with the addition of prosthetics and extra hair on my face, I also had one hand made up with wrinkles and pronounced veins etc. The other unmade-up hand remained as that of a thirty-year-old – and that was the one I had to fight the villain, Patrick Macnee, with. It was a one-handed fist-fight! The crew had 90 seconds to get the make-up off and clean me up, during the 'switch' of ages. When I 'switched', I had to be sure to use only the hand that was pertinent to my age, keeping the other hand hidden. It was quite complicated.

After the first rehearsal the rubber cement that was used to attach my prosthetics pulled a layer of my skin off. In the second rehearsal, when they put the make-up back on, the adhesive began to burn like hell. It was such agony: in fact I couldn't work for six or seven weeks afterwards until the wounds healed.

In another episode, *The Remarkable Jennie Jerome*, I played Randolph Churchill – Winston's father – with my on-screen wife played by Coleen Gray. My versatility knew no boundaries!

My divorce from Doorn was finalized in May 1953 and that July, Dot and I were married in Jersey City – in front of a very drunken Justice of the Peace. Our friend Joe Latona, a member of the knockabout comedy act Warren, Latona and Sparkes, was best man. It was a pretty strange wedding all in all. Apart from being undeniably drunk, the JP was extremely 'casual' in his approach to our solemn vows saying, 'Do you, Dot, take Rog? And, Joe, will you sign here?'

Dot had bought some new shoes for the wedding and they were killing her, so she took them off – and then left them in the JP's office. Guess who missed the wedding pictures as he gallantly ran back to reclaim the shoes?

We couldn't have a honeymoon as Dot was due back in Britain the next day for a TV appearance. I stayed on in New York to see what would happen next.

In addition to the TV plays, I'd also appeared in a few New York radio plays and, with a growing résumé, was therefore well placed to play the lead in the Broadway production of *A Pin to See the Peepshow*, by H. M. Harwood and F. Tennyson Jesse. A fictionalized dramatization of the famous Thompson-Bywaters murder trial, the story centred around the true-life case of two lovers who were convicted and hanged for murder. I was to play Leo, the Frederick Bywaters character. Peter Cotes – brother of British film-makers John and Roy Boulting – directed and his wife, Joan Miller, co-starred as Julia, based on Edith Thompson.

Because of its subject matter and the possible hurt it could cause to Thompson and Bywaters' living relatives, the play had never been given the Lord Chamberlain's licence in Britain, which meant that it couldn't be commercially performed. It had played a theatre club, I think, and the decision was then taken to move it to Broadway where it could be performed commercially.

We opened on 17 September 1953 . . . and closed on 17 September 1953.

There were only about eight critics in New York back then. If a production did not have a 'star' name, advance bookings were always slight and the play therefore relied on the 'press night' to generate publicity and bookings for the ensuing run. Our press night was also our first night. Unfortunately the critics were not particularly kind to us. A couple of rave reviews were negated by half a dozen mediocre ones. The audience reacted very positively – maybe because it included most of the cast's spouses – and certainly spurred us on. We were sure that given a few performances, they'd be queuing up outside.

The next night I arrived at the theatre. I wasn't on until the fifth scene, so came in fifteen minutes before curtain up to find the cast all hanging around the stage door. I asked what was happening and they pointed at the posters on the board. The show had closed, as there were not enough advance bookings to continue. Fortunately for us, the producer had given the cast two-weeks' guaranteed salary. We did at least get some pocket money.

I found a phone booth and called Squires. 'Let's go to the cinema.' We went to see *The Robe* with Dot's Welsh friend Richard Burton, which, incidentally, was the first film to shoot in Cinemascope. After the film we found ourselves going to see Mae West's stage show.

Mae was a great eccentric and launched her movie career on the back of these bawdy stage shows. On stage, one by one, Mae brought on a number of good-looking men, all dressed in long cloaks. One by one, they turned their backs to the audience and, one by one, flashed their bits at Mae. She reacted by holding her hands apart – suggesting the size of their appendages – while simultaneously adjusting the wideness of her open mouth.

Roll on a few years and I was invited to the cocktail party launch of what was to be Mae's last film, *Sextette*, directed my old friend Irving Rapper. Curiously enough, my fellow 007 Timothy Dalton was the male lead, along with George Hamilton. George later told me a wonderful story about the shoot. Apparently Mae couldn't remember a single line, and so they rigged up a little earpiece for her. Irving fed her direction and her lines via short-wave radio.

A couple of days in to the shoot George's character had to knock on Mae's character's trailer door. Mae was supposed to open the door and say 'Oooh, OOOh, OOOOH.'

Which she did, but then added, 'Move to your left.'

George moved.

'No, no,' she said, 'Mae, you move to your left.' She was speaking all the directions given to her!

Then on another day, in the middle of a scene, Mae said to George, 'Ten-Four, Ten-Four on the corner of Hollywood and Vine . . .' as she picked up a police radio frequency!

Back to 1953 and New York, where Dot kept herself very busy with all her friends in Tin Pan Alley, while I carved out a career in TV at the Brill Building on Broadway, where all the publishers and song-pluggers, the writers and the performers congregated in Jack Dempsey's bar on the ground floor. I don't think I've ever walked so far in my life as I did in those months in New York. I found that the pavements are very hard on shoe leather.

I did once take a cab from NBC at Rockefeller Plaza to my agents MCA at their offices on Madison and 58th Street; I had an appointment about a job and was running late. In my haste I pressed a dollar bill into the cabbie's hand and said, 'Keep the change.' The fare, according to the meter, was seventy-five cents.

There was the most horrendous squeal of tyres as the cab pulled away. Odd, I thought. At that same moment the blood rushed from my face: the bill I had given the cab driver did not bear the likeness of George Washington or even Jackson, NO it was a bloody Benjamin Franklin – one hundred dollars, if you please. It was small wonder that the cabbie could afford to burn ten dollars' worth of rubber on Madison. *And* I didn't get the job!

All of this pavement pounding and auditioning did lead to me being seen by Hollywood talent scouts, based in New York, which in turn led to me being 'optioned' for a contract by MGM.

Dot was not so fortunate with her record. Good songs are always recorded by a number of artistes, and in this instance Eddie Fisher, who was a very big star at the time, covered 'I'm Walking Behind You' and had a huge hit with it.

As MGM hadn't taken up their option on me, we decided to travel home to England where I was delighted to be cast in *I Capture the Castle*, a new play by Dodie Smith. I was even more delighted to be working with Virginia McKenna, whom I had seen a few months before in *The Cruel Sea*. Others in the cast included Andrew Ray, still in his early teens, Richard Greene – prior to *Robin Hood* – Yvonne Furneaux, Vivian Pickles and Bill Travers (who eventually became Virginia's husband).

Ahead of starting rehearsals, I told the producer-director, Murray McDonald, that MGM had an option on me but had shown little interest in exercising it to date. Even so, the fact remained that they *might* call me in. Murray told me not to worry: he would take the risk as long as I opened with the play in the West End.

I then heard from my agents that MGM were exercising the option of my contract and that I should be prepared to report to Culver City Studios imminently. Murray asked that I open with the play at the Aldwych Theatre and stay for three weeks. I did, but sadly the play didn't run for long after I left. No, it wasn't because the audiences missed me!

Typically, I had just received my first (and last) good notice for a play. The notice was so good that I was approached by the Royal Shakespeare Company in Stratford and invited to join them. In a matter of days, I went from being a bumming actor to having two offers on the table: Hollywood and the movies – or Stratford, where I could hone my craft and become an accomplished Shakespearean actor . . . A difficult decision? No, not really – I chose the one that paid the most!

Dot was playing at the Chelsea Empire the week that I left for MGM. I remember that on the same bill were singers Malcolm Vaughan and Kenny Earle. The night I flew, I left her at the theatre and a very talented young actress, Joan Dowling, who was married to a young actor Harry Fowler, was there visiting Malcolm and Kenny. A few weeks later, the day before I started at MGM, Joan committed suicide. It left me feeling very shaken.

FIVE

The MGM Years

'Is his cock all right?'

April Fool's Day, 1954, was the rather ominous day I said hello to Mr Hollywood, the appropriately named gatekeeper at Metro-Goldwyn-Mayer's Culver City Studios. I was reporting for my first day of shooting on *The Last Time I Saw Paris* and entering another new, exciting world.

I'd arrived at MGM at the very tail end of the contract system, and of the true glory days of Hollywood. People in the industry were feeling the effects of television, but refused to recognize it, or accept the growing importance of TV as a source of entertainment. Foolishly, the studios refused their contract players permission to appear in any television productions. Period. That was all to change, of course. Meanwhile, I was content with being a movie star.

I remember seeing the imposing Irving Thalberg Building, which dominated the MGM parking lot, for the first time. Through the studio gates and to the left were the offices of Al Trescony, Head of Talent, and Lillian Burns, the drama coach. I came to know these offices rather well.

As I walked from the parking lot I passed the wardrobe department with the great costume designers Walter Plunkett and Helen Rose in residence. Facing there was a passageway that led to the barber's shop – I never passed that shop without seeing Keenan Wynne getting a shave. Then there was the Commissary where stars such as Lana Turner, Debbie Reynolds, Jane Powell, Kathryn Grayson, Howard Keel, Glenn Ford, Eleanor Parker, Walter Pidgeon, Ava Gardner and a young Leslie Nielsen ate their lunch. MGM lived up to its slogan 'More stars than are in the heavens': all the stars could be seen dotted around the room. The writers, producers, composers and musicians would invariably sit at the same tables every day. I often sat with the composers who, I noted, had a wonderful mixture of mid-European accents. I wondered where Hollywood might have been had Hitler not forced so much talent to flee Europe.

In those days, MGM was divided by a number of lots. The back lots were amazing: railway tracks, New York Streets, lakes and streams, the Andy Hardy streets, remnants of sets from *Meet Me in St Louis* and *Showboat*, too. Some of the streets could be covered from above by giant tarpaulins making them weatherproof. Today those lots have become whole housing estates. Maybe at night one can hear the echoes of the fighting in *Gone with the Wind*, or Gene Kelly splashing his way down the street in *Singin' in the Rain*.

Aged twenty-six, a Hollywood virgin, and despite never having seen the workings of a US movie studio before, I did, however, feel a certain familiarity with the town through my countless visits to the Odeon cinema in Streatham. One couldn't help but marvel at the extraordinary stages that dominated the lot: huge window-less buildings with giant sliding doors numbered 1, 2, 3 and onwards, well into double figures. A world away from my early days in live TV at the two-stage Alexandra Palace.

As I walked down a corridor of dressing rooms, past bustling groups of people in various states of dress, I saw that all the doors were adorned with the names of the great actors of Hollywood. I reached the one with my name on, and it was spelled correctly. I stood admiring it for seconds, though it felt like many minutes. Roger Moore had arrived in Hollywood!

The size and position of your dressing room reflected your importance, or the size of the role you were playing – my room, for instance, was very small and quite a walk from the stage on which we were shooting.

Before I had a chance to admire myself in the brightly lit mirror, I was whipped down to make-up by the first assistant director, and then on to the stage. Strangely, I can't remember being nervous. I had actually reported to the studio three weeks previously, so I'd met a few people, but being pushed on to a fully dressed stage, with its wonderful smell of greasepaint, glue and timber, along with all manner of people carrying out their jobs, surely that should have unnerved me?

My first Hollywood film was directed by Richard Brooks. *The Last Time I Saw Paris* was an adaptation of F. Scott Fitzgerald's short story *Babylon Revisited*, updated from its 1931 setting to post-war Paris. Elizabeth Taylor and Van Johnson were the names above the title, and somewhere down the supporting players' list was mine.

The day's filming started with Elizabeth Taylor looking ravishing in a rather low-cut dress revealing a delightful swell of bosom. It was then I discovered that there was such a thing as front-office censorship, present that day in the form of a dour, drab-looking lady who objected to the neckline of Elizabeth's dress, and the fact that rather too much of the valley between the two hills of ripe young motherhood was being exposed for all and sundry to ogle and, indeed, for the camera to dwell upon.

Richard Brooks didn't take kindly to being told that his camera angle was too high and should be lowered immediately so as not to offend the sensibilities of Middle America. However, front-office politics won. The camera was lowered, the clapperboard clapped and I had to punch Van Johnson in the mouth. Recalling it now, I remember I was a little nervous at the thought that I might knock the great matinée idol's teeth out.

As shooting progressed, over the next few weeks I discovered the true power of stardom. Allow me to explain. I had a sort of semi-love scene with she of the mountains of desire, which was photographed first in what is called a master take: this meant that you could see the room and the two of us … then the camera moved in for Elizabeth Taylor's close-up, and then a wrap was called. Assistant director Bill Shanks told me that mine was the first shot in the morning, and I would be doing my close-up without Elizabeth's off-screen lines being delivered by herself in person, so to speak. Quite a blow for one as sensitive as me. I thought I'd maybe upset her. But no, it was just seen as being beneath her. I don't mean to criticize Elizabeth – she is a great actress and a great movie star – but I'm afraid she had been rather spoiled by the system. On that day I resolved that I would always be present to deliver off-screen lines.

One day during the shoot I met up with Eva Gabor for a coffee in the studio cafeteria. Before we'd finished, Bill Shanks came in and told Eva that she was needed for the next shot.

'Oh, darlink,' said Eva, pulling a huge diamond ring off her finger. 'I wasn't wearing this in the last shot. I'll have to take it off for continuity. Look after it for me.' She gave the ring to Bill, who duly popped it in his trouser pocket. As he was doing so, he asked if it was very valuable.

'Oh, it's worth about $40,000,' Eva replied.

'Oh, my God!' said Bill. 'Someone will cut my leg off for this!'

'Don't worry, darlink,' said Eva. 'It was only two nights' hard work.'

That was the difference between Eva and her sister. I am sure Zsa Zsa would have said it was only one night's hard work!

I was warmly welcomed by the cast and crew alike, and felt very secure in my new environment – almost untouchable, in fact. Van Johnson was particularly nice to me. When you were a featured player in a film, you had, on the stage or just outside, a trailer of your own: a solid, wooden-framed little room that rolled from one stage to another. If you had any clout you could arrange for your trailer to be decorated in any way you'd like. Johnson had clout. He'd been at MGM for seven years, though this was to be his last film for them. His trailer was full of memorabilia from his movies, and all the furniture and fittings were upholstered in rather lovely leather. I remember sitting with Van having a cup of coffee one morning when Edmund Purdom, who had also been under contract for some years with the studio and who was riding the crest of his Hollywood wave at that time, popped his head round the door.

'This is your last film here, isn't it, Van?' Purdom asked.

'Yes – yes, it is,' said Johnson, rather hesitantly.

'Oh good,' Purdom beamed. 'Well I'll ask for this woom after you've gone …' (He pronounced his 'r's as 'w's) '… I'll get wid of this … and keep this …' Through his freckles I could see Van's face getting paler and paler as Eddie went round the trailer detailing what he'd throw out and how he'd change things when Van was no longer there. It suddenly dawned on me that if Van Johnson could so easily be replaced, then maybe I wasn't untouchable after all.

Years later when I told Van that I'd never made a film before *The Last Time I Saw Paris*, he was mortified and begged my forgiveness, saying, 'If only I'd known you were green – I could have helped you so much more!' He was a very sensitive and caring man.

And the truth is, I was totally green. Of course, I was delighted that all this was happening to me, but I still couldn't quite believe it. As a contract actor, especially a British contract actor, I was pretty low on the ladder. Several British actors, including the aforementioned Eddie Purdom, were becoming what the studio bosses called 'temperamental', and the studios didn't like that one bit. Me? I was too new and too polite to even consider getting temperamental – even if I'd had anything to complain about.

The only person I knew in Hollywood, and I mean actually knew, rather than being familiar with from their big-screen appearances, was Jeff Hunter, a good-looking actor under contract to Twentieth Century-Fox. We'd met at a gymnasium in London during my time understudying Geoffrey Toone in *The Little Hut* on the West End stage. The role called for me to prance about in a loincloth, so I decided I ought to pump up some muscle. Jeff was en route to Malta to start filming the C. S. Forester story *Sailor of the King* and had had the same thought. A firm friendship was forged, and in fact I named my eldest son Geoffrey after him. In Hollywood, it was Jeff, who lived just over Coldwater Canyon with his wife the beautiful Barbara Rush, who showed Dot and me around and helped us in our quest to find a home in Westwood, our preferred area. There, we settled on a little apartment in Gayley Avenue, right in the heart of the sorority houses of the students of UCLA.

Before leaving England, I'd done a rather smart deal with the actor Richard Greene. He'd told me that he wasn't planning on going back to LA, but had a very nice Alvis car there, a silver-grey model with a red leather drop-down roof. In London, I'd just bought a new Vauxhall and so we did a straight swap. I certainly got the better deal. The drive from Gayley Avenue to Culver City took about ten minutes in my stylish car, with me posing at the wheel in true Hollywood beefcake style.

In my first week, Jeff took me to Rhonda Fleming's house for a party. She was one of the great Hollywood beauties and I was very excited to meet her. The house, white with great pillars around it, like something out of *Gone with the Wind*, was in the exclusive area of Bel Air, and was set against a cliff, enabling one of the internal walls to have an artificial waterfall running down it. Jeff rang the doorbell and out came this apparition all decked out in white, her red hair flowing down her back. 'I am Rhonda Fleming,' she said, shaking my hand.

'Yes, I know,' said I, rather awkwardly. Once inside she asked me if I wanted a drink. 'Yes, please,' I managed.

I was then handed some fruit juice and told to go outside to the patio where a large group of actors, agents and assorted Hollywood types were in a circle holding hands.

'Jesus, *already*?' I thought to myself. 'Everything I've heard about promiscuous Hollywood must be true!'

Alas, they were praying. As it turned out, they were praying against nuclear war. So I sat holding hands with Rhonda and prayed that the praying would soon stop.

I was in the publicity department at MGM one day when another great Hollywood beauty, Grace Kelly, came storming in. She was furious. Apparently, they'd put Ava Gardner's breasts on Grace's image for the posters of *Green Fire*. She objected to being given large breasts as she 'wasn't built like Ava'. (That was nothing. Later on they put my head on Steve Reeves's body – I never had muscles anything like his! Well, not then at least.)

It was in that publicity department that I met a fellow Brit who became one of my closest lifelong friends, a publicist named Jerry Pam. He lived in Dick Street, which I remember for some odd schoolboy reason. Jerry loved entertaining at his home, and it was the tiniest house you can imagine, often leaving me wondering just how he managed to squeeze us all in. Among many of his claims to fame, it was Jerry who orchestrated the Beatles' arrival in the USA and their subsequent media tour.

Not long after we met, Jerry went freelance as a publicist and I became one of his first clients. I am still a client and look forward to my visits to LA, or his to the South of France, where we have our Côte d'Azur Wine Club meetings. Fine wine, good conversation and delicious food are the order of those days.

★ ★ ★

My MGM contract was for the usual seven years, with 'options' – the options were very much on their side and I could have been dropped at any minute. All artists were contracted for forty weeks a year, but their salary was spread over the full year. I was receiving a princely $400 a week.

Money aside, I decided that Hollywood was marvellous. It was all I'd hoped it would be, and more. The sun always shone, unlike in London, and all the streets were lined with palm trees that seemed to reach to the sky. It felt very much like the land of opportunity. Added to that, I was young and lucky enough to make many friends right off the bat, thanks in the main part to Jeff Hunter. We went to all the nightspots and parties. We'd hang out at various bars, like The Luau, Don the Beachcomber – they made great rum drinks – or Scandia on the Strip, where they did great sausages on a Sunday morning.

Dot was still flitting between Hollywood and engagements in the UK, but in any spare time we'd go tenpin bowling with friends such as James Mason, Diana Dors and Eunice Gayson. A gang of us would meet up to have a beer and then play. Di was probably at the height of her fame at the time and became a good friend. We'd often meet up, for breakfast or lunch, or the aforementioned game of skittles.

Di had split with her first husband Dennis Hamilton, and one afternoon at my apartment I received a call from a *Daily Mirror* journalist

– I think it was Jack Bentley – to ask if I knew where Diana was. She was, in fact, sitting next to me. I asked why he wanted her.

'Dennis Hamilton has died,' he said, 'and we want to let her know.'

Bentley was obviously looking for a story, so I didn't let on that Di was with me, but then I had to break the news to her. Naturally, she wanted to return to London, so I arranged her flight and drove her right up to the steps of the plane at the airport so she could avoid the press – life at airports was easier then. Even though they had initiated divorce proceedings, Diana still cared deeply for Dennis.

In between films, contract players would be sent up for tests as a matter of routine. Thankfully I was not called for singing auditions for MGM musicals as, when I'd signed up, I'd made a point of saying I couldn't sing. To prove my point, I sang wildly off-key when the maestro played his first note. I didn't fancy being a part of musicals, and the feeling was mutual with my employers. I didn't know then how much I'd come to love watching them in later years.

A few months rolled by, along with several film tests and readings, and Dot and I were invited to a preview of *The Last Time I Saw Paris*, my eagerly anticipated Hollywood debut. It was quite a glitzy affair, an evening screening in a movie theatre on Olympic Boulevard. It was a huge thrill to sit there and see the famous lion roar, followed by the roll of names: Elizabeth Taylor, Van Johnson, Donna Reed, Walter Pidgeon, Eva Gabor, George Dolenz . . . and Roger Moore! Excitement soon turned to fear though, as I sank lower and lower into my seat waiting for my entrance. I suddenly felt very nervous. There was a murmur when I eventually walked on – a collective 'Get him off!' or 'Who let him in?' perhaps? I can't remember, I was too transfixed on the screen. It was a strange, strange feeling and rather intimidating to see myself and realize that I was not *quite* as good as I thought I was. However, I'd made it. I was on the big screen in Hollywood and in a speaking part.

Now that six months had passed and the first 'option' in my contract had been picked up, it looked like I would be at the studio for a while longer. Deciding to rent a slightly better apartment, we moved to a penthouse on the next street, Levering Avenue. There we had a large terrace all to ourselves, and a swimming pool shared with a few of the adjacent apartments. We had rather lovely neighbours too: young air hostesses. Oh, and another neighbour was William Shatner, later of *Star Trek* fame. We whiled away many an evening all sitting around the pool, having a drink or three. A little while later Christine Jorgensen moved into the block. She had been a he: a former army private from the Bronx who underwent surgery and hormone treatments in Denmark in 1952, in the very early days of gender realignment surgery. The joke going around was that Christine had announced she was going to star in H. Rider Haggard's *She* with me, but didn't say which part I was playing.

There was always a party going on somewhere in Hollywood, and we soon started building our circle of friends. There were three levels of parties, the A-list, B-list and C-list. If you were a contract player, you were immediately on the B-list. If you were just a jobbing actor, you were a C-lister. The A-listers were, of course, the big stars. Rarely would an A-lister attend a B-list party, but a B-lister would live in hope of being invited to an A-list party. We were all categorized and rarely did you move outside of your own listing.

Another friend in Westwood was the actor Red Buttons and his wife Helayne. One night I fixed a dinner date to take them both out, and I said I'd call to pick them up. Red had just returned from shooting a film in Africa with John Wayne. While there, he'd fallen in love with the bush babies – tiny little nocturnal animals, no bigger than squirrels, that have little suckers on the end of their fingers to help them grip as they bounce and leap around. Despite their small frame, bush babies are renowned for their very loud, shrill cries – just like those of a baby, hence their name. One method of catching these curious animals is by placing a saucer of beer on the ground. The bush baby comes down to investigate, pops its fingers into the booze to taste, and then falls over drunk.

Red decided to bring one back with him, and loved it dearly. They had to keep the doors and windows closed, as it flew around the rooms – jumping from wall to wall. On the evening of our date, I arrived to find Red and Helayne in tears. Apparently Red had popped to the bathroom, and after taking a leak pressed the flush button. At that moment their bush baby flew into the room and, plop, straight into the toilet bowl. Gone. In New York if people flush baby alligators down the toilet and the sewers are crawling with fully grown alligators, in Los Angeles there are colonies of bush babies!

My next film was to be *Interrupted Melody*, directed by Curtis Bernhardt, the true story of Marjorie Lawrence, the famous Australian soprano who fell victim to polio and, against the toughest of odds, fought back to make a full recovery. Eleanor Parker played Marjorie Lawrence, Glenn Ford was playing her husband, and I was cast as Paul, her younger brother.

The opening scene was shot a long way outside LA, up in a ranch. If you watch the film, you'll see the scene starts on a close-shot of a cock crowing and the camera moves across the frame revealing it to be a farm. I come out of a barn leading a horse, and Eleanor Parker rushes out of the house to get on the horse – a simple enough setup. While we were lining up the shot, the horse – which had clearly not read the script – decided to stand, and remain, on my foot. After eventually managing to free myself from its dead weight, I hopped around the ranch spouting a few choice words. There was obviously a reporter or publicist on set and, before I knew it, I was headline material. Somewhere along the line the message got a little garbled, though. The news in Hollywood was that I'd been trampled to death by wild horses. Later that night my phone rang. It was my mother from London. The story had gone transatlantic!

Eleanor Parker was very kind to me. She taught me a lot about screen-acting technique, which is very different from the skills required in the theatre. Raise an eyebrow on stage, and the front row might notice. Raise one on screen and it moves twenty-feet high.

During scene setups she'd say, 'Oh, I think you should move here, Roger. This is your scene.'

I'd reply that the director had asked me to stand somewhere else, but she would beckon me over and whisper, 'You go here, darling.'

One day, I said to Eleanor that I thought Glenn Ford was a really nice man and a terrific actor. In reply, she merely looked at me quizzically and said, 'Come and watch him tomorrow.'

The next day, Eleanor was in a big scene where she had to crawl across the floor, crying hysterically, dragging her legs. I watched as Glenn Ford deliberately killed every take until about the ninth, when he said 'Yeah, I like that – print it.' By this time Eleanor was absolutely exhausted. She'd given her all in the earlier takes and was now visibly flagging both in energy and in performance. Against his exhausted co-star, the energetic Ford looked very good indeed.

Eleanor looked at me and said, 'See what I mean?'

Glenn also taught me a trick or two though, one being, when in a two-person shot, always to point your downstage toe (the one closest to the audience or camera) to the middle of the camera, as this brings the shoulders round so that, rather than being in profile, it's your face that dominates the screen. His stand-in would always move his mark upstage of me, and my experienced stand-in would then move mine. I remember when we came to do the shot, Glenn would move upstage and I moved to follow him. The director eventually said, 'Would you *please* stop moving upstage – you're going to fall off the edge!'

By this time, I felt quite settled at MGM and thought I knew everyone around the studio. I'd say cheery hellos to Ava Gardner, Debbie Reynolds, Vic Damone, and the like. They probably wondered who the hell I was.

For me, one of the highlights of making *The King's Thief*, my next film for MGM, was working with and getting to know David Niven, who was playing the Duke of Brampton. As I mentioned earlier, I had met Niv during my time at Publicity Picture Productions in Soho in 1943, when he was adviser to the training film we were making, though then he wouldn't have noticed me, a lowly gofer. I was able to tell him about how, during my lean earlier years, I'd done some modelling, and how an artist had used me for reference stills in the serialization of his first book. A funny, funny man, Niv told great stories. However, he told them so often that he started believing them, and most were heavily embroidered. But it was during the making of *The King's Thief* that we forged a great friendship.

George Sanders was also in the picture, playing King Charles II. He was absolutely wonderful and had, of course, played the Saint in many films, though my haloed days were as yet some years away.

In life, there is a line that I am petrified of saying, at some point, to a fan. George and I were passing Mr Hollywood coming out of the studio gates one evening, and there was a group of people asking for autographs. I stood watching George diligently sign them when one, a young girl, said, 'Oh I've seen all of your movies, Mr Sanders.'

George looked down and snapped, 'Name one.' The look on that poor, crushed little girl's face was awful.

George was very sardonic. He was also very lazy. In his contract he had it written that he should get a thirty-minute break in between costume changes – and we were, of course, doing a costume picture! It was further stipulated that there should be a chaise longue in the room so he could rest whenever the mood took him. As he was playing Charles II, George spent most of his time sitting on the throne. So when they called, 'Cut!' and said, 'You can step out now, Mr Sanders,' he would say, 'No, I'll stay here, thank you,' and with that would close his eyes and fall asleep. It was amazing to watch.

I didn't see George again until I was shooting *The Saint* at ABPC Studios in Elstree and he was on another stage making a film. It was bizarre that I was now playing a part he had helped make famous. George was not at a happy point in his life. I know he had put a lot of his money into a company that produced sausages, and it had gone bust. All of a sudden, George was broke. It was very sad. He committed suicide at sixty-five. Hauntingly, he had previously told David Niven that he was going to kill himself when he reached pension age.

I think the entire Hollywood contingent of English actors, or those who played English roles, were employed on that movie. There was a long-established little clique of British artists based in Hollywood. I wasn't really part of it but would sometimes have dinner with Cecil Kellaway, and I'd find other people like Cedric Hardwicke, Gladys Cooper, Robert Hardy and so on, there too. I don't think I ever encountered any rivalry. There was more of a spirit of comradeship.

The King's Thief was written by Christopher Knopf, son of Edwin our producer, and directed by Robert Z. Leonard. Pop Leonard, as he was known, had actually retired but he came back to the studio as a favour. A real swashbuckler, the film was based on the story of Captain Blood, and Edmund Purdom and I played highwaymen.

Sydney Guilaroff, the hair stylist on the picture, who was a Hollywood legend in his own right, rather liked me and would always give me the longest wigs to wear. As I sat having my wig fitted one morning, a lady in the chair next to me was having an assortment of tapes attached to the back of her head, her neck, and over the top of her head, tightening up her facial skin. When they were all pulled together, the wig was put on and she turned towards me. It was Marlene Dietrich. She was filming *Around the World in 80 Days* at the Goldwyn Studios up the road, but would only have her hair done by Sydney.

While we were shooting, I was sent for by the head of MGM – the greatly feared Dory Schary, who had ousted former head Louis B. Mayer – and informed that my next role was going to be playing opposite Lana Turner in *Diane*. Edmund Purdom had worked with Lana in *The Prodigal*, a couple of years earlier. Returning to the set, I rather excitedly told Eddie about my upcoming starring part, which would surely see me on the party A-list.

'I guess that's OK if you don't mind a bit of booze and sex on set,' replied Eddie, which I thought was rather ungracious of him. I later learned later that he had been in discussions about the role in *Diane*, and had actually been expecting the part, but I gather Lana Turner did not want to work with him again.

During the making of *The King's Thief*, Eddie (who I think was married to his second wife at the time), was having an affair with Linda Christian (who was married to Tyrone Power). Who could blame him? Linda was one of the most beautiful women in Hollywood. On the sound stages, long before the days of mobile phones, there used to be a phone on a sort of stand that could be wheeled around as needed. Every time Edmund was called to set, it seemed that he would simultaneously receive a phone call, and would consequently hold everyone up. He wasn't malicious or nasty in doing it; his head was just up in the clouds. He was a very good actor, but his mind was in music ... and on Linda Christian.

One day, as he was about to hold us all up once again for the nth time, Niven looked at him, and said rather dryly, 'Bit of a cunt, isn't he?'

Unfortunately, during his successful years Edmund had made enemies of the two most influential journalists in Hollywood, Hedda Hopper and Louella Parsons. After he left MGM he was cast in a film to be directed by Irving Rapper. Irving brought Edmund in to have a meeting with the producer who was not sure about having him as Eddie's reputation had been sullied by the aforementioned hacks. Irving assured the producer that Edmund was a nice guy and much maligned. On meeting the producer the dialogue went thus: 'Eddie, I want you to meet with the producer Harriet, Harriet Parsons.' Pause. Edmund Purdom: 'No welation to that old cow, I twust?'

She was Louella's daughter. Oddly enough he did get the role. Good old Eddie.

We all knew *The King's Thief* was not going to win any Oscars. We didn't all choose to admit it, though. Reluctantly, I agreed to attend a test screening, where members of the cast, producers and studio executives attend a preview showing of the film to gauge the audience reaction. As the reels unspooled, the audience became increasingly restless. In fact, at one point, I thought they'd soon be throwing their seats at the screen if they had to sit through any more of this torture. Then a line came up that received a huge laugh, albeit unintentionally.

Edmund and I were chained in shackles in the Tower of London and Ann Blyth, who played Lady Mary, had come in to see Edmund's character, Michael. She slipped him a knife and after she left, Michael busied himself undoing his shackles from the wall, and then undid mine. We climbed into the chimney to make good our escape but discovered bars across it, preventing our exit. Michael picked away at one of them with his knife, loosened it and then handed the bar down to me, to undo his shackles on his wrist.

'Twist it open,' he said, dramatically.

'I'll break your arm!' I replied.

'It doesn't matter!' he airily replied, at which the audience hooted.

I anticipated the laugh at this awful line, but had not anticipated the crescendo it would reach when my character started climbing the chimney, behind Edmund, only to say earnestly, 'Careful, Michael,' as he kicked a pile of soot and a big brick, which bounced off my shoulders. Oh, such wonderfully clichéd dialogue.

Not feeling too bruised by the reviews of *The King's Thief*, I concentrated on more exciting times ahead – and Lana Turner.

Diane was directed by David Miller from a script by Christopher Isherwood. My character, Prince Henri, was a rough layabout of a man who liked to wrestle. In the costume fittings, which were endless, it was suggested that perhaps my legs were not muscular enough. Maybe I needed prosthetics on my legs? I had casts taken and these damn rubber things attached to my legs under my tights. I walked with my knees three feet apart because I couldn't close them. It looked ridiculous. I protested. The call came to go up to Benny Thor's office. He was the number two at MGM – and known as the hit man. It was he who would decide whether or not I needed to wear these false muscles.

I walked in and stood in the doorway, like a young boy visiting the headmaster's office. Benny Thor didn't look up at me.

'Has he got 'em on?' he growled to his people, who were obvious sycophants, there only to agree with everything Benny said.

'Yeah,' they confirmed.

He looked up. 'Well, tell him to take 'em off,' he growled, ignoring me completely.

I was ushered next door, to remove the leg pieces. I returned and stood in the doorway, looking at Benny Thor.

'Has he taken 'em off?' he asked his people.

'Yeah,' they said. He looked up.

Again, ignoring me, he turned to them and said, 'Well, he doesn't need them then, does he?'

Our very own Solomon had passed judgement. I was told my legs would appear unaided by prosthetics.

I've already mentioned how I understudied Geoffrey Toone on the stage. Well, I'd heard that he was coming back from Australia and stopping in LA. He'd always said that I'd be a star – 'All my understudies are now stars,' he used to say. 'Errol Flynn understudied *me*, you know.' Being now rather grand, I returned the favour, as it were, by suggesting him for the part of the Duke of Savoy. When Geoffrey came in to meet everyone, all seemed fine – he was perfect. They sent him off to wardrobe and kept putting different costumes on him. Each time he changed, he'd then have to walk half a mile from wardrobe to the Thalberg Building and the producer's office for the verdict. After about ten changes of costume, ten long walks to and fro, and being told he still didn't look like a duke, Geoffrey exploded.

'I've played more fucking dukes and fucking queens than you've had hot breakfasts!' he shouted. They cowered, agreed he looked perfect and he got the part.

The whole thing about the casting on the picture was bizarre. Pedro Armendariz, a Mexican, was playing a French king. I, an Englishman, was playing his French son, Henri. Lana, an American, in the title role, was also playing it French. When it came to my wife, Catherine de Medici, instead of going with Nicole Maurey, who had tested with me and was absolutely splendid, she was dismissed. Why? She was French and spoke with a French accent! They cast an Italian, Marisa Pavan – not that I minded as Marisa was lovely and a very good actress.

One good thing that came out of the film was that I learned to kiss. Though pushing twenty-eight, with two marriages under my belt, my technique was brought into question. In a dreadful scene, after Diane had been engaged by the king to turn his lout of a son into a gentleman, news of the king's death broke. I had to turn to Lana Turner and say, 'You made me a prince, now make me a king.' Our lips met and I gave her the kiss of all time.

She coughed, pushed me back and said, 'Cut, cut!' Then, 'Honey, you're a great kisser but when a lady's over thirty-five she has to be careful of her neckline. So, could you kiss with the same passion, but without the pressure?'

Passion without pressure. I'm forever grateful to Lana.

The soothsayer in the picture predicted that Henri would die 'in a cage of gold'. Cue the scene: we were in a boar hunt and I was to be savaged by a wild boar. They had a real live boar in the studio, none of your CGI or animatronic animals. The autumnal trees overhanging the set with their golden shades gave the impression of a cage of gold, hence the audience were supposed to think Henri was going to die.

As you cannot train pigs to jump, we had to improvise the attack sequence where the savage animal was to knock me off my feet. The prop boys rigged a plank in the bushes at 45 degrees, a sort of run-up for the boar – or rather a drop-off in this instance. They stood behind the boar with what looked like a soldering iron and, after a sudden whiff of cooking bacon and singeing hairs, the boar came flying over everything in its path!

Cut to me in the next scene. I'm underneath this creature, who had supposedly pinned me down. His back legs were tied down and his jaws were wired up with steel tusks on the outside. I had my arms around his neck. I was safe, he couldn't harm me. Oh no?

Suddenly, he picked me up and began thrashing me about like there was no tomorrow. The whole power of a boar is in its neck, I discovered. My back was black and blue for days.

Still, the steady supply of bacon sandwiches for breakfast for the rest of the week was a comfort.

Moving on, and out of continuity, we were to film the final sequence of the film next – the jousting. I was wearing the full regalia: the metal armour, hinged-finger gauntlets, metal foot and leg armour, the lot. Very handsome I looked too on horseback.

We were filming in cinemascope, which has a wide frame, and I, as King Henri, had to lead all the horses out and, fairly quickly, to bring them all into shot in time. I kicked the horse with my spurs to move forward, and somehow or other, because of the metal footwear, lost the stirrups. I tried to grip on with my metal knees and the horse was going flat-out as we approached the far end of the back lot. Realizing there was no more path lying ahead, the horse turned right … and, bless Isaac Newton, I continued straight ahead.

Coming to, it was as though as I was in an operating theatre with the sun beaming down, and all these faces looking at me. I heard them say, 'Cut his armour off!'Then Lana came into frame and said,'Is his cock all right?'

Let me explain.When we were filming, in between takes we would take it in turns to tell funny stories. One of our favourite stories was from director David Miller. Apparently the great opera singer Enzio Pinza was making his debut at the Met in New York. The auditorium was filled with tiaras, diamond chokers and gentlemen resplendent in white tie. As the music piped up, Pinza walked on to the stage, only for a drunk in the front row to shout out, 'Sing "Melancholy Baby".'

The music stopped. 'Ssh!' came the call from the management. The maestro tapped his baton, and the music started again.

'Sing "Melancholy Baby",' shouted the drunk again.Well, this happened three times before Pinza walked to the front of the stage, holding his hand below his eye level to stop the glaze of the footlights in his eyes.

'I do not know-a the "Melancholy Baby",' he said.

'Well, show us your cock then!' replied the drunk.

This story never failed to make the whole cast of *Diane* curl up with laughter. And it was to this that Lana was referring after my unfortunate accident. Thankfully, nothing was broken, not even my cock, but I was badly bruised, as was my ego. Having spent an uncomfortable night in the Queen of Angels hospital, I was discharged the next day, and the day after that reported back to the studio.

(Which reminds me … I'm not sure on which of my MGM films that I met 'OK Freddy' for the first time. He seemed to be a regular fixture on most film sets. OK Freddy was a terribly well-endowed film extra, if you get my drift. On crowd days he would get it out and show it around for fifty cents; and with a crowd of 1,000 on call, you can see how profitable an exercise it was for him.

Errol Flynn used to employ him for dinner parties. Freddy would dress in white tie and tails and would place his equipment on a silver tray, surrounded by a little watercress, and present it to the guests at the table.You can imagine the reactions. Mind you, on one occasion a girl, knowing full well what it was, stuck her fork in it. Errol was furious – it broke his fork!)

Dot's singing career was going great guns in Britain, so she continued to spend a lot of time in the UK while I stayed in Hollywood. She had sellout engagements all over the country and would fly over to join me whenever she could. I do remember one night during this shoot though, when Dot was with me in Hollywood. It was a night I learned one of life's small – but important – lessons. After a hard day's shoot, I went home tired and hungry, only to be told that dinner was going to be late. I replied with something like, 'What do you mean "late"? I've got to be up early in the morning!'

The Welsh firebrand looked at me furiously. 'Don't you come your fucking King Henri with me!' she snapped.

I promise you, ever since, I've always been *very* careful not to take my work home with me at the end of the day.

When shooting is over, there is usually a party and on this picture we used the MGM nightclub set from *Love Me or Leave Me*, which starred Doris Day and Jimmy Cagney. (I'd actually done a screen test for the film as they needed someone to test opposite Joanie James, but knew I wouldn't get it as Cagney was already lined up. But this is one of the tasks us contract players had to fulfil between films.)

I enjoyed visiting the set after for the lavish party though, and boy, what a wonderful setting it was! Being a nightclub, there were steps down to the dance floor and I sat on one of them with my drink in hand. Lana Turner came in behind me, sat down and started massaging my shoulders. I was rather enjoying it, to be honest, when I heard a male voice saying, 'Hi, honey.'

Lana immediately stopped massaging me. I turned around and there was Lex Barker, her husband – a six-foot-five giant. I got the message.

In the end, despite all of our high hopes, *Diane* was a huge flop and I was fired. It was 1956. I'd been at MGM for two years and I still had five years to run on my contract. Latterly I had been offered the lead in a big TV show but the studio wouldn't release me, or rather rent me out, saying, 'MGM contract players do not appear in TV'. Three months later, just before I was fired, they called for me and said I was going to appear in something called *MGM Presents*, a half-hour TV show using clips from MGM movies. The idea was used a few years later with terrific success by Jack Hayley Jr., who produced *That's Entertainment I* and *II*.

I was annoyed that they wouldn't let me do something really good but now wanted me to do this old rubbish – and it was rubbish. I became rather disconcerted. The films I'd made for MGM hadn't been that successful, and now I was categorized as an actor in costume pictures, which were falling out of favour with audiences. The announcement was made: 'By mutual agreement, MGM and Roger Moore have terminated their contract.'

What they'd actually said was, 'Fuck off'. Very publicly, too.

With prospects looking gloomy in Hollywood, I decided to pack up the apartment and return to England. Just then, the phone rang. It was Charles Russell and Lance Hamilton, Noël Coward's managers. They told me they'd just bought Robert Wagner's brand-new Thunderbird and wanted to ship it back to England for Coward. They asked me how I felt about driving it to New York and taking the *Queen Mary* to England. How did I feel? Delighted!

In tune with my luck at the time, it was my first, and last, trip on the *Queen Mary* – and the worst crossing ever. The weather was terrible: apart from me, everyone was seasick for the entire journey. One of my fellow passengers was a young Gore Vidal. In between heavy rolls of the ship, I managed to snap Gore with my camera – and he used that picture on the flyleaf of many of his books.

I moved back home to Bexley with Dot, wondering what might become of me, a failed Hollywood actor. Would I ever work again? Would I have to be a kept man?

Three long weeks later I received an offer to go back to New York to do a TV play of *This Happy Breed* with Noël Coward. He was obviously grateful I hadn't wrecked his car.

As the play was to be broadcast live, much like my old BBC days, we had a three-week rehearsal period to get it all spot-on. Edna Best was playing the mother, Coward the father, and I was playing Billy, who becomes engaged to Queenie, their daughter, played by Patricia Cutts. Coward liked everyone word-perfect for the first reading, not the rehearsal but the *reading*! He didn't like actors arriving, as was the norm, with a script to read through. It was fine for me as I knew the play: I'd done it at RADA and a few times in rep. I had the flight across the Atlantic to be word-perfect.

Patricia Cutts, however, was not word-perfect, she ummed and hesitated, and one day Coward leapt up and said, 'This scene should go "Pop! Pop! Pop!" but I've now had time to read a long book, do my knitting, drop into a deep curtsey and *then* you said your line.'

It was such an experience to work with 'The Master'. Noël Coward offered me a great deal of valuable advice and was always a mine of fabulous stories. One evening during rehearsals we ventured out on Broadway with him to see *The Diary of Anne Frank*. We had drinks before, and then dinner afterwards. Then we all went back to Coward's apartment. It must have been around 2 a.m. when I said I must go, but felt I must congratulate him first.

'We've been through a day of work, cocktails, theatre, dinner and now drinks afterwards, and you haven't stopped talking but you haven't once repeated yourself.'

'It's quite easy,' he said, 'when one talks about oneself.'

Very quick, very sharp. Volumes could be filled with his one-liners. In other valued words of wisdom, he told me never to turn down a job as, if one wasn't working, 'one was not an actor'.

One of my favourite Coward stories was when one of his many godchildren called him to the window, to witness two dogs procreating.

'What are they doing, Uncle Noël?' the youngster asked.

'The doggie in front has just gone blind,' replied Godfather Noël without hesitation, 'and his friend is pushing him all the way to St Dunstan's' (the famous hospital for the blind).

Another typical 'Cowardism' I was fortunate enough to witness was when he appeared on a TV series called *Person To Person*, in which Edward R. Murrow, one of America's finest broadcasters would, from the comfort of his studio, interview personalities in their homes. When Murrow interviewed Coward, I was present with Coward during the recording.

Coward was discovered sitting in the drawing room of his New York apartment and Murrow, with the ever-present cigarette burning from his fingers, after the usual platitudes of welcome said, 'Noël, you are an actor, a playwright, a composer, a director and also appear in cabaret, what is the secret of your tremendous energy?'

'In a word, relaxation, Ed,' came the reply.

'Then the burning question on America's lips is, what does Noël Coward do for relaxation?'

'If I were to answer that question this network would go off the air!' Coward replied.

'On the contrary, Noël, we would have great ratings.'

'Well, Ed, I do have a little secret for relaxation that I can share with you. I paint and, by chance, I have one of my paintings here.' With that, he reached down to the side of his chair and produced a rather nice watercolour of a harbour scene. 'Well, Ed, what do you think of that?'

'Very nice, Noël. What style would you call it?'

'My friends tell me that it is very touch and Gaugin!'

Another of Coward's productions around this time starred Claudette Colbert. Like Patricia Cutts, she also had problems learning the dialogue, and turned up for the dress rehearsal and blew all the lines.

'Oh, Noël! I am *terribly* sorry,' she said, turning to her director. 'I knew the lines backwards before I arrived!'

'I don't want you to say them *backwards*,' he replied, 'I want you to say them fucking *forwards*.'

Some years later in LA, my then wife Luisa and I, along with Greg and Veronique Peck, Kirk and Anne Douglas, and Frank Sinatra, went to see Claudette in a show. We all occasionally ventured out together. She was appearing opposite Rex Harrison. Rex was not a well-liked man and after the show we took Claudette out for dinner and left Rex at the theatre!

Which reminds me of a story that Stanley Holloway told me. He and Rex Harrison were out having dinner at a restaurant one night, when a chap approached them.

'Oh, Mr Harrison! Forgive me, but I'm a huge fan . . .'

'Fuck off then,' snapped Rex.

Later, as they were leaving, the same chap was standing outside. 'I'm sorry, Mr Harrison, I realize I shouldn't have interrupted your meal so I've waited for you to finish.' He proffered a piece of paper hoping for an autograph.

'Fuck off!' Rex snapped again.

Without blinking, the chap thumped Rex in the face and sent him flying backwards.

Stanley nearly wet himself with laughter. 'That's the first case of the fan hitting the shit I've ever witnessed,' he chuckled.

Back at the play, somehow or other I received rather good notices, and Coward referred to me as 'our little scene stealer'. I'd like to think those notices were instrumental in a couple of other TV films coming my way in the US. The shows were transmitted live, and recorded via a kinescope technique, which was a rather bad reproduction achieved by placing a 16mm or 35mm camera in front of a video monitor. I don't think any recordings have survived. One was the Goodyear Television Playhouse in which I found myself cast in a production of a Miss Marple story, *A Murder Is Announced*. Miss Marple was played by Gracie Fields, one of the great singing and theatrical personalities of the 1930s and 40s. She created quite a scandal at the beginning of the war, when she married an Italian,

Monty Banks, and they both went to America to escape internment. The British public never really stopped adoring Gracie, though. She wasn't pretty, but was very much the girl next door, the lass from Lancashire.

By 1956, Gracie was married to an Italian electrician by the name of Boris. We rehearsed in New York but then moved to the NBC studios out in Brooklyn, and Miss Fields and I were asked if we minded sharing a limousine, which I was delighted to do. I was quite aghast, though, to witness this mature lady putting her hand on her husband's knee in the car and saying, 'By heck, ma Boris is lovely.' Little did I know that I would share these passions, not for Boris's knee, but for my darling Kristina, into my late seventies and, goodness me, now my eighties.

★ ★ ★

After a few months in New York, autumn was approaching and I decided to return home to England and Squires once more. Word came from Noël Coward that there was a play he would like me to star in – *The Family Tree* at the Connaught Theatre in Worthing. Elspeth March and Daniel Massey were co-starring and it was written by Richard Buckle who was then the ballet critic for *The Times*. God, he was an eccentric, but a lovely one. He told me that he had been in the Scots Guards during the war, and at one point was dropped behind enemy lines. He didn't kill anyone or pull off any derring-do, but did come back with a looted wedding dress, which he proudly wore to dinner the same night.

Elspeth had spent many years married to my childhood hero, Stewart Granger, and naturally I was keen to talk about him. We all knew him as Jimmy Stewart, of course, but he had had to change his name because of the other famous Jimmy Stewart in America.

Fortunately, Elspeth took great delight in sharing stories about my idol, including this one. Apparently, just after Jimmy had completed *Waterloo Road*, one of his first big films, he and Elspeth were going to the hospital where she was to give birth. Although she'd had the most awful time conceiving, and had miscarried several times, they were waiting for a Green Line bus. Suddenly, the suitcase Jimmy was carrying burst open and everything fell out. There he was, trying to stuff Elspeth's bras and assorted baby clothes back in the case, when people gathered around, laughing. He whirled round and snapped, 'Don't laugh at me; I'm a fucking film star!' That made him *very* human in their eyes, I'm sure.

Baby Roger George Moore at about three months old, in early 1928.

With my father, George Alfred Moore, in the garden at Stockwell, south London.

I'm the handsome youth at the front, sitting next to my cousin Doreen. Her parents, my mother's brother Len and his wife Lily, are on the left, mum's sister Amy is centre right and my mum Lily is on the right. With so many 'Lily's' around, my dad called my mum 'Billy' whenever they came over.

A strapping young teenager in school uniform.

In the CSEU production of *The Shop at Sly Corner*, in Germany, 1946.

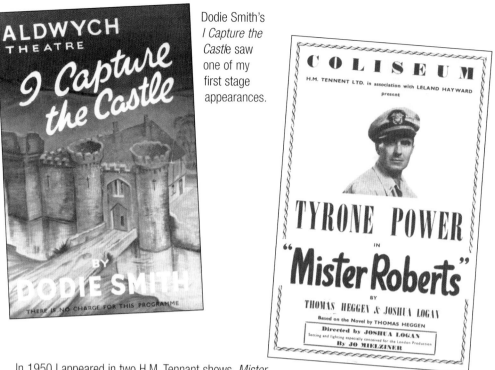

Dodie Smith's *I Capture the Castle* saw one of my first stage appearances.

In 1950 I appeared in two H.M. Tennant shows, *Mister Roberts* at London's Coliseum theatre in St Martin's Lane and *The Little Hut* at the Lyric Theatre in Shaftesbury Avenue – dashing between the two was called 'riding the Tennant's bicycle'.

To earn a few quid between shows in the early fifties, I did some modelling for knitwear catalogues – for which Michael Caine later dubbed me 'The Big Knit'.

My first Metro-Goldwyn-Mayer publicity portrait – the big-time beckoned, but note how they airbrushed my facial mole out of the shot.

Robert Brown (Gurth), Andrew Kier (Prince John) and Ivanhoe himself, 1958.

Ivanhoe, steering clear of water for fear of rusty armour.

Any initial fears I had of being typecast as a TV actor were proved unfounded when, with *The Miracle*, I found myself happily back in Hollywood, 1959.

Beau Maverick, Brett's English cousin, displaying his – and my – best poker face, 1960.

The intense heat of the desert brought on my first kidney stone problems when we shot *Gold of the Seven Saints* in 1961.

A passionate moment with the gorgeous Angie Dickinson in *The Sins of Rachel Cade*, 1961.

My Warner Brothers publicity portrait – with mole intact!

Dot Squires and I arriving back in the UK around 1960.

'Are you the famous Simon Templar?' *The Saint*, which ran for seven years, from 1962–8, was to be a large and wonderful part of my life.

The Variety Club of Great Britain is one of several charities with which I've been involved over the years. At the back, Jimmy Edwards, Max Bygraves, *middle row*, Sid James, Charlie Drake, Frankie Howerd, *front row*, me, Stanley Baker and Vera Lynn, bringing some Christmas cheer.

The famous Volvo P1800, of which there are about a dozen 'originals' out there somewhere.

Volvo also supplied 'half a car', for interior filming.

A scene from the first ever episode of *The Saint*, *The Talented Husband*, in which Derek Farr dragged up to play Mrs Jafferty, the scheming housekeeper.

'Where's my hairdresser when I need him?' A bad hair day on *The Saint*.

My first outing as director on *The Saint* was with *The Miracle Tea Party*. We filmed in Waterloo station in front of a large audience, who were rather more critical of my appearance than of my directing skills.

With my old RADA classmate Lois Maxwell in one of two episodes of *The Saint* in which she appeared.

No introduction necessary for Simon Templar, or the infamous stickman.

Always a charmer, Simon Templar takes tea with the ladies. Dawn Addams, right, was in fact an Italian princess by marriage.

In lugubrious mood in a shot filmed at Elstree Studios. *The Saint* may have run for seven years, but *El Santo* lives on around the world.

My 'partners in crime' on *The Saint*, Johnny Goodman (left), production executive, and Bob Baker (right) producer, fresh from recording a DVD commentary on the show in 2004.

Two shots from *The Man Who Haunted Himself*, 1970. Playing Harold Pelham was one of the first times in which I felt I was really allowed to act.

On the back lot at Elstree Studios during the shooting of *The Man Who Haunted Himself*, with my daughter Deborah and son Geoffrey pulling Luisa and myself.

Tony Curtis and I became firm friends during the making of *The Persuaders* in 1971. There was certainly never a dull moment when Tony was around!

High fashion and quintessential style were always my watchwords … *The Persuaders*, 1971.

With 'Uncle' Lew Grade, Tony and producer Bob Baker at Pinewood on the only visit Lew made to the set of *The Persuaders*. Much of my success is down to Lew, I will be forever grateful to him.

The famous La Croisette in Cannes, one of the many locations in the South of France we used in the series.

Is Joan Collins trying to ignore Tony Curtis in this break from filming? Joan, me, Johnny Goodman, Tony and Bob Baker.

Dame Gladys Cooper made her last screen appearance in *The Persuaders*, in an episode called *The Ozerov Inheritance*.

We persuaded many guest stars to come on the show, so I was very pleased when one of my heroes of comedy, Terry-Thomas, agreed to appear.

With Albert R. 'Cubby' Broccoli and Harry Saltzman on the set of *Live and Let Die* in 1973

This was my first Bond outing – I kept a keen lookout for Sean Connery, just in case.

In bed with Jane Seymour – but we kept our socks on. *Live and Let Die*, 1973.

Sherwood House, Denham, our first family home.

Filming *Gold* in South Africa, 1973. My first taste of the apartheid regime, and sadly not my last.

Although I'd given up cigarettes, I was still enjoying the odd cigar. In the back garden at Denham in the early 1970s.

Spurning the idea of going into local digs in Worthing, I opted to drive home to Bexley every night after the show. Back then, though there weren't any motorways, the roads were empty and I was back in no time. It was a happy few weeks travelling to and fro. I didn't know it but it was to be my last stage appearance for many decades – but perhaps the critics did?

Towards the end of 1956, my knight in shining armour, *Ivanhoe*, came along. There were pros and cons to taking on this role. The main pro was that it was to be a long-running series and a guaranteed year's work, with a holiday. The main con was that it was TV, rather than my preferred choice of a movie. However, bearing in mind what Coward had told me about not being an actor if I wasn't working, I accepted. There was a great deal of snobbery about being a film actor versus a television actor, but it was only when I was halfway through the series that I really started to worry about being typecast as a TV actor, and feared that I'd never work in film again. There was a great stigma in being branded a 'TV actor' in Britain back then, and whilst many crossed from film to TV, rarely did anyone go the other way.

We filmed a pilot for *Ivanhoe* at ABPC Elstree. We shot in colour, during November. I started smelling a rat there and then. They had an extra shouting a line down from the cardboard battlements, which was supposed to be, 'Lower the drawbridge for Sir Ivanhoe of Rutherwood!' and all he could get out was, 'Lower the bridge for Sir Robin of Ivanhood.' There were ten takes of various combinations, bar the correct one. No expense was lavished on talent. Was this my biggest mistake?

When it came to location work for this half-hour epic, there were no leaves on the trees in Sherwood Forest, so we upped and moved to California and shot out in the valley, and in their Sherwood Forest. Very extravagant, I thought, for a thirty-minute pilot. Perhaps things aren't so bad after all.

There wasn't any colour in television in 1956, and so when the decision was made to go to the series, we filmed in black and white – which was undoubtedly much less expensive and undoubtedly also why the show was never repeated in later years.

I had a couple of friends in LA whom I got on the show, one being an Irishman named Keith McConnell. When he was brought in for the reading he was asked if he could ride a horse. He replied, 'I'm Irish', which they took to mean he could ride like Gordon Richards.

It came to the scene where Ivanhoe is riding back home and is stopped by some soldiers. As they approached, with lances and swords drawn, the director David MacDonald said, 'OK, mount up, Keith.'

'I'm not getting up on that focking thing!' came the reply. Eventually, a small band of prop boys and assistants got Keith up on the horse, where he sat, rigid. 'I'm not focking moving on this focking thing,' he warned.

Then, when it was time to go for the take, a rather flustered Keith, instead of delivering his very English line of 'Sir Ivanhoe of Rutherwood, Sir Maurice of Beresford would speak with you,' said, in a very thick Irish accent, 'Ah, Sir Ivanhoe, Sir Maurice would have words wid yas.'

The other friend I got on the show was Tony Dawson, most famous for his role in *Dial M for Murder* and the first Bond movie. He was rather like George Sanders in that he could fall asleep at the drop of a hat. After one take, in which he was wearing full tabard, he decided to lie down in the long grass and dropped off to sleep. Nobody noticed him, and the unit moved on to another location in the forest. The next thing he knew, he was surrounded by children asking, 'Is he dead?' If you'd come across an ancient knight, in full armour, lying in a field, what would you think?

Robert Brown, who played Gurth, became a very close friend and we worked together on a number of things later, including a few Bond films. He was a bugger in that he was a giggler. In one episode, there was a master shot starting with Ivanhoe addressing a group of knights around a table; then a door in the background opens and the camera moves around over me, and Bob Brown – Gurth – walks up to me and the camera, which is pointing over my shoulder at him, and says:

'Sir Ivanhoe, Prince John has landed his forces at Runnymede.'

To which I had to reply with one of those awful bloody lines, 'Gurth, saddle up my horse. We must ride forth to meet him.'

When I started saying, 'Saddle up my horse,' Bob began smirking. The smirk became a laugh.

'Cut!' shouted Bernie Knowles, the director. 'We'll go again.'

Take two. We go through the scene again, and when I get to the said line, this time I burst out laughing.

After take eleven, Bernie was getting a little fed up. 'Right, we'll all sit down and have a nice cup of tea,' he suggested in his Yorkshire drawl, 'and then go back when we're all settled down.' A cup of tea, of course, was going to be the solution to all our problems.

After about fifteen minutes, we returned to the set. 'Have you all settled down then?' Bernie asked. 'Right, OK, we'll go again.'

'OK. Mark it.'

The clapperboard clapped.

'Right. And . . . Anxious! . . . Erm – no, I mean action!' We all fell about this time. The scene, such a simple one, was doomed and we didn't complete it until the next day.

I fell into a fairly quiet routine. Production was based at Beaconsfield. Throughout the week, I lived at the Crown Inn in Penn. I'd get up early and, trying not to disturb anyone, I'd go downstairs, make a light breakfast, then drive to the studio in my Ford Zodiac. In the evening, I'd eat either at the Crown or at one of the other local pubs. Then, at weekends, it was back to Bexley to spend time with family and friends. On Sundays Dot would often invite lots of friends for lunch – many of the characters she'd been working with in variety.

When we were shooting *Ivanhoe*, a suspected duodenal ulcer forced me to take a break. It was 1957, and Dot and I took off for a couple of weeks to Torremolinos – I don't think there was more than one hotel there then. It was a truly idyllic spot ... When Dot came back to England she wrote a song called 'Torremolinos' and all of a sudden everyone had heard of it. I mastered the Spanish language on that trip, two weeks of Berlitz Spanish, *Yo soy muy contento, dos huevos por favor...* what a linguist.

Schedules were tight on *Ivanhoe*. We only had five days to shoot an entire episode. They would be long days as each episode would feature three fights, lots of physical stuff and sword-fighting. Guest stars were often cast, usually in sinister roles, and would invariably say things like, 'I've done sword-fighting at Stratford and won't need a double.' My stunt double, Les Crawford, and I would run through a couple of quick routines, and when the actors saw how fast we were, they'd invariably say, 'Oh, OK, best have a double after all.'

We had one stuntman, Fred Haggerty, who worked all through the series. We knew him as 'Free Frust Fred', because in rehearsing sword-fighting routines he would say, 'One, en garde. Two, parry. Three, thrust!' Only, being a cockney, it came out, 'Free, frust!'

One day, out of the blue, I received a call from Lana Turner. She was in England making a film called *Another Time, Another Place*. One of her co-stars was a young, handsome Scottish actor by the name of Sean Connery. I often wonder what became of him . . . Lana said that she had rented a house on Bishop's Avenue, a rather swanky thoroughfare in North London. As a matter of fact, I already knew the house as it belonged to one of the Bernard Brothers, a very successful variety act, they were mime artistes and friends of Squires. Anyhow, Lana declared that she going to throw a party, and I was invited.

As the guests arrived, Lana pinned a label on them, mine read 'Roger Boy Knight', in reference to *Ivanhoe* of course. One of the other guests was a rather swarthy individual who carried the label Johnny Dago. I actually saw very little of him during the evening, which progressed from drinks to food to more drinks and music to dance . . .

At some point, as the guests started to thin out, Lana asked me to dance – not one of my talents I must admit. As I shuffled around the floor with her in my arms, probably standing on her toes several times, I felt a cold breeze on the back of my neck. I glanced over my shoulder to find 'Johnny Dago' leaning against the doorjamb and staring, unsmilingly, at Lana and me.

A little voice in my head said, 'Roger it is time you went home!' I didn't need a second prompt. I excused myself and made for the door.

A few weeks later I read that 'Johnny Dago' – better known as gangster Johnny Stampanato, with whom Lana was romantically involved, having recently divorced Lex Barker – had been deported by Scotland Yard for having physically abused Lana, and for having entered the UK illegally using a passport in the name of John Steele. He had, I read further, also turned up on the set of Lana's film and threatened Sean Connery with a gun. Sean wrestled the gun from him and decked him with a right hook; all very Bondian. Johnny was convinced that Sean was having an affair with Lana, also very Bondian.

A few months later we were all shocked, but not surprised, to learn that Stampanato had been stabbed to death; allegedly by Cheryl Crane, Lana's teenage daughter, after a huge fight at Lana's Beverly Hills home.

When he had first arrived in California, Stampanato worked for Micky Cohen, one of the West Coast's most notorious gangsters. I once met Cohen at a nightclub where I had gone to see the great Don Rickles, a fantastic comedian who became known as the 'master of the insult'. Gary Cooper was also there that night, and Rickles, having made a few cracks at Cooper and then dismissing me for being a pretty boy at Warner

Brothers, turned his attention to Cohen. He called him a dirty hood, then – obviously thinking better of it – dropped on his knees and held his hands together in prayer towards the gangster, saying that he was only joking and he loved MISTER Cohen SIR!

There were very few parts for women on *Ivanhoe*. Adrienne Corri was in one episode and I remember Jimmy Harvey, the cameraman, was obviously becoming a little frustrated with her. At one point she was sitting looking in the filter of the lens at her reflection. 'Oh, Jimmy, I have a double shadow here.'

'If you point your nose in the direction it should be pointing in,' he snapped, 'you'll only have *one* bloody shadow!'

On another occasion, our American producer from Columbia came over with a young would-be starlet with rather large mammary glands to be in an episode. The director tried to point out to our boss – who had a reputation for chasing any would-be starlet around the office – that there wasn't a part.

We were told to 'feature' this girl. OK. Well, in every scene her breasts framed either the left- or right-hand side of the screen. She never said a word, just appeared in profile with her 38D cups. As the floor had sand, straw and cork all over it, it was impossible to put chalk marks down for my toe to hit – so I'd know how far I should be from the lens. They therefore laid a baton for me instead, and this girl, who didn't have a word of dialogue, after a few days asked, 'Why can't I have one?'

The whole crew would have liked to have given her one . . . but anyway, they produced this baton in the shape of mammaries and put them down for her. I remember her saying, 'Do I put my toes in here?' One of the crew, in the rafters, shouted, 'No, love, your tits.'

As I've mentioned, we had quite a few guest stars on the show. Christopher Lee was cast as Otto the Hun in one episode. Lance Comfort was directing. We'd been on location for days and days; the weather was just awful. I was supposed to fight a duel with Otto to win the freedom of a serf – some thirteen- or fourteen-year-old child actor. Christopher was standing there waiting for the clouds to clear, and he came out with, '*Will dieses verfluchte Wetter, das überhaupt frei ist, ist es nicht genug gut,*' or words to that effect.

The kid looked at him, star-struck, and said, 'Cor, do you speak German?'

Without pausing for breath, Christopher said, 'Yes, and Portuguese, French, Italian, three dialects of Urdu, Swahili . . .' He went on and on – and yes, he does speak all these languages.

Finally, word came through from Wardour Street that we couldn't waste any more time and had to shoot regardless. It was drizzling and Lance said, 'Right, we're going to shoot.'

With that, Johnny Briggs, my dresser, came running forward and in a very camp voice said, 'Oh Mister Comfort! Mister Comfort! You can't shoot now!'

'Why not?' asked Lance.

'Because Roger's armour will get rusty!' said Johnny with a hand on his hip.

I worked with Johnny many times and he never failed to come out with some wonderful lines. On another occasion, a bunch of the stunt boys were sitting around in the wardrobe department and Johnny was sewing on buttons for someone. One of the boys read out the newspaper horoscopes and called, 'What's your birth sign, Johnny?'

'Hairy-arse, of course,' came the reply.

After a day of being buffered around on horses, being thrown into mud and so on, I'd get out of my costume and have a bath. Johnny would come in with a warm towel to put around me. There he'd stand, and murmur, 'Hmmm, not a bottom like my Hardy's.' He was referring to Hardy Kruger, the year before, on a film called *The One That Got Away*. I actually told Hardy that story years later when we were making *The Wild Geese*. He did have a nicer bum than me.

Oh, another Johnny Briggs story! I was having a cup of coffee in my dressing room one morning and we had a new assistant director who tapped on the door, opened it and said, 'They want you on the set, Roger.'

He was almost out of the door, when Johnny said, 'Call boy! Call boy, come back here!' The boy came back, and Johnny addressed him.

'When you come to a *fillum* star's dressing room you knock and wait to be bid enter. When you are bid enter you come in and say "*Sir*, when you are ready, *sir*, they are ready for you on set, *sir*." And then you exit.'

For three months the boy thought Johnny was the producer.

As the series drew to an end, I was worried about finding work as a television actor. It was my father who suggested I try and do my own thing, and he mentioned either John Creasey's series of adventure novels featuring the Hon. Richard Rollinson, *The Toff*, or Leslie Charteris's *The Saint* as being suitable for possible TV series. I liked the idea of *The Saint*, having seen the George Sanders movies, and so I made a half-hearted attempt at acquiring the rights. At that stage, author Leslie Charteris wasn't interested – in either me, or the idea of television, or perhaps both? I drew a blank.

Fortunately, a couple of jobs came up in the USA. Though, yes, they were TV and not film. Still, remember what Uncle Noël said. The first was an episode of *The Third Man* with Michael Rennie. Michael was about four inches taller than me, and of course he was the hero, which presumably meant I was a not-so-nice guy. In one scene he had to grab me by my sweater and pull me towards him, and so I made a point of wearing a loose-fitting sweater. But in every take, he would grab my rather well-developed pectorals. On the fifth take I let him have it in the shin with my boot. See how you like it, I said to myself.

Another British actor, Max Adrian, also in my episode, came in one day looking rather tired. He said he hadn't been sleeping at all well. 'Ah,' I said. 'Guilty conscience?'

He nodded.

'For things you've done?' I asked.

'No,' he replied, 'for things I haven't done. There were times when I could have called my mother, and didn't. Now it's too late. She's passed away.'

Hit suddenly by a combination of emotion, homesickness and maybe even guilt, I had to stop what I was doing, find a phone and call my parents. It was so good to hear their cheery hello on the other end of the line. From that day on, I always made a point of calling them whenever I could during my career and travels. I very much miss not being able to do it any more.

Alfred Hitchcock Presents was the second job out there. The series was topped and tailed by a speech from the great man himself, but of course he was never around the set. My episode was *The Avon Emeralds* with Hazel Court as my co-star. I don't think it was particularly memorable, but it did keep me in LA and in the thick of where it was all happening. I wondered if I might ever make a return to movies. Soon after that the phone rang. It was my agent. Could I report to Warner Brothers for a meeting? he asked. It seemed a contract was in the offing, along with – a movie . . .

SIX

The Warner Years

'Please, mush, any mush'

Warner Brothers Studio clearly didn't mind the fact that I'd been fired by MGM when they dangled another seven-year contract before my eyes in 1958. They had big plans for me. The first project on offer was *The Miracle* – hooray, I was back in movies! – to be directed by Irving Rapper. He had wanted Jean Simmons for the female lead, and she in turn suggested Stewart Granger to play opposite her. However, Irving wanted Dirk Bogarde. Everyone knew that the studio was offering it to one person, while the director was offering it to another, and they all got rather fed up.

Things were settled when Dirk wrote to Irving and suggested me, even though I'd never met him. I thought it was a very generous and gracious thing for him to do and for many years afterwards I tried to thank him in person. Even years later, in the 1970s when we lived in neighbouring villages in the South of France, Tony Forwood, Dirk's manager and partner, would never let me speak to him. It was all very odd. I never got to thank him and I regret it, as Dirk really was responsible for my being offered the Warner's contract.

I tested with Gladys Cooper and got the part, but Dame Gladys was then told that she wouldn't be hired. She adored the sun and did not have 'the pale white complexion' they'd envisaged for a nun. They thought I looked fine, but said that I was perhaps a little 'too English'. I didn't quite understand. I was playing the Duke of Wellington's nephew. How English was *he*? They asked if I'd mind working with Joe Graham, a dialogue director. I said no, I didn't mind.

Joe proved to be a wonderful, wonderful man. He'd also directed a couple of movies for the studio, and legend has it that when Jack Warner – the boss – said to him, 'You were made to direct films for me,' Joe replied, 'No, you were made so that I could direct films.'

They thought he was a little weird, what with that and being a vegetarian too.

Joe wore a hearing aid, and was always rather serious. I am known to clown and joke around, but that never seemed to bother Joe. One day I asked him, 'How can you put up with my awful jokes?'

He looked at me quizzically. I said it again.

'Hold on a minute,' he said, and turned his hearing aid on.

A very thoughtful man, Joe once asked me if I believed in God. I thought this was a bit odd coming from a dialogue director, but I said yes, 'But my vision of God isn't a man with a big white beard sitting in the clouds. I think God is intelligence. I think of God as the "brain" that created all of this.'

'Yes, you're on the right track,' he replied, enigmatically.

Joe reckoned that if I believed our universe was created by some intelligence, then there has to be a reason behind that intelligence – and the reason is that we are all required to acquire further knowledge. He added that if you then believe that what you have been given is only on loan, the biggest sin you can commit is not to use what you have been given.

Quite profound.

'You are six-foot-one,' he observed one day. 'Why do you only stand five-foot-ten? Stand six-foot-one. Did you ever go to university?'

I said no.

'Are you afraid if you say something you might use the wrong word?'

I said yes, I was.

'That's why they think you're too English. You don't open your mouth because you're subconsciously afraid of what might come out.'

Immediately, I felt my jaw loosen.

'It doesn't matter what you say or mispronounce when we're working together. I'll be there to make sure you get it right.'

Our conversations carried on in this vein over several sessions and Joe worked on every production at Warner's with me. I found that I began to speak more fluidly, no longer worrying about what people might think of me. Joe taught me so much about acting, about human nature, and about humanity. I always felt he was more psychiatrist than dialogue coach and remain eternally grateful for all the advice he gave me.

Virtually all of the exteriors of *The Miracle* were shot on the Warner Brothers' ranch in Calabasas, which at that time was just miles and miles of rolling hills, populated by horses. We also went to the MGM lot where they had a permanent bridge and river. We used it for a love scene between Carroll Baker, the female lead, and myself. No one noticed until rushes the next day that after our lips pressed together and we parted, a 12-inch stream of spittle from one lip to the other was left glistening in the sunshine. A retake was called. Not that I minded a retake with Baby Doll Baker.

Two major friendships were born for me on this picture: Irving Rapper and Gordon Douglas. Irving was a great actor's director but Gordon came in, as a favour to Irving, to handle the battle sequences and the action sequences. He didn't take a credit. We immediately hit it off.

For the Battle of Waterloo scene, I had a beautiful costume with white britches, a tight jacket and a brass helmet. The problem was I couldn't wear anything underneath the britches, such as an athletic support, as the line would show through. A solution was found in the shape of Rosalind Russell's toreador girdle from *Auntie Mame*. It was fine, but at the end of a hot day sitting on a horse, my arse was ribbed like a sheet of corrugated iron. I still carry the marks.

As the Duke's nephew, I had to lead the charge of a couple of hundred horses. I was positioned twelve lengths out in front and the special-effects guy said, very matter-of-factly, 'Now, Rog, there'll be a few explosions.'

It always unnerves me when the man who says this type of thing holds up his hand to reveal two missing fingers.

I asked where and he pointed out the trees that would blow up. 'When will they blow up?' I wanted to know.

'After you've gone past and before the others who are following.'

Great. I whispered in my horse's ear that this was what was going to happen. It seemed simple enough. We started off and, just as I reached the first tree, it blew up in front of me. Not behind, in front!

My horse shied and I lost my stirrups. I was shouting 'Help! Help!' but we were shooting without sound – MOS – and they all thought I was bravely laughing and smiling. There were no microphones to record my actual vocabulary. The buckles on my britches, meanwhile, were cutting into my knees and blood was pouring down into my boots. They were right, I was brave, but scared shitless. (MOS, by the way, came about when one of the Hungarian directors turned to his soundmen in Hollywood and said, 'We vill shoot zis mit out sound'.)

Torin Thatcher played Wellington, my uncle. (Squires told me that he had once tried to put his tongue down her throat – for which, I imagine, he got very short shrift.) Anyhow, he's looking down from his vantage point above the battle, and thinks he sees his nephew blown up. I'm now, in character, on the ground. The script says that my helmet has split in the explosion, and I am to reach forward for the helmet while being puzzled that I am alive and not dead.

Gordon, in his rough raspy voice, said, 'Roger, when I say action there'll be a few horses coming through, but they'll be behind you and in front of you.'

Two horses came in front and three behind, and as Gordon barked, 'Now reach for it. Reach for the helmet,' another horse came through, put its hoof on the helmet, which sank into the mud.

'Pick up the helmet, Rog,' he called.

'I can't find it! I can't find the bloody thing!'

That was a day I would not care ever to repeat.

I enjoyed making the picture, though. It was good to be in Hollywood again and on a movie. Movies generally have a little more time in their schedules, and a little more money. Breaking out from the constraints of TV felt quite liberating. I thought *The Miracle* was a happy start to my time at Warner's.

In 1959, Squires and I acquired a new neighbour. Josef Locke, the famous Irish tenor, arrived in LA with his new young bride from Manchester and moved into an apartment that directly faced our pool. Joe had worked in variety for years and so knew Squires and me. He would often come over to chew the fat, and one day admitted to us that his younger bride was driving him mad. He'd never actually wanted to move to LA, he claimed – it was her. Her mother had already moved to LA to be near her son, and so the daughter (Josef's wife), wanted to be there too, and encouraged Josef to uproot himself. He had recently received substantial tax demands from the British authorities and declined to meet them, so he probably didn't take too much persuading to leave for the US.

Joe was full of the Irish blarney. One night I was with him in his car driving home, and he was pulled over for some minor offence. He wound down the window and spoke in a three-times broader Irish accent than he had before – and as it happened the cop was Irish, so Joe got off scot-free.

As time went on, Joe became more and more determined to do something about his wife and her 'mother fixation'. 'She can't stand bad language,' he told me '. . . which is fecking terrible for me.'

He decided on a separation, but said that first he needed to recover some of the money he had deposited in a Dublin bank in her name. So he had her sign a piece of paper, which he told her was some customs document. Without thinking twice, she duly signed it. He then put in a letter above her signature, addressed to the manager of the bank in Dublin saying, 'please transfer all my assets into my husband's account'.

Every morning, Josef intercepted the mail, waiting for the reply to confirm the transfer, which eventually arrived. So he got his money back.

'You know, I bought her a lot of furs,' he told Dorothy one day. The very next morning, he turned up at our apartment carrying two suitcases. They were *stuffed* with fur coats.

'Would you look after these?'

The next morning he came in laughing. 'Oh it's all happened this morning!' he said. No doubt she'd noticed the absence of her furs. 'As a wife, she's never done anything for me. She's never made me breakfast. She is a lazy tart,' he claimed.

That and his wife saying, 'I think I'll go across town to see mother today,' started an almighty row.

'Fuck your mother! She's an old cunt and she's dying,' he shouted.

There was a scream and she rushed out the door, leaving him for ever. I don't think he minded.

A week or so later, Josef came over to join us for a drink on our terrace. 'You know, Roger, I gave her a lot of jewellery. I'd like to get that back.'

He had me drive him across town to the mother's apartment. Outside he used the phone booth to make a call. I'm not sure what he said, but minutes later the two women rushed out of the building and around the corner. Joe then dashed up the fire escape. Moments later he emerged clutching handfuls of jewellery. I was rather concerned that we were actually committing a robbery.

'Oh, fuck her!' said Joe.

'But how will she live? You've taken her money, clothes and now jewels,' I said.

'She'll become a whore,' he snapped.

Josef really was a bastard, but he had a charming side. He would always stage a terrific show, and delight audiences with his repertoire of songs. At the end of each one, he would say, 'Now any requests?' I was there one night when the cry went up, 'Mother Macree'.

'Did you say "I'll Take You Home Again Kathleen?"' . . . and he would launch into it. He'd launch into that song regardless of what was requested.

I don't think Josef stayed in LA for long. He returned to Ireland and laid low away from the tax authorities.

Dot continued to travel between Britain and America when I was out there, in between her tours and engagements. In LA, she appeared at the Moulin Rouge club in Hollywood. One of her biggest fans was a young Elvis Presley, who attended most of her performances and repeatedly asked her to sing 'This Is My Mother's Day!' He came backstage and, being very nervous, introduced himself to me – as though I didn't know who he was.

'Hello, I'm Roger,' I said.

'How are you, sir?' he asked. 'Lovely to meet you, sir.' He insisted on calling me 'sir' throughout our brief chat, and acted as though he was in awe of me. Him! In awe of *me*!

Elvis told Dot how much he admired her and hoped he might have just a little of the success she had achieved. If only he knew. If only I knew! I'd have signed him up, as I was, after all, an 'actor-manager'.

Like MGM, Warner Bros had its stable of contract players, but unlike MGM, most were employed in television productions. In fact, Warner's were the leading producers of TV and many TV shows were being made on the lot. When I signed with them it was discussed that I might go into TV, but during *The Miracle* my contract was rewritten and TV became part of the deal. So it was that, soon after *The Miracle*, I guested in an episode of *Maverick*, with Jim Garner and Jack Kelly – series regulars Brett and Bart. Little did I know that I was actually being lined up to take over from Jim. Les Martinson was the director and we nicknamed him 'Les the Weeper', because he would get very upset about everything and start crying.

'I've got the son of a bitch who doesn't want to make it [Garner], the other one who wants to clown all the time [Kelly] and *where is my sun?*' he would lament, when the sun went behind a cloud.

However, before I took over in *Maverick* came *The Alaskans*. After my spell in *Ivanhoe* I was familiar with the conveyor belt production system, limited budgets and tight schedules. But while *Ivanhoe* had been thirty-minute shows, *The Alaskans* was a series of one-hour shows. It would be tough going for a year, though my apprehension was appeased somewhat when I was told it was going to 'be a very big production'. It *was* big. Stage 12 at Warner's, in the heart of Burbank, was transformed into a Yukon setting, with fake mountains and trees that were nailed to the floor. There were giant boxes up in the roof that, on the flick of a switch, opened to jettison tons and tons of fake snow, made from gypsum and cornflakes, but which soon started including six-inch nails and lumps of wood. You wouldn't have wanted to be in an avalanche!

All was not happy or healthy, though. We soon realized that the air was full of choking dust particles, and I wouldn't be surprised if there had been asbestos in there. The crew were equipped with masks and goggles, but we actors were bare-faced. It meant that, at least twice a day, you had to go and see the nurse and have your eyes washed free of all the dirt and grit.

The champion dog-sled team from Sun Valley were signed up. They came down and looked very happy woofing and barking at the sight of all this snow in summer. The sleds had little wheels underneath, so it was relatively easy for the dogs to pull us along. I was taught to say, 'Gee, mush' to turn right; 'Haw, mush' to turn left; 'Mush' to go ahead; and 'Whoa' to slow or stop. 'Action!' was called and I mushed my way forward down the first slope. The lead dog immediately stopped at the first tree to relieve himself, followed in turn by the other eight. I was saying, nay, begging – 'Please, mush, *any* mush'. It really was a load of mush.

Then, out on the back lot, we had to shoot the Skagway streets, which were dressed with gypsum and fake snow: we were all dressed in giant snow boots, fur boots, gloves and parkas. Outside, the temperature was in the eighties. The smell would get pretty bad by the end of the day. Still, it kept my weight down.

The female lead in *The Alaskans* was Dorothy Provine, a highly attractive and talented young actress from Seattle. Jeff York, who had been under contract to Disney, was the other male lead. He was a lovely fellow but his one failing was that he liked a tipple, and if they weren't ready for him first thing in the morning, he'd stride out of the gate and across to the Ranch House, a bar opposite the studio. At one point the production manager, who was, I think, an ex-sergeant major from the marines, with a shaven head and a big moustache, went over to get Jeff. An hour and a half later he came back in Jeff's arms; Jeff carrying him, as drunk as a skunk. Jeff's excuse was that he had come into a big inheritance and was celebrating. I discovered he had invented this vast non-existent inheritance on at least three other occasions.

We had a wonderful series of directors on the show, including Robert Altman. However, there had been a writer's strike during the production, and so scripts would appear, written by 'W. Hermanos', the Spanish for Warner Brothers. They recycled scripts from other shows, but hardly bothered to change any dialogue, just the names. So here was I, Silky Harris, an Alaskan gold prospector, with lines like, 'As my old pappy used to say' which was a Jim Garner *Maverick* line. I'd change it to 'As my paternal grandmother would say . . .'

As in all episodic TV, we had several guest stars, and one in particular, an actress, was a great follower of the 'method' theory. It drove me mad. She had to be shot in one scene, and asked me, 'What happens if you're shot?'

'I guess you fall over,' I said.

'No, what happens *inside*?'

'You bleed, I presume.'

'No, what happens *mentally*?'

'Well, have you ever been kicked up the backside?' I said, doing so and running away rather quickly.

For all the high hopes the studio had for *The Alaskans*, there was an early thaw that year, and Warner's plans for a second season went with the snow.

With my newfound fame and fortune in Hollywood, I decided to buy a Jaguar XK150 car. I drove it proudly to Burbank every day, but it developed a nasty habit of stalling and stopping, and every damn day it would stop and wouldn't want to start again. One afternoon, just before closing time, I managed to get it into the Jaguar showroom on Hollywood Boulevard, which had a repair shop on the first floor. They said I'd have to leave it as they couldn't attend to it for a day or two. I was furious, and with my best Stewart Granger 'I'm a fucking film star' type attitude, I said, 'I'll tell you what, I'll just drive it through that window there and leave it on Hollywood Boulevard. I'm sure the press will be interested to hear that I did it because you wouldn't service it!'

They serviced it there and then. I don't recommend this approach in every instance, but do bear it in mind should you find yourself fobbed off.

There was some speculation about the nature of my relationship with my leading lady on *The Alaskans*, Dorothy Provine. Being young and unusually reserved for a beautiful woman in Hollywood, Dorothy was someone I warmed to and we became good friends on and off set. When Squires came to hear of our friendship she was naturally upset but, fortunately, some cabaret engagements in the UK meant that she had to leave Hollywood, and this gave us both some much needed time to calm down.

It was around this time that Dot and I had one our most embarrassing evenings. She was back in LA for a while and one Sunday, together with her agent, the legendary Billy Marsh, we went to see a new and very controversial American comedian called Lenny Bruce. I was quite enjoying Bruce's off-the-wall humour, until he made a negative remark about playing at the London Palladium. Suddenly, to my horror, Dorothy, who had by now consumed three large gin-and-tonics, screamed, 'You'd like the fucking chance to play there ... you cunt!'

'Fucking spell it!' countered Bruce, glowering in our direction.

This drew a 'Fuck you!' from Dot. Billy and I were trying desperately to shut her up, but she went into full sail and the insults were flying right, left and centre. In a bid to make an exit, I called for the bill. Lenny Bruce shouted that he wanted to pay, which infuriated Dot even more. Shouting and swearing reminiscent of that in a second-rate fish market ensued. And this on a Sunday too! We managed to flee, unscathed, dragging our Welsh diva behind.

I did pay the bill though. Fool that I am.

Having had a bellyful of fake snow, dogs that wouldn't mush and recycled scripts, I was rather relieved to hear that, next on my Warner's contract, was a film: *The Sins of Rachel Cade*. Better still, my mate Gordon Douglas was directing. Peter Finch and Angie Dickinson were the main stars. I wasn't in the film until the second part, as I was still shooting *The Alaskans* when they'd started, which meant all of my scenes were condensed into a fairly tight part of the schedule. My first day was also Peter Finch's last day. We never had a scene together, but they wanted us both there to pose for publicity stills. Finchie suggested that if they wanted him to do stills, they should send down a crate or two of Dom Pérignon. We proceeded to get totally pissed, and I can't quite recall how many crates we got through in the end ... but it's probably evident in the publicity stills ...

Although set in the Belgian Congo, the entire film was shot at Warner's and they used stock shots from *The Nun's Story* for the location footage! Can you spot the joins?

It was great to work with Gordie Douglas again though, and lovely to work opposite Angie Dickinson. Angie would come in everyday and say, 'Good morning, sweetheart,' to Gordie.

'Morning, Angie,' he'd rasp, and then they'd embrace and cough heavily, causing their hips to come into violent contact. I said to Gordie that I wouldn't mind having a go at that greeting the next morning, to which he rather dryly said he didn't fancy doing it with me . . .

With the end of shooting in sight, I made tentative enquiries as to what other properties Warner's might think me suitable for. Oh no! I was told that I would be starring in *Maverick* as Brett's English cousin, Beau. Jim Garner had done a walk at this point, and said, 'No more.'

They assured me that I wasn't replacing him. Oh, yeah? Then why did all of my costumes have 'Jim Garner' in them, semi-scratched out? They just took two inches out of the waist. I wasn't that thrilled about doing the show, particularly after I'd just served my time on *The Alaskans*, but the carrot of further films was dangled. *Maverick* was OK, as it happens, and I thought some of the scripts were quite funny.

One day we were sitting on the back lot doing one of those interminable interviews that we were forced to do to publicize the series, and I said to this faceless journalist, 'You know, the reason there were so many shootings and killings in the Old West was because of cowboy boots.' The reporter stared at me. Feeling fuelled by his gullibility, I continued, 'Because they pinch your feet and make you mean.'

When this story came out, William T. Orr, who was Jack Warner's son-in-law and in charge of TV, sent for me and gave me a right rollicking. 'Acme boots – who supply all of our boots – are very upset about this publicity,' he said.

Considering myself told off, I said I was terribly sorry. In my next interview I added that they *all* wore Acme boots!

Again, we had some lovely guest stars and when Lee Van Cleef was appearing in an episode my parents came to visit. It was their first visit to Hollywood, and quite an eye-opening experience for two ordinary folks from south London. My mother, in particular, was a huge Western fan, and Lee Van Cleef was one of her favourite actors. So to be in Hollywood, on a Western set, meeting Lee was a thrill and a half.

Incidentally, on arriving in LA, my parents were quizzed for some time by customs officers over the contents of their luggage. Back in London they'd been warned that American food was horrible and that there was no 'proper' food – like bacon and eggs – available. So they'd brought over tins of Walls sausages! So much for the British abroad. Mind you, I'm just as bad. One night during the 1980s, when I lived in glamorous Gstaad, my phone rang. It was Michael Caine.

'Hallo, Rog,' said the familiar voice. 'I'm here with Leslie Bricusse and Bryan Forbes. We were just talking about you and your posh lifestyle in Switzerland. What are you up to?'

'Actually, Michael,' I replied. 'I'm sitting in front of the telly watching a video of *Dad's Army*, eating baked beans on toast.'

Such glamour!

Back in Hollywood, meanwhile, Jack Kelly (Bart) remained a regular in the series after Jim Garner had departed. Jack and I got on really well, on and off set. In true *Maverick* style, I'd regularly join Jim Garner, Jack Kelly and their wives for a poker school at Jack's house on Sunset Boulevard. I was never particularly lucky in cards, but had my fair share of luck in the other side of the old adage.

We had five or six days to shoot an hour episode – the same time we'd had to shoot a thirty-minute episode of *Ivanhoe*. The hours we worked were long and arduous. OK, it wasn't as though we were digging roads or building houses, but it was tough. American crews were less unionized than their British counterparts, so there was none of the English, 'Charlie, it's 5.20 p.m., pull the plug.' We just shot until we'd finished what needed to be done.

We did protest at one point. Jim Garner, Clint Walker and I (all contracted players of Warner's) went up to meet Ronald Reagan who was then President of the Screen Actors' Guild. Others egged us on, but remained on the sidelines. What did we achieve? Well, we ruffled feathers and gained a sympathetic ear. Meanwhile, Warner's decided to punish us by putting in a time clock – in the make-up department. Actors had to punch in every morning. I refused to be part of such a stupid scheme. I bought my own make-up and never punched in.

'He hasn't punched in,' I'd hear them saying on set, as I stood in the wings. 'He hasn't punched in and wasn't in make-up.' I'd walk on the set and say, 'I'm ready to shoot.' Jack Kelly was similarly minded, and one day took the time clock and used it as a football.

As another form of punishment, Warner's would put an actor, (who shall remain nameless), whom I really hated into the shows. I'd had the misfortune to work with him on stage in London and then in Hollywood in my episodic TV series. He was very arrogant and downright rude. One of the hairdressing ladies was crying one morning, and I asked her what was wrong. She said Nameless had been very unpleasant to her. I didn't think that was very nice, so I went up to him and said, 'Listen, I'm breaking a rule here, as I told myself that I would never speak to you except in a scene, and I'm speaking to you now.' He looked at me with hatred. 'Why are you so goddamn rude to people?' I went on.

'I'm not in this business to win a goddamn popularity award,' he replied. 'I'm in it to be a good actor.'

That was my cue. 'Well, you've failed in that,' I told him. 'So why not go for runner-up in the popularity stakes?' He chased me all over the studio. If he'd caught me, he'd have killed me. Anyway, he's now gone to that great cutting room in the sky – as Tony Curtis used to say when he heard of a Hollywood personality passing away.

They say that England and America are two countries divided by a common language. This was really brought home to me on *Maverick* when, after being called to the dubbing theatre one day, I was asked to re-voice myself in quite a few scenes.

'Why?' I asked.

'You say been instead of *bin*,' came the reply.

'What?'

'You say been instead of *bin* . . . "I've just bin to the stables." You say, "I've just *been*". That's incorrect.'

Astounded by what I was hearing, I made my point by asking, 'Do you say Boston Baked Bins then?'

Around this fourth season of *Maverick* – my first and last – I was offered another film with Warner's, *Gold of the Seven Saints*. A rather prophetic title as it turned out, since I made *Gold* after that in South Africa; then I made *The Saint*; and double-o-seven played a big part in my life, and I made seven of them.

Gordie Douglas was directing, and Clint Walker was my co-star. Clint was a giant. He would curl enormous weights. Well, in fact, he'd just pick up cameras, and camera stands, and curl. Legend has it that he was once a skier – one day he fell on his ski pole and it penetrated his chest. He held the pole in front of him, still in his chest, skied down the hill and checked himself into hospital. It would have killed anyone else.

The film centred around two gold prospectors – Shaun Garrett, played by me, and Jim Rainbolt, Clint's character – who had found gold and were carrying it back to Seven Saints on a packhorse. Sadly the horse dies and Shaun is sent off to the nearest town to get another. He is caught trying to steal a horse, and ends up paying for it with a gold nugget. Rainbolt is horrified, as it means the whole town will know they have gold. Thus ensued a chase of the townsfolk, with the two prospectors trying to get to safety at Seven Saints.

We made good use of the terrain and locations. Moab was a curious place. They'd discovered uranium a few years before, and overnight they had three or four thousand people descend. They didn't build houses but lived in trailers. The place became a land of trailer parks. They had one restaurant that, during the day, was a courthouse and in the evening the judge became the cook. We used to go there and have two-pound steaks put on the fire, with a pile of French fries and we'd drink a lot of Jack Daniel's and beer – in an attempt to put fluid back into our bodies after gruelling days under the hot sun. It was a very hot, dry location and they had to oil our costumes to make it look like we were sweating. While you do sweat, it's so hot that the sweat dries before it reaches your skin. Your lips get dry and crack. For one sequence we scouted a high ledge between the junction of the Green River and Colorado River. It was 2,000 feet up, a sheer drop, and quite spectacular with it. Bill Kissell, our assistant director, got out of the car at the top, said, 'Whooah,' got back into the car and refused to get out again. Being brave actors, Clint and I dutifully stepped forward. We had to ride our horses into the scene; all the time, my character was cracking jokes and singing.

At one point, Gordie said to Clint, in his gravelly voice, 'Clint, when Rog says that line, give a little laugh.'

Clint, swallowing the words at the back of his throat, said, 'Can't do that, Gordie.'

'Why not?'

'I don't think it's very funny.'

'I don't care whether you think it's funny,' Gordie persisted. 'The *character* thinks it's funny, so give a chuckle.'

Clint took me to one side, put an enormous arm round my shoulders, and said, 'Rog, how do you laugh?'

'What? The technical trick of appearing to laugh?'

'Yeah.'

'Well, you let all your air out and on the intake of breath you catch your vocal cords – hahaha.'

'No, I can't do that,' said Clint. 'I find people expect me to laugh, and tell me jokes. A joke has to get me unawares.'

I started telling him jokes, trying to get him to chuckle. I eventually succeeded. It was bizarre. I mean, who doesn't know how to laugh?

Gordie of the raspy voice, by the way, had an extraordinary background. He was born in New York and started out as a child actor, before the legendary producer Hal Roach gave him his break as a gag writer on the *Our Gang (The Little Rascals)* series, and then on the Laurel & Hardy comedies. It was Gordie who came up with the classic thumb-lighting-the-pipe for Stan Laurel that was used in a few of their films.

Over dinner on one of our many evenings spent together during shooting, Gordie told me some wonderful stories about Hal Roach, who was a huge practical joker. One of my favourites was about a writer from New York whom Roach had invited to Hollywood for a few weeks to do some work on one of the company's films. One night Roach invited this chap to his house for dinner. He said it would just be Mary – his wife – himself and the writer. They have a nice dinner and after, when they're all sitting around chatting, Hal says to his wife, 'Have we got any of that Courvoisier left?'

'No,' she says, 'it's all gone.'

'Oh, OK then, I'll whip down to the liquor store to get some more,' says Roach. The writer offers to go with him, but Roach says, 'No, no. You stay and look after Mary. I won't be long.'

The minute Roach leaves, Mary eyes up the writer 'You look rather cute,' she says.

'Oh, well, thanks,' he replies, blushing.

Suddenly she lunges forward and shouts, 'Give it to me!', pulling up her skirt.

Excited, but terrified that his boss might come back at any moment, the young writer thinks 'what the hell!' and does it there and then on the carpet. However, by the time Roach returns, they are sitting up at the table, chatting quite normally. The writer can't wait to make his excuses and get away, as he is feeling pretty terrible by this stage, and petrified of being fired . . . or worse.

The following day, the writer is back in Roach's office, and the secretary buzzes through: 'Call for the writer on the line.'

'Hello,' the caller says. 'This is Mary.'

'Oh, um, hi, Aunt Winnie. How, um, how are you?'

'I want you to come over now, and give me some more of what you gave me last night.'

'Aunt Winnie,' he says, 'I'm in the middle of a script conference.'

'You get your ass over here now or I'll tell Hal about you,' Mary threatens.

The writer asks Hal Roach if he could be forgiven, but his Aunt is new in town and she has a few problems.

This torrid affair goes on for two weeks. As well as feeling absolutely terrible about what he is doing, the writer is becoming increasingly weaker and more tired as each day passes. Another script conference, and Roach says, 'You know where we're going with this story . . . I want to establish a relationship between these two fellas in the script. The sort a man can't have with a woman. You get my drift? Nothing homosexual, just something men have that binds them together. They trust one another, just as I can trust you.'

By this time the writer is going pale and wishing the ground would swallow him up.

'Trust,' Roach continues. 'You know? Just like I know I could trust you with my wife.' By now the writer is choking. 'Yes, with my wife. Not the hooker I'm paying $50 a day to pose as my wife!'

The writer leaps across the desk and tries to kill Roach! OK, he was the butt of a terrible practical joke, but the way I look at it is that he had terrific sex for two weeks and was getting paid.

Another wicked practical joke was one Roach played on Gordie himself. Apparently, when Gordie was quite new in town, Roach invited him over for dinner, telling him to arrive at 8 p.m. Meanwhile, Roach had also invited a dozen guests for 7 p.m., and he explained to them that the chap who was coming later had just been released from jail. But, he told them, they *can't* talk about that: he had actually murdered someone, but is a *terribly nice* person; it was really the drink's fault. He *mustn't* drink.

Gordie duly arrived and was introduced to everyone. They're all standing with drinks in their hands, and Gordie says, 'Oh, do you think I could have a drink?' A few people move away. By the time he asked for a second drink, the room had cleared!

Gold of the Seven Saints was a very happy film to shoot. I sang, I danced, and I played an Irish drunk. Fun to play, fun to do a dialect. I had a character to hide behind so I could act – though I've never been very guilty of doing that.

I hoped that it might lead to more collaborations with Gordie at Warner's. But, once again, my hopes were dashed when I was told my next job would be on *The Roaring Twenties*, a TV series that recounted the adventures of a newspaper journalist in 'cops and gangsters' 1920s Chicago. At this time, Warner's were making the bulk of the programmes for American television. They had 77 *Sunset Strip, Hawaii Five-O, The Alaskans, Maverick, Bronco, Bourbon Street Beat* . . . it was an extraordinary line-up, with fifty contract players who all looked alike – the boys and girls – and so we were all interchangeable. So fixated were they on finding me another television vehicle, that they came up with what they thought was hugely original – another damn Western series, only this time with an Englishman-turned-cowboy – at which point I said, 'I'm leaving'.

I think the feeling was mutual, actually. It saddened me that after just a couple of years, and some happy working experiences on movies, Warner's felt my future lay in TV. I wouldn't have minded if they'd come up with something original. As it was, and as much as I had come to love Hollywood, I was not prepared to sit out the remaining five years of my contract by accepting whatever was offered, good or indifferent. It was 1961, Hollywood was changing, and not for the better. Maybe it was time to try pastures new?

Squires, meanwhile, was enjoying huge success back in the UK, and in Australia and Europe. It was difficult to spend much time together – we were both dedicated to furthering our careers. I had a business manager at this point, Irving Leonard, who was also Jim Garner's manager. In fact, he handled most of the people who had been under contract to Warner's, and also Clint Eastwood. In fact it was he who persuaded Clint to go to Italy to do a picture for $15,000, which was a lot less than he was used to being paid in Hollywood. That was *The Good, the Bad and the Ugly*, the first of the Sergio Leone spaghetti westerns, which led to Clint becoming one of the biggest motion picture stars.

I had a certain profile in Italy by this point, and so when I was offered the lead in an Italian picture, Irving encouraged me to take it; even though the money wasn't brilliant. So I left Hollywood behind me, again, and departed for Rome to make *The Rape of the Sabine Women* or *Il Ratto delle Sabine*, as the natives say.

★ ★ ★

I received the script for *Sabines*, one of the scripts I should say, as many different language versions existed to accommodate the real Heinz 57 nationality mix of all the actors involved: English, French, German, Yugoslav, Italian and the rest. The film was about the founding of Rome, the story of Romulus and Remus. I was to play Romulus. Casting a blond, blue-eyed Anglo-Saxon as the twin of Remus, raised by a wolf and becoming the founder of Rome, seemed somewhat ambitious to me. However they were paying, so I said nothing.

I flew from LA to London, and then on to Paris to meet the producers, Enrico Bomba being the Italian one, and Alexander Salkind the French partner (Alex, and his son Ilya, went on to produce *Superman* among other films). After lunching with Alex, we walked along the Champs-Elysées – Alex lived just off the famously expensive thoroughfare, very near to the lavish George V Hotel – and as we passed a tailor's Alex said, 'Just a minute.'

He took me in with him and addressed the tailor in French; I gathered he said something about making a major movie, me being his star and that he wanted me fitted out. The tailor, obviously registering that this could be a very lucrative opportunity, wrote down all my measurements. Alex thanked him for his kind attention, picked up the measurements, and we walked out of the shop. He then called Rome and gave them my measurements to make my costumes – which were really just togas in any event. Maybe Alex's methods should have warned me how cheap this production was going to be!

I next flew to Rome for fittings and met some of the cast and crew. Richard Pottier was our director; he was Hungarian-born but had spent much of his working life in France. Mylène Demongeot was our French leading lady, Rea. Scilla Gabel was the Italian leading lady, Dusia. Then there was a very beautiful young lady named Luisa Mattioli, who was under contract to Enrico Bomba. Luisa was to play Silvia.

While we were in Rome, a press conference was set up for Italian television and Luisa, who had previously been a TV presenter in Italy, was asked to interview me. As I spoke no Italian and she spoke no

English, it was an interesting interview, as you might imagine. I still don't really know how we got through it, but we did. We seemed instantly able to communicate – language was no barrier between us.

I was fitted for my costumes and then we were shipped off to Zagreb in Yugoslavia. It wasn't a film studio, but a sort of converted warehouse, all very makeshift; and I felt rather lonely, as one of the few English-speaking people around the place. The first day's shooting was upon us. The Romans, under the leadership of yours truly, rode into the Sabinians' town with plentiful supplies of wine to get the menfolk drunk. Once they were incapacitated, the Romans carried the Sabine women off for the inevitable rape. The big problem was that my French was not very good; my Italian was non-existent and as for my German and Serbian, well, you can guess. Everyone was speaking in their own native language and it was chaos.

Our first assistant director was a lady called Beka. Never content with instructing the crowd and extras before calling 'Action', she would continually shout instructions, in her local dialect, at them during the scene and all over my and the other principals' dialogue. I found it very off-putting, but when I challenged her as to why she did this she replied, 'Because they are *stoopid.*'

'I may be stupid too,' I replied, 'but I find it very hard to concentrate.'

Anyhow, my first scene was with Mylène Demongeot, who spoke her lines in French. As soon as her lips stopped moving, I chipped in with, 'You mustn't be afraid, we mean no harm.' She then replied in French about all men being liars and, again as soon as her lips stopped moving, I knew it was my turn. We managed to get through some of this, with Beka continually shouting her Serbian directions in the background, when a man in the crowd wearing a white toga emerged and punched me squarely in the jaw; knocking me flat on my back.

'Cut! Cut!' called the director. 'Roger, where are you?'

'Here on the floor.'

'Why are you on the floor?'

'Because that man just punched me,' I replied.

'Beka! Why did that man punch Roger?' the director asked.

'Because he is drunk,' was her reply.

'Hang on,' I chimed in. 'He should be fired if he's drunk.'

'No,' said Beka. 'He's *acting* drunk.'

'Look, we normally discuss and rehearse things like this,' I said, 'so I'm prepared for someone to hit me!'

We broke off for lunch . . . with a lot of red wine. Then Pottier said, 'In this next scene you gallop in, your horse stumbles, you fall off your horse and you then get up and pull your sword –'

'Hang on!' I cried. 'I come riding in and then we cut to a *double* falling off the horse.'

'Ce qui? Un double? Je ne comprends pas.' All of a sudden, Pottier didn't speak English any more.

At first I didn't quite understand why my agent had specifically listed in the contract that I should have a dressing room, make-up and costumes supplied, as that was the norm I had come to expect. He'd also specified that a double should be available for stunt work. My agent was obviously wise to how Italians made movies. I reminded Pottier of this. He called Beka over, and they mumbled something between them. She then pulled a chap out of the crowd and said to me, 'Take your clothes off.'

'What?' I asked.

'Take your clothes off. If he is to double you, he needs your clothes.'

'Oh no. Oh no! If he is to double me, then you will make clothes for him,' I replied. It was an ordeal. And that was only the first day.

Folco Lulli was playing King Titus, and was always complaining about the cheap production. I remember we were in the back of a car together going to location one morning, and he was chattering away in Italian – and even though I spoke very little, I got the drift of what he was saying and it was none too complimentary. Just then he hacked phlegm from the back of his throat and spat it out of the window. Which would have been fine had the window been open. I was in hysterics.

As our shoot progressed on location, the beautiful Luisa Mattioli and I became more than just members of the cast. We were both away from our native lands and, as I said, language was no barrier. In fact we enjoyed many long conversations during which it didn't seem to matter whether the words made any sense whatsoever. I found out that a nod is, indeed, as good as a wink.

We somehow managed to complete the film and I have to say that the finished thing was really quite horrendous. Had my payment been forthcoming on time, it might have eased my disappointment and frustration. Eventually I did get paid but only, I suspect, because Bomba wanted to offer me a second picture, *No Man's Land*. Of course he dangled the fact that Luisa would again be co-starring, and as I wanted to stay on in Rome with her, it suited me. Our romance was developing and our feelings for each other growing stronger; soon we became quite inseparable.

In another wonderful bit of casting, I was to play an Italian soldier, a deserter. Max Schell's brother, Carl, played a Nazi villain and our leading lady was Pascal Petit. It was all haphazardly stitched together by director Fabrizio Taglioni. One wonderful actor who had a small role in the film was Memmo Carotenuto. He had a nose that didn't quite know which direction it should be pointing in. By this point I had picked up a little more Italian and was able to converse, so I asked how his nose had become broken in such a fashion. He said he had been playing Jesus in a production, and for the crucifixion he was tied to a cross, which was erected on top of a hill. All of the extras fell to their knees to worship Christ in his dying moments. The vibrations caused the cross to sway, but as he didn't want to draw too much attention and spoil the shot, he quietly called, 'Help me, help me!' The extras must have thought it was part of the script, so did nothing. At which point the cross fell forwards, and with him being tied he had nothing between himself and the rapidly approaching ground except his nose – which duly took the brunt of the impact.

Lack of communication and a bad script led to friction on the set. It wasn't a happy production. I wasn't in a position to turn the work down however, and so had to make the best of it. Mercifully I didn't have to think about a third Italian epic, as I received word from Britain about a new TV series that they wanted me to star in.

SEVEN

Enter the Saint

'You say, "Ladies and Gentlemen . . ." and then you're humble'

Having once tried to secure the rights to the character from Leslie Charteris, I was rather receptive to the offer of the lead in Lew Grade's new TV series of *The Saint*. The offer came through to me in Venice, via my agent Dennis van Thal, along with the script of episode one. My Italian films had certainly not catapulted me to international superstar status, as Clint Eastwood's did him, and, Luisa aside, I wasn't sure how much longer I wanted to spend in Italy pursuing a career in, shall we say, somewhat unremarkable films. Dennis flew out to discuss the deal. I said I felt the script was rather long for what was, like *Ivanhoe*, a half-hour show. 'Oh no, it's definitely half an hour,' he assured me, 'they'll cut it down.'

I wasn't convinced: it read very long to me. Dennis sent a telex to one of his assistants in London asking them to confirm the running time. The reply was 'half an hour'. Of course, this had a bearing on the contract and the offer. Satisfied that I was signing up for twenty-six half-hour shows, I met with the producers, Bob Baker and Monty Berman. They didn't ask me to screen test, the part was mine. I was very excited and looking forward to starting.

Not long after accepting the part, Lew Grade asked me to attend a press conference – Lew loved making press announcements, being the showman. I sat alongside him and the producers as he welcomed everyone and said that they were very excited about 'these twenty-six one-hour shows'.

'*Half-hour*,' I said from the side of my mouth.

Lew continued.

'Half-hours,' I said again.

'No, they're *one-hour* shows,' said Bob and Monty, firmly.

I had agreed my contract based on thirty-minute shows. 'We'll have to go back to the drawing board on this,' I said.

'What do you mean? You have a contract. You've signed it!' Fortunately there were a few revisions made, and Dennis van Thal's assistant was swiftly shown the door.

I thought the show would run for one series, possibly a second. I never dreamed it would run for seven years and 118 episodes. They were very, very happy days of playing a character to whom I easily adapted my limited ability.

Although the TV series was based on the stories and characters created by Leslie Charteris, rather cleverly in his agreement with Charteris, producer Bob Baker never actually gave Charteris script approval, only the right to 'comment' on the scripts. However, Leslie Charteris never held back in his criticism and was sometimes quite vitriolic – and often quite funny too – in his long memos, which were always delivered in a pre-used envelope. Of one episode, written by our story editor Harry Junkin, Charteris sent back the script with 'this is fit for junkin' written across it.

Charteris's stories were, in the main, all short stories. However we had a one-hour show to fill, and we found that while his stories offered material enough for a first and third act, there was no middle act. Which is what the show's writers were charged with creating. Obviously, in writing a new second part they'd often have to change details in the stories, the characters, and so on, and this is what Charteris objected to. He was extremely protective and possessive when it came to *The Saint*. In fact, he thought of himself as Simon Templar. He hated the production's invention and meddling with his stories, and never hesitated to tell us so. I'm not sure whether his criticisms eased or increased after the first series, as we created our own original stories. Bob handled everything with great diplomatic charm. Mind you, I think Charteris rather liked being able to protest.

There had been a number of films based on the Charteris stories in the 1930s, 1940s and even into the 1950s and while I was familiar with them, we were keen to try something different in terms of the style of our production. It was decided that, in the opening sequence, Simon Templar would talk to the camera and address the viewing masses. It set the scene, made the audience feel a part of the story and then moved to the now infamous raising of the eyebrow, and the skyward glance above my head to see the halo, while someone said, 'You're the famous Simon Templar!' or some such line, to introduce me. The episode would then launch into the opening titles and famous music by Edwin Astley. For many youngsters it was a Sunday night pre-bedtime treat. Even now, I'm often approached by people who say, 'I was allowed to stay up and watch you!' (Or rather, nowadays, they say their *grandmothers* were once allowed to stay up. It doesn't half make an old actor feel . . . old!)

As I said earlier, Luisa and I had been becoming closer, and when we were apart I realized just how much I missed her. I'm not particularly proud of the fact that I ended my marriage with Dorothy Squires to be with Luisa. Dot and I had been through a lot together and my actions around this time caused a lot of heartache and bad feeling. I didn't then realize it, but the long separations in the pursuit of our individual careers had obviously had an impact on me, on us both, perhaps. We had, quite simply, drifted apart without realizing it was happening.

But I felt I had to follow my heart, which now lay well and truly with Luisa. I have always been an incurable romantic.

I never stopped caring about Dot. I don't think you can ever stop caring about someone who was such a large part of your life, no matter how your relationship may have ended. I don't think she ever stopped caring about me either; which is undoubtedly why she refused me a divorce for so long.

Towards the end of her life, in 1998, when Dot fell ill and on hard times, she and I spoke on the telephone. We agreed that we'd shared some great and happy times and wouldn't have missed them for the world. I did what I could to make her remaining time more comfortable and while not asking her to ever understand what I did all those years earlier, she did say that she was pleased I had now found happiness with Kristina, my fourth wife.

'She's the one, Rog, isn't she?'

'Yes, Dot,' I replied, 'she really is.'

However, back in 1961, the breakdown of a marriage was not sufficient grounds for divorce, which could only be granted with Dot's consent – and that was not forthcoming.

After much agonizing on both our parts – Luisa because of her devout Catholic faith and me because I couldn't stand to see her so torn between that faith and her love for me – Luisa agreed to leave Rome and come back to Britain with me. We decided to set up home together and rented a three-bedroomed house with a rather nice garden in Mill Hill, about twenty minutes' drive away from Elstree Studios, where *The Saint* was based.

Our first day's shooting on episode one was on location in Cookham, Buckinghamshire, where Derek Farr – in drag as Mrs Jafferty – had to cross the road as Simon Templar drove by in his Volvo P1800. A simple enough shot. I parked around the corner waiting (as is the norm with British productions), for the sun to reappear from behind a cloud, which was to be signified by the drop of a hand on the opposite corner. Just then, a policeman pulled up on his bicycle. He looked at me and looked at the car, then got off his bike and walked over.

'That's a very interesting-looking car, sir,' he said. 'Interesting-looking number plate too.' Of course, it was the 'ST1' plate.

'Yes,' I said, not thinking. 'It's fake.'

The policeman reached into his pocket to pull out his notebook and pencil. At that very moment I saw the signal to go, so I sped off around the corner, did the circuit and returned to my starting point, where the policeman was still standing, scratching his head. Nobody had told him a film crew was in town.

Our schedules were invariably eight days per episode, and we rarely shot weekends. It allowed me a regular routine. Each day I'd get up at 6.00 a.m. to do my exercises – callisthenics, sit-ups and all sorts of other regimes as I hated gymnasiums and much preferred to keep fit at home – followed by tea and toast and the drive to the studio for 7.30.

I drove a Volvo P1800 in 'real-life', too. That all came about during pre-production, when we discussed what sort of car Simon Templar should drive. The general consensus was that it should be a Jaguar. I said that whatever car we had, I'd buy one as well – hoping for a favourable deal, naturally – so we'd have two; meaning that when we were shooting with the main unit, should the second unit require a car for establishing or pick-up shots they could use the production car and I'd use mine with the main unit.

Johnny Goodman, our production manager, placed a call to Jaguar in Coventry and explained that we were setting up a new TV series and required two cars.

'When do you need them, Mr Goodman?'

'Next week,' Johnny replied.

'Oh! We couldn't possibly do that.' came the reply. 'There's a six-month waiting list!'

'Yes, but this is for a *television* series,' added Johnny, 'that will be sold around the world. Think of the wonderful publicity it will generate for your company.'

'Publicity?' said Jaguar. 'What do we need publicity for? We have £250-million-worth of orders that we can't possibly fill as it is.'

That was the end of the conversation. Johnny then flicked through some car magazines and showed me a photo of the Volvo P1800. I thought it looked terrific. Johnny called them and within two days we had two cars at the studio, as well as the materials to mock up the interior of another car that we could use for close-ups in the studio. Every year Volvo changed the cars for us too. So there are a number of 'genuine Volvo P1800s as driven by *The Saint*' out there. It always amuses me when people write and say 'I own the original Volvo'. What they own is actually one of about twelve that we used over the years.

The lovely thing about *The Saint* was that our stories were often set in wonderful and glamorous countries. Television productions in those days, however, didn't have the vast budgets necessary, nor the schedules available, to actually film in these places. So we'd make British locations 'double' for more exotic foreign ones, which were not always entirely convincing. By wheeling out the odd plastic palm tree, affixing false car number plates and slapping up a caption across the bottom of the screen, the Elstree back-lot and surrounds would become France, Spain, Italy, Switzerland or even the Bahamas.

Invariably, in the middle of winter, I'd be in 'the Bahamas' or 'South of France' in a short-sleeved shirt with lights blazing down on me, a plastic palm in front of me, fronds blowing in the bitterly cold north wind. Ah, you say, don't they drive on the opposite side of the road in those countries? Yes, they do. That wasn't a problem for us either, as we simply flipped the film in the camera. Borehamwood High Street could have been anywhere.

I used to hate the thought of shooting on the back-lot and longed for days when I might be on location for real: those days came with *The Persuaders* and oh, how I missed being able to drive home at night. Actors are never content, you'll find.

The other nice thing about the show was that we had a terrific crew. Many, such as Alec Mills and Jimmy Devis our camera operators, June Randall our wonderful continuity girl, Johnny Goodman and Peter Manley our production managers, and Malcolm Christopher our invaluable location manager, have remained friends to this day. It was a huge family that gathered for ten hours of fun every day.

Time between series was actually limited. I think I might have had two months off before the next series started and often I'd be required to

go off to do a promotional tour somewhere, so Luisa and I would tie that
in with a holiday. We used to like going to Magaluf in Majorca, long
before it became spoilt by the masses of holidaymakers who descend
upon the over-developed coastline these days.

We also spent some time in Rome with my 'in-laws' when time
allowed. I remember on one occasion we were driving back from Rome
to England and went via Switzerland. I'd never been to Geneva before,
although the Saint had – thanks to a caption whacked across the bottom
of the screen in one episode – and thought it would make a good place
to stop off for a couple of days. We checked in to the Beau Rivage Hotel.
The manager asked if I would pose for a photograph with her daughter,
which I gladly did. When it came time to check out, I asked for the bill.
They said there was no charge; it had been their pleasure to welcome
Simon Templar. I experienced more kindness from a taxi driver in the
city. Having reached our destination, he refused to accept a fare.

I quite enjoyed being famous!

I must add here that, in later years, London taxi drivers – who are
undoubtedly the best in the world – have so often refused to charge me
saying, 'Give it to UNICEF, guv. We can't take your money.' It is hugely
touching to receive such generosity. The worst cab drivers I've come across
are definitely in New York. These days you have to put up with drivers
who talk on mobile phones all the time and don't know where they're
going, yet it's the easiest city in which to navigate – but then I could still
be smarting over the mistaken $100 dollar bill I paid out in 1953 . . .

One of our early guest stars in *The Saint* was Warren Mitchell, in fact
he popped up in a number of episodes, usually playing an Italian taxi
driver – though he didn't speak any Italian aside from the swear words
I taught him, courtesy of Luisa. I wonder if the audience ever picked up
on what he was saying? Another guest star was Jane Asher, who was
about sixteen when she guested. I remember we had a rack of black
painted tracking boards that were stacked against the wall, rather like
canvases in an artist's studio. I'd occasionally take a piece of chalk and do
sketches on these boards, and I did one of Jane with her then boyfriend,
a young musician named Paul McCartney. I put it in a heart with a bit
of holly around it and was so pleased with it that I announced it was to
be my Christmas card for that year.

'Oh no,' said Jane. 'Please don't do that. If it gets out that we're seeing
one another it will ruin his career.'

'What career?' I asked, in all ignorance. Little did I know!

Other wonderful leading ladies included the young Julie Christie, Jackie Collins, Erica Rogers, Annette Andre, Lois Maxwell, Nicola Pagett, Eunice Gayson, Jennie Linden, Sue Lloyd, Justine Lord, Suzanne Lloyd, Mary Peach, Jean Marsh, Imogen Hassall, Veronica Carlson, Samantha Eggar, Shirley Eaton, Kate O'Mara, Alexandra Stewart and so very many more. The subject of my leading ladies arose in a TV interview I did with HTV.

'You've played *Ivanhoe*, *Maverick* and now *The Saint*,' said the interviewer, 'you must have got through a lot of leading ladies in your time.'

'You can't say that!' I cried.

He didn't seem to realize what he was saying. I cringe whenever I see the clip. (It's on YouTube, by the way.)

A young actor named Oliver Reed was cast as a baddie in an episode called *The King of the Beggars*. Usually, in the penultimate scene of an episode, 'who did it' is all explained. In the beginning of this revealing sequence, the baddie was shot and the camera moved past him, on to me, for my summing-up. Oliver, knowing this would be his last chance to get his face on camera, took the gunshot and spun around, leapt up in the air and let his face linger in frame as he passed the camera on the way down to the floor.

We did about four takes, and each time he lingered a little longer. Running out of time – and patience – the director let it be and continued. I started summing up the plot, but all I could hear was a rasping sound coming from the floor. I thought Oliver was trying to break me up. I continued, but the noise got louder, and I looked down to see Oliver lying spark-out, with his purple tongue hanging from the side of his mouth. I dropped down to the floor to assist him.

'What have you stopped for?' cried the director.

'Oliver's concussed!' I shouted. 'He's going blue!'

'Oh yes. Fair enough. Call the unit nurse,' the director said calmly.

Luckily, Oliver survived that small trauma and his next appearance was in an episode I directed called *Sophia*. By now, Oliver had graduated to playing the main villain. What a terrific actor he was. I definitely thought that he was among the best 'villains' around at that time, and told him so.

Many years later, I was in Hollywood preparing to play Sherlock Holmes in a TV movie and our producer said, 'Oliver Reed's in town next week. He'd make a great Moriarty. You know him, don't you?'

I said yes on both counts.

'Give him a call at the Beverly Wilshire, would you?'

I called Oliver and explained what was afoot.

'Do you remember something you once said to me?' he asked.

'What?'

'We were at a BAFTA evening at the London Hilton and you said to me, "Stick to playing villains, because you can't do comedy".'

'Yeah, that's right,' I replied.

'Well, I've just done a comedy, and I was brilliant. So I don't think I want to play your Moriarty.'

Oops!

Another young actor I met during *The Saint*, though alas never worked with on it, later became one of my closest friends. It was around mid-1964, I was walking across Piccadilly and, coming towards me, were two actors: one was Terence Stamp and the other was a bespectacled, tall, good-looking blond chap whom I'd seen the night before in a TV play written by Johnny Speight.

'You're going to be a big star,' I dared to say to the blond actor.

'Fuck me! Roger Moore!' he replied. His name was Michael Caine. He was indeed to become a big star.

Conversely . . . I was asked to support a number of charity events, and one of my favourite charities was the Variety Club of Great Britain. During my *Saint* tenure I agreed to attend the races at York with a few ABPC actresses: Sylvia Syms, Rita Tushingham, Liz Fraser and a young starlet who made such an impression that I cannot remember her name. Anyhow, we all sat in the same compartment on the train and started playing poker – all but the starlet, that is. She sat admiring herself in two mirrors; one for the left profile and one for the right. It became rather obvious she had delusions of grandeur.

'Does my nose look big?' she asked, while manoeuvring her mirrors for the best angle.

Sylvia looked at her and said, rather loudly, 'I've never travelled with a fucking film star before.'

Ah, I wonder what ever happened to that starlet?

Harry Junkin, our story editor on *The Saint*, was a six-foot-six, garrulous Canadian and his idea of sophistication was reflected in the tag-line to almost all of his scripts. At the end of an episode, I'd be in the Volvo with my leading lady and she would ask, 'What shall we do now, Simon?'

My reply was, 'I'm going to take you to the best restaurant in town and then go dancing until dawn.' Maybe it was a chat-up line that worked for Harry?

When we filmed the car scenes, incidentally, we would shoot either with 'blue backing', which meant you couldn't wear anything blue as you'd become transparent, or with a revolving drum for shorter sequences. The drum had bits of silver paper on it to represent the city lights flashing past or, if we were in the country, we'd attach a few twigs to it. These were always shot MOS – mit out sound. One day, we were sitting in the screening room watching the previous day's rushes, and I appeared sitting in the driving seat of the Volvo. Without a cut, the camera operator was then sitting in the driving seat and I appeared to be running alongside the car. I held up a piece of paper that had 'Stop!' written on it.

He produced a piece of paper saying 'Why?'

'Because my dick's caught in the door!' said my next piece of paper. The boys in the room fell about. They thought it hilarious, as did the laboratory that processed the footage: it became the highlight of their Christmas blooper reel. The only person who didn't see the funny side was co-producer Monty Berman. He ordered the production manager to charge me for the film stock, saying I was wasting their money. That was really the beginning of the end between Monty and me, as far as I was concerned. We'd filmed two series and were completing the third. I really had no desire to go on to another.

When we were working on the second series, I said to Bob Baker one day that I'd rather like to direct.

'Oh yes,' said Bob, smiling. 'That'd be nice.' He obviously felt he should amuse his actor and not upset him. 'But alas there's a problem,' he added. 'The union. The ACTT. If you're not a member they won't let you step to the other side of the camera.'

'But I *am* a member,' I said.

'What?'

'I'm a member. From 1943 when I worked at PPP in d'Arblay Street.'

Bob could feel his argument failing. In all fairness, he knew I was professional enough not to screw things up, and we had such a professional crew around us that they would carry me, if needed. So, he agreed.

I enjoyed directing and went on to do a number of *Saint* and *Persuaders* episodes. I always figured I'd tell the story from Simon Templar's point of view, and from a master shot I'd have the camera over my shoulder, so then I was on screen for everything. I'd leave my close-ups until the end of the day, so I could let everyone else go home, and I'd do them with the script girl feeding me the lines.

I was fortunate in that I had learned a lot about directing from the many wonderful directors with whom I'd worked, both in Hollywood and the UK. I knew about lenses, cameras, a little about lighting and I think I had a certain sympathy for actors, being one myself. Anything I wasn't sure about I'd ask the crew. I found they were all very keen to help and offer advice.

I much preferred directing TV to film, if I'm honest. With a film you have six or eight weeks of pre-production, maybe ten weeks' shooting and then another ten weeks or more of post-production. When you're the director, you're required every step of the way. Typically, a film might take six or seven months of your life. Perhaps more. An ongoing TV series would take two or three. Maybe I'm lazy, or maybe I feel I'd just get bored with a long process. I declined quite a few offers to direct movies in later years.

The aspect I didn't relish about directing was the casting of the shows, believe it or not. I felt I knew a lot of actors and as I had a copy of *Spotlight* – the casting directory – I didn't feel the need to meet anyone, I'd just pick people I thought looked right. Alas no, it didn't work that way.

In the days when I was struggling, I'd have to give up a packet of cigarettes to be able to buy a train ticket out to Pinewood or Shepperton Studios, only to be told on arrival that I was either too thin, too fat, too short or too tall. It was a cruel and expensive process. I resolved that I would only ever hold interviews for anything I directed in London, and if I couldn't get a break in shooting for a few hours to see someone, then I'd do it on a Saturday.

Soon came the day when Bob presented me with the script of an episode called *The Miracle Tea Party*, which I was to helm. And so it was, that one Saturday morning, having already cast Bob Brown, Charlie Houston, Patrick Westwood, and Nanette Newman, I arrived at an office in Golden Square for further auditions. I asked the casting director who he had lined up for the part of Aunt Hattie. He said, 'X, Y, Z and Fabia Drake.'

'I can't interview Fabia Drake!' I spluttered. 'She was my teacher at RADA.'

'Well, she's here, you'll have to.'

I couldn't believe it. I felt so awkward and real fear set in. I called her in. 'Miss Drake . . .' I greeted her.

'No. I'm Fabia. You are Mr Moore,' she replied.

'I'm sorry, but I find this very embarrassing.'

'You shouldn't.'

'Have you read the script?' I asked.

'Yes, that's why I'm here.'

'Fine. There's no more to say. I'll see you on Monday,' I concluded.

All over the weekend I worried about how I was going to give Fabia Drake direction. My system of working was to draw sketches of the beginning and the end of each scene. I'd show the actors how I intended to start and end the scene, and then let them decide how they wanted to move around in between.

On the Monday, Fabia arrived and asked where I wanted her to go. I showed her the sketches.

'OK, darling, but do tell me if I'm doing anything wrong.' She made me feel so much at ease. It was lovely. From then on, I had no problems directing anyone else. Thank you, Fabia.

In this episode we had a location shoot at Waterloo Station. There was a whole day's filming scheduled, so I visited on the Sunday prior to prepare the various shots I knew I wanted and plan how to achieve them. Everything had to be timed with the trains arriving, and I wanted to shoot across the clock on the main concourse – as the story evolved, we would always see the time moving forward.

I found I had many sequences that I wasn't appearing in, so I didn't have to get made-up, and could wear old clothes and a hat to move around the station without being recognized. Unbeknown to me, my mother had come down that day to watch from the crowd. She heard a couple of people saying, 'Oh, that's Roger Moore. Don't half look scruffy, don't he? He don't look like he do on telly.' So much for disguise!

We had one difficult moment when I was standing on top of the station steps, shooting across one of the wonderful stone lions that grace the entrance to the station, when an Irish drunk came over. He really was rip-roaring drunk, and the railway police were not interested.

'I know who you are,' he said to me.

'Yes, thank you. Move along,' I said.

'I want to shake you by the hand.' He just wouldn't go until I shook hands and had a chat, which rather spoilt the shot.

That rather reminds me of another encounter I had with a drunk, this time a few years later when I was directing an episode of *The Persuaders* with Ian Hendry as our guest star. Our location was the Tower of London. I lined up a shot where Ian would pull up in a Mini, resplendent in a Gannex raincoat and trilby hat, and get out. Then Anna Palk would walk into frame and, through the car window we would see her walk towards the camera and Ian Hendry. We rehearsed; all was fine. In take one, however, it wasn't Anna Palk who walked into shot, but a seedy old tramp eating a bag of fish and chips.

The assistant director sprang over to move him on. The tramp proceeded to shout, 'I know my effing rights. I can stand where I want on a public effing thoroughfare . . .'

Just then, as quick as a flash, Ian Hendry, looking every inch the archetypal Scotland Yard inspector, walked over and said, 'I haven't seen you on my manor before, have I?'

'Sorry, inspector,' said the tramp, sheepishly, and shuffled off very quickly.

I rather enjoyed directing on location. There was a limited amount of time to film however many minutes of an episode, and you had to be very creative and versatile. As a director, you had to think on your feet and remain one step ahead at all times. We certainly didn't have the luxury of waiting for the weather, for example. I remember on one location, in Nice, it was raining and the crew thought we'd have to wait for it to stop, as we would do on a feature film. Bob Baker said, 'So, it never rains in Nice?' He was right. We carried on shooting and incorporated it into the story. That's what I mean about being versatile.

We were fortunate that Lord Grade of Elstree – or Lew, as he liked to be called by everyone from the tea-boy to top stars – insisted on shooting on 35 mm film. All his shows were shot on film, which gave them a longevity that so many other TV programmes, shot on video, failed to enjoy. Film added a great quality to a production, and I think that was one of the reasons we were able to secure such an impressive roster of directors, many of whom had enviable feature film credentials: Roy Ward Baker, Jeremy Summers, James Hill, Michael Truman, John Gilling, Leslie Norman, Peter Yates, John Moxey, Robert Asher, Freddie Francis and our own Bob Baker. Our shows were, in fact, seen and treated as mini-films.

Roy Ward Baker had learned much from working as Alfred Hitchcock's assistant in the 1930s, and taught me a very valuable trick in directing. He explained that you should never linger on a static shot for longer than needed, and you should always 'change the size' of the frame you're working with. For instance, if you go in for a close-up of one actor, then cut to a close-up of another, slightly change the size of the close-up framing on the second. That way people's eyes have to continually adjust, which in turn stops them becoming bored and falling asleep. Similarly, the sound volume should fluctuate, to prevent flatness. It keeps the viewers alert. All good advice for budding film-makers.

Escape Route was another fun episode I directed. Our guest star was a then relatively unknown actor called Donald Sutherland. The plot revolved around Simon being sent into a prison undercover and sharing a cell with a criminal – to pick his brains and organize an escape with him. We were shooting at a quarry in Rickmansworth (doubling for Dartmoor). Knowing little about prisons, having never been caught, I asked the assembled extras if any of them knew what happened on a work party. About four stepped forward and said, 'Yes, guv, we know.' They were invaluable!

Cue the escape. A helicopter comes down into the quarry and Donald Sutherland and I, who are part of the work party, make a run to it. Les Crawford, our stunt arranger came over.

'Roger, I've got a great idea,' he said. 'I'll be dressed as a warder and when the helicopter comes in, I'll come running after you. The helicopter will lift off and I'll grab a runner on the side, and try to pull myself up, and then we cut.'

Donald, I discovered, likes to throw himself well and truly into a character. So when we did the sequence and Les was hanging from the runners, Donald started kicking Les's fingers, trying to loosen his grip on the helicopter. Les was holding on for dear life and Donald started kicking harder as the helicopter rose higher. I was shouting, 'Cut! Cut! Donald, cut!'

We did get into bother later, when the episode was screened, as the Air Ministry contacted us to ask what safety precautions had been taken. We hadn't used any safety lines. We certainly wouldn't get away with such things nowadays.

A few weeks after filming, Donald contacted me and asked if it would be possible to show the episode to some producers. I said yes, sure. It was in a rough-cut state and not quite finished, but if they could come to the studio we would run it.

'No,' Donald interrupted. 'The film has to go to LA.'

I didn't quite know what to say.

'It's for a big part in a big film,' he told me.

'OK then,' I said, 'we'll send it.'

The film was *The Dirty Dozen* and I'd like to think, in some small way, that Les Crawford and I had been there at the birth of Donald's career. Mind you, had he knocked Les off that helicopter he wouldn't have done *The Dirty Dozen*, but a dirty dozen years!

In 1963, Luisa and I moved from Mill Hill to a bungalow in Totteridge. We didn't rent this one: with the financial security afforded to me by the show, I thought it was about time we bought. It was shortly after we moved that our daughter Deborah was born. I was filming when the news came through that Luisa was in labour. I rushed to her, and next thing I knew I was holding the most beautiful baby girl. I was thirty-six, and to have my first child was quite a moment. I had a perpetual smile on my face – an idiotic grin – that I wasn't really aware of until I pulled up at traffic lights one day on my way home and became conscious that someone was looking at me. They were obviously wondering why I had such a big grin on my face. She *was* a lovely baby.

I was working regular hours more or less every day, and so was able to spend my evenings and weekends with Luisa and Deborah, a luxury not afforded to many working actors. When, two years after Deborah made her debut, news of a further addition to the family came with the arrival of our first son, Geoffrey, we thought it time to move again. This time we chose a bigger house in Gordon Avenue, Stanmore – very close to where Bob Baker and his wife Alma lived.

Geoffrey was an equal delight. My wide grin returned.

I sometimes wondered if Deborah and Geoffrey understood what it was I did for a living, as they would often visit the set and see me prancing about in character, and then see me on the TV at home. One day, I overheard Deborah telling Geoffrey that they were lucky in having two daddies – daddy at home, and daddy Simon Templar on the TV.

Both Luisa and I were becoming more and more frustrated by Dot's refusal to grant me a divorce. I had money, I had fame, I had a beautiful 'partner' and two lovely children – it was domestic bliss. But there was always something 'unsaid' hanging over us. Again, it was worse for Luisa than it was for me. Back then it really wasn't the done thing to live together, and while most of our friends and colleagues were thrilled that we were so happy and thought of us as 'man and wife', there were a few snipes from newspapers and magazines – mainly on the continent – that never failed to hit their target. My attitude was always to keep a dignified silence on the matter. But there were times when I knew that Luisa was very hurt by what was said.

We attended a number of industry events, award shows and dinners throughout my time in the show – and ever after. It's all very nice, but sometimes you really do feel you'd rather just have a quiet night at home with the family.

One evening, I arrived back from the studio and Luisa said, 'Come on! We'll be late.'

'Late? What for?' I asked, hoping she was wrong.

'The British Film Producers' Association dinner!' she said.

I whipped into my black tie, and we dashed into town to The Dorchester, but we couldn't see our host, C. J. Latter, or anyone else I knew. We moved to the bar and grabbed a glass of champagne. Suddenly a lady appeared and asked if we'd like to sit at the top table. I explained that we were guests of C. J., and were waiting for him. A good few minutes passed. Glances were exchanged around the room, and then another lady approached us. 'I think you might have come on the wrong night,' she said.

'Isn't this the Film Producers' Association …?' I asked.

'No,' she said. 'This is the Ladies Underwear Manufacturers . . . but you're more than welcome to stay.'

We made a hasty retreat and rushed round to Curzon Street and the gambling tables, where I proceeded to lose. Oh, those bad old days of gambling. I did love the tables … but then I loved the horses and the dogs, too. I think it was domesticity that finally nailed my gambling bug, and now the odd game of poker among friends is the extent of my weakness.

While *The Saint* was hugely popular in the UK, it struggled to find a network to pick it up in America. Lew Grade had a partner out there who simply didn't share the faith that we had had in the series, and completely undersold it. Consequently, we went into syndication, and Lew had to sell the series to individual broadcasters all over the US, city by city, state by state. It was an enormously time-consuming way of doing business, and not a very satisfactory way of introducing a show to America, and a method that resulted in smaller financial returns, too.

However, that was all set to change. Lew had a very good friend named David Tebbet. David was vice-president in charge of talent at

NBC and later became a great friend of mine, and godfather to my youngest son, Christian. David recognized that in New York on the NBC station, out of prime time, *The Saint* was clearing the board in the ratings. He recommended that the series should go on to the NBC National Network, as a summer replacement for a show that was faring only moderately. And that's when it really took off. I think we were the first and only show ever to go from syndication to primetime networking. It usually worked the other way round.

Around the time we were coming to the end of the third series, Lew invited me for dinner. He asked how it was all going. I said fine. I told him that I loved the show and loved working with Bob Baker.

'What about Monty?' Lew asked intuitively.

'I don't have a good relationship with Monty,' I told him.

'What if we do another series, but in colour?' said Lew.

'I'd happily work with Bob, but not Monty,' I replied.

Lew was very keen to go to a new series and approached Bob with the problem I'd presented him with. He suggested that Bob should buy out Monty's share of the production company and offer Monty another series, which turned out to be *The Baron*.

I actually felt awful about it afterwards, as Bob and Monty had been partners since the war and had made a great many films together: here was I splitting them up. However, I couldn't see myself working with Monty again as there'd been too many instances where he'd really upset me. The final straw came when one day the schedule consisted of almost all blue backing shots. I was in a few scenes in the morning and then just a couple in the afternoon and I suggested to the director that if my afternoon scenes could be brought forward, it meant I'd have a half-day and could go home early. He said, 'Absolutely no problem, of course we'll change it.' All was OK with the production manager and the first assistant. Just then Monty came on set. 'What's happening?' he asked. They told him.

'Put it back the way it was,' was his order.

I was furious. I went over to the phone, called Bob and said, 'Get him off my back or there's likely to be a punch-up.'

I liked a fun atmosphere on set. I could never work if there was tension. Consequently, I'd sometimes keep the crew in a happy mood by screwing up the odd scene. It was great for morale but tended to aggravate Monty.

When the partnership was eventually dissolved, I had dinner with Bob and his wife Alma, who had both become great friends of mine. I didn't quite know what to say until Alma said, 'Thank you, Roger. Bob has wanted to get away from Monty for a long time but just didn't know how to do it.' I felt such elation.

Monty went off to make *The Baron* and left Bob to continue with *The Saint*. It was a fairly amicable split, though Monty did take Johnny Goodman, our production manager, with him, who in turn took some of the crew. That was a worry until Bob remembered a production manager he'd made a couple of movies with, Peter Manley. He recruited Peter for the first colour series and, as he had just finished working on some Disney films in London, Peter was able to bring most of his regular crew with him. They loved the security of a six-month engagement.

I don't think Johnny particularly wanted to leave our fold, and I know he had been uneasy about working with Monty, but work was work, and he had a start date with Monty long before we would be ready to start the next series of *The Saint*. He returned to work with us from the second colour series onwards and in fact became a junior partner in the new company Bob and I bought, TRI.

TRI Ltd or, to give it its full title, Television Reporters International Ltd, was a company formed by a group of distinguished television journalists, including Ludovic Kennedy, in an attempt to launch an ITV version of the successful BBC current affairs programme *Panorama*. However, at the eleventh hour, before the series made it to the screen, ITV backed down, leaving the partners high and dry. They had run up considerable expenditure, which was now never going to be recouped. In buying the company and producing future episodes of *The Saint* through it, we were able legitimately to offset any profits against accumulated losses within TRI. Later on Bob and I formed other companies such as BaMore (to produce the film *Crossplot*) and Copyright Exploitations Ltd. All the companies were Bahamas-based so that we could minimize our tax obligations. It was all perfectly above board.

In fact, it was while we were out in the Bahamas that Bob and I sat on the beach one afternoon, quite pleased with our financial arrangements, when Bob looked over to me and said, 'You know, Roger, sitting here on this idyllic beach is like being in an episode of *The Saint* – only if we were, a beautiful young girl would come up and ask "Aren't you the famous Simon Templar?"'.'

Realizing he had left his pipe in his hotel room, Bob popped back for it. When he returned he saw me sitting with a very pretty Swedish girl.

'Bob, you won't believe this,' I said, 'but after you left, this young lady came up to me and said "Aren't you Simon Templar?". I told her to sit down and wait for you as you wouldn't believe me otherwise!'

It wasn't the first time someone had mistaken the fictional character for one that actually existed. A call came through to the studio one morning from a man with a strong Italian accent. He demanded to speak to Simon Templar, not Roger Moore but Mr Templar. I declined to accept the call, and so Johnny was delegated to deal with it. Putting on a ludicrous phoney American accent, Johnny asked the guy what he could do for him. It turned out that this man suspected his wife was having a lesbian affair. He wanted the Saint to use his talent to set up a hidden camera to capture the evidence he required to file for divorce. Johnny turned on a mixture of charm and bullshit and eventually he rang off. Naturally, nothing more came of it, but it does make you wonder.

Lew Grade visited the set once during the whole seven-year run of *The Saint*; he was far more interested in making deals and doing business than getting bogged down in the production process. Stories of Lew and his brother Leslie were legendary, and long before Lew ventured into TV, he and Leslie were the two biggest artistes' agents in variety. I had known, and been very fond of, both of them since the early 1950s when they were Squires' agents. Sadly, Leslie died at an early age, just sixty-three. He'd had a bad heart for some years. Lew, meanwhile, had a good heart – in every sense – and was working right up until his death in 1998, aged ninety-two.

One weekend I joined Lew at a sales dinner in the South of France, where he was charming foreign TV buyers. As we drove back to the airport, I asked him if he'd heard any of the Lew and Leslie Grade stories.

'What stories?' he asked.

That then prompted me to tell him some of the stories I'd heard, several of which I cannot reproduce here I'm afraid, as they're far too rude. But here are a few that I can print.

Lew and Leslie were walking down Regent Street to lunch one day. Leslie stopped and said, 'Oh, my God! I've left the office safe open.'

'So?' said Lew. 'We're both here.'

Dennis Sellinger, an agent who worked for the Grades but later moved on to look after people such as Peter Sellers, Michael Caine and me, took a call from Lew one afternoon. 'What are you up to tonight, Dennis?'

'I'm going to the Finsbury Park Empire to see who's on the bill.'

'I'll come with you,' said Lew. He was particularly impressed with one of the acts, and went backstage. 'Tell me, how much do you earn?'

'Twenty quid a night, Mr Grade.'

'That's terrible!' Lew countered. 'I can get you £40. Who's your agent?'

'You are, Mr Grade,' was the reply.

Leslie Grade calls Lew in the office.

'Where are you speaking from?' asks Lew.

'From my car phone.' Now this was at a time when car phones were unheard of. A few days later, not to be outdone, Lew calls Leslie's car from *his* car phone.

'Hello, Leslie, I'm calling you from my car on my new car phone.'

'That's nice, Lew,' said Leslie. 'Hang on a minute, would you? I'm on the other line.'

Lew was a wonderful human being – ably supported in life by his darling wife Kathy. One critic asked him which of the shows he had made did he like best. Without hesitation, Lew said, 'All my shows are great. Some of them are bad, but they're all great.' His flagship programme was undoubtedly *Sunday Night at the London Palladium*. I was asked to be the guest presenter on two occasions and happily accepted. On it, I had the privilege of working with Rowan and Martin, and with great difficulty we learned a lyric that all three of us sang. It went, 'It looks like rain in Cherry Blossom Lane, in Cherry Blossom Lane it looks like rain, it looks like rain in Cherry Blossom Lane, in Cherry Blossom Lane it looks like rain ...' You try it. It's not the easiest of lines, but we did it.

The great Tommy Cooper was on the bill. We'd known each other for years, and before the show I sat with him and we began telling stories. I have a great capacity for, in the main, dirty stories, every one of which had Tommy in stitches. Afterwards, Tommy told me his agent, Miff Ferry, had overheard me telling him all these funny stories and said, 'Don't let him upset you, Tom,' as if Tommy Cooper might have felt he was less funny than me!

Also on the bill was a young comic named Jimmy Tarbuck. Live on stage, Tarbuck asked me if, as I played a secret agent and Sean Connery, Patrick McGoohan and Patrick Macnee all played agents too, we ever went out on the town together?

I said sure, occasionally.

'Pussy Galore?' he asked.

'Well, we don't go looking for it,' I replied. Amazingly, I got away with it on live TV without any complaints.

You know, when you're on a film set, it's very tempting to overeat all the bad things. Bacon rolls for breakfast, steak and kidney pie for lunch, bread pudding, tea and buns, and so forth. As you know, I've always loved food, and I realized at one point that I needed to lose a little weight, so I asked a doctor for something to help. He prescribed appetite suppressants: dospan tenuate. What I didn't know was that these were also fairly strong stimulants. They gave me enormous energy and I didn't need to sleep – I was drugged up to the eyeballs.

We were filming one episode in which the set was a bar filled with big, heavy barstools, and Simon Templar gets into a fight with the Irish doorman. I was throwing furniture around as if it was made of plywood. I'd already punched out the Irish doorman (in character), who was to fall back on to a mattress. He fell forwards as a matter of fact and injured his wrist – and swore a bit. Off he went to first aid and came back with the wrist bandaged up.

The second time around, he fell backwards all right, but one of the stools I then threw hit him head-on.

'Oh fuck! Oh shit!' he cried.

'Hey! Watch your language!' I said. I had a rather nice elderly lady on set doing an interview for a magazine aimed at the over-fifties.

'Oh, I'm sorry, dear,' he said apologetically to the lady, 'for my *fucking* language!'

Those tenuates were not to be recommended. At a dinner a few years later, Patrick Macnee was one of my fellow guests. He was always fighting his weight on *The Avengers* and I said to him that I thought he was taking drugs. He was most offended, and said he certainly was not.

'Do you find you have masses of energy and don't sleep well at night?' I asked him.

'As I matter of fact I do,' replied Patrick.

'You don't have any iris in your eyes, Patrick,' I explained, 'they're all pupil. Are you taking slimming pills?'

'Yes, I am,' he said.

'Tenuate?'

'Yes! How did you know?' I told him my story and got him off these highly addictive so-called slimming pills.

As I've mentioned, Harry Junkin was our story editor on *The Saint*. He was a very friendly man. You couldn't be in a restaurant with him for more than five minutes before he'd get up and go to another table; he loved talking to people. Harry and his wife lived at Albert Mansions, just behind the Royal Albert Hall in central London. The rooms were very high, with great views across the park. Every day, Harry would take a walk in the park and one afternoon he got chatting to a policeman. Christmas was approaching, and Harry asked him what he would be doing. The policeman explained that as he was unmarried, he lived in the Section House and would be spending Christmas there with the other policemen.

'How many of you will there be?' enquired Harry.

'Oh, about twenty,' the policeman replied.

'Well, you won't be in the Section House, you'll be at my place for a slap-up Christmas lunch.' Harry invited the whole Section House and such was his hospitality that they, C-Division, appointed him their head of special events. So whenever there was an occasion that involved a dinner or a speaker, Harry would coordinate it.

Accordingly, my call came. 'Roger, you're going to be the guest of honour at a police dinner,' Harry informed me.

'I am?'

'Yes, you are,' said Harry. 'And furthermore you're going to make a nice speech.'

'But, Harry,' I protested. 'I've never made a speech before.'

'Well it's time you did then.'

'OK,' I said, 'I'll tell you what. You write it and I'll do it.' It was agreed.

As the date drew nearer, I asked Harry for the speech. He kept putting me off, until finally, to put me out of my misery, he invited me round to his flat that night to write the speech. I arrived, had a Canadian Club . . . followed by another . . . The bottle was emptying rather quickly.

'Harry, where's my speech?' I begged while still preserving some modicum of sobriety.

Harry sat at his old Royal typewriter. With a flick of his wrist he started the first line, then another and then whipped out the paper and presented it to me. 'There you are!'

I looked at it. It said 'Ladies and Gentlemen, and then you're humble.'

'What sort of speech is this Harry – "and then you're humble"?'

'You know how to be humble, don't you?' Harry asked.

'I'll tell you what,' I said in desperation. 'I'll use this as my introduction and tell them you said I have to be humble. Then I'll just wing it.'

I did, and I still use that story to this day in starting speeches. 'I'm not very good at starting speeches, so I'll tell you a story about Harry Junkin and humility . . .'

Humility is an interesting subject. I know humility as an actor, as I believe any talent I have, any gift I possess, is merely loaned to me by a greater being. Every night before he goes to bed, the actor prays, 'Thank you, Lord, for giving me this gift . . . and thank you for making me better than anyone else.' That's humility! Or, as Michael Caine says, 'Enough of me talking about myself. What do *you* think of me?'

As I said earlier, I became rather well known for my love of practical jokes. Both as an actor and director I wanted to enjoy my work and create a good working atmosphere for all the cast and crew. Don't get me wrong, I was always professional, but a bit of levity in the right places was always appreciated . . . well, mostly . . .

Our production associate, Johnny Goodman, announced he was to marry his fiancée, the lovely Andrea. Her father was a commander in the London Flying Squad. Johnny was marrying into respectability. Their honeymoon was going to be spent in Majorca, but their wedding night was spent in Johnny's flat in Maida Vale. Around midnight on their all-consuming – or consummating – night, the phone rang. Andrea answered.

'Hello, is Bill Green there?' said the voice.

'You have the wrong number,' she said.

Five minutes later, it rang again. 'Hello, can I speak to Bill Green, please?'

'There is *no* Bill Green here,' Andrea said emphatically.

A few minutes later, the phone rang yet again. 'Is Bill in?'

'No he is not!' She slammed the phone down.

Ten minutes later, the phone rang again. This time Johnny took it.

'There is no bloody Bill Green here!' he barked.

'Oh no,' said the voice on the other end. 'This is Bill Green. Are there any messages for me?'

Johnny was furious. I do feel rotten for interrupting his wedding night, but hey, he did see the funny side of it later.

Camera operators spend most of their life looking through a lens, and therefore they have little idea about what is going on behind them. I used to love taking gaffer tape and tying them down to their chairs, or putting boot polish around the camera eyepiece. I really was quite awful.

Worse still, I would often give my stunt double, Les Crawford, some money to go across the road to the local newsagents and buy chocolate bars for the crew. On one show we had an actor called Tony Wager, who famously played Pip in David Lean's *Great Expectations*. We were filming at Watford Playhouse Theatre, and I dispatched Les across the road and told him to bring back some chocolates and some Exlax – chocolate laxative. I distributed the chocolates to the crew, but deliberately left out Tony Wager.

'Is there any for me?' Tony asked as he came over.

I handed him an unwrapped piece of chocolate – the Exlax. I then asked Les to nip out and buy some Diocalm, some toilet paper and a chamber pot. At the end of the day, I presented Tony with these items.

'What are these for?' he asked.

'You'll find out!' I said.

The next day he arrived on set and was furious with me. Apparently his wife had invited some friends over for dinner the previous night, and the Exlax struck halfway through! He got his own back though. A little while later I went to see Shirley Bassey at Caesar's Palace in Luton. Tony Wager was the MC, and he introduced me in the audience and proceeded to tell everyone the rather shitty story. I did not win friends that night.

Towards the end of the series' seven-year run, we decided to take advantage of the overseas popularity of *The Saint* by filming two two-part episodes, *The Fiction Makers* and *Vendetta for the Saint*. The plan was to screen them over two weeks in the UK, and edit them together for the international market to form a feature film for release in cinemas. They proved very popular.

In *Vendetta*, which had the subtitle 'Simon Templar Meets the Mafia' – that gives the story away! – we filmed in Malta, which doubled for Palermo. The interiors were shot at ABPC at Elstree. For the head of the

Mafia, the Don Corleone, Finlay Currie was cast. He was, shall we say, rather advanced in years at this point – ninety years old, I believe. The assistant director came over to me on the morning of Finlay's first scenes.

'Roger, Mr Currie is here,' he said. 'He looks rather frail. I've taken the liberty of removing his canvas chair and replaced it with a comfortable armchair and a footstool so he can rest between takes.'

Finlay came on to the set and sat in his chair. His hair was very long at this point, and quite yellow; I guess through the nicotine stains of his cigarettes. I went over to greet him.

'Mr Currie, I'm Roger Moore.'

'What?' he croaked. 'Eh?'

'I'm Roger Moore and I play the Saint,' I said.

'Aye, aye, aye,' he replied. 'I'm sorry about the hair.'

'Sorry? What do you mean?'

'It's long,' he added.

'That's all right,' I said. 'You look like a Beatle.'

'*What?*' he barked.

Realizing I might have said the wrong thing, I repeated, 'You look like a Beatle, sir.'

'WHAT?' he shouted.

'I said you look like a Beatle, sir.'

'Oh, aye. Aye. Yes, St Peter. I played him,' he replied.

I was biting my lip and trying not to burst out laughing. Rolling on a couple of hours, we reached Finlay's big death scene. He, as the Mafia boss, was lying in a big four-poster bed and was fading fast. Next to the bed was the family doctor and assembled other Mafioso types. If we'd been a big film we'd have had actors, but in our case we dressed the stunt boys up. It's always fatal to give stunt boys parts as they always get the giggles. This was no exception.

I arrived in the scene and Finlay Currie looked up at me, 'Simon Templar,' he said in his wonderful Scottish brogue. 'What are you daeing here in Palermo?' A Scottish Mafia boss! Please.

I said to the director, Jim O'Connolly, that we'd have to re-voice him.

'Re-voice Finlay Currie?' he protested. 'You can't re-voice Finlay Currie! He won the Oscar for playing St Peter with a Scottish accent! You'll go down in history as the man who had the temerity to dub this great actor.'

Finlay called me over. 'They think I'm ill,' he said.

'Why do you say that?' I asked.

'Well, they've got this doctor standing next to my bed,' he said, nodding at the actor playing the doctor.

My lip was sore from biting.

Finally, we reached the moment when Finlay had to expire. The doctor pulled the sheet up over his lifeless body and announced he had passed on. It was all very serious stuff. Finlay, meanwhile, started making more noise breathing when he was playing dead than when he was alive, and the sheet rose and fell in tandem with his breathing. The stunt boys started laughing and it all fell apart!

In another episode in the final series, we thought we might try teaming Simon Templar with an American partner. Bob Baker had the idea of a possible spin-off series, where a mismatching Brit and a Yank team up. A sort of 'buddy' series if you like. The episode was *The Ex King of Diamonds*. Stuart Damon played Rod Huston, a Texan. It worked very well and turned out to be the forerunner of *The Persuaders*.

I think it was a mutual feeling between Bob, me and everyone else as we approached the end of 1968 that we'd really done all we could with *The Saint*. One hundred and eighteen episodes is a lot. And so, the series and my tenure as Simon Templar came to an end. A decade later, Bob produced *Return of the Saint* with Ian Ogilvy, and I maintained my interest in the company. I didn't interfere though. That's the last thing they'd have wanted.

Then, throughout the late 1980s and into the early 1990s there was much talk of a *Saint* feature film. As Bob and I owned certain rights, the American studios involved us in discussions. Initially, scripts were written that included my involvement as an ageing Simon Templar who finds an illegitimate son and hands over the reins. A sort of *Son of the Saint*. It was a troubled production.

Paramount Pictures secured Robert Evans as producer, Steven Zaillian as writer and Sydney Pollack as the director. Ralph Fiennes, a wonderful actor who is also a UNICEF ambassador now, was courted to play the young Templar, but ultimately declined.

Robert Evans left the project, and David Brown replaced him. A new writer, Jonathan Hensleigh, was hired, and Philip Noyce boarded the project as director when Sydney Pollack left. Other leads reportedly linked with the film included Hugh Grant, Mel Gibson, Kevin Costner and Johnny Depp. Then Val Kilmer signed on. Another rewrite was called for by Wesley Strick, to tailor the script for Val.

In all of the rewrites and changes of management, any ideas relating to *The Son of the Saint* were abandoned. However, as I'd agreed my involvement with the studio some time earlier, they still had to compensate me. I think it was the first time I was paid *not* to act in a film; though I'm sure others have since said they'd have paid me not to. (I lie! I did appear in the film, briefly. Or rather my voice did. I pop up as a radio newsreader at the end.)

It was, in short, a bit of a mess and didn't perform well – critically or at the box office. A while later, I met with Val at a Cannes Film Festival.

'We really screwed that up, didn't we?' he said.

'Why do you say that?' I asked.

'I read all the books after we finished filming. They were damn good stories,' said Val.

I didn't argue.

Back to 1969, and I was not sorry to leave Simon Templar behind me to be honest; yes I'd had great fun over the seven years of making the series, enjoyed working with so many lovely people and now had financial security. But I felt it was time to move on to pastures new and stretch myself in new roles.

Things were about to change in my home life, too. It all began at a BAFTA awards dinner in 1968. My pal Kenneth More was the commentator for the event, which was being televised by ITV. In the course of his commentary, Kenny made an innocent – and, knowing him, very sweetly intended – remark about me and the fact that 'my wife' (referring to Luisa) was rather more attractive than me.

The next day all hell broke loose, and the papers all reported that Squires was going to sue both Kenny and ITV for libel. Of course, ITV broadcast an immediate apology, but the case did go to court. However, I think it was this furore that made Dot take stock and see just how ridiculous the situation was, some eight years after we had separated.

Word came through from mutual friends that Dot had decided to grant me a divorce.

★ ★ ★

When I left *The Saint* I wasn't walking into the wilderness without any prospect of work, you'll be reassured to read. Before we finished the last series, Bob Baker and I had been approached by United Artists with the offer of a three-film deal. They were keen to capitalize on the success of *The Saint*, as were Bob and I. And I was keen to get back into movies.

The first of these three films was *Crossplot*, written by Leigh Vance and John Kruse, two *Saint* regulars. The plot involved an advertising executive (me) hiring a model for a photo shoot. Unbeknown to the executive, the model has overheard an assassination plot and is being targeted by killers. Pretty much the same crew from *The Saint* joined us and I think we started production a month or so after finishing the TV series. It was probably slightly too soon as there were a few creaks in the script, and the production in general, that ought to have been fixed before we started shooting, but you live and learn.

Alvin Rakoff, who directed the buddy episode of *The Saint*, helmed the film and we assembled an impressive cast: Martha Hyer, Alexis Kanner, Claudie Lange, Bernard Lee, Francis Matthews and so on. Bernie Lee was a delight. I'd known him since my understudying days when I was in *The Little Hut* at the Lyric Theatre and he was next door in *Seagulls over Sorrento*. Those were the days when I used to frequent pubs, and we'd quite often meet up in the pub opposite the theatres. Alas, Bernie had a problem with the dreaded alcohol.

Rolling forward to *Crossplot*, one Sunday we had a sequence to shoot with the delightful Martha Hyer. Bernie was on first thing, clear-eyed and word-perfect. He then had a few hours to kill until his shots after lunch with Martha. He disappeared, and we couldn't find him anywhere. Runners were dispatched to local pubs but to no avail. We eventually found him in the first-aid room. I think he'd been sniffing the surgical alcohol, as he was pretty incoherent.

His one scene that afternoon involved him climbing into the back of a Rolls-Royce with Martha. Take one. Bernie sloped into the car looked at Martha and said, 'What a stupid fucking hat you're wearing, madam.' He laughed riotously.

Take two. 'OK, Bernie.'

He did exactly the same again. It tickled his funny bone you see, but after a few takes everyone else's patience was wearing a *little* thin.

Production wise, there are a few dodgy shots involving back projection in *Crossplot*, and a few dodgy hairstyles – from yours truly in particular in my efforts to get away from the famous Simon Templar bouffant.

I remember we were filming a sequence with the Royal Horse Artillery in Hyde Park. The piece centred around an assassination attempt on a foreign leader during celebrations for the Queen's birthday. My daughter Deborah was about six at the time, and she came with us on location for the day. The Hussars fired their twenty-one-gun salute and when the first gun went off, Deborah started to scream. I had to quickly take the poor hysterical child across Park Lane and realized that film sets are not always a place for children.

Despite our best efforts, the film wasn't very successful. I think people may have expected a *Saint* movie. It was certainly sold in some countries as 'Roger Moore aka Simon Templar' and had the famous stickman image on posters. United Artists were understandably not keen to progress on the other two projects under our deal.

Towards the end of 1968 my divorce from Dot finally came through, and at last Luisa and I were free to marry. It was an odd feeling: having waited so long and longed so much for this day, we had been expecting to be over the moon, cock-a-hoop, delighted, excited – but no, we actually felt rather deflated, as I remember. We did have a quiet celebration, though, with Kenny and Angela More, who both knew exactly what we'd been through as they, too, had waited some time before they could tie the knot.

On the night before the wedding I showed my bride-to-be just how romantic her hero could be ... and took her to the movies to see Richard Attenborough's *Oh! What a Lovely War*. It was the film premiere, I should add, not the early evening show at Streatham Odeon. When we left the premiere, Luisa went home and stayed with her sister, while I did the traditional thing and went out 'with the boys'. Being forty-one by this time – it's no age, I now realize, but it felt older then – it wasn't a raucous stag do, but, do you know, all these years later, I have absolutely no recollection as to who was there, aside from Kenny More, where we went or what we drank ... it must have been a very good night!

We were married at Caxton Hall in London on 11 April 1968, and literally hundreds of people came to watch. Kenneth More was my best man and the ceremony and the wedding luncheon after it were full of warmth and emotion. We had decided against having the children at the wedding – it just didn't feel right, somehow – so that night, back at home with the kids, we watched the television coverage. Suddenly, Deborah burst into tears.

'What's wrong, darling?' I asked her, giving her a hug.

'Oh, Daddy! You always said you'd marry me!'

I was lost for words.

In 1970, Luisa and I thought it was time for another move. A house with a few more rooms and a bigger garden for the children would be the ideal. Of course it had to be within an easy drive of London. We viewed numerous properties before finding the one – Sherwood House in Denham. It was perfect for a growing family. The upstairs had four main bedrooms, and at the end of a corridor there was a maid's room and nursery. There was also a room-size walk-in wardrobe. I had my own room off the bedroom and gained access, via a wrought-iron spiral staircase, to my study downstairs.

The front door led into a large wood-block floored hall (always beautifully polished). The main oak-beamed living-room area was straight ahead through double oak doors, it was split into two by back-to-back open fireplaces and both areas had French windows leading on to a patio. The dining room led off into the children's playroom and a country-style kitchen with an Aga, a wooden dresser and a scrubbed table. Most of our family meals were taken there. From the kitchen a door led to the main hall, and there wide oak polished stairs led to the bedrooms.

The patio outside looked on to a pond and trimmed lawns with clipped hedges. To the left was a tennis court and at the bottom of the gardens, a swimming pool. There was a wooded area where bluebells flowered in the spring.

I employed a driver at this time, John Bevan, as it wasn't always easy maintaining a social life after work while being one hundred per cent sober. The gravel drive curved to the left up to the house. The four-car garage at the end of the curved drive had the kitchen garden with greenhouse behind.

Sherwood House was to be our home until 1978 when, regrettably, we had to leave due to the punitive tax regime of the then government. We had a few famous neighbours: Cilla Black's land backed on to our land; Jess Conrad had a house just up the road – his children were of a similar age to Deborah and Geoffrey, so he'd often swing by to give the children a lift to school in the mornings. And just across the village were John Mills and Mary Hayley Bell.

The Millses had lived in Denham before moving away for a while, but they ended up returning and bought a lovely house on the edge of the village. I called them up soon after their return, and invited them out to dinner – a couple of new restaurants had come to the village since they had last lived there and I thought they might enjoy visiting one.

'Ah! Good evening, Mr and Mrs Moore . . . Mr and Mrs Mills,' said the restaurant manager. 'Lovely to have you with us again in Denham, Mr Mills and Mrs Mills. Are you ready to order, Mr Mills? ... Mrs Mills? . . . Thank you, Mr Mills . . .'

This went on for a couple of minutes, before Mary, who was becoming increasingly agitated, said, 'It is *Sir* John and *Lady* Mills.'

John hung his head, in semi-embarrassment, adding, 'I've waited long enough for it!' Ah, they were such a charming couple. I miss them both.

Meanwhile, I received a very exciting offer. *The Man Who Haunted Himself* was to be a film based on a short story by Anthony Armstrong, called 'The Case of Mr Pelham'.

'Have you read it?' asked Bryan Forbes, who had recently been appointed Head of Production at EMI Studios. Bryan, with the support of his backers, namely Lord Delfont, was embarking upon an ambitious programme of films, all to be produced on reasonable budgets, with the stars engaged taking lower salaries in order to get the studio back into sustainable film production. *The Railway Children, The Tales of Beatrix Potter, The Go-Between* and *The Raging Moon* were just a few of the successes Bryan achieved.

Basil Dearden and Michael Relph were to direct and produce respectively. They were two of Britain's most successful film-makers. I'd worked with Michael's father, stage actor George Relph, on *I Capture the Castle* some years earlier. That helped cement our new friendship.

It was one of the best scripts I'd ever read, and it was certainly a very intriguing story. Following a car accident, Harold Pelham momentarily 'dies' on the operating table, and his *doppelgänger* is released into the world. He begins assuming Pelham's identity among his friends, colleagues, and even his family. The real Pelham is plunged towards insanity, and thoughts of suicide. It was a role that called for emotion, drama and great intensity. In short – it was a role that needed an actor. I had that written in my passport, so felt somewhat qualified.

When asked about the movie nowadays, I always reflect that it was one of the few times I was allowed to act. It's a terrible admission from someone who has made a living from walking in front of cameras. Though, in my defence, I'd previously been cast in roles that were relatively straightforward in what was required of me, thank goodness – either as a romantic lead, heroic lead or just holding a spear, as I did in my first movie. I'd never been 'dramatically stretched' as they say. I committed to the film for £20,000 and a deferment.

A wonderful cast was assembled. Freddie Jones was a particular favourite of mine; he played the Kubrickesque psychiatrist, Dr Harris. Hildegarde Neil, a Royal Shakespeare Company actor, played my screen wife, Eve. Anton Rodgers, Thorley Walters and Charles Lloyd Pack (father of Roger, who stars in two of my favourite comedy series, *Only Fools and Horses* and *The Vicar of Dibley*) played my work compatriots and friends. We filmed extensively on location in the City of London, quite possibly where the Mayor's office now stands near Tower Bridge on the banks of the Thames. Our lighting cameraman Tony Spratling was very keen to use real daylight and real locations. It was all very inventive and clever, and gave the film an added quality and feeling of grandeur.

The sequences where I faced my alter ego were fun. I simply shot the scene as one character one way, and then the next week shot the other the other way, each time talking to thin air. The shots were then matched together. It's called a 'split screen' technique. It all works terribly well.

Basil Dearden was a wonderful director; both technically and dramatically. He gave me and the other actors a tremendous confidence. The great tragedy is that a short time after the film was released, when he was driving home on the very same stretch of the M4 where we'd filmed Pelham's accident in the opening sequence of the film, his car careered out of control. He was decapitated at the wheel. The film industry was robbed of a great talent that day.

I think there was a certain resentment in the hierarchy of EMI towards Bryan Forbes at that time. As well as being an accomplished director, producer, writer and actor, he was also Managing Director. There were noticeable undercurrents all around, not least in EMI's distribution arm. It was petty jealousy, I guess. Consequently, though, over all the films, the publicity machinery was cranked up in a rather amateurish way, sending out the message 'We've made a film for £200,000: aren't we clever?'

It was akin to EMI saying 'we're making cheap films', and when one hears the word 'cheap' one immediately thinks 'poor quality'. Audiences aren't foolish; they won't part with their money at the box office if they feel they're being sold a cheap film. What the marketing people should have said is that they made terrific films, and such was the principals' belief in them that they had taken reduced fees. The films were excellent but the publicity let them down, and as a result *The Man Who Haunted Himself* was not the commercial success it deserved to be. It saddened me greatly – not least because I owned a share of the profits!

Not long afterwards, Bryan Forbes resigned from his role. With promised funding not materializing and a lack of support from the company's distribution arm and a stoic board of directors, he was left with little choice.

As I've previously mentioned, during the final series of *The Saint*, Bob Baker and I tried out the 'buddy formula' in *The Ex King of Diamonds* episode. Nothing more came of the idea, until Bob started talking to Lew Grade in 1970 about a TV show format featuring an English toff and an American boy come-good. It was to be called *The Friendly Persuaders*. We'd moved on a couple of years by this time and, quite frankly, I'd cooled on the idea and, indeed, on the idea of doing more TV, having just made two movies.

Lew called me from New York. 'I want to see you at seven o'clock tomorrow morning.'

'I can't be in New York by tomorrow morning, Lew.'

'No, I'll be back in London,' he said.

'OK, but can we make it eight? Remember, I have to drive in from Denham.' I was only half joking.

Lew always arrived in his office at the crack of dawn. He liked to do all of his business early, before the phones started ringing. It also meant he could catch people in LA before they went to bed.

I arrived at eight o'clock. Lew sat me down and said, 'Roger, I've sold *The Persuaders* – with you in the lead.'

EIGHT

The Persuaders

'You can't sell a programme with me in, it's immoral'

The *Friendly* part of *The Persuaders* title was soon dropped; not that we were to be unfriendly but rather because it sounded too much like *Friendly Persuasion*, the Gary Cooper film. However, I was still adamant it was not for me.

'Lew! I said I didn't want to do it! You can't sell a programme with me in, it's immoral.'

Lew had just won the Queen's Award for Industry. So he played the patriot card. 'The country needs the money. Think of your Queen.'

'That's not a very convincing argument, Lew.'

He shoved a cigar in my mouth, and wrote out a rather large cheque. 'OK,' he said, 'how does that look for a start?'

I found that more convincing, and dutifully consented to star in the series. When I agreed to the show, I have to be honest and say that I didn't want to commit to several series. It's true that the Bond producers had made overtures towards me, and I didn't want to be tied to a three- or four-year TV contract. So, I never signed a contract. I shook Lew's hand and said I would do one series, and I honoured my word.

Our conversation came around to casting. 'I have three people who want to do it,' he told me. 'And I can get them: Rock Hudson, Glenn Ford and Tony Curtis.'

I explained to Lew that I'd worked with Glenn Ford in the past, and didn't think there'd be a happy chemistry. Glenn was quite selfish, not as a person but as an actor, and I didn't think it would work over a long period of time. Rock Hudson and I were really too alike; both six-foot-something, even-featured leading men. There would be no contrast. Tony, on the other hand, I thought would be brilliant. I remembered all too fondly *Some Like It Hot* and his terrific comedy timing. I was a fan of his, and thought him a very talented actor.

'OK, fine,' said Lew. 'You and Bob will go and have a meeting with him. But remember one thing, Tony is head of the anti-smoking lobby in America, so *don't* smoke.'

Bob, myself and Terry Nation, our story editor, flew to LA. Back then I smoked cigarettes, Bob smoked a pipe and Terry was a chain-smoker. It was to kill him in the end. We checked into the Beverly Hills Hotel, and the next morning drove over to Tony's house on Charing Cross Road.

We'd been chatting for about an hour and were getting on really well, when I ventured to say, 'Tony, Lew has told us that we shouldn't smoke, but I know Bob is dying for a pipe, Terry can't hang on another moment, and I'd rather like one myself.'

'Leslie! Oh dear, Leslie!' Tony called to his then wife, 'where is that ashtray we had?' The elusive ashtray was found, but meanwhile Tony slipped a book across the table to me. The front cover had a picture, quite difficult to describe, but it looked horrid. I asked what it was and he told me it was a diseased lung, caused by smoking. It turned my stomach and gave me the wake-up call I needed. I think it was at that moment I decided it was time to stop smoking cigarettes, and shortly after this I did. Admittedly, I continued smoking cigars for some years, but cigarettes were out. (However, while Tony was head of the anti-smoking lobby, I later discovered that the same ethics didn't apply when it came to marijuana.)

The deal was done with Tony and a start date was agreed for shooting in the South of France, the UK and at Pinewood Studios.

Unfortunately, just before Tony was due to arrive in the UK I had to go into hospital, suffering with a kidney stone. After an uncomfortable operation, I was still recuperating in bed on the day he flew in, so Johnny Goodman kindly agreed to step in for me and drove to Heathrow.

Tony arrived and was immediately arrested. He had cannabis in his luggage. He was hauled off to the Magistrates' Court and got us a heap of bad publicity in the process. Johnny was none too pleased, especially as he was the son-in-law of a commander in the Flying Squad. Being laid up in bed, I collected all the newspaper clippings and assembled them in a lovely scrapbook. I had a title put on the front, 'How to Enter a Country Quietly'. Bob Hope even worked a joke about Tony into his act: 'Tony Curtis has been flying around London for three months, waiting to land.'

Tony eventually placated the authorities and reached his lovely £48,000 house in Chester Square, Mayfair. That was part of the deal: Lew bought him a house.

We were to start filming in the South of France. After leaving hospital I stayed at a friend's house on Cap Ferrat, three doors down from David Niven, and had a whole month to recuperate before filming started. Joan Collins and Ron Kass came down to stay, and it was a happy month of swimming (albeit in a rather cold ocean) and getting fit.

Once Tony arrived, we moved into the La Voile d'Or hotel in St-Jean-Cap-Ferrat. We had identical suites. I guess we filmed for two or three months, enough material for six or seven episodes. Basil Dearden and Val Guest were the two location directors. Logistically, it's quite difficult to shoot exteriors for half a dozen or so different episodes of a TV series, as you're only filming part of a storyline before moving on to the next episode. Then we all reconvened at Pinewood some time later to film the remainder of the episodes. It also meant holding actors over a number of weeks, which can become quite expensive. A lot of detailed planning had to go into it.

But there were times in which all that careful planning came to nought, as Tony liked to wander off-script, ad-lib and go off at tangents. He felt he knew the character and, accordingly, put words in his mouth, which is fine, apart from when you're driving a story, and other actors are waiting for their specific cues. We only had forty-six minutes to set up the story and deliver all the answers in each show. I'd therefore find myself bringing the story back round from where Tony was taking it. Bob soon recognized this and, with Terry Nation, decided that – and if you watch the show you'll see – I should carry the storyline, or at least introduce it in each episode, while Tony carried the humour.

I had a car down there and would drive myself around, and to the daily locations. However, if we were filming somewhere I wasn't familiar with, I'd opt to drive with Tony in his chauffeured car. Every time I got in the car with Tony, his French driver would say, 'Where are we going today, Monsieur Curtis?'

'We're going to the location. Don't you know where it is?' Tony would reply.

'Yes,' said the driver.

'So what are you asking for?' shouted Tony. Every day the driver would go through this same routine and it really rather pissed Tony off.

When we finished shooting in the South of France the driver gave me an envelope. Inside was a photo of said driver and written across it was, 'This is for you, Mr Moore, but not for that prick Mr Curtis.' In fact, it was Tony who had written it and asked the driver to deliver it; he had a great sense of humour and knew this fellow was winding him up, so he just wanted to get his own back one more time – and make me laugh.

Walter Matthau told me a great story about Tony over dinner one night. He and Tony started out at the same time at the same drama school in New York, and they had a wager as to who would 'make it' in Hollywood first. A year or so later, Walter was walking down the street – having taken a little longer to get going as a character actor than Tony did as a leading actor – when a stretch limo pulled up opposite.

'Hey, Walter! It's me! Bernie, Bernie Schwartz!' Tony got out of the car. (He was Bernie Schwartz long before he adopted his new name.) 'I've made it in Hollywood! I fucked Yvonne de Carlo!'

One of the things that Tony had to overcome in doing the series was his attitude of being a big movie star in a TV show. Like many others, he felt TV was a step down from movies, and I don't think he realized just how popular television was. I remember when we were filming the car race sequence for the first episode, which became part of the title sequence too, both characters, Lord Brett Sinclair and Danny Wilde, arrived at Nice airport, and we both jumped into our respective cars – I drove a wonderful Aston Martin DBS and Tony a Ferrari. We were to end our friendly chase at the Hôtel de Paris in Monte Carlo, where we pulled up, nose to nose, outside the front steps. The hotel is directly opposite the Casino de Monte Carlo which attracts thousands of tourists each day; many flutter away some of their hard-earned cash, whereas others just pose for a photograph outside.

Anyhow, two coach-loads of Spanish tourists pulled up outside the casino and, looking across at the film crew opposite, obviously spotted us. They started walking over towards us.

'Oh, goddamn fans!' said Tony, as he saw them walking over. 'I don't want to have to sign autographs.'

But they all swept past Tony and came directly to me, saying 'El Santo, El Santo.' The Saint had been very popular in Spain. Tony realized at that point that working in television could increase one's popularity.

Tony and I shared a caravan on location. But being a TV show we couldn't afford the luxury of a fleet of trailers, and so just had two; one for Tony and me, and the other for the guest star. Joan Collins and Robert Hutton were guest-starring in one episode, and they took turns using the caravan to change. One afternoon, Joan needed to use the loo, and as Robert and his wife were chatting in the caravan between takes, she asked if they'd mind stepping out to allow her to use the facilities. Perfectly understandable. They readily agreed. At the moment that Joan asked, Tony was walking past the caravan, and came rushing over to me.

'What is it with that woman? Robert Hutton. Robert Hutton! She told him to get out of the trailer. Can you *believe* it?'

'Tony, Tony,' I said, 'calm down. This is a TV show. We're all in it together. We turn up on time, we learn our lines, say them, and then go home at 5.30. We don't make waves. We cash our cheques on Friday and we're all very happy.'

'Yes, dear sweet Roger. You're right. You're *always* right,' he replied.

Roll on twenty minutes. We were filming on the side of a mountain, trying to evade some Italian crooks in the story and we, in character, all took a breather by sitting on some rocks. The special effects chap came over and explained that there were going to be a few charges detonating, simulating gunfire.

'Where?' asked Joan.

'Oh! Goddamn leading lady!' said Tony, springing to his feet and mimicking a female voice. 'Where is there going to be an explosion?' he piped. 'Oh, my god! Oh, my god!'

'Tony! Stop it,' I reasoned. 'It's perfectly logical that if an explosion is going to go off near a lady's backside she would like to know exactly where. We've all been in explosions that have got a bit too close for comfort, and we've all seen people injured.'

'Yes, Roger, dear sweet Roger. You're right,' he said.

A few days later, I had a late call on set and was able to see my family off at the airport in Nice, for their return to London. The location was, conveniently, only half a mile from the airport, on the River Var. When I arrived, there was nothing happening. The whole crew was sitting around playing cards and Joan was sitting in a chair under a large tree. I thought it very odd. Then Tony appeared.

'Dear Roger,' he said, looking somewhat bashful. 'I let you down.'

I asked him what he'd done.

'I called Joan a cunt.'

'That's not very nice, Tony,' I said. I walked off to find her.

Joan leapt up when she saw me. 'He called me a cunt,' she cried.

'Yeah,' added her husband Ron Kass. 'He called Joan a cunt.'

Eventually I discovered that Tony and Joan had been in a truck together, filming a sequence where they drive down a very bumpy, rocky path and come to a halt on the dry riverbed, under a bridge. Unfortunately they drove a little too far, and missed their mark.

'Can we go again, please,' said the director. With that, Joan got out of the truck and started walking.

'Where are you going?' Tony shouted after her.

'I'm going to walk up to the starting point.'

'Goddamn chicken-shit actresses!' Tony added.

'I'll walk up, you drive the truck back up,' replied Joan.

Tony drove the truck, muttering all the way about women and actresses. He reached the start point and Joan hopped in.

'You know what, Joan?' he said. 'You're a cunt.'

The truck rolled down the path, came to a thundering halt and Joan wound down the window and shouted to the director, 'He called me a cunt.' She refused to film any more . . . which is where I came in, to smooth things over and get everyone back to work.

Tony had this little fixation with his character wearing leather gloves. It was obviously a trait that he thought suited Danny Wilde. But in one episode he had to wash his hands . . . and kept his gloves on to do it. Tony had a few odd ideas like that and, as much as I enjoyed working with him and admired him, he *was* eccentric.

One episode I directed had a scene in a gentlemen's club. Judge Fulton, the man responsible for teaming Brett and Danny, had his foot in plaster – due to gout – for this particular episode. I thought it would make an interesting shot to start on the judge's plastered foot resting on a low table, and then pull back to the rest of the scene. Tony was to walk in and, while talking to the judge, look around the room at all the mounted animal heads covering the walls.

Prior to shooting, I went down on set to line up the shots with my cameraman, Jimmy Devis, and asked the assistant director if he'd call Tony down from his dressing room to talk it through and do a quick line-up. Back came the word, 'Tell dear sweet Roger whatever he wants I will do, go ahead. I'll just get made-up and will join you on set.'

I said to Jimmy Devis that I thought we'd have problems with a line. He asked which one, and I showed him the line in the script. We placed a wager. Tony arrived.

'OK, dear sweet Roger. What do I do? Where do I go?'

'You come in through the door, Tony. You look at that head on the wall and see underneath that it was killed by General Bulstrode. Then you look at the second head and see that was also killed by General Bulstrode. You then grab a chair to stand on, and look at this head up here . . .'

'I wouldn't do that,' Tony interrupted.

'Pardon?' I asked.

'I wouldn't stand on a chair in a gentlemen's club,' replied Tony.

'But, Tony, you're not tall enough to see this head and the writing underneath it. What would you do?'

'I'd stand on a chair,' he said. Tony picked up the script and started reading the scene. 'Yeah . . . yeah . . . yeah . . . hang on! What's all this abatoy shit?'

'Abattoir, Tony,' I corrected him. The line was 'This General Bulstrode is a one-man abattoir.'

'Abatoy, abattoir – have it your way. But I can't say that,' Tony affirmed.

'Why not?' I asked.

'What *is* an *abatoy*?'

'An *abattoir* is where they slaughter animals,' I explained.

'You can't fool me!' he countered. 'It's where they wash their nunnies in France!' Anyhow, he finished his argument by saying that if he didn't understand it, nobody in America would. I thought it a very sweeping statement, but asked Tony what he would like to say instead.

'It's like a butcher's shop,' was his suggestion.

I didn't think it worked as a line, but gave in to Tony.

We both received invitations to the annual Royal Film Performance, which was and still is organized by the Cinema and Television Benevolent Fund, the only film trade charity in the UK.

The invitation said 'white tie'.

I had a very good white tie, as I used to share it with Monty Berman the costumier, and Richard Burton. Richard was a little shorter, so the legs had to be taken up for him, but we were the same chest size. It worked well, but if all three of us were invited to a premiere only one of us could have gone!

'Dear sweet Roger, what do we have to wear?' Tony asked me.

'White tie and tails.'

'Well, I haven't got that. I'll tell you what, I've got a very nice velvet jacket and a nice scarf, and with a nice shirt it'll be lovely.'

I suggested he stick to protocol, but no, on the night he turned up in his short velvet jacket with this long scarf, tied in a knot, and an open-neck shirt.

The Queen arrived. She made her way along the line-up, waiting to greet her in the Odeon foyer. She shook hands with me, had a few words, and moved straight on past Tony. Her eyes did not rest on him: she bypassed him totally.

Never mess around with the Queen is the moral here!

Being a great believer in getting the family on the payroll, I employed both Deborah and Geoffrey on *The Persuaders*. Well, you're never too young to learn the work ethic, are you?

Geoffrey, in fact, appeared only in the opening credits, which played over the terrific theme composed by John Barry. The credits set the back story to the characters and there were a couple of shots of them as children . . . as I didn't have a suitable photo of myself, I used one of Geoffrey. I'm not sure how much I paid the youngster. Too much, probably.

Deborah, who was about seven or eight, volunteered to play a little schoolgirl in one episode and, vital to the plot, had to drag a ruler along a set of railings in Gerrards Cross. I dressed her in her own school uniform and came in for a bit of an ear-bending from her headmistress afterwards for not clearing permission. Luisa came to the location that day and began telling Deborah what to do. Not having any of it, Deborah said, 'Daddy is the director, not you.'

That did *not* go down at all well, let me tell you.

As with *The Saint,* I was fortunate by virtue of directing (and producing) in that I was able to offer jobs to some of my old chums, colleagues and people I admired. I was able to offer Geoffrey Toone a role, for instance, and a great thrill for me was in casting the great Dame Gladys Cooper as a Grand Duchess in *The Ozerov Inheritance* episode. I was such an admirer of her work, for which she was three-times Oscar nominated. Sadly, it was to be her last screen appearance.

One scene with Gladys involved us walking into a rather grand room and towards her, sitting on a throne-like chair. Tony took her hand to kiss it.

'Tony,' I said. 'A gentleman would *never* kiss a lady's hand while he was wearing gloves.'

Tony thought for a moment. 'Yeah, well, she wouldn't know that, would she?' he declared.

On another occasion, we were working with a rather distinguished elderly actress and had to follow her character into a room. Unfortunately, both her hearing and her sense of smell were obviously diminished, as the said lady was unaware of the fact that she broke wind furiously as she walked. All the crew were hysterical, and it wasn't helped by Tony walking behind her, furiously waving his hand under his nose and pulling faces at us all as if to say, 'Gee, she stinks!' She did!

One of my favourite episodes of *The Persuaders* is *A Death in the Family*, which featured a terrific cast: Roland Culver, Willie Rushton, Diane Cilento, Denholm Elliot, and Ivor Dean. It was a homage to the Ealing comedy *Kind Hearts and Coronets*, and I played four roles, four members of the Sinclair clan. Apart from Brett himself, there was an old general who met his end by being shot via a remote-controlled model tank – that scene was filmed at Sherwood House in Denham; a crusty old admiral, who ended his days thanks to a loaded model boat; and Lady Agatha, Brett's aunt. (Eerily, when I dragged up to play Brett's Aunt, I looked like my mother. Not as pretty, mind.) One by one the relatives are bumped off.

When I was made-up as the Admiral I had a lot of facial padding and facial hair. I was really quite unrecognizable. We were filming the scene at the pond in the gardens at Pinewood and while we were waiting for the shot to be set up, I sidled up to Johnny Goodman who was overseeing everything. I moved in quite close and smiled broadly at Johnny before moving my hand across his bum and down the top of his leg. He moved away sharply and told the assistant director to get rid of the old extra who was trying it on with him!

Pinewood's gardens were very important to the show, as we filmed in just about every nook and cranny of them, and the studio itself, during the series. Heatherden Hall, the stately home at the centre of the studio, was used in quite a few episodes and just next door is a huge country park, Black Park, which, with the aid of a subtitle across the bottom of the screen, became an instant foreign locale. We took over two stages at the studio, L and M, which were relatively new – in fact I think we were the first production to use them – and they became our home for much of our fifteen-month schedule. I took an office at the studio, and maintain it as my base to this day.

Of course, the series' success was, in great part, was due to the writers and Terry Nation our script editor. We had a terrific team including

Brian Clemens, Donald James, Tony Barwick and Michael Pertwee. Without them, I wouldn't have had a word to say.

If you ever watch an episode of the show, aside from my *splendid* performance, you'll see that I am credited with designing my own clothes. That wasn't quite true. A year or two prior to *The Persuaders*, I had been approached by a milling company, Pearson and Fosters, to join their board of directors, which I did from 1968 to 1972. I turned up to board meetings, attended some Menswear Guild conferences and generally lent my name to the company and took an interest in textiles and fabrics, in exchange for a rather nice remuneration. It was all rather fascinating and I much enjoyed my visits to Bradford Mill. Consequent to my involvement, the company offered to outfit me for any films and TV shows. I took them up on it for *The Persuaders*, and made a few comments about the type of clothes I thought Brett Sinclair would wear. That secured me the credit.

Speaking of credits, I am often asked how Tony and I resolved the issue of who would get top billing on the show. To be honest, billing has never really worried me. I much prefer the cheque. However, when I was negotiating my deal with Lew Grade he promised I would receive top billing. Very nice, I thought. However, in his negotiations with Tony, Lew had promised *him* top billing. So we were both promised top billing. Lew was very clever in that respect: he didn't want to upset either of us, so tried to please us both. In the event we settled on 'Curtis & Moore'. I think it was more important to Tony that he received top billing, and I'm all for an easy life.

The Persuaders was a huge hit everywhere . . . except America. The problem there was that ABC pinned a lot of hopes on the show, and in the battle to top the Saturday night ratings, we were programmed against NBC's and CBS's top shows – shows that were already well established. They didn't win the ratings battle, and so moved us to another night against another big show, *Mission: Impossible*. When a network starts panicking and moves a show around, audiences sense there is something wrong and lose faith in you. Not every episode was broadcast on the first run – I think twenty-one of twenty-four were shown.

An American success, or lack of it, was a contributing factor in whether a show would be re-commissioned. Internationally, it was a very different story. In fact in some territories we stitched two episodes together to form a feature film – much like we had with *The Saint*.

Lew was keen to try a second season. He thought we could still pull round the American audiences. I was not keen though. I know discussions took place about bringing in an actor to replace me, but Bob Baker said no. He felt that we'd created a successful format and had made twenty-four great shows, and we should rest on our laurels.

★ ★ ★

Just before I started *The Persuaders* I had been invited to a reception at Buckingham Palace. There were quite a number of entertainment people there, and as I was going upstairs I saw Lew Grade was about a flight in front of me.

'Roger, Roger!' he shouted down. 'I've got a wonderful part for you in *The Bible*. You're going to play Gabriel! Larry Olivier wants to do it, but I want you.'

I managed to avoid giving an answer.

However, later on, Lew called me over. Oh no, I thought, not *The Bible* again. But no, he wanted to introduce me to George Barrie. George was the owner of Fabergé, the company that made Brut cologne. He was one of the moguls of the cosmetics world. He explained that Brut Films came about because he had been approached by Hollywood when *Valley of the Dolls* was being made, as the film-makers wanted to feature a commercial for a fictitious fragrance. George actually came up with a commercial for them. He realized the power of film and product placement when people started clamouring for this advertised, but non-existent, fragrance. Why not then, thought George, make films that can feature my own products? He formed Brut Films and Lew told him that I would be the ideal man to run the company.

Me? A film executive? I'd had some business experience in the textile industry, but this was rather different. OK, I thought, why not? I can give it at go and at worst he can fire me. Overnight, I became a movie mogul.

One of the first scripts to pass across my new desk at Brut Films came from Melvin Frank. It was called *A Touch of Class*. He had Glenda Jackson attached and said he would like George Segal to co-star . . . would Brut finance it?

I said I needed time. It wasn't a decision I could make quickly, or could I? I took the script home and read it within an hour. I called George Barrie in New York.

'George, I have a great script that I think we can do something with.'

'OK, I'll be there the day after tomorrow,' said George.

I called Mel and told him that I thought we had a deal. Everything started happening very quickly.

My ambitions as an actor were suddenly sublimated by my new ambitions as an executive. I could have pushed myself for the lead in the film, but didn't. George Segal was cast. The film went on to win great reviews, and was very successful, with Glenda Jackson ultimately winning the Best Actress Oscar.

The theme song, 'All That Love Went to Waste', was also massively popular. George Barrie indulged himself by writing the music with legendary songwriter Sammy Cahn, who was a mate of his. It was Oscar nominated, too.

What an auspicious beginning.

For many film-goers, if asked who was the epitome of sophistication, the response would undoubtedly be Cary Grant. Cary, though, had an amazingly ribald sense of humour, scatological to the nth degree. He loved fart stories, he had a collection of fart noise-making gizmos: ones that you held in your hand, whoopee cushions, the lot, all stacked in a cupboard and produced at the drop of a hat. I first met Cary in 1970 at Brut Films. Cary was on the board and I would often see him either in their London or New York offices. I kept distinguished company.

It was at Sammy's house that I heard Cary sing the Tin Soldier song for the first time. Sung to the tune of 'My Bonnie Lies Over the Ocean'.

I once had a box of tin soldiers,
I knocked off the general's head,
I broke all the sergeants and corporals,
Now I play with my privates instead.

Cary loved being rude!

I thought it would be a great coup if I could persuade Cary to make a movie for us. He had stopped making films a few years before, but I could imagine the headlines: 'Cary Grant Comeback!' However, Cary was having none of it. He said that he was simply not interested any more. When I pressed him on the subject he told me that he had 'enough of the bullshit of movie making'. I also suspect that, as he was very rich (being one of the first film actors to own the negatives of his films) he had no need to step in front of the cameras any longer. A clever man. The bullshit, he said, had manifested itself on his last film *Walk Don't Run*, when he was sitting in his trailer on location and overheard a conversation outside his window – which he knew was intended for him to hear – all about how nice he was and how good he was looking. That was it, he decided, he'd had enough of the bullshit of movies and decided to retire. However, he did very much enjoy switching to the other side of the camera and advising Brut Films. I greatly valued his wisdom and company. He was a most affable companion, and had such a great wit.

He would use his frequent trips to the UK for Brut as an excuse to visit his mother, who lived in Bristol and was well into her eighties. One day, sitting in his car, she said to him (he was born Archibald Leach), 'Arch, why don't you dye your hair?'

'Why should I, Ma? My hair is white and I like it.' He laughed as he told me her reply.

'You should dye it, Arch, because it makes me look so old!'

My first foray into being a movie mogul was enviable. Brut Films was a force to be reckoned with, and I – a boy from Stockwell – was socializing and in business with Cary Grant!

For our second venture we settled on a play adaptation. *Night Watch* had been written for the stage by Lucille Fletcher and adapted for the screen by Tony Williamson. It was to boast a starry cast, including Elizabeth Taylor, Laurence Harvey and Billie Whitelaw. Brian G. Hutton, hot on his success of *Where Eagles Dare*, was signed to direct. It seemed like a winning formula.

George, I, and a few other Fabergé people flew to Budapest in our private jet. This was while Hungary was still communist, you must remember. We left an airport of opulent jets, to land in one full of old Dakotas. Our reason for travelling there was twofold. Firstly we were involved with an animation film, *Hugo the Hippo*, which was being produced in Budapest. Secondly, we were to meet Elizabeth Taylor. She was there with her husband Richard Burton, who was making a movie with Raquel Welch. We booked into the same hotel, and eventually received word that we had an audience with Elizabeth at 4 p.m.

At the agreed time, we ventured up to the room. Richard was in the suite looking very solemn. He had good reason to be as his favourite brother, Ivor, had died a couple of days before.

'Richard,' George Barrie said. 'If you need my plane to travel back to

Wales, it is at your disposal.'

'*What* did he say?' snapped Burton.

George moved forward, offering his hand of friendship.

'*Don't* bloody move like that!' warned Burton.

Something had certainly gone on prior to our arrival. Burton was not happy, and we could feel the great tension in the air between him and Elizabeth.

We opened our conversation with Elizabeth, but when we mentioned Billie Whitelaw was going to play the other female lead, Burton's ears pricked up.

'I have a *much* better idea,' he said.

Elizabeth looked at him with her big violet eyes, 'Who else are you thinking of, dear?'

'Raquel Welch!' he shouted. 'A *fine* actress!'

I'll say no more.

I was glad to leave that hotel room. The tension in there was awful.

George Barrie was married to his second or third wife, Gloria, at this time. They would argue and argue all the time. It was a little like being with Richard and Elizabeth. Anyhow, we were going to Australia to do some publicity for Brut Films, and our wives were to accompany us. All through the journey, and all the time we were there, George and Gloria were arguing.

'I want a divorce!' he'd shout.

'It'll cost you ten million!' she'd shout back.

And so it went on.

I had to make a trip to Melbourne, and when I arrived back in Sydney I received a call from George at about two in the morning, 'It's great here in Tokyo!'

'What the hell are you talking about, George?'

'I'm in Tokyo,' he said. 'I left Gloria behind. You get tickets for the girls back to New York, OK?'

'Thanks loads, George. You are a bastard!' I said.

'Yeah, but a bastard with his own Lear jet! Ha ha!'

The nightmare journey of all time lay ahead of me. We had to change flights in Hawaii – US territory – where all bags had to be checked through customs. Without any helpers I had to lug about twelve suitcases from one end of the customs shed to the other. We then missed the connecting flight in LA, so checked into an airport hotel, where we had to be up for the 10 a.m. flight to New York. The conversation at check in went like this:

'See what the movie is, Roger,' said Gloria.

'What movies are playing on the flight? I asked.

'There are no movies on flights before midday,' the TWA flight attendant replied.

'Ask what's on the menu, Roger,' asked Luisa.

'What is on the menu?' I asked the attendant.

'I don't know, sir.'

'You don't *know*, Roger?' asked Gloria.

The ladies then jointly informed me that I was some sort of 'idiot' and I should have checked before booking this flight! When I told George this later, he laughed. Yes, well, it wasn't long after that when Mr and Mrs Barrie divorced.

George had a girlfriend who always appeared when he was in Europe; she was quite tiny, quite pretty, quite French and quite dumb. George would give her a piece of jewellery – usually gold and quite chunky – and she always wore everything that he gave her, and all at the same time. Consequentially, the weight made her shorter and shorter each time I saw her. George said one day, 'You know, she is really quite smart. She reads books in English all the time.'

I happened to notice at that moment that the book she was reading was upside down . . .

I was only involved with Brut for a year or so, and on those three mentioned productions (I was quite pleased to leave Gloria behind!). I felt I had to end my brief moguldom because Harry Saltzman and Cubby Broccoli had approached me with an interesting offer. I called George Barrie to explain why I was leaving Brut Films. When Lew Grade heard, he was furious. 'It'll ruin your career!' he said. Lew, of course, would have been quite happy if I'd stayed in TV for ever.

Far from ruining my career, however, James Bond was about to give my career a well-needed kick in the rear end.

NINE

And the Word was Bond

'There's only one thing I hate more than alligators'

I first met the producers of the James Bond films, Albert 'Cubby' Broccoli and Harry Saltzman, across the Curzon Street gambling tables in the mid-1960s. We became good friends and thereafter often socialized at home, as well as over the tables.

Harry and his wife, Jacqueline, had a grand country house at Iver, very close to Pinewood Studios, along with a mews house near the Connaught Hotel in the centre of London; while Cubby and his wife, Dana, had a town house in Green Street, Mayfair. Both were successful film producers before they joined up to form Eon Productions in 1962. Cubby, an American, had made films such as *The Red Beret, Cockleshell Heroes* and *The Trials of Oscar Wilde*; Harry a Canadian, made *Saturday Night and Sunday Morning* and *The Entertainer*. They had been lured to Britain to make films thanks to a favourable tax incentive called the 'Eady Plan', which diverted money raised via taxing cinema tickets into a fund that UK-based producers could call upon in order to make movies.

Harry had successfully negotiated an option on the James Bond books from Ian Fleming, but had struggled to raise the backing he needed to turn them into a film series. Around this time he was introduced to Cubby, who felt he could raise the necessary funding. They went to Columbia Pictures (for whom Cubby had made many films), but left empty-handed. However, a meeting was then set up with Arthur Krim at United Artists in New York, and a deal was struck to produce a series of Bond films.

In 1962, Cubby and Harry set up their production company and invested the rights they owned in a Swiss-based holding company, Danjaq, named after their wives. They each owned forty per cent of Danjaq shares, with Dana and Jacqueline holding the other ten per cent each.

Harry's two eldest children by the way, Hilary and Steven, became firm friends with Geoffrey and Deborah. Their house at Iver was just a short drive from us in Denham. We had a small pool, whereas the Saltzmans boasted a huge swimming pool. Our kids loved nothing more than to while away their school holidays around each other's pools. One day Geoffrey went to see Johnny Goodman at his house in Wembley. He looked into the back garden and asked, 'Where's your pool?' He thought every home had one!

Around the time of *You Only Live Twice* in 1967, when Sean Connery had made it known he didn't want to make another Bond film, Harry and Cubby spoke to me about the possibility of me taking over the role. Some people have since said to me that I was, apparently, on the shortlist of would-be 007 actors back in 1962, when they were casting for *Dr No*. I certainly wasn't aware of that, nor was I approached. The Bond adventure they discussed with me was planned for filming in Cambodia. I don't think preparations had got very far – was there even a script? – when all hell broke loose in that country and the plans were swiftly shelved. I continued making *The Saint* meanwhile, and was unavailable when they re-grouped and decided the next film would be *On Her Majesty's Secret Service*. George Lazenby was cast, and that was that; James Bond left my life.

Things didn't quite go as they'd hoped, though. George took some bad advice and decided that the Bond-gig was Sean's, and that he himself would never last beyond one more film in the role. He decided to get out while his fame was riding high and refused to sign the seven-picture contract Cubby and Harry waved under his nose. I knew George then, and have met him many times since. He admits he made a mistake – but then isn't hindsight a wonderful thing?

Cubby and Harry tried desperately to persuade Sean to return, but he was having none of it. The invasion into his private life that Bond had brought culminated in Japan, when a reporter followed him into a toilet and started snapping pictures. Sean compared Bond to a 'monster' that he had created. I know he also felt unhappy with his deal on the films. He believed the producers had taken advantage of him, and that they were earning many times what they had anticipated (and based his deal on) without increasing his share accordingly. Much legal wrangling ensued.

However, with the clock ticking and with United Artists keen to start on the next film, David Picker was dispatched from the studio to meet Sean. Sean demanded a fee of $1.25 million, a percentage of profits, and significant penalties for each day the film ran over schedule, along with UA's guarantee to back two other films of his choosing. He became the highest paid actor in the world and, very admirably, he used his entire salary to set up The Scottish International Education Trust, to help underprivileged Scots youngsters receive a better education.

Diamonds Are Forever was to be Sean's last Bond outing, though. He said 'never again' when asked if he'd be reprising the role.

I was at Pinewood filming *The Persuaders* when Sean was filming *Diamonds* there, and consequently I got to see a lot of Harry and Cubby around the studio. When Sean left the franchise, I knew the role was up for grabs again and declined Lew Grade's offer to make a second series of *The Persuaders*. Just as well I did, as my phone rang. It was Harry.

'Roger,' he said. 'Cubby and I have decided we want to go with you as the next James Bond.'

I was, naturally, ecstatic. They offered me a three-film contract, with options to do more. I let my agent sort out the nitty-gritty, but I think we all came away feeling happy.

I met with Cubby, Harry and their director, Guy Hamilton, at Scott's Oyster Bar in Mayfair. It hadn't been announced to the press yet, and Guy was keen we shouldn't all arrive or leave together for fear of someone putting two-and-two together.

It was Guy who showed the only trepidation about me playing Bond. He was anxious that I should not have any lines that were associated with Sean, such as 'Vodka martini, shaken not stirred'. Of course, I couldn't avoid the inevitable introduction, 'My name is Bond, James Bond' though I was conscious of maybe saying it with a Scots accent.

I'd be the first to admit that I'd been living the good life in the previous year or so, while making *The Persuaders* and being a movie mogul with Brut Films. That was brought home to me rather curtly when Harry called me one day.

'Cubby thinks you need to lose a little weight.'

Okay, I thought. So I started a strict diet.

The phone rang again. 'Cubby thinks you're a little out of shape.'

So I started a tough fitness regime.

Again the phone rang, this time it was Cubby. 'Harry thinks your hair's too long.'

'Why didn't you just cast a thin, fit, bald fellow in the first place and avoid putting me through this hell?' I replied.

Once I was announced as being the new 007, it started! The media interest was phenomenal. It should really have given me an inkling as to the relentless press interest that would follow throughout my whole tenure as Jimmy Bond, and beyond.

Live and Let Die began filming in New York in October 1972. I remember boarding the plane in London and Danny Kaye was on the same flight. He had everyone in hysterics as he did his own version of the safety demonstration. Little did I know then that Danny would later prove instrumental in my introduction to UNICEF.

In the Big Apple we staged a wonderful car chase and were fortunate to receive the complete and overwhelming cooperation of the Mayor, John Lindsay's, office and the Police Department. All our action vehicles were positioned on the slip roads leading on to the freeway. The authorities stopped the traffic on the freeway and allowed our vehicles to move on. The routine was that we were to drive along the freeway, dodging the action cars, and come off two exits later. Each time we did it, we moved forward two junctions from the previous start point. We soon discovered, though, that one key action vehicle was not in position on the slip road for take three.

The black stunt driver had noticed his car was getting a little low on fuel, so diverted to a gas station to fill up. His nice new Cadillac had false number plates on and so, as he pulled on to the forecourt to get his fuel, he attracted the attention of a couple of cops. They figured he was not the type to own such a nice car, and ran a check on the plates. They then duly arrested him, despite his protestations he was an actor working on a James Bond film . . . yeah, right.

We never got the vehicle back, but at least the driver was released when Cubby intervened!

A few more scenes were filmed around the city, including one where I spoke to Felix Leiter on a car radio – the microphone being the cigarette lighter. Our screenwriter Tom Mankiewicz – or Wanky Mitz as he was known on set by yours truly – used to come up with great one-liners and this was no exception. 'Ah! A genuine Felix Leiter,' I said.

Next on the schedule were a few scenes in Harlem. On our final afternoon of shooting in the district, word reached us that we had ten more minutes – that's how long our protection money had left to run. We didn't dawdle.

Music always plays a big part in any film, but particularly in the Bond films. From the opening 'gun barrel' sequence, featuring Monty Norman's James Bond theme, to the incidental music and title song.

Ron Kass, Joan Collins's husband, was instrumental – forgive the pun – in securing Paul and Linda McCartney for *Live and Let Die*. Ron was a lawyer and had represented the Beatles' company, Apple, and got to know the boys well. Paul agreed to write and perform the theme song with his group Wings, and asked if George Martin could be brought on as composer. Could he? He didn't need to ask twice!

I think I'm correct in saying that when Harry first heard the song, he said he didn't like it but – perhaps reserving final judgement – turned to George Martin and said, 'So, who are we gonna get to sing it?'

George Martin diplomatically told Harry that he already had one of the biggest recording artists of all time singing it . . . The song charted, became a huge hit, and Paul still performs it to rapturous applause to this day.

After New York, filming shifted to New Orleans, and it was here that I began to realize how my relationship with Harry had changed. It was no longer one of two friends, but rather that of an employer and employee. It was a subtle difference, but Harry liked me to be aware he was the boss, which I think he further demonstrated when my dear friend David Hedison (who was playing Felix Leiter in the movie) checked in to my hotel and Harry had him moved. Perhaps he thought we'd gang up on him? I don't know. Harry's relationship with Cubby was also becoming strained. Perhaps that had a bearing on things too? It seemed that while Cubby was content just to make Bond films, Harry was not and he produced the Harry Palmer films, *Battle of Britain* and others. I think that caused friction between them.

Cubby and Harry were two very different personalities. I liked them both, but found Cubby a little easier to get along with. Harry had a more fiery temperament and displayed it most often in restaurants. When the food came out Harry would always find fault. He'd let the waiter know – in no uncertain terms – what he thought of him and the chef, and send it all back. He'd then also send every one else's back as well!

'Harry, mine's *fine*,' I'd say, holding on to my plate for dear life. I had visions of the chef spitting in the re-served dishes. Cubby once quipped that if Harry had been at the Last Supper he'd have sent it back. Too true!

Harry was on the studio floor throughout *Live and Let Die*, while Cubby kept a lower profile. That was reversed on my next film, when Cubby was the one who spent more time on the floor. Director Guy Hamilton said that he could happily make a film with Harry, and happily make a film with Cubby – but not with the two of them together.

It was while filming in New Orleans that I suffered my first injury as Jimmy Bond – in the big jet-boat chase. The thing about jet boats is, although lovely to drive, to turn them you literally have to pile on the speed; a turn of the steering wheel then directs the extra power to one side of the boat or the other, and you change direction. I did quite a few run-throughs to practise my technique and while banking on one such run, I realized there wasn't much fuel left in the tank, as the engine cut out. I had no steering! I therefore continued in a straight line . . . directly into a wooden boathouse. On impact, I flew out of the boat and straight into a wall, cracking my front teeth and twisting my knee badly. I needed a walking cane for days afterwards, but fortunately most of the upcoming schedule involved me sitting down in the boat. There I was, a fearless 007, hobbling on a cane to my boat and then pretending to be indestructible for the cameras. Who says I can't act?

The odd accident aside, driving the boats was actually great fun and I was being paid to spend two weeks in Louisiana tearing around the bayous.

Our last sequence in New Orleans was the airfield sequence where Bond gives an unorthodox flying lesson to Mrs Bell. On my last scene, I suddenly felt a terrible pain in my groin. I asked to be excused and went to lie down in my trailer for a while. A short time later, assistant director Derek Cracknell came calling, took one look at his heroic star with knees under his chin – I was in *such* pain – and said, 'Right, doctor!'

They hitched up my trailer and towed me to the hospital, where they decided it was my kidney stone problem again. All sorts of painkilling drugs were administered. I was lying on my bed of pain, doped up to the eyeballs, when an officious little chap walked in with a clipboard.

'Name?' he asked.

'Roger Moore,' I moaned from my quivering lips.

'Who do you work for?'

'Eon Productions,' I said.

'What's their address?'

'I don't know,' I said, wondering what the hell this had to do with my recovery.

'You don't know who you work for?' he snapped. 'Where do you live?'

'Sherwood House, Tilehouse Lane, Denham,' I replied.

'What number?'

'I don't have a number, my house has a name.' He was really beginning to annoy me, delirious or not.

'OK, then,' he added smartly, 'how does the mailman find you without a number?'

'Because I'm fucking famous!' I shouted in the hope of silencing him once and for all.

'Oh. Oh!' he said sheepishly, sliding sideways out of my room, never to be seen again.

That evening they discharged me and I went back to my hotel carrying my various painkillers. One in particular – methylene – had the side effect of turning my urine bright blue, you'll no doubt be thrilled to hear. Well, I really was quite zonked out and in unfamiliar surroundings, so when I got up for a pee at two in the morning, I opened what I thought was the bathroom door and relieved myself. I later discovered it had in fact been the wardrobe door I'd opened, as all my lovely clothes had turned various shades of patchy blue!

The next location was Jamaica. It was my first time there and I was knocked out by the island's beauty. We stayed first at Montego Bay and then moved across to Ochos Rios. During our time there I visited Ian Fleming's home, Goldeneye, a sprawling, white bungalow. I was reminded of Noël Coward's quip when he was asked his impressions of Fleming's house, 'It's very golden eye, ears, nose and throat!' He was right – again.

Harry Saltzman said he would drive me to the first day's location shoot, and to be ready at eight o'clock the next morning. It was the one and only time I let him drive me anywhere. Harry, bless him, always drove as though everyone in Jamaica knew that an important film producer was heading down the road, on the wrong side, cutting every corner he took. Talk about a white-knuckle ride. We arrived on location, shaken and somewhat stirred, to be greeted by the friendly face of George Crawford, our catering manager. George was quite amazing. In the remotest location, anything you requested, he could find. If you said you liked HP or A1 sauce, then the next day it would be on the table. Anyway, when Harry and I arrived this day George had laid all the tables out with lovely white linen and the best china and silverware.

'You can tell we're a British film on location can't you, Harry?' I said.

'What do you mean?' he asked.

'Well, it's all very elegant. You don't get this on other films.'

'Goddammit! How much is this costing me?' he shouted at George. From then on, we had no such elegance. But worse was to come when Harry cut the per-person food allowance. George – realizing his protests would fall on deaf ears – bought in rotten green chickens and served them up to the crew, saying it was all he could afford. There was nearly a riot, and his budget was swiftly increased.

I'm afraid we played a terrible joke on our leading lady, Jane Seymour, who had joined us on location. Young Jane was then married to Michael Attenborough, Dickie's son. Before we started filming, Dickie wrote to me saying that Jane was going to be in the film, and would I please be nice to her. Well, I'm nice to everyone! However, Jane did have a funny little habit that we all noticed when we broke for lunch. At lunch, the lead cast, director, cameraman, etc. would sit on what was laughingly called the 'top table'. Every day, Jane would ask us to pass her the A1 sauce, *then* the ketchup, *then* the salt, then another sauce, one by one *ad infinitum*. This went on for days and – having spent half my lunch hours passing condiments to and fro – before Jane arrived the next day, I said to everyone, 'When she sits down, let's all stand up and walk away.' We did, and she burst into tears . . . Oh, how I regretted trying to play that joke on her.

As the 'star' of the film, I had my own caravan. I don't mean a luxury Winnebago, I mean a rickety old rust bucket – the sort of thing you see propped up in lay-bys these days, selling mugs of tea. To level it and keep it steady we had to put wedges under the corners. It was pretty basic but I did have the luxury of a bucket in the rear of the van in which to relieve myself. One afternoon I had just finished doing so – thank god – when an out-of-control truck came whizzing past, taking the rear of the caravan – and my bucket – with it. No shit!

One of the fun things I had to do in *Live and Let Die* was drive an old London bus, which, if you remember, goes under a low bridge that removes its upper deck. Before we all left London for Jamaica, I was dispatched to Hammersmith Bus Garage in west London, where they had a huge skidpan, to drive a bus and then apply the brakes hard on the slippery surface – as I was to do in the film. I was terrified the bus would turn over, but such is their design, I discovered, that they rarely ever do.

We sensibly employed a driving-double on location, but in many sequences I did drive the bus myself. I recall at one point I was waiting for the traffic to be cleared from a particular road, and was sitting in the cab of the Routemaster awaiting my call. A large Mercedes pulled up alongside me; it had been stopped like the other traffic. The driver, an Englishman, rolled down his window and said, in a rather upper-crust accent, 'Look, how long is this going on out here?'

'I'm terribly sorry,' I said. 'They're just getting ready for the shot, it shouldn't be too long.'

'It's too bad, you know. It *is* my land.'

It was his sugar plantation!

I've always thought that if times get hard in the future, I could do a bit of part-time bus driving.

Gloria Hendry played Bond's contact in Jamaica, Rosie Carver. She was wonderful to work with and carries the distinction of being the first black Bond girl. I think there was a bit of a hoo-ha in the press about Bond and a black girl – alas, racism was still commonplace then. Harry was very keen to quell such nasty press and was very helpful to and supportive of Gloria in coping with it.

Another of Mankiewicz's wonderful lines came when, in Rosie and Bond's hotel room, there is a small voodoo hat with a blood-soaked white feather in it – a voodoo warning sign – on the bed. Rosie screams, and Bond says, 'Don't worry, darling, it's just a small hat, belonging to a man of limited means, who lost a fight with a chicken.'

Yaphet Kotto played our villain, drug baron Mr Big aka Dr Kananga, Julius Harris played the metal-armed henchman Tee Hee, and Geoffrey Holder was the mysterious Baron Samedi, steeped in all things voodoo, in an attempt to ward off unwelcome visitors from the disguised poppy fields that yielded his heroin.

Dr Kananga was so named after Ross Kananga, the owner of an alligator farm that our art director Syd Cain stumbled upon in Jamaica. The warning sign outside the farm proclaimed, 'Trespassers will be eaten'. Ross's father had actually been eaten by one of them, he told me.

We thought it a very good name for a villain!

Those bloody alligators and crocodiles scared the you-know-what out of me. Even the little baby ones could snap your finger off. Ross had trained – as far as you can train these things – one to walk out of the water and into the hut, which was the HQ Bond had to destroy. I, meanwhile, had to stand and wait for this eating machine to crawl past me. And how could I be sure he was that well trained?

Foolishly, I made a wardrobe error. I thought it would be smart to wear crocodile-skin shoes. My beloved Italian croc-skin shoes probably had a few cousins and aunties in Ross's farm, but he assured me he had cleared all the alligators away from where we were filming. Yes, I thought, but did they *know* he had cleared them away?

I was standing on a little island in the middle of the small lake in Ross's farm; meanwhile the camera guys and crew, in boats, had pulled away leaving me on my own. All I could see were nasty eyes glinting in the undergrowth through the mangroves. Gulp.

I had to make a brave jump across the backs of a few alligators, like stepping stones, to the safety of the shore. Thankfully, rubber alligators were brought in and anchored in position for me. I ran across them pretty lively; if I'd slipped and tumbled into the water, there's no telling what might have happened to me.

Ross Kananga, meanwhile, in doubling for me and jumping with the real alligators in place, got tripped up on his first run across when one of his 'pets' snapped and caught his heel. He was wearing my croc-skin shoes too, and ruined them.

Tarot cards were also a feature of the film and as such we had a genuine card reader visit the set one day. He read my Tarot and said I was going to be involved in an accident with a black limousine. He also told me I had a son who was going to be a world leader. I did ask Geoffrey if he wanted to be prime minister, and he said 'Yes. OK.' He hasn't so far. Mind you, I avoided black cars for a while just to be on the safe side.

At that time Luisa and I weren't aware that she was expecting another baby; this was to be Christian, who was born on 18 August 1973, a month after this film's premiere. A joyous surprise – beyond the nappy-changing stage. How glad we were to have him though. Christian never became a world leader either, by the way, but is the next best thing – a property dealer.

I insisted that, whenever possible, Luisa and the children accompanied me on location shoots. We engaged a tutor to ensure the children's schooling didn't suffer, and a nanny or two to help out. We felt it important to try to maintain the family routine. Of course, it wasn't always possible, so my mum and dad moved in to Denham to look after the kids on those occasions – and spoilt them rotten.

I like to think we were a happy family and had fun. When on location, Luisa enjoyed exploring the local towns and markets, and loved cooking meals for the family and friends, such as dear Geoff Freeman, our publicist, whose idea of a sophisticated meal was always accompanied by a can opener.

Back at Pinewood Studios we completed work on the many interior sets, including that of James Bond's flat – where I was to be introduced to the cinema-going world as the new 007. All the sets were designed by art director Syd Cain, who had worked on a couple of earlier Bond films. I spent a very happy morning in bed with the exquisite Madeline Smith, who played Italian agent Miss Caruso. This scene featured my favourite Bond gadget of all, the magnetic watch, which I used to unzip Maddy's dress. I must admit that not all the gadgets in Bond films actually work. To achieve the impression that this one did, special-effects supremo Derek Meddings fixed a metal wire inside Maddy's dress and to the back of her zip. He then placed his hand up her dress and gently pulled as I ran my watch down her back saying, 'Sheer magnetism.' This *ménage à trois* wasn't as romantic as you might think. I believe Maddy dispensed with the services of special-effects men in subsequent romantic interludes.

It was also the scene where I got to play alongside my former RADA classmate, Lois Maxwell, in her role of Miss Moneypenny and, indeed, dear Bernie Lee as 'M'.

Another memorable interior set was the seduction of Jane Seymour, aka Solitaire. The scene had started in Jamaica, and then was completed on an interior stage at Pinewood. The temperature difference between the Caribbean in the summer and England in the winter was considerable, to say the least. I told Jane about a little trick Joan Collins had taught me – and we wore football socks to keep warm under the sheets.

The film's finale brought more horrible creatures on to the set at Pinewood ... If there's one thing I hate more than alligators, it's snakes. Geoffrey Holder shared my phobia and was horrified when he read in the script that he, as Baron Samedi, had to fall backwards into a box, a coffin, full of them.

'Don't worry,' came the reassurance of the crew. 'They're not biters, they're crushers.'

Oh! That's all right then ...

We'd heard Princess Alexandra was visiting the set that day and had already been told about this scene. Geoffrey knew there was no way out of it and he had to face his fears. He was very brave.

I think it was on this same set that Harry Saltzman brought a group of friends to show around. He was always doing it, and treated it very much like his own private sideshow: 'This is all mine ... my puppets are over there.'

The red light went up, meaning silence, then the bell sounded, but Harry took no notice and carried on talking – loudly.

'Quiet on the set!' shouted Derek Cracknell. 'Everybody! And that includes *you*, Mr Saltzman, sir.'

Ouch. Derek was a brave man!

It was then underground and into Mr Big's lair. I rescued my damsel in distress, dear Jane, blew up the villain and destroyed his lair. I'm good.

With the film in the can, I was free for a few months while the editing and other post-production work was completed. I wouldn't be needed, they told me, until around the end of June; the film was to premiere on 6 July 1973.

Come the end of June, it was time for the pre-premiere press junkets. The producers booked a number of hotel rooms, and placed a few large tables in each, where members of the lead cast and crew took turns to host journalists, moving the journalists around the tables in twenty-minute shifts. Invariably, they all asked the same questions:

'How does your Bond differ from Sean Connery?'

'Were you scared taking over from Sean Connery?'

'How many more will you make?'

'What did you think of your co-stars?' Along with other equally intellectual, far reaching, and thought-provoking questions.

We never had sneak previews with the Bond films, they were completed and went to premiere – usually a royal premiere – often with a press screening on the same morning. It was when I was on the way to the premiere press conference that I felt my first nerves. It finally dawned on me that my first James Bond adventure was going to be put to the ultimate test: the viewing public. But I was fairly philosophical. I imagine it's like having a baby, there's nothing you can do to stop it, the baby is going to come out no matter what.

'Ah, well,' I thought. 'I can always go back to modelling sweaters.'

The film, which was budgeted at $7 million, took $126 million at the worldwide box office. Not a bad return, is it? I think everyone was pleased.

★ ★ ★

Between getting *Live and Let Die* in the can and the film's premiere, I'd been in talks about my next film, *Gold*, based on a Wilbur Smith novel. I received the script from a producer named Michael Klinger. The film was to be shot in South Africa, where Michael had raised most of his £1-million budget.

I agreed to star as Rod Slater. However, before things got moving, a huge spanner was thrown into the works. Alan Sapper, head of the technician's trade union ACTT, of which I was still a card-carrying member, announced that his union would not allow us to film in South Africa due to the apartheid situation. He added, firmly, that should the producer ignore his ruling and try to set up the film in Africa, all further Roger Moore films would be 'blacklisted' by the union.

This was tantamount to blackmail, and the actors' union, Equity, stepped in and said that no one could threaten the livelihood of one of its members. The standoff was serious stuff and was grabbing the headlines. In an attempt to defuse the escalating situation, Michael Klinger asked Sapper for a solution. Where else might he film?

'Go to Wales,' replied Sapper smartly.

Michael tried to reason that coalmines were quite different to goldmines, and that the landscapes outside were completely inappropriate. Our story was set in Africa! Besides which, I'm not sure his backers would have remained on board the project. After much discussion, and bad press, Sapper said it was up to his members if they worked on the film or not. He certainly wasn't going to encourage them though.

In the end, a wonderful crew was assembled. They all felt it was better to defy the racist rulings and work in harmony with South Africans, than allow the government and blinkered unions the chance to continue fuelling apartheid.

Our director was Peter Hunt. He had been a first-class editor and a second unit director on the Sean Connery Bond films, setting the style of the movies, which continues to this day. He was then given a Bond to direct – *On Her Majesty's Secret Service*, with George Lazenby; a terrific film. It was a couple of years after *On Her Majesty's* that I first worked with Peter on an episode of *The Persuaders*. I found him to be a brilliant technical director and wonderful with actors. He had a very good eye for framing and knew exactly how a scene would cut together; consequently, he never wasted any time.

Our unit arrived in Johannesburg in September 1973 and we received a very warm welcome. The production employed a large number of local South Africans – black and white – and we never experienced a single apartheid issue. This was a film without any political message, nor did it portray blacks or whites in any controversial manner. Though one stark reminder of the political situation in South Africa arose at ten o'clock every night, when a siren wailed. We were told it was the curfew siren, and no blacks were allowed outside after it had sounded.

As Luisa and I didn't think the *Gold* locations were particularly suitable for children, and with Christian still a babe-in-arms, they all stayed home in Denham. So, in Johannesburg, I shared a hotel penthouse suite with Michael Klinger and his wife, Lilly. It was a huge suite with two bedrooms. The living area was divided into two for us, with a thin partition. I couldn't but help overhear some of their conversations in the morning when I was doing my exercises.

'Lil, make me a cup of tea,' called Michael, in his broad Cockney accent.

'Ring for room service!' Lil called back. For quite a large lady she had a rather thin voice.

'I don't want room service, Lil. I want *you* to make it.'

'Oh, you are a silly old man.'

So went the daily exchange.

Michael was a very entertaining man – rather rare in producers I thought. One day I asked him how he got his start in the business. He explained that he owned the Gargoyle Club, off Wardour Street in London, and allowed one member of the club to come in and use it as a backdrop to photograph models. His name was George Harrison Marks. A little while later, Marks said to Michael that he had an idea for a film based in a nudist colony in Cornwall, called *Naked as Nature Intended*. This was around 1960, when pornography was kept under a very tight lid in Whitehall, and consequently there was a huge market for it.

Marks said he needed some more money, and Michael readily agreed to back it. A few days later, Michael met up with a friend who asked him what he was up to and he mentioned he'd put some money into this film.

'Ah, so you're a film producer now.'

'Am I?' said Michael.

That's how it all started!

Michael was also a joy to have as a producer. He worried about his cast and crew endlessly, particularly on location, and was always hands-on. The goldmine sequences were filmed on location in Buffelsfontein and Randfontein – 160 kilometres and 45 kilometres west of Joburg respectively. They were working goldmines and were probably the two biggest in South Africa. At this time petrol restrictions were in force, and to ensure we had a plentiful supply Michael and our second unit director John Glen drove with huge empty cans over 250 miles to a pumping station to fill up. On another occasion we were shooting a couple of thousand feet down in the mine and had been told the lifts would be out of action for a few hours during routine maintenance work – that did wonders for my claustrophobia! However, Michael was determined his crew's tea break should not be affected and walked down about 2,000 steps carrying a huge tray of sausages, followed by tea urns. He really endeared himself to everyone.

To complement the wonderful crew, Michael assembled a wonderful cast: Susannah York, Ray Milland, Bradford Dillman, John Gielgud, while locally he cast Simon Sabela, a very fine Zulu actor.

One of the more pleasurable bonuses of being an actor is not only to meet but to work with actors whom you have admired in the past. For me, Ray Milland was one of those.

Ray was another source of extraordinary stories, and he told me this one while we were filming *Gold*. Once upon a time, not that long ago, aeroplanes did not fly nonstop from Europe to Los Angeles. They didn't even fly direct from New York to Los Angeles; flights would stop overnight in Chicago or Denver. It was on one such flight from NYC to LA that Ray Milland's plane parked up in Chicago.

Ray was sitting at a table in the hotel having supper, when a pretty member of the cabin crew sat down next to him. She appeared to be flirting with Ray, but he couldn't be absolutely certain that it would develop into anything more than that – though he hoped it would. He did a quick check on matters by saying that he'd forgotten his room number and asking Miss Pretty Cabin Crew if she could pop to the desk and get his key. She did so, returning with a smile and winsomely told Ray that he was in three-oh-nine.

'Ah, 309?' said Ray.

She nodded in affirmation with a flutter of eyelids and he bid her goodnight.

Leaving his door unlocked, Ray piled into bed and, not five minutes later, she appeared. In a very short space of time she was in the bed and straddling him.

'Oh, my God!' she screamed

'Uh, what's the matter?' asked Ray.

'Just think! I am fucking Ray Milland!'

It quite put him off his stroke.

When he had finished his tale of woe I said that nothing like that had *ever* happened to me.

'Really?' he said staring me in the eye, not quite believing I'd never received such an advance from a pretty girl.

'Yes, really,' I affirmed. 'Nobody in bed with me ever said that they couldn't believe they were fucking Ray Milland . . .'

Going down into the mine for the first time was quite an experience. The lift stopped on three levels: first to let the bosses in, then the next for the white miners, and on the third level the black miners stepped in. The descent was very fast into the mine, and when one of the biggest, strongest-looking miners grabbed a rail tightly as we shot down the shaft I must have looked rather worried.

'Look at him,' said one of the others. 'He's been going down this mine for thirty years and still shits himself each day.'

Comforting words!

Mind you, to be faced with those real conditions, as an actor, certainly helped me bring it all to life and enabled me to get under the skin of Rod Slater. You can't beat a bit of realism.

It was a little too real on one occasion, though, when my nipples started becoming rather sensitive, before turning a very odd colour. I popped into a chemist and asked what it might be. He told me it was arsenic poisoning. Apparently there's quite a lot of arsenic in mines, it's carried around in the water down there.

Speaking of water, in the final sequence where, following an explosion by the dastardly villains, the mine is flooded, we filmed at a surface training mine that was to be flooded by giant water tanks that were erected above it. However, no one took into account the fact that we were filming on sand, and as soon as the tanks were emptied, the water was absorbed into the ground like a sponge, leaving us standing in a few inches of mud to film the climatic scene. Michael Klinger was very worried about how we were going to film this sequence. Various suggestions were made before I raised my hand and said that the only way I could see us being able to do it, was by recreating the mine on a stage at Pinewood, where we could control the conditions. Klinger agreed.

'But I can't afford it, Roger,' he added. 'Our entire budget's almost spent.'

'Well, I'll work for free for the rest of the shoot,' I said, rather foolishly. 'I think it's important we get this right.' I did work for nothing over the two weeks we shot at Pinewood, and took a percentage share in the film for my efforts.

I won't bore you with the details, but some shrewd people became involved in the film later on and I never received any royalties from it. After much digging around by my assistant Doris Spriggs and business manager Tony Whitehouse, we legally seized the negative. I now own the film.

Keen to capitalize upon our success, Cubby and Harry fast-tracked the next Bond film, *The Man with the Golden Gun*, into pre-production. Much of the same creative team were on board – Guy Hamilton, Tom Mankiewicz and Ted Moore (our Director of Photography) – though it was to be the last film that Cubby and Harry made together.

Filming started in Hong Kong in the summer of 1974, and that's when I met my two lovely Swedish leading ladies: Maud Adams and Britt Ekland, whom I affectionately christened Mud and Birt. Well, it's easier to say, isn't it?

Dennis Sellinger – my agent as well as Britt's – did a very good selling job on Britt. Cubby always liked his leading ladies to be rather 'well-endowed'. He was, as we say in the trade, 'a tits man'. Dennis sent Cubby a copy of Britt's latest film, *The Wicker Man*, in which she appears nude and was, by the way, pregnant. She was also body-doubled for another nude sequence, or rather I should say 'arse doubled'. Britt is the first to admit that this particular posterior double was much bigger than she was. Cubby, of course, knew nothing of all this and got rather excited on both fronts, so to say, and agreed to her casting. By the time we started filming – a year after she had given birth – Britt's breasts were significantly reduced in size and her bum was nothing like the one he'd seen on screen. While I know Cubby loved Britt dearly, I can't help but think he felt just a *little* deflated when he saw her on set that first day.

Guy wanted to toughen up my Bond a little. I think it's most evident in the scenes I had with Maud Adams, where I twisted her arm and threatened – rather coldly – to break it unless she told me what I wanted to know. That sort of characterization didn't sit easily with me. I suggested my Bond would have charmed the information out of her by bedding her first. My Bond was a lover and a giggler. However, Guy was keen to make my Bond a little more ruthless, as Fleming's original had been. I went along with him – his instincts were always very good.

Guy told me a funny story about Cubby and Harry, and their increasing fortunes. They had separate offices, Harry's was in Tilney Street and Cubby's was in South Audley Street, but they faced each other. One day, at a time when the money was really flooding in faster than they knew what to do with it, Guy was in Cubby's office when Harry called, and was put on speaker-phone.

'Cubby, I've figured out what we should do with our money.'

'Oh yeah, what's that, Harry?'

'Buy gold bars!'

'But where would we keep them, Harry?' asked Cubby.

Guy envisaged hundreds of bars of gold piled up in their offices . . . of course they never did.

Jack Palance was rumoured at one point to have been approached to play the villain Scaramanga, but in the event we were fortunate to have my old friend Christopher Lee join us in the role. It seemed particularly fitting as he is a cousin of Ian Fleming.

This film was my first Bond with Desmond Llewelyn as Q. I'd known Desmond for many years, having worked with him in *Ivanhoe*, and often wonder why he wasn't in my first outing as 007. Poor Desmond was always saddled with the most technical dialogue you could imagine, and had reams of it to spew out. I think the writers took great joy in writing such daft lines for him. So, being ever-helpful, I frequently rewrote his dialogue. I'd ask one of the script girls to type it up for me, and then I'd pass it to whichever director we were working with, to hand on to Desmond.

Always very serious about his work, Desmond concentrated intensely. He'd go away and learn his new lines, not very happy at already having spent a month learning his previous lines, and then come on set. Meanwhile, I'd be giggling like mad, and Desmond would look at me, as though thinking, 'What is this bloody man laughing at? I'm giving my best performance and he thinks it's funny.'

Then the penny would drop!

We stayed at the Peninsula Hotel in Hong Kong. It was there that I first met Hervé Villechaize, the inimitable three-foot-eleven Nick Nack. Hervé loved the ladies, and would often go to the strip clubs in Hong Kong with a torch, which he used to point out the girls he wanted, 'You, you, and you . . . no, not you . . . you.' He'd then take them back to his hotel for the night.

When we were leaving Hong Kong, I asked him how many girls he'd had during our stay.

'Forty-five,' he replied in his squeaky French voice.

'It doesn't count,' I replied, 'if you paid for them.'

'Even when I pay, sometimes they refuse,' he told me, sadly.

Hervé tried it on with Maud Adams one day, in the lobby of the hotel. He walked over to her, his head only reaching the bottom of her skirt, looked up and said, 'Tonight, Maud, I am going to come into your room, climb under your sheets and make wild passionate love to you.'

'Yes,' said Maud, without missing a beat. 'And if I find out you have, I'll be *very* angry.'

Hervé told me another sad, funny thing. 'I can never stay on the second floor or above at a hotel,' he said.

'Why?' I asked.

'Because I cannot reach the buttons in the lift!'

We shot on the gambling boats in Macau, which have tables split over two floors – the roulette tables are on the lower floor, and from the next level up people are able to look down at the tables below and make bets by lowering little baskets down. On the upper floor they had blackjack tables too, where they always found Cubby and me between setups.

We were there for two or three nights in all and the crew would invariably end up in the casinos with Cubby and me; but because he was anxious that the boys didn't blow all of their wages he didn't let them claim their entire salary that week. Then, very generously, Cubby walked around with a huge handful of chips and gave them out to the crew.

Cubby and I never discussed business, we never had cause to get angry with each other. We were good friends and greatly enjoyed working together. We always had a backgammon game running throughout each film, and kept a book, which we'd then settle at the end of shooting. We would play for $1 a point, and then, if one person was racing ahead in the winning stakes, we'd up the ante to $5 or $10 a point to give the other player a chance to catch up. The call would come for me to return to the set, and Cubby would say, 'You can't have him yet – I'm playing him like an old banjo.'

Once, I remember I was on a great winning streak, and was up $200,000.

'OK,' Cubby said, 'next points are $100,000 each.'

Though competitive, we usually ensured that the pot was only worth a couple of thousand by the end of the schedule, which we didn't mind stumping up.

We were shooting on another boat, a Hong Kong Police boat, when a young inspector jumped on, dressed in his smart uniform with white shorts and socks. I said hello, and that I was pleased to meet him. He said that we'd actually met before. I asked where.

'You were directing in Downing Street,' he said. 'With Tony Curtis, and I was on duty outside number 10.'

'And you're only an inspector, three years later?' I asked cheekily.

'What do you mean?' he said. 'It's very good!'

'You could have been a commissioner,' I replied. 'Tony was smoking pot next to you outside number 10.'

Tony would say to me, 'Hey, Roger, look at this,' as he took a drag on his spliff – and that was *after* he'd been arrested on arrival in Britain.

Britt Ekland made me curl up one day. We were coming out of the Peninsula Hotel, filming the sequence where Bond gets into Mary Goodnight's (Britt's) little sports car. The hotel was surrounded by hundreds and hundreds of Chinese, all watching us and snapping away.

'Oh, I do like being a film star,' said Britt, in her Swedish lilt.

I laughed and moved quickly to kill any diva-like thoughts. 'They're here to see Maud and Hervé,' I said, 'now behave!'

Britt was divorced from Peter Sellers at this time. I'd known Peter for many years, through many wives, and consequently knew Britt before we worked together. There was talk that Britt had 'got to' Maurice Woodruff, a clairvoyant from whom Peter took advice. Maurice told Peter that he would meet a girl with the initials BE, and fall in love with her. I happened to know Maurice very well, and I think he was very genuine – but who knows about these things?

Just before leaving Hong Kong for a new location in Bangkok, Cubby called me in the hotel, sounding very excited. He'd found a fantastic tailor who'd made him a number of suits in twenty-four hours for a very good price. He wore one of the suits to the airport and as he was walking up the steps of the plane, the trousers split in two. Needless to say, he was ribbed mercilessly.

When we got to Bangkok we filmed another boat chase, this time on the klongs, the waterways found threading around the city. The word went round that, if we fell in, under no circumstances should we let any of the filthy water pass our lips. I did fall in myself, twice in fact. The first time was deliberate, but the second time was when I took a bend on the river – near an undertaker's – a bit too tight and lost my balance. I stayed under to avoid the rotor blade, but made the mistake of opening my eyes . . . I discovered what the undertaker did with some of the poorer people's bodies.

When I look back on the sequence now, I cringe when I think of pushing the little boy who climbed into Bond's boat trying to sell a wooden elephant, into the klong.

We were reintroduced to Clifton James, as Sheriff J. W. Pepper, in this sequence. He had played the red-necked sheriff so brilliantly in *Live and Let Die*. He just so happened to be inside a car Bond stole from a car showroom to chase Scaramanga. It led to one of the most fantastic car jump-stunts ever done on film. A 360-degree jump over a river. It was done for real, and calculated by mathematical geniuses. It worked on paper, but Cubby was sweating a bit on the day over whether it would work for real. W. J. Milligan was the stunt driver and I recall Cubby paid him a handsome bonus when he did it in just one take.

The whole unit then moved to Phuket, and a village called Pang Na. The art department had gone ahead of us to spruce up the one and only hotel in the town. There were only six, rather dilapidated, rooms. Cubby, Christopher, Guy, the girls and I each had a room. I had a rather large room with a ceiling fan – there was no such thing as air conditioning – and, down a step, was what they laughingly called a bathroom. The tiny room boasted a sink that was about six inches wide, a square with a hole in the centre, which was a toilet, above that was a shower and next to it was a bucket, which you filled with water to flush the toilet. I joked to Cubby that I could squat over the hole, clean my teeth, take a shower and shave all at the same time.

'That's nothing,' he said. 'I can do all that and shove a broom up my ass to sweep the room clean too.'

The walls were paper-thin. My room was next to Christopher's. What I didn't realize was that every day he used to like running through his favourite operatic songs, from *The Barber of Seville*, *Carmen* ('The Toreador Song'), and many others. As he had to wear Scaramanga's third nipple and look tanned, as though he'd been a long-time resident of

Phuket, Christopher had to apply full body make-up, every day. False tan, I think they call it. To wash it off at night, he used to carry over some hot water from George Crawford's kitchen. Every evening I'd see him coming across the road carrying two buckets of water and singing all the way. I knew he would become a successful recording artist.

Days shooting on location were long and quite hard. We had to get up very early, then faced a one-hour boat ride before we could get made up and changed into our costumes in our 'dressing-room' boat, which was moored nearby. As the sea was so flat we used to ride in a low-sided boat and would often have flying fish jump over the boat, or sometimes into it as we approached the group of island rocks, standing like erect penises in the sea.

Because we needed to leave equipment overnight, we employed a couple of security guards to stay on the island all night. We arrived one morning to find that, overnight, all the huge, heavy generators had disappeared from this twenty-foot wide location – and our guards saw nothing, they said. Something fishy was certainly going on.

On another day we had some aerial shots being taken from a helicopter. I said to Cubby that it would be nice to travel back to the mainland by helicopter at the end of the day, and avoid an hour in the boat. As we completed our final shots I saw Guy, Cubby and Derek Cracknell all jump in and wave at me as they took off. They were sods.

Of course, as with all the lovely Bond-villain lairs, the island had to be blown up. Guy and the special effects team explained that as Britt and I emerged from Scaramanga's lair, the explosions would be set off in sequence. The explosives consisted of huge skips full of all sorts of flammable material – and I'm talking big skips. The first ones were to go off behind us, and then as we ran clear and turned a corner, the big ones were to be set off.

'And where will you be?' I asked. There was no reply. I turned around to see they had all scarpered and were climbing on to the boat!

Word had got around that there was filming going on and consequently we endured many tourists coming on shore with their Nikons, spoiling several of our shots. When a group stepped on to the beach one morning and our explosions started, they must have wondered quite what they were getting into. They didn't hang around to find out!

Britt, in her skimpy bikini, and I, ran past the first explosion point ...

bang! We reached the point of the second explosion but I lost my grip on Britt's hand and she fell behind. I had two choices: leave her, as the harder-edged Bond probably would, or do what Roger Moore would do, and go back for her. I went back, grabbed her and just before we turned the corner the big bang went off. My arm was around Britt's back and I felt all of the tiny hairs on her skin burn.

Today the island is a huge tourist attraction. Kristina and I were in the area a few years ago, on a Star Clipper, with a group of Scandinavian friends – the King and Queen of Sweden and the Crown Princess among them. They wanted me to take them to the island. I'm here to tell you, when we were there in 1974 it was a deserted island. But on my return, there were landing piers all over the place, shops everywhere and nowhere to land. So we moved on.

The final scene that I filmed, by the way, appeared early on in the movie, where I meet a belly dancer in an attempt to retrieve a golden bullet. I was wearing a rather nice silk suit, and I was looking forward to being able to steal it at the end of the shoot. I couldn't understand why Cubby had climbed a ladder and was looking down on us.

'Have we got that?' asked Guy.

'Yes,' came the answer.

'Check for a hair in the gate.'

'All clear, guv.'

'OK,' added Guy. 'Print it. That's a wrap.'

Just then, a huge bucket of paste came down on top of me and all over my lovely new suit. Cubby looked down at what he'd achieved, and was wetting himself with laughter. So much for my new suit.

★ ★ ★

With my second Bond film in the can, it seemed that I was in demand! Scripts were coming in to my agent and offers were being made everywhere; whether they were backed-up with hard cash was another matter. One project that excited me, though, was called *That Lucky Touch*. Dimitri de Grunwald sent me the script of the comedy set in Brussels, in which Sophia Loren was going to play the female lead. I thought it a very amusing story and the prospect of working with one of the world's most beautiful women secured them my signature on the dotted line. Dimitri, director Christopher Miles and I travelled to Paris to have lunch with Sophia.

At the restaurant, Dimitri arrived after Christopher and I, and looked absolutely gaunt. He'd been to see Sophia and Carlo Ponti, her husband, and was due to bring them back with him.

'Sophia is not doing the film,' he said.

I don't know what happened. He didn't, or wouldn't, say. All I knew was we had two weeks until we started shooting and no female lead.

Fortunately, I suggested Susannah York, after my recent collaboration with her on *Gold*. A few hasty changes were made to the script and Susannah joined us, along with a great supporting cast: Shelley Winters, Lee J. Cobb, Donald Sinden, Sydne Rome and Jean-Pierre Cassel.

Shelley was great fun. Throughout the film we had an ongoing gin game taking place. When Lee J. Cobb asked to be included, she feigned ignorance about how to play. He saw a chance to win a few bucks – and Shelley took him to the cleaners; she was a seasoned and *very* competitive player.

Lee told me that he had been very ill and in hospital not that long before, where he became increasingly worried – and consequently felt even more ill – about how he was going to meet his medical bills. On checking out, the hospital administrator told Lee not to worry, as his bill had been paid.

'Paid? By who?' asked Lee.

'Mister Frank Sinatra,' he was told.

Lee phoned up Frank and said, 'Mister Sinatra, I'm afraid we've never met but I understand you have covered my hospital costs?'

'Yes, that's right,' Frank confirmed.

'Can I ask why?'

'Yeah, because I like your films.' That was typical of Frank. He did so much for so many people and so many charities without ever drawing attention to it.

I got to know Frank quite well in the 1960s, first meeting him during my Warner Bros days – at a charity dinner, in fact. A decade later I met up with him and his then wife, Mia Farrow, in London.

'We just love watching *The Saint*,' Mia said, taking me totally unawares.

'We watch it in bed, in our hotel room. It's the best thing on TV,' Frank added.

Not only did I admire him, I now realized what good taste he had too.

'How about dinner, tomorrow night?' Frank asked.

He didn't have to ask twice. We dined at Annabel's, and Frank asked me all about *The Saint* and was curious to know if I was still interested in making movies.

'Sure I am,' I told him. 'Why?'

'Well, kid,' he said, 'I get an awful lot of scripts coming over my desk. I'll find one for you.'

What a compliment! However, I should add that he never actually did find me a job.

Our friendship, though, lasted for the rest of his life. We spent Thanksgivings and Easters together, and Luisa and I attended many of his sell-out concerts all over the world. He was unlike any other performer I'd ever witnessed. He captivated everyone in his audience. Despite ailing health in later years, including deafness, Frank never stopped.

In one of our final conversations Frank said to me, 'You gotta love livin', kid. Because dyin's a pain in the ass.'

I loved working in Belgium on *That Lucky Touch*. The people are very friendly and have a rather nice sense of humour. I remember ordering fresh orange juice for breakfast at my hotel one morning. What arrived had clearly come out of a can, so I called down.

'I asked for fresh orange juice.'

'It is fresh,' said the waiter.

'No,' I said. 'It tastes like it's been poured from a can.'

'Yes,' the waiter said. 'Fresh from a can.'

I spoke to David Niven around this time and told him we had some filming to complete in Bruges. He told me that when the Allies advanced through Belgium at the end of World War II, he and a friend took a jeep and drove into Bruges, which had recently been liberated by the Allies. There, they enjoyed a sumptuous lunch by the canal, and so delighted was the restaurant owner to see them, that he produced a vintage wine from his cellar that had escaped the Germans' notice.

On returning to join their unit, Niv was stopped and asked where he'd been.

'To Bruges, for lunch,' he replied.

'Bruges? You've been to Bruges! It's in enemy territory!' came the reply.

'No, no,' assured Niv. 'We captured it three days ago.'

'Yes, and the Germans took it back one day later. You've been across enemy lines to eat lunch!'

Unfortunately, I don't think *That Lucky Touch* came off as a comedy.

Looking at the finished film, I felt that the pacing wasn't there. It had funny moments, but it wasn't the success I'd hoped it might be.

By late 1975, things between Harry and Cubby had come to a head. Harry had bought a lot of shares in Technicolor and he also bought the Debris Éclair camera company. He'd stretched himself financially and, in order to secure all the necessary funds he needed, Harry put up his stock in Danjaq – the holding company he owned with Cubby – as security with the banks. However, in the partnership agreement they'd drawn up in 1962, both men had said that they would never use Danjaq stock as security for other ventures. Things got complicated when shares in both of Harry's new companies dropped sharply. Fearing the worst, the banks foreclosed on their loans, meaning Harry was forced to sell his forty per cent share of Danjaq.

Cubby, being understandably concerned that he was about to get a new partner, launched legal proceedings against Harry. It all became very acrimonious and prolonged. Eventually it was agreed that United Artists should be offered the stock, and they would become Cubby's new partner. It seemed a good solution.

During this period plans for my third Bond were shelved. Guy Hamilton, who was going to stay on to direct, departed to start another film and it all looked rather uncertain. Being a great believer in the adage 'make hay while the sun shines', I continued working flat-out. Next on offer was a film in Rome. It allowed us a family Christmas in Denham and Luisa was delighted to think she could spend a few months with her family in Rome, so I accepted *The Sicilian Cross*. And, in early 1976, we packed our bags and the whole family shipped out to Italy.

When we first arrived in Rome we met up with Liza Minnelli – she was there shooting *A Matter of Time*, which her father was directing – and I invited her to see the film I'd made the year before which was about to be screened in the city.

'What's it called?' she asked.

'*Toccarlo porta Fortunato*,' I replied, in my best Italian.

She screamed with laughter. The literal translation of the Italian title of *That Lucky Touch*, was 'Touch It, It's Lucky'. Well, she didn't touch it, but I still live in hope!

TEN

Elementary, Dr Watson

'Say the marks and hit the lines'

My third, and alas final, collaboration with director Peter Hunt was the World War I drama set in Portuguese East-Africa, *Shout at the Devil*. Following *Gold*, producer Michael Klinger optioned another Wilbur Smith novel and set about assembling his preferred team. I was cast as Sebastian Oldsmith, an English adventurer and all-round rascal, and Lee Marvin was cast as Colonel Flynn O'Flynn, who was described as an American adventurer, but might well have been better described as a drunken opportunist and poacher.

A fifteen-week schedule was readied for South Africa and Malta, and yet again we flew straight into arguments about apartheid. It was a well-worn path in our case, and with British actors' union Equity on our side, Michael Klinger was soon able to counter the ACTT's threats of blacklisting the film – again.

Our location shoot was based out of Port St John, at the mouth of the Umzimvubu River, where we were billeted in little cottages overlooking the Indian Ocean. It was idyllic. The local mayor, however, made it known that if we threw a party and invited any of 'the blacks', then he would throw us out of town. What hospitality!

The movie was very much one of two parts. The first half was a catalogue of escapades in which Flynn O'Flynn and Sebastian Oldsmith try to get rich quick by scamming the local German commissioner, Herman Fleischer, and all with lots of humour and high jinx. However, the second half, after the Germans had attacked the O'Flynn family home, was much darker. There, my character now lived as man and wife with O'Flynn's daughter Rosa, played by Barbara Parkins, and our little baby girl. The Germans brutally murdered our daughter and so the story then became one of revenge.

The production team located a newly born baby in the area (in the story it's a girl, but the only baby available locally was a boy). I remember being terrified in the scene when grandpa O'Flynn was to pick up his young grandchild for the first time, as Lee, well-known for his hard-drinking, was six sheets to the wind and picked the child up without supporting his head. Let me assure you, my look of concern wasn't purely acting! The boy had been crying like there was no tomorrow but then suddenly, when Lee picked him up, he stopped. The reason? Lee breathed two hundred per cent vodka fumes all over him.

I often wonder if there is a thirty-something man in the Port St John area who has grown up an alcoholic.

Back to the story: when British intelligence try to recruit O'Flynn and Oldsmith to investigate a damaged German Blûcher battleship believed to be anchored in the area for repairs, with a view to them destroying it, the scene is set for revenge.

One of the hairiest sequences I filmed involved the initial surveillance of the transportation of parts for the damaged Blûcher battleship; namely steel plates, being towed on giant carts across part of Africa by hundreds of locals. The script called for O'Flynn, Rosa and Sebastian to sabotage this repair mission. As the convoy of huge plates moved towards a little valley, the characters positioned themselves at the foot of a hill with rifles in order to shoot some of the bearers, and in doing so ensuring the carts effectively run away downhill, sending the huge steel plates into trees and – hopefully – rendering them useless.

The brilliant John Glen was in charge of this particular sequence. We all stood at the foot of the hill, where a huge breakaway wheel from one of the carts was to roll. Even with my basic grasp of trigonometry I figured the trajectory of the wheel was one we ought to be concerned about. I picked up the radio to John and director Peter Hunt.

'There are an awful lot of people down here, and I think the wheel's going to come right through the middle of them. Can we move everyone that's not needed away to safety?'

'Good idea,' they replied. Moving people is not a quick business, so it took a good few minutes to move everyone to shelter under a large tree.

'Hang on,' I radioed. 'You've moved them to where the wheel is likely to end up – hitting that tree! We need to move everyone again.'

Peter was getting rather impatient with the delays, and was breathing down John Glen's neck; he in turn was somewhat pissed-off at this interfering actor, and Michael Klinger, meanwhile, thought I was simply amusing myself by wasting the whole unit's time. In the hope I might finally shut up, they moved the people again.

As the giant wheel broke away and came rolling down the hill, I was supposed to move in front of the camera so you effectively watch the sequence from over my shoulder. I couldn't see the crew behind me of course, but they promised to give me a call to 'move!' when it was prudent to do so.

'OK. Action!'

I stood there watching this thing rolling towards me . . . and stood there . . . and stood there. I remember thinking it was getting a bit close, but nobody told me to move, so I didn't like to for fear of spoiling the shot, which I knew would take an age to reset. My gurgling lower regions got the better of my head, so I turned around to find that the whole crew had taken to their heels, leaving me and a camera in the path of this self-propelled pulverizer. I didn't stay there to worry about the camera. The wheel bounced and rolled right down the valley and through the area where everyone had been gathered before I had them moved twice. Looks were exchanged, but nothing was said.

We filmed quite a lot in the Kruger National Park and in one scene had to incorporate an elephant shoot, as Flynn O'Flynn was an ivory poacher, among other things. With the aid of the park rangers, it was arranged that a helicopter would fly over the park, find the location of a herd and then drive a big bull elephant in our general direction.

There were three actors in the scene: Lee, myself and Ian Holm. To minimize any potential dangers, it was suggested that *only* we three and a minimal crew go into the park. When the bull was separated from the herd, the ranger said he would fire a tranquillizer at it, which would take about twenty minutes to take effect. In that time we had to rally ourselves to its position and, once the helicopter was well out of the way, simulate shooting blanks at this beast of burden when it was on the verge of collapse. It all worked remarkably well and after the elephant fell to the ground, we filmed Lee supposedly removing its tusks.

'OK. Clear the immediate area and then we'll wake the elephant up,' said the ranger. He gave it a jab behind the ear, where the veins are more accessible. 'When he wakes up we don't know what he'll do,' said the ranger. 'He might be very angry, but I need to see him conscious before we can leave.'

Oh great! I didn't particularly care to see how angry this huge animal might be, particularly as we'd been playing at shooting him. But Lee, on the other hand, was oblivious to the fact he had blanks in his gun, and thought himself the great white hunter. The beast woke up and we ran like hell for the car. I don't know if you've ever driven across scrubland, but let me assure you it is by far the most uncomfortable ride imaginable. Added to that, we had a rather angry elephant following us. We struggled to get up a decent speed and that day I learned that elephants can run rather fast – about twenty kilometres an hour, in fact. Suffice to say, I did not need a laxative for a week.

Speaking of hair-raising sequences, I should state that I don't mind doing stunts as long as I am in control of my own destiny. I always worry about it when a stuntman or effects boy tells me not to worry. In *Shout at the Devil*, in order to make an aerial recce of the possible location of the Blûcher, our characters are told a biplane will be at their disposal. The pilot of which, as per the script, came in to land on the beach – zooming down just above our heads – prompting O'Flynn to throw himself on the ground, while Sebastian – I – had to stand my full six-foot-two inches and appear unfazed. A few months later a similar stunt saw the pilot take an actor's head off . . . I no longer stand under planes.

Lee liked to do his own stunts. Quite whether it was because the alcohol he consumed in generous quantity had numbed his brain to any danger over the years, or whether he felt no one could possibly double him, I'm not sure. However, we stood on the bank of the Umzimvubu River which was, according to the locals, shark infested, as indeed are a number of the rivers there. In the scene, Lee's character was to swim out to the Blûcher on the opposite side of the river. Larry Taylor, an accomplished stuntman and swimmer, was brought in to double Lee.

Peter Hunt said he'd only need to film Lee getting into the water and starting to swim, for twenty or thirty yards or so. Larry would then go in and pick up the scene for the rest of the swim. Lee bravely dived in and started to swim. I don't think I've mentioned that Lee was a former marine, and was part of a rather elite group who were dropped behind Japanese lines. Consequently, he was quite a fit and tough old sod. He swam and swam and after he'd reached about 600 yards, an increasingly worried-looking Peter Hunt called:

'OK, that's far enough, Lee.'

Ignoring him, Lee continued all the way to the other side.

'There goes my fucking five hundred quid!' said Larry, putting his shirt back on. As he wasn't needed for the sequence, he didn't get paid.

Then there was the story of Nikos and the 'flightless' parrot. Nikos was Peter Hunt's Greek partner, and was with Peter throughout the shoot. Nikos took it into his head that he could train a parrot that was part of the O'Flynn house set, and which Michael Klinger had bought locally for 200 rand. It wasn't a particularly tame parrot, but having had its wings clipped, it couldn't fly. Before we knew it, Nikos had the bird out of the cage and, with a little stick, was attempting to train it.

The O'Flynn house was set on a hill high above an orange grove. Unfortunately none of the oranges were ripe at the time – they were bright green. You can't have green oranges, can you? So the art department were called in to paint them red (we didn't have orange paint) on the side that would be on camera; the other side remained green. They looked like a weird hybrid and were distinctly inedible.

Anyhow, I digress. The next thing we heard was Nikos shouting, 'C'mon back, c'mon back!' The 'flightless parrot' had somehow launched itself into the air, out of the house window and, above the orange grove, got itself into a bit of an upward thermal and floated across the river and into some trees.

As we'd shot a considerable amount at the house with the parrot in the background, it became a continuity issue. We couldn't have one shot of Lee Marvin sitting in his chair with the parrot behind him and then another shot with it gone. Michael Klinger was furious – not only about the continuity, but about his 200 rand.

'Nikos!' he barked in his Cockney swell. 'Get that fucking parrot back!'

Taking a couple of prop boys with him, Nikos crossed the crocodile-infested river in search of the feathered creature which, it turned out, had a great sense of humour. No sooner did Nikos approach it than the parrot – obviously thinking, 'Aye, aye, here's that Greek with a stick again' – immediately opened its wings, launched itself out of the tree, caught a bit of a breeze and flew back up the hill to the house!

That marked the end of Nikos's career as an animal trainer.

René Kolldehoff played the German commissioner, Herman Fleischer – a nasty piece of work. The climax of the film saw us destroy the Blûcher, but Fleischer, who was thought to be on board, actually escaped the explosion by jumping overboard. He then swam to shore and pulled himself out of the river. Rosa pulled her rifle to shoot him in revenge for murdering our child; but I took the gun from her and shot him myself, in what was quite an emotional climax.

René, resplendent in a now mud-stained off-white uniform, was wired with charges that were to detonate in coordination with my gunfire – each charge releasing a small pocket of stage blood.

Bang! The first charge detonated on Rene's left chest. He immediately clutched his right side, 'Ah, I have been *vounded*!' he said. 'I am *vounded*!'

Just then the second bang went off, and René really was wounded because his hand was directly over the charge. In anticipation of each shot, he then proceeded to place his hands, directly over all the places where shots were to hit ... and the charges were to explode. Poor René.

Lee Marvin was absolutely great throughout, though I remembered from my MGM days, legend had it that when Lee had a drink too many, his eyes would turn red. The centrepiece of the film was a glorious and bloody fist-fight between Sebastian and O'Flynn. It was reminiscent of the wonderful fight between John Wayne and Victor McLaglen in *The Quiet Man*. We rehearsed the routine but as we went for a take, I noticed Lee's eyes were turning red. He was drunk and clearly thought he was in a real fight. I moved damned fast to get out of the way of his fists. I forget exactly how long we filmed – it was probably at least five minutes – but I can still hear his fists whistling past my nose today.

A consummate professional, Lee was sometimes a bloody liability too. On days when he wasn't shooting he would come on set, squat on his heels and just watch. Then he'd put his arms around one of the many black actors, congratulating him and treating him like an old friend. Though as soon as Lee had a drink that very same person would become the enemy and he'd push them out of his way.

Lee told me that he absolutely hated the Japanese because of his wartime exploits, and this became apparent when we flew from Johannesburg to Malta for the final part of our schedule. We had a six-hour holdover in Rome, and unfortunately we'd all been exposed to a fair amount of alcohol on the flight and even more in the lounge at Fiumincino airport before we were called for our onward flight. When the flight was called, we exited the lounge straight into half the population of Tokyo, all carrying Nikon cameras.

'Ah, Ree Marvin!' they exclaimed. 'It's Ree Marvin!'

Suddenly, Lee found himself back in the war and, with bright red eyes, started throwing these poor tourists around the departure area. It very nearly became a diplomatic incident.

One day we were shooting in a hotel somewhere in Malta with Jean Kent and Maurice Denham, and Lee was squatting watching – as usual. He called me over.

'Roger,' he said, clearing the back of his nostrils with a low slow inhale, 'I'll give you a piece of advice,' as he threw his hands outwards from his body, 'if you know what I mean?'

'What's that, Lee?' I asked, poised to be offered career-changing information.

'Say the marks and hit the lines!'

'Oh, thanks, Lee.'

After filming wrapped, the family and I decided to head out to LA for a break and to catch up with some friends. We hadn't bought a house out there at that time – that came a year or so later. One of my chums in Hollywood was producer Jack Hayley Jr. He was the son of Jack Hayley Sr. – the actor who played the Tin Man in *The Wizard of Oz*. Curiously enough, Jack Jr. was married to Judy Garland's daughter, Liza Minnelli at this time – Judy, of course, played Dorothy in *The Wizard of Oz*.

Jack called me up and asked if I'd be interested in a TV movie for Fox called *Sherlock Holmes in New York*. Patrick Macnee was already cast as Watson. It was to film in LA, so that all rather suited me. It was actually shot on the *Hello, Dolly* sets at Fox's Hollywood studio.

I've already related the story of how I called Oliver Reed and asked if he was interested in playing Moriarty. Well, after he turned us down flat, Jack approached John Huston. As well as being a famous and accomplished director, writer and producer, Huston also turned his hand to acting in the odd film. He was wonderful to work with. On his arrival, John said to our director, Boris Sagal, 'My boy, I have a lot of these speeches to deliver. I may need some help in remembering them.' So, the art department made up beautiful prompt cards – or idiot boards as we call them – with the dialogue written on, and held them behind the camera at strategic points for John to refer to. He delivered every line perfectly, never looking at them once. The old cad.

John and I both enjoyed backgammon and fine cigars, so between takes we'd sit down to play and smoke. I never had the opportunity to work with Huston as a director. That would have been fun and is one of my few regrets.

Other casting fell into place: Charlotte Rampling, David Huddleston, Gig Young, Signe Hasso and my son Geoffrey, who was around ten, who played Irene Adler's (Charlotte Rampling's) son who is kidnapped by Moriarty. We later discover that the boy is in fact the result of a suggested liaison between Holmes and Irene Adler.

I won't say this is regarded as one of the most popular or warmly remembered Holmes films, but we certainly had fun making it.

Meanwhile, over in the world of 007, Harry Saltzman had sold his shares to United Artists for $20 million and dropped out of Danjaq and Eon Productions. He then experienced a number of business disappointments, which were all compounded by the death of his beloved wife, Jacqueline. Having then moved to Paris, Harry made only a couple more ventures into film production, which I don't think were very successful. He later remarried but suffered a number of health problems, which led to his death in September 1994.

In the summer of 1976, Cubby regrouped and commenced pre-production work on the biggest Bond adventure yet, *The Spy Who Loved Me*.

I wasn't too sure when things might kick off with the film, so when Richard Attenborough offered me one of the leads in *A Bridge Too Far* I had to say I was unavailable. However, when things dragged on a little longer than anticipated in setting up the Bond, suddenly I became available again. My agent got word to Dickie, who replied saying that there was only one role left to be cast, that of General Brian Horrocks – which I thought was very interesting as Brian Horrocks had been a general when I was serving in Germany.

'He has approval,' said Dickie when he called me up, 'and, unfortunately, he doesn't approve of you!'

The part went to Edward Fox.

I don't bear any grudges to Edward, but, you know, he got another part I wanted, too. In 1973, producer John Woolf asked if I would be interested in taking the lead in *The Day of the Jackal*. I said absolutely. Then I heard that the director Fred Zinnemann said he didn't want me. I was very upset at his snub.

Years later I attended a party in Paris at the home of Jean-Pierre Aumont and his wife Marisa Pavan, which Fred also attended, and I asked him why he didn't want me in the movie.

'It's not that I didn't want you,' he said. 'But the Jackal is a character who moves seamlessly through crowds. He goes unnoticed. You are six-foot-two, dashingly good-looking and internationally famous as Simon Templar and Brett Sinclair – how inconspicuous will you be to audiences?'

I took his point.

We moved back to Denham, and I awaited my start date on *The Spy Who Loved Me* which was 'imminent'. The film was big, even by Bond standards, and early on during preparations it became apparent that there was no stage large enough anywhere to house three nuclear submarines – the abduction of which is central to the plot. Cubby scoured potential locations, from aircraft hangers to overseas studios and couldn't find anything suitable. He turned to his production designer, Ken Adam, and asked if they could construct such a stage at Pinewood. In short, the answer was yes and so the famous 007 Stage came into being.

A number of writers had been involved in any number of script drafts before Christopher Wood was engaged by director Lewis Gilbert. Early drafts of scripts – before Christopher came on board – had Blofeld returning as our villain, along with his organization SPECTRE, but a lawsuit was filed by another producer, Kevin McClory, claiming that he had invented both Blofeld and SPECTRE when he collaborated with Ian Fleming on a story that was to become *Thunderball*. McClory became the bane of Cubby's attorney's life throughout this picture, primarily by claiming that Christopher Wood had plagiarized a Bond story he was preparing. Injunctions were launched, but eventually lifted.

Incidentally, the film was not based on Ian Fleming's book. When he wrote that particular adventure, Fleming told the story through the eyes of the female heroine, Anya Amasova. He didn't feel satisfied with the finished product and so declared that nothing, other than the title, could ever be used in a future film.

I expressed my concerns to Lewis about early drafts of the script. Not knowing him very well, I wasn't sure how this distinguished director would respond to an actor telling him where his script needed work. The problem was, I thought, that too much emphasis was placed on the extravagant and spectacular – the size of everything, the outlandish villainous plans and the gadgets – without too much thought to the dialogue. I knew the character by now, and knew what he would and wouldn't say.

Lewis looked at me. 'Well, dear,' he said in his typically vague manner. 'I'm sure we can make something up and improve on it on the day.'

I knew then that this was a man I was going to get on with. I love Lewis dearly. You see, we share the same childish sense of humour. The thing I also found with Lewis was that he got so involved in a scene that he paid little attention to anything else going on around him. We were filming across two rostrums (raised platforms) on one sequence, and Lewis was watching so intently that when he stepped sideways he didn't see the huge gap between the rostrums, and fell straight down, some twelve feet or so. He was so relaxed that he effectively bounced off the ground and pulled himself up to start again.

Cubby wanted to bring Bond back with a bang. The all-important pre-title sequence was going to be his chance. He'd seen a magazine advertisement for Canadian Club Whisky, which featured a chap called Rick Sylvester jumping off the edge of a perpendicular mountain in Greenland, Mount Asgard I believe. The ad read: 'If you Space Ski Mount Asgard . . . before you hit the ground, hit the silk!'

This was to be our opening.

Cubby recruited Rick Sylvester and dispatched him to Mount Asgard with a small team lead by second unit director John Glen to film a jump that was later to form the culmination of a ski-chase featuring yours truly (and my doubles!).

I know days went by and there was no word from John about completing a successful jump. Time was really marching on in our schedule, and Cubby thought he'd have to abandon the idea. But then, as the weather suddenly improved, John was able to call 'Action' and the jump was made. And along with claiming his $30,000 cheque, Rick Sylvester entered movie history by making one of the most spectacular movie openings of all time.

I remember so vividly attending the premiere in London's Odeon Leicester Square and the deathly hush that descended over the audience as Bond skied off the edge of the cliff. You could hear the proverbial pin drop. Then, as the Union Flag parachute opened and the Bond theme roared to a crescendo, the audience stood to offer an ovation. Never before have I witnessed such a thing. I felt enormously proud, and looked across at Cubby – who was smiling widely. If he ever had any doubts about going it alone with Bond, they were swiftly – and permanently – eradicated at that point. Mind you, Rick nearly came a cropper as a disengaged ski clipped the unopened chute as he was falling. The ski could easily have prevented the chute from opening, and you can see it clearly in the film.

A terrific cast was assembled: Curt Jurgens, Barbara Bach, Richard Kiel, and some of my old mates, Geoffrey Keen, Robert Brown and George Baker, not to mention Desmond Llewelyn as Q, Bernard Lee as M and Lois Maxwell as Miss Moneypenny again.

I was told that, for the first time ever, Bond would feature in the opening titles, as designed by Maurice Binder. Maurice was a wonderful, larger-than-life character. His opening titles featuring scantily clad females became legendary and he was also responsible for the famous gun barrel opening sequence. However, he always drove Cubby and the director mad, as he'd only complete his title sequence the day before the premiere, and even then he'd still have ideas to improve on parts. He was a perfectionist, you see. His late delivery occasionally caused us some trouble with the censors, as they deemed some of Maurice's images a little too racy for a PG certificate. However, by always having a charity premiere, Cubby was able to help influence the censor by saying the poor charity would end up losing a great deal of money if our date was put back, as organizing another premiere would be impossible.

Cubby and I visited Maurice on his shooting stage one day, and found him on his knees, lovingly spreading Vaseline over the private parts of one of his female nudes. He said it was to keep her pubic hairs flat in front of the wind machine, and thus not incur the further wrath of the censor.

I turned to Cubby, 'And I thought that was one of the producer's perks?'

The annual Royal Film Performance in 1977 was *Silver Streak* and I was invited as a guest. Broadway veteran Elaine Stritch was also attending, and she stood in the Royal line-up with me on one side of her and James Mason on the other. When the word came up that we should start forming our line in the upper balcony of the Odeon Leicester Square, with the people from the charity (the Cinema and Television Benevolent Fund) at the beginning of the line and then us actors, Stritch became very agitated.

'Oh my God!' she kept saying. 'This is so thrilling! Oh my God!'

Then came the announcement: 'The Queen Mother is in the theatre'. Off she went again about how exciting it all was. As Her Majesty started climbing the stairs, I thought Stritch would quiet down. Oh no!

Suddenly there was a screech. 'Oh my *God*! Look at that coronet! Oh my God! Look at that *darling* hairdo. Oh! What a *darling* dress! Isn't she a darling?'

James Mason was going, 'Ssh, ssh' and said to me out of the side of his mouth, 'Tell her to be quiet, would you.'

'I can't!' I replied from the side of my mouth. 'You tell her!'

Stritch twittered away until, finally, the Queen Mother arrived in front of her. She grabbed Her Majesty's hands with both of hers, and said, 'You are a darling. You *really* are a darling!'

The Queen Mother looked rather desperately at her escort, Lord Delfont. He, in turn, scowled at me – as though it was my fault.

'You know in the presentation on stage . . .' Stritch continued . . . 'I sing a song. I'll sing it for you now . . .'

She started singing this damn song, and the Queen Mother was trying very hard to pull her hand away. Oh, the embarrassment! I can imagine the Queen Mother going home later and saying, 'Some of these American girls are quite odd.'

Some of my early scenes in *Spy* were filmed up in Faslane, Scotland, at the nuclear submarine base. Filming with the submarines was all very interesting, and on board a sub Lewis thought it would be nice to have a hand-held shot of the interior of a torpedo tube, and it opening up to fire – as we could use that later on in the film. Cameraman Alec Mills was volunteered to carry a small Arri camera into the tube and capture the shot.

'Not until Roger is off this sub,' he said defiantly.

'Why?' asked Lewis.

'Because I know him, and once I'm in there he'll fire it for real.' Alec was adamant that he wouldn't do the shot unless I was well out of the way. Alec! As if I'd have fired you out of the tube! Hmmm. You know me too well, old friend.

I was feeling very rough by the time we returned to London, later realizing that I'd come down with shingles. I got home and collapsed into bed. Next morning I awoke with a very swollen face and slits for eyes. Unfortunately, I had a scene scheduled with Bob Brown and George Baker. I called Lewis to explain that I couldn't do it.

'Oh don't worry,' he assured me. 'I'll film over your shoulder dear, it'll be OK.'

So I went in and shot half of the sequence. If you look closely you can see, over my shoulder, my swollen face. I really wasn't well and after seeing the doctor was told to go home for complete rest. A few days later I had a call from Cubby saying that Prime Minister Harold Wilson was going to officially open the 007 Stage and would I go in? I dragged myself over – wearing dark glasses to disguise my slitty eyes – and had to marvel at this incredible structure containing the submarines, monorails, walkways and everything else.

David Niven was shooting a film called *Candleshoe* on an adjacent stage at Pinewood. We met one lunch time and he was raving about the young actress he was working with.

'You must come over and see her,' he said. 'She would like to see you, but I promise you'll like meeting her more. She's the most intelligent child I've ever met and without being precocious or presumptuous she's telling the director where he should place his camera.'

She was the young Jodie Foster. She was absolutely charming. I only wish she'd asked for me on one of her later films!

This was my first film with Ken, or Sir Ken Adam as he is now. He is, without doubt, one of the true geniuses of film-making. His sets are spectacular and extraordinary. His vision is awe-inspiring and almost every set of his that I walked on to took my breath away. The only sadness was seeing it all blown up at the end of films. But having said all that, I also used to love winding him up! United Artists were keen on staging press junkets in exotic locations, as invariably it meant a free trip for the media and such lovely surroundings often resulted in us receiving favourable write-ups. We were in a hotel in Sardinia when one such junket was arranged. A number of large tables were laid out: I hosted one, Cubby another, Barbara Bach another and then Ken had one, too. At mine, I had a large group of German press.

'Of course,' I told them. 'You know Klaus Adam was a great war hero, a famous pilot?'

'Oh, yah? Vos he?' they asked.

'Yes he shot down over thirty-two planes.'

They became rather excited and wanted to talk to him. Of course I failed to mention that Ken was on Britain's side during the war and they were German planes he destroyed.

On every Bond film, we had what I affectionately refer to as the 'wanker tape', that is, a tape containing some of the funniest gaffes. Our editor,

John Glen, compiled the clips, which I set to music. There had been a documentary made about the design and construction of the 007 stage, from which John copied bits and cut Ken in saying 'I did that,' after every clip, effectively claiming credit for everything. Ken is nothing if not immodest, but this went a bit too far. Added to this, John cut newsreel of the Third Reich marching in to some country or other and, yes, you've guessed it, Ken did that!

On the day we ran the tape, Ken couldn't understand quite why there were so many people in the theatre. He wasn't best pleased at first but eventually saw the funny side.

I shouldn't laugh. One of the other sequences on that damn tape was my final scene with our wonderful villain Curt Jurgens. He, sitting at his dining table, beckoned Bond to sit at the opposite end of the table, while all the time reaching underneath for his gun, which was attached to the underside. I was supposed to stand behind a chair at the opposite end to Curt, which in turn was to blow up when he fired his bolt.

'Lewis, wouldn't it add more suspense if I sat *in* the chair?'

'Yes, dear, that sounds like an idea,' he said.

So I did. Unfortunately for me, our special-effects man John Evans – a name I will never forget! – was a bit too quick on the button and my backside was only an inch off the chair when he blew it up. My rear end caught fire and it was pretty painful, as was my language. I had to have the dressing changed twice a day for weeks.

From Cairo to Luxor, the aforementioned Sardinia and Scotland to London and the Bahamas, we travelled the world. On arriving in Egypt – on my birthday – I remember walking on to our location set and being staggered by the number of huge tents that had been erected for the catering area. There in the middle was George Crawford, and he said he had a surprise for me.

'I've got some lobsters for the occasion.'

I looked down at these green crustaceans. They were moving. They were dead, but still moving.

'George!' I exclaimed. 'You don't get fresh lobsters out here, they've all gone off.'

Foreign locations often presented problems to the caterers. The British crews rarely ate any local foods 'Call this proper food?' you'd hear the cry go up, 'We want steak pudding, sausage and mash and treacle sponge with custard.' There was one day when something went wrong in Egypt and word reached us mid-morning that there wouldn't be any lunch. Cubby knew he'd have a revolt on his hands, and so – somehow – gathered together huge great cooking pots, bundles of pasta and meat, and made a wonderful pasta with meatballs and sauce. He served it up to the boys and girls himself too. Cubby liked nothing better than to cook, and the crew liked nothing better than to eat. You can see why everyone loved Cubby so much – and he was 'Cubby' to everyone. There was no 'Mr Broccoli' on his set.

One of the provisos to filming in Egypt was that we had to submit the script in advance to the Egyptian government, and whatever they approved could not be changed.

At the Temple of Karnak we had a wonderful fight scene between Bond and Jaws, the seven-foot-two giant of a henchman, resplendent with steel teeth and played by the wonderful Richard Kiel. I can't think of two more different characters – Richard is so kind, so gentle and indeed an accomplished writer as well as an actor, whereas Jaws is, well, a hired killer without much soul. Jaws did have a dry sense of humour, thanks to the little nuances Richard gave him. Despite being so tall, Richard is terrified of heights. When Lewis told him he would have to cross the top of some scaffolding high above the Temple ruins, he went pale.

'I don't even like being this tall,' he said.

In the event, Martin Grace – my stunt double – stood in for Richard and, despite being a foot or so shorter, I defy any of you to say it isn't Richard up there. Martin captured Richard's movements and the way he moves his head – being blind in one eye – so perfectly that even the man himself had to think twice about who it was when he saw the rushes.

Anyhow, we had this Egyptian government representative on the set, as he was throughout our shoot, closely watching our every move. At the climax of the fight sequence, I was to knock a piece of the scaffolding away, causing the whole structure to crumble on dear Richard.

'What are you going to say here, dear?' asked Lewis, aware of our Egyptian representative looking on.

'I'll say "Egyptian builders!" I think.'

'What about his nibs?' enquired Lewis, nodding at our friend.

'I'll just move my lips, and won't say anything aloud. We'll dub it back at Pinewood.'

So that's what I did, only for our sound recordist to come running over saying, 'We'll have to go again, I couldn't hear him.'

Lewis mouthed, 'Shut up!' at him.

I think it was just after this, when Bond and his female companion, Anya Amasova, played by my now neighbour in Monaco, Barbara Bach, start making their way back to Cairo that their van breaks down and they have to get out and walk across the sand dunes, with chimes of *Lawrence of Arabia* playing behind. As we walked across the frame in a David Leanesque shot, I'm afraid I let my trousers drop down. I had hoped they might leave it in, but it was vetoed.

In Cairo we had another fight scene, this time on the roof of the British Museum. Milton Reid was cast as the henchman who takes 007 on at this point. On the day of the fight, our stunt arranger Bob Simmons explained to Milton that he had to fall off the roof, with me snapping him away after he held on to my tie to prevent his fall.

'You're going to have to fall off this roof, Milton,' Bob said.

Milton – a burly, quite menacing-looking chap – took a quick peak over the edge. 'Oh! But it's six storeys, Bob! I can't do that.'

'No, we'll pile up boxes to the fourth storey, Milton, you just fall two,' added Bob, now determined to wind him up.

'Can't I fall just one storey?'

'No, no, we need a long scream.'

'Well,' reasoned Milton. 'Can't I do a short fall and long scream?'

Oh poor Milton, they did wind him up so much!

With villains defeated, Bond getting his girl, and the adventure over, we called a wrap. The film was certainly lighter than my previous two Bond efforts; I think largely due to Lewis wanting to have fun with it all, and make it slightly ridiculous – a giant with steel teeth for instance? It suited my style and my persona and I think I really settled into the role with this film. It's certainly my favourite of the Bonds I made.

I think it was on *The Spy Who Loved Me* that I first went to Japan on a promotional tour. It was wintertime, and the film was attracting full houses all over Tokyo and beyond. The manager of one cinema said to Cubby that he was sorry it wasn't a summer release. When Cubby asked why, he was told that in the winter everyone wore an overcoat; if it had been summer they could have squashed more people in without their shoulder pads!

Press conferences were hard going, a hundred or so journalists facing Cubby, Jerry Juroe (our chief of publicity) the interpreter and me. Every one of my joking answers to their very serious questions was greeted in po-faced silence: I obviously do not improve in the translation.

I'd brought Christian with me, who was about four. One evening a couple of United Artists' executives and Cubby asked me to join them in the sushi and sashimi bar of the hotel, so Christian came along too. He stared, swallowing very hard as he watched the *Ebi, Saba* and *Ika Tako*, (that is raw prawns, mackerel, squid and octopus) being prepared.

'You don't like this, do you?' I said.

'No, Daddy… I do not!' he replied, emphatically.

'OK. We'll find a hamburger at the hotel.'

Off we set in search of what a four-year-old English boy thinks of as 'proper' food. We did find a place in the hotel, full of Japanese parents with their children, all stuffing their faces with tomato ketchup-drenched burgers on buns.

Christian was quite a witty child, he always had a smart reply that would make us laugh. I remember Leslie Bricusse asked him one day, 'How old are you Christian?'

'Four!'

'And when will you be five?'

'When I have finished being four!'

Now that is either wit or logic, or both.

During the shoot of *The Spy Who Loved Me* I was persuaded to do something that I'd always said I wouldn't. I bought a Rolls-Royce. I thought them rather pretentious but my financial advisers said, 'You've earned it, and wouldn't you like to drive the family around in luxury, style and comfort?' It was just before Christmas that my shiny new brown Rolls was delivered to Pinewood. I was about to leave for the children's Christmas party, at which I was playing Santa. I asked my make-up artist and my dresser to make me up as Santa, with whiskers, the red suit and so on. I then hopped into my Rolls to drive home. I pulled up at the first set of red traffic lights only to see, out of the corner of my eye, people staring and pointing at me. I knew then that I should never have bought a Rolls, clearly they were all thinking what a pretentious twerp I was. I had completely forgotten what I was wearing!

The children rather enjoyed it, but young Christian later said to me 'you were inside him'. I had a mole on my face back then, and Christian spotted it on Santa's face. Clever boy.

All three children were all clever, in one way or another. In her teens, Deborah, much against my better wishes, decided she wanted to be an actress. Maybe after working with me on *The Persuaders* she thought it was a fun occupation? Being a hypochondriac, I had wanted her to study medicine: there's nothing like free medical care close at hand. However, I supported her decision and, having assured her that the negatives far outweighed the positives in this game, I was delighted when she was accepted at the London Academy of Music and Dramatic Art (LAMDA). One of her classmates was Rita Wilson, and she and her husband-to-be – a young actor named Tom Hanks – became close family friends.

I attended many of Deborah's performances at LAMDA. She made me feel very proud. She is a very good and talented actress and has appeared in film, TV, on stage and, famously, as the Scottish Widow in the insurance company's series of TV commercials. Each time I see her perform she gets better and better. Now all she needs is a bit of good luck; that one part that will take her to the great heights she deserves.

Geoffrey, a couple of years younger than his sister, is a handsome lad; taking after his mother. He was not the most academic of schoolboys though, and when a dreaded school report dropped on the doorstep I opened the envelope slowly. What low marks were going to be reported this time?

On one occasion, while we still lived in Denham, I called him into my study, and read down the list of subjects and the marks received.

'Maths… two out of ten,' I said. 'Geoffrey . . . that's awful!'

He was completely unperturbed and simply said, 'Read on.'

'Geography . . . three out of ten . . . *terrible!*'

'Read on.'

'History . . . two out of ten . . . hmmm!'

'Go on, Dad. Read on.'

I got to the end and the headmaster's remarks. 'Geoffrey is the most popular boy in the school and an asset to our academy.'

'See, Dad?' he said, triumphantly.

I wonder whether he was bribing the headmaster, or was he a master of forgery? But it's true, he is loaded with charm!

Ten years after Deborah appeared, around the same time that I was inflicted on the cinema-going public as James Bond, Christian came along. His schooling started in Paris. I was filming there and he came home from school one evening, absolutely furious.

'What's the matter, Christian?' I asked.

He glowered and said, 'They are *so* stupid in that school. They're trying to teach me English and I keep telling them that I *am* English!'

I explained that English is also a subject to study, learning grammar, comprehension, how to conjugate, etc.

It became easier when we moved to Gstaad and he went to the junior school in the next village, The Kennedy International School, under the guidance of a Canadian couple, Bill and Sandy Lovell. Christian adored the school and when he was too old to be a pupil there we entered him into Aiglon College in Villars. Christian didn't like it, and as a result failed to excel academically. I dreaded the end-of-term sessions when parents had to line up before each teacher and receive a verbal report as to their offspring's ability and performance. I would rather have been back at Hackford Road Elementary myself, being whacked on an extended palm with a cane. But, whatever his academic prowess, Christian, too, is full of charm. It must run in the family.

Though things were happy and harmonious at home, it was all about to change. By this time I had achieved a little success in my career, settled into our lovely family home in Denham and placed the children in good local schools. Then my accountants said I could no longer afford to live in Britain. No, they hadn't spent all my money. They were referring to the then labour government's tax policy. Earned income above a certain amount was to be taxed at eighty-seven per cent. That is to say, for every pound I earned, eighty-seven pence of it went to the Chancellor of Exchequer, Denis Healey. Unearned income – such as returns on investments and shares – was taxed even higher.

It sounds terribly greedy to say I didn't want to pay that much tax, but the fact is that an actor's life can be relatively short in terms of success and earning potential. It wouldn't be so bad if, on retirement, one could work out tax due over a long period of time as for many years I'm sure I earned relatively little, which would have balanced the more successful years out nicely. But no, tax was payable on *that* year's earnings, regardless of whether or not you worked again in ensuing years.

I agreed to put the house on the market. But then one morning I woke up and, indignantly, said no. I was staying put. I was happy in my country, my home, and with my family. In short, it was the ideal home and we were all very happy there.

I drove to Gerrards Cross, a few miles away, bought myself some new art material – paints, pencils, canvases – and settled down to enjoy my free time, determined to stay in *my* home, in *my* country.

However, romantic notions aside, with another Bond film in the offing – and an increased salary – my advisers reasoned with me that I would be working for virtually nothing if I continued living in the UK. A number of other actors had already left – Michael Caine and Sean Connery being two. (Michael later returned saying he couldn't bear living without English roast beef!) I talked about it all at length with Luisa, and made the tearful decision that we had to move. The house was put on the market again and we set about thinking just where we might relocate to.

Curt Jurgens, who had become a good friend after our Bond adventure together, suggested we might like to take his chalet in Gstaad for a couple of weeks while he was away, to think about Switzerland as an option. David Niven – another who had left the UK – was living nearby, in Château d'Oex and said he loved it there.

On arriving in Geneva, we drove up to Gstaad and immediately fell in love with the town. When the children learned that Swiss schools used to end lessons at lunch time to go skiing in the afternoons, that sealed it for them too! We found a place to rent for the following year and then, with summer approaching and the skiing season over, decided to spend some time at our home in LA, on Hidden Valley Road in Coldwater Canyon. It would be good, I thought, to reintroduce myself to the folks out there, now that I was 007, and maybe even get a job.

My career was, fortunately, going well. After the popularity of *Close Encounters* and *Star Wars*, Cubby had decided to postpone the announced *For Your Eyes Only* as the next Bond, and to get in on the space race with *Moonraker*. Lewis was asked to stay on board, and Christopher Wood was engaged to write the screenplay. Production was many months off, and so I was able to accept another project.

The Wild Geese was to be my third film in South Africa, and the third time the ACTT threatened to blacklist the film: it was becoming a bit of a bore, if the truth be known. Again, though, we won through.

The picture was produced by a wonderful man named Euan Lloyd and directed by Andrew V. McLaglen, a director for whom I have a tremendous respect, in fact we made two more films together after this. I wish it had been more. The script was based on a Daniel Carney book, adapted by Reginald Rose and initially it was going to star Robert Mitchum and Richard Burton. When Euan was in LA having one of the many meetings needed to set the film up, a particular agent who shall remain nameless said, 'Well, Euan baby, you've got Mitchum and Burton, who have you got lined up for Shawn Fynn?'

'Roger Moore,' Euan replied.

'Hold the phone, *hold the phone*! We pencilled in O. J. Simpson for that part!'

'Why would you pencil in O. J. Simpson for that role?' a rather bemused Euan asked.

'Well, in the script it says Shawn Fynn is black-Irish.'

Euan tried tactfully to explain what the term 'black-Irish' referred to . . . and the upshot was that it was me and not O. J. Simpson who was offered the part. I don't remember why Mitchum couldn't do it, but he dropped out and a last-minute replacement was found in Richard Harris.

At this time, Richard was considered a risk because of his slight alcohol problem. Film Finances, the company putting up the completion guarantee (which was required by the backers of the picture), resolved that they would only agree to his casting if, at five o'clock every evening, Andrew McLaglen would sign a chit to say Harris had turned up on time, knew his lines, and didn't drink. I felt it rather degrading, to be honest, but that was the only way they'd agree to his casting. His fee and some of Euan Lloyd's salary were held in escrow to further guarantee good behaviour. As it happened there was absolutely no problem with Harris. Richard Burton couldn't drink at that time either, though that was for medical reasons. Burton was suffering quite badly with his shoulders – I think it may have been arthritis.

The film's fourth lead was German actor Hardy Kruger, whom Burton referred to as 'Deadly Luger'.

In support was a cast to die for. And many did die . . . in the film. The wonderful Ronnie Fraser played Sergeant Jock McTaggart. Ron-Ron, as he called himself, was legendary. He had a little alcohol problem at this time too, and was quite literally poured on to a plane in London, poured off in Johannesburg, poured into a hotel and then poured on to a little Cessna and poured off in Tschepese on the border of the then Rhodesia, where we were filming.

Ronnie came over to me one morning and said, 'Ron-Ron is going to die if Ron-Ron has another drink, and so Ronnie will not have another drink.' He stopped drinking, but substituted his alcohol craving with ganja – the South African weed. However, whereas most people would roll up a joint with a single Rizla paper, Ronnie would take five or six papers and roll a joint the size of the tube in a toilet roll – and this would go on from the early morning. Ron-Ron was stone-stoned for most of the picture.

A few years later, Ronnie was appearing in a play at the Royal Court Theatre in Sloane Square. It was a matinée, which had followed a fairly good liquid lunch with his great mate the Honourable James Villiers. At the end of the first act Ronnie had a page-long speech. When he finished, a bemused audience of grey-haired old ladies heard a slow clapping coming from James, who added, 'Bravo, Ronnie! Bravo!'

Ronnie walked across stage to the footlights and said, 'Did you like that, Jimmy?'

'Yes,' came the reply.

'Shall I do it again?' he asked James.

'Oh yes!' So he did the whole thing again. What a wonderfully eccentric man.

I turned fifty during the production, and to mark it, the cast and crew organized a huge surprise party for me, miles out into the bush, where they lit six huge braais – barbecues – around ten feet high. I was rather sensitive about turning fifty, preferring to stay forty-nine forever, but it made headlines all around the world so there was very little chance of me avoiding it.

We shot in a spa resort with springs, sulphur baths and all sorts of other attractions; which had been closed to the public for our use. Most of the crew and cast stayed in the rondavels (round houses) and there were a few other houses that were rented to the lead actors, director and producer. I had a rather nice house on a hill and Richards Burton and Harris were next door.

I knew Harris was up to something one evening. I returned to my house and could hear a lot of giggling between him and his wife Ann. I looked around and at the foot of my bed lay a snake – a rubber one. I pulled the sheets off the bed and there lay a tarantula – again, rubber. Aha! Harris is up for some fun, I thought. I didn't scream or react in any way whatsoever, which must have annoyed him no end.

However, there were loud screams the next night, from the Harris household, as he went to put on his boots and discovered snakes in them – real snakes. The moral of this story? 'Don't fuck around with Moore!'

In the film, the 'Wild Geese' are double-crossed by Sir Edward Matherson, played by Stewart Granger. The last scene was set in

Matherson's London home. I looked at the script, dying to see the exchange between my character and my childhood hero. Alas, there wasn't any. I wasn't in the scene at all, having taken a bullet in the leg sometime earlier.

Richard Burton suggested that I really should be in this scene as otherwise there was rather a loose end, as we wouldn't know if Shawn had made it back to England alive. While I wouldn't actually share any screen time with Granger, at least I'd be at the tail-end of the sequence.

They were filming the sequence at a big house in Belgrave Square, on the opposite corner to the Spanish Embassy, and I wasn't needed until late evening. I had lunch with Elliot Kastner who was over here to discuss an upcoming film he was producing, *North Sea Hijack*, but I was at the location in time to sit outside the house in the car, for when Burton's character came out, having shot Matherson.

Burton exited. 'By heck,' he said in his wonderful Welsh lilt. 'That Jimmy Granger. He hasn't made a film for fifteen years and he's still a bugger!'

Burton said they did one take on the scene, in which Granger was very elegant in evening dress, and Granger started taking off his tie and shirt. Burton said, 'Jimmy, I think we're going to go another take on this.'

'Fuck 'em!' replied Granger, who – as Burton said – hadn't made a film for a decade-and-a-half. No wonder he was short on offers. It brought back to mind the 'Don't laugh at me, I'm a fucking film star' line he'd uttered many years before.

Richard, as I've mentioned, did have a lovely turn of phrase. One day, a member of the production crew upset him by not allowing Stanley Baker's son, Glyn, to sit on the top table at lunch. Later that day, the same production person was driving out of the parking lot, and, passing Burton, stopped and said, 'Would you like a lift, Richard?'

'If I were dead and you were a fucking hearse, I wouldn't ride in you!' came the reply.

The film was quite successful and a few years later Euan Lloyd started work on a sequel, *Wild Geese II*. I was asked to reprise my role of Shawn Fynn, with Richard Burton returning as Faulkner. I didn't particularly want to do it. It was all about springing Rudolph Hess from jail and I just didn't think I was right for it, plus I was being rather grand at that time too, playing Bond.

Tragically, Burton died a week or two before filming commenced. Hasty re-casting saw Edward Fox sign on as Faulkner's younger brother.

With Sherwood House up for sale, it was agreed that as soon as I'd finished shooting *The Wild Geese* we would go, house sold or not. I remember getting into our car and driving along the long gravel drive for the last time. I didn't look back, it was too painful. Mum, Dad and my assistant Doris Spriggs, waved us off and then handled the later sale of the house for us, to producer Ken Hyman – who subsequently sold it to magician Paul Daniels.

David Niven had made many, many pictures before he won both the Golden Globe and Oscar for 'Best Actor' in *Separate Tables*. In fact his performance that year pretty much swept the board of all awards and plaudits. It was a well-deserved win that was built on solid foundations with his prior body of work. However, Niv told me that when the Critics Awards nominations were announced, there was one New York critic who voted against him and publicly dismissed his performance.

Niven was really rather curious as to why this one man so disliked him. I think it niggled away at David to the point that when he was in New York, on the promotion trail, he asked the United Artists' press officer to invite the critic to lunch. Niv wanted to talk to him.

I need to tell you here that when Niv came out of the army, as a young lieutenant, he found himself in Bermuda. There he met two young ladies, both of whom were without their husbands; had a wild affair with both of them before moving on to America and leaving them brokenhearted.

At the lunch, Niv came straight out with it, 'Can you tell me why you made such a point, in your column, of saying that you voted against my nomination? I'd like to know.'

The critic said, 'There was a young lieutenant in Bermuda who had his way with my wife and her friend.'

'Ah, we'll say no more,' replied Niv.

In between my last Bond and *The Wild Geese*, David Niven Jr. came to visit us in Denham. One morning he said, 'Come on, let's go to Switzerland to see Dad.'

'Okay,' I said, 'why not?' We loaded up the car and Niv Jr., Luisa and I drove across to Château d'Oex. Just before we pulled into the town, he produced a blonde wig and suggested Luisa put it on.

Niv's wife, Hjordis, came to the door. Junior said, 'Hjordis, can I introduce my date . . . Roger's here, too, but Luisa couldn't make it.'

As Junior was saying this, Niv came down the stairs. He took one look at Luisa, turned on his heel and disappeared back upstairs *very* quickly. Later on, when all was revealed and the wig removed, Niv explained his actions to me, 'I knew the face but I couldn't remember where I'd had her!'

Where was the regiment then, I wonder?

Actually, Niv was the one who first introduced me to many things and people in Switzerland. It was on my first visit out there to see him that he took me across to Gstaad, and the very exclusive Eagle Club. He was on the committee. When I moved to Gstaad I became a life member of the club, and later was voted on to the committee to replace Niv when he died. I seem to replace everyone.

I was once called, at very short notice, to give the Loyal Address at a Royal Film Performance when Charlton Heston had to pull out. I explained that I was replacing Moses, but that was nothing new as I replaced George Sanders in *The Saint*, Jim Garner in *Maverick*, Sean Connery as Bond . . . you get my point.

Niven Jr., by the way, was dubbed 'The Ponce' by his father. He was always finding ways of making money, you see, which caused Niv to say, 'He's really a bit of a Ponce, isn't he?' The name stuck, and thereafter he was known as Poncey.

Anyhow, after his great success as a producer with *The Eagle Has Landed*, I said to Poncey that I found it odd that here I was, supposedly one of his best friends, and there was his father, an Academy Award-winning actor, and he'd never once offered either of us a job! About a month later, when I was out in LA, Poncey called me and invited me over to lunch in the Polo Lounge at the Beverly Hills hotel. I'd forgotten all about my leg-pulling with him, when he said, 'I have someone here I'd like you to meet.'

A rather strange, chain-smoking Greek stepped forward. His name was George Pan Cosmatos. Forever after I dubbed him Cosmatosis. He produced a script and said there were parts for both me, and Niven Sr. It was called *Escape to Athena*. Poncey had secured financing via Lew Grade, and all was set to roll. The other cast members included Telly Savalas, Stephanie Powers, Claudia Cardinale, Elliott Gould, Anthony Valentine, Sonny Bono, Richard Roundtree and Michael Sheard. Quite impressive!

Filming was to take place entirely on the isle of Rhodes and I was to play a camp commandant – no, not that sort of 'camp' – who was an Austrian; when they wanted to attract sympathy for a German character, they'd always make him an Austrian. I looked terrific, my uniform resplendent with swastikas, as Major Otto Hecht.

On the island there was a rather nice little casino – and this was in the days when I gambled. Telly Savalas was also a great gambler and we'd find ourselves at the tables together most nights. One evening I struck lucky and won $25,000. I felt so damn guilty about hitting this casino for that much money, and the German manager was such a nice man, I felt I was robbing his modest living from him. I'm too soft for my own good. Anyway, on my next visit my luck had turned. I started losing. When I'd lost $25,000 I thought it was time to stop. The manager, knowing I was good for the money had extended me a credit line. I told him that I would bring the money to him the next day on my way to location – at noon.

Next day, I got dressed and made-up in my hotel, as I always did before going to location, and pulled up to the casino. It must have been rather an odd sight, thinking about it: me in full Nazi uniform bearing a large briefcase, banging on a casino front door.

It was noon exactly. The manager came to the door. He didn't react to my dress. He looked at the case, took it off me and said, looking at his watch, '*Mein liebergott*! You English are so precise.'

He didn't say a word about the money, so I clicked my heels and got back into my car.

After a quick trip to see the new home we had taken in Gstaad and ensure that everything was OK, I received the script for *Moonraker*, my next Bond film. My agent negotiated the deal as we were now moving forward on a film-by-film basis, rather than signing up for another three films.

ELEVEN

It's Bond and Beyond

'Well, we shall air our crotches'

By this time, Cubby had also left the UK due to the tax laws; and while Lewis Gilbert maintained his home in London, he had a home in France too, and was rather keen, if at all possible, not to work in Britain. The decision was made to base *Moonraker* in Paris, between three film studios.

Doris Spriggs went ahead of us to find an apartment in Paris for the whole family, and came up with a wonderful one, tucked away in a quiet side street in the centre of the city. We moved in during August and all was fine; but come September, when the school holidays ended, we discovered it was actually one of the noisiest thoroughfares in the city.

I loved the French way of working in studios. We'd start around noon and shoot for seven or eight hours, then go home. Gone were the early-morning calls to get to make-up in time for an early shoot on the stage floor. I did miss a few of my home luxuries, though. Our stunt arranger, Bob Simmons, went home to London most weekends, coming back on the Monday with a lovely bowl of pork or beef dripping from his Sunday lunch. Oh, the heaven of dripping-on-toast.

We shot a number of set pieces before moving to South America. I remember one set in particular, the interior of the Iguazú Falls sequence, was erected on a big stage in Paris, and we then went on to pick up the exterior on location. Going back to the studio a few months later, that stage then contained our villain Drax's mission-launch centre set. Walking on to the stage, one of the pretty 'Bond girls' who had appeared in the previous Iguazú Falls sequence said, 'Oh! It's different.' I don't think she was used to working in films.

Michael Lonsdale played our Mr Nasty, Drax, who was intent on destroying earth in favour of a new settlement in space. I did think it was all a little far-fetched, but hey, it made a fortune at the box office, becoming the most successful Bond film – and remaining so for two decades.

Incidentally, making the Bond films I developed a technique with the villains of imagining that they had halitosis. Watch them and you'll see I look mildly repulsed whenever I'm in a scene with a baddie. Mind you, in some other films I made I didn't have to act it, they really *did* have bad breath.

He didn't have breath problems, but I'd have hated to be the dentist for our steel-toothed friend, Jaws, who was back for another go at Bond – though this time mellowing, thanks to his love interest with the diminutive Dolly, as played by Blanche Ravalec. My leading lady, meanwhile, was the lovely Lois Chiles. Oh what a wonderful character name she had – Dr Holly Goodhead.

Lois, bless her, had something of a fixation with her hair. She had the most lovely, naturally curly hair . . . but the hairdressing department wanted it straight! Before every take they would iron and and straighten it out. Then Lois would dash off after the take and wash it, making it all curly again. I've met Lois many times since and she now cringes with embarrassment at the thought of her demands concerning her hair, such as having her hairdresser flown in by Concorde.

One of the more memorable scenes in the film was where Dr Goodhead invites Bond to have a spin in the gravitational simulator – a sort of giant spin dryer. Thanks to Ken Adam it actually worked, like a huge fairground ride, though the speeds at which I travelled in it were somewhat slower than it appears on film. To achieve the skin-rippling effects, as I passed through any number of G-Force increments, the prop boys rigged small high-pressure hoses that jetted air over areas of my face – some parts of which ended up around the back of my head and haven't been seen since!

I always got on well with the prop boys, and consequently they were always up for a laugh when I suggested something. I had a pretty intense – or as intense as I get, at least – scene with Lois in the final reel of the film. We are on board Drax's space station looking out to Earth and at the pods – loaded with a deadly nerve gas – hurtling towards the planet; upon impact they are set to kill millions. As I say, fairly intense stuff. Our dialogue exchange was all about the aforementioned pods and how we could stop them, but Lois wasn't feeling particularly easy about it all and we couldn't seem to get it right. It was obvious that I needed to help relax her!

A couple of takes later, Lois was again looking out to space and just before she could deliver her line, a little green-suited Martian popped up – complete with antennae – and started washing the Plexiglas windows on the space station. We all fell about laughing. It did the trick and helped relax

On location in Thailand in 1974 filming *The Man With the Golden Gun* with Britt Ekland, my stand-in John Wood and director Guy Hamilton.

A 'Saintly' encounter with Maud Adams in *The Man with the Golden Gun*.

Ian Fleming's cousin, Christopher Lee, playing Scaramanga, the only operatic Bond villain I worked with.

Deborah, Geoffrey (front) and Christian with Grandma and Grandpa Moore, Denham, 1975.

Confusion reigned as Sacheen Littlefeather took to the stage to announce that Marlon Brando was refusing the Best Actor Oscar for *The Godfather*, 1973.

On location in South Africa with *Shout at the Devil* in 1975, nervously waiting for the elephant to come round.

Packing a punch with co-star Lee Marvin in *Shout at the Devil*.

Lt Shawn Fynn, ready for anything in *The Wild Geese*, 1978.

My fellow Wild Geese, Richard Harris, Richard Burton and Hardy Kruger, mercenaries for hire in Africa, 1978.

Towards the end of 1977 I took up my pencil to sketch the children – from left to right, Christian, Deborah and Geoffrey – for our family Christmas card. I am available for commissions.

Walter Gotell, Bernard Lee, myself and Barbara Bach in a scene from *The Spy Who Loved Me*. Bernie Lee had appeared in all the previous Bonds, but this was to be his penultimate one with me, as sadly he died in 1981.

Moonraker, 1979. Lois Chiles played Dr Goodhead, which ranks alongside Pussy Galore as one of the more risqué Bond Girl names.

Moonraker saw the gentle giant Richard Kiel make his second appearance as the formidable Jaws.

'Ah, Miss Moneypenny … What would I do without you?' My dear friend, the late Lois Maxwell.

Escape to Athena with Elliott Gould and Stephanie Powers, 1979.

Rufus Excalibur ffolkes (*sic*), cat-loving misogynist, in *North Sea Hijack*, 1979.

On the set of *North Sea Hijack* with another great friend, Andrew V. McLaglen, who directed me on three occasions.

What a line up! With Henry Kissinger, Lord Mountbatten and Cary Grant in Monaco for a Variety Club presentation.

Four old friends mixing it up a bit on the set of *The Sea Wolves* in 1980.

ROGER MOORE   GREGORY PECK   TREVOR HOWARD   DAVID N

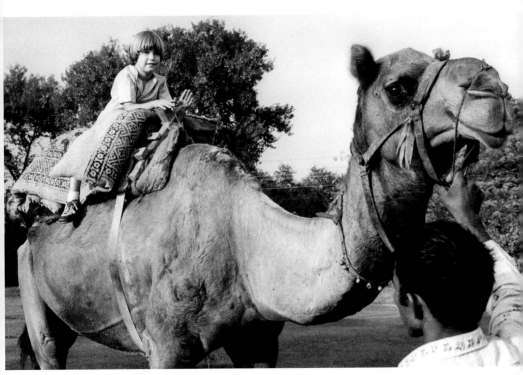

Christian on the camel specially laid on for him the day producer Euan Lloyd made us attend a mysterious party while on location in India for *The Sea Wolves*.

My darling daughter, Deborah, aged seventeen – still the apple of her daddy's eye.

Jimmy Bond was beginning to feel his age the day he was seduced by Lynn Holly Johnson's sixteen-year-old Bibi Dahl in *For Your Eyes Only*, 1981.

I never missed an opportunity to wind up dear Desmond Llewelyn, who often had the most technical dialogue imaginable thanks to my 'rewrites'.

Two years after breaking most of the bones in his body, my stunt double, Martin Grace, was back on the job. I'm the handsome one on the right.

The Irving G. Thalberg Award, the highest honour that the American Academy can bestow, was given to my great friend Cubby Broccoli in 1981.

No hard feelings … dancing with former Chancellor of the Exchequer Denis Healey, the man responsible for me having to leave the UK, and the wonderful Les Patterson, cultural attaché to the Court of St James, on the *Dame Edna Show*, 1987.

At Buckingham Palace in 1999 with Geoffrey, Deborah and Christian, to receive my CBE.

'Has anybody seen Sean?' Pierce Brosnan, me, Michael Parkinson, George Lazenby and Timothy Dalton at the BAFTA 'Forty Years of Bond' tribute in 2002. (© BAFTA 2002)

David 'Poncey' Niven Jr, Christian, Joan Collins and Kristina at my birthday party in LA in 2005.

'All good friends ...' *back row, l to r*, Leslie Bricusse, Terry O'Neill, Johnny Gold, me, Michael Caine, and *front row*, Andrew Lloyd Webber and the 'birthday boy' himself, Michael Winner, at Michael's birthday party in Venice in 2006.

Since 1991, my work with UNICEF has taken me and, later, Kristina all around the world. These days, our lives revolve around UNICEF and its ongoing work — it's the most rewarding thing I've done.

TOP, El Salvador, 1991 (© UNICEF/Horst Cerni);
BELOW, Jaipur, India, 2005 (© UNICEF/Sanjit Das);
RIGHT, Macedonia, 1999 (© UNICEF /Mark Thomas).

'Flossie' and me. It saves confusion with Kristina's daughter being named Christina too!

One of our favourite photographs, taken in Monaco in 2007. (© Anthony Osmond-Evans)

My Hollywood 'Walk of Fame' star, outside 7007 Hollywood Boulevard, October 2007, with my wonderful family and friends. Kristina, kneeling next to her son Hans-Christian, is holding hands with his adorable baby, Kathrine, whose mother, Henriette sits behind them.

My son Geoffrey and his beautiful family – the lovely Loulou, and daughters Ambra and Mia – with Kristina in Switzerland, 2006.

When did Christian grow up? My youngest boy with his gorgeous daughter, Jessie, St Paul de Vence, July 2008.

everyone and we got the scene in the bag on the next take.

We next moved to Venice, and to gain the necessary permissions for the silly things we needed to do, local government officials were befriended and Cubby arranged substantial donations to the 'Save Venice Fund'. It obviously did the trick, as we were allowed to film boats tearing up and down the canals, gunfire, explosions, a mock funeral, and even a hovercraft crossing St Mark's Square – not your typical day in Venice.

There was a quite embarrassing moment in the funeral sequence. It was felt that more wreaths and flowers were needed to dress the boat carrying our coffin – inside of which a real-live nasty was ready to pop out and throw a few knives at 007. Within a few minutes the prop boys had gathered up a number of wreaths. Where from? From outside a church quite near to St Mark's Square where a *real* funeral was taking place.

One evening I was volunteered to attend a function at a huge house just off the Grand Canal, in aid of the 'Save Venice' campaign. Ken Adam offered to come with me. We eventually found the bar and soon realized that we were the youngest people there. We'd just taken a sip of our drinks when a white-haired old lady, in a very strangulated upper-class English country voice, asked, 'What are you doing here in Venice?'

'We're making a film,' I said.

'Oh a fillum, eh? What sort of fillum?'

'It's James Bond, 007.'

'Ohhh! And what do *you* do?' she asked.

Ken was now snorting with laughter behind her back – I could have killed him.

'Well, I sort of try to play James Bond,' was my considered reply.

She paused, moved back a foot or two, looked me up and down, then announced, 'You'll be very good. I know Ian Fleming, you know.'

I wondered if she knew he'd been dead fifteen years?

We were joined in Venice by Bernard Lee and Geoffrey Keen. Dear Bernie was a lovely, lovely man but I'm afraid he became quite impossible after he'd had a drink. Now more so than ever. As he was usually in the same scenes as Bernie, Geoffrey became Bernie's keeper, in the sense of 'keeping Bernie off the sauce', while shooting. However, he wasn't always successful.

My hotel, the Gritti Palace, was just around the corner from one particular location we were shooting at and I could literally walk there in thirty seconds. I came down after breakfast and was told they weren't ready for me, so I popped back a short time later to be told, again, they were not ready. This went on for over an hour and I couldn't quite understand what the problem was. Lewis then admitted that props had lost a piece of equipment vital to the scene.

'Where is it?' I asked.

'Well, you know this is the high tide and equinox? They tied up the prop boat alongside the hotel and when the tide went down, one of the submerged wooden piles in the canal pushed up through the floor of the boat and sunk it.'

'Oh no!' I exclaimed.

'It's OK, Roger,' said Lewis.

'No!' I cried, 'you don't understand. The wonderful Ferragamo luggage that Bond has was on that boat, and I was promised it after filming!' Anyhow, divers were sent down to retrieve the prop. By the time it arrived on set, we had one rehearsal and a rather red-eyed Bernie just managed to hit his mark. Geoffrey had done his best to keep Bernie sober, and felt so relieved that he'd got him to set ready to film the sequence.

'OK,' said Lewis, 'let's go for a take. Everyone ready? Action!'

Just then, all we could hear was *Bo-ing, bo-ing, boi-ing* ... Masses of bells, all over Venice, rang simultaneously and showed no sign of being silenced.

'Will somebody stop those bells!' Lewis shouted.

I sidled up to Lewis. 'Lewis, the Pope has just died. He was Cardinal of Venice. You won't shut those bells up.'

'Ah, we'd better rest then,' he said. The upshot was, after all Geoffrey's efforts, Bernie dashed off to the bar, and we lost the light so definitely couldn't finish the scene. Fortunately, the next day we regrouped early to shoot it, before Bernie had a chance to have a drink.

You might recall the gondola, or Bondola, that 007 was issued with – it turned into a speedboat of sorts, and then into a hovercraft. It did actually work, but in its transformation from a water- to a land-going vehicle, it inflated in a non-uniform manner. That is to say, the left side inflated quicker than the right, and duly tipped me into the water.

'It worked earlier, guv,' said props.

Meanwhile, a sea of Nikon cameras appeared – tourists! The inflate-tip-soak routine was repeated another four times, much to the amusement of the tourists, to the frustration of the prop boys, and to the utter despair of the make-up and wardrobe department who, each time, had to dry me off, make-me-up and change my clothes.

I said we really had to get it on take six, as there were no more dry suits. Thankfully, we did and I was able to tear across St Mark's Square in my Ford-chassis mounted gondola. The only problem was that as we couldn't totally close the square off, we had to shoot around the tourists, but they had no way of knowing what was heading towards them. I therefore asked for a horn to be installed, as I didn't want to hit any of them – imagine the inconvenience.

For two days we shot in the cloisters of a monastery on the Lido Island. I was sitting in my canvas chair in between takes on the first morning when a chap dressed in jeans and T-shirt came over and asked if I'd like to have lunch with him. I stalled, before he said 'I'm Father so-and-so, forgive the informal look, but we only wear our cassocks for meals and prayers, and these are my working clothes.'

'Ah,' I said, 'the thing is we have United Artists executives here today, could we do it tomorrow?'

'Father Abbott did say he'd like you to join us today,' he replied.

I agreed I would, and as it turned out I had a most delicious lunch, sitting in the chair that was reserved for the Cardinal of Venice – the Pope – each Friday. Monks eat very well, you know, God's work obviously gives you an appetite. We sampled many delicious wines from each of the monk's home towns (and there were lots of monks!), and all the time throughout my long boozy lunch I could see assistant directors waving frantically at me from the wings. I figured I wasn't going to get a line out that afternoon, so might as well carry on and get totally plastered. All in the name of public relations, naturally.

I absolutely adore Venice and have returned many times since – once to shoot a commercial for Lark cigarettes for Japanese TV. As opposed as I am to smoking, I'm a bit of a ponce when it comes to earning a few quid – but I was never shown smoking a cigarette, if that mitigates me slightly?

I always make a point of visiting the Cipriani, on Torcello, for lunch when I'm there. It's the most magical place and they serve one of my favourite dishes, black squid. Then there's Harry's Bar which my friend Michael Winner rates as the best restaurant in the world.

On one trip I remember going to the Fenice Theatre with Gregory and Veronique Peck, Walter and Carol Matthau and Liza Minnelli, for a tribute evening to Ingrid Bergman. We spent a splendid night in Harry's

Bar, and after a rather large dinner took to the canals in two gondolas. We were joined by Jack Basehart, the son of actors Richard Basehart and Valentina Cortese, who had a fine baritone voice. At two o'clock in the morning it became quite a cacophony, and at one point Liza started singing 'Start spreading the news . . .' when a window opened and a chap shouted out, 'Shut-a up, who do you think-a you are? Liza Minnelli?'

If only he knew!

From Venice, we returned to Paris, and Charles De Gaulle airport where we were to board the Concorde for Rio. The main unit had left a day earlier and were setting up down there to film my arrival, or rather that of 007, on the Concorde.

Luisa and I, Lewis and Hylda Gilbert and Ken and Letitzia Adam all boarded the wonderful aircraft, only to be asked to disembark due to a mechanical error. We were offered lunch while we waited, but I didn't feel hungry, which was unlike me. Then I felt the onset of that awful pain I had so hoped to avoid ever experiencing again – a renal colic. Knowing I had barely minutes to seek help, I grabbed Lewis and told him to get me to the chemist in the airport. I was almost white by the time we arrived. I asked for morphine. The pharmacist refused, and said he couldn't give me anything without a prescription. He said I should go and see the airport doctor. The pain was now almost unbearable. I stumbled into the doctor's office, with my knees almost touching my chin. Above the pain, I couldn't even summon the energy to tell him what was wrong. The doctor never spoke a word. He reached down into a drawer, pulled out a hypodermic and gave me a huge shot of morphine. Lewis, on seeing the needle, went white himself and shuffled out sideways, saying something about how he'd let the ladies know. He left me!

The doctor called for an ambulance and I was whipped away to the American Hospital. Ken and Letitzia said they would stay to look after Luisa, and I entered a drug-filled daze for three days.

Feeling better, and no longer in pain, I declared myself fit enough to travel and we duly boarded the Concorde for Rio. We touched-down, got off and after a quick change, I got on again to be filmed coming down the steps as James Bond. All very heroic stuff.

At the welcome party that evening I was still taking muscle relaxants and painkillers, and mixing them with some booze was probably not a good idea. I suffered a colic attack, but eventually did pass the stone.

The next day, publicist Jerry Juroe had organized a press call and informed the assembled reporters that there was good news, 'Roger Moore has passed his kidney stone,' then added, 'but the bad news is that Lois Chiles has swallowed it!'

Speaking of the press, I remember on this film that a young reporter from *Newsweek* interviewed me.

'When are you going to make a serious movie?' she asked.

I replied that they were spending $35 million on the picture – 'that's pretty serious!'

Lewis did many interviews too, and his bugbear was always being referred to as a 'veteran film-maker'. The press do have some strange ideas, bless them.

Rio wasn't the easiest of locations. All necessary permissions were sought, palms were crossed with dollars, and all was agreed in advance of our arrival. But after we had touched down the powers that be – in a very Brazilian way – decided that they wanted more money. At that point we were shooting on the funicular, high above Rio and were threatened with not being able to complete the cable-car fight sequence, which was staged by Martin Grace and Richard Graydon. I don't envy stuntmen, I think they're all mad! High level conferences were called and Cubby used a combination of charm and firm words to resolve everything.

Back in Paris, we launched ourselves into space for the finale of the film on Ken Adam's terrific space-station sets.

The weightless scenes were not particularly easy, nor comfortable, to film. Lots of wires were attached to us, slow motion was required and the very worst moment was when I had to seduce Lois. Not literally, but in terms of the rig, you understand. We were suspended on a base – in mid-air – which was moulded to the shape of our bodies, and supported by fine wires. A sheet was strategically draped over us, as we were supposedly making love. I lay face-down with blood running to my nose and about to pour out of my eyes. Try it! It's the most unromantic thing you can do.

Lois had the line, 'Take me round the world one more time,' but I think the best line came from Desmond Llewelyn who, looking at some computer screen or other while everyone else in MI6 was watching Bond and Goodhead getting it on, determined that I was 'attempting re-entry'.

During my stay in Paris, at the Plaza Athénée, I bumped into a young director named Steven Spielberg. He was a huge Bond fan and said that he would love to direct one of the films. He'd recently had great success with *Jaws* and *Close Encounters* and was considered a very hot property. I was rather excited at this news and went looking for Cubby to tell him.

'Do you know how much of a percentage he'd want?' Cubby asked me, shaking his head.

It's always been policy that no Bond director ever got a slice of the box office profits. So, Spielberg went off and made *Indiana Jones* who I reckon to be a period James Bond!

Like David Niven, I'd grown to love the South of France and, in particular, the hilltop village of St Paul de Vence – dubbed 'Hollywood on the Hill' by Dirk Bogarde. My old friends Leslie and Evie Bricusse had a house there and allowed us to stay during the summer while we looked around for a plot of land to buy. We duly found one, and commissioned the building of what was to be our new French home, La Torretta. Many happy summers were spent there with the family and friends, with whom we enjoyed our favourite pastimes of playing tennis, eating delicious foods, drinking fine wines and swimming. It's not a bad life, is it?

While La Torretta was being built, we returned to life in Gstaad. However, with barely any time to ski, I was off to the airport again to board a plane to Galway for *North Sea Hijack*, which is also known as *ffolkes* in some countries.

Originally, the film was to be called *Esther, Ruth and Jennifer* but the people at Universal thought it sounded 'too biblical', though I've yet to come across Jennifer in the Bible. In fact I badgered the writer, Jack Davies – a neighbour of ours in the South of France – to let me play the lead. He first thought me unsuitable, but I succeeded in changing his mind. Thank goodness I did, as it was of the most enjoyable roles I've played. Rufus Excalibur ffolkes (with two small f's, if you please), was a misogynist of the highest degree, and a cat-lover. It was lovely being rude.

We were shooting at a castle in Galway, where Elliot Kastner, our producer, had succeeded in negotiating a better deal than he had been offered in Scotland, so now Galway was doubling for Scotland. It was fine in every aspect. The castle was a museum, with ladies spinning yarn as they did in the olden days. Much to the fury of these Irish ladies, however, we flew the British flag over the castle.

A terrific cast was assembled, including my old mucker Jack Watson. The set of a ship, the *Esther*, that featured in the film, was constructed on the edge of some rocks in Galway and Jack was playing the ship's captain. To set the backcloth, some villain had hijacked this ship, hit Captain Jack Watson over the head and planted charges under two drilling platforms in the North Sea. A helicopter, carrying ffolkes – who had been engaged by the government to foil this dastardly plot – and Admiral Sir Francis Brinsden (James Mason), was to land on the deck of the ship, in an attempt to do a deal. It was a night shoot, raining heavily – in fact Galway fire brigade were supplying the driving rain from their hoses on our behalf.

As the helicopter came in to land, Andrew McLaglen shouted over to Jack. 'Jack, you are still the captain of this boat and you hear the helicopter coming in, and you look down, see an admiral and another high-ranking naval officer and you come out to see what's going on.'

'Oh. Well I must have a plaster on my head.'

'Yeah,' said Andrew, 'that's a very good idea. Get a plaster on his head.'

Jack came out sporting his plaster, and called down to Andrew, 'Should I be holding a cup of cocoa?'

A second assistant director shouted out, 'A cup of bleeding cocoa, who do you think you are, bloody Cary Grant?'

Poor Jack.

When we finished this sequence it was around four in the morning, and we began making our way back to central Galway. I was fortunate in having my dear friend David Hedison on this picture with me, and it was David's birthday. We passed a pub that had all its lights on, and I suggested we might have something to warm us up, and celebrate David's birthday. We were in Ireland, remember, and the pub was doing a roaring trade at five o'clock in the morning. We had a few drinks and sloped back into the back of the car, when I realized I needed to relieve myself. I asked the driver to stop, stepped out and in the dark tripped over a rock, slashed my shin and became covered in blood. The next night I apologized to the driver for making a mess and for falling over, to which he said, in his broad Irish lilt, 'Oh, sir, but there was a very strong wind blowing.'

Anthony Perkins played the villain, Kramer, and was a great authority on film trivia. He knew every film, every film title and anything else you'd care to know. The other leading cast member was, of course, James Mason. As I said earlier, ffolkes is a cat lover and in every scene at the castle, there were cats everywhere. Admittedly, the cats had never been in a film before – or even been to drama school. They were completely unaware of things such as cameras or lights, and actors. In order to get all these cats together an advert was placed in the Galway press under the headline, 'James Bond Looks for Pussy Galore'. A lot of pussy duly arrived. Anyhow, to the point: James Mason was a well-known cat lover. In my first scene with him and the cats, Andrew McLaglen leaned over and whispered to me, 'I'm afraid we're going to have a little trouble with the pussies today, as the vet couldn't come by.'

'What does the vet do?' I asked, innocently.

'He comes by and gives them a little shot to calm them down; so today they're a little frisky.'

James heard just a little of this conversation. 'You're not doing anything to the pussies, are you, because I couldn't bear to be in a scene when something has been done to them.'

'No, James,' I lied convincingly. 'Nothing has been done to them. We're just talking about that now.'

'Oh, fine,' says James.

So, I was standing with James, waiting for Andy to call 'Action!' when one of our, what we call hairy-arsed sparks (electricians) calls out, 'Cats a bit frisky, ain't they? Why don't they give them another shot?'

'What? What was that?' said James.

'Oh! I've no idea,' I said quickly, and looked at Andy, who called 'Action!' and we did the scene. We were such bloody liars!

I had, in fact, known James Mason socially, for a number of years and while his screen persona was often quite hard and villainous, he was quite the opposite in real life. Along with being a cat lover, he devoted much of his free time to indoor games such as chess, backgammon and ninepin bowling. The fact I knew James probably made me even more nervous about working with him. He was married rather famously to actress Pamela Kellino, daughter of Maurice Ostrer who in the 1930s and 1940s controlled Gaumont British Studios in London. When she met James in 1939, Pamela was married to director Roy Kellino, whom she left for James. There was much speculation and amusement in Hollywood about Roy Kellino living in the guest house of the Mason's home. James would refer to Roy as, 'my ex-husband-in-law'.

Pamela was so funny. I once sat next to her at a tribute, where we were all deposited in rows of plastic chairs facing the speaker. Someone finished speaking and Pamela said, 'Let's give them a standing ovation.'

'But it was a terrible speech,' I replied.

'Well, we shall air our crotches!'

It was a relief to get off the cheap plastic seats.

I must preface this part of my reminiscences by advising you, dear reader, that I was called to LA. The reason? I was awarded the Golden Globe for being 'World Film Favourite' – they added '(male)' afterwards just to be sure!

What a great honour it was to be recognized by the distinguished group of critics who voted on such matters. You'll recall that, during my Warner days, I once gave an actor the advice that, as he'd never be a great actor, why didn't he go for the runner-up popularity prize? It was advice I myself obviously followed rather well!

I never lost touch with Lew Grade after finishing *The Persuaders* and I think, over the years, I must have appeared in just about every variety type show he produced, from *Sunday Night at the London Palladium*, to *Millicent Martin*, to *The Burt Bacharach Show* and one of the highlights of my career, *The Muppets*. *The Muppet Show* was recorded at ATV studio in Borehamwood, and Lew asked if I would guest-star in an episode.

It was funny to see that more work went on around my knees than anywhere else, as that is where all the Muppeteers sat, crouched and hidden with their hands up in the air, breathing life into puppets such as the wonderful Kermit the Frog and Miss Piggy.

I was rather excited about my appearance, and prepared all my best Muppet jokes for when I met the team:

'What's green and smells of pork?'

'*Kermit's finger.*'

'What's green and red and spins at 150 mph?'

'*Kermit in a dishwasher.*'

Let's just say they didn't appreciate them in the way I thought they might! They looked as me as though I was something the cat had brought in. I resisted making any more jokes. Instead, I suggested I might sing one of Leslie Bricusse's lyrics in a really funny sketch, *Talk to the Animals*. It was a bit of a send-up of me and my supposed suave image, and great fun to do.

I've not told anyone this before. I ask you to understand that I was in Borehamwood alone, away from my wife and family. I was feeling a little lonely and, well, it was inevitable that when she made her advance, I would crumble. I'm not proud of what happened.

It was a one-night thing. I never heard from her again – not a letter, text, email or even a phone call.

So much for Miss Piggy saying she loved me!

Euan Lloyd, producer on *The Wild Geese* gave me a call. He flew to America to discuss a picture with me and to tie up the deal. He wanted me to play one of the male leads in a World War II drama called *The Sea Wolves*. Gregory Peck had committed to playing the other lead, Lewis Pugh – an announcement which pleased me no end. During our script discussions Greg said to Euan, 'I think the third lead, Bill Grice could be the ideal part for our friend David Niven.' I don't think Euan had budgeted for the likes of Niv and he winced a little at the suggestion, but was so convinced that Niv would be perfect that he deferred his own fee in order to accommodate David's.

Our film became a gathering of old friends, including several survivors from *The Wild Geese*: Kenneth Griffith, Jack Watson and Patrick Allen to name but three. They were augmented by Patrick Macnee, whom I'd known from a hundred years before; Trevor Howard, who was a neighbour in St Paul; John Standing; Michael Medwin; Glyn Houston and Donald Huston. Donald, as you'll remember, was the one who got the part I tested for in *The Blue Lagoon* back in 1946. To be honest, those bronzed, topless parts terrified me. At one point in my career I was offered Tarzan but turned it down as I didn't think I could hold my stomach in for twenty-six weeks.

Although I'd known Greg Peck for many years, it was the first time we'd worked together and the first time he'd been exposed to my terrible practical jokes and schoolboy humour. He'd often shake his head at me in slight disappointment, 'Oh, Roger . . . Roger . . . Roger.'

The shoot was based in Goa, where our merry band of old-timers were brought in, undercover, to put out of action three German ships that had been transmitting to U-boats the locations of Allied ships from the neutral port. Britain could not officially be seen to do anything.

We all had bungalows in the grounds of a hotel called the Fort Aguada and each of those bungalows had a young man who served as a butler/waiter. Our particularly young man, who was about sixteen, told me that he had not seen his parents since he was seven or eight, as he had run away. I asked what had made him leave home at such a young age. He said he had been taken on a camping trip by an 'uncle' and some other boys into the hills – with their parents' full knowledge – where he was served a meal that tasted odd. The boy declined to eat it. Just as well, as the food had been drugged. During their drug-induced sleep, the other boys were taken away and had limbs amputated so they could become beggars for their families.

Our butler ran for his life, and never returned home again. His story horrified me. I never thought human beings could be so cruel to their fellow man. Alas, since joining UNICEF I have discovered that they can indeed be extremely cruel, particularly where children are concerned.

Just across from the hotel was fifteen miles of golden beach. At the far end was a hut called 'Paradise Pharmacy'. They sold everything from heroin to toothpaste over the counter. I gave it a wide berth after learning about the former! I've always said if I could own a shop it would be a pharmacy, but only dealing in prescription drugs. That's the hypochondriac in me, I guess.

There was a large hippy community in the area, mainly German, who would stride from one end of beach to the other – naked – to the excitement of some and disgust of others. I often wondered what they might buy at the pharmacy.

One of the joys of working on this beautiful location was to try to get back to the hotel before sunset each evening, and to the wonderful beach where I loved swimming with the sea snakes, or was it the naked Germans again?

Goa had been a Portuguese colony and is very different from the rest of India. There are many, many Catholic churches and all of the architecture is influenced by the Portuguese style, as is the food, I'm afraid to say. I'm not a huge fan of Portuguese cuisine and I've always found that when you visit an ex-colony you usually find the food pretty bad, as it's very much a hangover from those colonial times and nothing like their traditional home cooking.

With Christmas looming, Greg, Niv, Andy McLaglen and I enquired as to what the culinary arrangements might be, and suggested that we would like to organize a typically English Christmas dinner. As we only had Christmas Day off we wanted to make it a special one for the cast and crew – with turkey, stuffing, Christmas pudding and all the trimmings. Euan asked us not to put orders through to Fortnum & Mason's in London.

'Politics are very important here in Goa,' he said. Instead of bringing in supplies, he told us, he had been in touch with the Canadian Embassy, and the ambassador had assured him that Indian turkeys were very good. We were forced to capitulate. A dress rehearsal was called with a local chef who was going to serve us our Christmas lunch. The lumps of lard that he served as turkey were quite disgusting and totally undercooked. After a 'good old talking-to' he assured us all would be fine on the day and that we'd also have a lovely Christmas pudding.

The big day arrived, and so again did the lumps of undercooked lard. Never mind, we had pudding to follow! Yes, and that pudding was cut up in front of us and resembled slices of the great pyramids – there was nothing but sand and a few dried sultanas inside. The custard, meanwhile, had never seen an egg, or fresh milk for that matter. It was awful! To cap it all, a few weeks later the bill arrived . . . for an astronomical amount. We decided to appoint Greg – as he'd been president of the Motion Picture Academy and had held all sorts of high-ranking appointments – our negotiator. He managed to get about twenty-five per cent knocked off, but we still felt insulted.

During the production my family were with me, including seven-year-old Christian. One day the cast were all invited out for lunch, Euan said. It was 'political' that we went to this lady's house in Delhi. I've no idea who she was, but apparently one did not turn down an invitation from her. I said I'd rather have the day off and spend it with the family, to which Euan said, 'she's laid on a camel and an elephant for Christian.'

What could I say? Yes . . . what *could* I say?

Greg Peck was the only one who was smart enough to get out of it. The rest of us were bundled into Mercedes cars. I was curious as to why the trunks were all being filled with crates of beer. I later discovered that it was one of several days when they had a 'dry day' without alcohol.

We duly arrived at this mystery house, which looked like a mid-1930s Odeon cinema. A Sikh manservant opened the door, pointed and simply said, 'Down by the pool, down by the pool,' as if we were a travelling ENSA (Entertainments National Service Association) party. Trevor, Niv and the rest of us went down to the mosquito-infested pool where nothing was served until Euan had the beer brought out of the car. There was still no sign of a host or hostess.

Eventually a gentleman turned up, and told us that he was a very important high-ranking Indian Army Officer. I think he said his name was something like Raincoat, prompting me to call him Aquascutum thereafter (I later learned he was Field Marshal Sam Manekshaw, whose obituary I read in *The Times* only recently). An hour later, nothing was really happening apart from us all getting rather merry and schoolboyish. Then, at last, the hostess finally arrived and ushered us in for lunch. We were still only offered our own warm beer to drink, but the hostess managed to get herself vodka-tonics by holding her hand aloft behind her back, into which an ice-packed gimlet was duly pressed. She had no idea who any of us were. It was mutual.

When it was eventually time to go – after what seemed like a very long afternoon – David Niven said, 'Well, madam, we must leave.'

'Oh, aren't you staying for dinner?' she asked.

'No, madam,' replied Niven, and with a beatific smile added, 'and I hope I never see you again in my life.'

'Oh, thank you very much,' she said. Which goes to show, people never listen to what you say.

How Euan got us involved in that I do not know.

The film took its toll on David Niven. His eldest adopted daughter, Kristina, had been involved in a car accident in Switzerland and whenever he wasn't shooting he flew back to be with her. David loved to walk and in Goa he would often do so with Patrick Macnee, along the wonderful beach. A couple of years earlier during *Escape to Athena*, I'd marvel at David walking back to the hotel – sometimes many miles – after shooting. I never had the energy to do anything but slump into the back of a waiting car. But in Goa he confided in me that he had a problem, as he couldn't lift his heel off the ground. It was the beginning of motor neurone disease.

It then manifested itself in his speech patterns. During an interview on British TV, he began slurring his words. Viewers called in saying he was drunk and should be taken off air. He was not drunk. David Niven was far too professional to ever appear in a state of inebriation; the disease was attacking all of his functions, and it was the beginning of a couple of agonizing years for his family and friends. He made a few more films, but in his last couple he was dubbed. Fortunately, we were near neighbours in both Switzerland and France, and that meant we could see a great deal of each other.

I'd only had opportunity to work with Bryan Forbes once, and that's when he was head of EMI Films and offered me *The Man Who Haunted Himself*, but he'd never directed me in anything. That opportunity arose with the comedy *Sunday Lovers* in 1980. It was a film in four parts: four writers, four directors and four leads. As I'd been spending more and more time in America, I welcomed any opportunity to work in Europe; particularly with friends.

My segment was written by my mate Leslie Bricusse and co-starred another old mate, Denholm Elliot. Priscilla Barnes and Lynn Redgrave provided glamour and beauty. It was a story of a chauffeur (me), a sort of 'Alfie' character, who worked for an English businessman living in France. When the boss was away, the chauffeur slipped off his chauffeur's cap and slipped into the back seat – with the butler, Denholm Elliot, driving – and played a millionaire in search of a girlfriend at a hotel favoured by air hostesses. On the boss's next trip away, the butler and chauffeur swapped roles and it was the butler's turn to be driven around and take his pick of the cabin crew.

I thought it was a very funny story, stylishly directed, but I'm not sure the paying cinema-going audience agreed that the sum of its parts worked. My next comedy film was somewhat more successful, *The Cannonball Run*. I'd always resisted sending up my Bond image in other films, after all, I always treated it slightly tongue-in-cheek as it was, and accordingly always turned such 'spoof' projects down. I met with Hal Needham and Hal told me about his next film, and about the character who thought he was James Bond.

'No, I won't do that,' I told him. 'I won't send up Bond, but I'll tell you what I would do . . . I would send up Roger Moore.'

'Uh-huh?'

'I'd love to play someone who thought he was Roger Moore, particularly if I had a name like Seymour Goldfarb and a mother played by Molly Picon.'

'OK,' said Hal.

I thought that would be the last I heard, but no, a script arrived with the character Seymour Goldfarb Jr. written in: a would-be actor who thought he was Roger Moore. It was hilarious. What's more, Molly Picon had agreed to play Mrs Goldfarb.

It was the hugest fun to make and I got to drive the Aston Martin DB5, allegedly driven by Sean Connery in *Goldfinger*, and in each scene I had a different female passenger alongside me – very Bondian. Hal would have two or three cameras running at the same time, so as not to miss any of the comedy ad libs – and with the cast he had lined up, who could blame him: Burt Reynolds, Dom DeLuise, Dean Martin, Sammy Davis Jr., Jack Elam, Peter Fonda, Jackie Chan, Farrah Fawcett and so many more.

I loved the scene when I tackled a group of Hell's Angels saying, 'I must warn you, I am Roger Moore . . .' and duly got knocked out cold!

As we completed shooting, word reached us from the studio that a sequel was being considered. My final shot was standing with my back to camera, near the Aston, saying something or other. Hal asked – in post-production – if I would re-dub the line with, 'This has been such fun, I think I'll do it again next year.' However, when the sequel did come about – three years later – I didn't feel the 'I am Roger Moore' joke could really go any further. Added to that, the end of shooting of the first film was tarnished for me when my last on-screen female companion was seriously injured in a car crash when a stunt double was brought in to complete a driving sequence with her and lost control. It rather upset me to be honest.

One regret I did have about saying 'no', though, was when I later heard my friend Frank Sinatra was cast in the sequel. Had I agreed to do it, I could have worked with him, and that would have been a dream come true. Alas, it wasn't to be. Regrets, yes I've had a few, but then again, too few to mention . . .

As I've mentioned, after my third Bond film, my contract with Eon was renewed on a film-by-film basis. Cubby and I discussed most things in life, but we never discussed financial matters. In fact, the only time Cubby ever made reference to business with me was around the time of pre-production of *For Your Eyes Only*. We were playing backgammon and it was Cubby's turn to throw the dice. He picked them up, popped them in the cup and hesitated.

'You can go tell your agent to shit in his hat,' he said, rolling his dice.

He was referring to the ongoing negotiations on whether I would join the movie. I never got involved in that side of things. I left it to my agent who, of course, pushed for the best deal possible – he was on ten per cent of it, after all. I understand that Eon had been holding casting sessions where would-be James Bonds were tested with a view to replacing me. It didn't bother me, as I knew Cubby would never find anyone who would work as cheaply as I did. To be honest, I *did* want to do another film. This was all part of the bargaining ploy on Eon's side – let it be known they were testing others so I'd take the deal on the table for fear of losing the part. Fair enough, we all enjoy a game of poker. I'm quite principled about not undervaluing my worth. If someone wants me for a job then I believe they should pay me a fair fee. My agent usually haggles it up a bit, the producer usually haggles it down a bit and a happy middle ground is found. If someone undervalues me, I simply walk away. I have no qualms about it.

Meanwhile, my agent called to say a deal had been struck and I opened a new book for the backgammon games.

Our new director was to be John Glen with whom I had very happily worked on so many other films. I felt I knew John well enough to express a few concerns about the script. He paused, looked at me, and said it wasn't up for discussion, as he had orders from above 'not to change any dialogue'.

I guess when one of the writers is also one of the producers, orders like this have more sway over the director. However, having played Jimmy Bond for eight years in four films, I felt I knew the character – just as I'd known Simon Templar and Brett Sinclair – and knew that some of the lines were not ones Bond would say. But rather than argue in advance, I decided just to get on with it and address each issue as it arose.

People have since said to me that *For Your Eyes Only* is a much more 'serious' and 'realistic' Bond film. Looking at it again today, I guess there is a slightly different tone to it, with a little less humour and a little more grit; but I wasn't really conscious of it at the time. John felt this – his first – Bond should get back more to the spirit of the Ian Fleming novels and develop a harder edge. Times and situations had changed, and Bond needed to react accordingly.

All of the elements were there as far as I was concerned – action, adventure, gadgets, exotic locations and girls. The story centred on a top secret ATAC computer – a device used to order submarines to launch ballistic missiles. An undercover British trawler, armed with the device, had been sunk in the Greek islands when it accidentally hit an old World War II sea mine. Should anyone but the British recover it, we were told, our whole defence system could be rendered useless, as our own subs could be ordered to destroy one another. Bond to the rescue!

Many years earlier, when I was playing Simon Templar in fact, I was invited to the first night of *Fiddler on the Roof* in the West End, and was knocked out by Chaim Topol's performance. You can imagine my glee on hearing that Topol was joining the cast, along with Julian Glover, whom I'd also known for many years. Their characters were cleverly scripted as we were never quite sure which of them was the good guy and which was the bad guy working for the KGB; they kept us guessing.

Topol's character, Columbo, chewed pistachio nuts throughout the film and I drove our camera operator Alec Mills mad by throwing the shells under his camera. You'd hear them crunching as the camera moved, swiftly followed by choice words from Alec!

My leading lady was French actress Carole Bouquet. She was delightful and one of the most beautiful Bond girls ever. Sadly, she was attached to a troubled young man, a film producer who was also a heroin addict. I liked Carole and enjoyed working with her, especially in the wonderful car chase where we had to outrun some henchmen in a 2CV. Not a car of Bond's choice, by any means.

I felt terribly sad when Bernard Lee arrived on set. By this time Bernie was dying from stomach cancer and was very weak. He insisted on coming in and filming a sequence to see if he could carry it off, but I'm afraid he couldn't get through the scene. Reluctantly he bowed out of playing 'M', and died a short time afterwards, in January 1981. I have lost so many dear friends to this awful disease; I feel so angry with life at times.

Out of respect for his great contribution to the series, Cubby refused to re-cast and instead brought in James Villiers to play the Chief of Staff, Bill Tanner, changing the script to explain that, 'M is on leave'. Desmond Llewelyn, meanwhile, took on an extra scene as a Priest in a confessional, which was originally written for 'M'.

Looking back, we had a rather excellent cast on this film. Jill Bennett, an old RADA friend of mine, joined the cast as skating coach Jacoba Brink, to Lynn-Holly Johnson's skating protégée Bibi Dahl. I think Bond started feeling his age when sixteen-year-old Bibi tried to seduce him! Meanwhile, accompanying his wife Cassandra Harris – who played the ill-fated Countess Lisl – was a young Irish actor named Pierce Brosnan. Whatever happened to him? And Charles Dance played a henchman in the picture, which I believe was his first film, and a few years later went on to play Ian Fleming in a TV film about the author's life; with my daughter Deborah playing his secretary.

However, perhaps the most important henchman, as far as my portrayal of Bond is concerned, was Michael Gothard. He played Locque and his demise changed the way I played Bond. In the story, Locque had killed my ally, Ferrara, leaving his calling card of a pin badge in the shape of a white dove. Bond later chased Locque's car on foot, and after a few well-aimed shots from my faithful Walther PPK, forced the car off the road and into a cliff-top wall. There, delicately balanced on the edge of the cliff, Locque looked to Bond for help.

The script said Bond was to 'toss the dove pin at Locque and then kick the car hard to force it over the cliff'. I said that my Bond wouldn't

242 IT'S BOND AND BEYOND

do that. It would be far better, I reasoned, if in tossing the badge in I caused Locque to move, thus unsettling the balance of the car, and sending him over that way. John Glen was adamant that this man had killed my friend and now I should show my anger and a more ruthless side to my character. It didn't sit happily with me, so we compromised – I tossed the badge in and gave the car a not-so-hard kick to topple it.

Many critics and Bond-experts have highlighted that scene as being an important one in the evolution of Bond on film. So maybe I was wrong?

From these scenes in Corfu we moved on to Tofana, Cortina, and the snow. Or rather, lack of snow! We had a sequence in a town square where Carole Bouquet and I did battle with a couple of motorcycle-riding nasties. Despite the cold, the snow in the town had melted. Despair! Orders were given to send some trucks further up into the hills to load-up and bring the white stuff down to the square where it could be scattered. It just goes to show that you can never rely on the weather.

I was a pretty adept cross-country skier, but I didn't attempt any of the downhill activities – not that the insurance company would have allowed it – they were all handled by the most extraordinary skier and director, Willy Bogner. He filmed my close-ups with me strapped to a sled being pulled, while he skied backwards looking into his camera.

It was this experience that really made me think I should now tackle downhill skiing – aged fifty-four, and suffering from vertigo – so I bravely set about learning in my home town of Gstaad. My children, meanwhile, had school afternoons on the ski slopes and implored me not to venture to certain mountains where they'd be, as they were so ashamed of the fact that I kept falling over. It really is a wonder they grew up to be as tall as they did!

I persevered and became quite a reasonable downhill skier. I began enjoying it so much that I found myself saying to my agent what Niven used to say to his, 'I don't work January and February as that's when we have the snow. Then in the summer I like to go to the South of France to swim and sail.'

'That doesn't leave much time to work,' was his reply.

My vertigo wasn't helped by the fact that most of the climax-building third act of the movie was spent with Bond climbing a rock face. I overcame my fears with a valium and a large glass of beer. Rick Sylvester doubled for me, as he had done in the pre-title sequence on *The Spy Who*

Loved Me, for the various dangerous slips and falls on the location – for which I then filmed some close-ups back at Pinewood. I had to suffer a four-foot drop at one point. I don't know what happened to Rick Sylvester's testicles when he did the full twenty-foot drop, but for my little close-up part of it ... well let's just say they were so flat you could have slipped them into a child's money box.

There was lots of underwater work too, which I didn't mind, but Carole discovered she couldn't dive due to a sinus problem. This created some potential difficulties. However, the film-makers came up with an ingenious solution. Using doubles, the second unit filmed various sequences in the water tank at Pinewood, and then John and his first unit filmed Carole and me 'dry' on another stage. They used a wind machine to blow our hair, and turned the camera over at seventy-two or eighty-four frames per second, which, when it was played back at the regular speed of twenty-four frames per second, simulated underwater inertia. Derek Meddings then took the negative, and with the aid of some Alka Seltzers and airlines, produced a stream of bubbles that was imposed over the negative when we opened our mouths. All clever stuff.

Given that the film was shot in a more serious tone, it seemed rather unfitting that the finale featured a scene with the then prime minister, Margaret Thatcher, or rather impersonator Faith Brown. It was funny, but did it devalue the seriousness of the movie, I wonder? That and the damn talking parrot in the movie that was responsible for delivering a clue to Bond, 'ATAC to St Swithins'.

And *I'm* criticized for being too light as Bond!

My contention about my 'light' portrayal of Bond is this: how can he be a spy, yet walk into any bar in the world and have the bartender recognize him and serve him his favourite drink? Come on, it's all a big joke.

Sheena Easton was engaged to sing the title song, and when she arrived at Pinewood to meet the team, John and Maurice Binder were so taken by her beauty that they thought of including her in the opening titles. She became the first ever singer to feature and, as such, Cubby had the publicity people engage her for promotional interviews. I did a number of interviews in New York too, and was always asked if I'd be back for another film. I think I was generally diplomatically vague, as if I'd said yes and *For Your Eyes Only* was a flop they wouldn't want me back. However while taking part in an interview at NBC, the journalist asked that same question.

'Well,' I said, in an attempt to pretend I hadn't been asked it a hundred times before. 'At the end of every film they say "James Bond will return" but don't go as far as to say Roger Moore will!'

'Oh,' she said. 'And what will James Bond be returning in?'

'*Octopussy*,' I replied.

There was a pause. 'WHAT?' she asked.

'*Octopussy*,' I said again.

'You can't be serious!'

'What's wrong with *Octopussy*?' I asked. 'It's an Ian Fleming title.'

She seemed very embarrassed and really thought I was fooling around. Would I?!

The premiere of *For Your Eyes Only*, in aid of the Royal Association for Disability and Rehabilitation, was held at the Odeon Leicester Square and was attended by Princess Margaret and the newly engaged Prince Charles and Lady Diana Spencer. I believe it was their first film premiere and certainly one of their first public events since becoming engaged.

At Topol's bidding, Cubby invited Harry Saltzman to the premiere. The two former partners had not split on the most amicable of terms, but they greeted each other as old friends. I know Harry was touched to be there and to feel he was still a part of Bond. That was a very nice, and a very *big*, gesture from Cubby.

After *For Your Eyes Only* I spent some time in America, and then moved to Gstaad for Christmas and the ski season. It was wonderful to relax with the family. We then headed out to LA again, in time for the annual Oscars ceremony. One of the occupational hazards of being an actor is being invited to awards ceremonies, and I have been to more than I care to remember. By far the most glitzy were, and still are, the Oscars.

I've never been invited as a nominee or winner, I should add. Though I am open to that opportunity, producers please note. I have presented best actor and supporting actor, and in 1982 was asked to bestow the highest honour in the academy's gift, the Irving G. Thalberg Award, to Cubby Broccoli. There had been only twenty-six recipients of the award in its forty-four year history, and have been only nine more since 1982. The Bond films had often been thought overlooked by the academy, with only two wins in the series' history. This was the night the oversight was corrected. It meant a huge amount to Cubby, and consequently he and his wife Dana were terrified that I would make light of the situation and say something silly. Me?

In rehearsals, Dana sat right at the front of the auditorium to ensure I stuck to the script. I did indeed stick to the script, and Cubby accepted his award with great pride and modesty.

I think the funniest ever experience I had at the Oscars was a few years earlier, in 1974. David Niven was making his introduction to presenting an award, when a naked man streaked across the stage behind him. Without missing a beat, Niv deadpanned, 'The only laugh that man will ever get in his life is by stripping and showing his shortcomings.'

Conversely, the most awkward experience ever came in 1972 when I was co-presenting the best actor award with Liv Ullman. The winner was Marlon Brando for *The Godfather*. I was holding the statuette, and when Brando's name was called, a girl dressed in Indian clothes, whom I refer to as Mini Ha Ha, came up to the stage. She held her hand up, and thinking it was a greeting I did similar and said, 'How.'

'No,' she shouted, before launching in to an impassioned speech about Native American Indians. Brando had refused his Oscar and sent this girl, Sacheen Littlefeather (who was later discovered to be an actress), to state his reasons – which were based on his objections to the depiction of American Indians on film by Hollywood.

In all the confusion, nobody actually took the Oscar from me. I left the stage with it firmly clenched in my sweaty palm, before immediately being pushed back on stage with John Wayne, and all the other assembled presenters and winners, to sing, 'There's no business like show business'. Still humming the tune, I left the stage for the second time. Everyone was leaving and there was no one to take the Oscar from me. What else could I do but leave with it?

As I left the theatre, walking up the red carpet to my car, the crowd outside – who had no idea about what had gone on inside – saw me carrying the statuette.

'Hey, Rog, congratulations!' . . . 'Rog you've won the Oscar, great going!' . . . 'Good on you, Rog!' were the collective cries.

I was staying, with the family, at Cubby Broccoli's house – I'd just agreed to play Bond. There, I placed the Oscar on the hall table and went to bed. The next morning my daughter came in to the bedroom, 'Oh, Daddy! You won the Oscar!'

I explained that I hadn't and despite her suggestions I should keep it, I said I couldn't really.

'Well, why don't you give it to Michael?' Meaning Michael Caine. He had been nominated that night but didn't win. The thought crossed my mind to take it back to England – with it being such a famous Oscar, it would raise a small fortune in a raffle for a children's charity, I thought. Unfortunately, the academy had other ideas and soon sent armoured cars to collect their valued prize.

One year, when I wasn't attending, Greg Peck suggested we should go to watch the show on TV at his house. There were six of us: Greg and Veronique, Jimmy and Gloria Stewart, Luisa and myself. After drinks and snacks, we settled down to watch the show. Jimmy Stewart was rather hard of hearing at this time and would, in that unique voice of his, say, 'G-g-gloria, w-w-w-ho is that?' when some young person went up on stage.

'That's Raquel Welch, honey,' she'd say.

'O-o-h, yes.' Then he'd ask it again for the next award, and the next . . . and you know in my dotage I find myself saying the same thing, as I don't recognize half the people who win – or even present – the awards these days.

I received word that the next Bond film, the aforementioned *Octopussy*, was being put into pre-production in the late spring for a summer 1983 release. John Glen had signed to direct and I heard that they were, again, testing other potential Bonds. Maybe they'd heard I was ill?

TWELVE

A Farewell to Bond and Niv

You wanna be careful, mate, your lot are dropping like fucking flies'

A deal was struck and I agreed to star as Bond, for what I thought would be the last time. Six films and ten years was a good run. Other casting news filtered through. The delightful Maud Adams was back, this time as the female lead – Octopussy herself. My old friend Louis Jourdan was also announced as the villain, followed by Steven Berkoff – whom I'd worked with on *The Saint* – as a power-crazed Russian general. However, when it was announced that tennis ace Vijay Amritraj was going to be in the movie, the actor's union Equity threw up their arms and said 'no way'. As he wasn't a card-carrying actor, they argued, and as there were plenty of actors who could play the part, why should he be allowed to?

A compromise was reached when we said we'd split his part into two characters, meaning an Indian actor could be cast alongside him. That's how Albert Moses got the job of playing Sadruddin.

Of course, with Bernie Lee's death there was a gap in the family. I suggested my old mate Robert Brown might be the ideal 'M'. Bob came in, met John Glen and Cubby, and was offered the job.

Locations included Berlin – at Checkpoint Charlie – India, Oxford and London. The pre-title sequence was supposedly set in Cuba, but was actually filmed at Northolt Airport in West London. John Wood, my stand-in, was promoted: he played Toro, whom I was impersonating in order to access a military hangar and blow it up. As in my Saint days, they wheeled in a few palm trees and made Northolt look rather exotic!

In naturally exotic India, however, we first stayed in Udaipur – at the Palace in fact, part of which had been converted into a hotel. There was only one telephone there then and when Maud arrived, more often than not she'd hog it each night to talk to her boyfriend in America. I didn't know at the time but this boyfriend was actually Steven Zax – a doctor I'd met some years before – who went on to save my life some years later.

We had a local doctor assigned to the unit, and he took great pride in presenting his card to whomever he was administering aid. On it he'd written, 'Personal Physician to James Bond'. He'd acquired an ECG machine from somewhere and followed me around, asking if he could use it on me. To shake him off, I agreed, and he ran his test. He then said I should seek immediate cardiology assistance when I returned to Britain. By that time, however, Steven Zax had arrived and to my relief reassured me that everything was fine – the doctor seemingly did not know how to use his new toy.

Throughout *Octopussy*, Cubby was often diverted by his legal team and their ongoing battle with Kevin McClory. Kevin, with whom I had played backgammon, had befriended Ian Fleming in the late 1950s and together they worked on a screenplay – with Jack Whittingham – for what Fleming hoped would be the first in a series of Bond films. When financing failed to materialize, Fleming used the script as a basis for his book *Thunderball*. McClory sued and was awarded the film rights. He later collaborated with Cubby and Harry Saltzman, and *Thunderball*, released in 1965, became Sean Connery's fourth film in the franchise.

The upshot of all this was that Cubby had agreed with McClory that no remake of *Thunderball* would be permitted within ten years of the film's release. And, sure enough, from 1975 onwards McClory kept trying to mount a remake. Eventually, he involved Sean in writing a script and then persuaded him to return as Bond for one last time. Cubby fought it all the way, and when he heard McClory had raised the finance to shoot his remake at the same time that *Octopussy* was due to commence production, he became concerned. The press hailed it as 'Battle of the Bonds'.

Cubby launched several lawsuits, but eventually backed down after agreeing he would take a profit share in Connery's Bond, now entitled *Never Say Never Again*, and that the film's release would be delayed until three months after *Octopussy's* release.

There was no animosity between Sean and me. We didn't react to the press speculation that we had become competitors in the part. In fact we often had dinner together and compared notes about how much we'd each shot and how our respective producers were trying to kill us with all the action scenes they expected us to do. I never actually saw Sean's film. I'm told it did very well, but not quite as well as *Octopussy*!

Unfortunately there was a terrible accident during the filming. We were shooting at the Nene Valley Railway in Peterborough, and my stunt double, Martin Grace, was standing in for me in a sequence where Bond climbs on the outside of a moving train, and pulls himself along the side to the next carriage window. Martin rehearsed the scene and checked the line was clear of obstructions. Soon after starting out though, on the pre-checked length of track, a halt was called for some technical reason. A few minutes later they resumed. However, they didn't go back to the start of the track, which meant they overshot the piece of track that Martin had inspected. The train hurtled along and Martin hit a huge concrete post, side-on.

I can't imagine the number of bones it shattered, but Martin continued holding on to the side of the train for dear life as, had he let go, he would have fallen under the wheels. He was in hospital for months and when I visited him I really thought he'd never work again. But such was his determination to recover that he put himself through a strict fitness regime and was back to work incredibly quickly.

I remember when we were at Pinewood, filming my close-ups for the sequence, I had to hang on the underside of a coupling and behind me was a rolling drum simulating the moving track. It wasn't the most comfortable of mornings. King Constantine of Greece visited the set that day and watched me complete this scene. He came over afterwards.

'I don't know how much they pay you,' he said. 'But it's not enough.'

I didn't disagree.

The King was one of many, many visitors who used to come on set. There would generally be members of the press or other media there each day too. In between takes I'd go over to my canvas chair and have a chat with them, or perhaps a lunch in the Pinewood dining room. Often sponsors (such as Seiko, Bollinger and so on) would come down for the day and be entertained. So, from the moment I set foot on the stage until the moment I left, I was very much working. Occasionally I'd slip back to my dressing room for a snooze, or go off for a game of backgammon with any unsuspecting victim, if I knew I wouldn't be required for a while.

Octopussy was a joy to film. The cast were wonderful, as were the crew. It was a fitting farewell to my tenure; in my mind I was preparing to bid farewell to Bond.

Blake Edwards and his wife Julie Andrews were neighbours of ours in Gstaad. For some time Blake had spoken of making a new *Pink Panther* film. Sadly, Peter Sellers had died in 1980, but Blake felt he had enough material in the can from previous adventures to make a movie called *The Trail of the Pink Panther* in which, halfway through, Clouseau disappeared (i.e. when Blake had run out of material!). Blake wanted to shoot another movie alongside it, a sort of follow-on, where the search for Clouseau was continued – and he asked me to play Clouseau.

I'd known Peter Sellers, and his wives, for many years – going back to when he appeared on a variety bill with Squires, in fact. Both Peter's third wife, Miranda Quarry, and his widow, Lynne Frederick, had heard about Blake making another film and, not knowing that I was in discussions about the role, they each came to me, saying how upset they were and that Blake shouldn't do it. It was quite embarrassing.

In *The Curse of the Pink Panther*, Clouseau is tracked down, in the final reel, to some mountain-top lair guarded by Joanna Lumley. There, having stolen the Pink Panther diamond and with his head bandaged after the plastic surgery that gave him a new identity, I was to be revealed as the new look of post-surgery Clouseau.

Blake said they could film at Pinewood at the tail end of *Octopussy*. I figured it would be a five-day engagement, and as they were offering $100,000 a day, it seemed pretty attractive. However, the buggers worked me from morning till night and filmed it all in just one day. I enjoyed hamming it up and attempting the funny French accent. I don't think the film received much of a release though, and that was that.

Incidentally, my old friend David Niven appeared in both these new Panther films but the motor neurone disease was making him very ill. Nobody knew just how short a time he had left. During his final months, Niv bumped into an old acquaintance in Gstaad.

'How are you, David?' he asked.

'Afraid I have m-m-motor n-n-n-neurone,' he stuttered.

'Oh really, well I've just bought a new Mercedes,' replied his friend.

Niv laughed so much when he told me. He never did lose his sense of humour, even in his darkest hours.

Around seven o'clock on the morning of 29 July 1983, I received a call at my home in St Paul de Vence from David Bolton, a physiotherapist in Gstaad. He said he was waiting for the doctor to come over and sign Niv's death certificate. I asked who was there at the house. He said only Fiona, Niv's youngest adopted daughter. He thought there was a nephew of Hjordis, Niv's wife, around but couldn't be sure.

Hjordis was in the South of France. I said I'd go over straight away. I couldn't bear the thought of my dear friend being alone, even in death.

Deborah and I drove from St Paul to Château d'Oex in five and a half hours, a record time. I prepared the best I could for Hjordis's arrival, and that of Niv's other children, who were flying in from around the world. I liaised with everyone who needed to know. By this time, the press were starting to congregate, and in order to spare her the ordeal of having to face the TV cameras I suggested that the car take Hjordis around to the back of the house, where they could drive straight into the underground garage.

As she arrived, I went down to the garage. She, meanwhile, decided to enter by the front door. The car door opened and, with her wig slipping and an empty bottle of vodka rolling around her feet, Hjordis looked up at me and slurred, 'Here for the press, are you?'

I could hear myself saying, 'Just get in the fucking house.'

It had been no secret that she and David didn't get on in later life. In fact, she was a bitch to him. I say that with all the conviction it deserves, as David was a dear, dear friend of mine who did nothing but try to please her. In return, Hjordis showed him nothing but disdain. Hjordis never wanted or encouraged people to visit David at the house in the South of France when he became ill. She seemed to resent his friends and the affection they held for him.

Earlier that summer, Bryan Forbes was staying with me in St Paul. Bryan knew Niv of old and he desperately wanted to visit, but Hjordis made it clear he was not welcome.

'We'll just drive over, knock on the door and go in,' I suggested.

And that's what we did. I can't recall if Hjordis said anything, nor would I have taken any notice. By this time Niv had a terrible speech problem as the disease had affected his vocal chords. He would speak slowly and very hesitantly. Bryan, bless his heart, like all Englishmen speaking to foreigners or people with an impediment, spoke very loudly.

'D-d-on't shout, I am not deaf,' said Niv.

Bryan considered himself chastised, though as we were leaving he looked at the swimming pool and – gesturing the breaststroke with his arms – said, 'Getting plenty of swimming in are you, David?'

Niv began to laugh. The laughter turned into tears. He enjoyed our visit. We were both feeling as emotional as he was.

I visited him two weeks before he died. The only exercise he could manage was swimming with the aid of an inflatable ring. He had a very attentive Irish nurse who would patiently help him. As he came in from the pool that day, Hjordis appeared.

His voice was weak, but Niv proudly said, 'I swam two lengths.'

In a cutting voice she replied, 'Aren't we a clever boy?'

Niv then asked to go back to his home in Switzerland. I arranged for a friend, Gunther Sachs, who had a pool in Gstaad to allow him to swim there but he became too weak to do so.

In the midst of this sadness, I must tell you that David's home in the South of France, on Cap Ferrat, was one of the most beautiful you can imagine. When he bought it he had a swimming pool built. He gave the builders his desired measurements and disappeared off to shoot a movie. However, not realizing that French builders work in metres, he had given his measurements in feet … so the planned fifteen foot deep pool was actually fifteen *metres* deep and hence Niv had the deepest pool in Europe!

The day of Niv's death, Deborah and I left the house knowing we'd done all we could. Writer and journalist Alistair Cameron Forbes, who had lived in the town for many years and befriended Niv, helped Fiona with all the funeral arrangements in the absence of her siblings. I stayed clear because of my deep dislike of Hjordis.

Prince Rainier, God bless him, came up from Monaco for the funeral and ensured Hjordis made it to the church. I'm not sure she'd have got there otherwise in her drunken state. Audrey Hepburn also attended.

David's body remains in the churchyard at Château d'Oex. I would sometimes drive past, but felt unable to stop. His death had such an effect on me that I could not watch any of his films for many, many years.

I must just add a story here that Geoffrey Keen told me. He played the minister in most of my Bond films, and said after the *Octopussy* premiere he was at home and called a plumber to do some work. This was around the time when a number of notable actors had died, including Ralph Richardson, David Niven and James Mason. The plumber did his job and then, looking around, spotted some theatrical mementos.

'Are you an actor?' he enquired.

'Yes, I am,' said Geoffrey.

'You wanna be careful, mate, your lot are dropping like fucking flies.'

Indeed.

A short time after Bryan Forbes resigned as head of production at EMI, the studio and library was purchased by Cannon Films, which was run by the

Go-Go Brothers – as they were called – Menahem Golan and Yoram Globus. They approached me and said they'd like to make a movie with me.

Since first reading Sidney Sheldon's book *The Naked Face* I had felt it would lend itself to a very good film. I suggested this was a project I'd like to do with them. They asked if I had any ideas about who should direct. I said Bryan Forbes, as I knew he'd do a terrific job but could also adapt the script. When you're working with a director who is also the writer, it saves on so many arguments and discussions between these creative partners. A deal was struck.

The Go-Go Brothers loved to announce projects at the Cannes Film Festival with a big splash, and part of my deal was that I, Bryan and Sidney Sheldon should join them there for a press conference. We arrived at a room with about sixty journalists packed in, and sat on a podium. Menahem stood up.

'We have the writer of writers, Sidney Sheldon . . .' he said. 'We have the director of directors, Bryan Forbes . . . and we have the actor of actors, Roger Moore . . .'

It was quite hysterical.

The story was, in my opinion, a very clever one. I played Dr Judd Stevens, a psychiatrist who specialized in listening to other people's problems. One day, a woman walked into his office just to talk. Unfortunately, she was the wife of the local Mafia boss and was thought to be telling all the family's secrets to Dr Stevens. Consequently, he had to die. The tag line was 'What he doesn't know can get him killed.'

Production was based in Chicago and was a total delight. We – Luisa and I – lived there for two months and grew to love the city. Other casting was soon confirmed: Anne Archer, Elliott Gould, Art Carney, Rod Steiger and my old pal David Hedison. The only fly in the ointment was the production manager, who seemed intent on cutting every corner possible. He slashed the twelve-week schedule to eight, and put a lot of pressure on Bryan to work faster, which I felt was very unfair given the sterling results we were producing.

When Rod Steiger turned up on the first day the make-up man came in to my trailer.

'I can't make him up!' he said. 'He needs a surgeon to touch him up! He has running wounds – he's just had a face-lift.'

He had literally come straight from the clinic!

I had known Rod quite well from my gambling days, when he, Telly

Savalas and I used to meet up. He was known as a bit of a 'scenery chewer' and hadn't changed. Poor Bryan had quite a job trying to keep control of his performance.

One morning I received a phone call from home. My blood ran cold. It was to say that my mother had suffered a heart attack and was in Colchester hospital, which was the nearest infirmary to my parent's retirement home in Frinton-on-Sea. Mum was stable, but they were obviously very concerned for her.

I went to see Bryan. Without hesitation he said I must get on the next plane home. I knew the producers and the production manager were breathing down his neck, but he said that'd he'd shoot around me and I shouldn't worry. British Airways were fantastic and transferred me across airports in order to get to London in the fastest time, and then up to Colchester. I know my father feared the worst. But, fortunately, by the time I arrived, Mum was off the danger list. I stayed for a couple of days, and when my mother's condition improved further, I felt able to return to the set. Meanwhile, the producers had not taken kindly to Bryan's actions.

'How can you release the lead actor? We have a film to make.'

'But his mother is dying,' reasoned Bryan, to deaf ears.

I looked at them in a different light from then on.

The film turned out well, but sadly gained an '18' certificate and came in for a little criticism in that the hero – that's me – got beaten up at the end. It limited the number of cinemas prepared to take it and consequently the release felt a little half-hearted.

I was asked to record the talking book which was to tie in with the release of the movie. That's the sort of work I love – sitting in a small recording theatre, reading the lines without the aid of make-up and going home at night to cash the cheque. I was either rather good, or too cheap, as I was asked to read a couple more talking books; one being a Jack Higgins story.

Being the consummate ponce, I never read the book before I turned up at the studio. They weren't paying me enough for that. I always remember Robert Morley saying to a producer, 'If you want me to do the film it's £500,000 but if you want me to read the script first it'll be £750,000.'

Anyhow, it started off in Germany, in Hitler's bunker, and I loved playing all the parts *wiz my German accent* but then noticed a character from Northern Ireland appeared. I'm not bad at the old Belfast accent, and can keep it up for a short while, so launched into it. Only then did I realize the rest of the book was set in Northern Ireland! Now I always glance through voice-over scripts.

It was about this time, during a lovely family Christmas at our home in LA, that I started to reflect on my life to date. I'd had a pretty good run in movies, but it seemed as though I was now working to maintain the lifestyle of owning three houses. I loved them all, but I couldn't see myself maintaining this pace forever. Perhaps my mother's illness made me sit up and take stock?

However, I didn't have much time to think about it all too much as the phone rang. It was Cubby. He wanted me to play Bond again in *A View to a Kill*.

At fifty-seven, I felt a little long in the tooth, a bit like Gary Cooper in *Love in the Afternoon*, but I was pretty fit and still able to remember lines. A rather nice deal was agreed with my agent, and once again I slipped into the tuxedo – admittedly it had been let-out a bit since my first film – to play Jimmy Bond one last time.

John Glen was back for his third successive film as director, as were most of the familiar crew – Peter Lamont as production designer, Alan Hume as director of photography, 'Randy' June Randall as continuity girl, Alec Mills as camera operator and so forth. It was very much like reuniting with the family.

Christopher Walken was cast as the villain Zorin: the first Oscar-winning actor to date to play in an 007 adventure. Chris had a bit of a reputation for being 'difficult'. I never found him so. He liked to be prepared and he liked everyone else to be prepared – so maybe he didn't suffer fools and they branded him difficult? Tanya Roberts was cast as Stacey Sutton. Then there was singer Grace Jones, who was cast as May-Day. I've always said if you've nothing nice to say about someone, then you should say nothing. So I'll say nothing.

One thing that drove me mad was that between every take my leading ladies would both rush over to their handbags and pull out a lipstick and mirror. Time after time they did it, and time after time we had to wait for them. So, when they weren't looking, I reached into their bags, pulled out the lipstick and mirrors and hid them. A few minutes later they returned, reached in and pulled out a lipstick and mirror . . . They apparently had half a dozen of each – just in case! They worried more about appearance than performance.

Meanwhile, another old chum, Patrick Macnee, called.

'I've heard there could be a part in the film that would suit me,' he said.

'Yes,' I agreed, 'and Cubby has already said he's going to approach you.'

How great minds think alike.

During pre-production, word reached us that tragedy had struck at Pinewood. The 007 Stage had burnt down. How can a steel structure of such size burn down, you ask? Well, it actually melted in the intense heat caused by the explosion of a gas canister during a lunch break on Ridley Scott's film, *Legend*. Within a couple of hours, the once-grand structure that dominated the Pinewood skyline was a moulded mound of smouldering black metal.

Shooting was weeks away and the huge mineshaft sequence was due to be housed on that stage. Cubby surveyed the site, turned to our production designer Peter Lamont and asked, 'How long to rebuild?'

Peter said something like sixteen weeks. Without flinching, Cubby said to go ahead. Peter did some fairly quick recalculations, meanwhile, and split his planned setup into segments that could be housed on other stages, until the new 007 Stage was in operation where the finale flooding of the mine could take place.

In recognition of Cubby's significant contribution to the British film industry, and in particular Pinewood, the new stage was named in his honour – The Albert R. Broccoli 007 Stage.

You can imagine how my stomach turned on 30 July 2006, when I heard that Cubby's famous stage was on fire again. The second incarnation of the huge structure, like its predecessor, all but melted in the heat during a fire that started while the *Casino Royale* sets were being dismantled. However, within six months, a new 007 Stage, the third one, was ready for business.

There were some terrific locations in *A View to a Kill*, including Iceland, Royal Ascot, Paris, Chantilly and San Francisco. We had some terrific location difficulties too, especially at the Eiffel Tower. The script called for Grace Jones's character, May-Day, to leap off the Eiffel Tower, open a parachute and land on a boat on the Seine. However, while the authorities had given permission for takeoff, we didn't have permission to land. Apparently, the river came under the remit of another authority and only on the day of the shoot was permission forthcoming. What fun.

Grace Jones had her boyfriend with her, Dolph Lundgren. He was a very nice guy and John Glen cast him in a small role – his first film role in fact – and had lots of stills taken of Dolph for publicity. Next thing we knew, he'd been cast in *Rocky IV*. He never asked for me though.

Barbara Broccoli, Cubby's daughter, joined the production team for her second film after *Octopussy*, as an assistant director. One of her duties was to collect Grace every morning, as our star wasn't a fan of early starts. Barbara ensured Grace arrived on time each day, and I believe she developed much of her diplomatic charm on those early-morning car journeys.

Barbara always seemed destined to follow in her father's footsteps. She studied film at university and joined the family firm in positions of increasing importance on each film she worked on. She now co-produces the Bonds. I love Barbara: she is a wonderfully warm character and a deeply caring one, much like her father. She is now steering the franchise into new, exciting territory with Daniel Craig. I know Cubby would be very proud of her, and her stepbrother, Michael Wilson.

I'm afraid my diplomatic charm was stretched to the limit with Grace. Every day in her dressing room – which was adjacent to mine – she played very loud music. I was not a fan of heavy metal, so didn't quite appreciate it vibrating through the walls whenever I returned to my room. An afternoon nap was well and truly out of the question. I did ask Grace to turn it down several times, to no avail. One day I snapped. I marched into her room, pulled the plug out and then went back to my room, picked up a chair and flung it at the wall. The dent is still there.

And so to bed. Yes, my love scene with Grace. I slipped between the sheets, followed by her and her rather large black dildo. I'm glad she thought it was funny.

Barbara told me that the producers had a meeting with the Mayor of San Francisco, Diane Feinstein, to explain what they'd like to do – set City Hall on fire, drive a fire engine through the streets, car chases and so on – but got a rather cold reception to it all.

'Who's playing Bond?' ask Mayor Feinstein.

'Roger Moore,' replied Cubby.

'Ah, I like him!' All permissions were immediately forthcoming. I became very good friends with Diane and her husband Dick, and they were absolutely wonderful in facilitating our every request. We literally got away with anything we wanted. I was like a boy in a toyshop when I drove a fire engine around the streets! Nowadays, Diane is Senior Senator in California – I have friends in influential places.

The day before our night shoot at City Hall, where we set a section of the roof on fire (in the film, not for real!), Diane sent a memo instructing everyone to close their windows before they left the office. Someone didn't read the memo, and one particular office was soaked when they opened it the next morning – the smoke that came in through the windows had triggered the fire sprinkler system.

The Golden Gate Bridge shots, by the way, were filmed with doubles – Martin Grace being mine – and then part of the bridge was recreated at Pinewood for close-ups with me, Chris Walken and Tanya Roberts. I wasn't paid enough to climb the real one. Peter Lamont did a fantastic job in his production design, despite the big setback of the fire at the 007 Stage. I so admire Peter and his colleagues – Syd Cain, Peter Murton and dear Ken Adam. They make the impossible possible and the unbelievable believable.

The film premiered in May 1985 in San Francisco, as a small token of our thanks for the city's help and co-operation, swiftly followed by Prince Charles and Princess Diana honouring us with their presence at the film's Royal Premiere in London.

I knew this would be my last Bond film.

Cubby and I sat down one day afterwards, reflecting on its success and mutually agreed that it was time for a younger actor to pick up the Walther PPK. There was no drama, no tears (aside from my agent) and there was certainly no big discussion where Cubby told me that it was all over and I had to accept it. That however was not the case as reported in his autobiography, completed by Donald Zec after Cubby's death.

I felt very hurt by the claims that Cubby had to effectively tell *me* it was all over, and how I wouldn't accept it at first. Then he claimed I had started making 'neurotic demands' and had become difficult in so much as I refused to attend charity events or make personal appearances. I always did what I was asked – after all I had a percentage of the film – but obviously there is a limit to what one can do, and occasionally it was not always possible to do *everything*. I've always prided myself on being an unspoilt, down-to-earth individual. I like the finer things in life, sure, but I've never forgotten my roots and how lucky I have been.

THIRTEEN

Taking Stock

'I'd gladly piss in your ear any time'

A huge blow hit me after completing my last Bond film – the death of my mother. She died on 22 June 1985, and I was not there. I received a call in France to say she was in hospital but it turned out to be too late for me to be able to get there for her. It was her heart. I was devastated, as was my poor father. I spent a week with Dad afterwards. His world had been shattered and he was totally lost.

Even before I left, I became rather irked to see the spinsters and widows of Frinton descending upon the house and my helpless father, who could not so much as boil an egg.

'Can we help you, George?' ...'Anything we can do, George?' ...'Can we cook you a meal, George?'

All perfectly innocent and neighbourly, you might think, but they were in fact jostling for the position they saw as vacant, as became evident very shortly afterwards when one particular lady moved in and then persuaded my father to marry her in order that she could care for him and keep it 'all above board'. He maintained he was very happy.

After I achieved some success in life, I regularly put aside a little money for my mother to help her eke out her pension. When her will was read, we discovered that she had saved all of my contributions and never spent a penny. She left it all to be split between my children.

My father continued to enjoy his retirement years in Frinton, and whiled away many hours in his workshop at the end of his garden – turning wood and making models, and suchlike. I know my mother often said to him, 'Come on, George, let's go for a walk.'

'Lil,' he'd reply, 'I've done enough walking in my life. Now the end of the garden is as far as I go.'

I think it was around summer 1994 when Dad called me in France.

'That was very bad last night, son.'

'What was, Dad?'

'There was a talk show on television and they said that you were on the way, but you never got there. That's not good, son. Not good at all.'

'What show, Dad?' I asked.

'It was on the BBC,' he replied.

Anyway, I called Doris Spriggs – my wonderful assistant who looked after us all for twenty-nine years, before Gareth Owen took over on Doris's retirement in 2002 – and she said she'd find out. It turned out to be the Alan Partridge *Knowing Me, Knowing You* chat show with Steve Coogan, a spoof show and the joke in that episode was that I didn't get to the studio in time for the recording. Doris got me a tape. It was a hysterically funny send-up. I called Dad to explain.

'Yes, but it's still bad, son, still bad,' he said.

As he got older, Dad's hearing started to deteriorate. I bought him various hearing aids, but like most deaf people who wear them he would boom his voice when talking. I was in a restaurant in Frinton with him, and told him a funny story. He shouted, 'YES, SON, VERY GOOD. THAT REMINDS ME OF ANOTHER ONE.'

'Sssh, Dad! You're shouting,' I said.

He then started telling me a joke, gradually increasing the volume. 'There's this woman WHO IS HAVING IT OFF . . .'

'Dad! Crank it down a few decibels.'

I visited him and his new wife as often as I could; however in late 1997 his health took a turn for the worse. This time I was there, with my darling Kristina. I don't know how I would have coped without her love and support.

After my mother's death I decided it was time to take a little time off and re-evaluate things. I'd always enjoyed producing and working behind the scenes, and when the opportunity arose to option James Clavell's *Tai-Pan,* I jumped at it. John Guillermin signed on as director, and together we began developing the script, raising the finance, talking about casting – it even reached the point where sets were being built in Croatia. Then the finance fell through. The whole production collapsed. Months if not years of my life had been wasted. I didn't get a penny in fees either. Dino De Laurentiis later bought up what assets were left in the company and went on to make the film a few years later.

I remained good friends with Cubby in my post-Bond years, and often visited and dined with him and Dana. I occasionally met Timothy Dalton at their house after he took over the role, though I had never seen either of Timothy's films. I'm often asked if I have seen subsequent 007 adventures, and what I thought of subsequent Bond actors. I always replied the same – 'Sorry I've not seen them'. That saves lying!

Well, I did, in fact, see a reel of Pierce's first one, *Goldeneye*, when I visited my son Christian at Leavesden Studios, where he was working with the location department. I had a chat with Pierce, saw a few old friends and then they ran some of the film for me. I thought he looked terrific. In 2002 I was invited to the Royal Premiere of Pierce's fourth film *Die Another Day*, which also marked the fortieth anniversary of the first Bond adventure. My daughter Deborah had a small part in the film as a BA air hostess, so that was a double excuse to attend. George Lazenby, Timothy and Pierce were also present and we were all presented to Her Majesty the Queen. I was somewhat disappointed that Kristina was not allowed to be in the line-up with me and that we former Bonds were kept down the line from the current one. How soon they forget.

In the early 1990s, after winning a long-drawn-out legal battle with MGM – whose new management were selling off the TV rights at knockdown prices – Cubby began suffering ill health. It was a very sad time. He was too ill to produce *Goldeneye* and handed the reins over to Michael and Barbara. A short time after the film's release, he sadly died. I lost a great friend and mentor that day.

There was a memorial service at The Odeon, Leicester Square shortly afterwards, presented by Iain Johnston. It was a huge event for a huge man – in heart that is.

Many people spoke including me, Timothy Dalton and the newly announced 007, Pierce Brosnan. Sadly, neither George Lazenby nor Sean Connery attended, though I know Sean had not remained on the best of terms with Cubby.

Some years previously, I attempted to bring Sean and Cubby together at a party at our house in LA, hoping they might settle their differences. I should add that, a couple of weeks prior to the party, there had been a newspaper article in which Sean was quoted as saying that if Cubby Broccoli's brain was on fire, he 'wouldn't piss in his ear to put it out'.

At the party, I sat them both down with a drink. I heard Cubby – who was very much a gentleman Don Corleone – say, 'Sean, did you really say if my brains were on fire you wouldn't piss in my ear? I found that very upsetting.'

'Cubby,' replied Sean, 'I'd gladly piss in your ear any time.'

End of conversation!

In 1986, entirely unworthy and unjustified, the Friars Club of New York announced that I was to be their 'Man of the Year'. It was an honour previously bestowed on the likes of Dean Martin, Frank Sinatra, Sammy Davis Jr. and Tom Jones. It was a great honour but I did wonder if they'd asked me by mistake, instead of Sean Connery. Fortunately, they did mean it for me and I was thrilled to be 'roasted' by so many of my distinguished friends and peers. I myself attended a number of such 'roasts' to other people. One of the most memorable for me was also in 1986 in LA.

Milton Berle, the famous actor who was perhaps best known as Uncle Miltie, asked what I was doing one evening.

'Nothing in particular,' I replied.

'Right. You're coming with me,' he said. 'We have a roast to Arnold Schwarzenegger.'

This was long before Arnie was governor, of course, and just after he had married Maria Shriver. I guess he was then best known for having starred in *The Terminator*. I later worked with Maria Shriver by the way, and for ABC Television, at the time of the Duke of York's wedding to Sarah Ferguson in 1988. Maria was a presenter for the network and I was a sort of witness and commentator on the wedding with her: presumably they thought me the expert on British royalty? I've known a few queens in my time, so maybe I was.

As far as I recall, at the roast it was a completely male audience, apart from – at the rear of the Beverly Hilton ballroom – what looked like a solitary female silhouette. All of the invited speakers were huge hulking musclemen, who spouted choice comments such as, 'Wouldn't half like to give Maria one, Arnie'. All in good spirits, of course.

Milton Berle took to the stage. Ah, I thought, the voice of respectability.

His opening line was, 'Arnold Schwarzenegger's schlong is so big, it has its own heart and lungs.'

Oh-oh, I thought, I'm not in for a Salvation Army evening here.

Back in Gstaad for the winter, I received a call from *The Dame Edna Show* asking if I would appear. I love Barry Humphries, so readily agreed. But I laid down a proviso – I wanted to appear with Les Patterson, his bad-taste *alter* alter ego, whom I absolutely adore. They agreed, but said as it took many hours in make-up, Barry proposed we film a Les Patterson sequence on the Friday and then the next day pick it up for the Dame Edna chat sequence.

Denis Healey was also going to be on the show – he didn't know that he was the man who effectively made me leave the UK – and they asked if we'd both maybe do a song-and-dance routine with Les Patterson?

OK, why not? It was to be 'You've Either Got or You Haven't Got Style'.

I arrived at the studio and met Les Patterson for the first time, resplendent in his food-stained suit.

''Ere, Rog, watch this. You've gotta make it shine, old mate,' he said. With that he started 'adjusting' something in his trouser leg.

'Props, bring me the Vaseline, will you?' He then popped some Vaseline on the trousers over the false penis strapped to his leg, polished it up and said, 'There you are, it stands out from the front.'

It was so damn funny.

We did the song and dance, received a huge applause and resumed the next night for the chat with Dame Edna.

The next thing I knew, Andrew Lloyd Webber called me. He'd seen the show and wanted to discuss me starring in his next West End production, *Aspects of Love*. I was flattered and, cutting a long story short, agreed. I was introduced to Ian Adam to begin my vocal training and joined the lovely cast, headed by a young Michael Ball. It was like being in rep again. Trevor Nunn was directing and Gillian Lynn choreographing. Over many weeks rehearsals we came up with a pretty good show.

Advance bookings were looking good and we were all feeling excited. However, as the opening drew nearer I started having nightmares about forgetting my lines and having to sing without a note to key me in. I guess it had been many years since I was last on stage, so I was feeling a bit jittery. At the final run-through I sensed Andrew wasn't happy. Maybe he was having those same nightmares about me? The long and short of it was that Andrew didn't want me to open in the show.

I was very, very disappointed and felt very sad. It was agreed that I would issue a statement saying I was backing out. I guess I can still say that

I appeared in a hit West End musical . . . through all of its rehearsals!

I'd known Willy Bogner for a number of years, going back to *The Spy Who Loved Me*. He called me up one day and said he had an idea for a film, could we talk? Sure, I said. At that point, my older son, Geoffrey, was thinking about pursuing a career in acting and Willy knew this. 'There'd be a part for Geoffrey, too,' he said.

The film was *Fire, Ice and Dynamite* and we shot in St Moritz. It was the first film I'd shot in five years and news reports said I had come out of retirement to make it. See! If you're not on the screen on a regular basis, they assume you've retired. I had, of course, been busy with *Tai-Pan*, but nobody realized that.

Geoffrey had rather a good part in this film, and after it he went on to make a couple of other movies in America. But he soon rather wisely decided it wasn't going to be an actor's life for him. He turned his attentions to the music industry instead, and was signed by EMI. His first (and only) record did quite well, before he began pursuing another interest. In 1999, Geoffrey and a friend joined forces to open a restaurant in London's Mayfair, and soon turned it into one of the must-eat places in town. I don't think the film bug ever quite left Geoffrey though, and he grew restless to return to the business – though on the other side of the camera. In 2004 he and Bill Macdonald acquired the film rights to *The Saint* and set about bringing Simon Templar to the small screen once again. Not an easy process, but hopefully it will prove a rewarding one for him.

Immediately after working with Geoffrey on *Fire, Ice and Dynamite* I found myself working with my daughter Deborah, who had just graduated from LAMDA, on a Michael Winner film. My old mate Leslie Bricusse co-wrote a script called *Train of Events* which was a vehicle (forgive the pun) for Michael Caine and myself. When Michael Winner joined as producer and director, things started moving, with the new title *Bullseye!*. Michael Winner was hilarious to work with, but he screams at everyone on set. He never did with me or Caine, as the truth is he's scared of us. I used to warn people joining us for a day or two what they were in for but would reassure them we were all on the same side, and told them to watch for the red rings forming in his cheeks, which were the sign to take cover!

Winner was a great *bon viveur*, and would send location scouts out to find the best restaurants in the area, and we'd always dine supremely.

Food has always been a passion of his, as it is mine – see the waistline for proof.

The original story was set on the Orient Express travelling through Europe, but by the time the financiers had cut every corner possible we ended up on a train going through the Scottish highlands.

There was one actress on the film though who had, shall we say, ideas above her station and asked why she was not getting as many close-ups as Michael and I. This served to anger Mr Winner, who shouted, 'Close-ups? Close-ups! Another word out of you and I'll cut you out of this film like butter – no one will know you were there!'

Bullseye! wasn't a bad film. It wasn't the greatest either, but it did have funny moments. It was huge fun to make and I think my 'blind piano tuner' was one of the funniest things I've done on film. I love dressing up.

From the Scottish highlands, I moved immediately to New England in the United States to start another film, my third in two years. *Breakfast in Bed*, as it was known then, became *Bed and Breakfast* and was a rather intriguing project featuring three generations of women in one family and how their lives changed when a stranger was quite literally washed up on shore. Colleen Dewhurst, Talia Shire and Nina Siemaszko were those three generations. I was lured in as an executive producer, which is a ploy producers often use to get actors to work on a film for a scaled-down fee in exchange for a piece of said film. I should have held out for a better fee and given up the credit. So much for profit participation.

One of the nicer things that happened was when the commander of the Maine State Police Force came down to visit the set and he made me a captain in the police. I have the badge to prove it, along with the power of arrest! Be warned.

When one of the world's great beauties calls you and asks if you would like to go somewhere with her, what do you say? No? Of course not! You ask where and when?

The 'where' was Amsterdam, and the 'when' was the first week in May 1991. The 'beauty' was my near neighbour in Switzerland, Audrey Hepburn. She told me that I was going to co-host, with her, the Danny Kaye International Children's Awards for UNICEF. I said that I would arrive there on the morning of the transmission but she said no – I had to be there the day before in order to take part in a press conference.

'Dear Audrey, I don't know enough about UNICEF to handle a press conference; I know that UNICEF looks after children . . .'

'Roger,' she interjected. 'The press will not want to talk about UNICEF, they will want to talk about movies!'

She was right, they did – but she wouldn't let them. Every question that was asked, Audrey turned around to the problems facing the world's children. She was so passionate and so eloquent on the subject that I felt compelled to learn more about the workings of this organization – the United Nations International Children's Emergency Fund. The next day, we taped the show with some quite extraordinarily talented children. Though I had known her for many years, I couldn't quite believe that I was on stage co-starring with the wonderful Audrey Hepburn. I felt so honoured and humbled that she had asked me – little realizing that she was, in fact, intent on recruiting me.

Audrey's amazing passion for UNICEF, I discovered, stemmed mainly from her being helped as a child by the organization at the end of the Second World War.

'They came to the aid of thousands of children like myself, famished victims of five years of German occupation in Holland,' she said. 'We were reduced to near total poverty as is the developing world today – for it is poverty that is at the root of all their suffering – the not having, not having the means to help themselves. And that is what UNICEF is all about – helping people to help themselves – giving them the aid to develop, thereby allowing them to become self-reliant and live with dignity.'

On our way back to Switzerland, Audrey suggested that I might like to attend a seminar taking place in Geneva shortly afterwards. There, I would have the opportunity of hearing and meeting some other goodwill ambassadors, and hearing UNICEF staff discuss the various programmes and goals. I accepted without hesitation.

In Geneva, I talked with Sir Peter Ustinov – a longtime ambassador – and lunched with one of the great minds of UNICEF, the executive director, James Grant. I knew that I wanted to help, but how? Mr Grant asked me to meet him in New York, at UNICEF headquarters to discuss just how I could help. Audrey smiled, knowing her job was done. I attended a meeting in New York with Jim Grant, along with an old friend and his wife, Harry and Julie Belafonte. They too spoke with the same passion as Peter and Audrey did. I didn't need any further persuading, I wanted to get involved and help.

I said I needed to learn first-hand about the problems, and about how

UNICEF was trying to solve them – I needed to go into the field. Jim agreed, but said first it was necessary for me to sign a contract and become an accredited representative of the organization. By signing on the dotted line, I became a 'UNICEF Special Representative'. I discovered it came with an added bonus – a salary!

Yes, I am paid the princely sum of one US dollar per year. It has to do with something about the legality of a contract and insurance. The main advantage of it is that I don't have to give my agent ten per cent. It is the smallest pay packet that has ever come my way: mind you, there are those who believe that it would have been a more than adequate fee for some of my movies.

I decided to take my son Christian with me on my first field trip; he had just turned eighteen and I thought that apart from improving his knowledge of geography it would allow him to see what privileged lives we led in the developed world. Our first stop was Guatemala.

The regional director for UNICEF in Central America, Per Engebak, met us at the airport and Horst Cerni, who was on the UNICEF staff in New York, accompanied us for the whole of my inaugural trip. Horst was of German origin, while Per was a Norwegian. I was beginning to see how the 'UN' in 'UNICEF' really did mean United Nations. Having dropped our bags at the hotel, Per took us to the UNICEF office to meet the local committee staff and for me to be briefed as to what I would be doing and what was expected of me. I was told we would be visiting daycare centres where working mothers left their babies, after which we would travel north of Guatemala City to Santabal, in the El Quiche area, where we would inaugurate a new water system.

There were also a few trips planned to communities where the ladies of the villages made a living from weaving cloth, which is sold in major US cities – the profits coming back to those communes to fund a village store that stocks basic food items such as flour, meal, sugar and oil. We would then, I was told, return to Guatemala City where I would be shown Mezquital, the slum area. I would visit many of these favelas over the coming years in my trips around the world, and it never becomes any easier to see people living in absolute and total poverty.

The Guatemalan leg of my first field trip concluded with an audience at the Presidential Palace; followed by a fund-raising dinner at which I would have to make my very first UNICEF speech, but thankfully the area office said they'd provide some notes for me to refer to.

It was to be quite an itinerary.

The first day and the care centre at La Verbana witnessed my first ever contact with children as a UNICEF representative. I wished that I could have been as funny as Danny Kaye was when he met with children. I felt awkward in being asked to pose for pictures with them all as I thought that the press would see it as 'just another film actor trying to get his picture in the papers'. It took many years of travelling and posing before I started to feel comfortable.

The journey to the El Quiche area seemed to take forever – it was a very long, bumpy and hot drive, interrupted by frequent stops to allow me to find a convenience. My film-location experiences of alien food always taught me to find the quickest route to the 'thunder box' – or else. That first journey introduced me to the most primitive of 'glory holes', inhabited in the main by giant spiders, mosquitoes and snakes.

On our arrival in the village of Santabal, we were greeted by what appeared to me to be literally hundreds of singing and dancing children. That day was a 'feast day'; with music, dancing and then the turning on of the first tap that anybody in that remote part of the world had ever seen. UNICEF had supplied the know-how and the equipment, and the villagers supplied the labour in laying PVC tubing from a water source high in the surrounding jungle-covered hills. To the cheers of the children and exploding firecrackers, I turned the tap and clean, drinkable water came spurting out. I felt as if I'd performed some sort of miracle. I was filled with gratitude to Audrey for her introduction to this new world.

Later that day we were entertained by a group of health workers who performed a playlet illustrating, to stress the importance of sanitation, the washing of hands which – with their standpipe in the centre of the village – was not now such a problem. What happened if food was prepared with unclean hands was demonstrated hilariously, with much rolling around on the floor, clutching of guts and screams of pain. It was a very effective message.

The next day we visited another village where I learned about 'ORT' or 'OR' salts. 'Oral Rehydration Therapy' is, as it suggests, a treatment for the rehydration of diarrhoea-related dehydration. In other words, it gets fluids back into the system. It is commonly used around the world, but in the Third World it has saved millions of children from the effects of diarrhoea – which is still one of the leading causes of death. UNICEF distributes these salts in the developing world.

One fascinating fact is that practically anywhere one goes in the world you can always find a bottle of Coca-Cola or Pepsi. It's true! UNICEF was quick to recognize this, and the distributors of these drinks have been tremendously helpful in getting OR salts to the remotest corners of the world. James Grant, the then executive director of UNICEF never went anywhere without a packet in his pocket. He would produce it at the drop of a hat, and wade into a lecture on this simple, effective treatment, '*And* it only costs twenty-five cents a pack. Save the life of a child for just a quarter!' was his war cry. He would often add, 'It is also a good cheap cure for a hangover!'

The next day, back in Guatemala City, we visited the slum area. For the first time in my life I witnessed poverty such as I had never seen before, nor thought possible. It was a heart-wrenching experience.

There was no running water, no sanitation and no electricity. Entire families existed – I don't think you could call it living – in shacks built from waste materials.

There I learned of how UNICEF endeavours to immunize all the children against diseases such as measles, polio, tetanus, tuberculosis, diphtheria and whooping cough: these run rife in shanty towns and areas of extreme poverty. Not one child can afford to be missed, as failure to give at least one dose of the measles vaccine, for example, would result in an estimated 1.6 million deaths worldwide.

The following day, after very little sleep thinking about the sights I had witnessed in the slums, we paid an official visit to president Jorge Serrano Elías. So how does middle-aged English actor get into a president's palace, you ask? The answer, I believe, is that every president has a wife and in many cases children who have seen 007 movies or *The Saint*, and they're curious to meet you, if only to see whether you actually have your own teeth! That's when 'celebrity' proves useful – if I can use what celebrity I have to open doors for the betterment of children's lives, then my career in movies has produced an added bonus.

The meeting started off very formally, with the president sitting stage-centre, officials sitting to his left and the guests facing him on the right. Then we all posed for photographs with, of course, the shaking of hands. We thanked the president for his country's co-operation with UNICEF, and congratulated him on the daycare centres that we had seen. At that point, the First Lady arrived. Magda Bianchi de Serrano was very charming and attractive and we spoke about her involvement with mothers and children and their issues. I've discovered that president's and prime minister's wives – in practically every country – are very active in supporting their country's impoverished children.

After tea, we said our farewells to the president and acknowledged the fact that we would be seeing his wife again that evening for the fund-raising dinner, where I was very relieved to put my first UNICEF speech to bed, so to speak. I then put myself to bed, ready for an early rise to fly to El Salvador.

Arriving at El Salvador's international airport reminded us that this was not exactly a peaceful paradise. Military uniforms were very much in evidence and the drive to the capital, San Salvador, was made under military escort. On the outskirts of the city stood a large circular hotel, its walls pitted with bullet and shell holes; there wasn't one unbroken window in sight. Apparently, this hotel changed hands between the rebel and government forces with great frequency.

Before I left for the trip, a friend of mine, Emilio Azcarraga, who owned Televisa, the biggest Latin television company in Latin America, suggested that I really shouldn't go, but if I insisted, he would be happy to supply some bodyguards to look after me. I declined the offer, saying that I was sure UNICEF would do that job, but then in El Salvador I started to wonder whether I should call him – and take him up on his offer after all!

Our first field trip was to the Travesia region, to visit the Hospital Benjamin Bloom. Many years before, while living in England, I had visited the burns unit at East Grinstead Hospital and I shall never forget the smell of burnt flesh. As we got out of the car that morning in San Salvador I recognized that very same awful smell, and tried to prepare myself for what we were about to see.

There was no way I could have prepared myself, though, for seeing a young girl with various limbs missing, propped up on the bed and moaning to herself, an eerie sound that seemed to come from the bottom of her soul. She was not conscious of our presence and the doctor said that they didn't know what she was thinking, or if she was even conscious of her surroundings. She was possibly still in shock over the landmine that had killed her sister and destroyed most of her young body with its blast.

We then moved into a sluice room that was being prepared for an expected cholera epidemic, where everything could be hosed away down the slightly sloping floor into the central drain. Hearing how many human lives were expected to end in this room was a spine-chilling experience. I felt sick, but dared not show it.

Next came the children's ward.

We received a heart-warming greeting from the unfortunate youngsters – a few were standing, others were in wheelchairs and some were still in their beds, with those in front holding a banner with a greeting to 'El Santo'. I did not feel like a Saint that day. It was shocking to see so many young children with horrendous burns, and a number with a limb missing; yet all with smiles on their little faces.

One of the doctors took me to a cot on the far side of the ward where there was a baby of indeterminate months, desperately, heart-breakingly thin, with pallid skin and an IVF drip attached to her arm, which itself was barely as thick as the tubing. The doctor, speaking in Spanish, said that this sad little creature might last another twenty-four hours; she was suffering from acute anaemia and had been brought in a few days before, 'If only we had received her sooner,' Per chokingly translated.

Christian remained at my side, regarding the horror in silence.

We were relieved to step out into the heavy Salvadorian air, with eyes blinking from holding back tears. I felt so full of rage against my fellow man. How could man be so inhumane that he could create weapons that tear children's bodies and lives apart? I was angry at the ignorance of parents who had not had the sense to seek help for their offspring before they could waste away with malnutrition. Most of all, I think my fury was aimed at the governments that allowed the manufacture of mines designed to resemble a child's toy, and at the governments that would not create a worldwide ban on such things.

With heavy hearts, we got back into our cars and drove on to visit a house that, with UNICEF financial and practical support, supplied a day refuge for street boys; a shelter where they could wash and maybe get a change of clothing, try their hands at making wooden boxes that would carry shoe cleaning equipment in order for them to earn money instead of having to beg or steal. They were also given a midday meal. Sadly, however, they could not be accommodated overnight and the majority slept rough on the streets.

We shared a meal with them, and Per translated the answers they gave to our questions on the circumstances that had brought them to the centre: parents dead; parental abuse; no food at home for them and their maybe ten brothers or sisters. Too-large families, I'm sad to say, are the common problem factor in the poorest areas of the world.

We visited a number of similar establishments and that evening as we made our way back to the hotel, Per apologized to me. He said that he had a problem translating some things because he was choked up. He thought that after the number of years he had been with UNICEF, he would have become hard-headed.

'That's the answer, Per,' I said. 'When you become hard-headed you get out!' I have now been working with UNICEF for nineteen years and have yet to meet a hard-headed person within the organization.

That evening, I was a guest at another fund-raising dinner. After the First Lady, President Alfredo Cristiani's wife, Margarita, had spoken, I told the other dinner guests of our reactions to what we had witnessed that day. I said we would leave their country with the fervent prayer that they would soon find peace, and that all Salvadorian children would live in good health and with the prospect of bright futures.

We retired to the bar for a nightcap with President and Señora Cristiani. The señora did not stay long but the president was quite willing to continue bending elbows with us. He was a tall, handsome, distinguished gentleman who wanted to talk about his days in the USA studying at Georgetown University. I looked at my watch and saw that we would only have about four hours' sleep before our early departure.

'Señor Presidente,' I said, throwing protocol to the wind. 'I'm afraid we have to make our excuses, as we fly in the morning to Honduras.'

He asked at what time. I told him we had to be up at half past four in order to get to the airport for the seven o'clock flight – it was a long drive to the airport. He gazed down at me with a smile and beckoned to an aide. He said something in Spanish, the aide clicked his heels and left. The president then told us that there would be two helicopters in front of the hotel at six in the morning.

'Gracias, and the next drink's on me, Señor Presidente!'

Surprisingly bright and fresh at six o'clock the next morning, we were in front of the hotel, and there, as promised, were our helicopters. I flew with Christian and Per in the president's own helicopter, while poor Horst Cerni had to settle for the other one, which had no doors and was obviously only ever used for low-level flying and combat. We did fly low, as it happens, and very fast due to hostile forces in the woods below. Have no fear James Bond is here!

The airport in Tegicugalpa may have changed since we landed there in 1991, but I know that our landing was quite scary. It seemed to me that the airstrip finished up a few feet from the base of a cliff that rose up into the sky. The pilot's foot was on the brakes before we'd even touched down, or maybe I was still recovering from the late drinks with the president and the helicopter ride?

As ever, the routine was to drop the bags at the hotel, meet the local UNICEF staff and pay a visit to a facility, this time run by Save the Children. Here, street children had classes in reading and writing and rudimentary mathematics. I sat with a maths class and found that they were all smarter than me! Again, as in San Salvador, the boys also had the opportunity to do woodwork and, of course, they were all making shoe-boxes.

The next morning we had an early meeting with President Rafael Leonardo Callejas Romero, which went very well and in discussing our itinerary – which was to finish with a day off – he suggested that we might like to visit Roatan, located near the largest barrier reef in the Caribbean Sea (the second largest worldwide after Australia's Great Barrier Reef). Furthermore, he said, he would take us there in his own plane. Things were really looking up and I could see that being a UNICEF representative had other benefits too.

Having bid our farewells to the luxury of the presidential offices, we next headed for the region of San Pedra Sula, where we were to again spend some time in the slum area. I was horrified to see that the walls of one of the shacks were made from X-ray plates; one can only imagine the exposure the inhabitants had to radiation. As with other favelas, there was no running water and certainly no sanitation. Gutters dug in the earth carried rotting vegetation amid the human effluence, and any scraps were being picked over by rabid-looking dogs. UNICEF and other NGOs had a presence in the area, with health clinics taking care of children and young pregnant mothers, who were old before their time. It was very difficult to leave this minor hell knowing that we were going back to our comfortable hotel. We sat silent in our people carrier on the journey home

The following day we were escorted to the airport and boarded the presidential plane: but this was no Air Force One, or even Two, Three, or Four. It was a twelve-seater, with twin propellers that spluttered into life as soon as the president was aboard. As we headed westward, the president explained how he had acquired his aircraft: it had strayed into Honduran airspace while ferrying drugs to the USA, and the air force had been scrambled to persuade the intruder to land immediately – with further encouragement added by a few bursts of gunfire, which actually put a couple of holes in one wing. We were assured that the repairs were perfect and that the plane was as good as new.

That evening, we were invited to dine aboard a presidential yacht – not our flying host's but that of his neighbour, President Jorge Serrano Elias from Guatemala. He had sailed to Roatan for discussions with President Callejas Romero. The yacht, like the plane that brought us there, had also been confiscated from drug runners. Whether it had bullet holes in the hull I do not know. In any event, we had a delicious dinner, retired to our hotel, and left the presidents to get on with their affairs of state. The next day we left for Costa Rica, and then on to Dallas where we had a three-hour stopover, during which a press conference had been arranged. I spoke to the assembled media and the UNICEF Dallas staff of the things I had seen. I spoke of my reasons for having become a volunteer and for making this first field trip. I think I said that all I had previously known about the situation in the developing world had come from the fact sheets that were compiled by UNICEF and the World Health Organization. They were merely statistics, however, the one that stood out and shook me most was that 40,000 children die every day from preventable causes. But I wanted to put faces to those numbers and, as horrifying as it was, I succeeded. I saw hundreds and thousands of faces: sad ones, smiling ones, hungry ones and expectant ones. All those faces made me determined to continue in my capacity as a representative of the world's leading organization that cares for children and mothers.

Returning from Dallas to my summer home in St Paul de Vence in the South of France, I realized how damned fortunate we who lived in Europe are – especially those, like myself, who because of a little luck are able to lead such privileged lives. We have ample food on the table, a roof over our heads, excellent health services and most basic of all, with just a twist of the wrist, a limitless supply of safe drinking water. I can now never leave the tap running while cleaning my teeth; if I ever forget, I see the dozens of taps that I have been able to turn on in the developing world, and see the women and children without that most basic facility, who have to carry water, sometimes for many, many miles.

It was without the slightest hesitation that I answered the next request from UNICEF – to visit Brazil. It was not, of course, my first trip to the world's fifth largest – and fifth most populous – country. I had seen Brazil through the eyes of the privileged tourist when making *Moonraker* twelve years earlier.

This trip took me to the capital city of Brasilia, a very impressive architecturally modern city. UNESCO has named it as a World Heritage Site, and quite rightly so in my opinion. Our UNICEF group was shown into the elegant office of the president, Fernando Collor de Mello. A tall, handsome man, who was sincerely interested in UNICEF's work in his country. His support of our programmes for lay midwives and measles eradication was to win Brazil a UNO award for its 'best in South America vaccination programme' and, in 1993, a year after he had left office, Collor's project Minha Gente (My People) also won a UNO award.

We were invited to participate in a discussion called 'The Rights of a Child' – which set the minimum standards a child should expect from their home country in terms of education, healthcare and so forth – along with a large number of parliamentarians, which for us was most encouraging.

From Brasilia we moved to Fortelaza in the state of Ceara – possibly an even lovelier spot than Rio – where I heard one of the ugliest tales ever.

A nun was brought to the UNICEF office to meet me. Accompanied by two children, a boy and a girl of approximately twelve years, the nun started to relate the children's stories. They were street children. The girl was the eldest of a family of ten brothers and sisters. She chose not to live at home because of the abuse she was threatened with by her stepfather. At the age of eight she had been raped by a policeman. Policemen in Brazil have name-tags on their uniforms. This brave officer of the law had removed his; he did not want his victim to identify him. Being a policeman's son I felt even more outraged. She now lived on the streets and went with men, or rather scum, to earn a little money. After four years of abuse I asked what she had to show for it? What did she do with the money she earned? She took it and gave it to her mother, she said.

'Do you ever keep any for yourself?' I asked.

'Yes, to buy food. I want to save some to buy a bicycle too.'

I found it very difficult to continue, but I had to listen to the boy's story. It was more or less the same pattern, he too was forced to go with men. These 'men' were usually foreigners, and mainly European paedophiles. To this day I am filled with disgust at the behaviour of my fellow man.

The Sister of Mercy then made an extraordinarily profound remark. 'It is strange,' she said. 'The world is talking about saving the rainforests, but what is the use of a forest without children to live and play in it?'

I gave the UNICEF rep two hundred dollars and asked him to make sure that the girl got her bicycle. But I know I can't go round the world buying bicycles.

Rio, with its Copacabana Beach, its Sugar Loaf Mountain, and its luxury hotels, was just a façade behind which there was – is – great poverty; poverty that I had not seen when filming there. This time I met many of the street children, who were despised by the local shopkeepers and, I learned, sometimes became victims of the death squads who were allegedly employed to discourage youngsters from harassing shop customers.

UNICEF had just appointed a very talented Brazilian entertainer, Renato Aragão, as a national goodwill ambassador. Together we were able to exchange some useful ideas and opinions relating to the welfare of children. We visited one home run by the local Catholic Church, which supplied shelter for street boys. The one thing that struck me was how these youngsters wanted to be close to visitors, not to pick their pockets but to be close and feel some affection. All through Central America and Brazil I had been impressed by the aid given by the Catholic Church to youngsters and their support with health clinics. However, in view of overpopulation and now the worldwide HIV/AIDS epidemic, I could not agree with their attitude to contraceptives.

In Brazil, it seems almost every child is born with a football at the end of his or her foot. It's played everywhere – from stadiums to dusty fields and paved areas. In a favela I saw it played with a ball made of paper and string. I went along to see Renato and a group of his show-business friends play one of their regular games against a team of professionals, to raise money for children's projects. Worldwide, football has an important part to play in the welfare of children: for the young themselves it is great exercise, it teaches team spirit and it is also used in the rehabilitation of children in unfortunate circumstances, particularly those who, even as young as eight, have been taken and trained by militias to maim and kill. Over the years I have participated in the opening of dozens of makeshift pitches that townships in the developing world have put aside for their young.

UNICEF has had a long affiliation with soccer around the world and uses games to create UNICEF awareness as well as raise funds. In 2002 I was at Old Trafford to watch Manchester United play Boca Juniors from the Argentine. The event was in aid of UNICEF, of course, and, together with Sir Alex Ferguson, both teams and I came out of the tunnel on to the great pitch. It was an extraordinary sight for me to see sixty thousand spectators gathered in the stands. I was handed a microphone and I announced that Sir Alex had become a goodwill ambassador. I presented him with my own UNICEF badge and then told the crowd that I had participated in many 'stadium waves' but had never seen one from a player's point of view, so would they start a wave for Sir Alex? What a sight! What a roar!

Manchester United has done so much for children around the world. The UK National Committee for UNICEF works in partnership with the club and has raised millions – the match that I attended raised an incredible half a million pounds.

I started off 1992 in my capacity as a UNICEF representative with fund-raising trips to Kiel and Berlin – where I had not been since shooting *Octopussy* in 1983. The wall was still standing back then, however in 1992 I was able to cross freely into East Berlin without passing through Checkpoint Charlie.

I have written about ORT and the twenty-five cent packets James Grant always had in his pocket. Now, my UNICEF colleague from New York, Horst Cerni, and I were in East Berlin visiting the factory that made and packaged the salts. In less than a year I had seen them in use, being distributed and now manufactured. On top of that I was now helping raise the money to purchase them. You might say I had gone the full circle.

I travelled with Audrey Hepburn to the Hague for my second Danny Kaye International Children's Awards. Greg and Veronique Peck came along, as well as Joel Grey, Ben Vereen and Natalie Cole. There may well have been more stars there, but after Greg and Audrey, the stars of *Roman Holiday*, who needs to mention more?

I should have been more aware of Audrey's failing health at that time. She was always desperately thin, but now she seemed to be very fragile too, and had to sit down quite often. What Audrey knew herself about her deteriorating condition, I do not know. I do know, however, that it did not deter her from continuing her field trips – the following month she went to Somalia and Kenya.

Audrey's dedication to UNICEF was recognized and rewarded when, in December 1992, she received the Medal of Freedom, the highest civilian award in the USA. By this time she was at home in Tolochenaz. Her remaining pleasure was being able to walk in her garden but that was taken away from her, as her dear friend from UNICEF, Christa Roth, told me, by the paparazzi and their long-distance lenses revealing her wasting disease. When she saw those images she knew that she could never walk in that garden again. How cruel and irresponsible the press were to publish such photographs.

On 20 January 1993 the world's children lost their greatest champion. Audrey died at home, with her sons Sean and Luca and her devoted companion Robert Wolders with her to the end. Four days later, on 24 January, Audrey was laid to rest in the village cemetery in Tolochenaz, in the canton of Vaud. The burial followed a service in the village church, at which Sean Ferrer read Audrey's favourite poem 'Time Tested Beauty Tips', by Sam Levenson.

Alain Delon was at the funeral, he said that he had never met Audrey but thought that she was such a lovely human being he felt compelled to come from Paris just to pay his respects. Mel Ferrer, Audrey's first husband, was there too and it saddened me greatly to learn of his death earlier this year.

Audrey had asked me to do a couple of things for her, as she didn't feel she'd be able. I had no idea that it would be death that would stop her. One was to receive a doctorate and the other to receive the World Service Medal from the Kiwanis. The latter event took place in Nice in June 1993.

The Kiwanis International is an organization of service clubs, of which there are about 8,000 in ninety-six countries. Their main object is to improve the quality of life for the world's children, and it was little wonder that Audrey had been selected for their World Service Medal. That day in June marked the beginning of a new chapter in my work with UNICEF. David Blackmer, Kiwanis' International Director of Public Relations, had been in discussions with UNICEF regarding a project that Kiwanis could be involved with, such as Rotary International's Polio Elimination Project, which had been very successful. They came up with IDD: Iodine Deficiency Disorders.

In its most extreme form, the lack of iodine in our diet can be the cause of hypothyroidism, a severe lack of thyroid hormone, which used to be known as cretinism. It also raises the risk of stillbirth and miscarriage. In adults, the goitre, or enlarged thyroid gland, is an obvious sign of iodine deficiency, but the lack of iodine in childhood reduces intellectual ability, resulting in an IQ ten to twelve per cent below the norm. We only actually need the equivalent of a teaspoon of iodine throughout our life, but it does have to be spread out. I learned that, in 1990, thirty per cent of the world's population lived at risk of IDD; 750 million people suffered from goitre; and 43 million had brain damage. These were people who lived in mountainous or flood-plain areas, where erosion bled the soil and crops of sufficient iodine.

This was to be my project – encouraging Kiwanis worldwide to support the initiative and raise at least $75 million for salt iodization equipment and awareness. It also fell on my shoulders to speak with presidents and ministers in affected countries, so they could understand the seriousness of iodine deficiency. After all, what chance had a country if its population lacked ten per cent of their brain cells?

The most simple method of combating this scourge is by iodizing salt, then by encouraging people to buy only that salt. The first two countries in the world to iodize their salt were Switzerland and the USA. Now so many more do, in no small part thanks to the Kiwanis. I'm proud to be associated with them.

In the spring of 1993 I took my daughter Deborah with me to the windy city, Chicago, for a fund-raising event and to raise UNICEF awareness. While there, my old friend and publicist Jerry Pam asked me to record a guide to the Forbidden City in Beijing. I thought, in addition to a few dollars, it would mean a free trip to the Far East! Ever the ponce, I readily agreed. However, the nearest I got to China was a taxi ride to an address on Michigan Boulevard. I then had to walk up ten flights of stairs and sit in front of a microphone, trying to sound authoritative in describing this great place – which I'd never seen. It was only in 2002, a few months after we were married, that Kristina and I, in Beijing for UNICEF, were able to listen to my guide as we moved around that extraordinary structure. Would you believe it – we didn't get lost once!

Back in 1993, meanwhile, I spent the summer travelling – for both UNICEF and work – to and from London, the USA, Athens and Nice.

Along the way I met with the Kiwanis for events, attended the Montreal Film Festival and finally ended up at a big fundraiser in Los Angeles. It was while I was in LA, that my very good friend and doctor Steven 'Stevo' Zax insisted that I should pay more attention to my health – I hadn't told him I was a closet hypochondriac.

Apart from having a mutual friend, cardiologist Selvyn Bleifer, run his rule over me and make sure that my heart kept the correct time, Steven also had his urologist, Rick Erlich, make regular checks on my PSA – prostate-specific-antigen – with tests. PSA is a protein produced by the cells of the prostate and, via a blood test, you can use it as a biological marker for the early stages of prostate cancer. I'm told that when the PSA level starts to rise on subsequent blood tests then it is time for a further investigation. That investigation – apart from the finger up the rectum – can also mean taking a number of microscopic samples, through a needle penetrating the prostate gland and taking eight to ten particles for biopsy.

Needless to say, it's as painful and irritating as it sounds – a pain in the arse, you might say.

I had two of these well-meaning investigations, and on each occasion Rick called me the same evening and said all was OK; or else Stevo would ring me in the morning to confirm a clean report. The day after the third such test I remember it was a sunny September morning in Beverly Hills and I was about to start my morning workout, when I heard a ring at the door. Stevo was standing there with a faint smile on his face. He said he'd decided to come by the house instead of phoning because the news was not good. We went into my study. Strangely, I started to feel so sorry for him, as he had bad news to impart and clearly did not know how to start to tell me. His eyes began to well up with tears and I could only make a joke, saying something fatuous.

'Well, we have got a little time,' said Stevo. 'This operation can't be done until you give four units of blood in reserve; that's going to take a month.'

I felt very calm. After all, he hadn't said I had cancer, only that I was going to give a couple of pints of blood ready for an operation.

Whoa! Just a minute, what operation exactly?

Stevo then explained that they would open my abdomen and remove the offending prostate. Only then would they be able to check whether the cancer had spread to other tissues or the bones.

Cancer. The dreaded C word. I had cancer.

FOURTEEN

The Health Scare

'In Kristina I had found my soul mate and it has made me happier than words can ever express'

'Stevo, let's look on the bright side,' I said, somewhat more concerned than I was letting on. 'It won't have spread, so how long will I be out of action?'

He reckoned a good six weeks. I knew that in the autumn I had an important trip to make for UNICEF, to Sweden and then Finland. It was all still possible he said, assuming there were no complications. I never let on to anyone but my closest family and my assistant Doris Spriggs. The following week I started the blood-letting. I kept thinking of the marvellous Tony Hancock and *The Blood Donor* sketch, 'So *now* do I get a cup of tea?'

The date for the knife was set. By now I had given three units of blood and I was free to fly to Stockholm. As usual, Ingvar Hjartsjo, UNICEF's director in Sweden, met me at Arlanda airport. He had a number of engagements lined up for me, which we discussed on the way to the Grand Hotel, the most important of which was for the next evening – presenting a 'Baby-Friendly Hospital' award to one of Sweden's leading hospitals. During my brief tenure as a UNICEF representative, not only had I learned about immunization, OR salts and Iodine Deficiency Disorders; I'd also learned how to construct bio toilets and how to make bricks, how to dig a well, how to lay PVC tubing, how to turn on taps and make speeches (without notes) – and now it was baby-friendly hospitals. I know it is an extremely important factor in the rearing of healthy babies, but the irony of an ex-James Bond going around the world advocating the benefits of breastfeeding was not lost on me.

I was taken around the hospital by the dedicated nursing staff. All the time, at the back of my mind was the thought that the following week I'd be in an establishment similar to this one, although different insofar as I would not be delivering a baby, but a rather precious part of my anatomy . . .

One of the big thrills for me was being shown into room where a young mother who had just had her first child was about to give her first breastfeed. I was horrified, though, to see half the press and TV people had followed me into the room. I said I couldn't inflict this invasion of the press, and Lord alone knows what germs, on a baby only a few hours old. Everyone was hustled out, but the mother said that she'd be happy to allow a photographer and myself to be present. On leaving the room a mass of microphones were shoved in my face and to my disgust I heard a Swedish journalist asking, 'So Mister Bond, vat you think of Sveedish teets?'

'Swedish teeth?'

'No, Swedish tits?'

I told the journalist that he was trying to make a poor joke out of a quite serious subject. I wanted to add 'Piss off' but that would have been playing his game. However, later, Ingvar spoke with the director of that particular TV station, and they made a generous contribution to the UNICEF Swedish Fund.

The next day I left for a two-day visit to Finland and then it was back to LA and on to Cedars-Sinai Hospital. I was checked in under a false name, so as not to alert the press. However, these things always have a habit of reaching the media, as it did in my case. This time round in the hospital there were no red and yellow tunnels, and no boom-bams; there were socks though, but they were not the woolly ones of my childhood, these were tight and very long – the sort to wear in aeroplanes. All was hazy. I slipped in and out of pain, and remember a terrible ache in the bones of my pelvic area. I was in a sort of cotton cloud shattered only occasionally by stabs of pain.

In slowly coming round, I remember the hospital room and my family coming in and out, along with nurses and doctors. I wanted nothing more than to have the hose-pipe, which had been so inelegantly shoved into my bladder via my 'little friend', removed. Alas, this was not to be and it accompanied me back to the house in Hidden Valley where my bedroom had become an extension of Cedars-Sinai Hospital.

I tumbled over and over into a well of self-pity and anger. It was the sight of my body limping its way to the bathroom with a great plastic bag attached to the other end of the garden hose that gave me the despair of inadequacy. I felt emasculated. I know I must have been completely impossible to live with – the more I complained as I wallowed in self-pity, the more Luisa started snapping back. When feeling fine I was quite capable of handling outbursts of Italian temperament – I had been for a number of years. However, these new and unwanted circumstances left me unable to cope. Between visits from Stevo and Sel Bleifer, and my daughter Deborah, I had plenty of time to think about my life and how close I had been to losing it. It was not very admirable behaviour I admit, but the seeds for life change had been planted and were beginning to grow.

One day, Stevo told me that he had spoken on the telephone to my friend Kristina Tholstrup, a neighbour of ours in the South of France, whom he had helped through her double mastectomy some time previously. Kristina asked him to pass on her love to me and said she hoped that all would be well, and that I'd have a speedy recovery. I knew that I wouldn't be seeing her until after spring the following year, when we moved back to St Paul, and I found myself starting to think about her a lot. She knew what I was going through and, as it happens, was thinking about me a lot.

The day came when Stevo had to take me over to Rick's offices in Westwood, to examine the scar tissue. In a scene reminiscent of my time at Westminster Hospital sixty years previously, I stood – feet apart – in front of the seated Rick. He removed the dressing, deemed all satisfactory and then he took hold of the hose-pipe, which now seemed to resemble a fireman's hose in length. With an enormous jerk he detached the offending waste disposal unit from its moorings. All I remember is sheer, dark, bright, screaming pain! As I fell back on to the chair, I was positive that I'd lost my liver, kidneys, spleen and possibly my passport together with my Screen Actor's Guild card.

As my breathing returned to normal and my blood pressure lowered, I felt a new surge of relief. No more hose-pipe! No more plastic bag! It was joy untold, apart from then receiving the news that I would now have to be trussed up with waterproof pants and frequently change the disposable pads.

Luisa and I started planning our departure from the Hills of Beverly and getting ourselves to Gstaad for the winter.

'Before you leave,' said Stevo, 'Rick and I think that you should have a bone scan, just to make sure that nothing's spread.'

That was nice – a couple more sleepless nights before finally getting the 'all clear'. We then left, before they decided there should be some other blooming test! It was to be my last winter in Gstaad with Luisa.

UNICEF kept me very busy, but I realized that I was only of value to them if I maintained a profile in the public eye. That is to say, made the occasional film to show I was still alive! When *The Man Who Wouldn't Die* landed on my desk, I was intrigued. Bill Condon sent me the script and said it was to be shot as a TV movie in Vancouver for Universal Studios, with Malcolm McDowell and Nancy Allen co-starring.

It was interesting because I got to play two parts: that of an author, and that of the fictional police inspector he wrote about. The story concerns Thomas Grace, an author of mystery stories, who based his villain on a criminal – played by Malcolm – who was at the time incarcerated. However, when the arch-criminal escapes during a fierce prison fire, he plans to take revenge on Grace for 'stealing his personality' by carrying out a number of murders based around the novels. Grace is unable to convince the authorities of the identity of the true murderer and, alerted by an avid fan (Nancy Allen) who has psychic powers, seeks to trap McDowell into giving himself away.

It was a hugely enjoyable experience. I returned to Gstaad feeling rather proud of myself for returning to work, but I walked straight in to another row about something or other. And that was it. With the children all grown up, I knew that I would leave Luisa. I took the coward's way out, rather than face yet another confrontation, and just left with the clothes I was standing up in.

In Kristina I had found my soul mate and it has made me happier than words can ever express. I couldn't bear to be apart from her any longer. We have been inseparable ever since, and married in 2002 in a small ceremony in Denmark – just us, two witnesses and a priest, Peter Parkov, who had been a friend for some time. Our love grows stronger each day and the years since we have married have been even happier, if that's possible.

I only dislike, and I mean really *dislike* two people in this business. Both were involved with my next film, *The Quest*, on either side of the camera.

Jack Gilardi, my agent in the US, called to say Jean-Claude Van Damme had written a script and he wanted to meet me to discuss it. I duly met with him and he enthused about how much he liked me, how good I would be for the part of Lord Edgar Dobbs and generally did a very good salesman act on me. I thought the script was pretty reasonable and when Van Damme said that he wanted to direct it, I had no issue with that either. Our main location, he said, was to be Thailand. I knew it well and thought it would be the perfect opportunity to spend some quality time with Kristina on my days off. I signed on the dotted line.

I then met the chap who called himself our producer, Moshe Diamant. I have nothing nice, or even anything vaguely redeeming, to say about him, I'm afraid. So, in the best tradition, I'll say nothing.

My sanity was preserved on the film thanks to the casting of Janet Gunn and the wonderfully funny Jack McGee, whose humour was very off-the-wall – and I loved it! Halfway through a scene, he'd belch or fart; much to the annoyance of our director but to the delight of silly schoolboy Moore. Jack and I shared most of our scenes together and also lunched in my trailer, as I preferred to be there than have to mix with certain other members of the cast and crew.

I remember on one night we had a long drive to a location and I was wedged into the back of a small car. When we finally arrived, my knee had locked. It was agony! For the rest of the film I had my leg in a cast and had to use a cane or lean up against walls and posts for support. That wasn't the only long drive we had to a night location either, the other being in Mai Hon Song near the Burmese border. They'd built a fort on a hill up there. It was a good ninety minutes' drive from our unit base and it seemed crazy to me that we should drive all the way up there because we could have frankly shot anywhere; after all it was pitch dark – who'd have known? That was symptomatic of our producer's lack of planning I'm afraid.

Anyhow, with time being wasted hand-over-fist, one night the crew took exception to being told they would have to work overtime on this location, without pay. Our producer told the second unit director to speak to Jean-Claude and the crew and say he wanted to shoot until six o'clock the following morning.

'Why should we work for nothing, mate?' said a gaffer, quite reasonably in my view. 'Give us one good reason.'

Our fearless producer stepped forward, and with a quivering bottom lip said, 'For the glory of the film!'

'OK, boys! Pull the plugs,' the gaffer called.

I met the producer some years later in Monaco, and politely ignored him. On another occasion – having not taken the first hint – he called me.

'I am in Monaco . . .' he said.

'That's nice,' I said and replaced the handset.

Much of the credit for making and finishing the film goes to our second unit director Peter MacDonald. He and his wonderful Australian crew did wonders under the most difficult of conditions and leaderships. I enjoyed the film insomuch as my fellow supporting cast members and the crew were great fun to work with, plus I spent my days off with Kristina, which was wonderful.

When release-publicity for the film finally emerged though, I was rather disappointed to see that my promised 'above-the-title' billing had changed. I've never been overly bothered about billing, but Van Damme had made such a fuss about having me in the movie and told me that I'd be up there above the title with him, so I expected it. Now I saw my name was in small text below the title. It was a bit of a snub to be honest. Thankfully I didn't have any more dealings with Mr Van Damme or his producer friend, and won't waste any more printers' ink on writing about them.

There hadn't been a new terrestrial TV channel in the UK since Channel 4 launched in 1982. Therefore news of Channel 5's launch in March 1997 was greeted with great enthusiasm. For some reason, the powers that be asked me to be part of the first night's festivities with an up-and-coming girl band. I reported to the Whitehall Theatre in central London, and to a tiny dressing room. There was a knock on the door.

'Can we talk to you?' they said.

'Sure!' I replied.

In walked five young girls. I had no idea who they were, but realized they must be the girl band.

'We're going to make a film,' one said. 'Will you be in it?'

'Sure, I'd love to,' I said, not taking them very seriously.

'Would you send me a signed picture?' said another.

'What's your name,' I asked.

'Victoria.'

I felt such a fool when, a few months later, the Spice Girls were topping the charts! The next thing I knew, though, my London agent, Dennis Sellinger, called to say that they'd sent a script and wanted me for a day's filming. He then told me how much they'd offered. Wow! Let's just say I didn't have to think for long.

I arrived at Twickenham Studios to be greeted by the girls and the lovely director Bob Spiers. I was familiar with him from his work directing many episodes of *Fawlty Towers*. My scene was as a Blofeld-type character with a white cat, and it was essentially spent on the phone to

Richard E. Grant. What impressed me greatly was Richard insisted on coming in, on his day off, to feed me his lines off-set. If you remember, it was something I always used to do on *The Saint*. I liked Richard immensely after that.

The last time I saw young Victoria was with her husband David Beckham at the Colombe d'Or in the South of France – David didn't ask me for a picture, I might add – when they were dining with Elton John. I'm such a name-dropper.

Following my separation from Luisa, I had set up home with Kristina in Monaco – where she was a resident – during the summer months, and for the winter months we decided to look for a new home in Switzerland – where I was a resident. We visited a number of ski resorts but didn't find anything that really grabbed us, until it was suggested we visit Crans-Montana.

We drove to the resort and booked in at the Crans Ambassador hotel as our base for a few days. Having viewed a number of properties, we again thought that we'd be leaving without finding one we liked. But then, a stroke of luck came our way. We were told about a chalet that was for sale, which actually backed on to a ski slope. It sounded perfect and as soon as we saw it, we knew it was for us. After a little building work and a few internal improvements, Kristina set about furnishing and making it not only our home, but a retreat for all our children to escape to as well.

Crans has everything you could wish for: great restaurants, varied shops, wonderful skiing, an amazing doctor – Ariane Kunz (being the old hypochondriac I always find the best doctor) – and friendly, warm people. There are numerous pharmacies too.

We have many dear friends in the town, but one of the first people we met was ski guide Jorg Romang. Not only did Jorg introduce us to the best pistes with virgin snow, he helped us house-hunt and in the ensuing years has become an invaluable font of knowledge and help for Kristina and I. If only every town could have a Jorg!

My engagements for UNICEF continued apace, and Kristina joined me on every trip and is just as passionate about the children, if not more so, than I am. I often say that she makes a far better ambassador than I do. Our wonderful UNICEF friends Mary Cahill in New York, and Christa Roth in Geneva were a great help to us in organizing our field trips and helping to plan our programmes with the Committees of each country we visited. Mary's delightful Irish lilt was always a pleasure to hear on the telephone, and though she has now retired – or rather had been retired at sixty, as is UN policy despite whether or not an individual still wants to remain on staff – we keep in touch and try to see each other when we're in New York.

From Dublin to Amsterdam, from Tirana to Saarbrücken and on to New Orleans and Hong Kong and then on to London in 1995 to launch 'Check Out For Children', our schedule remained very busy.

'Check Out' was the brainchild of Robert Scott at Starwood – the large hotel and leisure group that owns, among other hotels and resorts, the world-famous Sheraton chain. I was privileged to be asked to take part in the launch of the very successful partnership between Starwood and UNICEF at the Sheraton Park Towers in Knightsbridge. Robert's idea was that guests would be invited to give a dollar or a pound each time they check out after a stay at a Sheraton Hotel. Entirely voluntary on the part of the guest; on the in-house television, guests would see exactly how the money collected would work for UNICEF.

I was asked to film the introduction to the images of the children. The camera was set up in a suite at the Sheraton Belgravia, and when I was given the nod to start recording, I said words more or less to this effect: 'Ladies and gentlemen, and dear guests, the film you are watching is showing how the work of UNICEF affects the lives of the world's most precious commodity, the children . . .' and so on.

I then finished by saying, 'You will find that one pound has been added to your bill. If you are not happy about this, just tell the cashier and we will be happy to remove it from your bill and the cashier will look at you and say, "You are a mean insufferable bastard and you can stick your pound . . ." Cut!'

The director and crew looked horrified. 'Only a joke!' I said. I can't imagine anybody ever refusing, and to the best of my knowledge when I've asked in the many Starwood Hotels that I've visited, over the intervening years there have only been a handful of refusals.

A short time afterwards, Kristina and I helped the UK Committee celebrate their raising of £2-million through their partnership with British Airways, and the 'Change for Good' campaign, whereby passengers can donate their small change in unwanted currency to UNICEF. At the time of writing, the continuing partnership has raised over £25 million.

I've often been asked just how much UNICEF receives from the United Nations and why we need to raise funds. The answer is UNICEF receives nothing from the UN, it is completely self-funded and that is why I – and others like me – go out banging the drum. Of the money we raise, less than nine per cent goes in administration costs around the world; the rest goes directly to the children. That's an enviable amount. We are so very fortunate in UNICEF to have regular supporters, both large and small. Sure, the big corporations are very important and valued by us for their substantial and generous contributions, but equally important are the individuals who support UNICEF by buying greetings cards, making modest donations or a regular contribution from each month's salary. It is those tens of thousands of people who make much of UNICEF's work possible – every penny counts.

The tail end of 1998 brought both great and sad news. I received a letter from the Honours Committee confirming that I was to be appointed a Commander of the British Empire (CBE). The citation specified it was for my work for charity, which was particularly humbling. Two weeks before that became public news, however, one of my dearest friends and mentors passed away. Lord Grade – Lew – died on 14 December 1998, following complications after a routine operation. He was ninety-two and had still been working up until the day of his admittance to hospital. The news was a great shock to me. Without doubt, I owe much of my success to Lew. There has never been, nor will there ever be, a man quite like him.

On 9 March the following year, I collected my CBE from Buckingham Palace. You are allowed to take three guests with you, but before I had time to think who the other two should be, Kristina said that I should take all three of my children, and not her. I never, not even for a moment, envisaged collecting this important honour without her by my side, but she insisted it was right that my children should be there to share the day with me. It was just typical of how Kristina always puts others before herself. You can understand why I love her so very much.

I was terrified on the day, and thought I might trip over or walk in the wrong way, but it's actually run like a military operation and you're given very clear directions as to what will happen. Guests are shown to their seats and recipients of honours are shown into separate rooms according to their presentation – MBEs, OBEs, and CBEs. There you are told by an equerry to call Her Majesty 'Ma'am as in ham, not Ma'am as in harm' and 'When the Queen shakes your hand that is the end of the conversation.'

Afterwards, Kristina hosted a lunch at Harry's Bar for me and we were joined by Michael and Shakira Caine and Kristina's daughter Christina (I call her Flossie to save any confusion).

A few years later, in 2003, at Heathrow airport, I received a call from my assistant, Gareth.

'How would you like to be a knight?' he asked. I thought he was playing one of his jokes on me. He had to read the letter from the Honours Office to me twice before I believed him. It said that the government wished to offer me a knighthood for my services to UNICEF and please would I let them know if I'd like to accept it. I was dumbstruck! It also said that I wasn't to tell anyone until the official announcement in June. Naturally, I told Kristina, who was sitting beside me, and I suddenly realized that she would become Lady Moore; it was certainly an honour she greatly deserved for all of her tireless work for UNICEF. We wrote back and said I would be delighted to accept. I didn't tell anyone else, not even the children, until the day before it was announced. I was terrified the government might change its collective mind.

When I was invited to the palace to accept my KBE I insisted Kristina join me this time, with Deborah and Geoffrey. Christian was then living in LA, so he didn't feel too left out. It was a very proud day.

Traffic on the Mall was horrendous that morning and we were all conscious of running late. I wasn't too worried, as I knew from my previous experience that knighthoods were awarded at the end of the morning, after the MBEs, CBEs and so forth. My only real worry was having to kneel in front of Her Majesty, and not be able to get up again. I phoned Michael Caine.

'Michael, when you were knighted did you have to kneel right down on the floor?'

'No,' he laughed. 'There is a sort of kneel stool there with a handle on the side to push yourself up on.' That was a relief. I mean, think how embarrassing it would be for a former 007 who had saved the world so many times not to be able to get up off the floor.

When we eventually arrived, I was shown into a room with six or seven others, including Union Chief Bill Morris and my old friend Ken Adam, who was also receiving a knighthood. The equerry said that I would be first on, and on my own. First on! On my own! I had no one to follow. First night nerves took over. I think he then said something like, 'When your name is called you leave this room, follow this corridor and turn left, then you walk to Her Majesty . . .'

In truth I heard nothing. I think I slipped into autopilot mode. Thankfully, Her Majesty didn't slice my head off, nor did my knee lock. I have been very fortunate to have met the Queen on many occasions, and am always as nervous as I was that first time, however she quickly puts one at ease and I think she rather enjoys the occasions just as much as we recipients do.

Though I had three of my nearest and dearest with me, I remember thinking, 'I wish Mum and Dad were here.' I know they'd have been so proud to see their son receive this tremendous honour. I was told that, after I was told to arise, I should leave the room without looking at anyone. I knew where Kristina was sitting though, and couldn't resist a little wink at her.

Downstairs, my medals were placed into a box and I was escorted through to meet the press – flash, flash, chat, chat – and then I was taken back upstairs to the inauguration room and watched everyone else. Our great friend Sirdir Ali Aziz then hosted lunch at the Ritz for us, and gave us the most wonderful suite to stay in. I enjoy swanking every now and again and, boy, was this the place to swank.

Later in the evening, my son Geoffrey welcomed us to his new restaurant, Shumi, for a wonderful dinner party with friends including Michael and Shakira Caine, Sean and Michelene Connery, Barbara Broccoli, Bob Baker, David and Carina Frost, Michael Winner, Bryan and Nanette Forbes, our very good friends Raja Sidawi and Monique Duroc-Danner, along with many others. It was the perfect way to end a perfect day, among so many wonderful people.

Back to 1999, and I was approached with an American TV series called *The D.r.e.a.m. Team*. It was a sort of *Charlie's Angels* type premise, only with one male and three female agents who masqueraded as fashion models. I was to play Desmond Heath, the chap who coordinated the team. They said I could film my sequences in the South of France, and with it a rather large pay cheque would be attached. It felt very much like a d.r.e.a.m. job. But you know how you were always told that if something seemed too good to be true, then it probably was? That applied to this show. I filmed, I think, for a day before rumours of financial difficulties began circulating. I was assured that all was OK and my next filming day would come after some press and PR at the TV festival in Cannes — where they hoped to secure more sales for the show.

Meanwhile, just as the TV festival at Cannes was starting, I was invited to Paris to the French TV Awards, to accept yet another honour. This time it was for *The Persuaders* — which had always been huge in France. Tony Curtis had recorded a tribute and it all went down rather well. Kristina and I had arranged to meet our friends Ricky and Sandra Portanova at Régine's restaurant afterwards, but on arriving — rather late — we thought that they might have tired of waiting for us and left. In fact, they were en route and running late too. However, we decided to return to our hotel and went out to find our driver. I could see the car was across the road, so we crossed over and I opened the back door for Kristina to step in. At that precise moment, the driver put the car into reverse and drove backwards with great speed; the door hit Kristina and knocked her flat on the ground. He drove with such speed that he smashed up four cars behind him before coming to a halt. How he didn't drive over Kristina's arm I'll never know. He later claimed that his foot had slipped. What, into reverse? He was in fact found to be drunk.

Kristina lay with blood pouring from her head, unconscious. I took off my dinner jacket and put it behind her head. On looking down, I saw my hand was covered in blood. Régine came running out of the club and called the paramedics, who seemed to take forever to arrive. Kristina remained unconscious and my heart was thumping like I'd never felt before. I ran the whole gamut of emotions. When the ambulance arrived there was a further delay for a discussion about which hospital they would take her to. Finally, they agreed it should be the American Hospital. It was now about two o'clock in the morning and Kristina was regaining consciousness. Various tests and scans were taken at the hospital, but, thank the Lord, the doctors felt there was no brain damage.

The police meanwhile arrived and said the driver was in a cell, and was three times over the limit. I sat in a chair next to Kristina all night. I never left her side.

I had committed myself to visiting Cannes the next day for *The D.r.e.a.m. Team* show. I really didn't want to go. Kristina had stabilized and insisted I should. The production arranged a private jet to fly me to Cannes and back later that day.

A couple of days later, Kristina was discharged. However, while the physical scars have mended, the mental ones have not. To this day Kristina will not drive nor will she cross the road alone. After months of wrangling, the French insurance company shrugged it all off, saying that it was an accident. The driver was not prosecuted. Was this fair justice, I asked?

The D.r.e.a.m. Team became a Nightmare Team as far as I was concerned, and when their extra finance failed to materialize, I walked away from the project. Some things are just not worth the hassle. I decided it was time to take a break and concentrate on looking after Kristina. It wasn't until 2001 that I felt like working again.

When a script called *The Enema* arrived, I thought, 'Oh goodie a medical drama.' Alas I misread: it said *Enemy*. A story by Desmond Bagley, *The Enemy* was set to star Luke Perry, Olivia d'Abo, Tom Conti, and Horst Buchholz, Tom Kinninmont was directing. Filming was all to take place in Luxembourg, which I found to be a wonderful country. Fortunately my schedule was such that I had many days off and could enjoy exploring the country and its many restaurants. My old friend John Glen was setting up a film there at the same time, so we were able to get together – another excuse to visit yet more restaurants.

Having never turned my back on Bond after I hung up the Walther PPK, I often introduced TV documentaries or took part in promotional interviews. However when Disney approached me to film a number of introductions to an upcoming season of my Bond films on their ABC TV Network in the USA, I realized just how lucrative my association could be. A huge cheque was dangled before me, and they agreed that we could film it at Ardmore Studios in Ireland, thereby avoiding any issues about me working in the UK. Being a tax exile has its advantages, but you have to be careful how many days you spend in the UK.

I've shot a few things at Ardmore over the years, mainly commercials. One was for a Midlands' beer, Banks' Bitter, and another was for one of Lord Hanson's companies, but it was never shown. Apparently MGM said it was a rip-off of Bond, and put an injunction in. I remember Lord Hanson saying to Frank Low, who set up the deal, that he was aghast to see I was 'being paid that much for just three days' work'. Frank said, 'No, it's for a lifetime's work'. How true, hence I never undervalue myself.

While working at Ardmore in 2001, one of the Disney executives approached me about a series they were making called *Alias*. He asked if I might be interested. 'Sure,' I said, not realizing it was one of the hottest shows on TV. A number of scripts arrived, and the show's writer and creator, J. J. Abrams, called me. We discussed several characters and I agreed to guest star as Edward Poole, a sort of 'M' type figure. I filmed my scenes in LA and really, really enjoyed it. JJ said that the character would reappear throughout the next season and he'd love me to return. 'Sure, I'm available,' I said.

However when they did approach me, the pay cheque on offer was slashed to a fraction of the previous one. Never being one to undersell myself, I said 'no thanks'.

As I've said earlier, being a UNICEF ambassador really does benefit from me maintaining a profile as an actor, well, of sorts. I enjoy working too so was intrigued to hear about *Boat Trip* in 2002 – it was certainly a little step to the left for me. I read it and thought the idea of two butch guys booking themselves on a gay cruise by mistake was very funny. Added to that, it was all filmed around the Greek islands! What more did I need?

Cuba Gooding Jr. and Horatio Sanz were the leads; and were terrific fun to work with. We kicked off with interiors in Cologne and then hopped on board ship in Athens for a two-week cruise. I played Lloyd Faversham, an ageing queen who rather took a shine to Horatio's character. Kristina joined me throughout the shoot, and we thoroughly enjoyed the cruise; as not being on call every day meant that we had quite a few days off to enjoy – with the added bonus of being paid to do so.

The critics weren't too kind to us, and the film didn't do well at the box office. However I'm told it's a big success on DVD and, aside from receiving one rambling homophobic letter, I don't think my swinging the other way had much of an impact on the world. Mind you, I do wonder what Brian Desmond Hurst might have thought about it all.

During one of our subsequent trips to London, Kristina and I went to see a play. We both love theatre, and London undoubtedly hosts some of the finest productions, so it's always a treat we look forward to. This particular play was *The Play What I Wrote*. No, I didn't write it, it was called that. In fact, it was really a sort of tribute to the spirit of Morecambe and Wise, written by and starring Sean Foley and Hamish McColl, and directed by Kenneth Branagh. It also starred Toby Jones, the son of my old mate Freddie Jones and I'm so delighted that Toby has now gone on to great things in Hollywood.

One of my few regrets in this business was being invited to take part in the *Morecambe and Wise Christmas Show*, several times, and never being able to make it. I was always either working or on the far side of the world. This was my nearest chance to doing it.

The play was hugely funny. In the second half, a guest was introduced – much like they did on the *M&W Show* – but here it was kept a secret. Throughout the run people such as Ralph Fiennes, Dawn French, Honor Blackman, Ewan McGregor, Daniel Radcliffe, Kylie Minogue, Charles Dance and Glenn Close guest-starred and camped it up in the final 'play within a play' segment, 'A Tight Squeeze for the Scarlet Pimple'. On the night I attended, Jonny Lee Miller was the guest star. What I didn't know then was that he is Bernie Lee's grandson. I wish I'd known.

They obviously noted that I was in that night, and laughed my socks off as, a few days later my London agent – who was now Jean Diamond, as both dear Dennis Sellinger and Dennis van Thal had passed away – called to say the producer had asked if I might like to guest star for a few performances (guests only ever did three nights to help preserve the 'mystery guest' angle). I agreed immediately.

I probably ended up guest-starring more than anyone else, over a period of a year or so in the West End then on tour in Woking, Milton Keynes and Belfast. The show was so successful that it then transferred to Broadway. David Pugh asked if I would appear in some of the previews. I couldn't star in the opening night performance, as that had to be an American – they'd lined-up Kevin Kline – but I came back to do a few performances a short while afterwards, which tied in with a UNICEF gala one Friday night.

It was during the Wednesday matinée performance, before the gala, that the curse of Broadway struck me again. I'd made it past the opening night this time, unlike *A Pin to See the Peep Show*, and was dressed in the full Marie-Antoinette garb. I got through the song-and-dance routine but I then suddenly heard a tremendous bang. It was my head hitting the stage. Then next thing I realized, Hamish was standing over me asking if I was OK.

'What the heck is he doing in my bedroom?' I thought. I then registered the stage, the audience and the curtains closing.

Kristina, meanwhile, was in the front row. She'd been to every performance, and knew this was not in the script. After a few moments I felt fine and we continued with the show. Kristina insisted I should see a doctor after I came offstage though. The next thing I knew, there were two enormous paramedics shoving needles in my arm, putting me in a chair and carrying me – in costume – down the spiral staircase into an ambulance. They raced me to the Roosevelt Hospital. In ER, a very nice young Indian doctor did a number of tests and then called my friends and doctors Steven Zax and Selvyn Bleifer in LA. I then spoke to Sel.

'They're going to give you a pacemaker. You're being transferred to the Beth Israel Hospital. And, before you say it, don't even think about getting on a plane to head here to LA, they won't let you. You need a pacemaker, and you need it now or you could die.'

Sobering words! I felt slightly removed from it all, as though I was observing all this going on and it wasn't really happening to me.

Christian was already en route from LA to see us, and when he arrived at our hotel he was told I was in hospital. Christian is very good in a crisis, and is very level-headed, so it was good to have him around to support Kristina and to reassure me. The next morning I was wheeled into theatre for the operation and left in the capable hands of surgeon Darryl Hoffman. The next thing I remember, as I came round, was a theatre nurse asking for my autograph. Barely conscious I scribbled something on a bit of paper, relieved that all had gone well.

Afterwards, I had a long conversation with the cardiologist, Steven Evans, who ran through what had happened with the pacemaker implant, and the dos and don'ts of living with a pacemaker, such as not holding a mobile phone nearby, not walking through metal-detecting machines in airports and the like. He then asked what I was doing in New York. I explained I was in the play and the next evening had a UNICEF gala. It seems I must have talked to him a lot about UNICEF as when he discharged me on the Friday morning, he said I could attend the UNICEF gala so long as it was a brief visit, and then added, 'Most doctors present you with a bill when you leave. I'm going to give you a cheque.'

It was for $10,000 and was made payable to UNICEF. 'I'm sorry I'm not a Beverly Hills doctor, as then it would have been for $100,000.'

Our wonderful friend Mary Cahill at UNICEF ensured my appearance at the gala would be short and not taxing. It was important I went, as attendees had spent a lot of money to be there and were promised I would be too. I hate letting people down. It also satisfied the media that I was not on my deathbed and all was fine.

A couple of days later, I was pronounced fit enough to fly home to Monaco. What a joy it was to return to my own bed.

The pacemaker hasn't adversely affected my life. In fact my father had one for many years, and he lived very happily with his. It was comforting to receive messages of goodwill from other carriers too, such as Elton John. He reckoned he had a designer zip to access his. I'm not sure I believe him.

Hopefully the batteries in mine are good for a few more years. They have to be changed after around seven to ten years. I remember Dad – who'd had his a few years – saying to me one day, 'I don't think I'll bother about the new battery, son, waste of money. This'll last me out.'

One other thing that came out of this episode was a letter from a small charity called STARS. Its founder Trudie Lobban wrote to say she had set up a 'blackout awareness' campaign after her daughter was misdiagnosed with epilepsy some years earlier. Trudie was not satisfied with the diagnosis and investigated further. It was then that a neurologist in Glasgow, Professor Stephenson, said she had the condition known as Reflex Anoxic Seizure. So many people are misdiagnosed and incorrectly treated for this condition. If you suffer a blackout it is probably due to a sudden shortness of blood to the brain, caused by a problem with the heart. This is exactly what happened to me. My diagnosis was swift, and I'm forever grateful I was in New York City and not on a field trip in a third-world country.

There are many ways to treat RAS, including as in my case having a pacemaker fitted. Trudie decided to do something about the lack of understanding in both the medical profession and indeed amongst the likes of you and me, and formed STARS. She asked if I would become a patron. I have been one ever since, and help out when I can in raising awareness and recruiting others, such as Sir Elton John, to the cause. Has my involvement helped? Well, let me tell you that my assistant Gareth Owen picked up a parcel one day soon after my appointment, and the man who served him said that I had saved his daughter's life. Startling words.

Apparently she had been treated for epilepsy for a number of years, but when she read my story in the newspaper in an interview for STARS, she asked for a second opinion; her attacks were growing more regular and serious at this point. RAS was duly diagnosed and now she is living a healthy, normal life. If I have helped just one person through banging the drum for STARS, then it has been worth it.

I've always liked gadgets. Even before I was armed with the latest from Q-Branch, I loved anything I could lay my hands on such as the newfangled electronic calculator, digital watches and the like. When the home computer became available, I bought one and now, with my much more powerful PC and laptop, I've become one of the growing band of 'silver surfers'. I love the immediacy of the internet in being able to find out practically anything – always handy when flying to new countries to learn about them, or to research notes for a UNICEF speech. I've become an avid e-mailer and keep in touch with friends, family and even my bank manager via the medium. And as for Skype (which my step-daughter's boyfriend, Janus Friis, invented, by the way), well, that's saved me a fortune in phone calls and I regularly converse with friends and family around the world using it. Kristina often has to pull me away from my screen as I could quite happily spend hours there. But at least I now have the excuse of saying I'm writing.

I do have a website out there in cyberspace, run by two fans – Alan Davidson and Marie-France Vienne – and they work tirelessly in promoting what I'm up to, as well as running an interactive forum for fans. It's a very friendly community and I'm touched that anyone would be so interested in an aspiring actor such as me.

Speaking of websites and e-mails, I received one from Marcia Stanton, Lew Grade's former assistant, telling me that a friend of a friend of hers had done a funny little tribute to me on the internet. The animator, Dan Chambers, claimed it was to keep his sometime writing buddy Olly Smith amused. I thought it was very funny and let them know. I've always had a soft spot for animation. They in turn asked if I would voice a special animation they were thinking of doing for UNICEF. It was called *The Fly Who Loved Me* and was about a fly saving Christmas after Santa's reindeer was taken ill. I was intrigued!

The boys came to meet me the next time I was in London and I recorded the voice of Santa. It became one of UNICEF's most popular e-cards of the season, and you can still find it on the internet.

Olly and Dan, meanwhile, have gone on to great things. In fact Olly is more famous than me nowadays, what with his wine programmes and fondling Anne Robinson on *The Weakest Link*. And to think I was there at the beginning of his burgeoning career.

Soon after *The Fly*, another couple of animation projects came my way. *Here Comes Peter Cottontail* being the first. I was asked to lend my tonsils to the voice of villainous Irontail. I was able to record in a beautiful studio in St Paul, in the South of France, which is sadly now closed. We were treated royally and I realized just how much I enjoyed voiceover work. My ultimate role would be *The Invisible Man*, as I could phone the dialogue in.

My tonsils were in fact lent, a year or so later, to another animation project – this time a feature. Two other boys, brothers in this case, Sean and Barrie Robinson sent me a script for *Agent Crush*. They had trained under Derek Meddings, and loved the *Thunderbirds* style of puppeteering, only this time the wires wouldn't be visible. I recorded the dialogue for my character, again a sort of M-type one who kept our gallant hero in check, in Geneva. I think it all went rather well as there is talk of a sequel.

In May 2004, Kristina and I were delighted to be part of the tenth anniversary celebrations for UNICEF and British Airways' 'Change for Good' project. To mark the occasion, BA invited HM the Queen to unveil a specially inaugurated plane.

UNICEF UK's Chairman Lord Puttnam, BA's Lord Marshall, myself and members of UNICEF staff, greeted Her Majesty at Heathrow and she was escorted to the commemorative plaque that was to be unveiled. She pressed the button to open the curtains. Nothing. The curtains did not open. There was a pause; nobody really knew what to do. I stepped forward, gave the curtains a little tug, and suggested Her Majesty try now. It worked. Well, as I said afterwards, James Bond had to do something.

We then climbed some steps for a photo opportunity at the door of the special UNICEF-emblazoned plane. I followed Her Majesty up the steps and I couldn't help but notice what fantastic legs Her Majesty has – I hope I'm not sent to the Tower for saying that.

'Change for Good' has had a marked impact on the world. For example, through the money raised, UNICEF rebuilt a dilapidated primary school in Nigeria, including furniture, toilets and running water for 3,000 pupils. It sponsored an immunization campaign in Zambia where 1.2 million children were inoculated against polio. In Mexico, over £1-million has been donated to help protect street children and vital emergency work in India, El Salvador, Kosovo, Iraq and Iran has been made possible.

When I fly BA, I sometimes make the announcement about the 'Change for Good' envelopes in the seat pockets, and how any unwanted change popped into them can save lives. I'm never less than touched by people's generosity. On one recent flight, Jonathan Ross was on board. As I made the announcement, he walked the length of the plane collecting the envelopes.

In addition to UNICEF trips, I've also kept myself busy in recent years hosting and fronting a number of TV documentaries for David McKenzie and his wife Laura, who were introduced to me by Jerry Pam. *The Secret KGB Files, In the Footsteps of the Holy Family, The World Magic Awards* and so many more shows have been great fun to make, with short schedules, nice locations and they've helped me earn a few bob to pay the gas bill. What more could I ask?

I remember when we were in Moscow filming one of the *KGB Files*, David – who is a bit of a wine connoisseur – was told by a Russian waiter that we Westerners always rave about French wines, yet Georgian wines are just as good. So we ordered a bottle. It was like drinking red rust – absolutely disgusting. On a later trip to St Petersburg, Kristina and I gave it a second chance, just in case we'd been served a bad bottle in Moscow. Alas no, it tasted just the same!

A few years ago, Josephine Hart (Lady Saatchi) – whose writing I admire greatly – asked if I might participate in one of her regular, non-profit making, poetry readings at the British Library. The idea behind it was to introduce people – who might not otherwise have the chance – to great poetry. The lure of a celebrity reading undoubtedly helped. I said I'd be delighted, and only afterwards thought what might happen if I messed up!

I've always loved Rudyard Kipling's writing and suggested to Josephine that I'd like to read a selection of his poems. Josephine introduced each of her evenings, and provided biographical and informative narration between sections of poetry. It was all hugely effective. I've read at the British Library a couple of times and it then led, in 2007, to me receiving an invitation from the Nobel Museum in Sweden to help celebrate the 100th anniversary of Kipling receiving the Nobel Prize in literature in 1907.

To stand in the room where the Nobel Prizes are awarded was a breathtaking experience in itself. I opened with 'If' – which I know off by heart – and then referred to my notes for a ninety-minute lecture on Kipling, intertwined with a number of his poems – 'The Mary Gloucester' I like to think of as my tour de force . . . although it could make me be forced to tour!

People do occasionally ask if I've retired; namely my bank manager and agent. I haven't. I'm still available should the right offer and script come along, but I am, I guess, more choosy. These days life is good. While I remain busy with UNICEF work and the occasional bit of paying work, I am fortunate in being able to spend time with my darling Kristina and our children and grandchildren.

As I've previously mentioned, my first child was born when I was thirty-six. That was Deborah. I'm so proud of her, despite her choosing a career in acting over medicine. She is very talented.

My next child, a couple of years later, was Geoffrey. A handsome lad, took after his mother. He is loaded with charm, and today has a beautiful wife, Loulou and two absolutely ravishing daughters, Ambra and Mia. After taking a turn as a restaurateur, Geoffrey is now turning his attentions to producing, and is one of the new producers on *The Saint* starring James Purefoy – hopefully it will lead to a series of TV movies featuring the character.

Ten years after Deborah came Christian, and although he may not have excelled academically, Christian too is full of charm and is now based in Europe working in the property business. He has a beautiful daughter, Jessie, whom we love spending time with.

On marrying Kristina I acquired two stepchildren, I had known them as children, of course, very often we all played tennis together and I had seen them grow up into adulthood; they are Hans-Christian and his sister Christina. Despite the fact that her name is spelt with a C and not a K, as in my Kristina, I found that I confused them when I said 'Christina or Kristina'. Thus young Christina became Flossie. I should add that Flossie's a very lucky girl – she looks like her mother.

Hans has a son, Lucas, and a beautiful young daughter Kathrine. Flossie lives in London and Hans, Henriette and family in Copenhagen.

My routine these days invariably starts off with BBC News and a glance through the newspapers. I find myself drawn to the obituary columns, for some macabre reason. Morbid curiosity, I guess.

A. E. Matthews, a fine English actor who specialized in playing bumbling old eccentric Englishmen, had an enormous appetite for work, and at one time not only was he appearing on stage in the West End in *The Chiltern Hundreds*, but he was also making a film of it at Denham Studios, where my career started. A journalist asked AE how, at his advanced age, being as he was in his eighties (well?), how could he film all day then go out and perform a play at night.

'Quite simple, my boy. At seven o'clock the butler comes in with my breakfast, boiled egg, tea, toast, marmalade and a folded, neatly pressed copy of *The Times*. I open it to the obituaries, and if I am not mentioned, I have m' breakfast, get dressed and go to work!'

That's my philosophy too.

I keep physically active and keep my mind active too. Having had a few back problems over the years, I don't do my old daily exercise regime in the mornings and I do feel the difference, I must admit. The old limbs creak a bit. I walk, though. In Switzerland we do Nordic Walking across snow with poles – and when in Monaco I like early-morning walks along the front before it gets too hot, or we drive to Fontvielle and then walk to Cap d'Ail. It's such a beautiful stretch of coastline.

I enjoy cooking too: the wok being my favourite cooking utensil. If we eat at lunch-time, then in the evening we just have a piece of fruit or a boiled egg and retire early to watch TV in bed.

It's not a bad life.

In 2007 I celebrated my eightieth birthday. Can it be? Eighty!

David McKenzie asked me to host the *Magic Awards Show* in LA around the same time, so we decided that we'd all head out there for a few weeks and celebrate together – all the children came – and Kristina hosted the most fabulous dinner for me and so many of my lovely friends. It was a hugely memorable night. The trip was made more memorable by me being awarded a star on the Hollywood Walk of Fame. Outside number two thousand and seven, 2007, I knelt down to unveil the star, surrounded by my family and friends. Unfortunately there wasn't a stool with a handle, as at Buckingham Palace, to help me get up!

Fifty years earlier I'd arrived in Hollywood an unknown, full of hopes, aspirations and ambitions (and with knees that worked); now I was being hailed by huge crowds. It's funny how life goes, isn't it?

I don't think I feel any different having turned eighty. Then again, age is just a number, isn't it? It's what's inside that counts and I feel just the same as ever, albeit with a few extra creaks.

One thing's for sure, I realize just how lucky I've been in life and how fortunate I am to have such a wonderful family and terrific friends. I've not done badly for a boy from Stockwell, where I used to gaze at the silver screen in wonderment; little realizing I'd be a part of this magical world. It's been fantastic.

I've often been asked what I might like my epitaph to be. Well, that's easy. I've no intention of going anywhere so won't need one!

Around the World in Eighty Years

My travels with UNICEF

The other day it occurred to me that in my eighty years I must have been around the world at least once. I've already documented some of my travel experiences, but with UNICEF my travelling increased dramatically, as did the number of countries I visited. It would be impractical to list every single field trip and UNICEF initiative I was involved with, however I thought it might be an idea to recollect some of the more memorable ones for you in a whistle-stop tour.

ALBANIA The trip, in 1994, was a short two years after the election of the first non-communist president since World War II, Sali Berisha, a doctor of medicine. He was in control of a country that, since 1939, had suffered with annexation by Italy, occupation by the Nazis and, after the Second World War, affiliation by two oppressive regimes, first the USSR and Stalinism, then China and Maoism.

On this trip, accompanied by my UNICEF colleague and friend, Horst Cerni, I was working on behalf of the Kiwanis (a global organization of volunteers dedicated to changing the world, one child and one community at a time) to raise funds and awareness for the elimination of Iodine Deficiency Disorders (IDDs).

Driving away from the airport, I noticed that all the factories we drove past had their windows smashed. It was an overhang from occupation, we were told; apparently, on liberation from the communist regime, the workers had put the windows out in an act of defiance against their managers. The countryside, meanwhile, was covered with thousands of pillboxes and antitank constructions, set against invasion by Lord knows whom, while other infrastructure was practically non-existent. We drove out of Tirana to visit a salt plant, and on the way stopped off at a so-called 'health centre'. A more depressing sight than this you could not imagine: a filthy delivery room, dominated by a rusting metal table with stirrups; a refrigerator with the door hanging off and, in the other room (there were only two) were four cots with dirty mattresses and four grubby, stained blankets. The air was foul. It was a relief to get back in the car and continue our journey.

When we arrived at the salt plant, it had the all-important iodization equipment, but it was in complete disrepair and had not been used for twenty years. It needed replacing completely. I felt disheartened. The following day we visited a hospital near Tirana where they treated out-patients suffering from IDD. I remember thinking that all this could have been avoided if only the salt factory's equipment was up and running – it would probably have worked out cheaper too.

That night I dined with President Berisha and his charming wife Liri. They were both very much aware of the country's IDD problems and I tried to highlight for them how the problem could be minimized. They reacted positively and said they looked forward to any assistance that might be forthcoming from UNICEF.

ANDORRA In 1961 I had driven from Barcelona to Andorra – just out of curiosity – and, forty-six years later, I was back again with Kristina. On the second trip I noted that this small mountainous country has the highest life expectancy of any country in the world: 83.52 years. But this wasn't a trip on which we hoped to gain a couple more years of mortal coil: it was a UNICEF fund-raising visit. There, we had the pleasure of meeting many of our UNICEF colleagues and being entertained royally at the same time as imposing on the generosity of the good people of Andorra in raising funds for the disadvantaged children in the world.

ARGENTINA Oh, how we loved our trip to Buenos Aires. The tango has to be the most exciting dance form ever and we were privileged to be taken to the dress rehearsal of a new Tango show with Juan Carlos Copez, where he danced, with his daughter, just for us. What a thrill! Kristina and I were there to film some TV interviews and heighten UNICEF awareness. This was my second time in Argentina. My first had been in 1979 filming *Moonraker*. At that time I was ignorant of the poverty in certain areas of the country and the problems facing young children and their mothers; my only worries were where we'd be eating and whether I had enough clean shirts for the next day. UNICEF certainly focussed my mind on the really important things in life.

AUSTRALIA I have made a number of trips to Australia. The first time on a promotional visit for the textile company Pearsons, when I was on the board. Another time I collected the Logie TV award for *The Persuaders* in Melbourne. Then there was unforgettable trip with George Barrie and Brut Films. Happily, Australia has little child poverty and much of UNICEF's work there is in raising funds for less fortunate countries.

The last time I was in Sydney, during the late 1990s, Kristina and I were invited to meet Ken Done. As well as being a very talented artist he was also appointed a UNICEF ambassador in 1988. We boarded a boat to cross Sydney harbour to his office and experienced the wettest, roughest crossing ever – we'd obviously brought the British weather with us! I trust on our next visit the weather will be as hospitable as the country folk have always been!

Much as I hate to name drop – let alone Queen drop – but four years ago Kristina and I were invited to the future Queen of Denmark's wedding in Copenhagen. Mary Donaldson from Hobart, Tasmania, married a long-time friend of ours, Crown Prince Frederik of Denmark. A right royal do you might say, with the father of the bride resplendent in his kilt of the Donaldson clan. By the way, Mary is beautiful, the Crown Prince is a lucky man.

BELGIUM I know that I'll bring the wrath of French cooks on my head, but I truly find Belgian cuisine first class. The Belgians have an excellent UNICEF committee, and Brussels is the European HQ for Starwood Hotels and the 'Checkout for Children' campaign.

BRAZIL Kristina and I made one trip here entirely for pleasure, as guests of Ivo Hélcio Jardim de Campos Pitanguy, a world-famous plastic surgeon and his family, on his private island. It was, I thought, a perfect setting for a Bond villain's hideout. Ivo is no villain though, his humanitarian record is exceptional. Just one example of his altruism happened in 1961, when a burning circus tent fell on 2,500 men, women and children enjoying a pre-Christmas treat. For weeks afterwards, Ivo worked nonstop treating the burn victims. Now at the Santa Casa da Misericodia Hospital in Rio, for the last forty years he has operated, free of charge, on impoverished patients.

CAMBODIA In the autumn of 2003 we made our first visit to this fascinating but impoverished country. UNICEF has a difficult task in trying to ensure that Cambodia's children have lives that can compare with their peers in industrial nations. The principal objective of this field trip was for IDD awareness. Our UNICEF representative there, Rodney Hatfield, very English and very good company, took us on some long drives through the Killing Fields. He took us south of Phnom Penh to Kampot, at the base of the Elephant Mountains on the Kampong River. On the evening of our arrival, we were taken by the governor of the province to a riverside restaurant, where we ate the best shrimps I have ever had.

One of the problems for children in Cambodia is malnutrition. In the villages around Kampot we didn't have to look far to see both children and adults suffering with iodine deficiency. With that in mind, on arriving back in Phnom Penh for an audience with HM King Norodom Sihanouk the following morning, we took with us a presentation box of iodized salt. We had thought that presenting this symbolic gift would give me the opportunity to leap into my, 'the reason why salt has to be iodized ...' speech. But the King was way ahead of us. He was an expert on the subject and welcomed UNICEF's initiative, saying he looked forward to working with us. We talked for a while and then the King raised his hand.

'As it is eleven o'clock, it's time for champagne'.

Well, all that talk of salt made us thirsty!

CANADA I have a soft spot for Canada – and I can't recall the exact number of times I've visited this wonderful country. For many years Harry Black was head of the UNICEF Committee, but my first contact was a lovely lady called Olive Sloane. Olive went with me to Prince Edward Island (known as PEI), which was joined to the mainland by a long green bridge, known as the Bridge of Green Cables, a play on words, of course.

When travelling, I have a little trick for arriving at the next venue looking as if I had just stepped out of Burton's window, and I employed it on this occasion. As soon as I get my bags to the hotel room, I take my suits out and hang them in the bathroom, where I turn on the hot tap in the bath, then close the door, allowing the room to fill with steam and remove any unsightly wrinkles in the suits. The first stop of this particular evening was to make a speech to the local dignitaries and the kind and generous supporters of UNICEF who paid quite a lot of money to have me stand up and bore them for a couple of hours. Having looked at my notes and put on my shirt and tie, I opened the bathroom door to discover that three pairs of trousers had slipped off their hangers and were now floating in the boiling hot bath. Donning my only pair of dry trousers – the ones I had arrived in – I slung on a blazer and went down to the lobby, where Olive was waiting for me. We raised quite a lot of money that night I believe. Perhaps my wrinkled trousers made them think I needed the money?

CHILE It may be the longest country in the world but it was the shortest visit to a country that we have ever experienced for UNICEF. We were in and out in a day just to record a TV programme. A short trip, a short report!

CHINA There were two reasons for visiting China in August 2004. The first was to address the Asian Football Confederation and China Football Association, and to see China play Japan. The Asian Football Confederation and the CFA very generously presented me with a cheque for UNICEF of $100,000. The second, and far more serious, reason was to help in the HIV/AIDS campaign and in particular to support the UNICEF China initiative in bringing children orphaned by HIV/AIDS to summer camps.

The morning after the presentation, Kristina and I visited Tiananmen Square to make a tour of the Forbidden City, for which I had made the audio guide in Chicago years before. I listened to my recording and was impressed with how much I knew about the place. Let me rephrase that, I was impressed by how well written the material was that I had recorded. From there we went to see the Summer Palace. The guidebook said that it is an ideal place to avoid the sun ... we discovered that it wasn't quite an ideal place to avoid the torrential rain though, which greeted us when we were halfway around the grounds.

We visited a summer camp just outside Beijing, where a group of seventy children orphaned by HIV/AIDS had gathered together from twelve different regions. In an afternoon of both joy and tears, Kristina and I sat in the garden surrounded by the children and their chaperones. We took pictures and they were fascinated to see how my latest gadget could show their images immediately. The youngsters were looking forward to seeing the Great Wall, Tiananmen Square, the Forbidden City and other Chinese treasures.

There was one very pretty child of eleven or twelve years. She was full of laughter and bursting with personality. Through the interpreter, we asked if she and the others could sing for us – which they all did, without further prompting. It was a song that all children in China are familiar with, and suddenly our pretty girl's eyes welled up with tears, which then started to roll down her cheeks. I asked what the words of the song were and we were told that it was something like, 'The best thing in life is your mummy'.

Kristina started crying, as did I. I wasn't the tough British agent 007 by any means. It was such a beautiful yet such a sad song. These poor children had no mummies. It was very hard saying goodbye to our new young friends who dazzled us further before our departure with traditional dancing.

On the way back to the hotel Charles Rycroft, UNICEF'S press officer in China, told us why the children had been billeted so far from the centre. Apparently none of the hotels or youth hostels in Beijing would accept them. They were stigmatized. I thought it was disgraceful. The next morning we went to a press conference with Charles, the UNICEF China representative Dr Christian Voumard, and Chinese actor and National Goodwill Ambassador, Pu Cunxin. Charles introduced us to the assembled press corps but, still furious about the treatment of the orphans, I remarked that the Beijing hoteliers should hang their heads in shame. I thought that maybe I had gone too far with my scathing comments, and so did UNICEF New York, apparently, but the following day the National Chinese Press agreed with me.

CROATIA My first ever glimpse of Croatia was from a cruise ship, The Sea Goddess, which had been chartered by Dame Vivien Duffield who took some friends on a seven-day cruise to celebrate her fortieth birthday. Being the gentleman that I am, I shall refrain from saying how many years ago that was. I was married to Luisa at the time; in fact I was given the award at the end of the trip for being 'The most henpecked husband on the ship'. I had to beat off some pretty heavy competition, I might add.

On landing in Dubrovnik and in stepping into its medieval streets, the first sign I saw was advertising a Bond film, which may have been the reason that, a few years later, the Serbs were lobbing bombs at this UNESCO World Heritage Site.

I have been back many times since the fighting and I am so happy to be able to say there is no evidence of the damage that was inflicted on those hapless inhabitants.

CZECH REPUBLIC My son Christian decided to spend some time in Prague in the early 'noughties', and became involved in the setting up of a film studio in the historic and beautiful city. Our first trip there was, of course, to see Christian, but shortly after that I was asked by UNICEF and the Kiwanis to spend a little time there again. I shall never forget that week in winter, crossing the Vitiva River by way of Charles Bridge, with giant flakes of snow falling and a complete silence that one only becomes aware of during a heavy snowfall. We were completely alone and yet only a few hours before the bridge had been packed with tourists and memorabilia and trinket sellers.

DENMARK I have been visiting Denmark on-and-off for sixty years and I still cannot say more than, 'Hej, mina damer og herrer, jeg er meget glad for at vaere her I dag!' As the Danes are far more adaptable than the English and can in the main speak better English than the English, then my few words are sufficient. Sixty years ago I posed for a photograph by the famous Hans Christian Andersen statue in the Rad Hus Pladsen in Copenhagen; five years ago I was honoured to be appointed an Ambassador for Hans Christian Andersen, along with Harry Belafonte and a number of other distinguished artistes. This initiative was to encourage young people the world over to read the master and raise funds for the education of the millions of children who cannot read or write and have no access to primary education.

Denmark has a very active UNICEF committee and although it is a small country, it ranks in the top five of per capita donations. UNICEF's Global Supply headquarters is also in Copenhagen. Kristina and I found it absolutely fascinating to see the place in action; in an emergency situation, a large number of volunteers report immediately and start packing emergency requirements, such as blankets, tents, medical kits, some essential equipment for primary health care workers, midwifery kits, 'Schools in a Box' ... the list seems endless. One could say practically everything from a pin to an elephant can be found there. I heartily recommend a visit to the warehouse to any prospective UNICEF representative.

EGYPT I've paid many visits to the Land of the Pharoahs, but Kristina and I returned more recently with David and Laura McKenzie when we were making two documentaries, and we also enjoyed the bonus of a magical cruise down the Nile from Cairo to Luxor and back. On-board, we had a terrace above the bow of the boat and each evening, with a warm, gentle breeze embracing us, we watched the feluccas sliding by. It was if time had stood still and we were back in the days of Cleopatra. We then visited Karnak, the Valley of the Kings and, back in Cairo, we had a personal tour of The Egyptian Museum of Antiquities. Personally, I thought I was rather brave going into this museum, as there's always the risk that they might keep me.

UNICEF is very active in Egypt and has many problems to address, not least those of street children, education, immunization and, what I find most repellent, the circumcision of young girls. Kristina and I had a meeting with the first lady, Suzanne Mubarak. In one of the elegant reception rooms of her home in Cairo, she spoke very frankly and agreed that the custom of female genital mutilation (or, in UN speak, FGM/C) was one of her great concerns too. However, she told us that this was a problem not easily resolved as, though it was no longer allowed to be performed in hospitals, the procedure was being undertaken by backstreet doctors, often in unhygienic conditions. Many young women had died as a result of infections.

FINLAND There was not a great deal to see as the plane approached Helsinki; I know that Finland boasts clean air and no smog, but unfortunately there was a lot of the dark grey stuff around as I came down the steps from the plane. Professor Lindström, Executive Secretary at UNICEF, was waiting for me in the fog and we drove to his house, there was not much to see on the way there either! His home was hidden away in a forest of trees, where his charming wife had prepared a dinner for the three of us. I then hopped into a taxi and had another dark drive to the hotel. So far I hadn't seen much of the country.

The hotel lobby seemed to be a rather depressing establishment, and on entering my room it turned out to be even more depressing. The floor was wood, with wafer-thin rugs scattered about, the bed had greyish sheets and there was one pillow, also wafer thin. The bathroom was tiled with white enamelled tin, the section by the sink curling upwards in the corners. A tap dripped into the bath, leaving a long red rusty stain down to the plughole (I'm beginning to sound like Michael Winner). It was not my idea of heaven. When morning came, I dressed ready for action. The good professor was in the lobby and off we set. As we turned the corner, driving along the seafront on the right, the professor pointed out a large rather modern elegant hotel.

'That's the best hotel in Helsinki.'

'Oh really? Couldn't I have stayed there?' I said. 'I can pay for it.'

'No, I am afraid you don't understand the reasoning here,' the professor said. 'If you are raising money for charity, it must not appear that you live in luxury!'

Suitably chastized, we moved on to our first school visit. I was going to address the senior students and there would also be a press conference to handle. It was most interesting, because every question was loaded.

'How much money do you earn?'

'Do you give to charity?'

'Why do you do this?'

I, of course, replied truthfully to every question realizing that, at that time, Finland was a country with socialist leanings and in actual fact they were quite entitled to ask those questions. I was almost ashamed of myself to the point where I thought I might leave the hotel and sleep in a tent.

FRANCE Like the majority of Englishmen of my era, the French language was a compulsory subject in school and I spent three or four years, 'J'ai, tu as, il a, nous avoning . . .' However, it was taught in such a boring fashion that I developed a mental block and oh, how I regret it. Even now, I struggle manfully in shops and restaurants and dread the dinner parties where I'm seated among people who do not converse in English. I have tried the Berlitz method and all the others that *en trouve sur l'Internet*, but without success. That mental block persists. Maybe now that I have arrived at my three score and ten, plus another ten, I shall be excused if I make the odd mistake!

GERMANY Modesty almost forbids me to mention that in 2005 the then President, Johannes Rau, awarded me the *Bundesverdienstkreuz*, the Federal Cross of Merit. His charming wife, sadly now his widow, Christina Delius, was very active in her support of UNICEF, maybe she had nudged the president to give me such an award?

GHANA Our trip to Ghana actually started in Zurich, in 1999. We had been invited to a dinner with a number of potential donors and, after dinner, I was invited to talk about UNICEF. Returning to our table, I sat with Mark Makepeace, the FTSE Group's Chief Executive, who was very sympathetic towards the aims and needs of UNICEF. The outcome of our post-dinner conversation was that I would investigate the possibility of taking a number of likely donors on a field trip. It would be called a Flight to Reality.

It was Abraham Lincoln who said, 'A commitment is what turns a promise into a reality'. It did become a reality, and the first of these flights was in 2000 when, together with Mark, Gordon Glick from UNICEF UK and corporate partners and representatives of the UK National Committee, we arrived in Ghana. The first day, we flew north by helicopter, landing somewhere in a jungle where we transferred to four-wheel drive trucks. We bumped and bounced our way to a village on the shore of Lake Volta, where we spent a few hours talking with children and their parents. It was interesting to find out what their priorities were: here the children wanted light. They said that they walked miles to school and when they came home it was dark and they couldn't see to do their homework. We take it for granted don't we?

Accompanied by all the villagers, we walked down to water's edge where a long wooden boat was waiting to take us further down the lake and to another village. The lake was studded with broken trees, some above and some below the surface; the water, I'm sure, was crocodile infested. I should add now that one member of our party had been quite green in the face on the helicopter, and the thought of a watery grave did not appeal to him either. He was very, very silent. Fortunately we arrived – dry – at our next destination, where the male village elders were all sitting in a line in the shade of a giant tree. The children, as always, sung a song of welcome and we then moved to shake hands with the men. It was very strange; they would not take the hands of the ladies in our party. A religious thing? Or were women still seen as inferior to men?

When it became time to leave our helicopter took us to an airfield further north, where a plane was waiting to take us to another destination even further north! My green-faced friend went a very pale shade of green. He told me he hated helicopters. He was going to hate the next form of transportation even more I thought! With our seat belts fastened and the twin engines roaring, we climbed slowly and banked to the left. Pale Green Face was definitely not keen on this either, and as the night gradually drew in on us I saw his lips moving as if in prayer. Then, the plane started to buck and the engines took on a different sound. All around us were big, black thunderclouds and the lightning cracked as the pilot tried to climb and bank out of the storm. PGF's lips were moving overtime. After being tossed around the heavens, the pilot's voice came over the speaker to tell us that it was not possible to continue and we would have to fly back to Accra, from where we had started our tour early that morning. It occurred to me that we couldn't have that much fuel left as we had been tossed around for what seemed hours. PGF had the same thought. With eyes tightly closed he silently prayed and I believe that he did a deal with God right there and then: if we came home safely he would be a VERY generous donor. He still is!

The following day we visited various projects in and around Accra. We stopped at a UNICEF-supported school that was run by a Ghanian couple, who had sold their family business to buy this property to help in the education of the underprivileged children. Our next stop was in a stone quarry where, after breaking away large boulders, the men would struggle up the hill with them to where women and children were sitting with hammers, breaking the large rocks into gravel. This back-breaking toil went on day after day for hours on end. Their reward? One measly dollar a week. Many of the women were sightless in one eye, and many, like their children, were missing toes and fingers, or had ugly scars on their exposed limbs. It was a heart-breaking sight. Disgusted with the insufferable conditions, Kristina commented to a camera crew accompanying us that she felt a deep shame that we lived in a world that permitted this form of slavery. These people should at least be given protective goggles. She repeated this when we later met with the minister of health. His reply was that they were lucky to receive a dollar a week. Such heartlessness.

Back in Accra the next day we took part in a celebration of 'Kick Polio Out of Africa' in the presence of the then first lady Mrs Jerry

Rawlings. Not forgetting my promises to the Kiwanis we also spent time at a salt iodization plant close to Accra, and I am happy to say that it was more functional than the one I had seen years before in Albania. The 'flight to reality' had been very real.

GREECE In September 2005, we flew from Helsinki to Athens – where we were going to attend a gala dinner to celebrate the tenth anniversary of Check Out For Children, the brainchild of Robert Scott. Robert and Christina Papathassiout the hotel's public relations manager had arranged that we should stay in the royal suite. Four hundred square metres of sheer luxury, entrance hall, gigantic bedroom, bathroom and dressing rooms, steam room and gym, a grand piano that was dwarfed in the enormous sitting room, a dining room for at least twenty people, and a kitchen, plus a library-come-office in which part of the bookcased wall slid to one side to reveal the bedroom. A terrace ran the entire length of the suite and overlooked Constitution Square. To our left, the high-stepping white-skirted guards in front of the government building that was once, I believe, the Royal Palace. HM King Constantine visits quite often and stays at the Grande Bretagne but always declines the royal suite, preferring a view in the other direction!

HUNGARY My first time in Budapest was for Brut Films. The second was after the 'red menace' had left, and Budapest seemed a very different place. The architecture was the same, apart from some new hotels and office buildings, but the atmosphere was very different and the violins heard in practically every restaurant seemed to play sweeter, which is the only way that I can describe it. Now, it had a democratically elected government and the city had returned to some of its former glory. On my last trip I had stayed on the flat side of the Danube, the Pest, but this time Kristina and I were to stay at the Hilton Budapest Hotel on the Buda side in the Castle district. It has become one of our favourite hotels and we look forward to every visit.

We went back in 2006 and visited a number of children's homes, one a kindergarten for children of homeless parents. I was surprised to discover that, despite Hungary being democratic, there is still a strong prejudice against the gypsy community. It seems that there are parents who will not let their children go to the same schools as, or mix with, children of gypsy blood. It seems very sad that, after all the country has suffered under restrictive regimes, there should be prejudice of any sort. We met many brilliant musicians, themselves gypsies, who are only accepted for their musical talent and not for their God-given right to exist as normal human beings.

Also during this visit, we met the members of the Hungarian National Philharmonic Orchestra and their musical director, the most talented Zoltan Kocsis. I had the privilege of announcing their appointments as Goodwill Ambassadors and we then announced that in 2007 we would give two concerts in aid of UNICEF and also that I would narrate Saint Saens' 'The Carnival of the Animals', which would be recorded on DVD and sold for the benefit of UNICEF. On the nights of the recordings, Zoltan was suffering very badly with flu, but it did not affect the energy that he applies to his conducting – and that was despite the fact that I skipped one entire movement and in the second concert someone forgot to call the pianists! Amazingly no tempers were lost, Zoltan did not hit me over the head with his baton, and I personally had a wonderful evening.

I don't know whether the wives of the president and the prime minister and also of the minister of foreign affairs had anything to do with it, but between the time of the 2006 and 2007 visits, the Hungarian government tripled it's donation to UNICEF. Köszönöm. (Thank you in Hungarian.)

ICELAND Stefan Stefansson, the executive director of UNICEF Iceland, was waiting at the foot of the steps of the private jet that had picked us up in Sion, Switzerland, half an hour's drive from our Crans-Montana home, and brought us to Reykjavik. Not, I hasten to add, the usual form of transportation for UNICEF ambassadors, it was thanks to the generosity of the Bauger Group, an International Investment Company in retail and fashion. It was the very first UNICEF fundraiser that had ever been held in Iceland.

INDIA In November 2005 I went back to India for the third time, but this time as someone who felt that he was giving a little back for all the good luck that he had enjoyed. Landing in Delhi, it had been arranged that I should address the Hindustan Times Leadership forum, together with the Indian Prime Minister, Manmohan Singh, the former US secretary of defence, William Cohen, and the finance minister, P. Chidambaram, among others, on IDD awareness.

I was in my first year of playing *The Saint* when Mrs Pratibha Patil entered the world of politics. Today she is the twelfth president of India, but the day we met in Jaipur she was the governor of Rajisthan. In fact she was not only the first female governor of Rajisthan but also was to become the first female president. No wonder we were impressed with her knowledge and empathy for the Iodization of Salt and for its universal usage. She had authorized the free distribution of iodized salt in remote areas: more politicians of her kind would make the WHO and UNICEF's jobs a lot easier.

In Jaipur, we didn't have time to visit the Pink Palace, just enough time to admire it from afar as we visited various salt manufacturers and salt projects. We took a long drive to visit a primary school. As we had in Indonesia, two young girls sat at a table with testing kits and demonstrated to us and the other children how to check the iodine levels in the family salt. A cheery farewell, and off we went to a project that feeds 300,000 children a midday meal every day.

Back to the reality of India, it's very hard to drive through Mumbai without being accosted at every stop sign by pathetic beggars holding babies and pleading for money. India is the seventh largest country in the world, it is the second most populous, the largest democracy, and has the second fastest growing economy, but it still has unacceptable levels of poverty, malnutrition and illiteracy. We had flown from Jaipur to Mumbai to have the opportunity of meeting with a large number of Bollywood personalities and enlist their support for UNICEF's goals. A very enthusiastic and supportive group, and who knows? They might just offer me a Bollywood movie.

INDONESIA We entered the grand Presidential Palace for an audience with President Abdurrahman Wahid of Indonesia, and after the usual ritual of being received by aides we were ushered into a very ornate, indeed palatial, reception room. This UNICEF visit was for the IDD campaign and I was to discuss the iodization of salt in Indonesia with His Excellency. Kristina, myself and the UNICEF Indonesia representative were invited to sit on a sofa and chairs placed to the left of the president's chair; facing us would be the aides and interpreters. The door behind the president's chair opened and, as we rose from our seats, a frail almost blind gentleman entered and took his seat, having given a nod of greeting in our direction. It was a pleasant meeting with Mr Wahid, he agreed that there was indeed a problem with Iodine Deficiency Disorders and welcomed our efforts.

Our next meeting was to be with Mme Megawati Sukarnoputri, the vice-president. It was a less formal affair than the presidential meeting, and I had been told that it was more than likely that she would soon be replacing President Wahid and thus it was more important that we should stress the seriousness of our campaign with her. She was indeed interested in our reasons for being there and promised that she would actively support us.

Pupils at a school we were going to visit had been asked to bring salt from their homes for us to check with our test kits to see whether the salt their mothers bought was iodized. Our little party was seated behind a table in the playground and, one by one, the boys and girls came up to see us do the tests. A number showed no iodine content whatsoever, but the children assured us that their mothers had bought salt that said on the packaging that it was iodized. Their faces were so sad, it was if we'd told them that they had failed in maths or geography.

Our next stop was Surabaya. We arrived at the Surabaya Sheraton Hotel, always happy to see the Check Out for Children information displayed in reception. We were to lunch with the governor of Surabaya and then visit one of the most important salt factories in the region. There, we were shown their packaging and then the fake packaging that purported to contain iodized salt. Their salt – the iodized salt – cost one cent more than the un-iodized salt, and for this the customers in the markets were being swindled. A point I raised in letters to the governors of all the provinces, asking them to carry out checks in the marketplaces.

IRELAND In March 2001, Kristina and I went to Dublin and, staying as guests of the Conrad Hotel, we attended the Mother's Day luncheon organized by Maura Quinn who was at that time the director of UNICEF, Ireland. On my left at the luncheon was the mother of one of Ireland's best contributions to cinema, Liam Neeson, the Big Man who is a National Goodwill Ambassador for Ireland, along with another feller who played Bond, Pierce Brosnan, and two other fine actors, Gabriel Byrne and Stephen Rea. So why with all these Irish actors did they ask me to speak? Maybe they thought that as my name is Moore I must have a bit of the old sod in me. I love Ireland: great food, the Guinness, and what's more it was the first country to ban smoking in restaurants, good for them.

JAMAICA At the end of October 2001 we were lucky enough to be invited to the Jamaican Film and Music Festival and, even nicer, we were able to take Deborah and Christian. We were given a villa in the Half Moon Rose Hall resort – with our own pool and a twenty-yard walk to the beach, a bay with golden sands and palm trees gently swaying in the breeze. Well that's how it was the day we arrived. However, the following morning the wind was howling, the pool thick with leaves, the palm trees no longer gently swaying. Oh no! They were being whipped by the wind and the golden sands were hidden under the crashing surf which ended its onward rush at the edge of our pool. It was hurricane season and we were on the edge of a big one.

Mercifully, it passed but it had left in its wake seas that made it impossible to bathe and a beach littered with mounds of flotsam. Braving the elements, we ventured forth to attend a luncheon together with the Mayor of Montego Bay and the British High Commissioner, it was a UNICEF lunch to benefit Street Children, and later that day we were able to meet with some of them. The following day while I was dealing with some UNICEF meetings, Kristina was taken to visit a home far from the tourist areas where children suffering with severe disabilities were cared for. She returned badly shaken by what she had seen, not that the care was inadequate, it was the heartlessness found in so many places believing that by hiding these unfortunate young human beings away from sight, then the rest of us could forget them. Fortunately there are dedicated, selfless people in this world who make it their business to care.

Before we took our leave of Jamaica, I was presented with the Marcus Garvey Lifetime Achievement Award by the creator and organizer of the festival, Sheryl Lee Ralph, a very talented actress and singer.

JAPAN For me there are two Japans. There is the Japan I've visited in order to publicize a movie and there is the UNICEF Japan, trips we look forward to with great anticipation. The Japanese National Committee is, or was back in 2004, the most successful of the UNICEF family in being the first one to donate more than US $100,000,000. This not only reflects on the generous nature of the Japanese people, but also the tireless work of the committee under the leadership of Yoshihisa Togo, a wonderful Goodwill Ambassador, actress Tetsuko Kuroyanagi, who has been with UNICEF since 1984, and Dr Agnes Chan Miling, a popular singer and television personality, who has been active as the Japan Committee's Ambassador since 1998.

KOREA In 2001, together with Sam Koo, we arrived in Seoul from Tokyo. Sam was all smiles as he was going to see his wife again: she is the world famous cellist, Myung-wha Chung. Also waiting to meet us was our friend Reiko from Japan, she was in Korea in her UNICEF capacity, to help us through the South Korean formalities. This was going to prove to be one of the busiest legs of our tour.

LUXEMBOURG Europe's best-kept secret is the Grand Duchy of Luxembourg; one of the forty-four landlocked countries in the world with a population of just under half a million. My knowledge of Luxembourg, up until 1994, was really rather sketchy. Before the war I listened as did hundreds of English children to the Ovaltinies on Radio Luxembourg, 'We are the Ovaltinies, Happy boys and girls…la la la!' My friend and fellow actor Pete Murray did a DJ show from there, and that was about it, I'm ashamed to say.

That changed in 1994 when, together with Horst Cerni from UNICEF NYC, I arrived in Luxembourg from a rain-soaked Saarbrücken where, apart from launching millions of plastic ducks into the river − a race to win funds for UNICEF − we had a ceremony creating Saarbrücken as the fourth German twin town with UNICEF. On this trip we had already visited Amsterdam, Hanover, Tirana and Munich. So when the car disgorged us in Luxembourg I was sporting clothes that were badly in need of a press, as was my body. The reps from the Luxembourg committee met with us and I did the usual round of interviews, 'Who was your favourite Bond girl?' etc.

'So now let me tell you a little more about UNICEF . . .'

'How do you like Luxembourg?'

Fortunately this was all taking place at the airport and consequently we did not have far to step for the relative safety of a LUXAIR jet.

Six years were to pass before Kristina and I returned to Luxembourg as I had been offered a film with Tom Conti, Luke Perry, Olivia D'Abo and Horst Bucholtz there. The film unit put us into the Intercontinental Hotel, I believe it is now a Hilton, which was set in a lovely wooded area of Luxembourg – and that is what Luxembourg has in abundance. Outside the city there are some spectacular sights to see, old castles, quaint little towns and some of the best restaurants to be found anywhere, and one more thing: they produce some excellent wines.

MEXICO I've paid many visits to Mexico over the years, to some of the most beautiful places – and people – one can imagine. However, some of our other trips to Mexico were on a far more serious note. In 1998 Kristina and I made our first field trip, which started off at Health Ministry level, and we also promoted the Sheraton Hotels, Check Out for Children fund-raising initiative. We have found that it's important to enthuse the hotel staff with the idea, after all it's the maid who turns the beds down that places the UNICEF information on the pillows. It is important that everyone connected to the hotel group knows that they are helping to make life better for children.

We spent a couple of days in Mexico City and then left for the south, to visit a children's project in Oaxaca. This was a very successful project for this poor region: before it began the children didn't get a midday meal and they didn't get schooling, now they ate and they were being educated. It was very popular. We sat at long tables placed in the shade of a building and, with some apprehension, having seen the vast number of flies buzzing around the kitchen, started to eat. It was delicious but I was anxious we might have a little problem on the return drive. The end of the meal was signalled by everyone raising their glasses of the local tequila, swallowing it down and taking a second glassful . . . no problem, then or on the way back. I wish I had a bottle of that now, I could make a fortune, either curing all digestive disorders or stripping paint off furniture.

On our return to Mexico City we visited a large medical establishment and participated in a discussion of the IDD problems in Mexico, including villages with one hundred per cent dwarfism. The film we were shown was most disturbing.

In 2004, together with Lord Marshall, who was then chairman of British Airways, we flew to Mexico City. This being a part of the 'Change for Good' partnership with BA we naturally had a collection on the aircraft flying down. I made the appeal and then went around the plane hustling the BA customers to dig deep in their pockets, and they did. In Mexico City, Lord Marshall pledged £150,000 to go with the £1,000,000 that BA had already given to assist in the drive to educate the children in the city.

There are thousands of children living on the streets of Mexico City and it is estimated that over 60,000 are not even enrolled in schools. There are many projects that have UNICEF and BA support in the city, places where they can eat, get an education and, sometimes, be saved from the violence that stalks these youngsters. It is very gratifying to see the beneficial results of many of these schemes.

MACEDONIA In May 1999, Macedonia was trying to cope with the influx of about a quarter of a million refugees from the conflict in Kosovo. We had been asked by Carol Bellamy, UNICEF's Executive Director, to fly into Skopje to raise awareness of UNICEF's mission and to raise funds. We were able to visit three different camps erected by the UNHCR and within these camps UNICEF had set up tented schools, which were trying to bring some form of normal education to the hundreds of unfortunate children. The teachers were all refugees themselves, and so great was the number of children that the teachers had to have three sessions of classes a day.

It was heart-warming for us to see how clean and well turned out these pupils were – and so well mannered, we couldn't enter a class without them all standing up. An image that will stay with me for ever, is of a handsome young refugee with a shaven head. It transpired that she was a girl and the teacher told us that the girl's father had shaved her for fear that she would be raped.

In Skopje itself we were taken to a house where the owner had taken in forty-two refugees. I heard some horrific and harrowing stories that day. Through an interpreter, one middle-aged refugee told us about his circumstances. Three months before, some Serbs had held him at gunpoint while they raped his teenage daughter, he was then taken and thrown from a truck in the middle of nowhere and told that if he showed his face in the town again he would be killed. He stayed in the woods for a couple of months, meeting up with others in similar straits. They heard that the border was going to be opened and they could get to Macedonia, but to get to the border he had to pass near where he had lived, and in a field he saw evidence of where his family had been massacred. Blinded by tears and rage he had left the country of his birth.

The following day we had a meeting with the president, Kiro Gligorov. At eighty-two, he was the oldest president in the world, but we were warned not to be surprised by his appearance. In 1995 he was the victim of a car bomb assassination attempt. It left him blind in one eye, with a deep scar, almost a crater, in his forehead. His one good eye, however, seemed to have a permanent twinkle. He talked a great deal about the Kosovo situation and how his country needed aid because of revenue lost through being unable to export their fruit and vegetables.

Our last evening in Skopje was spent together with another Goodwill Ambassador, Vanessa Redgrave, along with friends she had made while touring the camps. They were musicians and actors, all refugees themselves and all with terrifying tales to tell of atrocities witnessed.

MOROCCO Morocco was the destination of the first 'Flight to Reality'. We flew from Gatwick and there I met for the first time the incredible Lord Bill Deedes. He would have been eighty-eight when we made that trip, and he left us all standing when it came to energy. The purpose of this field visit was to show our FTSE friends and some of our donors how UNICEF made a difference in the lives of villagers who lived in the southern Atlas mountains. From Marrakech, we drove to the first of a group of villages that UNICEF had provided with water points and small schools. When it had started a few years before, the first school they saw had about forty boys, no girls, but since water had been provided they were able to have separate toilet facilities for girls and at the time of our visit there were an equal number of girls and boys. Another factor that got the girls into school was because now that there was water on tap, they did not have to spend half the day carrying containers over great distances.

The next part of the trip was a mile-long trek over a mountainous track, either on foot or on mules. Bill decided on a mule, and sat behind a young Moroccan boy. Either the mule or its driver had been influenced by Kamakazi pilots, as one or other them was determined to go over the edge of the track. Bill slid further and further back over the mule's rump as it nosed its way towards instant death. I had elected to walk, which was just as well as I was able to support Bill as he fell back into my arms. After that experience he plumped for walking with Kristina and me. UNICEF had supplied the village we visited with cooking ovens that required very little wood. Before they had these ovens, the women of the village would have to leave their huts and clamber for miles over the mountains, scouring for anything combustible and staggering back to their homes weighed down with these enormous bundles of sticks. For the benefit of our visit they had one of these bundles for our group to try to lift. Not many of us could do it.

Our trip finished in Casablanca, and a lunch party held on the roof terrace of the Royal Mansour in the presence of the British Ambassador, to encourage support for UNICEF from Moroccan businessmen.

THE NETHERLANDS It is always a pleasure to be in the Netherlands and I have lost count of the number of times I have visited either Amsterdam or The Hague, after all it is where Audrey Hepburn first inspired me to become a part of UNICEF.

In June 2005, the Dutch National Committee for UNICEF celebrated its fiftieth year. Part of the celebration was a gala tribute to the Convention on the Rights of a Child. The event took place in the Royal Theatre and, appropriately enough, it was in the presence of HM Queen Beatrix of the Netherlands. It was an excellent chance for Kristina and me to get together with UNICEF's new executive director, Ann Veneman, and a very productive meeting it was. It was also the start of wonderful friendship.

The following year we were back again, this time for the Starwood Hotels and the Starwood Bicycle Challenge, in which three hundred and sixty employees and associates in sixty teams rode the 360km from Amsterdam's Passenger Terminal to Brussels. Good for them, they raised an astonishing US $250,000 for the children of Ethiopia. Needless to say, we did not cycle, I just said 'GO!'

NORWAY I have visited Norway several times, the first being in the 1960s when I was invited to do some PR for *The Saint*. Many years passed before returning to Norway, but in 1985 I went back as a guest of the Haugesund Film Festival. I took Geoffrey with me, and a Danish artist friend, Jurgen Waring. My work with the festival was very easy and Geoffrey, Jurgen and I were able to take a few boat trips, and try our hands at fishing . . . don't offer me the part of St Peter, the world would starve.

Kristina and I visited Bergen a number of times as her son, Hans-

Christian, was studying marine biology there for a number of years and lived there with his then wife, Jane and their son, Lucas. A couple of years ago we were in Bergen again with Julian Rachlin and Friends and I performed 'Carnival of the Animals', we raised money and awareness for UNICEF Norway.

THE PHILIPPINES In 1996, as part of our tour of Australia and Hong Kong, we went to the Philippines for the first time. We were to spend many days visiting various UNICEF-supported initiatives, I also had meetings with the local Kiwanis and saw some of the salt iodization in progress in Cebu City. We spent an afternoon with Sister Mary Marcia Antigua of the good Shepherd Convent and her young charges, all girls, some ex-street children, some orphaned, and all in need of aid. We sat on chairs in the garden and the girls, ranging from eight to fourteen, performed three little pageants. The first depicted what their lives had been before they came to this place, the second, what they did on a daily basis and the final story showed what they would like to become. It was fascinating and some of it was terribly moving. One child of eleven had been found three years before in a hovel, where she had lived with her mother, who was a drug dealer in trouble with one of the pushers. This child was playing under the table when these despicable thugs entered and chopped the mother in pieces. Fortunately, these bastards were unaware of the child's presence. She was discovered later, unable to speak, and brought to the convent. This was the first time in the three years that she had regained her power of speech.

After the second pageant we discovered that all the girls either wanted to enter the convent and become nuns themselves, or to be nurses or doctors, all callings that devote their lives to others. At the end of the play we were invited by the children to come and see where and how they lived, they all wanted to hold our hands as, with great pride, they showed us their bedrooms and their precious possessions – dolls, pictures and the like. We took refreshments with them – some of the cakes had been prepared by the children and they were delicious. It was hard leaving them that day but I am so grateful to Sister Mary Marcia for what she had accomplished and for letting us pass such an afternoon.

POLAND In 2004 I was delighted to be invited to Poland for the first time. You know when you are getting old because you start receiving

'Lifetime Achievement Awards', which obviously mean that you are still alive, but (and it is a big but), you have to be capable of getting up to receive it. The Polish TV guide, *Tele Tydzien*, had selected me for their Telekamera award, and Kristina and I were able to see Warsaw and meet many of its friendly citizens. Our hotel was situated right across the road from the Palace of Culture and Science, a gigantic neogothic structure, and despite the fact that our room was at the top of the hotel, we were still dwarfed by this massive concrete gift from Joseph Stalin sometime in the 1950s. I imagine that the best spot in Warsaw is the thirty-fifth floor terrace of this architectural nightmare, because from there you can see all of the beautiful city spread out below you and not have your view impeded by this legacy of one-time Soviet domination. We were able to find time to contact our UNICEF friends in Poland, and I look forward to a return visit – even though they have relocated to the Palace of Culture and Science.

RUSSIA I've made several trips to Russia over the years. The first time was en passant, on a BOAC flight that touched-down on the way to Hong Kong: either we needed fuel or the pilot wanted to stock up on caviar and vodka. In any event, it was a very depressing airport, a shop that appeared to only have one camera and some old binoculars for sale. My most recent trip, however, was under entirely different circumstances, it was for UNICEF, to coincide with the G8 summit. UNICEF's Ann Veneman met up with Kristina and me there, together with more than sixty young people aged between thirteen and seventeen, selected from the eight countries in the G8: Canada, France, Germany, Italy, Japan, the Russian Federation, the UK and the USA. The young people were there to put forward their points of view to the world leaders gathered: after all, it's important that the leaders hear what the young have to say, they are the ones who have to live with decisions their elders make. Of course, I was particularly interested in the UK delegation, eight of them from the Caedmon School in Whitby, led by a bright young man by the name of James Goodall, he gave me the school badge and I trust that when he becomes prime minister he will give me a seat in the House of Lords.

SLOVENIA I reckon that Slovenia is one of the world's best-kept secrets. In 1998 I knew that Slovenia had been a part of the former Yugoslavia, and that was about it. Mary Cahill at UNICEF in New York had suggested that it would be a good idea for us to accept an invitation to visit Slovenia and assist the Slovenian Committee in a fund-raising and awareness initiative. Mary explained that, having been formed in 1993, it was one of the youngest committees (there had been a UNICEF presence since 1947, in the shape of a country office). Since they had formed a National Committee and were now selling greetings cards, we discovered a most impressive fact: here was a country with, in 1998, a population of almost 1,900,000, yet this very young 'Natcom' had managed to sell over two million greetings cards. This demonstrated that they were go-getters and that the Slovenian citizens and companies supported the UNICEF principle. Unfortunately for us, this was a very short visit as it had to be squeezed between fund-raising events in Zurich and then Houston Texas, but we were able to elicit another invitation from the committee, for a visit that took place eighteen months later, in June 2000.

Kristina and I were so happy to be visiting our new friends in Slovenia again, and it was with great anticipation that we waited for the door of our aircraft to open. Usually such arrivals lead to bags and self being hustled into cars and swished away, not this time, however. We ascended the steps of a flower-bedecked carriage to be pulled by an equally florally bedecked horse and then clip-clopped our way through the lush green countryside to Cerklje. There we were welcomed by the Mayor of Cerklje, Mr Janez Cebulj, and the pupils of the Davorin Jenko Primary School, the school that had raised the most funds for the Drop of Water campaign.

USA In previous chapters I have written of much of my life in the USA, but it occurred to me that I owe a large debt of gratitude to the Kiwanis, not only for what they do to help the children of the world but also for the wonderful geography lessons they have given me by allowing me to join them all over the States as well as abroad. After I had attended their annual International Convention in Nice in 1993 and agreed to become honorary chairman of their committee to raise US $75,000,000 to help in the elimination of Iodine Deficiency Disorders, I then started to attend their annual conventions, starting off with New Orleans in 1994.

Since then, we have made countless visits in support of the Kiwanis, all over America and beyond. The battle for the elimination of IDD continued and the Kiwanis did reach their goal in raising the US

$75,000,000. Kristina and I always place IDD at the top of our agenda as we continue to travel the world. But it does not end there, other life and death struggles in the world may have taken the highlight off the IDD problem, but we must not forget it, not if we are going to have a world with all people being able to think and work at their full potential.

ZAMBIA In November 2002 Kristina and I, with UNICEF colleagues from the UK Committee, arrived in Lusaka, Zambia, another of the Southern African landlocked countries. We had been informed that 2.4 million people faced a long-term and rapidly growing humanitarian crisis. Stella Goings, the UNICEF representative, told us that they estimated 650,000 children had lost a parent to AIDS in Zambia. The first village we went to we found plenty of children, indeed as we looked around it was mainly children in the group gathered around us, and some old people. The elderly people had lost their children to AIDS and were left to care for the grandchildren. There had not been anyone able-bodied enough to plant seeds or plough the fields, and now there was the drought as well. I gazed into the eyes of an old lady, I couldn't hazard a guess as to her age, she was probably years younger than me, but disease and hunger had taken their toll, they were the saddest eyes I have ever had to witness. At a little classroom, Kristina asked one girl when she had last eaten. The child replied it had been breakfast the previous morning. it is very difficult to study on an empty stomach.

We visited a number of other outlying households and communities, and everywhere we were conscious of the lack of parents. In an effort to find food, some of the girls would walk to areas where truckers stopped to refuel and, of course, the inevitable happened and their young bodies were abused by those to whom they had turned for help . . . and consequently HIV/AIDS was carried back into their communities.

In Southern Province we were shown how UNICEF was expanding its HIV/AIDS awareness. The children had formed an AIDS club, where they were taught about the spread and prevention of AIDS. They showed us their art impressions of life, disease and hunger and then presented us with a choral rendering of an Anti-AIDS song. With their voices ringing in our ears, we bid a rather tearful goodbye to those youngsters, who we hope will survive and be a part of a stronger, wiser and pestilent-free Zambia.

The End

and with thanks

What I really mean is, the beginning of the rest of my life. I never had to buy a ticket to go on this voyage around the world, and when I started I had no idea that the first stop for reflection would be here in Monaco, in July 2008. Quite honestly, I'm glad of the rest. I've had time to reflect on the people and events that made it all possible. I've examined my true feelings and had a chance to remember those steps I shared with some; the laughs and tears I shared with others. I've said goodbye to so many and written far too many letters of condolence.

Like my friend Max Adrian, I've thought of what I didn't do, and regretted some of the things I did do. I've been thankful for the great fortune in my private and professional life, and the exceptional people I've met along the way: Nelson Mandela, who put his arm around Kristina's shoulder in the UN; Bill and Melinda Gates, again at the UN, who said they'd thought they would leave their philanthropic activities until they were in their sixties, but then they realized that the children cannot wait; the hundreds of dedicated UNICEF staff, the volunteers and the other NGOs in the field, all giving their skills – and lives – for the needy.

There have been so many people I didn't have a chance to say goodbye to, but I do have the memories and, shutting my eyes, sometimes I see their faces. Among them, great minds and talented writers, Bill Buckley and his wife Pat, James Clavell, David Niven – who didn't lend me the title of my voyage, I took it – Charlie Isaacs, darling Audrey Hepburn, Sir Peter Ustinov, my other actor friends Bob Brown, Bernie Lee, Francis Albert Sinatra, Cary Grant, Gregory Peck, Milton Berle, Red Buttons, Leslie Norman, Laurence Harvey, Mary and John Mills. Then there were associates, as well as friends, Cubby Broccoli and Dana, Harry Saltzman, Peter Hunt, Michael Klinger, Lew Grade, his brothers Leslie and Bernie, David Tebet, Gordon Douglas, Irving Rapper, Helmut Newton, Marvin Davis, Richard Cohen, Oscar Lerman and this year a tailor, a friend, a tennis partner and an all-round good bloke, Doug Hayward. Last but not least, I reflect fondly on a lady who was a friend of Dot Squires and also of my parents, the mother of the very talented composer Ernie Dunstall and one of the funniest women in the world, my dear departed friend Floss Dunstall. Lord, how she made us laugh.

Big regrets? That I never had the chance to know Kristina's parents and I never got to know my Aunts Lily, Nelly, Isabel, Amy, Uncle Jack and cousin Bob better – they will never have the chance to read this. Maybe Mum and Dad will be able to tell them about it and not tut-tut too much over some of the bad language. I am sorry for some of the heartache I have given, for the occasional lapse in good manners and any debt I didn't repay.

There are many people to thank for making this book possible, not least the kind producers who have employed me in the past and who might still do in the future. To the directors, the writers, my co-stars, the stuntmen, in particular Martin Grace, and all the crews I have worked with, I offer my wholehearted thanks for making this boy from Stockwell look like a hero.

I would also like to thank: Gareth Owen for sprinkling some literacy on to my recollections; Lesley Pollinger and all at Pollinger Limited; Michael O'Mara and all of his team; my lovely editor Louise Dixon; Bruce Nichols and everyone at Collins; Dan Strone of Trident Media Group in New York; my long-time business partner Bob Baker; Johnny Goodman; Harry Myers; Dave Worrall and Lee Pfeiffer at www.cinemaretro.com; Jaz Wiseman at www.itc-classics.com; my long-time assistant and friend Doris Spriggs; Barbara Broccoli and Michael Wilson at Eon Productions; Andrew Boyle; Ann and David Blackmer and the Kiwanis; Ann Veneman; Dheepa Pandian; Mary Cahill; Fran Silverberg; Christa Roth; and everyone at UNICEF.

I would like also to thank the doctors who have kept me going over the last eighty years: Dr Desmond Hall, my GP in Gerrards Cross; Dr Trevor Hudson, my GP in London; Dr Camel, my GP in St Paul de Vence; Barry Savory, who kept my back from collapsing; Selvyn Bleifer, my cardiologist in Beverly Hills; Steven Evans, my cardiologist in NYC; Darryl Hoffman MD, my cardiothoracic surgeon, who put in the pacemaker with the good batteries; Dr Bourlon, my cardiologist in Monaco; Dr Nabil Sharara my GP in Monaco; Dr Simsbler my dermatologist in Monaco; Dr Gilkes London, the dermatologist who burns off the bits that might have escaped the eagle eye of Dr Simsbler; Dr Ariane Kunz, my GP in Crans Montana; Rick Erlich, my urologist in Los Angeles; and, of course, Stevo, Dr Zax, of Beverly Hills. Also, though I can't remember seeing his face, my proctologist Dr Frielich in Beverly Hills (I promise I did not make up the name). Dr Singh in the ER room at the Roosevelt Hospital in NYC – he diagnosed the problem with my ticker – and Michael Mcnamara, a brilliant radiologist in Monaco.

I told you I was a hypochondriac!